Elizabeth George is an internationally acclaimed and best-selling author who divides her time between Huntington Beach, California, and London. *In Pursuit of the Proper Sinner* is her tenth novel.

'A compelling mystery, intricately plotted, with multiple twists and a satisfyingly devious finale. George is brilliant at juggling so many motives and so many suspects, keeping the reader enthralled, and coming up with such a clever solution.' Marcel Berlins, *The Times*

'Elizabeth George is in the front rank of modern crime writers, and with good reason. She spins a page-turning, multi-layered yarn set in dramatic surroundings involving people with vivid, believable characters. She is, in short, a class act.' *Daily Mail*

In Pursuit of the
Proper Sinner

Elizabeth George

NEW ENGLISH LIBRARY
Hodder & Stoughton

First published in 1999 by Hodder and Stoughton
First published in paperback in 2000 by Hodder and Stoughton
A division of Hodder Headline
A New English Library paperback

13 15 17 19 20 18 16 14

A CIP catalogue record for this title is available
from the British Library.

ISBN 0 340 68884 X

Typeset by Palimpsest Book Production Limited,
Polmont, Stirlingshire
Printed and bound in Great Britain by
Mackays of Chatham PLC, Chatham, Kent

Hodder and Stoughton
A division of Hodder Headline
338 Euston Road
London NW1 3BH

In loving memory of my father

Robert Edwin George

and with gratitude for
roller skating on Todd Street
trips to Disneyland
Big Basin
Yosemite
Big Sur
air mattress rides on Big Chico Creek
the Shakespeare guessing game
the raven and the fox
and most of all
for instilling in me
a passion for our native language

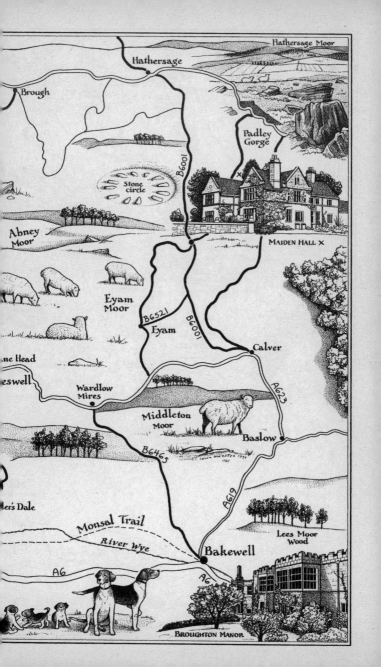

How sharper than a serpent's tooth it is
To have a thankless child

King Lear

JUNE

The West End

Prologue

What David King-Ryder felt inside was a kind of grief and a secondary dying. He felt overcome by a gloom and despair completely at odds with his situation.

Below him on the stage of the Agincourt Theatre, Horatio was reprising Hamlet's 'Divinity That Shapes Us' while Fortinbras countered with 'O Proud Death.' Three of the four bodies were being borne off the stage, leaving Hamlet lying in Horatio's arms. The cast – thirty strong – were moving towards one another, Norwegian soldiers coming from stage left, Danish courtiers coming from stage right, to meet up-stage from Horatio. As they began the refrain, the music swelled and the ordnance – which he'd initially argued against because of the risk of begging comparisons with the *1812* – boomed out in the wings. And at that precise moment, the stalls began rising beneath David's box. They were followed by the dress circle. Then the balconies. And over the music, the singing and the cannons, thundered applause.

This was what he had craved for more than a decade: a complete vindication of his prodigious talent. And by God, he finally had it before him. He had it below him and everywhere round him as well, for that matter. Three years of mind-crushing, body-numbing labour were at this moment culminating in the standing ovation that had been denied him at the conclusion of his two previous West End productions. For those extravaganzas, the nature of the applause and what followed the applause had said it all. A polite and perfunctory recognition of the cast members had preceded a hasty exodus from the theatre, which itself had been followed by an opening night party not unlike a wake. After that, the London reviews had finished what the first night word-of-mouth had begun. Two hugely expensive productions sank like concrete battleships. And David King-Ryder had the dubious pleasure of reading countless analyses of his creative decline. *Life Without Chandler* was the sort of headline he'd read from the reviews of the one or two theatrical critics possessing an emotion akin to sympathy. But the rest of them – the types who crafted vituperative metaphors over their morning Weetabix and spent months waiting for the opportunity to plug them into a commentary more noted for its vitriol than its information – had been merciless. He'd been called everything from an 'artistic charlatan' to a 'vessel buoyed by past glories', with those glories ostensibly burgeoning from a single source: Michael Chandler.

David King-Ryder wondered if other musical partnerships had undergone the scrutiny that his collaboration with Michael Chandler had. He doubted it. It seemed to him that musicians and lyricists from Gilbert and Sullivan to Rice and Lloyd-Webber had bloomed, had faded, had risen to prominence, had flourished, had failed, had vanquished critics, had stumbled, and had gloried all without the accompanying baying of the jackals that had snapped at his own heels.

The romance of his association with Michael Chandler had called for this analysis, naturally. When one partner of a team who mounted twelve of the West End's most successful productions dies in such a ghastly, stupid way, then a legend is going to be born from that dying. And Michael had died just that sort of death: becoming lost in an underwater Florida cave that had claimed three hundred other divers, violating every rule of diving by going alone, going at night, going inebriated, and leaving only an anchored fifteen-foot boat to mark the spot where he'd entered the water. He left behind a wife, a mistress, four children, six dogs, and a partner with whom he'd dreamed of fame, fortune, and theatrical success from their shared childhood in Oxford, sons of assemblymen at the Austin Rover plant.

So there had been a logic to the interest that the media had displayed in David King-Ryder's emotional and artistic rehabilitation following Michael's untimely death. And while the critics had battered him for his first solo attempt at pop opera five years later, they'd used fleece-covered clubs, as if in the belief that a man who lost both his long-time partner and his lifelong friend in one fell swoop deserved at least a single opportunity to fail without being publicly humiliated in his effort to find the muse by himself. These same critics hadn't been so merciful upon his second failure, however.

But that was over now. That was the past.

Next to him in the box Ginny cried out, 'We did it! David! We bloody well did it!' as she doubtless realised that – all charges of nepotism be damned when he'd chosen his own wife to direct the production – she'd just risen to the sort of heights occupied by artists like Hands, Nunn, and Hall.

David's son Matthew – as his father's manager, knowing only too well how much they had at stake in the production – grabbed David's hand hard and said gruffly, 'Damn. Well done, Dad.' And David wanted to warm to those words and to what they implied, a firm withdrawal of the initial doubts that Matthew had expressed when told of his father's intention to turn Shakespeare's greatest tragedy into his own musical triumph. 'You're *sure* you want to do this?' he'd asked and the rest of his remarks had remained unspoken: *Aren't you setting yourself up for a final deadly fall?*

He was indeed, David had confirmed at the time, if only to

himself. But what other option did he really have than to try to restore his name as an artist?

He'd managed to do just that: Not only were the audience on their feet, not only were the cast members ecstatically applauding him from the stage, but the critics – whose seat numbers he had memorised, 'the better to blow them up', Matthew had noted sardonically – were also standing, making no move to depart and joining in the sort of approbation that David had come to fear was as lost to him as was Michael Chandler.

That approbation only grew in the ensuing hours. At the opening night party at the Dorchester, in a ballroom creatively converted into Elsinore Castle, David stood at his wife's side, at the end of a receiving line comprising the production's leading actors. Along that line stepped London's foremost glitterati: Stars of stage and screen gushed over their colleagues and privately gnashed their teeth to conceal their envy; celebrities from all walks of life pronounced King-Ryder Productions' *Hamlet* everything from 'top notch' and 'just fab, darling' to 'kept me on the abso*lute* edge of my seat;' It girls and Sloanes – slinkily attired, displaying an astonishing degree of cleavage, and famous either for being famous or for having famous parents – declared that 'someone finally made Shakespeare *fun*'; representatives from that notable drain on the nation's imagination and economy – the Royal Family – offered their best wishes for success. And while everyone was pleased to press the flesh of Hamlet and his thespian cohorts, and while everyone was happy to congratulate Virginia Elliott for her masterful direction of her husband's pop opera, everyone was also most eager to talk to the man who'd been vilified and pilloried for more than a decade.

So there was triumph to be felt in spades, and David King-Ryder wanted to feel it. He was starved for a sensation that would tell him life was opening before him instead of closing. But that was the feeling that he couldn't escape. *It's over* boomed like the cannon in his ears.

If he had been able to talk to her about what he'd been going through since the curtain call, David knew that Ginny would tell him his feelings of depression, anxiety, and despair were perfectly normal. 'It's the natural letdown after opening night', she would have said. Yawning as she padded round their bedroom, dropping earrings on her dressing table and kicking shoes carelessly into the cupboard, she would have pointed out that she had far more reason to be let down than he had, anyway. As director, her job was over now. True, there were various components of the production to be tweaked – 'It *would* be satisfying if the lighting designer would cooperate and get the last scene right, wouldn't it?' – but by and large, she had to let go, to begin the process all over again on another production of another play. In *his* case, the morning would bring a flood of congratulatory phone calls, requests for interviews, and offers to mount the pop opera all over the world. Thus, he could dig into another staging of *Hamlet* or go on to something else. She didn't have that option.

If he had confessed that he just didn't have it in him to go on to anything else, she would have said, 'Of course, you haven't at the moment. That's normal, David. How could you right now? Give yourself some leeway to recover, won't you? You need time to refill the well.'

The well was the wellspring of creativity, and if he'd pointed out to his wife that she never seemed to need to refill her own supplies, she would have argued that directing was different from creating the product in the first place. She, at least, had raw materials to work with – not to mention a score of fellow artists with whom to knock heads as the production took shape. He had only the music room, the piano, endless solitude, and his imagination.

And the world's expectations, he thought morosely. They would always be there as the price of success.

He and Ginny left the Dorchester as soon as they were able to manage it surreptitiously. She'd protested at first when he'd indicated that he wanted to leave – as had Matthew who, always his father's manager, had argued that it wouldn't look good for David King-Ryder to depart the party before the party's end. But David had claimed exhaustion and strung-out nerves and Matthew and Virginia had accepted that self-diagnosis. After all, he hadn't slept well in weeks, his complexion was jaundiced, and his demeanour throughout the production – alternating between standing, sitting, and pacing in their box – strongly suggested a man whose personal resources had finally been depleted.

They rode from London in silence, David with a vodka curved into his palm and his thumb and forefinger pressed into his eyebrows, Ginny making several attempts to draw him into conversation. She suggested a holiday as a reward for their years of endeavour. Rhodes, she mentioned, Capri, and Crete.

The jolly-hockey-sticks tone of her voice told David that she was becoming increasingly concerned with her failure to reach him. And considering their history together – she'd been his twelfth mistress before he'd made her his fifth wife – there was good reason for her to suspect that his condition had nothing to do with first-night nerves, letdown after triumph, or anxiety about critical reaction to his work. The past few months had been rough on them as a couple, and she knew quite well what he'd done to cure himself of the impotence he'd experienced with his last wife, since he'd done it by moving on to Ginny herself. So when she finally said, 'Darling, it happens sometimes. It's *nerves*, that's all. It'll all come right at the end of the day,' he wanted to reassure her somehow. But he didn't have the words.

He was still trying to find them when their limousine entered the tunnel of silver maples that characterised the woodland in which they lived. Here, not an hour from London, the countryside was thickly grown with trees, and footpaths trod by generations of foresters and farmers disappeared into an undergrowth of ferns.

The car turned between the two oaks that marked their drive. Twenty yards along, an iron gate swung open. The road beyond curved beneath alders, poplars, and beeches, skirting a pond where the reflection of stars made a second sky. It climbed a slight rise, swung past a row of silent bungalows, and pooled out suddenly into the alluvial fan of the entrance to the King-Ryder mansion.

Their housekeeper had laid out supper for them, assembling an array of David's favourite foods. 'Mr Matthew did phone,' Portia explained in her quiet, dignified voice. A runaway from the Sudan at the age of fifteen, she'd been with Virginia for the last ten years and she had the melancholy face of a beautiful, sorrowing black Madonna. 'My warmest congratulations to both of you,' she added.

David thanked her. He stood in the dining room where the windows stretched from floor to ceiling and reflected all three of them in the glass. He admired the epergne that spilled white roses onto plaits of ivy. He fingered one of the thin silver forks. He used his thumbnail against a drip of candle wax. And he knew he wouldn't be able to force a morsel of food past the constriction in his throat.

So he told his wife that he needed a bit of time alone to unwind from the evening. He would join her later, he said. He just needed a while to decompress.

One always expected an artist to retreat to the heartbeat of his artistry. So David went to his music room. He flipped on the lights. He poured another vodka and placed the tumbler on the unprotected top of the grand piano.

He realised as he did it that Michael would never have done such a thing. Michael had been careful that way, realising the value of a musical instrument, respectful of its boundaries, its dimensions, its possibilities. He'd been careful about most of his life as well. It was only on one crazy night in Florida that he'd got careless.

David sat at the piano. Without thinking or planning, his fingers sought out an aria he loved. It was a melody from his most auspicious failure – *Mercy* – and he hummed as he played it, trying and failing to recall the words to a song that had once held the key to his future.

As he played, he let his gaze travel the walls of the room, four monuments to his success. Shelves held awards. Frames enclosed certificates. Posters and playbills announced productions that even to this day were mounted in every part of the world. And photographs by the silver-framed score documented his life.

Michael was there among them. And when David's glance fell on his old friend's face, his fingers shifted – of their own accord – from the aria he'd been playing to the song he knew was destined to be the hit of *Hamlet*. 'What Dreams May Come' was its title, taken from the prince's most famous soliloquy.

He played it only halfway through before he had to stop. He found that he was so monumentally tired that his hands fell from the keys and his eyes closed. But still he could see Michael's face.

'You shouldn't have died,' he told his partner. 'I thought a success would make everything different, but it only makes the prospect of failure worse.'

He took up his drink again. He left the room. He tossed back the vodka, set the tumbler next to a travertine urn in a recessed alcove, and didn't notice when he failed to push the glass in far enough and it fell to the carpeted floor.

Above him in the enormous house, he could hear a bath running. Ginny would be soaking away the stress of the evening and the tension of the months that had preceded it. He wished that he could do the same. It seemed to him that he had so much more cause.

He allowed himself to relive those glorious moments of

triumph a final time: the audience rising to its feet before the curtain call had begun, the cheers, the hoarse shouts of 'Bravo.'

All that should have been enough for David. But it wasn't. It couldn't be. It fell, if not on ears that were deaf, then on ears that were listening to another voice entirely.

'Petersham Mews and Elvaston Place. Ten o'clock.'

'But where . . . ? Where are they?'

'Oh, you'll work that out.'

And now when he tried to hear the praise, the excited chatter, the paeans that were supposed to be his air, his light, his food and his drink, all David could hear were those last four words: *you'll work that out.*

And it was time.

He climbed the stairs and went to the bedroom. Beyond, behind the closed door to the bathroom, his wife was enjoying her soak. She was singing with a determined happiness that told him how worried she actually was: about everything from the state of his nerves to the state of his soul.

She was a good woman, Virginia Elliott, David thought. She was the very best of his wives. It had been his intention to stay married to her till the end of his days. He simply hadn't realised how abbreviated that time would turn out to be.

Three quick movements did the job neatly.

He took the gun from a drawer in the bedside table. He raised it. He pulled the trigger.

SEPTEMBER

Derbyshire

Chapter One

Julian Britton was a man who knew that his life thus far had amounted to nothing. He bred his dogs, he managed the crumbling ruin that was his family's estate, and daily he tried to lecture his father away from the bottle. That was the extent of it. He hadn't been a success at anything save pouring gin down the drain, and now, at twenty-seven years old, he felt branded by failure. But he couldn't allow that to affect him tonight. He knew that he had to prevail.

He began with his appearance, giving himself a ruthless scrutiny in his bedroom's cheval glass. He straightened the collar of his shirt and flicked a piece of lint from his shoulder. He stared at his face and schooled his features into the expression he wanted them to wear. He should look completely serious, he decided. Concerned, yes, because concern was reasonable. But he shouldn't look agonised. And certainly he shouldn't look ripped up inside and wondering how he came to be where he was, at this precise moment, with his world a shambles.

As to what he was going to say, two sleepless nights and two endless days had given Julian plenty of time to rehearse what remarks he wished to make when the appointed hour rolled round. Indeed, it was in elaborate but silent fantasy conversations that Julian had spent most of the past two nights and two days that had followed Nicola Maiden's unbelievable announcement. Now, after forty-eight hours engaged in endless colloquies within his own skull, Julian was anxious to get on with things, even if he had no assurance that his words would carry the weight he wanted.

He turned from the cheval glass and fetched his car keys from the top of the chest of drawers. The fine sheen of dust that usually covered its walnut surface had been removed. This told Julian that his cousin had once again submitted to the cleaning furies, a sure sign that she'd met defeat yet another time in her determined course of sobering up her uncle.

Samantha had come to Derbyshire with just that intention eight months previously, an angel of mercy who'd one day shown up at Broughton Manor with the mission of reuniting a family torn asunder for more than three decades. She hadn't made much progress in that direction, however, and Julian wondered how much longer she was going to put up with his father's bent towards the bottle.

'We've *got* to get him off the booze, Jules,' Samantha had said to him only that morning. 'You must see how crucial it is at this point.'

Nicola, on the other hand, knowing his father eight years and not merely eight months, had long been of a live-and-let-live frame of mind. She'd said more than once, 'If your dad's choice is to drink himself silly, there's nothing you can do about it, Jules. And there's nothing that Sam can do either.' But then Nicola didn't know how it felt to see one's father slipping ever more inexorably towards debauchery, absorbed in intensely inebriated delusions about the romance of his past. She, after all, had grown up in a home where how things *seemed* was identical to how things actually *were*. She had two parents whose love never wavered, and she'd never suffered the dual desertion of a flower-child mother flitting off to 'study' with a tapestry-clad guru the night before one's own twelfth birthday and a father whose devotion to the bottle far exceeded any attachment he might have displayed towards his three children.

In fact, had Nicola ever once cared to analyse the differences in their individual upbringings, Julian thought, she might have seen that every single one of her *bloody* decisions—

At that, he brought his thoughts up short. He would *not* head in that direction. He could not *afford* to head in that direction. He could not afford to let his mind wander from the task that was immediately at hand.

'Listen to me.' He grabbed his wallet from the chest and shoved it into his pocket. 'You're good enough for anyone. She got scared shitless. She took a wrong turn. That's the end of it. Remember that. And remember that everyone knows how good the two of you always were together.'

He had faith in this fact. Nicola Maiden and Julian Britton had been part of each other's lives for years. Everyone who knew them had long ago realised that they belonged together. It was only Nicola who, it appeared, had never come to terms with this fact.

'I know that we were never engaged,' he'd told her two nights previously in response to her declaration that she was moving away from the Peaks permanently and would only be back for brief visits henceforth. 'But we've always had an understanding, haven't we? I wouldn't be sleeping with you if I wasn't serious about . . . Come on, Nick. Damn it, you *know* me.'

It wasn't the proposal of marriage he'd planned on making, and she hadn't taken it as such. She'd said bluntly, 'Jules, I like you enormously. You're terrific, and you've been a real friend. And we get on, far better than I've ever got on with any other bloke.'

'Then you see—'

'But I don't love you,' she went on. 'Sex doesn't equate to love. It's only in films and books that it does.'

He'd been too stunned at first to speak. It was as if his mind had become a blackboard and someone had taken a rubber to it before he had a chance to make any notes. So she'd continued.

She would, she told him, go on being his girlfriend in the Peak District if that's what he wanted. She'd be coming to see her parents now and again, and she'd always have time – and be happy, she said – to see Julian as well. They could even continue as lovers whenever she was in the area if he wished. That was fine by her. But as to marriage? They were too different as people, she explained.

'I know how much you want to save Broughton Manor,' she'd said. 'That's your dream, and you'll make it come true. But I don't share that dream, and I'm not going to hurt either you or myself by pretending I do. That's not fair on anyone.'

Which was when he finally repossessed his wits long enough to say bitterly, 'It's the God damn money. And the fact I've got none, or at least not enough to suit your tastes.'

'Julian, it isn't. Not exactly.' She'd turned from him briefly, giving a long sigh. 'Let me explain.'

He'd listened for what had seemed like an hour, although she'd likely spoken ten minutes or less. At the end, after everything had been said between them and she'd climbed out of the Rover and disappeared into the dark gabled porch of Maiden Hall, he'd driven home numbly, shell-shocked with grief, confusion, and surprise, thinking No, she couldn't . . . she can't mean . . . *no*. After Sleepless Night Number One, he'd come to realise – past his own pain – how great was the need for him to take action. He'd phoned, and she'd agreed to see him. She would always, she said, be willing to see him.

He gave a final glance in the mirror before he left the room, and he treated himself to a last affirmation: 'You were *always* good together. Keep that in mind.'

He slipped along the dim upstairs passage of the manor house and looked into the small room that his father used as a parlour. His family's increasingly straitened financial circumstances had effected a general retreat from all the larger rooms downstairs that had slowly been made uninhabitable as their various antiques, paintings, and *objets d'art* were sold to make ends meet. Now the Brittons lived entirely on the house's upper floor. There were abundant rooms for them, but they were cramped and dark.

Jeremy Britton was in the parlour. As it was half past ten, he was thoroughly blotto, head on his chest and a cigarette burning down between his fingers. Julian crossed the room and removed the fag from his father's hand. Jeremy didn't stir.

Julian cursed quietly, looking at him: at the promise of intelligence, vigour, and pride completely eradicated by the addiction. His father was going to burn the place down someday, and there were times – like now – when Julian thought that complete conflagration might be all for the best. He crushed out Jeremy's cigarette and reached into his shirt pocket for the packet of Dunhills. He removed it and did the same with his father's lighter. He grabbed the gin bottle and left the room.

He was dumping the gin, cigarettes, and lighter into the dustbins at the back of the manor house when he heard her speak.

'Caught him at it again, Julie?'

He started, looked about, but failed to see her in the gloom. Then she rose from where she'd been sitting: on the edge of the drystone wall that divided the back entrance of the manor from the first of its overgrown and untended gardens. An untrimmed wisteria – beginning to lose its leaves with the approach of autumn – had sheltered her. She dusted off the seat of her khaki shorts and sauntered over to join him.

'I'm beginning to think he wants to kill himself,' Samantha said in the practical manner that was her nature. 'I just haven't come up with the reason why.'

'He doesn't need a reason,' Julian said shortly. 'Just the means.'

'I try to keep him off the sauce, but he's got bottles everywhere.' She glanced at the dark manor house that rose before them like a fortress in the landscape. 'I do try, Julian.

I know it's important.' She looked back at him and regarded his clothes. 'You're looking very smart. I didn't think to dress up. Was I supposed to?'

Julian returned her look blankly, his hands moving to his chest to pat his shirt, searching for something that he knew wasn't there.

'You've forgotten, haven't you?' Samantha said. She was very good at making intuitive leaps.

Julian waited for elucidation.

'The eclipse,' she said.

'The eclipse?' He thought about it. He clapped a hand to his forehead. 'God. The *eclipse*. Sam. Hell. I'd forgotten. Is the eclipse tonight? Are you going somewhere to see it?'

She said with a nod to the spot from which she'd just emerged, 'I've got us some provisions. Cheese and fruit, some bread, a bit of sausage. Wine. I thought we might want it if we have to wait longer than you'd thought.'

'To wait . . . ? Oh hell, Samantha . . .' He wasn't sure how to put it. He hadn't intended her to think he meant to watch the eclipse with her. He hadn't intended her to think he meant to watch the eclipse at all.

'Have I got the date wrong?' The tone of her voice spoke her disappointment. She already knew that she had the date right and that if she wanted to see the eclipse from Eyam Moor, she was going to have to hike out there alone.

His mention of the lunar eclipse had been a casual remark. At least, that's how he'd intended it to be taken. He'd said conversationally, 'One can see it quite well from Eyam Moor. It's supposed to happen round half past eleven. Are you interested in astronomy, Sam?'

Samantha had obviously interpreted this as an invitation, and Julian felt a momentary annoyance with his cousin's presumption. But he did his best to hide it because he owed her so much. It was in the cause of reconciling her mother with her uncle – Julian's father – that she'd been making her lengthy visits to Broughton Manor from Winchester for the past eight months. Each stay had become progressively longer as she found more employment round the estate, either in the renovation of the manor house proper or in the smooth running of the tournaments, fêtes, and reenactments that Julian organised in the grounds as yet another source of Britton income. Her helpful presence had been a real godsend since Julian's siblings had long fled the family nest and Jeremy hadn't lifted a finger since he'd inherited the property – and proceeded to populate it with his fellow flower-children and run it into the ground – shortly after his twenty-fifth birthday.

Still, grateful as Julian was for Sam's help, he wished his cousin hadn't assumed so much. He'd felt guilty about the amount of work she was doing purely from the goodness of her heart, and he'd been casting about aimlessly for some form of repayment. He had no available money to offer her, not that she would have needed or accepted it had he done so, but he did have his dogs as well as his knowledge of and enthusiasm for Derbyshire. And wanting to make her feel welcome for as long as possible at Broughton Manor, he'd offered her the only thing he had: occasional activities with the harriers as well as conversation. And it was a conversation about the eclipse that she had misunderstood.

'I hadn't thought . . .' He kicked at a bare patch in the gravel where a dandelion was shooting up a furry stalk and leaves. 'I'm sorry, I'm heading over to Maiden Hall.'

'Oh.'

Funny, Julian thought, how one syllable could carry the weight of everything from condemnation to delight.

'Stupid me,' she said. 'I can't think how I got the impression that you wanted to . . . Well, anyway . . .'

'I'll make it up to you.' He hoped he sounded earnest. 'If I hadn't already planned . . . You know how it is.'

'Oh yes,' she said. 'Mustn't disappoint your Nicola, Julian.' She offered him a brief, cool smile and ducked into the hollow of the wisteria vine. She hooked a basket over her arm.

'Another time?' Julian said.

'Whatever.' She didn't look at him as she walked past, slipped through the gateway, and disappeared into the inner courtyard of Broughton Manor.

He felt the breath leave him in a gusty sigh. He hadn't realised he'd been holding it back. 'Sorry,' he said quietly to her absence. 'But this is important. If you knew how important, you'd understand.'

He made the drive to Padley Gorge swiftly, heading north-west towards Bakewell where he spun across the old mediaeval bridge that spanned the River Wye. He used the journey for a final rehearsal of his remarks, and by the time he'd reached the sloping drive to Maiden Hall, he was fairly sure that before the evening was out, his plans would bear the fruit he wanted.

Maiden Hall sat midway up a slope of woodland. Here the land was thick with sessile oaks, and the incline leading up to the Hall was canopied with chestnuts and limes. Julian cruised up this drive, negotiated the serpentine turns with the skill of long practice, and chugged to a stop next to a Mercedes sports car in the gravelled enclosure that was reserved for guests.

He skirted the main entrance and went in through the kitchen, where Andy Maiden was watching his chef put the flame to a tray of crème brûlée. The chef – one Christian-Louis Ferrer – had been brought on board from France some five years previously to enhance the solid if not inspired reputation of Maiden Hall's food. At the moment, however, with culinary blow lamp in hand, Ferrer looked more like an arsonist than *un grand artiste de la cuisine.* The expression on Andy's face suggested that he was sharing Julian's thoughts.

Only when Christian-Louis had successfully turned the coating into a perfect, thin shell of glaze, saying, '*Et la voilà, Andee,*' with the sort of condescending smile one gives to a doubting Thomas who's once again had his doubts proven groundless, did Andy look up and see Julian watching.

'I've never liked flame throwing in the kitchen,' he admitted with an embarrassed smile. 'Hello, Julian. What's the news from Broughton and regions beyond?'

This constituted his usual greeting. Julian made his usual response. 'All's well with the righteous. But as for the rest of mankind . . . Forget it.'

Andy smoothed down the hairs of his greying moustache and observed the younger man in a friendly fashion while Christian-Louis slid the tray of crème brûlée through a serving hatch to the dining room. He said, '*Maintenant, on en a fini pour ce soir,*' and began removing the white apron that was stained with the evening's sauces. As the Frenchman disappeared into a small changing room, Andy said, '*Vive la France,*' wryly and rolled his eyes. Then to Julian, 'Join us for a coffee? We've one group left in the dining room and everyone else in the lounge for the after-dinners.'

'Any residents tonight?' Julian asked. An old Victorian lodge once used as a hunting retreat by a branch of the Saxe-Coburg family, Maiden Hall had ten bedrooms. All had been individually decorated by Andy's wife when the Maidens had made their escape from London a decade previously; eight were let out to discerning travellers who wanted the privacy of a hotel combined with the intimacy of a home.

'Fully booked,' Andy replied. 'We've had a record summer, what with the fine weather. So what's it to be? Coffee? Brandy? How's your dad, by the way?'

Julian winced inwardly at the mental association behind Andy's words. Doubtless the whole blasted county paired his father with one type of booze or another. 'Nothing for me,' he said. 'I've come for Nicola.'

'Nicola? Why, she isn't here, Julian.'

'Not here? She's not left Derbyshire already, has she? Because she said—'

'No, no.' Andy began storing the kitchen knives in a wooden stand, sliding them into slots with a neat *snick* as he continued talking. 'She's gone camping. Didn't she tell you? She set out mid-morning yesterday.'

'But I spoke to her . . .' Julian thought back, reaching for a time. 'Early yesterday morning. She wouldn't have forgotten that quickly.'

Andy shrugged. 'Looks like she has. Women, you know. What did you two have on?'

Julian sidestepped the question. 'Did she go alone?'

'Always has done,' Andy replied. 'You know Nicola.'

How well he did. 'Where? Did she take the proper gear?'

Andy turned from storing his knives. Obviously, he heard something worrying in Julian's tone. 'She wouldn't have gone without her gear. She knows how fast the weather changes out there. At any rate, I helped her stow it in the car myself. Why? What's going on? Did you two have a row?'

Julian could give a truthful answer to the last of the questions. They hadn't had a row, at least not what Andy would have considered a row. He said, 'Andy, she should've been back by now. We were going to Sheffield. She wanted to see a film—'

'At *this* time of night?'

'A special showing.' Julian felt his face getting hot as he explained the tradition behind the *Rocky Horror Picture Show*. But Andy's time undercover in what he always referred to as his Other Life had exposed him to the film long ago, and he waved the explanation off. This time, when he reached for his moustache and stroked it thoughtfully, he frowned as well.

'You're certain about the evening? She couldn't have thought you meant tomorrow?'

'I should have preferred to see her last night,' Julian said. 'It was Nicola who set the date for tonight. And I'm certain she said she'd be back this afternoon. I'm *certain*.'

Andy dropped his hand. His eyes were grave. He looked

beyond Julian to the casement window above the sink. There was nothing to see but their reflections. But Julian knew from his expression that Andy was thinking about what lay beyond them, in the darkness. Vast moors populated only by sheep; abandoned quarries reclaimed by nature; limestone cliffs giving way to screes; prehistoric fortresses of tumbling stone. There were myriad limestone caves to entrap one, copper mines whose walls and ceilings could collapse, cairns whose hotchpotch of stones could snap the ankle of an unwary hiker, gritstone ridges where a climber could fall and lie for days or weeks before being found. The district stretched from Manchester to Sheffield, from Stoke-on-Trent to Derby, and more than a dozen times each year Mountain Rescue was called to bring in someone who'd broken an arm or a leg – or worse – in the Peaks. If Andy Maiden's daughter was lost or hurt somewhere out there, it was going to take the effort of more than two men standing in a kitchen to find her.

Andy said, 'Let's get on to the police, Julian.'

Julian's initial impulse also was to phone the police. Upon reflection, however, he dreaded the thought of everything phoning the police implied. But in this brief moment of hesitation, Andy acted. He strode out to the reception desk to make the call.

Julian hurried after him. He found Andy hunched over the phone, as if he intended to shelter himself from potential eavesdroppers. Still, only he and Julian stood in reception, while the Hall's guests lingered over coffees and brandies in the lounge at the other end of the corridor.

It was from this direction that Nan Maiden approached just as Andy's connection to the Buxton police went through. She came out of the lounge bearing a tray that held an empty cafetiere and the used cups and saucers of coffee for two. She smiled and said, 'Why, Julian! Hullo. We weren't expecting

. . .' but her words petered out as she took in her husband's surreptitious appearance – huddled over the phone like an anonymous caller – and Julian's accomplice-like hovering nearby. 'What's going on?'

At her question, Julian felt as if the word *guilt* were tattooed on his forehead. When Nan said, 'What's happened?' he said nothing and waited for Andy to take the lead. However, Nicola's father spoke in a low voice into the phone, saying 'Twenty-five,' and completely ignored his wife.

But, *twenty-five* seemed to tell Nan what Julian wouldn't put into words and what Andy was avoiding. 'Nicola,' she breathed. And she joined them at the reception desk, sliding her tray onto its surface where it dislodged a willow basket of hotel brochures that tumbled to the floor. No one picked them up. 'Has something happened to Nicola?'

Andy's answer was calm. 'Julian and Nick had a date this evening, which she's apparently forgotten,' he told his wife, left hand over the mouthpiece of the phone. 'We're trying to track her down.' He offered the lie ingenuously, with the skill of a man who'd once made falsehood his stock in trade. 'I was thinking that she might have gone to see Will Upman on her way home, to pave the way for another job next summer. Everything all right with the guests, love?'

Nan's quick grey eyes darted from her husband to Julian. 'Exactly who're you talking to, Andy?'

'Nancy . . .'

'Tell me.'

He didn't do so. On the other end of the line, someone spoke, and Andy looked at his watch. He said, 'Unfortunately, we're not altogether sure . . . No. Thanks. Fine. I appreciate it.' He rang off and picked up the tray that his wife had placed on the desk. He headed towards the kitchen. Nan and Julian followed.

Christian-Louis was just leaving, his chef's whites changed for jeans, trainers, and an Oxford University sweatshirt with its sleeves cut off. He grabbed the handlebars of a bicycle that was leaning against the wall and, taking a moment to measure the tension among the other three people in the kitchen, he said, '*Bonsoir, à demain*,' and quickly left them. Through the window, they saw the white glow of his bicycle lamp as he pedalled off.

'Andy, I want the truth.' His wife planted herself in front of him. She was a small woman, nearly ten inches shorter than her husband. But her body was solid and tightly muscled, the physique of a woman two decades younger than her sixty years.

'You've had the truth,' Andy said reasonably. 'Julian and Nicola had a date. Nick's forgotten. Julian's got himself into a twist and he'd like to track her down. I'm helping him out.'

'But that wasn't Will Upman on the phone, was it?' Nan demanded. 'Why would Nicola be seeing Will Upman at—' She glanced at the kitchen clock, a functional and institutional timepiece that hung above a rack of dinner plates. It was eleven-twenty, and all of them knew that the hour was unlikely for paying a social call on one's employer, which was what Will Upman had been to Nicola for the last three months. 'She said she was going camping. Don't tell me that you actually think she stopped to have a chat with Will Upman in the middle of a camping trip. And why would Nicola fail to turn up for a date with Julian? She's never done that.' Nan shifted her sharp gaze. 'Have you two had a row?' she asked Julian astutely.

Julian's immediate discomfort came from two sources: having to answer the question another time and realising that Nicola hadn't yet told her parents of her intention to leave Derbyshire permanently. She would hardly have been seeking her next summer's employment if she'd been planning to leave the county.

'Actually, we talked about marriage,' Julian decided to say. 'We were sorting out the future.'

Nan's eyes widened. Something akin to relief wiped the

worry from her face. 'Marriage? Nicola's agreed to marry you? When? I mean, when did all this happen? And she never said a word. Why, this is wonderful news. It's absolutely brilliant. Heavens, Julian, it makes me feel giddy. Have you told your dad?'

Julian didn't want to lie outright. But he couldn't bring himself to tell the full truth. He settled on the precarious middle ground. 'Actually, we're just at the talking stage. In fact we were supposed to talk again tonight.'

Andy Maiden had been watching Julian curiously, as if he knew very well that any talk of marriage between his daughter and Julian Britton would be as unlikely as a discussion on raising sheep. He said, 'Hang on. I thought you were going to Sheffield.'

'Right. But we planned to talk on the way.'

'Well, Nicola would never forget that,' Nan declared. 'No woman is likely to forget she has a date to talk about marriage.' And then to her husband, 'Which is something you ought to know very well, Andy.' She was silent for a moment, dwelling – so it seemed – on that final thought while Julian dwelt on the uneasy fact that Andy still had not answered his wife's questions about the phone call he'd just made. Nan reached her own conclusion about this. 'God. You've just phoned the police, haven't you? You think that something's happened to her. And you didn't want me to know about it, did you?'

Neither Andy nor Julian replied. This was answer enough.

'And what was I to think when the police arrived?' Nan demanded. 'Or was I just supposed to keep serving the coffee?'

'I knew you'd worry,' her husband said. 'There may be no cause.'

'Nicola could easily be out there in the dark, lying hurt or trapped or God knows what else and you – both of you – didn't think I should know? Because I might *worry*?'

'You're working yourself into a state right now. That's why

I didn't want to tell you till I had to. It may be nothing. It's probably nothing. Julian and I agree on that. We'll have it all sorted out in an hour or two, Nancy.'

Nan attempted to shove a handful of hair behind her ear. Cut in a strange fashion that she called a beret – long on the top and clipped on the sides – it was too short to do anything but flop back into place. 'We'll set out after her,' she decided. 'One of us must start looking for her at once.'

'One of us looking for Nicola isn't going to do much good,' Julian pointed out. 'There's no telling where she went.'

'But we know all her haunts. Arbor Low. Thor's Cave. Peveril Castle.' Nan mentioned half a dozen other locations, all of them inadvertently serving to underscore the point that Julian had been attempting to make: There was no correlation between Nicola's favourite spots and their locations in the Peak District. They were as far north as the outskirts of Holmfirth, as far south as Ashbourne and the lower part of the Tissington Trail. It was going to take a team to find her.

Andy pulled a bottle out of the cupboard, along with three tumblers. Into each he poured a shot of brandy. He handed round the glasses, saying, 'Get that down you.'

Nan's hands circled her glass, but she didn't drink. 'Something's happened to her.'

'We don't know anything. That's why the police are on their way.'

The police, in the person of an ageing constable called Price, arrived not thirty minutes later. He asked the expected questions of them: When had she left? How was she equipped? Had she set off alone? What seemed to be her state of mind? Depressed? Unhappy? Worried? What had she declared as her intentions? Had she actually stated a time of her return? Who spoke to her last? Had she received any visitors? Letters? Phone calls? Had anything happened recently that might have prompted her to run off?

Julian joined Andy and Nan Maiden in their efforts to

impress upon Constable Price the gravity of Nicola's failure to reappear at Maiden Hall. But Price seemed determined to go his own way, and a painstaking, hair-tearingly slow way it was. He wrote in his notebook at a ponderous pace, taking down a description of Nicola. He took them through her activities during the last two weeks. And he seemed terminally fascinated by the fact that, on the morning before she'd left for her hike, she'd received three phone calls from individuals who wouldn't give their names so that Nan could pass them along to Nicola before she came to the phone.

'One man and two women?' Price asked four times.

'I don't know, I don't *know*. And what does it matter?' Nan said testily. 'It may have been the same woman calling twice. What difference does it make? What's that got to do with Nicola?'

'But just one man?' Constable Price said.

'God in heaven, how many times am I going to have to—'

'One man,' Andy interposed.

Nan pressed her lips into an angry line. Her eyes bored holes into Price's skull. 'One man,' she repeated.

'It wasn't you who phoned?' This to Julian.

'I know Julian's voice,' Nan said. 'It wasn't Julian.'

'But you have a relationship with the young lady, Mr Britton?'

'They're engaged to be married,' Nan said.

'Not exactly engaged,' Julian quickly clarified, and he cursed in silence as the damnable heat rose from his collar bone to suffuse his cheeks yet again.

'Had a bit of a quarrel?' Price asked, voice shrewd. 'Another man involved?'

Jesus, Julian thought grimly. Why did everyone assume they'd rowed? There hadn't been a single harsh word between them. Indeed, there hadn't been time for that.

They hadn't quarrelled, Julian reported steadily. And he

knew nothing about another man. Absolutely nothing, he asserted for good measure.

'They had a date to talk about their wedding plans,' Nan said.

'Well, actually—'

'D'you honestly know any woman who'd fail to turn up for that?'

'And you *are* certain she intended to return by this evening?' Constable Price asked Andy. He shifted his eyes over his notes, going on to say, 'Her gear suggests she might have intended a longer outing.'

'I hadn't thought much about it till Julian stopped by to fetch her to Sheffield,' Andy admitted.

'Ah.' The constable eyed Julian with more suspicion than Julian felt was warranted. Then he flipped his notebook closed. The radio receiver that he wore from his shoulder buzzed with an incomprehensible stream of babble. He reached up and turned down the volume. Easing his notebook into his pocket, he said, 'Well. She's done a runner before, and this's no different to that, I expect. We'll have ourselves a wait till—'

'What're you talking about?' Nan cut in. 'This isn't a runaway teenager we're reporting. She's twenty-five years old, for heaven's sake. She's a responsible adult. She has a job. A boyfriend. A family. She hasn't run off. She's disappeared.'

'At the present, p'rhaps she has,' the constable agreed. 'But as she's bunked off before – and our files do show that, madam – till we know she's not doing another runner, we can't send a team out after her.'

'She was seventeen years old when she last ran off,' Nan argued. 'We'd just moved here from London. She was lonely, unhappy. We were caught up getting the Hall in order and we failed to give her the proper attention. All she'd needed was guidance so that—'

'Nancy.' Andy put his hand gently on the back of her neck.

'We can't just do nothing!'

'No choice in the matter,' the constable said implacably. 'We've got our procedures. I'll make my report, and if she's not turned up by this time tomorrow, we'll have ourselves another look at the problem.'

Nan spun to her husband. '*Do* something. Phone Mountain Rescue yourself.'

Julian interposed. 'Nan, Mountain Rescue can't begin a search unless they have an idea ...' He gestured towards the windows and hoped she would fill in the blanks. As a member of Mountain Rescue himself, he'd been on dozens of cases. But the rescuers had always had a general idea of where to begin looking for a hiker. Since neither Julian nor Nicola's parents could even generalise about Nicola's point of departure, the only avenue left to them was to wait until first light when the police could request a helicopter from the RAF.

Because of the hour and their lack of information, Julian knew that the only possible activity that actually could have grown from their midnight meeting with Constable Price would have been a preliminary phone call to the closest mountain rescue organization, telling them to assemble their volunteers at dawn. But clearly they had failed to impress upon the constable the gravity of the situation. Mountain Rescue responded only to the police. And the police – at least at the moment and in the person of Constable Price – weren't themselves responding.

They were wasting time talking to the man. Julian could see from Andy's expression that he'd arrived at this same conclusion. He said, 'Thank you for coming, Constable,' and when his wife would have protested, Andy went on. 'We'll phone you tomorrow evening if Nicola hasn't turned up.'

'Andy!'

He put his arm round her shoulders and she turned into his chest. He didn't speak until the constable had ducked out of the kitchen door, gone to his panda car, switched on the ignition, and flicked on the headlamps. And then he spoke to Julian, not Nan.

'She always likes camping in the White Peak, Julian. There're maps in reception. Would you fetch them please? We'll each want to know where the other's searching.'

Chapter Two

———◆———

It was just after seven the next morning when Julian returned to Maiden Hall. If he hadn't explored every possible site from Consall Wood to Alport Height, he certainly felt as if he had. Torch in one hand, loud hailer in the other, he'd gone through the motions: He'd trudged the leafy woodland path from Wettonmill up the steep grade to Thor's Cave. He'd scoured along the River Manifold. He'd shone his torchlight up the slope of Thorpe Cloud. He'd followed the River Dove as far south as the old medieval manor at Norbury. At the village of Alton, he'd hiked a distance along the Staffordshire Way. He'd driven as many as he could manage of the single lane roads that Nicola favoured. And he'd paused periodically to use the loud hailer in calling her name. Deliberately marking his presence in every location, he'd awakened sheep, farmers, and campers during his eight hours' search for her. At heart, he'd known there was no chance that he would find her, but at least he'd been *doing* something instead of waiting at home by the phone. At the end of it all, he felt anxious and empty. And completely fagged out, with throbbing eyeballs, bruised calves, and a back that ached from the night's exertion.

He was hungry as well. He could have eaten a leg of lamb had one been offered. It was odd, he thought. Just the previous night – wrought up with anticipation and nerves – he'd barely been able to touch his dinner. Indeed, Samantha had been a bit put out at the manner in which he merely picked at her fine sole amandine. She'd taken his lack of appetite personally, and while his father had leered about a man having other appetites to take care of, Sam, and wasn't their Julie about to do just that with we-all-know-who this very night, Samantha had pressed her lips together and cleared the table.

He'd have been able to do justice to one of her table-groaning breakfasts now, Julian thought. But as it was ... Well, it didn't seem right to think about food – let alone to ask for it – despite the fact that the paying guests in Maiden Hall would be tucking into everything from corn flakes to kippers within the half hour.

He needn't have worried about the propriety in hoping for food under the circumstances, however. When he walked into the kitchen of Maiden Hall, a plate of scrambled eggs, mushrooms, and sausage sat untouched before Nan Maiden. She offered it to him the moment she saw him, saying, 'They want me to eat, but I can't. Please take it. I expect you could do with a meal.'

They were the early kitchen staff: two women from the nearby village of Grindleford who cooked in the mornings when the sophisticated culinary efforts of Christian-Louis were as unnecessary as they would be unwanted.

'Bring it with you, Julian.' Nan put a cafetiere on a tray with coffee mugs, milk, and sugar. She led the way into the dining room.

Only one table was occupied. Nan nodded at the couple who'd placed themselves in the bay window overlooking the garden and after politely inquiring about their night's sleep and their day's plans, she joined Julian at the table he'd chosen some distance away by the kitchen door.

The fact that she never wore make-up put Nan at a disadvantage this morning. Her eyes were troughed by blue-grey flesh. Her skin, which was lightly freckled from time spent on her mountain bicycle when she had a free hour in which to exercise, was otherwise completely pallid. Her lips – having long ago lost the natural blush of youth – bore fine lines that began beneath her nose and were ghostly white. She hadn't slept; that much was clear.

She had, however, changed her clothes from the night before, apparently knowing that it would hardly do for the proprietress of Maiden Hall to greet her guests in the morning wearing what she'd worn as their hostess at dinner on the previous night. So her cocktail dress had been replaced by stirrup trousers and a tailored blouse.

She poured them each a cup of coffee and watched as Julian tucked into the eggs and mushrooms. She said, 'Tell me about the engagement. I need something to keep from thinking the worst.' When she spoke, tears caused her eyes to look glazed and unfocused, but she didn't weep.

Julian made himself mirror her control. 'Where's Andy?'

'Not back yet.' She circled her hands round her mug. Her grip was so tight that her fingers – their nails habitually bitten to the quick – were bleached of colour. 'Tell me about the two of you, Julian. Please. Tell me.'

'It's going to be all right,' Julian said. The last thing he wanted to force upon himself was having to concoct a scenario in which he and Nicola fell in love like ordinary human beings, realised that love, and founded upon it a life together. He couldn't face that at the moment. 'She's an experienced hiker. And she didn't go out there unprepared.'

'I know that. But I don't want to think about what it means that she hasn't come home. So tell me about the engagement. Where were you when you asked her? What did you say? What kind of wedding will it be? And when?'

Julian felt a chill at the double direction Nan's thoughts were taking. In either case, they brought up subjects he didn't want to consider. One led him to dwell upon the unthinkable. The other did nothing but encourage more lies.

He went for a truth that both of them knew. 'Nicola's been hiking in the Peaks since you moved from London. Even if she's hurt herself, she knows what to do till help arrives.' He forked up a portion of egg and mushrooms. 'It's lucky that she and I had a date. If we hadn't, God knows when we might've set out to find her.'

Nan looked away, but her eyes were still liquid. She lowered her head.

'We should be hopeful,' Julian went on. 'She's well-equipped. And she doesn't panic when things get dicey. We all know that.'

'But if she's fallen . . . or got lost in one of the caves . . . Julian, it happens. You know that. No matter how well prepared someone is, the worst still happens sometimes.'

'There's nothing that says anything's happened. I only looked in the south part of the White Peak. There're more square miles out there than can be covered by one man in total darkness in an evening. She could be anywhere. She could even have gone to the Dark Peak without our knowing.' He didn't mention the nightmare Mountain Rescue faced whenever someone *did* disappear in the Dark Peak. There was, after all, no mercy in fracturing Nan's tenuous hold on her calm. She knew the reality about the Dark Peak, anyway, and she didn't need him to point out to her that while roads made most of the White Peak accessible, its sister to the north could only be traversed by horseback, on foot, or by helicopter. If a hiker got lost or hurt up there, it generally took bloodhounds to find him.

'She said she'd marry you, though,' Nan declared, more to herself than to Julian, it seemed. 'She *did* say that she'd marry you, Julian?'

The poor woman seemed so eager to be lied to that Julian found himself just as eager to oblige her. 'We hadn't quite *got* to yes or no yet. That's what last night was supposed to be about.'

Nan lifted her coffee with both hands and drank. 'Was she

. . . Did she seem pleased? I only ask because she'd seemed to have . . . Well, she'd seemed to have some sort of plans, and I'm not quite sure . . .'

Carefully Julian speared a mushroom. 'Plans?'

'I'd thought . . . Yes, it seemed so.'

He looked at Nan. Nan looked at him. He was the one to blink. He said steadily, 'Nicola had no plans that I know of, Nan.'

The kitchen door swung open a few inches. The face of one of the Grindleford women appeared in the aperture. She said, 'Mrs Maiden, Mr Britton,' in a low, hushed voice. And she used her head to indicate the direction of the kitchen. *You're wanted*, the motion implied.

Andy was leaning against one of the work tops, facing it, his weight on his hands and his head bowed. When his wife said his name, he looked up.

His face was drawn with exhaustion, and his growth of peppery whiskers fanned out from his moustache and shadowed his cheeks. His grey hair was uncombed, looking windblown although there wasn't any wind to speak of this morning. His eyes went to Nan, then slid away. Julian prepared himself to hear the worst.

'Her car's on the edge of Calder Moor,' Andy told them.

His wife drew her hands into a fist at her breast. 'Thank *God*,' she said.

Still, Andy didn't look at her. His expression indicated that thanks were premature. He knew what Julian knew and what Nan herself might well have acknowledged had she paused to probe for the possibilities that were indicated by the location of Nicola's Saab. Calder Moor was vast. It began just west of the road stretching between Blackwell and Brough, and it comprised endless expanses of heather and gorse, four caverns, numerous cairns and forts and barrows spanning time from Paleolithic through Iron Age, gritstone outcroppings and limestone caves and fissures through which more than one foolish tripper had crawled for adventure and become hopelessly stuck. Julian knew that Andy was thinking of this as he stood in the kitchen at the end of his long night's search for Nicola. But Andy was thinking something else as well. Andy was *knowing* something else, in fact. That much was evident from the manner in which he straightened and began slapping the knuckles of one hand against the heel of the other.

Julian said, 'Andy, for God's sake, *tell* us.'

Andy's gaze fixed on his wife. 'The car's not on the verge, like you'd think it should be.'

'Then where ... ?'

'It's out of sight behind a wall, on the road out of Sparrowpit.'

'But that's good, isn't it?' Nan said eagerly. 'If she went camping, she wouldn't want to leave the Saab on the road. Not where it could be seen by someone who might break into it.'

'True,' he said. 'But the car's not alone.' And with a glance towards Julian as if he wished to apologise for something, 'There's a motorcycle with it.'

'Someone out for a hike,' Julian said.

'At this hour?' Andy shook his head. 'It was wet from the night. As wet as her car. It's been there just as long.'

Nan eagerly said, 'Then she didn't go onto the moor alone? She met someone there?'

'Or she was followed,' Julian added quietly.

'I'm calling the police,' Andy said. 'They'll want to bring in Mountain Rescue now.'

When a patient died, it was Phoebe Neill's habit to turn to the land for comfort. She generally did this alone. She'd lived alone for most of her life, and she wasn't afraid of solitude. And in the combination of solitude and a return to the land, she received consolation. When she was out in nature, nothing manmade stood between her and the Great Creator. Thus on the land, she was able to align herself with the end of a life and the will of God, knowing that the body we inhabit is but a shell that binds us for a period of temporal experience prior to our entering the world of the spirit for the next phase of our development.

This Thursday morning things were different, though. Yes, a patient had died on the previous evening. Yes, Phoebe Neill turned to the land for solace. But on this occasion, she hadn't come alone. She'd brought with her a mixed breed dog of uncertain lineage, the now-orphaned pet of the young man whose life had just ended.

She'd been the one to talk Stephen Fairbrook into getting a dog as a companion during the last year of his illness. So when it had become clear that the end of Stephen's life was fast approaching, she knew that she'd make his passing easier if she reassured him about the dog's fate. 'Stevie, when the time comes, I'm happy to take Benbow,' she'd told him one morning as she bathed his skeletal body and massaged lotion into his shrunken limbs. 'You're not to worry about him. All right?'

You can die now was what went unspoken. Not because words like *die* or *death* were unmentionable round Stephen Fairbrook, but because once he'd been told his disease, been through countless treatments and drugs in an effort to stay alive long enough for a cure to be found, watched his weight decline and his hair fall out and his skin bloom with bruises that turned into sores, *die* and *death* were old companions to him. He didn't need a formal introduction to guests who were already dwelling within his house.

On the last afternoon of his master's life Benbow had known Stephen was passing. And hour after hour, the animal lay quietly next to him, moving only if Stephen moved, his muzzle resting in Stephen's hand until Stephen had left them. Benbow, in fact, had known before Phoebe that Stephen was gone. He'd risen, whimpered, howled once, and was silent. He'd then sought out the comfort of his basket, where he'd stayed until Phoebe had collected him.

Now he raised himself on his hind legs, his plumed tail wagging hopefully as Phoebe parked her car in a lay-by near a drystone wall and reached for his lead. He barked once. Phoebe smiled. 'Yes. A walk shall make us right as rain, old chap.'

She clambered out. Benbow followed, leaping agilely from the Vauxhall and sniffing eagerly, nose pressed to the sandy ground like a canine Hoover. He led Phoebe directly to the wall and snuffled along it until he came to the stile that would allow him access to the moor beyond. This he leapt over easily, and once on the other side he paused to shake himself off. His ears pricked up and he cocked his head. He gave a sharp bark to tell Phoebe that a solo run, not a walk on a lead, was what he had in mind.

'Can't do it, old boy,' Phoebe told him. 'Not till we see what's what and who's who on the moor, all right?' She was cautious and overprotective that way, which made for excellent skills when it came to nursing the house-bound dying through their final days, particularly those whose conditions required hyper-vigilance on the part of their care giver. But when it came to children or to dog ownership, Phoebe knew intuitively that the natural hovering born of a cautious nature would have produced a fearful animal or a rebellious child. So she'd had no child – although she'd had her opportunities – and she'd had no dog till now. 'I hope to do right by you, Benbow,' she told the mongrel. He lifted his head to look at her, past the scraggly kelp-coloured mop of fur that flopped into his eyes. He swung back round towards the open moor, mile after mile of heather creating a purple shawl that covered the shoulders of the land.

Had the moor consisted of heather alone, Phoebe would not have given a second thought to letting Benbow have his romp unrestrained. But the seemingly endless flow of the heather was deceptive to the uninitiated. Ancient limestone quarries produced unexpected lacunae in the landscape, into which the dog could tumble, and the caverns, lead mines, and caves into which he could scamper – and where she could not follow – served as a siren enticement for any animal, an enticement with which Phoebe Neill didn't care to compete. But she was willing to let Benbow snuffle freely through one of the many birch copses that grew in irregular clumps on the moor, rising like feathers against the sky, and she grasped his lead firmly and began heading northwest where the largest of the copses grew.

It was a fine morning, but there were no other walkers about yet. The sun was low in the eastern sky, and Phoebe's shadow stretched far to her left as if it wished to pursue a cobalt horizon that was heaped with clouds so white they might have been giant sleeping swans. There was little wind, just enough of a breeze to slap Phoebe's windcheater against her sides and flip Benbow's tangled fur from his eyes. There was no scent on this breeze that Phoebe could discern. And the only noise came from an unkindness of ravens somewhere on the moor and a flock of sheep bleating in the distance.

Benbow snuffled along, investigating nasally every inch of the path as well as the mounds of heather that edged it. He was a cooperative walker, as Phoebe had discovered from the thrice-daily strolls she and he had taken once Stephen had been completely confined to bed. And because she didn't have to tug him along or pull him back or encourage the little dog in any way, their jaunt on the moor gave her time to pray.

She didn't pray for Stephen Fairbrook. She knew that Stephen was now at peace, quite beyond the necessity of an intervention – Divine or otherwise – in the process of the inevitable. What she prayed for was greater understanding. She wanted to know why a scourge had come to dwell among them, felling the best, the brightest, and frequently those with the most to offer. She wanted to know what conclusion she was meant to draw from the deaths of young men who were guilty of nothing, of the deaths of children whose crime was to be born of infected mothers, and of the deaths of those unfortunate mothers as well.

When Benbow wanted to pick up the pace, she was willing to do so. In this manner, they strode into the heart of the moor, ambling along one path, forking off onto another. Phoebe wasn't worried about becoming lost. She knew that they'd begun their walk southeast of a limestone outcrop that was called Agricola's Throne. It was the remains of a great Roman fort, a windswept outlook shaped not unlike an enormous chair that marked the edge of the moor. It towered above a valley of pastures, villages, and derelict mills, and anyone sighting off the throne during a hike was unlikely to get lost.

They'd been trekking for an hour when Benbow's ears pricked up and his stance altered. From shuffling along happily, he came to a sudden halt. His body elongated, back legs stretching out. His feathery tail stiffened into an immobile quill. A low whine issued from his throat.

Phoebe studied what lay before them: the copse of birches she'd intended to allow Benbow to gambol in. 'Gracious me,' she murmured. 'Aren't you the clever one, Bennie?' She was deeply surprised and just as deeply touched by the mongrel's ability to read her intentions. She'd silently promised him freedom when they reached the copse. And here the copse was. He read her mind and was eager to be off the lead. 'Can't blame you a bit,' Phoebe said as she knelt to unhook the lead from his collar. She wound the rope of braided leather round her hand and rose with a grunt as the dog shot ahead of her into the trees.

Phoebe walked after him, smiling at the sight of his compact body bouncing along the path. He used his feet like springs as he ran, bounding off the ground with all four legs at once as if it were his intention to fly. He skirted a large column of roughly hewn limestone on the edge of the copse and vanished among the birches.

This was the entrance to Nine Sisters' Henge, a Neolithic earth-banked enclosure that encircled nine standing stones of varying heights. Assembled some thirty-five hundred years before the time of Christ, the henge and the stones marked a spot for rituals engaged in by prehistoric man. At the time of its use, the henge had been standing in open land that had been cleared of its natural oak and alder forest. Now, however, it was hidden from view, buried within a thick growth of birches, a modern encroachment on the resulting moorland.

Phoebe paused and surveyed her surroundings. The eastern sky – without the clouds of the west – allowed the sun to pierce unimpeded through the trees. Their bark was the white of a seagull's wing, but patterned with diamond-shaped cracks the colour of coffee. Leaves formed a shimmering green screen in the morning breeze, which served to shield the ancient stone circle within the copse from an inexperienced hiker who didn't know it was there. Standing before the birches, the sentry stone was hit by the light at an oblique angle. This deepened its natural pocking, and from a distance the shadows combined to effect a face, an austere custodian of secrets too ancient to be imagined.

As Phoebe observed the stone, an unaccountable chill passed through her. Despite the breeze, it was silent here. No noise from the dog, no bleating of a sheep lost among the stones, no call of hikers as they crossed the moor. It was altogether too silent, Phoebe thought. And she found herself glancing round uneasily, overcome by the feeling that she was being watched.

Phoebe thought herself a practical woman, one not given to casual fancies or an imagination run riot with ghosties and ghoulies and things that go bump in the night. Nonetheless, she felt the sudden need to be away from this place, and she called for the dog. There was no response.

'Benbow!' she called a second time. 'Here, boy. *Come.*'

Nothing. The silence intensified. The breeze stilled. And Phoebe felt the hair stirring on the back of her neck.

She didn't wish to approach the copse, but she didn't know why. She'd walked among the Nine Sisters before. She'd even had a quiet picnic lunch there one fine spring day. But there was something about the place this morning . . .

A sharp bark from Benbow and suddenly what seemed like hundreds of ravens took to the air in an ebony swarm. For a moment they entirely blocked out the sun. The shadow they cast seemed like a monstrous fist sweeping over Phoebe. She shuddered at the distinct sensation of having been marked somehow, like Cain before being sent to the east.

She swallowed and turned back to the copse. There was no further sound from Benbow, no response to her calling. Concerned, Phoebe hurried along the path, passed the limestone guardian of that sacred place, and entered the trees.

They grew thickly, but visitors to the site had trod a path through them over the years. On this, the natural grass of the moor had been flattened and worn through to the earth in spots. To the sides, however, bilberry bushes formed part of the undergrowth, and the last of the wild purple orchids gave off their characteristic scent of cats in the tough moor grass. It was here beneath the trees that Phoebe looked for Benbow, drawing nearer to the ancient stones. The silence round her was so profound that the very fact of it seemed like an augur, mute but eloquent all at once.

Then, as Phoebe drew near the circle's boundary, she finally heard the dog again. He yelped from somewhere, then emitted something between a whine and a growl. It was decidedly fearful. Worried that he'd encountered a hiker who was less than welcoming of his canine advances, Phoebe hastened towards the sound, through the remaining trees and into the circle.

At once, she saw a mound of bright blue at the inner base of

45

one of the standing stones. It was at this mound that Benbow barked, backing off from it now with his hackles up and his ears flattened back against his skull.

'What is it?' Phoebe asked, over his noise. 'What've you found, old boy?' Uneasily, she wiped her palms on her skirt and glanced about. She saw the answer to her question lying round her. What the dog had found was a scene of chaos. The centre of the stone circle was strewn with white feathers, and the detritus of some thoughtless campers lay scattered about: everything from a tent to a cooking pot to an opened rucksack spilling its contents onto the ground.

Phoebe approached the dog through this clutter. She wanted to get Benbow back on the lead and get both of them out of the circle at once.

She said, 'Benbow, come here,' and he yelped more loudly. It was the sort of sound she'd never heard from him before.

She saw that he was clearly upset by the mound of blue, the source of the white feathers that dusted the clearing like the wings of slaughtered moths.

It was a sleeping bag, she realised. And it was from this bag that the feathers had come, because a slash in the nylon that served as its cover spat more white feathers when Phoebe touched the bag with her toe. Indeed, nearly all the feathers that constituted its stuffing were gone. What remained was like a tarpaulin. It had been completely unzipped and it was shrouding something, something that terrified the little dog.

Phoebe felt weak-kneed, but she made herself do it. She lifted the cover. Benbow backed off, giving her a clear look at the nightmare vignette that the sleeping bag had covered.

Blood. There was more in front of her than she'd ever seen before. It wasn't bright red because it had obviously been exposed to air for a good number of hours. But Phoebe didn't require that colour to know what she was looking at.

'Oh my Lord.' She went light-headed.

She'd seen death before in many guises, but none had been

as grisly as this. At her feet, a young man lay curled like a foetus, dressed head-to-toe in nothing but black, with that same colour puckering burnt flesh from eye to jaw on one side of his face. His cropped hair was black as well, as was the pony tail that sprang from his skull. His goatee was black. His fingernails were black. He wore an onyx ring and an earring of black. The only colour that offered relief from the black – aside from the sleeping bag of blue – was the magenta of blood, and that was everywhere: on the ground beneath him, saturating his clothes, pooling from scores of wounds on his torso.

Phoebe dropped the sleeping bag and backed away from the body. She felt hot. She felt cold. She knew that she was about to faint. She chided herself for her lack of backbone. She said, 'Benbow?' and over her voice, she heard the dog barking. She realised that he'd never stopped. But four of her senses had deadened with shock, heightening and honing her fifth sense: sight.

She scooped up the dog and stumbled from the horror.

The day had altered completely by the time the police arrived. In the way of weather in the Peaks, a morning that had been born into sunshine and perfect sky had reached its maturity in fog. It slithered over the distant crest of Kinder Scout, creeping across the high moors from the northwest. When the Buxton police set up their crime scene tape, they did it with the mist falling on their shoulders like spirits descending to visit the site.

Before he went out to join the scenes of crime team, Detective Inspector Peter Hanken had a word with the woman who'd come upon the body. She was sitting in the back of a panda car, a dog on her lap. Hanken normally liked dogs a great deal: He was the master of two Irish setters who were almost as much his pride and joy as were his three children. But this pathetic-looking mongrel with his unkempt coat of mangy fur and his sludge-coloured eyes looked a likely candidate for the dog-meat factory. And he smelled like a dustbin left in the sun.

Not that there was any sun, which lowered Hanken's spirits even further. On every side of him, he encountered grey – in the sky, on the landscape, and in the grizzled hair of the old woman before him – and grey had long had the capability of sinking his ship faster than the realisation of what a murder investigation was going to do to his weekend plans.

Over the top of the car Hanken said to Patty Stewart – a WPC with a heart-shaped face and breasts that had long been the objects of fantasy for half a dozen of the younger DCs – 'Name?'

Stewart filled in all the blanks in her typical competent manner. 'Phoebe Neill. She's a home nurse. From Sheffield.'

'What the hell was she doing out here?'

'Her patient died yesterday evening. She took it hard. She brought his dog out here for a walk. It helps, she said.'

Hanken had seen plenty of death in his years of policing. And in his experience, nothing helped. He slapped his palm against the roof of the car and opened the door, saying to Stewart, 'Get on with it, then.' He slid inside.

'Is it Miss or Missus?' he said after introducing himself to the home nurse.

The dog strained forward against her hands, which she'd placed on his chest just above his legs. She held him in position firmly. She said, 'He's friendly. If you'd just let him smell your hand . . .,' and she added, 'Miss,' when Hanken obliged.

He excavated the particulars from her, trying to ignore the mongrel's rank odour. When he was satisfied that she'd seen no other sign of life besides the ravens who'd fled the scene like the marauders they were, he said, 'You didn't disturb the area?' and narrowed his eyes when she flushed.

'I know what's appropriate in the situation. One does watch police dramas on the television occasionally. But, you see, I

didn't *know* there would be a body beneath the blanket . . .
only it wasn't a blanket at all, was it? It was a sleeping bag
that'd been slashed to bits. And as there was rubbish all round
the site, I suppose that I—'

'Rubbish?' Hanken interrupted impatiently.

'Papers. Camping things. Lot of white feathers. There were
bits and pieces everywhere.' The woman smiled with a pitiful
eagerness to please.

'You didn't disturb anything, did you?' Hanken asked.

No. Of course, she hadn't done that. Except for the sleeping
bag. Which was where the body was. Beneath the bag. As she'd
just said . . .

Right, right, right, Hanken thought. She was a real Aunt
Edna. This was probably the most excitement she'd had in
her life and she was determined to prolong the experience.

'And when I saw it . . . him . . .' She blinked as if afraid to
cry and recognising, correctly, how little stock Hanken put
in women who shed tears. 'I believe in God, you know, in a
greater purpose behind all that happens. But when someone
dies in such a way, it tests my faith. It really does.' She lowered
her face to Benbow's head. The dog squirmed round and licked
her nose.

Hanken asked her what she needed, if she wanted a WPC
to take her home. He told her that there would likely be more
questions. She was not to leave the country. If she travelled
from Sheffield, she was to let him know where she could be
reached. Not that he thought he'd need her again. But there
were some parts of his job that he did by rote.

The actual murder site was irritatingly remote and inac-
cessible by any means other than foot, mountain bike, or
helicopter. Given these options, Hanken had called in a few
favours at Mountain Rescue and had managed to hijack an
RAF chopper that was just concluding a search for two lost
hikers in the Dark Peak. He used the waiting helicopter now,
to ferry himself to Nine Sisters' Henge.

The fog wasn't heavy – just wet as the dickens – and when they made their approach, he could see the popped lightning of flash bulbs as the police photographer documented the crime scene. To the southeast of the trees, a small crowd milled. Forensic pathologist and forensic biologists, uniformed constables, evidence officers equipped with collection kits, they were waiting for the photographer to finish his work. They were also waiting for Hanken.

The DI asked the helicopter's pilot to hover above the birch copse for a minute prior to landing. From two hundred and fifty feet above the ground – sufficient distance so as not to disturb the evidence – he saw that a campsite had been set up within the perimeter of the old stone circle. A small blue tent domed against the northern face of one stone, and a fire ring burned black like the pupil of an eye in the circle's centre. On the ground lay a silver emergency blanket and nearby a square sit mat coloured bright yellow. A black and red rucksack spat out its contents, and a small camping cook stove tumbled onto its side. From the air, it didn't look like the nasty piece of business that it was, Hanken thought. But distance did that to you, giving a false assurance that all was well.

The chopper set him down fifty yards to the southeast of the site. He ducked beneath the blades and joined his team on the ground as the police photographer strode out of the copse. He said, 'Ugly mess.'

Hanken said, 'Right,' and 'Wait here,' to the team. He slapped his hand against the limestone sentry marking the entrance to the copse, and alone he started down the path beneath the trees where the leaves dripped condensation from the fog onto his shoulders.

At the entrance to Nine Sisters' proper, Hanken paused and let his gaze roam where it would. From the ground now, he saw that the tent was a size suitable for one, and that fact was in keeping with the rest of the gear scattered round the circle: one sleeping bag, one rucksack, one emergency blanket, a single sit mat. What he hadn't seen from the air he saw now. A map case gaped open with its contents half torn. A single ground sheet crumpled against the solitary rucksack. One small hiking boot toppled into the charred remains of the central fire and another lay nearby discarded. White feathers clung wetly to everything.

When at last he moved from the entrance, Hanken engaged in his usual preliminary observation of a crime scene: He stood over each noticeable physical item and considered it, with his mind clear of possible explanations. Most officers, he knew, went directly to the body. But it was his belief that the sight of a body – brought to its death through human brutality – was traumatic enough to deaden not only the senses but also the intellect, leaving one incapable of seeing the truth when it lay openly before him. So he went from one object to the next, studying it without disturbing it. And thus he made his initial examination of the tent, the rucksack, the mat, the map case, and the rest of the equipment – from socks to soap – that was tossed round in the inside of the circle. He took the most time over a flannel shirt and the boots. And when he'd seen enough of these objects, he turned to the body.

It was one of the more gruesome corpses in his experience, a boy of not more than nineteen or twenty. He was thin, almost skeletal, with delicate wrists, dainty ears, and the wax-like skin of the dead. Although one side of his face was badly burnt, Hanken could still tell that the boy had a finely bridged nose and a well-shaped mouth and an overall appearance of femininity that he seemed to have tried to alter by growing a wispy black goatee. He was drenched with blood from numerous wounds, and beneath the mess he wore only a black T-shirt, with no pullover or jacket of any kind. His jeans had faded from black to grey in spots where the wearing was most apparent: along the seams, the knees, and in the seat. And he wore heavy boots on his overlarge feet, Doc Marten's by the look of them.

Beneath these boots, half-hidden now by the sleeping bag that had been carefully moved to one side by the police photographer in order to document the body, a few sheets of paper lay stained with blood and limp with fog-born condensation. Crouching, Hanken examined these, separating them carefully with the tip of a pencil, which he removed from his pocket. The papers, he saw, were common anonymous letters, crudely written, creatively spelled, and assembled with letters and words cut from newspapers and magazines. Thematically they were all of a piece: They threatened death, although the means that were suggested differed each time.

Hanken directed his gaze from these papers to the boy on the ground. He wondered if it was reasonable to conclude that the recipient of them had met the end augured by the messages left at the scene. The deduction would have seemed reasonable had not the interior of the old stone circle told another tale entirely.

Hanken strode out of it, along the path beneath the birches.

'Start a perimeter search,' he told his team. 'We're looking for a second body.'

Chapter Three

———————◆———————

Now Scotland Yard's Barbara Havers took the lift up to the twelfth floor of Tower Block. This housed the extensive library of the Metropolitan Police, and, among the scores of reference books and police reports, she knew that she would be safe. She very much needed safety at the moment. She also needed privacy and time to recover.

In addition to more volumes than anyone had time to count – much less look at – the library offered the finest view of London in the entire building. This view spread to the east, encompassing everything from the neo-Gothic spires of the Houses of Parliament to the south bank of the River Thames. It spread to the north, where the dome of St Paul's dominated the City skyline. And on a day like this one, when the bright hot sunlight of summer was finally altering to the subtle glow of autumn, the sheer scope of the view became secondary to the beauty of everything touched by that light.

Here on the twelfth floor, Barbara thought that if she concentrated on identifying as many of the buildings below her as she could, she might be able to calm herself and forget the humiliation through which she'd just lived.

After three months' suspension from work, she'd finally received a cryptic phone call at half past seven that Thursday morning. It was an order thinly disguised as a request.

Would Detective Sergeant Barbara Havers join Assistant Commissioner Sir David Hillier in his office at ten a.m.? The voice was scrupulously polite and even more scrupulously careful to betray no knowledge of what lay behind the invitation.

Barbara, however, had little doubt about the purpose of the meeting. She'd been the object of an enquiry by the Police Complaints Authority for the last twelve weeks, and once the Crown Prosecution Service had declined to instigate legal proceedings against her, the machinery of the Metropolitan Police's internal affairs division had begun to grind. Witnesses to her behaviour had been called. Statements from those witnesses had been taken. Evidence – a high-powered motor boat, one MP5 carbine and a Glock semiautomatic pistol – had been examined and evaluated. And Barbara's fate had long been due to be revealed.

So when the phone call had finally come, interrupting her increasingly fitful sleep, she should have been prepared. After all, she had known all summer that two aspects of her behaviour as an officer were under scrutiny. Facing criminal charges of assault and attempted murder, facing disciplinary charges that ran the gamut from abuse of authority to failure to obey an order, she should have begun the process of putting her professional life in order prior to what anyone with a teaspoonful of sense would have called its ineluctable demise. But police work had been Barbara's life for a decade and a half, and she couldn't imagine her world without it. So she had spent her suspension telling herself that every day that passed without her being sacked made it more likely that she would emerge from the investigation unscathed. That hadn't been the case, of course, and a more realistic officer would have known what to expect when she walked into the Assistant Commissioner's office.

She'd dressed with care, eschewing her usual drawstring trousers for a skirt and jacket. She was hopeless with clothes, so the colour didn't suit her, and the *faux* pearl necklace was a ludicrous touch that merely emphasised the thickness of her neck. Her shoes, at least, were polished. But getting out of her old Mini in the Yard's underground car park, she'd scraped her calf on a rough edge of door metal and a ladder in her tights had been the result.

Not that perfect tights, a decent piece of jewellery, and a suit of a hue more flattering to her complexion would have altered the inevitable. Because as soon as she'd entered AC Hillier's office, with its four windows indicating the Olympian heights to which he'd risen, she'd seen the writing on the wall.

Still, she hadn't expected the castigation to be so vitupera-tive. AC Hillier was a pig – always had been and always would be – but Barbara had never before been on the receiving end of his brand of discipline. He'd seemed to feel that a vigorous upbraiding wasn't sufficient to relay his displeasure with her comportment. Nor was sufficient a blistering letter that utilised such terms as 'disgracing the reputation of the entire Metro-politan Police' and 'bringing the service of thousands of officers into disrepute' and 'a disgraceful brand of insubordination unlike anything in the history of the force', which would be placed in her permanent file and left there through the years for every officer with suzerainty over Barbara to see. AC Hillier had also felt the need to interject his personal commentary on the activities that had brought about her suspension. And knowing that, without witnesses, he could be as free as he wanted to reprimand Barbara in whatever language he chose, Hillier had included in that commentary the sort of risky invective and innuendo that another subordinate officer – with less at stake – might well have taken as crossing over the line that separated the professional from the personal. But the assistant commissioner was nobody's fool. He was perfectly aware that, thankful her punishment did not include being sacked, Barbara would adopt the wise course of action and take whatever he chose to dish out to her.

But she didn't have to like hearing herself referred to as

a 'bloody stupid slag' and a 'sodding minge bag'. And she didn't have to pretend that she was unaffected by having her physical appearance, her sexual proclivities, and her potential as a woman brought into Hillier's ugly monologue.

So she was shaken. And as she stood by the window in the library and observed the buildings that rose between New Scotland Yard and Westminster Abbey, she tried to control the trembling of her hands. She also tried to eliminate the waves of nausea that kept causing her breath to come in great gulps, as if she were drowning.

A cigarette would have helped, but in coming to the library where she wouldn't be found, she'd also come to one of the many locations in New Scotland Yard where smoking was prohibited. And while at one time she would have lit up anyway and damned the consequences, she wouldn't do that now.

'Once more out of order and you're finished,' Hillier had shouted in conclusion, his florid face grown as maroon as the tie that he wore with his bespoke suit.

That she hadn't been finished already – considering the level of Hillier's animosity – was a mystery to Barbara. Throughout his speech, she'd prepared herself for her inevitable sacking, but it hadn't materialised. She'd been dressed down, slagged off, and vilified. But the peroration of Hillier's remarks hadn't included her termination. That Hillier wanted to sack her as much as he wanted to abuse her was clear as could be. That he didn't do so told her that someone of influence had taken her part.

Barbara wanted to be grateful. Indeed, she knew she ought to be grateful. But at the moment all that she could feel was a monumental sense of betrayal that her superior officers, the disciplinary tribunal, and the Police Complaints Authority hadn't seen things her way. When the facts are in, she'd thought, everyone would see that she'd had no choice but to take up the nearest weapon to hand and fire it in order to save a life. But that wasn't the way her actions had been viewed by those in power. Except for someone. And she had a fairly good idea who that someone was.

Detective Inspector Thomas Lynley had been on his honeymoon during the birth of Barbara's troubles. Her longtime partner, he'd come home with his bride from ten days in Corfu to find Barbara on suspension and an investigation being mounted into her conduct. Understandably confounded, he'd driven across town that same night, seeking an explanation from Barbara herself. While their initial conversation hadn't gone as smoothly as she would have wished, Barbara had known at heart that, at the end of the day, DI Lynley would never stand by and let an injustice be done if there was any way that he could prevent it.

He'd be waiting in his office now to hear about her meeting with Hillier. As soon as she recovered from that meeting, she'd go to see him.

Someone came into the quiet library. A woman said, 'I'm telling you he was born in Glasgow, Bob. I remember the case because I was at the comprehensive and we were doing reports on current events.'

Bob replied, 'You're daft. He was born in Edinburgh.'

The woman said, 'Glasgow. I'll prove it.'

Proving it meant having a browse through the library. *Proving it* meant that Barbara's solitude was at an end.

She left the library and descended by the stairs, buying more time to recover and to come up with the words to thank Inspector Lynley for interceding. She couldn't imagine how he'd done it. He and Hillier were at each other's throats most of the time, so he must have asked a favour of someone above Hiller's head. She knew that doing so would have cost him dearly in professional pride. A man like Lynley wasn't used to going cap in hand, to anyone. Going cap in hand to those who openly begrudged him his aristocratic birth would have been especially trying.

She found him in his office in Victoria Block. He was on the phone with his back to the door, his chair swung round to face the window. He was saying lightly, 'Darling, if Aunt Augusta's declared that a visit's in order, I don't know how we can actually avoid it. It's rather like trying to stop a typhoon . . . Hmm, yes. But we should be able to keep her from rearranging the furniture if Mother's agreed to come with her, shouldn't we?' He listened, then laughed at something his wife said on the other end of the line. 'Yes. All right. We'll announce the wardrobes off-limits in advance . . . Thank you, Helen . . . Yes. She does mean well.' He rang off and swivelled his chair to face his desk. He saw Barbara in the doorway.

'Havers,' he said, surprise in his tone. 'Hullo. What're you doing here this morning?'

She entered, saying, 'I had the word from Hillier.'

'And?'

'A letter in my file and quarter of an hour's speech that I'd like to forget. Cast your thoughts to Hillier's propensity for seizing the moment and throttling it and you'll have a good idea of how things played out. He's a flamer, our Dave.'

'I'm sorry,' Lynley said. 'But that was all? A lecture and a letter in your file?'

'Not all. I've been demoted to detective constable.'

'Ah.' Lynley reached for a magnetic container of paper clips sitting on his desk. Restlessly, his fingers explored the tops of the clips while he apparently gathered his thoughts. He said, 'It could have been worse. Far worse, Barbara. It could have cost you everything.'

'Right. Yes. I know.' Barbara tried to sound expansive. 'Well, Hillier had his fun. No doubt he'll replay his speech for the big boys at lunch with the commissioner. I thought about telling him to screw himself about half way through, but I held my tongue. You would've been proud of me.'

At this, Lynley moved his chair away from the desk and stood at the window, looking out at its indifferent view of Tower

Block. Barbara saw a muscle move in his jaw. She was about to venture into the arena of gratitude – his uncharacteristic reserve suggested the price he'd paid interceding on her behalf – when he finally spoke, introducing the topic himself by saying, 'Barbara, I'm wondering if you know what had to be gone through to keep you from getting the sack. The meetings, the phone calls, the agreements, the compromises.'

'I reckoned as much. Which is why I wanted to say—'

'And all of it to keep you from getting what half Scotland Yard think you richly deserve.'

Barbara shifted uncomfortably on her feet. 'Sir, I know you put yourself out for me. I know I would have been given the sack if you hadn't interceded. And I just wanted to tell you how grateful I am that you recognised my actions for what they were. I wanted to tell you that you won't have any reason to regret taking my part. I won't give you a reason. Or anyone else, for that matter. I won't give anyone a reason.'

'I wasn't the one,' Lynley said, turning back to her.

Barbara looked at him blankly. 'You . . . ? What?'

'I didn't take your part, Barbara.' To his credit after making the admission, he kept his eyes on hers. She would think of that later and grudgingly admire it. Those brown eyes of his – so kind and so at odds with his head of blond hair – settled on hers and just stayed there, openly.

Barbara frowned, trying to assimilate what he'd said. 'But you . . . you know all the facts. I told you the story. You read the report. I thought . . . You said just now the meetings and the phone calls—'

'They weren't mine,' he cut in. 'In conscience, I can't let you think that they were.'

So she'd been incorrect. She'd jumped to a conclusion. She'd presumed their years of partnership meant that Lynley would automatically take her part. She said, 'Are you with them, then?'

'Them? Who?'

'The half of the Yard that thinks I got what I deserve. I only ask because I s'pose we ought to know where we stand with each other. I mean if we're going to work—' Her words were starting to tumble together, and she forced herself to slow down, to be deliberate. 'So are you? With them? That half? Sir?'

Lynley went back to his desk and sat. He regarded her. She could easily read the regret on his face. She just couldn't tell where it was directed. And that frightened her. Because he was her partner. He *was* her partner. She said again, 'Sir?'

He said, 'I don't know if I'm with them.'

She felt deflated, Just a shrivelled bit of her skin remained, lying there on the office floor.

Lynley must have read this because he continued, his voice not unkind. 'I've looked at the situation from every angle. All summer long, I've examined it, Barbara.'

'That's not part of your job,' she told him numbly. 'You investigate murders, not . . . not what I did.'

'I know that. But I wanted to understand. I still want to understand. I thought if I went at it on my own, I could see how it happened, through your eyes.'

'But you couldn't manage that.' Barbara tried to keep the desolation from her voice. 'You couldn't see that a life was at stake. You couldn't get your mind round the fact that I wasn't able to let an eight year old drown.'

'That's not the case,' Lynley told her. 'I understood that much and I understand it now. What I couldn't get round was that you were out of your jurisdiction, and, given an order to—'

'So was she,' Barbara broke in. 'So was everyone. The Essex police don't patrol the North Sea. And that's where it happened. You know that. On the sea.'

'I do know that. All of it. Believe me, I know. How you were chasing a suspect, how that suspect dropped a child from his boat, what you were ordered to do when he took that action, and how you reacted when you heard the order.'

'I couldn't just toss her a life belt, Inspector. It wouldn't have reached her. She would have drowned.'

'Barbara, please hear me out. It wasn't your place – or your responsibility – to make decisions or reach conclusions. That's why we have a chain of command. Arguing about the order you'd been given would have been bad enough. But once you fired a weapon at a superior officer—'

'I expect you're afraid I'll do that to you next, given half a chance,' she said bitterly.

Lynley let the words hang there between them. In the silence, Barbara found herself wanting to reach into the air and unspeak them, so untrue did she know them to be. 'Sorry,' she said, feeling that the huskiness in her voice was a worse betrayal than any action she herself had taken towards anyone else.

'I know,' he said. 'I do know you're sorry. I'm sorry as well.'

'Detective Inspector Lynley?'

The quiet interruption came from the door. Lynley and Barbara swung to the voice. Dorothea Harriman, secretary to their divisional superintendent, stood there: well-coifed with a helmet of honey blonde hair, well-dressed in a pin-striped suit that would have done service in a fashion advert. Barbara all at once felt what she always was in the presence of Dorothea Harriman, a sartorial nightmare.

'What is it, Dee?' Lynley asked the younger woman.

'Superintendent Webberly,' Harriman replied. 'He's asked for you. As soon as you can make it. He's had a call from Crime Operations. Something's come up.' And with a glance and a nod at Barbara, she was gone.

Barbara waited. She found that her pulse had begun throbbing painfully. The request from Webberly couldn't have come at a worse time.

Something's come up was Harriman shorthand for the fact that the game was afoot. And in the past that summons from Webberly had generally preceded an invitation from the inspector to accompany him in his discovery of what the game was.

Barbara said nothing. She just watched Lynley and waited. She knew very well that the next few moments would constitute the stand he took on their partnership.

Outside his office, business went on as usual. Voices echoed in the lino-floored corridor. Telephones rang in departments. Meetings began. But here, inside, it seemed to Barbara as if she and Lynley had taken themselves into another dimension altogether, one into which much more than merely her professional future was tied.

He finally got to his feet. He said, 'I'll need to see what Webberly has going.'

She said, 'Shall I . . . ?' despite his use of the singular pronoun that had already said it all. But she found that she couldn't complete the question because she couldn't face the answer at the moment. So she asked another. 'What would you like me to do, sir?'

He thought about it, looking away from her at last, seeming to study the picture that hung by the door: a laughing young man with a cricket bat in his hand and a long rip in his grass-stained trousers. Barbara knew why Lynley kept the photo in his office: It served as a daily reminder of the man in the photo and what Lynley had done to him on a long ago drunken night in a car. Most people put what was unpleasant out of their minds. But DI Thomas Lynley didn't happen to be most people.

He said, 'I think it's best that you lie low for a while, Barbara. Let the dust settle. Let people get past this. Let them forget.'

But you won't be able to, will you, she asked silently. What she said, however, was a bleak, 'Yes, sir.'

'I know that isn't easy for you,' he said, and his voice was so gentle that she wanted to howl. 'But I haven't got any other answer to give you at the moment. I only wish that I had.'

And again, the few words she could manage were, 'Sir. I see. Yes sir.'

'Demotion to detective constable,' Lynley said to Superintendent Malcolm Webberly when he joined him. 'That's thanks to you, isn't it, sir?'

Webberly was ensconced behind his desk, smoking a cigar. Mercifully, he'd kept the door to his office closed to spare the other officers, the secretaries, and the clerks from the fumes emanating from the noxious tube of tobacco. This consideration, however, did little to deliver anyone who had to enter from experiencing and breathing the fug of smoke. Lynley tried to inhale as little as possible. Webberly used his lips and tongue to move the cigar from one side of his mouth to the other. It was the only response he gave.

'Can you tell me why?' Lynley asked. 'You've gone out on a limb for officers before. No one knows that better than I. But why in this case, when it seems so cut and dried? And what're you going to have to pay for having saved her?'

'We all have favours,' the superintendent said. 'I called a few in. Havers was in the wrong, but her heart was in the right.'

Lynley frowned. He'd been trying to work himself round to this same conclusion from the moment he'd learned about Barbara Havers' disgrace, but he hadn't been able to manage the feat. Every time he came close, the facts reared up at him, demanding acknowledgment. And he'd gathered a number of those facts himself, driving out to Essex to talk to the principal officer involved. Having talked to her, he couldn't understand how – let alone why – Webberly was able to condone Barbara Havers' decision to fire a rifle at DCI Emily Barlow. Disregarding his own friendship with Havers, even disregarding the very basic issue of chain of command, weren't they responsible for asking what sort of professional mayhem they were encouraging if they failed to punish a member of the force who'd taken part in such an egregious action? 'But to *shoot* at an officer . . . Even to pick up a rifle in the first place when she had no authority . . .'

Webberly sighed. 'These things just aren't black and white, Tommy. I wish they were, but they never are. The child involved—'

'The DCI ordered a life belt thrown to her.'

'Right. But there was doubt as to whether the girl could swim. And beyond that . . .' Webberly removed the cigar from his mouth and examined its tip as he said, 'She's someone's only child. Evidently, Havers knew it.'

And Lynley knew what that fact meant to his superintendent. Webberly himself had a single light in his life: his one daughter Miranda. He said, 'Barbara owes you on this one, sir.'

'I'll see that she pays.' Webberly nodded at a yellow pad that lay before him on the desk. Lynley glanced at it to see the superintendent's scribbling rendered in black felt-tip pen. Webberly said, 'Andrew Maiden. D'you remember him?'

At the question – the name – Lynley sat in a chair near Webberly's desk and said, 'Andy? Of course. I'd not be likely to forget him.'

'I thought not.'

'One operation in SO10 and I made a hash of it. What a nightmare that was.'

SO10 was the Crime Operations Group, the most secret and secretive collection of officers in the Met. They were responsible for hostage negotiation, witness and jury protection, the organisation of informants, and undercover operations. Lynley had once aimed to work among them in the latter group. But at twenty-six years old, he hadn't possessed either the sangfroid or the performance ability to adopt a persona other than his own. 'Months of preparation went straight down the drain,' he recalled. 'I expected Andy to string me up.'

Andy Maiden hadn't done so, however. That wasn't his

style. The SO10 officer was a man who knew how to cut his losses and that's what he'd done, not assigning blame where it was owed but instead matching his moves to the moment's need: He quickly withdrew his officers from the undercover operation and waited for another opportunity to introduce them, months later, when he could join them and assure that no outrageous *faux pas* such as Lynley's could undermine their efforts again.

He'd been called Domino – Andy Maiden – so adept had he been at assuming the character of everyone from hit men to American backers of the IRA. His primary field had ultimately become drug operations, but before he arrived there, he made his mark in murder for hire and organised crime as well.

'I used to run into him from time to time on the fourth floor,' Lynley told Webberly. 'But I lost track of him once he left the Met. That was ... when? Ten years ago?'

'Just over nine.'

Maiden, Webberly said, had taken early retirement and moved his family to Derbyshire. In the Peaks, he'd poured his life savings and his energy into the renovation of an old hunting lodge. It was a country hotel now, called Maiden Hall. Quite the spot for walkers, holiday-makers, mountain bikers, or anyone looking for an evening out and a decent meal.

Webberly referred to his yellow pad. 'Andy Maiden brought more louts to justice than anyone else in SO10, Tommy.'

'It doesn't surprise me to hear that, sir.'

'Yes. Well. He's asking for our help, and we owe him.'

'What's happened?'

'His daughter was murdered in the Peaks. Twenty-five years old and some bastard left her in the middle of nowhere in a place called Calder Moor.'

'Christ. That's rough. I'm sorry to hear it.'

'There was a second body as well – a boy's – and no one knows who the devil he is. No i.d. on him. The girl – Nicola – had gone out hiking and camping and she was geared up for the works: rain, fog, sun, or anything else. But the boy at the site hadn't got any gear at all.'

'Do we know how they died?'

'No word on that.' And when Lynley raised an eyebrow in surprise, Webberly said, 'This is coming our way via SO10. Name the time those bastards made fast and loose with their information.'

Lynley couldn't do so. Webberly went on.

'What I know is this: Buxton CID's got the case, but Andy's asking for more and we're giving it to him. He's asked for you, in particular.'

'Me?'

'That's right. You may have lost track of him over the years, but it seems he hasn't lost track of you.' Webberly plugged his cigar into his mouth, clamping it into the corner and referring to his notes. 'A Home Office pathologist is on his way up there for a formal by-the-books with scalpel and recorder. He's set to do the autopsy sometime today. You'll be on the patch of a bloke called Peter Hanken. He's been told that Andy's one of us, but that's all he knows.' He removed the cigar from his mouth again and looked at it instead of Lynley as he concluded, 'Tommy, I'll make no pretence about this. It could turn dicey. The fact that Maiden's asked for you by name . . .' Webberly hesitated before finishing with, 'Just keep your eyes open and move with caution.'

Lynley nodded. The situation was irregular. He couldn't remember another time when a relative of the victim of a crime had been allowed to name the officer who would investigate it. That Andy Maiden had been allowed to do so suggested spheres of influence that could easily encroach upon Lynley's efforts to manage a smooth investigation.

He couldn't handle the case alone, and Lynley knew that Webberly wouldn't expect him to do so. But he had a fairly good idea of what officer the superintendent, given half the chance, would assign as his partner. He spoke to circumvent that assignment. She wasn't ready yet. Neither – if it came down to it – was he.

'I'd like to see who's on duty to take with me,' he told Webberly. 'Since Andy's a former SO10 officer, we're going to want someone with a fair amount of finesse.'

The superintendent regarded him directly. Fifteen long seconds ticked by before he spoke. 'You know best who you can work with, Tommy,' he finally said.

'Thank you, sir,' Lynley said. 'I do.'

Barbara Havers made her way to the fourth floor canteen, where she bought a bowl of vegetable soup which she took to a table and tried to eat while all the time imagining that the word *pariah* hung from her shoulders on a sandwich board. She ate alone. Every nod of recognition she received from other officers seemed imbued with a silent message of contempt. And while she tried to bolster herself with an interior monologue informing her shrinking ego that no one could possibly yet know of her demotion, her disgrace, and the dissolution of her partnership, every conversation going on round her – particularly those flavoured by light-hearted laughter – was a conversation mocking her.

She gave up on the soup. She gave up on the Yard. She signed herself out – 'going home ill' would doubtless be welcomed by those who clearly saw her as a form of contagion anyway – and made her way to her Mini. One half of her was ascribing her actions to a mixture of paranoia and stupidity. The other half was trapped in an endless repetition of her final encounter with Lynley, playing the game of what-I-could-have-would-have-and-should-have-said after learning the outcome of his meeting with Webberly.

In this frame of mind, she found herself driving along Millbank before she knew what she was doing, not heading for home at all. Her body on automatic pilot, she came up to Grosvenor Road and the Battersea Power Station with her brain engaged in a mental castigation of DI Lynley. How easy it had been for him to cut her loose, she thought bitterly. And what an idiot she had been, believing for weeks that he was on her side.

Obviously, it hadn't been enough for Lynley that she'd been demoted, upbraided, and humiliated by a man whom both of them had loathed for years. It seemed now that he'd also needed an opportunity to do some disciplining of his own. As far as she was concerned, he was wrong wrong *wrong* taking the direction he'd chosen. And she needed an ally straightaway who would agree with her point of view.

Spinning along the River Thames in the light midday traffic, she had a fairly good idea where to find just such a confederate. He lived in Chelsea, little more than a mile from where she was driving.

Simon St James was Lynley's oldest friend, his schoolmate from Eton. A forensic scientist and an expert witness, he was regularly called upon by defence lawyers as well as Crown Prosecutors to bolster one side or the other of a criminal case that was relying on evidence rather than eyewitnesses to win a conviction. Unlike Lynley, he was a reasonable man. He had the ability to stand back and observe, disinterested and dispassionate, without becoming personally embroiled in whatever situation was roiling round him. He was exactly the person she needed to talk to. *He'd* see Lynley's actions for what they were.

What Barbara didn't consider in the midst of her turbulent mental gymnastics was that St James might not be alone in his house in Chelsea's Cheyne Row. However, the fact that his wife was also at home – working in the dark room that adjoined his own top floor laboratory – didn't make the situation nearly as delicate as did the presence of St James's regular assistant. And Barbara didn't know that St James's regular assistant was there until she was climbing the stairs behind Joseph Cotter: father-in-law, housekeeper, cook, and general factotum to the scientist himself.

Cotter said, 'All three of them's at work, but it's time to break for lunch and Lady Helen, for one, 'll be glad of the diversion. Likes her meals regular, always 'as done. No change there, married or not.'

Barbara hesitated on the second floor landing, saying, 'Helen's here?'

'She is.' Cotter added with a smile, ''S nice to know some things's the same as ever, isn't it?'

'Damn,' Barbara muttered under her breath.

For Helen was the Countess of Asherton, titled in her own right, but also the wife of Thomas Lynley who – although he made no bones about preferring it otherwise – was the other half of the Asherton equation: the official, belted, velvet-and-ermine-clad Earl. Barbara could hardly expect St James and his wife to join her in a round of denigration doo-dah with the wife of the object of denigration in the room. She realised that retreat was in order.

She was about to beat a hasty one when Helen came onto the top floor landing, laughing over her shoulder into the lab as she said, 'All right, all right. I'll fetch a new roll. But if you'd claw your way into the current decade and replace that machine with something more up to date, we wouldn't be out of fax paper at all. You'd think you'd notice these things occasionally, Simon.' She turned away from the door, began to come down the stairs, and spied Barbara on the landing below her. Her face lit up. It was a lovely face, not beautiful in any conventional sense, but tranquil and radiant, framed by a smooth fall of chestnut hair.

'My Lord, what a wonderful surprise! Simon. Deborah. Here's a visitor for us, so you'll absolutely have to break for lunch now. How *are* you, Barbara? Why haven't you called round in all these weeks?'

There was nothing for it but to join her. Barbara nodded her thanks to Cotter, who called up, 'I'll lay another place at the table, then,' in the general direction of the lab and headed back down the way they'd come. Barbara climbed upwards and took Helen's extended hand. The handshake turned into a swift kiss on the cheek, a welcome so warm that Barbara knew Lynley hadn't yet contacted his wife about what had occurred at Scotland Yard that day.

Helen said, 'This is brilliant timing. You've just saved me from a slog down the King's Road in search of fax paper. I'm famished, but you know Simon. Why stop for anything as incidental as a meal when one has the opportunity to slave for a few more hours? Simon, detach yourself from the microscope, please. Here's someone more interesting than fingernail scrapings.'

Barbara followed Helen into the lab where St James regularly evaluated evidence, prepared reports as well as professional papers, and organised materials for his recently acquired position as a lecturer at the Royal College of Science. Today he appeared to be in expert witness mode because he was perched on a stool at one of the work tables, and he was assembling slides from the contents of an envelope that he'd unsealed. The aforementioned fingernail scrapings, Barbara thought.

St James was a largely unattractive man, no longer the laughing cricket player but disabled now and hampered by a leg brace that made his movements awkward. His best features were his hair, which he always wore overlong with complete disregard for whatever current fashion dictated, and his eyes, which changed from grey to blue depending on his clothing, which was itself nondescript. He looked up from the microscope as Barbara entered the lab. His smile humanised a lined and angular face.

'Barbara. Hullo.' He eased himself off the stool and came across the room to greet her, calling out to his wife that Havers had joined them. At the far end of the room, a door swung open. In cut off blue jeans and a olive T-shirt, St James's wife stood beneath a line of photographic enlargements that hung from a cord running the length of the darkroom and dripped water onto the rubber-matted floor.

Deborah looked quite well, Barbara noted. Renewing her commitment to her art – instead of brooding and mourning the string of miscarriages that had plagued her marriage – obviously agreed with her. It was nice to think of something going well for someone.

Barbara said, 'Hullo. I was in the area and . . .' She glanced at her wrist to see that she'd forgotten her watch at home that morning, in her haste to get to the Yard for her meeting with Hillier. She dropped her arm. 'Actually, I didn't think about what time it was. Lunch and everything. Sorry.'

'We were about to stop,' St James told her. 'You can join us for a meal.'

Helen laughed. '"About to stop?" What outrageous casuistry. I've been begging for food these last ninety minutes and you wouldn't consider it.'

Deborah looked at her blankly. 'What time *is* it, Helen?'

'You're as bad as Simon,' was Helen's dry reply.

'You'll join us?' St James asked Barbara.

'I just had something,' she said. 'At the Yard.'

All three of the others knew what that last phrase meant. Barbara could see the underlying connotation register on their faces. It was Deborah who said, 'Then you've finally had word,' as she poured chemicals from their trays into large plastic bottles that she took from a shelf beneath her photographic enlarger. 'That's why you've come, isn't it? What happened? No. Don't explain yet. Something tells me you could do with a drink. Why don't the three of you go downstairs? Give me ten minutes to clean up here and I'll join you.'

Downstairs meant Simon's study, and that's where St James took Barbara and Helen, with Barbara wishing that Helen and not Deborah had been the one to stay above and continue working. She thought about denying that her visit to Chelsea had anything to do with the Yard, but she realised that her tone of voice had probably given her away. There was certainly nothing buoyant about it.

An old drinks trolley stood beneath the window that overlooked Cheyne Row and St James poured them each a sherry as Barbara made much of inspecting the wall on which Deborah always hung a changing display of her photographs. Today these were more of the suite she'd been working on for the last nine months: oversize enlargements of Polaroid portraits taken in locations like Covent Garden, Lincoln's Inn Fields, St Botolph's Church, and Spitalfields Market.

'Is Deborah going to show them?' Barbara asked, gripping the sherry she'd been given and stalling for time. She nodded towards the pictures.

'In December.' St James handed Helen her sherry. She slid out of her shoes and sat in one of the two leather chairs by the fireplace, drawing her slender legs underneath her. She was, Barbara noted, watching her steadily. Helen read people the way other people read books. 'So what's happened?' St James was saying as Barbara wandered from the photo wall to the window and looked out at the narrow street. There was nothing to hold her attention there: just a tree, a row of parked cars, and a line of houses, two of which were currently fronted by scaffolding. Barbara wished she'd gone into *that* line of work. Considering how frequently it was employed in everything from gentrification projects to washing windows, erecting scaffolding as a career would have kept her busy, out of trouble, and extremely well-oiled with lolly.

'Barbara?' St James said. 'Have you heard something from the Yard this morning?'

She turned from the window. 'A letter in my file and demotion,' she replied.

St James grimaced. 'Are you back on the street, then?'

Which had happened to her once before in what felt like another lifetime. She said, 'Not quite,' and went on to explain, leaving out the nastier details of her meeting with Hillier and mentioning Lynley not at all.

Helen did it for her. 'Does Tommy know? Have you seen him yet, Barbara?'

Which brings us to the point, Barbara thought morosely. She said, 'Well. Yes. The inspector knows.'

A fine line appeared between Helen's eyes. She placed her glass on the table next to her chair. 'I'm getting a bad feeling about what's happened.'

Barbara was surprised at her own response to the quiet sympathy in Helen's voice. Her throat tightened. She felt herself reacting as she might have reacted in Lynley's office that morning had she not been so stunned when he'd returned from his meeting with Webberly and explained that he was setting out on a case. It wasn't the fact of his assignment to a case that struck her momentarily wordless and emotionless, however. It was the choice he'd made of a partner to accompany him, a partner who was not herself.

'Barbara, this is for the best,' he'd told her, gathering materials from his desk.

And she'd gulped down what she wanted to say in protest and stared at him, realising that she'd never known him before that moment.

'He doesn't seem to agree with the outcome of the internal investigation,' Barbara concluded her story for St James and Helen. 'Demotion and all. I don't think he believes I've been punished enough.'

'I'm so sorry,' Helen said. 'You must feel as if you've lost your best friend.'

The authenticity of her compassion burned against the back of Barbara's eyelids. She hadn't expected Helen – of all people – to be the source. So deeply did it touch her to have the surprising sympathy of Lynley's wife that she heard herself stammering, 'It's just that his choice . . . To replace me with . . . I mean . . .' She fumbled for the words and instead encountered that rush of pain all over again. 'It felt like such a slap in the face.'

All Lynley had done, of course, was to make a selection among the officers available to work with him on an investigation. That his choice was itself a wound to Barbara wasn't a problem he was required to address.

Detective Constable Winston Nkata had done a fine job on two cases in town on which he'd worked with both Barbara and Lynley. It wasn't unreasonable that the DC would be offered an opportunity to demonstrate his talents outside London on the sort of special assignment that had previously gone to Barbara herself. But Lynley couldn't have been blind to the fact that Barbara saw Nkata as the competition nipping at her heels at the Yard. Eight years her junior, twelve years younger than the inspector, and more ambitious than either Lynley or Barbara had ever been. He was a self-starter, a man who anticipated orders before they were spoken and seemed to fulfil them with one hand tied behind his back. Barbara had long suspected him of showboating for Lynley, trying to outdo her own efforts in order to replace her at the inspector's side.

Lynley knew this. He *had* to know it. So his choice of Nkata seemed an instance of outright in-your-face cruelty.

'Is this Tommy in a temper?' St James asked.

But it hadn't been anger behind Lynley's actions, and desolate as she was, Barbara wouldn't accuse him of that.

Deborah joined them then, saying, 'What's happened?' and fondly kissing her husband on the cheek as she passed him and poured herself a small sherry.

The story was repeated, Barbara telling it, St James adding details, and Helen listening in thoughtful silence. Like Lynley, the others were in possession of the facts connected to Barbara's professional insubordination and her assault on a superior officer. Unlike Lynley, however, they appeared capable of seeing the situation as Barbara herself had seen it: unavoidable, regrettable, but fully justified, the only course open to a woman who was simultaneously under pressure and in the right.

St James even went so far as to say, 'Tommy'll doubtless come round to your way of thinking at the end of the day, Barbara. It's rough that you have to go through this, though.' And the other two women murmured their agreement.

All of this should have been intensely gratifying to Barbara. After all, their sympathy was what she'd come to Chelsea in order to gather. But she found that their sympathy merely inflamed her pain and the sense of betrayal that had driven her to Chelsea in the first place. She said, 'I guess it boils down to this: The inspector wants someone he knows he can trust to work with him.'

And no matter the ensuing protests of Lynley's wife and Lynley's friends, Barbara knew she was not, at the present time, anywhere close to being that someone.

Chapter Four

❧━━━━◆━━━━❧

Julian Britton could picture exactly what his cousin was doing on the other end of the telephone line. He could hear a steady *thwack thwack thwack* punctuating her sentences, and that sound told him that she was in the old, ill-lit kitchen of Broughton Manor, chopping up some of the vegetables that she grew at the bottom of one of the gardens.

'I didn't say that I was unwilling to help you out, Julian.' Samantha's comment was accompanied by a *thwack* that sounded more decisive than the earlier ones. 'I merely asked what's going on.'

He didn't want to reply. He didn't want to tell her what was going on: Samantha, after all, had never made a secret of her aversion for Nicola Maiden.

So what could he say? Little enough. By the time the police in Buxton had made the assessment that it might behoove them to phone the force headquarters in Ripley, by the time Ripley had sent two panda cars to examine the location in which Nicola's Saab and an old Triumph motorcycle were parked, and by the time Ripley and Buxton in conjunction reached the obvious conclusion that Mountain Rescue was needed, an old woman on a morning stroll with her dog had stumbled into the hamlet of Peak Forest, pounded on a door, and told a tale about a body she'd come across in the ring of Nine Sisters' Henge.

The police had gone straight there, leaving Mountain Rescue waiting at their meeting point for further directions. When those directions came, they were ominous enough: Mountain Rescue would not be needed.

Julian knew all this because as a member of Mountain Rescue, he'd gone to his team's rendezvous site once the call had come through – passed along that morning by Samantha who intercepted it at Broughton Manor in his absence. So he was standing among the members of his team, checking his equipment as the leader read from a dog-eared checklist, when the mobile phone rang and the equipment check was first interrupted and then cancelled altogether. The team leader passed on the information he was given – the old woman, her dog, their morning walk, the body, Nine Sisters' Henge.

Julian had returned immediately to Maiden Hall, wanting to be the one to break the news to Andy and Nan before they heard it from the police. He intended to say that it was only a body after all. There was nothing to indicate that the body was Nicola's.

But when he arrived, there was a panda car drawn up to the front of the hunting lodge. And when he dashed inside, it was to find Andy and Nan in a corner of the lounge where the diamond panes of a large bay window cast miniature rainbows against the wall. They were in the company of a uniformed constable. Their faces were ashen. Nan was holding onto Andy's arm, her fingers creating deep indentations in the sleeve of his plaid flannel shirt. Andy was staring down at the coffee table between them and the constable.

All three of them looked up when Julian entered. The constable spoke. 'Excuse me, sir. But if you could give Mr and Mrs Maiden a few minutes . . .'

Julian realised that the constable assumed he was one of the guests at Maiden Hall. Nan clarified his relationship to the family, identifying him as 'my daughter's fiancé. They've only just become engaged. Come, Julian,' and she extended a hand to him and drew him down onto the sofa so that the three of them sat together as the family they were not and could now never be.

The constable had just got to the unsettling part. A female body had been found on the moor. It might be the Maidens' missing daughter. He was sorry, but one of them was going to have to accompany him to Buxton to make an identification.

'Let me go,' Julian had said impulsively. It felt inconceivable that either of Nicola's parents would have to be subjected to the grisly task. Indeed, it felt inconceivable that the identification of Nicola's body should fall to anyone but himself: the man who loved her, wanted her, and tried to make a difference in her life.

The constable said regretfully that it had to be a member of the family. When Julian offered to go along with Andy, Andy demurred. Someone needed to stay with Nan, he said. And to his wife, 'I'll phone from Buxton, if . . . if.'

He'd been as good as his word. It had taken several hours for the call to come through, owing to the time involved in getting the body from the moor to the hospital where the postmortems would be performed. But when he'd seen the young woman's corpse, he'd phoned.

Nan hadn't collapsed as Julian thought she might do. She'd said, 'Oh no,' shoved the phone at Julian, and run from the lodge.

Julian had spoken to Andy only long enough to hear from his own mouth what Julian already knew to be the fact. Then he'd gone after Nicola's mother. He found her on her knees in Christian-Louis's herb garden behind the Maiden Hall kitchen. She was scraping up handfuls of the freshly watered earth, mounding them round her as if she wished to bury herself. She was saying, 'No. No', but she wasn't weeping.

She fought to break loose when Julian put his hands on her shoulders and began to lift her to her feet. He'd never suspected how strong such a small woman could be and he'd had to shout for help from the kitchen. Both of the Grindleford women had come running. Together with Julian, they'd managed to get Nan back into the lodge and up the staff stairs. With their help, Julian got her to drink two shots of brandy. And it was at this point that she began to weep.

'I must do . . .' she cried. 'Give me something to *do*.' The last word rose on a chilling wail.

Julian was aware of being out of his depth. She needed a doctor. He went to phone one. He could have left it to the Grindleford duo. But making the decision to call in a doctor got him out of Nan and Andy's bedroom, a space suddenly so close and confined that Julian felt in another minute he would be unable to breathe.

So he'd descended the stairs and commandeered the telephone. He rang for a doctor. And then, finally, he rang Broughton Manor and spoke to his cousin.

Whether they were appropriate or not, her questions were logical. He'd failed to come home on the previous night, as his unusual absence at breakfast had no doubt telegraphed to his cousin. It was now midday. He was asking her to take on one of his responsibilities. Naturally, she would want to know what had occurred to spur him to behaviour as uncharacteristic as it was mysterious.

Still, he didn't want to tell her. Talking to her about Nicola's death was something he couldn't do at the moment. So he said, 'There's been an emergency at Maiden Hall, Sam. I need to hang about. So will you see to the puppies?'

'What sort of emergency?'

'Sam . . . Come on. Will you do me this favour?' His prize harrier Cass had recently whelped, and the puppies as well as their dam needed to be monitored. The temperature of the kennel needed to be kept constant. The puppies needed to be weighed and their manner of nursing needed to be noted in the book.

Sam knew the routine. She'd watched him perform it often

enough. She'd even helped him on occasion. So it wasn't as if he was asking her to perform the impossible or even, for that fact, the unusual or the unknown. But it was becoming clear that she wasn't going to accommodate him without being told why she was being asked to do so.

He settled on saying, 'Nicola's gone missing. Her mum and dad are in a state. I need to be here.'

'What d'you mean "gone missing"?' *Thwack* served as punctuation. She would be standing at the wooden work top beneath the kitchen's ceiling-high single window, where generations of knives cutting up vegetables had worn a shallow trough into the oak.

'She's disappeared. She went hiking on Tuesday. She didn't turn up last night when she was supposed to.'

'More likely that she met up with someone,' Samantha announced in that practical way of hers. 'Summer's not over yet. There're thousands of people still hiking in the Peaks. How could she have gone missing, anyway? Didn't the two of you have a date?'

'That's just the point,' Julian said. 'We did have a date, and she wasn't here when I came to fetch her.'

'Hardly out of character,' Samantha pointed out.

Which made him wish she were standing in front of him so that he could slap her freckled face.

She must have heard how close he was to breaking. She said, 'I'm sorry. I'll do it. I'll do it. Which dog?'

'The only one with new puppies at the moment. Cass.'

'All right.' Another *thwack*. 'What shall I tell your father?'

'There's no need to tell him anything,' Julian said. The last thing he wanted was Jeremy Britton's thoughts on the topic.

'Well, I take it you won't be back for lunch?' The question was tinged with that particular tone that bordered on accusation: a blend of impatience, disappointment and anger. 'Your dad is bound to ask why, Julie.'

'Tell him I was called out on a rescue.'

'In the middle of the night? A mountain rescue hardly explains your absence at the breakfast table.'

'If Dad was hung over – which, as you've noticed, is usually the case – then I doubt my absence at breakfast was noted. If he's in any condition to realise I'm not there at lunch, tell him Mountain Rescue called me out mid-morning.'

'How? If you weren't here to take the call—'

'Jesus, Samantha. Would you *stop* splitting hairs? I don't care what you tell him. Just see to the harriers, all right?'

The *thwacking* ceased. Samantha's voice altered. Its sharpness dissipated and left in its place were apology, hollowness, and hurt. 'I'm just trying to do what's best for the family.'

'I know. I'm sorry. You're a brick and we wouldn't be able to cope without you. *I* wouldn't be able to cope.'

'I'm always glad to do what I can.'

So do *this* without making a bloody court case out of it, he thought. But all he said was, 'The record book for the dogs is in the top drawer of my desk. That's the desk in the office, not in the library.'

'The library desk's been sold at auction,' she reminded him. He received the underlying message this time: The Britton family's financial condition was a perilous one; did Julian truly wish to jeopardise it further by committing his time and his energy to anything other than the rehabilitation of Broughton Manor?

'Yes. Of course. Whatever,' Julian said. 'Go easy with Cass. She's going to be protective of the litter.'

'I expect she knows me well enough by now.'

Do we ever know anyone? Julian wondered. He rang off. Shortly thereafter the doctor arrived. He wanted to give Nan Maiden a sedative, but she wouldn't allow it. Not if it meant leaving Andy to face the first terrible hours of loss alone. So the doctor wrote out a prescription instead, which one of the Grindleford women set off to have filled in Hathersage, where the nearest chemist was. Julian and the second Grindleford woman remained, to hold the fort at Maiden Hall.

It was, at best, an effort patched together with Sellotape. There were residents wanting lunch as well as non-residents who'd seen the restaurant sign on the gorge road and had innocently followed the winding drive upward in the hope of having a decent meal. The serving girls had no experience in the kitchen and the housekeeping staff had the rooms to attend to. So it was left to Julian and his companion from Grindleford to see to what Andy and Nan Maiden usually did themselves: sandwiches, soup, fresh fruit, smoked salmon, paté, salads . . . Julian knew within five minutes that he was out of his depth and it was only when a suggestion that Christian-Louis might be called in supervened upon Julian's dropping a plate of smoked salmon that he realised there was an alternative to trying to captain the ship alone.

Christian-Louis arrived in a flurry of incomprehensible French. He unceremoniously threw everyone out of his kitchen. A quarter of an hour later, Andy Maiden returned. His pallor was marked, worse than before.

'Nan?' he asked Julian.

'Upstairs,' Julian said. He tried to read the answer before he asked the question. He asked it anyway. 'What can you tell me?'

Andy's answer was to turn, to begin heavily climbing the stairs. Julian followed.

The older man didn't go directly to the bedroom he shared with his wife. Instead, he went to the cubicle next to it, a part of the attic that had been fashioned into a lair-like study. There, he sat at an old mahogany desk. It was fitted with a secretaire drawer, which he pulled out and lowered into a writing surface. He was taking a scroll from one of its three cubicles when Nan joined them.

No one had been able to prevail on her to wash or to change, so her hands were filthy and the knees of her trousers were caked with earth. Her hair was tangled as if she'd been pulling at it by the fistful.

'What?' she said. 'Tell me, Andy. What happened?'

Andy smoothed the scroll against the secretaire drawer's unfolded writing surface. He weighed down the top end with a Bible. The bottom end he held in place with his left arm.

'Andy?' Nan said again. 'Tell me. Say something.'

He reached for a rubber. It was stubby and marked with the blackened remains of hundreds of erasures. He bent over the scroll. And when he moved, Julian was able to see the contents of the scroll.

It was a family tree. At the top were printed the names *Maiden* and *Llewelyn* and the date 1722. At the bottom were the names *Andrew, Josephine, Mark,* and *Philip*. With them were the names of their spouses and below that their issue. There was only a single name beneath those of Andrew and Nancy Maiden, although space for Nicola's spouse had been provided and three small lines branching beneath Nicola's name indicated Andy's hopes for the future of his immediate family. He cleared his throat. For a moment, he appeared to be regarding the genealogy in front of him. Or perhaps he was only garnering courage. For in the next moment he erased those over-sanguine marks reserved for a future generation. And once he'd done that, he picked up a calligraphy pen, dipped it into a bottle of ink, and began to write beneath his daughter's name. He formed two neat parentheses. Inside them, he penned the letter *d*. He followed that with the year.

Nan began to weep.

Julian found that he couldn't breathe.

'A fractured skull,' was all that Andy said.

Detective Inspector Peter Hanken was less than chuffed when his CC at the Buxton nick informed him that New Scotland Yard was sending up a team to assist in the investigation into the Calder Moor deaths. A native of the Peak District, he possessed an inherent distrust of anyone who hailed from south of the Pennines or north of Deer Hill Reservoir. The oldest son of a Wirksworth quarryman, he also possessed an inherent dislike of anyone whom their class-weighted society told him he was supposed to consider his social better. The two officers of the Scotland Yard team thus garnered his double animosity.

One was a DI called Lynley, a bloke tanned and fit and with hair so gold that it had to be courtesy of the nearest bleach bottle. He had an oarsman's shoulders and a posh public school voice. He wore Savile Row, Jermyn Street, and the scent of old money like a second skin. What the hell was he doing in the police force? Hanken wondered.

The other was a black, a detective constable called Winston Nkata. He was as tall as his superior officer, but with a tensile rather than a muscular strength. He had a long facial scar that put Hanken in mind of the manhood ceremonies undertaken by African youths. In fact, aside from his voice that sounded like a curious mixture of African, Caribbean, and South London, he reminded Hanken of a tribal warrior. His air of confidence suggested he'd been through trials by fire and had not been found wanting.

Aside from his own feelings in the matter, Hanken didn't particularly like the message it sent to the rest of his team, having New Scotland Yard involved on their patch. If there was a question about his competence or the competence of his officers, then he would have vastly preferred to be told so to his face. And no matter that having two more bodies in on the action meant he could end up with time to put together Bella's surprise swing set in advance of her fourth birthday next week. He hadn't *asked* his CC for help, and he was more than just a little annoyed to have help thrust upon him.

DI Lynley appeared to take the measure of Hanken's irritation within thirty seconds of meeting him, which somewhat elevated Hanken's opinion of the man, despite his upper ten voice. He said, 'Andy Maiden's asked for our help. That's why we're here, Inspector Hanken. Your CC told you the dead girl's father retired from the Met, didn't he?'

The chief constable had done, but what anyone's working for the Met in his salad days had to do with Hanken's ability to get to the bottom of a crime without assistance was an issue that hadn't yet been clarified. He said, 'I know. Smoke?' And he offered his packet of Marlboros to the other two. Both demurred. The black looked like he'd been offered strychnine. 'My blokes aren't going to like it much, having London breathing and peeing for them.'

'I expect they'll adjust,' Lynley said.

'Not bloody likely.' Hanken lit his fag. He took a deep drag and observed the other two officers over the cigarette.

'They'll follow your lead.'

'Yeah. Like I said.'

Lynley and the black exchanged a look. It said kid glove treatment was called for. What they didn't know was that kid gloves, silk gloves, or chain mail gauntlets wouldn't make a difference to their reception in Hanken's office.

Lynley said, 'Andy Maiden was an SO10 officer. Did your CC tell you that?'

This *was* news. And the mild animosity Hanken had felt towards the London officers was immediately redirected towards his superiors who'd apparently and deliberately kept the information from him.

'You didn't know, did you?' Lynley said. He dryly directed his next comment to Nkata. 'Politics as usual, I expect.'

The DC nodded – his expression disgusted – and crossed his arms. Although Hanken had offered both men chairs when they'd entered his office, the black officer had chosen to stand. He was lounging at the window from which he had a bleak view of the football grounds across Silverlands Street. It was a stadium structure topped by barbed wire. It couldn't have offered a less pleasing prospect.

Lynley said to Hanken, 'Sorry. I can't explain why they hold back information from the officer in charge. It's some sort of power game. I've had it played on me once too often to like it.' He went on to fill in the missing information. Andy Maiden had worked undercover: drugs, organised crime, and contract killings. He'd been highly respected and exemplarily successful during a thirty-year career. 'So the Yard feels an obligation to one of its own,' Lynley finished. 'We're here to fulfil that obligation. We'd like to work as part of a team with you, but Winston and I will stay out of your way as much as possible if that's how you prefer it. It's your case and your patch. We're well aware that we're the interlopers here.'

Each of the statements was graciously made, and Hanken felt a slight de-icing of his attitude towards the other DI. He didn't particularly want to like him, but two deaths and one unidentified body were unusual in this part of the world, and Hanken knew that only a fool would object to having two more minds sorting through the facts in the investigation, especially if both the minds in question were absolutely clear about who was giving the orders and making the assignments in the case. Besides, the SO10 detail was an intriguing one that Hanken was grateful to have passed his way. He needed to ponder it when he had a moment.

He twisted his cigarette down into a spotless ashtray, which he then emptied and cleaned thoroughly with a tissue, as was his custom. He said, 'Come with me, then,' and took the Londoners to the incident room, where two of his uniformed WPCs were at computer terminals – apparently doing nothing save chatting to each other – and a third male constable was making an entry on the china board where Hanken had neatly penned assignments earlier in the day. This last constable nodded and left the room as Hanken walked the Scotland Yard officers over to the china board. Next to it, a large diagram of the murder site was hanging alongside two pictures of the Maiden girl – in life and in death – as well as several pictures of the second – and hitherto unidentified – body, and a line of photos of the murder scene.

Lynley put on a pair of reading spectacles to have a look at these as Hanken introduced him and Nkata to the others in the room. Hanken said to one of the WPCs, 'The computer still down?'

'What else?' was her laconic response.

'Bloody invention,' Hanken muttered. He directed the Londoners' attention specifically to the diagram of Nine Sisters' Henge. He pointed out the spot where the boy's body had been found within the circle. He indicated a second area some distance away from the henge, to the northwest. 'The girl was here,' he said. 'One hundred and fifty-seven yards from the birch copse where the standing stones are. She'd had her head bashed in with a chunk of limestone.'

'What about the boy?' Lynley asked.

'Multiple stab wounds. No weapon left behind. We've done a fingertip search for it but come up cold. I've constables out scouring the moor right now.'

'Were they camping together?'

'They weren't,' Hanken told them. The girl had gone to Calder Moor alone according to her parents, and the facts at the crime scene backed them up. It was apparently her belongings – and here he indicated the photograph that would document his words – that were strewn round the inside of the stone circle. For his part, the boy seemed to have nothing with him aside from the clothes on his back. So it appeared that, setting out from wherever he'd set out, he hadn't intended to join her for his own night under the stars.

'There was no identification on the boy?' Lynley asked. 'My super told me no one can place him.'

'We're running the plates of a motorcycle through the DVLA, a Triumph found near the girl's car behind a wall on the road outside Sparrowpit.' He pointed out this loca- tion, using an ordnance survey map that was unfolded on a desk that abutted the wall holding the china board. 'We've had the bike staked out since the bodies were discovered, but no one's come to claim it. It looks like it probably belongs to the kid. Once our computers are up and running again—'

'They're saying any minute,' one of the WPCs called from across the room.

'Right,' Hanken scoffed, and went on with 'We'll have the registration information from the DVLA.'

'Bike could be stolen,' Nkata murmured.

'Then that'll be on the computer as well.' Hanken fished out his fags and lit another.

One of the women officers said, 'Have a heart, Pete. We're in here all day,' an entreaty which Hanken chose to ignore.

'What are your thoughts so far?' Lynley asked, his inspection of each of the photographs complete.

Hanken rustled under the ordnance survey map for a large manila envelope. Inside were photocopies of the anonymous letters found at the feet of the dead boy. He kept one back, said, 'Have a look at these, then,' and handed the envelope over to Lynley. Nkata joined his superior officer as Lynley began to flip through the letters.

There were eight communications in all, each fashioned from large letters and words that had been clipped from newspapers and magazines and Sellotaped to sheets of plain white paper. The message on each was similar, beginning with YOUR GOING TO DIE SOONER THEN YOU THINK; continuing with HOW DOES IT FEEL TO KNOW YOUR DAYS ARE NUMBERED?; and concluding with WATCH YOUR BACK BECAUSE WHEN YOUR NOT READY FOR IT, I WILL BE THERE AND YOU WILL DIE. THERES NOPLACE TO RUN AND NOPLACE TO HIDE

Lynley read every one of the eight letters before he finally raised his head, removed his glasses, and said, 'Were these found on either of the bodies?'

'Inside the stone circle. Near to the boy, but not on him.'

'They could have been directed to anyone, couldn't they? They may not even be related to the case.'

Hanken nodded. 'My first thought as well. Except they appear to have come from a large envelope that was on the scene. With the name *Nikki* printed straight across it in pencil. And they had blood on them. That's what those dark smears are, by the way: places where our copy machine couldn't register red.'

'Prints?'

Hanken shrugged. 'Lab's going through the exercise.'

Lynley nodded and reconsidered the letters. 'They're threatening enough. But sent to the girl? Why?'

'The why's our motive for murder.'

'Do you see the boy involved?'

'I see some thick yobbo in the wrong place at the worst possible time. He complicated matters, but that's all he did.'

Lynley returned the letters to the envelope and handed the envelope over to Hanken. He said, 'Complicated matters? How?'

'By making it necessary for reinforcements.' Hanken had had the day to evaluate the crime scene, to look over the photographs, to view the evidence, and to develop an idea of the events from what he'd seen. He explained his theory. 'We've got a killer who knows the moors well and who knew exactly where to find the girl. But when he got there, he saw what he hadn't expected to find: She'd got someone with her. He had only one weapon—'

'The missing knife,' Nkata noted.

'Right. So he had one of two choices. Either separate the boy from the girl somehow and knife them one at a time . . .'

'Or bring in a second killer,' Lynley finished. 'Is that what you're thinking?'

It was, Hanken told him. Perhaps the other killer was waiting in the car. Perhaps he – or she – went out to Nine Sisters' Henge in the company of the other. In any case, when it became clear that there were two able-bodied victims to dispose of instead of just one and only a single knife with which to do the job, the second killer was called into action. And the second weapon – a chunk of limestone – was used.

Lynley went back for another look at the pictures and the site plan. He said, 'But why are you marking the girl as the main victim? Why not the boy?'

'Because of this.' Hanken handed over the single sheet of paper that he'd held back from the anonymous letters in anticipation of Lynley's question. Again it was a photocopy. Again, it was taken from another note. This one, however, had been scrawled by hand. THIS BITCH HAS HAD IT snaked across the page, the penultimate word underlined three times.

'Was this found with the others?' Lynley asked.

'It was on her body,' Hanken said. 'Tucked into one of her pockets nice and neat.'

'But why leave the letters after the murders were done? And why leave the note?'

'To send someone a message. That's the usual purpose of notes.'

'I'll accept that for a note on her body. But what about the cut-and-paste letters? Why would someone have left them behind?'

'Consider the condition of the crime scene. There was rubbish everywhere. And it was dark.' Hanken paused to crush out his cigarette. 'The killers wouldn't even have known the letters were there in all the mess. They made a mistake.'

At the other end of the room, the computer finally came to life. One of the WPCs said, 'About time, that,' and began inputting data and waiting for responses. The other constable did likewise, working with the activity sheets and reports that the investigative team had already turned in.

Hanken continued. 'Think about the killer's state of mind, the principal killer that is. He tracks our girl to the stone circle, all set to do the job, only to find her with a companion. He's got to bring in help, which throws him off his stride. The girl manages to run off, which throws him off further. Then the boy puts up a hell of a fight, and the camping site is turned into a shambles. All he's worried about – this is the killer, not our boy – is dispatching the two victims. When the plan doesn't go smoothly, the last thing on his mind is whether the Maiden girl brought his letters with her.'

'Why did she?' Like his superior, Nkata had gone back to look at the crime scene photos. He turned from them now as he spoke. 'To show the boy?'

'There's nothing to indicate that she knew the boy before they died together,' Hanken said. 'The girl's dad saw the boy's body, but he couldn't put a name to him. Had never seen him before, he said. And he knows her friends.'

'Could the boy have killed her?' Lynley asked. 'And then inadvertently become a victim himself afterwards?'

'Not unless my pathologist had the times of death wrong. He puts them both dying within an hour of each other. How likely is it that two completely unrelated killings would occur in a single location on a Tuesday night in September?'

'Yet that's what appears to have happened, isn't it?' Lynley said. He went on to ask where Nicola Maiden's car had been in relation to the stone circle. Had plaster impressions of tyre prints been taken from that location? What about footprints in the circle itself? And the boy's face . . . What did Hanken make of the burns?

Hanken fielded the questions, using the map and the reports that his men had compiled thus far in the case. From the other end of the room, WPC Peggy Hammer – whose countenance had always reminded Hanken of a shovel with freckles – called out, 'Pete, we've got it. Here's the DVLA.' She copied something from her terminal's monitor at the far end of the room.

'The Triumph?' Hanken said.

'Right. Got it.' She handed over a slip of paper.

Hanken read the name and the address of the motorcycle's

owner and when he did so, he realised that the London detectives were going to turn out to be a godsend. For the address he was looking at was in London, and using either Lynley or Nkata to handle the London end of things would save him manpower. In these times of budget cuts, belt tightening, and the sort of fiscal responsibility that made him shout about 'not being a bloody accountant for God's sake', sending someone out on the road was a manoeuvre that had to be defended practically all the way to the House of Lords. Hanken had no time for such nonsense. The Londoners made such nonsense unnecessary.

'The bike,' he told them, 'is registered to someone called Terence Cole.' According to the DVLA in Swansea, this Terence Cole lived in Chart Street in Shoreditch. And if one of the Scotland Yard detectives didn't mind taking on that end of things, he'd send him back to London straightaway to find someone at that address who could make an i.d. of the second body from Nine Sisters' Henge.

Lynley looked at Nkata. 'You'll need to head back immediately,' he said. 'I'll stay. I want a word with Andy Maiden.'

Nkata seemed surprised. 'You don't want London yourself? You'd have to pay me a bundle to stay up here if I was you.'

Hanken glanced from one man to the other. Lynley, he saw, was colouring slightly. This surprised him. Until that moment, the man had seemed utterly unflappable.

'Helen can cope for a few days without me, I expect,' Lynley said.

'No new bride ought to have to do that,' was Nkata's rejoinder. He explained to Hanken that 'the 'Spector got himself married three months ago. He's practically fresh from the honeymoon.'

'That'll do, Winston,' Lynley said.

'Newlywed,' Hanken acknowledged with a nod. 'Cheers.'

'I'm afraid that's quite a moot point,' Lynley replied obscurely.

*   *   *

He wouldn't have said so twenty-four hours earlier. Then, he had been blissful. While there were numerous rough edges of adjustment that had to be smoothed as he and Helen established their life together, nothing they had come across so far had seemed so scabrous that it couldn't be levelled through discussion, negotiation, and compromise. Until the Havers situation had come along, that is.

In the months since their return from the honeymoon, Helen had maintained a discreet distance from Lynley's professional life, and she'd merely said, 'Tommy, there must be an explanation,' when he'd returned from his only visit to Barbara Havers and reported the facts behind her suspension. After that moment, Helen had kept her own counsel, relaying telephone messages from Havers and others interested in the situation but always remaining an objective presence whose loyalty to her husband was beyond question. Or so Lynley had assumed the case to be.

His wife had disabused him of the notion when she'd returned from the St James house earlier that day. He'd been packing for the journey to Derbyshire, tossing some shirts into a suitcase and rooting out an old waxed jacket and hiking boots for using on the moors, when Helen had joined him. In a departure from her usual more oblique manner of addressing herself to a delicate subject, she'd taken the bull by the horns, saying, 'Tommy, why've you chosen Winston Nkata rather than Barbara Havers to work this case with you?'

He said, 'Ah. You've spoken to Barbara, I see,' to which she replied, 'And she practically defended you, although the poor woman's heart was clearly breaking.'

'Do you want me to defend myself as well?' he'd asked mildly. 'Barbara needs to keep her head down at the Yard for a while. Taking her along to Derbyshire wouldn't have accomplished that. Winston's the logical choice if Barbara's unavailable.'

Elizabeth George

'But, Tommy, she adores you. Oh, don't look at me that way. You know what I mean. You can do no wrong in Barbara's eyes.'

He'd placed his last shirt into the suitcase, stuffed his shaving gear in among his socks, closed the case, and draped his jacket on top of it. He'd faced his wife. 'Are you here as her intermediary, then?'

'Please don't patronise me, Tommy. I hate it.'

He'd sighed. He didn't want to be at odds with his wife and he thought fleetingly of the compromises one made in attaching another life to one's own. We meet, he told himself, we want, we pursue, and we obtain. But he wondered if the man existed who, caught up in the heat of desire, still managed to consider whether he could possibly *live* with the object of his passion before he was actually doing so. He doubted it.

He said, 'Helen, it's a miracle that Barbara still has her job, considering the charges she was facing. Webberly went to the wall for her and God only knows what he had to promise, give up, or compromise on in order to keep her in CID. At the moment, she ought to be thanking her lucky stars that she wasn't sacked. What she shouldn't be doing is looking for support in a grievance against me. And, frankly, the last person on earth she should be trying to set against me is my own wife.'

'That's not what she's doing!'

'No?'

'She came to see Simon, not me. She didn't even know I was there. When she saw me, she wanted to turn tail and run. And she would have done had I not stopped her. She needed someone to talk to. She felt terrible, and she needed a friend, which is what you always used to be in her life. What I want to know is why you're not being a friend to her now.'

'Helen, this isn't about friendship. There's no place for friendship in a situation in which everything depends on an

94

officer obeying an order. Barbara didn't do that. And what's worse, she nearly killed someone in the process.'

'But you know what happened. How can you not see—'

'What I see is that there's a purpose to a chain of command.'

'She saved a *life*.'

'And it wasn't her place to determine that life was in danger.'

His wife had moved towards him then, coming to grasp one of the posts at the end of their bed. She said, 'I don't understand this. How can you be so unforgiving? She'd be the first person to forgive you anything.'

'In the same circumstances, I wouldn't expect it. She shouldn't have expected as much of me.'

'You've bent the rules before. You've told me so.'

'You can't think attempted murder is bending the rules, Helen. It's a criminal act. For which, by the way, most people go to prison.'

'And for which, in this case, you've decided to be judge, jury, and executioner. Yes. I see.'

'Do you?' He was beginning to get angry and he should have held his tongue. Why was it, he wondered, that Helen could rattle his cage in ways no one else ever could? 'Then I'll ask you to see this as well. Barbara Havers doesn't concern you. Her behaviour in Essex, the subsequent investigation, and whatever medicine she's asked to swallow as a result of that behaviour and investigation are none of your business. If you're finding your life so circumscribed these days that you need to champion a cause to keep yourself busy, you might consider aligning yourself with me. To be honest, I'd appreciate coming home to support and not to subversion.'

She was as quick to anger as was he and just as capable of expressing it. 'I'm not that sort of woman. I'm not that sort of wife. If you wanted an obsequious sycophant to marry—'

'That's tautology,' he'd said.

And that terse statement finished their argument. Helen had snapped, 'You *swine*,' and left him to gather the rest of his belongings. When he had done so and had gone in search of her to say goodbye, she was nowhere to be found. He'd cursed: her, himself, and Barbara Havers for being the source of a disagreement with Helen. But the drive to Derbyshire had given him time to cool off as well as time to reflect upon how often he hit below the belt. This contretemps with Helen was one of those times, and he had to admit it.

Now, standing on the pavement in front of Buxton police station with Winston Nkata, Lynley realised there was a way to make amends to his wife. Nkata would be waiting for him to assign another officer to accompany him on any rounds he might have to make in London, and both of them knew who the logical selection was. Yet Lynley found himself temporising by turning the Bentley over to his subordinate officer. He couldn't commandeer a car from the Buxton police for his DC to drive all the way to London, he explained to Nkata, and the only alternative to having him take the Bentley was directing him to return to London by plane from Manchester or by train. But by the time he got himself to the airport and caught a flight or waited for a train and changed from one line to another in God only knew how many towns between Buxton and London, he could have driven the distance.

Lynley hoped Nkata had more finesse behind the wheel than Barbara Havers had employed the last time she happily ran over an old milestone and threw out the car's front suspension. He informed the younger man that he was to drive the Bentley as if he had a litre of nitroglycerin in the boot.

Nkata grinned. 'Don't you think I know how to treat a motor this fine?'

'I'd just prefer it survive its adventure with you unscathed.' Lynley disarmed the car's security system and handed over his keys.

Nkata cocked his head at the front of the station. 'Think he'll play our game? Or're we playing his?'

'It's too soon to tell. He's unhappy about our being here, but I would be as well, in his position. We'll need to tread softly.' Lynley glanced at his watch. It was nearly five. The postmortem had been scheduled for early that afternoon. With any luck, it would be completed by now and the pathologist would be available to share his preliminary findings.

'What d'you think of his thinking?' Nkata reached into his jacket pocket and brought out two Opal Fruits, his vice of choice. He examined their wrappers, made his flavour selection, and passed the other sweet over to Lynley.

'How Hanken sees the case?' Lynley unwrapped the sweet. 'He's willing to talk. That's a good sign. He seems able to shift gears. That's good too.'

'Something edgy about him, though,' Nkata said. 'Makes me wonder what's eating at him.'

'We all have private concerns, Winnie. It's our job not to let them get in the way.'

Nkata adroitly tagged a final question onto Lynley's thought. 'D'you want me working with someone back in town?'

Still, Lynley avoided. 'You can call in help if you think you need it.'

'Sh'll I make the choice, or d'you want to do it yourself?'

Lynley regarded the other man. Nkata had made the queries so casually that it was impossible to read into them anything other than a request for direction. And the request was perfectly reasonable considering the fact that Nkata might well have to return to Derbyshire shortly after his arrival in London, bringing someone North with the purpose of identifying the second body. If that happened, someone else in London would be needed to look into Terence Cole's background and business in town.

Here was the moment, then. In front of Lynley was the opportunity to take the decision that Helen would approve of. But he didn't take it. Instead, he said, 'I'm not up to date with who's available. I'll leave it to you.'

Samantha McCallin had learned early into her extended stay at Broughton Manor that her uncle Jeremy didn't discriminate when it came to drink. He imbibed anything with the potential to obliterate his sensibilities quickly. He seemed to like Bombay gin the best, but at a pinch when the nearest off licence was closed, he wasn't finicky.

As far as Samantha knew, her uncle had been drinking steadily since adolescence, having taken a brief few years away from booze during his twenties to do drugs instead. Jeremy Britton had been – according to family legend – the once shining star of the Britton clan. But his marriage to a fellow flower-child who had what Samantha's mother euphemistically and archaically called A Past, had caused him to fall into disfavour with his father. Nonetheless, the laws of primogeniture couldn't prevent Jeremy's inheriting Broughton Manor and all its contents upon his father's death, and the realisation that she'd lived her life as the 'good child' for naught – while Jeremy had the time of *his* life among fellow ingesters of hallucinogenic substances – had planted in the breast of Samantha's mother more seeds of disharmony between her and her brother. That disharmony had only grown throughout the years as Jeremy and his wife produced three children in rapid succession and drank and drugged Broughton Manor into the ground while in Winchester Jeremy's only sister Sophie hired investigators to provide her with periodic reports on her brother's dissolute life and wept, wailed, and gnashed her teeth when she received them.

'Someone's got to do something *about* him,' she cried, 'before he destroys our family's entire history. The way he's carrying on, there'll be nothing left to pass on to *anyone*.'

Not that Sophie Britton McCallin needed her brother Jeremy's money, which he'd long ago run through anyway.

98

She herself was rolling in it since her own husband had worked himself into an early grave to keep her supply line running.

During that period when Samantha's father had been healthy enough to adhere to a schedule at the family factory that would have felled an ordinary mortal, Samantha herself had ignored her mother's soliloquies on the topic of her brother Jeremy. Those soliloquies changed in both tone and content, however, when Douglas McCallin was felled by prostate cancer. Faced with the grim reality of earthly mortality, his wife had been reborn to a fervent belief in the importance of family ties.

'I want my brother here,' she'd wept in her widow's weeds at the wake. 'My only living blood relative. My brother. I *want* him.'

It was so like Sophie to forget that she had two children herself – not to mention those belonging to her brother – who served as blood relatives. Instead, she seized on a rapprochement with Jeremy as the only solace in her present grief.

Indeed, her grief became *so* present that it soon was apparent that Sophie was setting herself up to outdo Victoria's mourning for Albert. And when she finally saw this, Samantha decided that the only road to peace in Winchester was decisive action. So she'd come to Derbyshire to collect her uncle once she deduced from incoherent phone conversations with the man that he was in no condition to get himself south unaided. And once she'd arrived and had seen his condition for herself, Samantha had known that carting him down to his sister in his present state would probably send Sophie to her grave.

Besides that, Samantha found it a relief to be away from Sophie for a time. The drama of her husband's death had provided her with more fodder than she usually had, and she'd been using it with a gusto that had long left Samantha too exhausted to deal with her.

Not that Samantha didn't mourn her father's passing herself.

She did. But she'd long ago seen that Douglas McCallin's first love was the family biscuit factory – not the family itself – and consequently his death seemed more like an extension of his normal working hours than a permanent parting. His life had always been his work. And he'd given it the dedication of a man who'd had the luck to meet his one true love at the age of twenty.

Jeremy, on the other hand, had chosen drink as his bride. On this particular day, he'd started with dry sherry at ten in the morning. During lunch, he'd worked his way through a bottle of something called the Blood of Jupiter, which Samantha assumed from its colour was red wine. And throughout the afternoon, he'd plied himself with one gin and tonic after another. The fact that he was still ambulatory was, to Samantha, remarkable.

He usually spent his days in the parlour, where he shut the curtains and used the ancient eight millimetre projector to entertain himself with endless meanderings down memory lane. In the months that Samantha had been at Broughton Manor, he'd gone through the Britton family's entire cinematic history at least three times. He always did it the same way: beginning with the earliest films that one Britton or another had shot in 1924 and watching them in chronological order to the point at which there was no Britton with sufficient interest in the family to record their doings. So the pictorial record of fox hunts, fishing expeditions, holidays, pheasant shoots, birthdays, and weddings ended round the time of Julian's fifteenth birthday. Which, according to Samantha's calculations, would have been just the time that Jeremy Britton had fallen from his horse and compressed three vertebrae, for which long ago injury he religiously plied himself with pain killers as well as intoxicants.

'He's going to kill himself mixing pills with booze if we don't watch him,' Julian had told her soon after her arrival. 'Sam, will you help me? With you here, I can get more work done on the

estate. I might even be able to put some plans in motion . . .
if you'll help me, that is.'

And within days of meeting him, Samantha had known
that she would do anything to help her cousin Julian. Anything at all.

Which was something that Jeremy Britton obviously knew
too. Because hearing her return from the vegetable garden
in the late afternoon and clomp across the courtyard ridding
her boots of soil, he'd actually emerged from the parlour and
sought her out in the kitchen where she was beginning to
prepare their dinner.

'Ah. Here you are, my flower.' He leaned forward in that
gravity-defying posture that seemed second nature to drunks.
He had a tumbler in his hand: Two small pieces of ice and a
slice of lemon were all that remained of his latest gin and tonic.
As usual, he was dressed up to the nines, every inch of him
the country squire. Despite the late summer weather he was
wearing a tweed jacket, a tie, and heavy wool plus fours that
he must have resurrected from a predecessor's wardrobe. He
might have passed for an eccentric albeit well-to-do landowner
in his cups.

He placed himself at the old wooden work top, precisely
where Samantha wished to work. He jiggled the ice in his
tumbler and drained what little liquid he was able to coax
from the melting cubes. That done, he set the glass next to
the large chef's knife that she'd removed from its stand. He
looked from her to the knife to her once again. And he smiled
a slow, happy inebriate's smile.

'Where's our boy?' he inquired pleasantly, although it came
out as *whairshare boy?* His eyes were so light a grey that their
irises might not even have existed, and the whites of them had
long since gone yellow, a colour that was beginning to suffuse
most of his skin. 'Haven't noticed Julie skulking about today,
don't you know. Fac' tis, I don't believe he was home last night
at all, our little Julie, because I don't recall seeing his mug at

breakfast.' Except it was *hishmuggabrekkest*, and having said this much, Jeremy waited for her reaction to his remarks.

Samantha began emptying the vegetable trug of its contents. She placed lettuce, a cucumber, two green peppers, and a cauliflower into the nearby sink. She began to wash them free of soil. To the lettuce she gave particular attention, bending over it like a mother examining her infant child. There was nothing quite as irritating as having one's salad taste of grit, she thought.

'Well,' Jeremy went on with a sigh, 'I s'pose we know what Julie was up to, don't we, Sam?' *Doe-we-Sham?* 'That boy won't see what's before his face. I don't know what're we going to do with him.'

'You haven't taken any of your pills, have you, Uncle Jeremy?' Samantha asked. 'If you mix them with spirits, you could be in trouble.'

'I was born for trouble,' Jeremy said – *I-sh born f'trouble* – and Samantha tried to discern if his slurring was any worse than usual, an indication of an assault on his consciousness. It was just past five o'clock, so he'd be slurring anyway, but the last thing Julian needed to contend with was his father's usual drunken slumber working its way into a coma. Jeremy sidled along the work top till he was standing next to her at the sink. 'You're a good looking woman, Sammy,' he said. His breath was a study in mixing his drinks. 'Don't you think I'm ever so many sheets to the wind that I don't notice what a looker you are. Thing is, we've got to make our little Julie see that. No point showing off those legs of yours if the only one looking is this old sod. Not that I don't appreciate the sight, mind you. Having a nice young thing like you running about the house in those tight little shorts is just the very thing that—'

'These are hiking shorts,' Samantha interrupted. 'I wear them because it's been warm, Uncle Jeremy. Which you'd know if you ever left the house during the day. And they aren't tight.'

'Jus' a compliment, girl,' Jeremy protested. 'Got to learn to accept a compliment. And who better to learn from than your own blood uncle? Christ, it's good to know you, girl. 'Ve I mentioned that?' He didn't bother to wait for a response. He leaned even closer for a confidential whisper – 'Now let's figure what to do about Julie.' *Less figger whatta do bow Julie.*

'What about Julian?' Samantha asked.

'We know what we're dealing with, don't we? He's been mounting the Maiden girl like a randy donkey since he was twenty years old—'

'Please, Uncle Jeremy.' Samantha could feel her neck getting prickly.

'Please Uncle Jeremy what? We got to look at the facts so we know what to do with them. And fact number one is that Julie's been tupping the Padley Gorge ewe every chance he's had. Or, better said, every chance she's given him.'

For a drunk, he was remarkably observant, Samantha thought. But she said, rather more primly than she intended, 'I really don't want to talk about Julian's sex life, Uncle Jeremy. It's his business, not ours.'

'Ah,' her uncle said. 'Too nasty a topic for Sammy McCallin? Why's it that I don't think that's the case, Sam?' *Thassacase Sam.*

'I didn't say it was nasty,' she replied. 'I said it wasn't our business. And it isn't. So I won't discuss it.' It wasn't that she felt odd about sex – embarrassed, shy, or anything like that. Far from it. She'd had sex when it was available to her ever since getting past the awkward inconvenience of virginity by pressing one of her brother's friends into service when she was a teenager. But this . . . talking about her cousin's sex life . . . She just didn't want to discuss it. She couldn't *afford* to discuss it and run the risk of giving herself away.

'Girly girl, listen,' Jeremy said. 'I see how you look at him, and I know what you want. I'm on your side. Hell, keep the family for the family *in* the family's my motto. You think I want him chained to the Maiden tart when there's a woman like you hanging round, waiting for the day when her man'll wise up?'

'You're mistaken,' she said although the pounding just beneath her skin told her how her blood was giving the lie to her words. 'I'm fond of Julian. Who wouldn't be? He's a wonderful man—'

'Right. He is. And d'you actually— *ackshully* – 'think the Maiden sees that in our Julie? Not on your life. She sees a bit of fun when she's hereabouts, a bit of tumble-in-the-heather-and-poke-me-if-you-can.'

'But,' Samantha went on firmly as if he hadn't spoken, 'I'm not in love with him and I can't imagine ever being in love with him. Good grief, Uncle Jeremy. We're first cousins. I think of Julian the way I think of my brother.'

Jeremy was silent for a moment. Samantha took the opportunity to move past him, cauliflower and peppers in hand. She placed them into the cutting trough and began slicing the cauliflower into florets.

'Ah,' Jeremy said slowly, but his tone was sly, which told Samantha for the first time that he wasn't as drunk as he seemed. 'Your brother. I see. Yes. I do see. So he wouldn't interest you in the other way. Wonder how I got the idea . . . ? But no matter. Give your uncle Jer a touch of advice, then.'

'About what?' She fetched a colander and scooped the cauliflower into it. She turned her attention to the green peppers.

'About how to cure him.'

'Of what?'

'Of her. The cat. The mare. The sow. What you will.' *Whachewill.*

'Julian,' Samantha said in a last ditch effort to divert her uncle from his course, 'doesn't need to be cured of anything. He's his own man, Uncle Jeremy.'

'Bollocks, that. He's a man on a string, and we both

know where it's tied. She's got him so he can't see up for down.'

'Hardly.'

'Hard's the word, all right. He's been hard so long that his brain's made a permanent journey into his dick.'

'Uncle Jeremy—'

'All he thinks about is having a suck on those pretty pink teats of hers. And once he gets his prong inside her and has her moaning like a—'

'All *right*.' Samantha drove the chef's knife through the green pepper like a cleaver. 'You've made your point thoroughly, Uncle Jeremy. I'd like to get on with making dinner now.'

Jeremy smiled slowly, that inebriate's smile. 'You're meant for him, Sammy. You know that as well as I.' *Swellseye*, he said. 'So what're we going to do to make it happen?'·

He was suddenly looking at her steadily, quite as if he were not drunk at all. What was the mythological creature that could fix you in its stare and kill you? Cockatrice, she thought. Her uncle was a cockatrice.

'I don't know what you're talking about,' she said, but she sounded, even to herself, much less assured and far more afraid.

'Don't you.' He smiled and when he left the room, he didn't walk the walk of a man who was remotely tipsy.

Samantha kept determinedly chopping the peppers until she heard his footsteps on the stairs, until she heard the kitchen door latch shut behind him. Then, with a careful control that she was proud to be able to muster in the circumstances, she set the knife to one side. She put her hands on the edge of the work top. She bent forward over the vegetables, inhaled their scent, directed her thoughts into a self-created mantra – 'Love fills me, embraces me. Love makes me whole' – and tried to regain a sense of serenity. Not that she'd had any serenity since the previous night when she'd realised what a mistake she'd made in conjunction with the lunar eclipse. Not that she'd had much serenity before that moment. Not that she'd had serenity at all once she'd realised what Nicola Maiden was to her cousin. But forcing herself to whisper the mantra was habit, so she used it now, despite the fact that love was the very last feeling of which she pictured herself capable at the moment.

She was still attempting the meditation when she heard the dogs barking from their kennels in the converted block of stables just to the west of the manor house. The sound of their sharp, excited yelping told her that Julian was with them.

Samantha looked at her watch. It was feeding time for the adult harriers, observation time for the newly born pups, and rearranging time for the play runs in which the older puppies were beginning the socialisation process. Julian would be out there for at least another hour. Samantha had time to prepare herself.

She wondered what to say to her cousin. She wondered what he'd say to her. And she wondered what it mattered anyway with Nicola Maiden to consider.

From the moment she'd met her, Samantha hadn't liked Nicola. Her dislike wasn't grounded in what the younger woman represented to her, though – primary competition for Julian's affections. It was grounded in what Nicola so patently was. Her easiness of manner was an irritant, suggesting a self-confidence entirely at odds with the girl's appalling roots. The daughter of little more than a publican, graduate of a London comprehensive and a third-rate university that was no better than an ordinary polytechnic college, who was she to move so easily through the rooms of Broughton Manor? Decrepit as they were, they still represented four centuries of unbroken possession by the Britton family. And that was the kind of lineage that Nicola Maiden could hardly claim for herself.

But this knowledge didn't seem to faze her in the least. Indeed, she never acted as if she was in possession of the knowledge at all. And there was a single good reason for this: the power that went with her English-rose looks. The Guinevere hair – unnatural in colour though it doubtless was – the perfect skin, the dark-lashed eyes, the delicate frame, the seashell ears ... She'd been given every physical advantage a woman could be given. And five minutes in her presence had been enough to tell Samantha that she bloody well knew it.

'It's brilliant to meet one of Jule's relatives at last,' she'd confided to Samantha on their first meeting seven months earlier. 'I hope we'll become the best of friends.' Half term for Nicola, she'd come to spend her holiday with her parents. She'd rung Julian on the morning of her arrival, and the moment he pressed the telephone receiver to his ear, Samantha had seen which way the wind was blowing and for whom. But she hadn't known how strong that wind was till she met Nicola herself.

The sunny smile, the frank gaze, the shout of pleased laughter, the artless conversation ... Although she'd rather more than mildly disliked her, it had taken several meetings with Nicola for Samantha to make a full evaluation of her cousin's beloved. And when she did, the realisation she reached did nothing but add to Samantha's discomfort whenever they met. For she saw in Nicola Maiden a young woman completely content with who she was, offering herself to the world at large without the slightest care as to whether the offering would be accepted. Not for her were the doubts, the fears, the insecurities, and the crises of confidence of the female in search of a male to define her. Which was probably why, Samantha thought, she had Julian Britton so hot and bothered to do just that.

More than once in the time she'd been at Broughton Manor, Samantha had come upon Julian engaged in an act that was testimony to the thrall into which Nicola Maiden drew a man. Hunched over a letter he was writing to her, sheltering the telephone receiver from unwanted eavesdroppers as he talked to her, staring sightlessly over the garden wall at the footbridge that spanned the River Wye as he thought of her, sitting in his office with his head in his hands as he brooded about her, Samantha's cousin was little more than the prey of a huntress he couldn't begin to understand.

There was no way that Samantha could make him see his beloved as she truly was, however. There was only the option of allowing his passion to play itself out, to culminate in the marriage he was so desperate to attain, or to lead to a permanent break between him and the woman he desired.

Having to accept this as her only course had brought Samantha face to face with her own impatience, and it accosted her at her every turn at Broughton Manor. She fought her longing to beat the truth into her cousin's head. Time and again she deliberately turned from the appetite for derogation that rose in her whenever the subject of Nicola came up. But these virtuous efforts at self control were taxing. And the price she was beginning to pay was anger, resentment, insomnia, and fraying nerves.

Uncle Jeremy didn't help matters. By him, Samantha was daily regaled with lubricious innuendoes and direct assaults, all circling or landing upon the subject of Julian's love life. Had she not quickly seen upon her arrival how necessary was her presence at Broughton Manor, had she not needed a respite from her mother's incessant displays of lugubrious mourning, Samantha knew that she would have decamped months ago. But she maintained her position and held her peace – most of the time – because she'd been able to see the bigger picture: Jeremy's sobriety, the blessed distraction that a reunion with him would provide her mother, and Julian's gradual awakening to the contribution Samantha was making – and was fully capable of continuing to make – to his well-being, his future, and his hope of transforming the derelict manor house and the estate into a thriving business.

'Sam?'

She raised her head. So deeply had she been into her attempt to release the tension of having a conversation with her uncle, she'd failed to hear his son come into the kitchen. Stupidly she said, 'Aren't you with the dogs, Julian?'

'Short shrift,' he said in explanation. 'They need more but I can't give it to them now.'

'I did see to Cass. Do you want me to—'

'She's dead.'

'My God. Julian, she *can't* be,' Samantha cried. 'I went out as soon as I spoke to you. She was fine. She'd eaten, the puppies were all asleep. I made notes of everything and left them on the clip board. Didn't you see it? I hung it on the peg.'

'Nicola,' he said tonelessly. 'Sam, she's dead. Out on Calder Moor where she'd gone camping. Nicola's dead.'

Samantha stared at him as the word *dead* seemed to echo round the room. He isn't crying, she thought. What does it mean that he isn't crying? 'Dead,' she repeated, careful with the word, certain that saying it the wrong way would give an impression that she didn't want to give.

He kept his eyes on her and she wished he wouldn't. She wished he'd talk. Or scream or cry to do something to indicate what was going on inside so that she would know how to behave with him. When he finally moved, it was to walk to the work top where Samantha had been chopping the peppers. He stood examining them as if they were a curiosity. Then he lifted the chef's knife and inspected it closely. Finally, he pressed his thumb firmly against the sharp blade.

'Julian!' Samantha cried. 'You'll hurt yourself!'

A thin line of crimson appeared on his skin. 'I don't know what to call how I feel,' he said.

Samantha, on the other hand, didn't have that problem.

Chapter Five

DI Peter Hanken apparently decided to show mercy when it came to the Marlboros. The first actions he took when they were on the road from Buxton to Padley Gorge were to lean over, flip open the Ford's glove compartment, and pluck out a packet of sugarless gum. As he folded a stick of it into his mouth, Lynley blessed him for his willingness to abstain from tobacco.

The DI didn't speak as the A6 began its course through Wye Dale, hugging the placid river for several miles before dipping slightly to the southeast. It wasn't until they passed the second of the limestone quarries scarring the landscape that he made his first comment.

'Newlywed, is it?' he said with a smile.

Lynley steeled himself for the ribald humour that was doubtless coming, the price one generally paid for legitimising a relationship with a woman. 'Yes. Just three months. That's longer than most Hollywood marriages, I expect.'

'It's the best time. You and the wife starting out. There's nothing else like it. Your first?'

'Marriage? Yes. For both of us. We got a late start.'

'All the better,' Hanken said.

Lynley glanced at his companion warily, wondering if the fallout from his parting argument with Helen could be read on his face, acting on Hanken as an inspiration for a tongue-in-cheek panegyric to the blessings of the marital state. But all he saw in Hanken's expression was the evidence of a man who seemed content with his life and his partner of choice.

'Name's Kathleen,' the DI confided. 'We've got three kids. Sarah, Bella, and PJ. That's Peter Junior, our newest. Here. Have a look.' He pulled a wallet from his jacket pocket and handed it over. In pride of place was a family photo: two small girls cuddling a blue-blanketed newborn on a hospital bed with Mum and Dad cuddling the two small girls. 'Family's everything. But you'll be finding that out for yourself soon enough.'

'I dare say.' Lynley tried to picture himself and Helen similarly surrounded by winsome offspring. He couldn't do it. If he summoned up his wife's image at all, it was as it had been earlier that day, pale-faced a moment before she left him.

He stirred uncomfortably in his seat. He didn't want to discuss marriage at the moment, and he offered a silent imprecation to Nkata for having brought up the subject at all. 'They're brilliant,' he said, handing the wallet back to Hanken.

'Boy's the image of his dad,' Hanken said. 'Hard to tell from that snap, of course. But there you have it.'

'They're a handsome group.'

To Lynley's relief, Hanken took this as sufficient closing comment on the subject. He returned his full attention to the driving. He gave the road the same concentration that he appeared to give everything else in his immediate environment, a characteristic of the man that Lynley had had little difficulty in deducing. After all, there hadn't been a paper out of place in his office, he was running the most orderly incident room in Lynley's memory, and his clothes made him look as if his next destination were a photo shoot for *GQ* magazine.

They were on their way to see the parents of the dead girl,

having just met the Home Office pathologist who'd travelled up from London to perform the postmortem. They'd had their conference with her outside the postmortem room, where she was changing from trainers into court shoes, one of which she was in the process of repairing by pounding its heel into the metal plate on the door. Announcing that women's shoes – not to mention their handbags – were designed by men to promote the enslavement of the female sex, she had eyed the DIs' comfortable footwear with undisguised hostility and said, 'I can give you ten minutes. The report'll be on your desk in the morning. Which one of you is Hanken, by the way? You? Fine. I know what you want. It's a knife with a three inch blade. Folding knife – pocket knife – most likely, although it could be a small one used in the kitchen. Your killer's right handed and strong, quite strong. That's for the boy. The girl was done in with that chunk of stone you had off the moor. Three blows to the head. Right-handed assailant as well.'

'The same killer?' Hanken asked.

The pathologist gave her shoe five final pounds against the door as she reflected on the question. She said brusquely that the bodies could only tell what they'd told: how they'd been robbed of life, what sort of weapons had been used against them, and whether a right or left hand had wielded those weapons. Forensic evidence – fibres, hairs, blood, sputum, skin and the like – might tell a longer, more precise story but they'd have to wait to get the reports back from the lab for that. The naked eye could only discern so much, and she'd told them what that *so much* was.

She tossed her shoe onto the floor and introduced herself as Dr Sue Myles. She was a stout woman with short-fingered hands, grey hair, and a chest that resembled the prow of a ship. But her feet, Lynley noted as she slid them into her shoes, were as slender as a debutante's.

'One of the boy's back wounds was more of a goudge,' she went on. 'The blow chipped the left scapula, so if you find a likely weapon, we can go for a match from the blade to the bone.'

That wound didn't kill him? Hanken wanted to know.

'The poor sod bled to death. Would've taken some minutes, but once he took a wound to the femoral artery – that's in the groin, by the way – he was done for.'

'And the girl?' Lynley asked.

'Skull cracked like an egg. The post cerebral artery was pierced.'

Which meant what exactly, Hanken enquired.

'Epidural haematoma. Internal bleeding, pressure on the brain. She died in less than an hour.'

'It took longer than the boy?'

'Right. But she'd have been unconscious once she was hit.'

'Could we have two killers?' Hanken asked directly.

'Could have, yes,' Dr Myles confirmed.

'Defensive wounds on the boy?' Lynley asked.

None that were obvious, Dr Myles replied. She settled her trainers into a sports bag and zipped it smartly before giving them her attention again.

Hanken asked for confirmation on the times of the deaths. Dr Myles narrowed her eyes and enquired what times his own forensic pathologist had given him. Thirty-six to forty-eight hours before the bodies had been discovered, Hanken told her.

'I wouldn't argue with that.' And she scooped up her bag, nodded a curt farewell, and headed towards the hospital exit.

Now in the car Lynley reflected on what they knew: that the boy had brought nothing with him to the camping site; that there were anonymous and threatening letters left at the scene; that the girl was unconscious for close to an hour; that the two means of murder were entirely different.

Lynley was dwelling on this last thought when Hanken swung the car to the left, and they headed north in the direction of a town called Tideswell. Along this route they

ultimately regained the River Wye, where the steep cliffs and
the woods surrounding Miller's Dale had long since brought
dusk to the village. Just beyond the last cottage, a narrow lane
veered northwest and Hanken steered the Ford into it. They
quickly climbed above the woods and the valley and within
minutes were cruising along a vast expanse of heather and gorse
that appeared to undulate endlessly towards the horizon.

'Calder Moor,' Hanken said. 'The largest moor in all the
White Peak. It stretches from here to Castleton.' He drove
another minute in silence till they came to a lay-by. He pulled
into it and let the engine idle. 'If she'd gone camping in the
Dark Peak, we'd have had Mountain Rescue going after her
eventually, when she didn't turn up. No old bat with a doggy
to walk would've taken her constitutional up there and found
the bodies. But this—' He swept his hand in an arc above the
dashboard – 'is accessible, all of it. There's miles and miles
to cover if someone gets lost, but at least those miles can be
handled on foot. Not an easy walk and not entirely safe. But
easier to tackle than the peat bogs you'll find round Kinder
Scout. If someone had to be murdered in the district, better
it happened here, on the limestone plateau, than the other.'

'Is this where Nicola Maiden set off?' Lynley asked. There
was no track that he could see from the car. The girl would
have had to fight her way through everything from bracken
to bilberry.

Hanken rolled down his window and spat out his chewing
gum. He reached over Lynley and flipped open the glove
compartment to fish out another stick. 'She set off from the
other side, northwest of here. She was hiking out to Nine
Sisters' Henge, which's closer to the western boundary of
the moor. Rather more of interest to be looked at on that
side: tumuli, caverns, caves, barrows. Nine Sisters' Henge is
the highlight.'

'You're from this area?' Lynley asked.

Hanken didn't answer at once. He looked as if he was

considering whether to answer at all. He made the decision at last and said, 'From Wirksworth,' and appeared to seal his lips on the subject.

'You're lucky to live where your history is. I wish I could say the same for myself.'

'Depends on the history,' Hanken said and shifted gears abruptly with, 'Want to have a look at the site?'

Lynley was wise enough to know that how he met the offer to look over the crime scene would be crucial to the relationship he developed with the other officer. The truth was that he did want to see the site of the murders. No matter the point at which he joined an investigation, there was always a time during the course of the enquiry when he felt the need to look things over himself. Not because he didn't trust the competence of his fellow investigators but because only through a first hand viewing of as much as possible of what related to the case was he able to become a part of the crime. And it was in becoming a part of the crime that he did his best work. Photographs, reports, and physical evidence conveyed a great deal. But sometimes the place where a murder occurred held back secrets from even the most astute observer. It would be in pursuit of those secrets that Lynley would inspect a murder scene. However, inspecting this particular murder scene ran the risk of unnecessarily alienating DI Hanken, and nothing Hanken had said or done so far even hinted that he might overlook a detail.

There would be an occasion, Lynley thought, when he and the other officer wouldn't be working this case in each other's presence. When that occasion arose, he would have ample opportunity to examine the location where Nicola Maiden and the boy had died.

'You and your team have covered that end of things, as far as I can see,' Lynley said. 'It wastes our time for me to go over what you've already done.'

Hanken gave him another lengthy scrutiny, chewing his gum

in staccato. 'Wise decision,' he said with a nod as he put the car back into gear.

They cruised northwards along the eastern edge of the moor. Perhaps a mile beyond the little market town of Tideswell, they turned to the east and began to leave the heather, bilberry and bracken behind. They drove a short distance into a dale – its gentle slopes dotted with trees that were only just beginning to display the foliage of the coming autumn – and at a junction that was curiously sign posted to the 'Plague Village', they headed north again.

Less than quarter of an hour took them to Maiden Hall, situated in the shelter of limes and chestnut trees on a hillside not far from Padley Gorge. The route coursed them through a verdant woodland and along the edge of an incision in the landscape made by a brook that tumbled out of the woods and cut a meandering path between slopes of limestone, fern, and wild grass. The turnoff to Maiden Hall rose suddenly as they entered another stretch of woodland. It twisted up a hillside and spilled out into a gravel drive that swung round the front of a gabled stone Victorian structure and led to a car park behind it.

The hotel entrance was actually at the back of the building. There a discreet sign printed with the single word *reception* directed them through a passage and into the hunting lodge itself. A small desk stood just inside the lodge proper. Beyond this a sitting room apparently served as the hotel lounge, where the original entrance to the building had been converted to a bar and the room itself had been restored with oak wainscotting, subdued cream and umber wallpaper, and overstuffed furniture. As it was too early for any of the residents to be gathering for preprandial drinks, the lounge was deserted. But Lynley and Hanken hadn't been in the room for a minute before a dumpling-shaped woman – red-eyed and red-nosed from weeping – came from what appeared to be the dining room and greeted them with some considerable dignity.

There were no rooms available for the evening, she told them quietly. And as there had been a sudden death in the family, the dining room would not be open tonight. But she would be happy to recommend several restaurants in the area should the gentlemen require one.

Hanken offered the woman his police identification and introduced Lynley. The woman said, 'You'll be wanting to speak to the Maidens. I'll fetch them,' and she ducked past the officers, hurried through the reception area, and began climbing the stairs.

Lynley walked to one of the lounge's two alcoves, where late afternoon light was filtering in through lead-paned windows. These overlooked the drive that curved round the front of the house. Beyond it, a lawn had been reduced to a heat-baked mat of twisted blades in the previous months' drought. Behind him, he could hear Hanken moving restlessly round the room. A few magazines shifted position and slapped down onto table tops. Lynley smiled at the sound. His fellow DI was doubtless giving in to his restless need to put things in order.

It was absolutely quiet inside the hunting lodge. The windows were open, so the sound of birds and a distant plane broke the stillness. But inside, it was as hushed as an empty church.

A door closed somewhere and footsteps crunched across gravel. A moment later, a dark-haired man in jeans and a sleeveless grey sweatshirt pedalled past the windows on a ten-speed bicycle. He disappeared into the trees as the Maiden Hall drive began to descend the hill.

The Maidens joined them then. Lynley turned from the window at the sound of their entrance and Hanken's formal, 'Mr and Mrs Maiden. Please accept our sympathies.'

Lynley saw that the years of his retirement had dealt with Andy Maiden kindly. The former SO10 officer and his wife were both in their early sixties, but they looked at least a decade younger. Andy stood a good ten inches taller than his wife, and he'd developed the appearance of an outdoorsman: a tanned face, a flat stomach, a brawny chest, all of which seemed suited to a man who'd left behind a reputation for disappearing chameleon-like into his environment. His wife matched him in physical condition. She too was tanned and solid, as if she took frequent exercise. Both of them looked as if they'd missed more than one night's sleep, though. Andy Maiden was unshaven, in rumpled clothing. Nan was haggard, beneath her eyes a puckering of skin that was purplish in hue.

Maiden managed a painful half smile. 'Tommy. Thank you for coming.'

Lynley said, 'I'm sorry it has to be under these circumstances,' and introduced himself to Maiden's wife. He said, 'Everyone at the Yard sends condolences, Andy.'

'Scotland Yard?' Nan Maiden sounded somewhat dazed. Her husband said, 'In a moment, love.' He made a gesture with his arm, indicating the alcove behind Lynley where two sofas faced each other across a coffee table that was spread with copies of *Country Life*. He and his wife took one of the sofas, Lynley the other. Hanken swivelled an armchair round and positioned himself just a few inches away from the central point between the Maidens and Lynley. The action suggested that he would play a mediating influence between the parties. But Lynley noted that the DI was careful to place his chair several inches closer to Scotland Yard of the present than to Scotland Yard of the past.

If Andy Maiden was aware of Hanken's manoeuvre and what it implied, he gave no sign. Instead, he sat forward on the sofa with his hands balanced between his legs. Left hand massaged right. Right massaged left.

His wife observed him doing this. She passed him a small red ball that she took from her pocket. She said quietly, 'Still bad? Shall I phone the doctor for you?'

'You're ill?' Lynley asked.

Maiden squeezed the ball with his right hand, gazing at the spread fingers of his left. 'Circulation,' he said. 'It's nothing.'

'Please let me phone the doctor, Andy,' his wife said.

'That's not what's important.'

'How can you say—' Nan Maiden's eyes grew suddenly bright. 'God. Did I forget even for a moment?' She leaned her forehead against her husband's shoulder and began to cry. Roughly, Maiden put his arm round her.

Lynley cast a look at Hanken. You or I? he asked silently. It's not going to be pleasant, whoever takes it on.

Hanken's reply was a sharp nod of his head. It's yours, the nod said.

'There isn't going to be an easy time to talk about your daughter's death,' Lynley began gently. 'But in a murder investigation – and I know that you're already aware of this, Andy – the first hours are critical.'

As he spoke, Nan raised her head. She tried to speak, failed completely, then tried again.

'Murder investigation,' she repeated. 'What are you saying?'

Lynley looked from husband to wife. Hanken did likewise. Then they looked at each other. Lynley said to Andy, 'You've seen the body, haven't you? You've been told what happened?'

'Yes,' Andy Maiden said. 'I've been told. But I—'

'*Murder?*' his wife cried out in horror. 'Oh my God, Andy. You never said that Nicola was murdered!'

Barbara Havers had spent the afternoon in Greenford, making the decision to use the rest of her sick day to visit her mother in Hawthorn Lodge, a misnamed postwar semi-detached where Mrs Havers had lived as a permanent resident for the last ten months. In the way of most people who attempt to gain support from others for a position that might well be untenable, Barbara had found that there was a price to pay for successfully cultivating advocates among Inspector Lynley's friends and relatives. And because she didn't want to face any more price paying in one afternoon, she sought a distraction.

Mrs Havers was nothing if not adept at providing escape hatches from reality, since she herself no longer lived in that realm on a regular basis. Barbara had found her in the back garden of Hawthorn Lodge, where she was engaged in putting together a jigsaw puzzle. The puzzle's box top had been propped up against an old mayonnaise jar that was filled with coloured sand holding five tasteful plastic carnations in position. On this lid, a smarmy cartoon prince – perfectly proportioned and demonstrating a sufficient amount of adoration for the occasion – was slipping a high-heeled glass shoe onto the slender and curiously toeless foot of Cinderella while the girl's two cowlike and resentful stepsisters watched jealously to one side, culling a richly deserved comeuppance.

With the tender encouragement of her nurse and keeper Mrs Flo – as Florence Magentry was called by her three elderly residents and their families – Mrs Havers had managed successfully to assemble Cinderella, part of the stepsisters, the Prince's shoe-wielding arm, his manly torso, and his bent left leg. However as Barbara joined her, she was in the midst of attempting to pound the Prince's face onto one of the stepsister's shoulders and when Mrs Flo gently guided her hand towards the proper placement of the piece, Mrs Havers shouted, 'No, no, no!' and pushed the whole puzzle away, knocking over the jar, scattering its plastic carnations, and spilling sand across the table.

Barbara's intervention didn't help matters. Whether her mother recognised her during visits was always a matter of chance, and on this day Mrs Havers' clouded consciousness attached Barbara's face to someone called Libby O'Rourke who apparently had been the school temptress during Mrs Havers' childhood. It seemed that Libby O'Rourke had operated in a female version of Georgie Porgie mode most of the time, and one of the boys whom she'd kissed was none other than Mrs Havers' own beau, an act of effrontery that Mrs Havers felt compelled to avenge on this very day by throwing puzzle pieces, shouting invective coloured by the sort of language Barbara wouldn't have thought part of her mother's vocabulary, and ultimately crumpling into a weeping heap. It was a situation that had taken some handling: persuading her mother to leave the garden, urging her upstairs to her room, coaxing her to look through a family album long enough to see that Barbara's round and snubby face appeared on its pages far too often for her to be the loathsome Libby.

'But I don't have a little girl,' Mrs Havers protested in a voice more frightened than confused when she'd been forced to agree that Libby O'Rourke's being given a position of prominence in the family album made no sense, considering the offence she had once given. 'Mummy won't *let* me have babies. I c'n only have dolls.'

Barbara had no answer for that. Her mother's mind made the tortuous journey into the past too often and with so little warning that she'd long ago forgiven herself her inability to deal with it on any extended basis. So, after the album was set aside, she hadn't made any further attempts to argue, persuade, dissuade, or appeal. She'd merely selected one of the travel magazines that her mother loved to thumb through and she'd spent ninety minutes sitting shoulder to shoulder on the edge of the bed with the woman who'd forgotten she'd ever given birth, looking at photographs of Thailand, Australia, and Greece.

That was when her conscience finally gained some dominance over her resistance, and the internal voice that had earlier decried Lynley's actions was confronted by a voice that suggested her own actions might have been wanting. What ensued was a nonverbal argument taking place in her head. One side insisted that Inspector Lynley was a vindictive prig. The other informed her that – prig or not – he didn't deserve her disloyalty. And she *had* been disloyal. Trotting round to Chelsea in order to denounce him to his intimates was not the behaviour of a steadfast friend. On the other hand, *he'd* been disloyal as well. Taking it upon himself to amplify her formal punishment by overlooking her on a case, he'd more than illustrated whose side he was on in her battle to save her professional hide, no matter *what* he claimed about her need to keep a low profile for a while.

Such was the argument that raged within her. It began as she leafed through the travel magazines and murmured comments about fantasy holidays her mother had taken to Crete, Mykonos, Bangkok and Perth. It continued unabated on her drive from Greenford back into London at the end of the day. Not even an old Fleetwood Mac tape playing at maximum volume could subdue the disputing parties inside Barbara's head. Because throughout the drive, singing harmony with Stevie Nicks was the mezzo soprano of Barbara's conscience, a sententious cantata that stubbornly refused to be excised from her brain.

He deserved it, he deserved it, he deserved it! she silently screamed at the voice.

And where did giving him what he deserved get *you*, my darling? her conscience replied.

She was still refusing to answer that question when she pulled into Steeles Road and slid the Mini into a parking space that was being conveniently vacated by a woman, three children, two dogs, and what appeared to be a cello with legs. She locked up and trudged in the direction of Eton Villas, gratified that she was feeling tired because tired meant sleep and sleep meant putting an end to the voices.

She heard other voices, however, as she rounded the corner and came upon the yellow Edwardian house behind which sat her mousehole dwelling. These new voices were coming from the flagstone area in front of the ground floor flat. And one of the voices – a child's – cried out happily when Barbara came through the bright orange gate.

'Barbara! Hullo, hullo! Dad and I are blowing bubbles. Come and see. When the light hits them just exactly right, they look like round rainbows. Did you know that, Barbara? Come and see, come and see.'

The little girl and her father were seated on the solitary wooden bench in front of their flat, she in the fast fading light, he in the growing shadows where his cigarette glowed like a crimson firefly. He touched his daughter's head fondly and rose in the formal fashion that was his by nature. 'You'll join us?' Taymullah Azhar asked Barbara.

'Oh do, do, do,' the child exclaimed. 'After the bubbles, we're watching a video. *The Little Mermaid.* And we've got toffee apples for a treat. Well, we've only got two, but I'll share mine with you. One's too much for me to eat anyway.' She scooted off the bench and came to greet Barbara, dancing across the lawn with the bubble wand and creating a trail of round rainbows behind her.

'*The Little Mermaid*, is it?' Barbara said thoughtfully. 'I don't know, Hadiyyah. I've never thought of myself as a Disney sort of bird. All those skinny Sloane-types being rescued by blokes in suits of armour—'

'This is a *mermaid*,' Hadiyyah interrupted instructively.

'Hence the title. Yeah. Right.'

'So she *can't* be rescued by someone in armour 'cause he'd sink to the bottom of the sea. And anyway no one saves her at all. *She* saves the Prince.'

'Now there's a twist I might be able to live with.'

'You've never seen it, have you? Well, tonight you can. Do come.' Hadiyyah whirled round in a circle, surrounding herself with a hoop of bubbles. Her long thick plaits flew about her shoulders, the silver ribbons that tied them glittering like pale dragon flies. 'The little mermaid's prettier'n anything. She has auburn hair.'

'A good contrast to her scales.'

'And she wears the sweetest little shells on her chest.' Hadiyyah demonstrated with two small dark hands cupped over two non-existent breasts.

'Ah. Strategically placed, I see,' Barbara said.

'Won't you watch it with us? Please? Like I said, we've got to-ffee ap-ples ...' Coaxingly, she drew out the last two words.

'Hadiyyah,' her father said quietly, 'an invitation once extended needn't be repeated.' And to Barbara, 'Nonetheless, we'd be most happy to have you join us.'

Barbara considered the proposition. An evening with Hadiyyah and her father offered the potential for more distraction, and she liked the thought of that very much. She could sit with her little friend, comfortably lounging on enormous floor pillows, their heads in their palms and their feet in the air, swaying side by side as they kept time to the music. She could chat to her little friend's father afterwards, when Hadiyyah herself had been sent off to bed. Taymullah Azhar would expect that much. It was a habit they'd developed during the months of Barbara's enforced leave from Scotland Yard. And in the past few weeks especially, their dialogue together had moved from the banalities of relative strangers being polite to the initial delicate conversational probing of two individuals who might become friends.

But in that friendship lay the rub of the matter. It called for Barbara to reveal her encounters with Hillier and Lynley. It required the truth of her demotion and her estrangement from the man she'd sought to emulate. And because Azhar's own eight-year-old daughter was the child whose life had been saved by Barbara's impetuous actions on the North Sea – actions that she'd managed to keep from Azhar in the three months since the chase had occurred – he would feel a responsibility for the fallout to her career that wasn't his to bear.

'Hadiyyah,' Taymullah Azhar said when Barbara didn't answer at once, 'I think we've had enough bubbles for the evening. Return them to your room and wait for me there, please.'

Hadiyyah's small brow furrowed, and her eyes looked stricken. 'But, Dad, the little mermaid . . . ?'

'We shall watch it as previously decided, Haddiyah. Put the bubbles in your room now.'

She gave Barbara an anxious glance. 'More'n half the toffee apple,' she said. 'If you'd like, Barbara.'

'Hadiyyah.'

She smiled impishly and dashed into the house.

Azhar reached into the breast pocket of his spotless white shirt and brought forth a packet of cigarettes, which he offered. Barbara took one, said thanks, and accepted his light as well. He observed her in silence until she grew so restive that she was compelled to speak.

'I'm knackered, Azhar. I'll have to cry off tonight. But thanks. Tell Hadiyyah I'm happy to watch a film with her another time. Hopefully when the heroine isn't as skinny as a pencil with a silicone chest.'

His gaze was unwavering. He studied her the way other people studied the labels on tins in supermarkets. Barbara wanted to writhe beneath his gaze, but she managed to restrain herself. He said, 'You must have returned to work today.'

'Why d'you think—'

'Your clothing. Has your—' he searched for a word, a euphemism undoubtedly – 'situation been resolved at New Scotland Yard, Barbara?'

There was no point in lying. Despite the fact that she'd been able to keep from him the full knowledge of what had occurred to put her there, he knew that she'd been placed on home leave. She was going to have to start dragging herself out of bed and down to work each morning, beginning with the very next day, so he would deduce sooner or later that she wasn't spending her waking hours feeding the ducks in Regent's Park any longer. 'Yeah,' she said. 'It was resolved today.' And she drew in deeply on her cigarette so that she'd have to turn her head and blow the smoke away from his face, thus hiding her own.

'And? But what am I asking? You're dressed for work, so it must have gone well.'

'Right.' She offered him a spurious smile. 'It did. All the way. I'm still gainfully employed, still in CID, still have my pension intact.' She'd lost the confidence of the only person who counted at the Yard, but she didn't add that. She couldn't imagine an occasion when she would.

'This is good,' Azhar said.

'Right. It's the best.'

'I'm happy to know that nothing from Essex affected you here in London.' Again, that level gaze of his, dark eyes the colour of chocolate drops in a face with nut brown skin that was amazingly unlined on a man of thirty-five.

'Yeah. Well. It didn't,' she said. 'Everything worked out brilliantly.'

He nodded, looking past her finally, above her head and up into fading sky. The lights from London would hide all but the most brilliant of the coming night's stars. Even those that shone would do so through a thick pall of pollution and haze that not even the growing darkness could dissipate. 'As a child, I drew my greatest comfort from the night,' he told her quietly. 'In Pakistan, my family slept in the traditional way: the men together, the women together. So at night, in the presence of my father, my brother, and my uncles, I always believed that I was perfectly safe and secure. But I forgot that feeling as I came into adulthood in England. What had been reassuring became an embarrassment from my past. I found that all I could remember were the sounds of my father and my uncles snoring and the smell of my brothers breaking wind. For some time when I came to be alone, I thought how good it was to be away from them at last, to have the night for myself and for whomever I wished to share it with. And that's how I lived for a while. But now I find that I would willingly return to that older way, when whatever one's burdens or secrets were, there was always a sense – at least at night – of never having to bear them or keep them alone.'

There was something so comforting in his words that Barbara found herself wanting to grasp the invitation to disclosure that they implied. But she stopped herself from doing so, saying, 'P'rhaps Pakistan doesn't prepare its children for the world's reality.'

'What reality is that?'

'The one that tells us we're all alone.'

'Do you believe that to be the truth, Barbara?'

'I don't just believe it. I know it. We use our daytimes to escape our nighttimes. We work, we play, we keep ourselves busy. But when it's time to sleep, we run out of distractions. Even if we're in bed with someone, their act of sleeping when we can't manage it is enough to tell us that we've got only ourselves.'

'Is this philosophy or experience speaking?'

'Neither,' she said. 'Just the way it is.'

'But not,' he said, 'the way it has to be.'

At the comment, alarm bells went off in Barbara's head, then quickly receded. Coming from any other bloke, the remark could have been construed as a chat up line. But her personal history was an illustration of the fact that Barbara wasn't the type of bird blokes chatted up. Besides, even if she'd ever had the odd moments of Aphrodisian allure, she knew that this wasn't one of them. Standing in the semi-dark in a rumpled linen suit that made her look like a transvestite toad, she knew quite well that she was hardly a paragon of desirability. So, ever articulate when it counted, she said, 'Yeah. Well. Whatever,' and tossed her cigarette to the ground where she mashed it with the sole of her shoe. 'Goodnight, then,' she added. 'Enjoy the mermaid. And thanks for the fag. I needed it.'

'Everyone needs something.' Azhar reached into his shirt pocket again. Barbara thought he was going to offer his cigarettes another time in response to her remark and in support of his. But instead he extended to her a folded piece of paper. 'A gentleman was here looking for you earlier, Barbara. He asked me to make sure you got this note. He tried to fix it to your door, he said, but it wouldn't stay in place.'

'Gentleman?' Barbara knew only one man to whom that word would automatically be applied by a stranger after a mere moment's conversation. She took the piece of paper, scarcely daring to hope. Which was just as well because the writing on the note – a sheet of paper removed from a small spiral notebook – wasn't Lynley's. She read the eight words: *Page me as soon as you get this.* A number followed them. There was no signature.

Barbara refolded the note. Doing so, she saw what was written on the outside of it, what Azhar himself must have seen, interpreted, and understood the moment it had been handed over. *DC Havers* was printed in block capitals across it. *C* for *Constable.* So Azhar knew.

She met his gaze. 'Looks like I'm back in the game already,' she said as heartily as she could manage. 'Thanks, Azhar. This bloke say where he'd be waiting for the page?'

Azhar shook his head. 'He said only that I should make sure you had the message.'

'Okay. Thanks.' She gave him a nod and turned to walk away.

He called her name – sounding urgent – but when she stopped and glanced back, he was studying the street. He said, 'Can you tell me . . .' and then his voice died away. He drew his eyes back to her as if the effort cost him.

'Tell you what?' she asked, though she felt the prickles of apprehension along her spine when she said the words.

'Tell me . . . How is your mother?' Azhar asked.

'Mum? Well . . . She's a bloody disaster when it comes to jigsaw puzzles, but otherwise I think she's okay.'

He smiled. 'That's good to know.' And with a quiet goodnight, he slipped into the house.

Barbara went to her own lodgings, a tiny cottage that sat at the bottom of the back garden. Sheltered by the limbs of an old false acacia, it was not much larger than a potting shed with mod cons. Once inside, she peeled herself out of her linen jacket, tossed the string of *faux* pearls onto the table that served purposes as diverse as dining and ironing, and went to the phone. There were no messages on her machine. She wasn't surprised. She punched in the number for the pager, punched in her own number, and waited.

Five minutes later, someone phoned. She made herself wait through four of the double-rings before she answered. There was no reason to sound desperate, she decided.

Her caller, she discovered, was Winston Nkata, and her back went up the instant she heard that unmistakable mellifluous voice with its mixed flavours of Jamaica and Sierra Leone. He was in the Load of Hay Tavern just round the corner on Chalk Farm Road, he told her, finishing up a plate of lamb curry and rice that 'was not, do believe me, something my mum would ever put on the table for her favourite son, but it's better than McDonald's although not by much.' He would set off directly for her digs. 'Be there in five minutes,' he said and rang off before she had a chance to tell him that his mug was just about the last one she wanted to see putting in an appearance on her doorstep. She hung up the phone, muttered an expletive, and went to the refrigerator to graze.

Five minutes stretched to ten. Ten minutes to fifteen. He didn't show up.

Bastard, Barbara thought. Fine idea of a joke.

She went to the bathroom and turned on the shower.

Lynley tried to adjust quickly to the astonishing fact that Andy

Maiden hadn't told his wife that their daughter had been the victim of a crime. Since Calder Moor was a location replete with potential sites of accidents, Lynley's former colleague had apparently and unaccountably allowed his wife to believe that their daughter had fractured her skull in a fall in an area too remote for immediate help to reach her.

When she learned otherwise, Nan Maiden crumpled forward, elbows pressed into her thighs and fists raised to her mouth. Either shocked, too stricken with grief to comprehend, or comprehending something only too well, she didn't weep further. She merely muttered a guttural 'Oh God, oh God, oh God.'

DI Hanken appeared to take a fairly quick measure of what was implied by her reaction. He was observing Andy Maiden with a decidedly unsympathetic eye. He asked no questions in immediate response to Nan's revelation, though. Like a good cop, he merely waited.

In the aftermath of all this, Maiden waited as well. Still, he apparently reached the conclusion that something was required of him by way of explanation for his incomprehensible behaviour. 'Love, I'm sorry,' he said to Nan. 'I couldn't . . . I'm *sorry*. Nan, I could barely cope with the fact that she'd died, let alone tell . . . let alone have to face . . . have to begin to deal with . . .' He spent a moment rigidly marshalling the inner resources a policeman learned to develop over time, in order to live through the worst of the worst. His right hand – still in possession of the ball his wife had given him – clutched and released it spasmodically. 'I'm so sorry,' he said brokenly. 'Nan.'

Nan Maiden raised her head. She watched him for a moment. Then her hand – shaking as it was – reached out and closed over his arm. She spoke to the police.

'Would you . . .' Her lips quivered. She didn't go on until she had the emotion under control. 'Tell me what happened.'

DI Hanken obliged with minimal details: He explained

where Nicola Maiden had died and how, but he told them nothing more.

'Would she have suffered?' Nan asked when Hanken had concluded his brief remarks. 'I know you can't be positive. But if there's anything that might allow us to feel that at the end ... anything at all ...'

Lynley recounted what the Home Office pathologist had told them.

Nan reflected on the information for a moment. In the silence, Andy Maiden's breath sounded loud and harsh. Nan said, 'I wanted to know because ... D'you think ... Would she have called out for one of us ... Would she have hoped ... or needed ...?' Her eyes filled. She stopped talking.

Hearing the questions, Lynley was reminded of the old moors murders, the monstrous tape recording that Myra Hindley and her cohort had made, and the anguish of the dead girl's mother when the recording had been played at the trial and she'd had to listen to her child's terrified voice crying out for her mummy in the midst of her murder. Isn't there a certain kind of knowledge, he thought, that shouldn't be revealed publicly because it can't be borne privately? He said, 'The blows to the head knocked her unconscious at once. She stayed that way.'

Nan Maiden nodded, assimilating this. 'On her body, were there other ... Had she been ... Had anyone ...?'

'She wasn't tortured.' Hanken cut in as if he too felt the need to show some mercy to the dead girl's mother. 'She wasn't raped. We'll have a fuller report later, but at the moment it seems that the blows to the head were all that she—' He paused, it seemed, in the search for a word that connoted the least pain – 'experienced.'

Nan Maiden's hand, Lynley noted, tightened its grip on her husband's arm. Maiden said, 'She looked asleep. White. Like chalk. But still asleep.'

'I want that to make it better,' Nan said. 'But it doesn't.'

And nothing will, Lynley thought. 'Andy, we've got a possible identification on the second body. We're going to need to press forward. We think the boy was called Terence Cole. He had a London address, in Shoreditch. Is his name familiar to you?'

'She wasn't alone?' The glance Nan Maiden cast at her husband told the police that he'd withheld this information from her as well. 'Andy?'

'She wasn't alone,' Maiden said.

Hanken clarified the situation for Nan Maiden, explaining that the camping gear of one person only – which he would later ask Maiden to identify as belonging to his daughter – had been within the enclosure of Nine Sisters' Henge along with the body of a teenaged boy who himself had no gear other than the clothes on his back.

'That motorcycle by her car.' Maiden pulled his facts together quickly. 'It belonged to him?'

'To a Terence Cole,' Hanken affirmed. 'Not reported stolen and so far not claimed by anyone coming off the moor. It's registered to an address in Shoreditch. We've a man heading there now to see what's what, but it seems likely that we've got the right i.d. Is the name familiar to either of you?'

Maiden shook his head slowly and said, 'Cole. Not to me. Nan?'

His wife said, 'I don't know him. And Nicola ... Surely she would have talked about him if he was a friend of hers. She would have brought him round to meet us as well. When did she not? That's ... It was her way.'

Andy Maiden then spoke perspicaciously, asking a logical question that rose from his years of policing. 'Is there any chance that Nick ...' He paused and seemed to prepare his wife for the question by laying a hand gently on her thigh. 'Could she just have been in the wrong place? Could the boy have been the target? Tommy?' And he looked to Lynley.

'That would be a consideration in any other case,' Lynley admitted.

'But not in this case? Why?'

'Have a look at this.' Hanken produced a copy of the hand-written note that had been found on Nicola Maiden's body.

The Maidens read the five words on it – THIS BITCH HAS HAD IT – as Hanken advised them that the original had been found tucked into their daughter's pocket.

Andy Maiden stared long at the note. He shifted the red ball to his left hand and clutched it. 'Jesus God. Are you telling us someone *went* there to kill her? Someone *tracked* her to kill her? That this wasn't just a case of her meeting up with strangers? A stupid argument breaking out over something? A psychopath killing her and that boy?'

'It's doubtful,' Hanken said. 'But you know the procedure as well as we do, I expect.'

Which was, Lynley knew, his way of saying that as a police officer Andy Maiden would know that every avenue potentially related to the killing of his daughter was going to be explored. He said, 'If someone went out to the moor specifically to kill your daughter, we must consider why.'

'But she didn't have enemies,' Nan Maiden declared. 'I know that's what you expect every mother to say, but in this case, it's the truth. Everyone liked Nicola. She was that kind of person.'

'Not everyone, apparently, Mrs Maiden,' Hanken said. And he brought forth the copies of the anonymous letters that had also been at the site.

Andy Maiden and his wife read these in silence and without expression. She was the one who finally spoke. As she did so, her husband's gaze remained locked on the letters. And both man and woman sat still, like statues.

'It's impossible,' she said. 'Nicola can't have received these. You're making a mistake if you think that she did.'

'Why?'

'Because we never saw them. And if she'd been threatened – by anyone, by *anyone* – she would have told us at once.'

'If she didn't want to worry you—'

'Please. Believe me. That wasn't how she was. She didn't think like that: about worrying us and such. She only thought about telling the truth.' Nan moved at last, reaching for her hair and shoving it back as if the single movement would emphasise her remarks in a way that her voice couldn't. 'If something had been going wrong in her life, she would have told us. That's how she was. She talked about everything. *Everything.* Truly.' And with an earnest look at her husband, 'Andy?'

With an effort, he took his eyes off the letters. His face, which had appeared bloodless before, was now even more so. He said, 'I don't want to think it. But it's the best possible answer if someone actually tracked her . . . if someone wasn't with her already . . . if someone didn't just stumble upon her and kill her and the boy for the sick fun of it.'

'What?' Lynley asked.

'SO10,' he said heavily, looking as if the words cost him dearly. 'There were so many cases over the years, so many yobs put away. Killers, drug dealers, crime bosses. You name them, I rolled in the muck with them.'

'Andy! No,' his wife protested, apparently understanding where he was heading. 'This has *nothing* to do with you.'

'Someone out on parole, tracking us down, hanging round long enough to get to know our movements—' He turned to her then. 'You see how it could have happened, don't you? Someone out for revenge, Nancy, striking at Nick because he knew that to hurt my daughter – my girl – was to kill me in stages . . . to sentence me to a living death . . .'

Lynley said, 'It's a possibility that we can't rule out, can we? Because if, as you say, your daughter had no enemies, then we're left with the single question: Who had? If you put away someone who's out on parole, Andy, we're going to need the name.'

'Jesus. There were scores.'

'The Yard can pull all your old files in London, but you can help by giving us some direction. If there's a particular investigation that stands out in your memory, you could halve our work by listing the players.'

'I've got my diaries.'

'Diaries?' Hanken asked.

'I once thought—' Maiden shook his head self-derisively. 'I thought of writing after retirement. Memoirs. Ego. But the hotel came along, and I never got round to it. I've got the diaries, though. If I have a look through them, perhaps a name ... a face ...' He seemed to crumple slightly then, as if the weight of responsibility for his daughter's death bore down on him.

'You don't know this for certain,' Nan Maiden said. 'Andy. Please. Don't do this to yourself.'

Hanken said, 'We'll follow whatever leads turn up. So if—'

'Then follow Julian.' Nan Maiden spoke defiantly, as if determined to prove to the police that there were other avenues to explore beyond the one that led to her husband's past.

Maiden said, 'Nancy. Don't.'

'Julian?' Lynley said.

Julian Britton, Nan told them. He'd just become engaged to Nicola. She wasn't suggesting him as a suspect, but if the police were looking for leads, then they certainly would want to talk to Julian. Nicola had been with him the night before she left for her camping trip. She might have said something to Julian – or done something even – that would result in another possibility for the police to explore in their investigation.

It was a reasonable enough suggestion, Lynley thought. He jotted down Julian's name and address. Nan Maiden supplied the information.

For his part, Hanken brooded. And he said nothing more until he and Lynley had returned to the car. 'It may all be a blind, you know.' He switched on the ignition, reversed out of their parking space, and turned the car to face Maiden Hall. There, he let the engine idle while he studied the old limestone structure.

'What?' Lynley asked.

'SO10. This business of someone from his past. It's a bit too convenient, wouldn't you say?'

'*Convenient* is an odd choice of words to describe a lead and a potential suspect,' Lynley said. 'Unless you yourself already suspect . . .' He looked towards the Hall. 'Exactly what is it that you suspect, Peter?'

'D'you know the White Peak?' Hanken asked abruptly. 'It runs from Buxton to Ashbourne. From Matlock to Castleton. We've got dales, we've got moors, we've got trails, we've got hills. This—' with a gesture at the environment – 'is part of it. So's the road we came in on, for that matter.'

'And?'

Hanken turned in his seat to face Lynley squarely. 'And in all this vast amount of space, Andy Maiden managed to find his daughter's car hidden out of sight behind a stone wall. All on his own. What would you say the odds are on that, Thomas?'

Lynley looked to the building, to its windows reflecting the last of the daylight like row upon row of shielded eyes. 'Why didn't you tell me?' he asked the other DI.

'I didn't think of it,' Hanken said. 'Not till our boy brought up SO10. Not till our Andy got caught out keeping the truth from his wife.'

'He wanted to spare her as long as he could. What man wouldn't?' Lynley asked.

'A man with nothing on his conscience,' Hanken said.

Showered and changed into the most comfortable elastic-waisted trousers that she possessed, Barbara was back to grazing – on leftover take-away pork fried rice which, unheated, wasn't about to make it onto anyone's culinary top ten – when Nkata arrived. He announced himself with two sharp raps on the door. She swung it open, take-away container in hand, and levelled a chopstick at him.

'Your watch stopped or something? What goes for five minutes in your book, Winston?'

He stepped inside unbidden and flashed her the full wattage of his smile. 'Sorry. Got another page before I could clear out. The Guv. I had to phone him first.'

'Of course. Can't keep his lordship waiting.'

Nkata let the comment go. 'Damned lucky that service is slow at the pub. I should've been out of there thirty minutes ago, which would've put me too close to Shoreditch to come back here for you. Funny, isn't it? Like my mum always says. Things work out exactly the way they're s'posed to work out.'

Barbara stared at him, eyes narrowed, wordless. She felt nonplussed. She wanted to tell him off for the note he'd left her – and for the letter C so prominent on it – but his air of ease stopped her. She couldn't explain his nonchalance any more than she could explain his presence inside her dwelling. He could at least look bloody uncomfortable, she decided.

'We got two bodies in Derbyshire and a London angle that needs playing on the case,' Nkata said. He sketched in the details: a woman, a young man, a former SO10 officer, anonymous letters assembled from newsprint, a threatening note written by hand. 'I got to get over to an address in Shoreditch where this dead bloke might've come from,' he told her. 'If someone's there who can i.d. the body, I'm on my way back to Buxton in the morning . . . But the Yard end of things'll need looking into. The 'spector just told me to set that up. That's why he paged.'

Barbara couldn't hide her eagerness when she said, 'Lynley asked for me?'

Nkata's glance shifted away for an instant, but that was enough. Her spirits came to earth.

'I see.' She carried her take-away container to the kitchen work top. The pork sat heavily on her stomach. Its flavour clung to her tongue like fur. 'If he doesn't know you're asking me, Winston, I can refuse with no one the wiser, can't I? You can pass me by and get someone else.'

'Can do, sure,' Nkata said. 'I can check the rota. Or I can wait till morning and let the super make the call. But doing all that leaves you free to get assigned to Stewart, Hale, or MacPherson, doesn't it? And I didn't much think you'd want to go that way if you didn't have to.' He left unsaid what was legend in CID: Barbara's failure to establish a working relationship with the DIs he'd mentioned, her subsequent return to uniform from which she had only been elevated by her partnership with Lynley.

Barbara swung around, perplexed by what appeared to be the other DC's inexplicable generosity. Another man in his position would have left her hanging in the wind, the better to improve his own position and to hell with what she might have to face. That Nkata wasn't doing so made her doubly cautious,

He was saying, 'It's computer work the guv wants. On CRIS. Not your thing, I know. But I thought if you wanted to come to Shoreditch with me – which is why I was in your neighbourhood in the first place – I could drop you at the Yard afterwards and you could get onto Crime Recording straightaway. If you pull something good from the records quick, who knows?' Nkata shifted on his feet. His air of ease diminished slightly as he concluded, 'It could go some distance to setting you right.'

Barbara found an unopened packet of cigarettes wedged between the crumb-dusted toaster and a box of watermelon Pop Tarts. She lit up, using one of the gas burners on the cooker, and she tried to make sense of what she was hearing. 'I don't get it. This is your chance, Winston. Why don't you take it?'

'My chance for what?' he said, looking blank.

'You know for what. To climb the ladder, to ascend the mountain, to fly to the moon. My stock with Lynley couldn't be much lower. Now's your chance to break out of the pack. Why aren't you taking it? Or rather, why're you taking the risk that I might do something to untarnish myself?'

'The 'spector told me to bring in another DC,' Nkata said. 'I thought of you.'

And there they were, those two ugly letters once again. DC. And there was the nasty reminder as well: of what she had been and what she had become. Of course Nkata would have thought of her, she realised. What better way to rub her face in her loss of position and authority than by bringing her in as a fellow DC, his superior no longer?

'Ah,' she said. 'Another DC. As to that . . .' She scooped up the note from where she'd left it on the dining table next to her necklace. She said, 'I guess I've got to thank you for this, haven't I? I'd been thinking about taking out an advert in the paper to inform the general public, but you've saved me the trouble.'

Nkata's eyebrows knotted. 'What're you on about?'

'The note, Winston. Did you honestly think I might forget my position? Or did you just want to remind me that we're equals now, players on a level field lest I forget?'

'Hang on. You've got it dead wrong.'

'Have I?'

'Right.'

'I don't think so. What other reason could there possibly be for you to address me as DC Havers? *C* for *constable*. Just like you.'

'Most obvious reason in the world,' Nkata said.

'Really? What's that?'

'I've never called you Barb.'

She blinked. *'What?'*

'I've never called you Barb,' he repeated. 'Just Sarge. Always that. And then this . . .' He used his wide hands in a gesture that encompassed the room but meant the day, as she very well knew. 'I didn't know what else. The name and everything.' He grimaced and rubbed the back of his neck, which lowered his head and ended eye contact. He said, 'DC's only your title, anyway. It's not who you are.'

Barbara was struck dumb. She stared at him. His attractive face with its nasty scar looked unsure at the moment, which had to be a first. She thought back and relived in an instant the cases on which she'd worked with Nkata. And in reliving them, she was a witness to the truth.

She covered her confusion with her cigarette, inhaling, exhaling, studying the ash, flicking grey flakes of it into the sink. When the silence between them became too much for her, she sighed and said, 'Jesus. Winston. Sorry. Bloody hell.'

'Right,' he said. 'So are you in or out?'

'I'm in,' she answered.

'Good,' he said.

'And, Winnie,' she added, 'I'm Barbara as well.'

Chapter Six

It was dark by the time they cruised into Chart Street in Shoreditch and sought out a parking space along a pavement that was lined with Vauxhalls, Opels, and Volkswagens. Barbara had felt a distinct twinge in her gut when Nkata had led her to Lynley's sleek silver car, a possession so prized by the inspector that merely to have been handed its keys was an eloquent statement of Lynley's confidence in his subordinate officer. She herself had been casually tossed that key ring on only two occasions, but both had come long after she'd worked her first case as the inspector's partner. Indeed, reflecting upon her association with Lynley, she found that she couldn't begin to imagine him passing his car keys over to the person she'd been on the first investigation they'd worked together. That he'd given them so easily to Nkata spoke volumes about the nature of their relationship.

Fine, she thought with resignation, that's just the way it is. She studied the neighbourhood through which they were driving, looking for the street address that the DVLA had listed as belonging to the owner of the motorcycle found near the murder scene in Derbyshire.

Like so many of its sister districts in London, Shoreditch may have been down at one time or another, but it could never be counted fully out. It was a densely populated area comprising a narrow appendix of land that dangled from the greater body of Hackney in northeast London. Since it formed one of the boundaries of the City, some of Shoreditch had been encroached upon by the sort of financial institutions one expected to see only within the Roman walls of old London. Other parts of it had been taken over by industry and commercial development. But there were still vestiges of the former villages of Haggerston and Hoxton in Shoreditch, even if some of those vestiges merely took the form of commemorative plaques marking the spots where the Burbages had plied their theatrical trade and where associates of William Shakespeare lay buried.

Chart Street appeared to represent the history of the district in one brief thoroughfare. Forming a dogleg that stretched between Pitfield Street and East Road, it contained commercial establishments as well as residences. Some of the buildings were smart, modern, and new and consequently they expressed the abundance of the City. Others awaited that miracle of London neighbourhoods – gentrification – which could take a simple street and transform it from slum into yuppie paradise within the space of a few short years.

The address produced by the DVLA took them to a line of terraced houses that, in appearance, were somewhere between the two extremes of disintegration and renovation. The terrace itself was flat-fronted and constructed of brick, and while the woodwork of the house in question badly needed painting, its windows were hung with white curtains that, at least from the exterior, looked crisp and clean.

Nkata found a parking space in front of the Marie Lloyd pub. He slid the Bentley into it with the sort of concentration that Barbara imagined a neurosurgeon giving to a patient's exposed brain. She shoved open the door and clambered out the third time the other DC meticulously straightened the car. She lit a fag and said, 'Winston. Bloody hell. You're not clocking on and neither one of us is getting any younger. Come *on.*'

Nkata chuckled affably. 'Giving you time to see to your habit.'

'Thanks. But I don't need to smoke a whole packet.'

The car finally parked to his satisfaction, Nkata eased out of it, locked it, and set its alarm. He checked scrupulously to make sure the doors were secured before joining Barbara on the pavement. They walked to the house, Barbara smoking and Nkata ruminating. At the yellow front door, he paused. Barbara thought he was giving her time to finish off her fag, and she puffed away, bulking up on the nicotine as she usually did before embarking on a task that could turn unpleasant.

But when she finally tossed the burning stub of the cigarette into the street, Nkata still didn't move. She said, 'So? Are we going in? What's up?'

He roused himself to answer, saying, 'This's my first.'

'First what? Oh. First time as the bearer of bad tidings? Well, take comfort. It doesn't get any easier.'

He shot her a look, smiled ruefully. 'Funny when you think,' he said quietly, the Caribbean in him coming out in his pronunciation of the final word. *T'ink*, he said.

'Think what?'

'Think how many times it could've been my mum getting a visit like this from the rozzers. If I'd kept on walking the path I was walking.'

'Yeah. Well,' she jerked her head towards the door and mounted the single step. 'We've all got blots on our copybooks, Winnie.'

The faint sound of a child's crying seeped round the cracks in the doorjamb. When Barbara rang the bell, the crying approached. It intensified, a woman's harassed voice said, 'Shush now. Shush. That's quite enough, Darryl. You made your point,' and then called through the panels, 'Who's there?'

'Police,' Barbara answered. 'Can we have a word?'

There was no response at first, other than Darryl's crying which went unabated. Then the door swung open and they were confronted by a woman with a small boy on her hip. He was in the act of rubbing his running nose against the collar of the green smock she wore. *The Primrose Path* was embroidered on the left breast of this, along with the name *Sal* beneath it.

Barbara had her warrant card ready. She was showing it to Sal when a younger woman came dashing down the narrow stairs that rose about nine feet from the entry. She wore a chenille dressing gown with one chewed up sleeve. Her hair was wet. She said, 'Sorry, Mum. Give him here. Thanks for the break. I needed it. Darryl, what're you *on* about, luv?'

'Da',' Darryl sobbed and reached a grimy hand towards Nkata.

'Wanting his daddy,' Nkata remarked.

'Not likely he'd be wanting *that* bloody bastard,' Sal muttered. 'Give your granna kiss, then, darling boy,' she said to Darryl, who in his distress didn't oblige her. She bussed him noisily on one wet cheek. 'It's his tummy again, Cyn. I made him a hot water bottle. It's in the kitchen. Mind you wrap it in a towel before you give it him.'

'Thanks, Mum. You're a queen,' Cyn said. Her son on her hip, she disappeared down the corridor towards the back of the house.

'What's this about, then?' Sal looked from Nkata to Barbara, not moving from her position by the door. She hadn't invited them to step inside. It was clear that she didn't intend to do so. 'It's gone ten. I expect you know that.'

Barbara said, 'May we come in, Mrs . . . ?'

'Cole,' she said. 'Sally Cole. Sal.' She stepped back from the door and scrutinised them as they crossed the threshold. She folded her arms beneath her breasts. In the better light of the entryway, Barbara saw that her hair – cut bluntly just below her ears – was streaked on either side of her face with panels of white blonde. These served to emphasise irregular and incongruous features: a broad forehead, a hooked nose, and a tiny rosebud mouth. 'I can't cope with suspense, so tell me what you got to tell me straightaway.'

'Could we . . . ?' Barbara nodded towards a door that opened to the left of the stairs. Beyond lay what appeared to be the sitting room, although it was dominated by a large and curious arrangement of gardening tools that stood in its centre. A rake with every other tine missing, a hoe with its edge turned inward, and a blunted shovel all formed a teepee over a cultivator whose handle had been split in half. Barbara examined this curiosity and wondered if it had anything to do with Sal Cole's manner of dress: The green smock and the words embroidered on it *did* suggest a source of employment that leaned towards the floral, if not the agricultural.

'He's a sculptor, my Terry,' Sal informed her, coming to stand at Barbara's side. 'That's his medium.'

'Gardening tools?' Barbara said.

'He's got a piece with secateurs that makes me want to cry. Both my kids're artists. Cyn's doing a course at the college of fashion. Is this about my Terry? 'S he in some sort 'f trouble? Tell me straightaway.'

Barbara glanced at Nkata to see if he wanted to do the dubious honours. He raised the fingers of one hand to his scarred cheek as if the cicatrix there had begun to throb. She said, 'Terry isn't home, then, Mrs Cole?'

'He doesn't live here,' Sal informed her. She went on to say that he shared digs and a studio in Battersea with a girl called Cilla Thompson, a fellow artist. 'Something's not happened to Cilla, has it? You're not looking for Terry because of Cilla? They're only friends, the two of them. So if she's been roughed up again, you best talk to that boyfriend of hers, not to my Terry. Terry wouldn't hurt a flea if it was biting him. He's a good boy, always has been.'

'Is there a . . . Well, is there a Mr Cole?' If they were about to suggest to this woman that her son was dead, Barbara wanted another presence – a potentially stronger presence – to help absorb the blow.

Sal gave a hoot. 'Mr Cole – as he *was* – did a Houdini on us when Terry was five. Found hisself a little bit of fluff with a nice set of kitties down in Folkestone and that was that for Mr Family Man. Why?' Her voice had begun to sound more anxious. 'What's this all about, then?'

Barbara nodded at Nkata. He, after all, had come to London to fetch the woman should it be necessary. It was in his hands how to break the news that the unidentified body they had might well be her son's. He began with the Triumph. Sal Cole confirmed that her son owned such a motorcycle, and as she did so, she also made the logical leap to a traffic accident. She went on so quickly to ask what hospital he'd been taken to that Barbara found herself wishing that the news they bore was as simple as a crash on the motorway.

There was no easy way. Barbara saw that Nkata had moved to a photograph-laden mantel that spanned a shallow embrasure where a fireplace once had been. He lifted one of the plastic-framed pictures, and the expression on his face told Barbara that carting Mrs Cole all the way to Derbyshire was probably going to be a mere formality. Nkata had, after all, seen pictures of the corpse if not the corpse itself. And while murder victims sometimes bore little resemblance to their living selves, there were usually enough areas of commonality for the astute observer to make a tentative identification from a photograph.

Seeing the picture appeared to give Nkata the courage to tell the tale, which he did with a simplicity and sympathy that impressed Barbara more than she would have thought possible.

The police needed someone to accompany them to Derbyshire in an attempt to identify the body, he told Mrs Cole in conclusion. She could be that someone. Or if she believed it would be too traumatic, then someone else – perhaps Terry's sister ... It was up to Mrs Cole. Nkata gently replaced the photograph.

Sal watched him, looking stunned. She said, 'Derbyshire? No. I don't think so. My Terry's working on a project in London, a big money project. A commission taking up all his time. It's why he couldn't be here last Sunday for lunch like he usually is. He dotes on our little Darryl, he does. He wouldn't miss his Sunday afternoon with Darryl. But the commission ... Terry couldn't come because of the commission. That's what he said.'

Her daughter joined them then, having donned a blue track suit and slicked back her hair. She paused in the doorway and appeared to take a reading of the room. She went hastily to Sal's side, saying, 'Mum. What's wrong? You've gone dead white. Sit down or you'll faint.'

'Where's our baby? Where's our little Darryl?'

'He's settled. That hot water bottle did the trick. Come on, Mum. Sit *down* before you fall over.'

'You wrapped it in a towel like I said?'

'He's fine.' Cyn turned to Barbara and Nkata. 'What's happened?'

Nkata explained briefly. The second time through seemed to deplete not his resources but those of Mrs Cole. When he reached the body another time, she grasped the handle of the hoe in the odd teepee sculpture, said, 'It was to be three times this size, his commission was. He *told* me so,' and made her way to a threadbare overstuffed chair. A small child's toys encircled this, and she reached for one of them: a bright yellow bird that she held to her chest.

'Derbyshire?' Cyn sounded incredulous. 'What the hell's our Terry doing in Derbyshire? Mum, he probably borrowed the motorcycle to someone. Cilla would know. Let's phone her.'

She strode to do so, punching in the numbers on a phone that stood on a squat table at the foot of the stairs. Her end of the conversation was simple enough: 'Is that Cilla Thompson?

... This is Cyn Cole, Terry's sister ... Yeah ... Oh, right. Proper little monster, he is. Got us all running round for him whenever he blinks. Listen, Cilla, 's Terry about? ... Oh. D'you know where's he gone off to, then?' A sombre glance over her shoulder at her mother as Cilla's answer told them the tale. Cyn said, 'Right then ... No. No message. But if he turns up in the next hour or so, have him phone me at home, okay?' And then she rang off.

Sal and Cyn communicated wordlessly in the way of women long used to each other's company. Sal said quietly, 'He's set on that commission heart and soul. He said, "This'll bring destination art into being. Just you watch, Mum." So I don't see why he would've left.'

'"Destination art?"' Barbara asked.

'His gallery. That's what he wants to call it: Destination Art,' Cyn clarified. 'He's always wanted a gallery for moderns. It was to be – *is* to be – on the south bank near the Hayward. It's his dream. Mum, this could be nothing. You hold onto that. It could be nothing.' But the tone of her voice sounded as if she'd have loved nothing more dearly than to convince herself.

'We'll need the address,' Barbara told her.

'There isn't any gallery yet,' Cyn replied.

'For Terry's digs,' Nkata clarified. 'And the studio he shares.'

'But you just said—' Sal didn't finish her remark. A silence fell among them. The source of it was obvious to them all: What could have been nothing was probably something, the worst sort of something that a family like the Coles might ever have to face.

Cyn went in search of the exact addresses. As she did so, Nkata said to Terry Cole's mother, 'I'll fetch you first thing in the morning, Mrs Cole. But if Terry should ring you sometime tonight, you page me. Right? Don't mind the time. Just page me.'

He wrote out his pager number on a sheet of paper that he removed from his neatly kept notebook. He was ripping it out and handing it over to Sal Cole when Terry's sister returned with her brother's information. She gave it to Barbara. Two locations were listed next to the words *flat* and *studio*. Both, Barbara saw, were in Battersea. She committed them to memory – just in case, she told herself – and she gave the paper to Nkata. He nodded his thanks, folded it, and shoved it into his pocket. A time was agreed upon for the morning's departure, and the two police constables found themselves out in the night.

A mild wind gusted on the street, blowing a plastic carrier bag and a large Burger King cup down the pavement. Nkata disarmed the security system on the car, but he didn't open the door. Instead, he looked at Barbara over the roof, then beyond her to the dismal council housing on the other side of the street. His face was a study in sadness.

'What?' Barbara asked him.

'I killed their sleep,' he said. 'I should've waited till morning. Why didn't I think of that? No way could we have driven back there tonight. I'm too shagged out. So why'd I rush over here like there was a fire I had to put out? They got that baby to see to, and I just killed their sleep.'

'You didn't have a choice,' Barbara said. 'If you'd waited till morning, they'd probably both've been gone – to work and to school – and you'd've lost a day. Don't drive yourself round the bend on it, Winston. You did what you had to do.'

'It's him,' he said. 'The bloke in the picture. He's the one got the chop.'

'I reckoned as much.'

'They don't want to believe it.'

'Who would?' Barbara said. 'It's the final goodbye without a chance to say it. And there can't be anything more rotten than that.'

Lynley chose Tideswell. A limestone village climbing two opposing hillsides, Tideswell sat virtually at the midway point between Buxton and Padley Gorge. Housing himself in the Black Angel Hotel – with its pleasing view of the parish church and its surrounding green – would provide him during the investigation with easy access both to the police station and to Maiden Hall. And to Calder Moor, if it came to that.

Inspector Hanken was agreeable to the idea of Tideswell. He would send a car round for Lynley in the morning, he said, pending the return of Lynley's own officer from London.

Hanken had thawed considerably in the hours they'd spent in each other's company. In the bar of the Black Angel Hotel, he and Lynley had tossed back two Bushmills apiece before dinner, a bottle of wine with the meal, and a brandy afterwards which also gave some assistance in the matter.

The whiskey and wine had elicited from Hanken the sort of professional war stories that were common to most interactions between policemen: rows with superiors, cock-ups in investigations, rough cases he'd been unhappily lumbered with. The brandy had provoked more personal revelations.

The inspector from Buxton pulled out the family photograph he'd shown Lynley earlier and gazed upon it long and silently. His index finger tracing the bundled shape of his infant son, he finally said the word *children* and went on to explain that a man changed for all time the moment a newborn was placed into his arms. One wouldn't expect that to be the case – that sort of alteration in persona was women's stuff, wasn't it? – but that's what happened. And what resulted from that change was an overwhelming desire to protect, to batten down every hatch in sight, and to secure every route of access into the heart of the home. So to lose a child despite every precaution . . . ? It was a hell beyond his imagining.

'Something Andy Maiden is currently experiencing,' Lynley noted.

Hanken eyed him but didn't argue the point. He went on to confide that his Kathleen was the light of his life. He'd known from the day they'd met that he wanted to marry her, but it had taken five years to persuade her to agree. What about Lynley and his new bride? How had it been for them?

But marriage, wife and children were the last subjects Lynley wanted to entertain. He sidestepped adroitly by claiming inexperience. 'I'm too wet behind the ears as a husband to have anything remarkable to report,' he said.

But he found that he couldn't avoid the subject when he was alone with his thoughts later that night. Still, in an attempt to divert them – or at least to postpone them – he went to the window of his room. He notched open the casement an inch and tried to ignore the strong scent of mildew that seemed to permeate his lodgings. He was as successful at this, however, as he was at overlooking the bed with its concave mattress and its pink duvet covered with a slick pseudo-satin material that promised a night of wrestling to keep it on the bed. He'd at least been equipped with an electric kettle, he observed gloomily, with a wicker basket of P.G. Tips, seven plastic thimbles of milk, one packet of sugar, and two fingers of shortbread. And he had a bathroom as well, although it had no window and it was fitted out with a water-stained tub encased in linoleum and lit by a single light bulb of candle-strength wattage. It could have been worse, he told himself. But he wasn't sure how.

When he could no longer avoid doing so, he glanced at the telephone on the iron-legged outdoor table that did service next to the bed. He owed Helen a call, at least to give her his whereabouts, but he was reluctant to punch in the numbers. He considered the reason.

Certainly, Helen was more in the wrong than he. He may have lost his temper with her, but she'd crossed a line when she'd taken the part of Barbara Havers' advocate. As his wife, she was supposed to be *his* advocate. She might have asked why he'd chosen Winston Nkata to work with and not Barbara Havers, instead of attempting to argue him into altering a decision that he had felt compelled to take.

Of course, upon reflection, he recalled that Helen's conversational opening had indeed been to ask him why he'd selected Nkata. It was his series of responses that had led them from a reasonable discussion into a row. Yet he'd responded as he had done because she'd provoked in him a sense of marital – if not moral – outrage. Her questions implied an alliance with someone whose actions couldn't begin to be justified. That he was being asked to justify his *own* actions – which were reasonable, allowable, and completely understandable – was more than mildly annoying.

Policing worked because of its officers' adherence to an established chain of command. Senior officers gained their positions by proving themselves capable of performance under pressure. With a life at stake and a suspect fleeing, Barbara Havers' superior officer had made a split second decision, giving orders that were as pellucid as they were reasonable. That Havers had contravened those orders was bad enough. That she'd taken matters into her own hands was very much worse. But that she'd wrested power to herself by using a firearm was a violation of their entire oath of office. It wasn't a simple bending of rules. It was a mockery of everything they stood for. Why hadn't Helen understood all this?

'*These things aren't black and white, Tommy.*' Malcolm Webberly's comment came back to him, as if in answer to his mental question.

But Lynley had to disagree with his superintendent. It seemed to him that some things were.

Still, he couldn't work his way round the fact that he owed his wife a telephone call. They didn't need to pursue their argument. And he could at least offer an apology for losing his temper.

Instead of Helen, however, he found himself talking to Charlie Denton, the young frustrated thespian who played the role of manservant in Lynley's life, when he wasn't haunting the half-price ticket booth in Leicester Square. The countess wasn't at home, Denton informed him, and Lynley could tell how much the maddening man enjoyed giving Helen the title. She'd phoned round seven o'clock from Mr St James's house, Denton went on, and said she'd been asked to stay to dinner. She hadn't yet returned. Did his lordship wish—

Lynley cut him off wearily. 'Denton,' he warned.

'Sorry.' The younger man chuckled and dropped the servility. 'D'you want to leave her a message, then?'

'I'll catch her in Chelsea,' Lynley replied. But he gave the Black Angel's number to Denton all the same.

When he phoned the St James house, however, he discovered that Helen and St James's wife had gone out straight after dinner. He was left talking to his old friend.

'They mentioned a film,' St James told him vaguely. 'I got the impression it was something romantic. Helen said she could do with an evening looking at Americans rolling round on a mattress with sculpted bodies, fashionable hair, and perfect teeth. That's the Americans, not the mattress, by the way.'

'I see.' Lynley gave his friend the number of the hotel with a message for Helen to phone if she returned at a reasonable hour. They hadn't had a proper chance to speak before he'd taken off for Derbyshire, he told St James. Even to his own ears, it sounded a lame explanation.

St James said that he'd pass the message to Helen. How was Lynley finding Derbyshire? he wanted to know.

It was a tacit invitation to discuss the case. St James would never inquire directly. He had too much respect for the unwritten rules that governed a police investigation.

Lynley found himself wanting to talk to his old friend. He reviewed the facts: the two deaths, the differing means by which they'd come about, the absence of one of the weapons, the lack of identification on the boy, the anonymous letters assembled from cut-outs, the scrawled suggestion that 'this bitch has had it'.

'It puts a signature on the crime,' Lynley concluded, 'although Hanken thinks the note could be part of a blind.'

'Misdirection on the part of the killer? Who?'

'Andy Maiden, if you go along with Hanken's thinking.'

'The father? That's a bit rough. Why is Hanken heading that way?'

'He wasn't, at first.' Lynley described their interview with the dead girl's parents: what had been said and what had been inadvertently revealed. He ended with, 'So Andy believes there's an SO10 connection.'

'What do you think?'

'Like everything else, it needs checking out. But Hanken didn't trust a word Andy said once we learned that he'd been keeping information from his wife.'

'He could merely have been trying to protect her,' St James offered. 'Not an unreasonable thing for a man to do for a woman he loves. And if they were really looking for a blind, wouldn't they misdirect you into considering the boy?'

Lynley agreed. 'There's a real bond between the two of them, Simon. It appears to be an extraordinarily close relationship.'

St James was silent for a moment on the other end of the line. Outside Lynley's hotel room, someone walked down the corridor. A door shut quietly.

'Then there's another way to look at Andy Maiden protecting his wife, isn't there, Tommy?' St James finally said.

'What's that, then?'

'He may be doing it for another reason. The worst possible reason, in fact.'

'Medea in Derbyshire?' Lynley asked. 'Christ. That's horrific. And when mothers kill, the child's generally young. I'll be pressed for a motive if things go that way.'

'Medea would have argued that she had one.'

In the midst of dealing with one of Nicola's many disappearances prior to the family's move to Derbyshire, Nan Maiden would have been incredulous had anyone suggested to her that there would come a day when she would yearn for something as simple as a teenager's running away from home in a fit of temper. When Nicola had disappeared in the past, her mother had reacted the only way she knew: with a mixture of terror, anger, and despair. She'd phoned the girl's friends, she'd alerted the police, and she'd taken to the streets to track her down. She'd been capable of nothing else until she'd known her child was safe.

That Nicola would vanish into the streets of London always intensified Nan's worry. For anything could happen on the streets of London. A teenage girl could be raped; she could be seduced into the nether world of narcotics; she could be beaten; she could be maimed.

There was one prospective consequence of Nicola's running off that Nan never considered, however: that her daughter had been murdered. The thought simply didn't bear dwelling upon. Not because murder never happened to young girls, but because if it happened to this particular young girl, her mother had no idea how she herself would go on.

And now it had happened. Not during those tempestuous teenage years when Nicola was insisting on autonomy, independence, and what she'd called 'the right to self-*determination*, Mum. We're not living in the Middle Ages, you know.' Not during that torturous period when making a demand of her parents – whether it was for something simple and concrete like a new CD or something complex and nebulous like personal freedom – was no less than an unspoken threat to vanish for a day or a week or a month if that demand wasn't met. But now, when she was an adult, when locking her door and nailing closed her window were actions that were supposed to be not only unthinkable but also unnecessary.

Yet that's exactly what I should have done, Nan thought brokenly. I should have locked her in, tied her to her bed, and refused to let her out of my sight.

'I know what I want,' Nicola had declared so many times throughout the years. 'And this is it.'

Nan had heard that in the voice of the seven year old who wanted Barbie, Barbie's house, Barbie's car, and every item of clothing that could be slid onto the impossibly shaped plastic figure that was supposed to be the epitome of femininity. In the cry of the twelve year old who could not exist another moment unless she was allowed to wear make-up, stockings, and four-inch-high heels. In the black moods of the fifteen year old who wanted a separate telephone line, a pair of in-line skates, a holiday in Spain without the burden of her parents along. Nicola had always wanted what Nicola wanted at the moment that Nicola wanted it. And many times over the years, it had seemed so much easier just to give in than to face a day, a week, or a fortnight of her disappearance.

But now, Nan wished with all her heart that her daughter had simply chosen to run off again. And she felt the hundred-weight of guilt dragging down on her for the occasions during Nicola's adolescence when, faced with yet another of her daughter's petulant flights from home, she'd even for an instant harboured the notion that it would have been better to have Nicola die at birth than not to know where she was or if she'd ever be found at all.

In the laundry room of the old hunting lodge, Nan Maiden clutched one of her daughter's cotton shirts to her chest as if the shirt could metamorphose into Nicola herself. Without a thought that she was doing so, she raised the collar of that shirt to her nose and breathed in the scent that was her child, the mixture of gardenias and pears from the lotions and shampoo that Nicola had used, the acrid odour of perspiration from a body used to brisk activity. Nan discovered that she could visualise Nicola on the last occasion when she'd worn the shirt: on a recent bike ride with Christian-Louis once the Sunday afternoon lunches had all been served.

The French chef had always found Nicola attractive – what

man hadn't? – and Nicola had observed the interest in his eyes and had not ignored it. That was her talent: pulling men without effort. She didn't do it to prove anything to herself or to anyone else. She simply did it, as if she gave off a peculiar emanation that was transmitted solely to males.

In Nicola's childhood, Nan had fretted over her sexual powers and what price they might exact from the girl. In Nicola's adulthood, Nan saw that the price had finally been paid.

'The purpose of parenthood is to bring up children who stand on their own as autonomous adults, not as clones,' Nicola had said four days ago. 'I'm responsible for my destiny, Mum. My life has nothing to do with you.'

Why did children say such things? Nan wondered. How could they believe that the choices they made and the end they faced touched no lives other than their own? The way that events had unfolded for Nicola had everything to do with her mother simply because she *was* her mother. For one did not give birth and then spare no thought to the future of one's treasured child.

And now she was dead. Sweet Jesus, there would never be another crash-bang entrance of Nicola coming home for a holiday, of Nicola returning from a hike on the moors, of Nicola slugging her way inside the lodge with carrier bags of groceries dangling from her arms, of Nicola back from a date with Julian all laughter and chatter about what they'd done. Sweet Jesus, Nan Maiden thought. Her lovely tempestuous incorrigible child was truly gone. The pain of that knowledge was an iron band growing tight round Nan's heart. She didn't think she'd be able to endure it. So she did what she had usually done when the feelings were too much to be borne. She continued to work.

She forced herself to lower the cotton shirt from her face and went back to what she had been doing, removing from the laundry all of her daughter's unwashed clothing as if by keeping the scent of her alive, she could also forestall the inevitable acceptance of Nicola's death. She mated socks. She folded jeans and jerseys. She smoothed out creases in every shirt, and she rolled up knickers and matched them to bras. Finally, she slid the clothing into plastic carrier bags from the kitchen. Then she methodically Sellotaped these bags closed, sealing in the odour of her child. She gathered the bags to her and left the room.

Upstairs, Andy was pacing. Nan could hear his footsteps above her as she moved noiselessly down the dimly lit corridor past the guest rooms. He was in his cubbyhole of a den, walking from the tiny dormer window to the electric fire, backwards and forwards, over and over again. He'd retreated there upon the departure of the police, announcing that he would start looking through his diaries immediately in an attempt to find the name of someone with a score to settle against him. But unless he was reading those diaries as he paced, in the intervening hours he'd not begun the search.

Nan knew why. The search was useless. For Nicola's death had nothing to do with anyone's past.

She *wouldn't* think of it. Not here, not now, and possibly not ever. Nor would she think what it meant – or didn't mean – that Julian Britton claimed to be engaged to her daughter.

Nan paused at the staircase that led to the private upper floor of the house where the family's quarters were. Her hands felt slick on the carrier bags, which she held to her chest. Her heart seemed to pound in tandem with her husband's tread. Go to bed, she told him silently. Please, Andy. Turn out the lights.

He needed sleep. And the fact that he was starting to go numb again told her just how badly he needed it. The advent of a detective from Scotland Yard hadn't resulted in a mitigation of Andy's anxiety. The departure of that same detective had only increased it. The numbness in his hands had begun to travel up his arms. A prick of a pin brought no blood to the surface of his skin, as if his whole body were shutting down. He'd managed to hold himself together while the police were present but once they'd left, he'd fallen apart. That was when he'd said he wanted to start going through the diaries. If he withdrew from his wife into his den, he could hide the worst of what he was experiencing. Or so he thought.

But a husband and wife should be able to help each other through something like this, Nan argued in the stillness. What's happening to us that we're facing it alone?

She had tried to replace conversation with concern earlier in the evening, but Andy had sloughed off her solicitous hovering, consistently refusing her offers of heating pads, brandy, cups of tea, and hot soup. He'd also avoided her attempts to massage some feeling back into his fingers. So ultimately, everything that might have been spoken between them went unsaid.

What to say now? Nan wondered. What to say when dread was among the emotions raging inside like innumerable battalions from a single army, out of control and combating one another?

She forced herself to mount the stairs, but instead of going to her husband, she went to Nicola's bedroom. There, she moved across the green carpet in the darkness and opened the clothes cupboard that was tucked under the eaves. Eyes used to the gloom, she could make out the shape of an old skateboard pushed to the back of a shelf, of an electric guitar leaning long unused against the far wall where it was draped by trousers.

Touching these with the tips of her fingers, saying idiotically, 'Tweed, wool, cotton, silk' as she felt the material of each, Nan became aware of a sound in the room, a buzzing that came from the chest of drawers behind her. As she turned, puzzled, the sound stopped. She had almost convinced herself that she'd imagined it, when it occurred again.

Curious, Nan set her Sellotaped packages on the bed and crossed the room to the chest. There was nothing on top of it to make such a noise, just a vase of drooping bladder campion and nightshade collected on a walk through Padley

Gorge. These wildflowers were accompanied by a hairbrush and comb, three bottles of scent, and a small beanbag flamingo with bright pink legs and large yellow feet.

With a glance towards the open bedroom door as if she were engaged in a surreptitious search, Nan slid open the top drawer of the chest. As she did so, the buzzing sounded for a third time. Her fingers moved in the direction of the noise. She found a small plastic square vibrating beneath a stack of knickers.

Nan carried this plastic square to the bed, sat, and switched on the bedside lamp. She examined what she'd taken from the drawer. It was Nicola's pager. On the top of it were two small buttons, one grey and one black. Across the end of it a thin screen held a brief message: *one page.*

The buzzer sounded again, startling Nan Maiden. She pushed down one of the two buttons in response. The thin screen shifted to another message, this a telephone number with an area code that Nan recognised from central London.

She swallowed. She stared hard at the number. She realised that whoever had paged her daughter had no idea that Nicola was dead. It was this thought that took her automatically to the telephone in order to make a reply. But it was another set of thoughts that took her to a telephone in the reception area of Maiden Hall when she could have as easily phoned the London number from the bedroom that she shared with Andy.

She drew a long breath. She wondered if she would have the words. She considered the possibility that having the words would make no difference to anyone. But she didn't want to think about that. She just wanted to phone.

Rapidly, she punched in the numbers. She waited and waited for the connection to be made, till she became lightheaded and realised that she was holding her breath. Finally, with a click, a phone somewhere in London began sounding. Double ring, double ring. Nan counted eight of them. She had started to think she'd misdialled the number when she finally heard a man's gruff voice.

He answered in the old way, marking his generation: He gave the last four digits of his number. And because of that fact, and because his way of answering reminded her so much of her own father, Nan heard herself saying what she would not have believed herself capable of saying an hour earlier. A whisper only, 'Nicola here.'

'Oh, so it's *Nicola* tonight, is it?' he demanded. 'Where the hell've you been? I paged you over an hour ago.'

'Sorry.' And in her daughter's abbreviated style of talking, 'What's up?'

'Nothing, and you damn well know it. What've you decided? Have you changed your mind? You can do that, you know. All will be forgiven. When're you back?'

'Yes,' Nan whispered. 'I've decided yes.'

'Thank God.' It was fervent. 'Oh Jesus. Thank *God*. Damn. It's become impossible, Nikki. I'm missing you too much. Tell me at once when you're coming back.'

'Soon.' The whisper.

'How soon? Tell me.'

'I'll phone you.'

'No! Good God. Are you mad? Margaret and Molly are here this week. Wait for the page.'

She hesitated. 'Of course.'

'Darling, have I made you angry?'

She said nothing.

'I have done, haven't I? Forgive me. I didn't mean to.'

She said nothing.

Then the voice altered, becoming suddenly and bizarrely childlike. 'Oh Nikki. Pretty Nikki of mine. Say you're not angry. Say *something*, darling.'

She said nothing.

'I know what you're like when I've made you angry. I'm a wicked boy, aren't I?'

She said nothing.

'Yes. I know. I'm wicked. I don't deserve you, and I must

take the medicine. You've got my medicine, haven't you, Nikki? And I must take it. Yes, I must.'

Nan's stomach heaved. She cried out, 'Who *are* you? Tell me your name!'

A muted gasp was the answer. The line went dead.

Chapter Seven

At the end of her third hour at the computer, Barbara Havers knew she had two alternatives. She could continue with the SO10 files in CRIS and possibly end up blind. Or she could take a break. She chose the latter option. She flipped her notebook closed, made an exit from the search she'd been conducting, and inquired where the nearest office was in which she could indulge her habit. With New Scotland Yard giving itself ever more over into the eager embrace of ASH, she was told that everyone on this particular floor was abstemious.

'Bloody hell,' she muttered. There was nothing for it but to backslide into behaviour from her schooldays. She slouched towards the nearest stairwell and plunked her squat body onto the stairs where she lit up, inhaled, and held the wonderful, noxious fumes within her lungs for so long that her eyeballs felt ready to pop from their sockets. Pure bliss, she thought. Life didn't get much better than a fag after three hours away from the weed.

The morning had gained her nothing of scintillating substance. On CRIS she'd discovered that Detective Inspector Andrew Maiden had served with the force for thirty years, and he'd spent the last twenty with SO10, where only Inspector Javert could have had a more resplendent career. His record of arrests was transcendent. The convictions that followed those arrests were themselves a marvel of British jurisprudence. But those two facts created a nightmare for anyone looking into his history undercover.

Maiden's convicts had gone through the system and ended up being detained at Her Majesty's pleasure in virtually every one of Her Majesty's prisons within the UK. And while the files gave details of undercover operations – most of them having been named by someone with a distinct taste for loony acronyms, she found – and complete reports into investigations, interrogations, arrests, and charges, the information became sketchy when it came to prison terms and sketchier still in the area of parole. If a ticket-of-leave man was on the streets and after the bloke who caused the silver bracelets to be slapped on him in the first place, he wasn't going to be easy to find.

Barbara sighed, yawned, and tapped her cigarette against the sole of her shoe, dislodging ash onto the step beneath her. She'd abjured her trademark high-top red trainers in deference to her new position – all spit and polish for AC Hillier should he happen past, eager to give her another wigging – and she found that her feet had begun to throb, so unaccustomed had they become to formal footwear. Indeed, sitting on the step in the stairwell, she became aware of entire areas of her body that were screaming discomfort and had doubtless been doing so for most of the morning: Her skirt felt as though an anaconda had taken position round her hips, her jacket appeared to be chewing large bites from her underarms, and her tights had dug so far into her crotch that she'd never need an episiotomy.

She'd never been one for high fashion during her working hours, choosing drawstring trousers, T-shirts, and jerseys over anything that might be construed as remotely related to haute couture. And used to seeing her more casually arrayed, more than one person this day had encountered Barbara with a raised eyebrow or a stifled grin.

Among this lot had been her near neighbours, whom Barbara had encountered not twenty-five yards from her own front door. Taymullah Azhar and his daughter had been loading themselves into Azhar's spotless Fiat when Barbara trundled round the corner of the house that morning, fighting her notebook into her shoulder bag, a half-smoked fag dangling from her lips. She hadn't been aware of them at first, not till Hadiyyah called out happily, 'Barbara! Hullo, hullo! Good morning! You shouldn't smoke so awfully much. It'll make your lungs all black and nasty if you don't stop. We learned that in school. We saw pictures and everything. Did I tell you that already? You look quite nice.'

Half in and half out of the car, Azhar extricated himself and nodded at Barbara politely. His gaze travelled from her head to her toes. 'Good morning,' he said. 'You're off early as well.'

'The bird, the worm, and all that rubbish,' Barbara replied heartily.

'Did you reach your friend?' he inquired. 'Last night?'

'My friend? Oh. You mean Nkata. Winston. Right? I mean Winston Nkata. That's his name.' She winced inwardly, wondering if she always sounded so lame. 'He's a colleague from the Yard. Yeah. We got in touch. I'm back in the game. It's afoot. Or whatever. I mean, I'm on a case.'

'You aren't working with Inspector Lynley? You've a new partner, Barbara?' The dark eyes probed.

'Oh no,' she said, partial truth, partial lie. 'We're all working the same case. Winston's just part of it. Like me. You know. The Inspector's handling one arm. Out of town. The rest of us're here.'

He said reflectively, 'Yes. I see.'

Too much, she thought.

'I only ate half my toffee apple last night,' Hadiyyah informed her, a blessed diversion. She'd begun to swing on the open door of the Fiat, hanging from the lowered window with her legs dangling and her feet kicking energetically to keep up the momentum. She was wearing socks as white as angel's wings. 'We c'n eat it for tea. If you like, Barbara.'

'That'd be nice.'

'I have my sewing lesson tomorrow. Did you know? I'm making something awfully special but I can't say what it is right now. *Because.*' She cast a meaningful look at her father. 'But *you* can see it, Barbara. Tomorrow, if you like. Do you want to see it? I'll show it to you if you say you want to see it.'

'That sounds just the ticket.'

'But only if you can keep a secret. Can you?'

'Mum's the absolute word,' Barbara vowed.

During this exchange, Azhar had been regarding her. His professional field was microbiology, and Barbara was beginning to feel like one of his specimens, so intense was his scrutiny. Despite their conversation of the previous night and the conclusion he'd reached upon seeing her manner of dress, he'd witnessed her setting off in her normal work togs long enough to know that the alteration in her get up had a significance beyond a woman's fancying a fashion make over. He said, 'How content you must be, on a case again. After the weeks of idleness, it's always gratifying to engage one's mind, isn't it?'

'It's definitely the cat's jim-jams.' Barbara dropped her cigarette to the ground and crushed it out, kicking the dog end into the flower bed. 'Biodegradable,' she said to Hadiyyah, who was obviously about to reprimand her. 'Aerates the soil. Feeds the worms.' She settled the strap of her bag more comfortably on her shoulder. 'Well. I'm off. Keep that toffee apple fresh for me, okay?'

'Maybe we can watch a video as well.'

'No damsels in distress, though. Let's do *The Avengers.* Mrs Peel's my idol. I like a woman who can show off her legs and kick gentlemen's bottoms simultaneously.'

Hadiyyah giggled.

Barbara nodded her goodbye. She was on the pavement, making her escape when Azhar spoke again. 'Is Scotland Yard undergoing a reduction in force, Barbara?'

She stopped, puzzled, and answered without thinking of the intent behind the question. 'Good grief, no. What made you ask that?'

'Autumn, perhaps,' he said. 'And the changes it brings.'

'Ah.' She sidestepped the implication behind the word *changes*. She avoided his eyes. She took the statement at its most superficial and dealt with it accordingly. 'The bad guys want nabbing no matter the season. You know the wicked. They never rest.' She smiled brightly and went on her way. As long as he never confronted her directly with the unpleasant word *constable*, she knew that she wouldn't have to explain to him how it had come to be attached to her name. She wanted to avoid that explanation as long as possible, forever if she could, because explaining to Azhar ran the risk of wounding him. And for reasons she didn't care to speculate upon, wounding Azhar was unthinkable to her.

Now, in the stairwell of New Scotland Yard, Barbara strove to put the thought of her neighbours out of her mind. That's all they were at the end of the day anyway: a man and a child whom she had come to know by chance.

She glanced at her watch. It was half past ten. She groaned. The thought of six or eight more hours staring at a computer screen was less than exciting. There had to be a more economical way to delve into DI Maiden's professional history. She tossed round several possibilities and decided to try the most likely one.

In her perusal of the files, she'd come across the same name time and again: DCI Dennis Hextell, with whom Maiden had worked in partnership as an undercover cop. If she could locate Hextell, she thought, he might be able to put her onto a lead that was stronger than something she would have to interpret from reading twenty years of files. That was the ticket, she decided: Hextell. She shoved herself off the stairs and went in search of him.

It turned out to be easier than she had anticipated. A phone call to SO10 gained her the information that DCI Hextell was still in the department although now as detective chief superintendent he directed operations instead of taking part in them on the street.

Barbara found him at a small table in the cafeteria on the fourth floor. She introduced herself, asking if she could join him. The DCS looked up from a set of photographs. His face, Barbara saw, wasn't so much lined as it was gouged, and gravity had taken its toll on his muscles. The years certainly hadn't been good to him.

The chief superintendent gathered his photographs together and didn't answer. Barbara said helpfully, 'I'm working on the Maiden killing in Derbyshire, sir. Andy Maiden's daughter. You were a team with him, right?'

That got a response. 'Sit.'

She could live with monosyllables. Barbara did his bidding. She'd fetched herself a Coke and a chocolate donut from the cafeteria, and she set these down on the table in front of her.

'Rot your teeth, that,' Hextell noted with a nod.

'I'm a victim of my addictions,' Barbara replied.

He grunted.

'That your plane?' she asked, with a nod at the picture on the top of his stack. It featured a yellow bi-plane of the sort that had been flown in World War I when aviators wore leather helmets and flowing white scarves.

'One of them,' he said. 'The one I use for aerobatics.'

'Stunt pilot, are you?'

'I fly.'

'Oh. Right. Must be nice.' Barbara wondered if the years undercover had made the man so loquacious. She launched into the purpose behind tracking him down: Was there any case, any stake out, any operation that leapt to mind as being particularly important in the history of his association with Andy Maiden? 'We're looking at revenge as a possible motive for the girl's murder, someone that you and DI Maiden put away, someone wanting to settle the score. Maiden's trying to come up with a name on his own in Derbyshire, and I've been scrolling through the reports all morning on the computer. But nothing's ringing my chimes.'

Hextell began separating his pictures. He appeared to have a system for doing so, but Barbara couldn't tell what it was since each shot was of exactly the same plane, just of varying angles: the fuselage here, the struts there, the wing tip, the engine, and the tail. When the piles were arranged to his liking, he took a magnifying glass from his jacket pocket and began studying each photograph under it. 'Could be anyone. We were rubbing elbows with real scum. Pushers, addicts, pimps, gun runners. You name it. Any one of them would have walked the length of the country to do us in.'

'But no one's name comes to mind?'

'I've survived by putting their names behind me. Andy was the one who couldn't.'

'Survive?'

'Forget.' Hextell separated one picture from the rest. It documented the plane head on, its body truncated by the angle. He applied his magnifying glass to every inch of it, squinting like a jeweller with a diamond in question.

'Is that why he left? He was out of here on early retirement, I've heard.'

Hextell looked up. 'Who's being investigated here?'

Barbara hastened to reassure him. 'I'm just trying to get a feeling for the man. If there's something you can tell me that'll help . . .' She made a that-would-be-great gesture and gave her enthusiasm to her chocolate donut.

The DCS set down his magnifying glass and folded his hands over it. He said, 'Andy went out on a medical. He was losing his nerves.'

'He had a nervous breakdown?'

Hextell blew out a derisive breath. 'Not stress, woman. *Nerves.* Real nerves. Sense of smell went first. Taste went next, then hands. He coped well enough, but then it was his vision. And that was the end of him. He had to get out.'

'Bloody hell. He went blind?'

'Would have done, no doubt. But once he retired, it all came back. Feeling, vision, the lot.'

'So what'd been wrong with him?'

Hextell looked at her long and hard before answering. Then he raised his index and middle fingers and tapped them lightly against his skull. 'Couldn't cope with the game. Undercover takes it out of you. I lost four wives. He lost nerves. Some things can't be replaced.'

'He didn't have wife problems?'

'Like I said. It was the game. Some blokes keep their peckers up fine when they're pretending to be someone they're not. But for Andy, that's not how it was. The lies he had to tell out there on the street . . . Keeping mum about a case till it was over . . . It knocked the stuffing out of him.'

'So there was no one case – one big case, perhaps – that cost him more than the others?'

'Don't know. I put it behind me. If there was one case, I couldn't name it.'

With that sort of memory, Hextell would have been a pearl of low price to the crown prosecutors in his salad days. But something told Barbara that the DCS didn't care whether the prosecutors found him useful or not. She packed the rest of her donut into her mouth and washed it down with Coke.

'Thanks for your time,' she told him and added in a gesture of friendliness, 'Looks like fun,' with a nod at the bi-plane.

Hextell picked up the propeller picture, held it top to bottom with the edges of his thumb and his index finger so as not to smudge it. 'Just another way to die,' he said.

Bloody hell, Barbara thought. What people do to put the job out of mind.

No closer to the name she was looking for but wiser to the potential pitfalls promised by a lengthy career in police work, she returned to the computer. She'd just begun revisiting Andrew Maiden's history when a phone call interrupted her.

'It's Cole.' Winston Nkata's voice came over a line that was thick with static. 'Mum took one look at the body, said "Right. That's my Terry," walked out 'f the room like she was going for groceries, and just hit the floor. Flat on her face. We thought she'd had a heart attack, but she'd just checked out. She had to be sedated once she came to. She's taking it hard.'

'Rough go,' Barbara said.

'She doted on the bloke. Makes me think of my mum.'

'Right. Well.' Barbara couldn't help thinking of her own mother. *Doting* certainly wouldn't be the word to describe her maternal deportment. 'Sorry and all that. Are you bringing her back?'

'Be there by mid-afternoon, I expect. We stopped for coffee. She's in the loo.'

'Ah.' Barbara wondered why he was phoning. Perhaps to serve as intermediary between herself and Lynley, passing along information so that the inspector would have as little contact with her as he apparently deemed necessary at the moment. She said, 'I haven't got anything on Maiden's arrests yet. At least not anything that *looks* useful.' She told him what DCS Hextell had confided about Maiden's nervous complaints, adding, 'Whatever the inspector wants to make of that.'

'I'll give him the information,' Nkata told her. 'If you c'n break off, there's Battersea to look at. It'd save us some time.'

'Battersea?'

'Terry Cole's digs. His studio as well. One of us needs to get over there, talk to his roommate. This Cilla Thompson, you recall?'

'Yeah. But I thought . . .' What had she thought? Obviously, that Nkata would keep as much to himself as he could, leaving the grunt work to her. The other DC continued to nonplus her with his easy generosity. 'I can break off,' Barbara said. 'I remember the address.'

She heard Nkata chuckle. 'Now, why'm I not surprised at that?'

Lynley and Hanken had spent the first part of the morning waiting for Winston Nkata to deliver Terry Cole's mother to them for the purpose of identifying the second body found on the moor. Neither man had much doubt that the procedure would be a mere formality – devastating and anguished, but still a formality. When no one had come off the moor by dawn to claim the motorcycle and no one else had reported it stolen, it seemed fairly conclusive that the mutilated male and the owner of the motorcycle were one and the same.

Nkata reached them by ten, and the answer was theirs by quarter past the hour. Mrs Cole verified that the boy was indeed her son Terry, after which she collapsed. A doctor was summoned, sedative in hand. He took over where the police left off.

'I want his effects,' Sal Cole had sobbed, by which they understood that she meant her son's clothes. 'I want his effects for our Darryl. I mean to have them.'

And she would do, they told her, once forensics had completed their analysis, once the jeans and T-shirt and Doc Martens and socks were no longer deemed necessary for a successful prosecution of whoever had committed the crime. Until that time, they would give her receipts for each garment that the boy had been wearing, for his motorcycle as well. They didn't tell her that it could easily be years before the ensanguined clothing was released to her. And for her part, she didn't ask when she might expect it. She just clutched the envelope of receipts and wiped at her eyes with the back of her wrist. Winston Nkata escorted her from the nightmare, into the extended nightmare to come.

Lynley and Hanken withdrew to the DI's office in silence. Prior to Nkata's arrival, Hanken had spent the time reviewing his notes on the case thus far, and he'd had another look at the initial report compiled by the constable who'd first talked to the Maidens about their daughter's disappearance. 'She had several phone calls on the morning of her hike,' he told Lynley. 'Two from a woman, one from a man, neither giving their names to Nan Maiden before she fetched Nicola to take the call.'

'Could the man have been Terence Cole?' Lynley asked.

It was more grist for the mill of their suspicions, Hanken concluded.

He went to his desk. At its precise centre, someone had placed a sheaf of papers while they'd been with Mrs Cole. It was, Hanken told Lynley upon taking them up, a document relating to the case. Owing largely to the services of an excellent transcriptionist, Dr Sue Myles had managed to be as good as her word: They had the autopsy report in hand.

Dr Myles had been as thorough as she'd been unconventional, they discovered. Her findings upon external examination of the bodies alone took up nearly ten pages. In addition to a detailed description of every wound, contusion, abrasion, and bruise on both corpses, Dr Myles had recorded each minute particular associated with a death on the moor. Thus, everything from the heather caught up in the hair of Nicola Maiden to a thorn pricking one of Terry Cole's ankles was assiduously noted. The detectives were made aware of infinitesimal fragments of stone embedded in flesh, evidence of bird droppings on skin, unidentified slivers of wood in wounds, and the postmortem damage done to the bodies by insects and birds. What the detectives didn't have at the end of their reading, however, was what they hadn't had at the beginning of it: a clear idea of the number of killers they were seeking. But they *did* have one intriguing detail: Aside from her eyebrows and the hair on her head, Nicola Maiden had been completely shaved. Not born hairless, but deliberately shaved.

It was that interesting fact that suggested their next move in the investigation.

Perhaps it was time, Lynley said, to talk to Julian Britton, the grief-stricken fiancé of their primary victim. They set off to do so.

The Britton home, Broughton Manor, sat midway up a limestone outcrop just two miles southeast of the town of Bakewell. Facing due west, it overlooked the River Wye, which at this location in the dale cut a placid curve through an oak-studded meadow where a flock of sheep grazed. From a distance, the building looked not like a manor house that had once been the centre of a thriving estate but instead an impressive fortification. Erected from limestone that had long ago gone grey from the lichen that thrived upon it, the house comprised towers, battlements, and walls that rose twelve feet before giving way to the first of a series of narrow windows. The manor's entire appearance suggested longevity and strength, combined with the willingness and the ability to survive everything from the vicissitudes of weather, to the whimsies of the family who owned it.

Closer, however, Broughton Manor told a different tale. Glass was missing from some of its diamond-paned windows, part of its ancient oak roof appeared to have caved in, a forest of greenery – everything from ivy to old man's beard – seemed to be pressing against the remaining windows of the southwest wing, and the low walls that marked a series of gardens falling towards the river were crumbling and gap-ridden, giving wandering sheep access to what had probably once been a descending array of colourful parterres.

'Used to be the showplace of the county,' DI Hanken said to Lynley as they swung across the stone bridge that spanned the river and became the sloping drive up to the house. 'Chatsworth aside, of course. I'm not talking about palaces. But once Jeremy Britton got his maulers on it, he ran it straight to hell in less than ten years. The older boy –

that's our Julian – has been trying to bring the place back to life. He wants to make it pay for itself as a farm. Or a hotel. Or a conference centre. Or a park. He even lets it out for fêtes and tournaments and the like, which probably has his ancestors spinning in their graves. But he's got to stay one step ahead of his dad, who'll drink up the profits if he's got the chance.'

'Julian's in need of funds?' Lynley asked.

'Putting it mildly.'

'And there are other children?' Lynley asked. 'Julian's the eldest?'

Hanken pulled past an enormous iron-studded front door – its dark oak dun with age, indifferent care, and bad weather – and drove them round to the back of the house where an arched gate big enough for a carriage to pass through had an additional human-size door cut into it. This stood open, beyond it a courtyard between whose paving stones weeds sprung like unexpected thoughts. He switched off the ignition. 'Julian's got a brother permanently at university. And a sister married and living in New Zealand. He's the oldest child – Julian is – and why he doesn't go along the same path as the others and clear out is beyond me. His dad's a nasty piece of work, but you'll see that for yourself if you meet him.'

Hanken shoved open his door and led the way into the courtyard. Excited howling came from what seemed to be the stables, which stood at the end of an overgrown gravel lane shooting north from a curve in the nearby drive. 'Someone's with the hounds,' Hanken told Lynley over his shoulder. 'Probably Julian – he breeds the dogs – but we may as well check inside first. This way.'

This way took them into a courtyard, one of two, Hanken informed him. According to the DI, the imperfect rectangle in which they stood was a relatively modern addition to the older four wings of the building which comprised the west façade of the house. *Relatively modern* in the history of Broughton

Manor, of course, meant that the courtyard was just under three hundred years old and as such it was called the new court. The old court was mostly fifteenth century, with a fourteenth century central portion that constituted the shared boundary between the courts.

Even a cursory inspection of the courtyard was enough to reveal the decay that Julian Britton was attempting to counter-act. But there were indications of occupancy intermingling with those of decrepitude: A makeshift clothesline waving incongru-ous pink sheets had been rigged in one corner, extending in a diagonal between two wings of the house and tied onto two paneless windows by means of their rusting iron casements. Plastic rubbish bags waited to be carted off alongside antique tools that probably hadn't been used for a century. A shiny aluminium walking stick lay near an old discarded mantel clock. Past and present met in every corner, as something new tried to rise from the detritus of the old.

'Hullo there. Can I help you?' It was a woman's voice, calling to them from above. They looked towards the windows, and she laughed and said, 'No. Up here.'

She was on the roof, with a rubbish sack slung over her shoulder, giving her the appearance of a decidedly unseasonal and even more outsized Christmas elf in the midst of a delivery. But she was a particularly dishevelled elf: her bare arms and legs were streaked with grime.

'Gutters,' she said cheerfully, in apparent reference to her current occupation. 'If you'll wait a moment, I'll be right down.'

Clouds of filth and decomposing leaves rose round her as she worked, her head turned away to keep the worst of the mess from alighting on her face.

'There. That's that,' the young woman said when she reached the gutter's end. She yanked off a pair of gardening gloves and came across the roof to an extension ladder that rested against the building, behind the line of pink sheets. She climbed down agilely and came across the courtyard. She introduced herself as Samantha McCallin.

In an environment so conducive to historical reflections, Lynley saw the young woman as she would likely have been seen in the distant past: extremely plain but hardy, of peasant stock, a perfect specimen for childbearing and labour on the land. In modern terms, she was tall and well-built, with the physique of a swimmer. She wore no-nonsense clothes that were suited to her activity. Old cut-off blue jeans and boots were topped by a T-shirt. A bottle of water hung from her belt.

She'd pinned her mouse brown hair to the top of her head in a coil, and she loosed it as she observed them frankly. It fell in a single thick plait to her waist. 'I'm Julian's cousin. And you, I expect, are the police. And this visit, I imagine, is about Nicola Maiden. Am I right?' Her expression told them that she generally was.

'We'd like a chat with Julian,' Hanken told her.

'I hope you're not thinking he was involved in her death in some way.' She unhooked the water bottle and took a slug of it. 'That's impossible. He adored Nicola. He played knight to her damsel and all that nonsense. No distress was too much of a challenge for Julie. When Nicola called, he was into his armour before you could say Ivanhoe. Metaphorically speaking, naturally.' She offered them a smile. It was her only mistake. Brittle, it revealed the anxiety beneath her friendly demeanour.

'Where is he?' Lynley asked.

'Gone to the dogs. Fitting, isn't it, for the environment we're in? Come along. I'll show you the way.'

Her guidance wasn't necessary. They could have followed the noise. But the young woman's determination to monitor their meeting with Julian was an intriguing circumstance that a wise investigator would want to toy with. And that she was determined to monitor that meeting was evidenced in the long, sure stride she employed, charging briskly past them out of the courtyard.

They followed Samantha up the overgrown lane. The branches of unpruned limes overhung it, offering an idea of what the leafy tunnelled path to the stables had once been like.

The stables themselves had been converted to kennels for the breeding of Julian Britton's harriers. There were dogs in abundance in a number of curiously shaped runs, and all of them broke into cacophonous barking as Hanken and Lynley approached with Samantha McCallin.

'Quieten down, you lot,' Samantha shouted. 'You, Cass. Why aren't you with the pups?'

In reply, the dog spoken to – stalking back and forth in a separate run from the others – trotted back to the building and disappeared through a dog-size door that had been hewn into the limestone wall. 'That's better,' Samantha remarked. And to the men, 'She whelped a few nights ago. She's protective of the pups. Julie'll be with them, I expect. It's just inside.' The kennels, she told them as she swung open the door, consisted of exterior and interior dog runs, two birthing rooms, and a dozen puppy pens.

In contrast to the manor house, at the kennels the accent was on the clean and the modern. Outside, the runs had been swept, the water dishes had sparkled, and the chain link fence had borne not a fleck of rust. Inside, the detectives found that the walls were whitewashed, the lights were bright, the stone floor was polished, and music played. Brahms, by the sound of it. The thick walls of the building provided an insulation against the noise of the dogs outside. Because they also intensified the damp and the cold, central heating had been installed.

Lynley glanced at Hanken as Samantha led them towards a closed door. It was clear that the other DI was thinking the same thing: The dogs were living better than the humans.

Julian Britton was in a room identified on its door as 'Pup

Room One.' Samantha knocked twice and called his name. She said, 'The police want a word, Julie. Can we come in?'

A man's voice said, 'Quietly. Cass's uneasy.'

'We saw her outside.' And to Lynley and Hanken, 'Act reassuring if you will. Towards the dog.'

Cass set up a ruckus when they entered the room. She was in an L-shaped run that gave on to the exterior run by means of the door through the wall. At the far end of this – well away from the draught – a box contained her new litter of puppies. Four heat lamps shone over this section of the run. The box itself was insulated, sided with sheepskin, and floored with a thick padding of newspaper.

Julian Britton stood inside the run. He held a puppy in his left hand while he offered his right index finger to the tiny dog's mouth. Eyes still closed, the animal sucked eagerly. After a moment, Julian disengaged him, returned him to the nest, and made a note in a three-ring binder. He said, 'Easy, Cass,' to calm the dog. She remained wary, though, merely exchanging the bark for low growls.

'All mothers should take such an interest in their brood.' It was impossible to tell to whom Samantha was referring: the dog or Julian Britton.

As Cass settled herself in the nest of newspapers, Julian watched. He said nothing until the pup he'd been examining had found its place on one of the teats. Then he merely murmured to the dogs as the rest of the litter nosed into position to nurse.

Lynley and Hanken introduced themselves, producing warrant cards. Julian looked these over, which gave them time to look him over. He was a good size man, hefty without being overweight. His face bore the sort of irregular freckles on the forehead that were indications of a life spent out of doors as well as the precursors of skin cancer, and an additional patch of freckles across his cheeks gave him the appearance of a ginger-haired bandit. In combination with the unnatural pallor of his skin, though, the freckles enhanced a look of malaise.

After he had inspected the detectives' identification to his satisfaction, he removed a blue handkerchief from his trouser pocket and wiped his face with it, although he didn't appear to be perspiring. He said as he wiped, 'I'll do anything I can to help you. I was with Andy and Nan when they got the news. I had a date with Nicola that night. When she didn't turn up at the Hall, we phoned the police.'

'Julie went out looking for her himself,' Samantha added. 'The police weren't willing to do anything.'

Hanken didn't look pleased with this oblique criticism. He cast a sour glance at the woman and asked if they could have their conversation somewhere where the bitch wouldn't be growling at them. He was referring to the dog. But Samantha didn't miss the *double entendre*. She gave Hanken a narrow glance and pressed her lips together.

Julian obliged them by leading the way to the puppy runs in a separate section of the building. Here, older pups were engaged in play. The runs were cleverly devised to keep them challenged and entertained, with cardboard boxes to tear apart, complicated multi-level mazes to wander in, toys to play with, and hidden treats to search out. The dog, Julian Britton informed them, was an intelligent animal. Expecting an intelligent animal to thrive in a concrete run devoid of distraction was not only stupid, it was also cruel. He'd talk to the detectives while he worked, he said. He hoped that would be all right.

So much for the grieving fiancé, Lynley thought.

'That'll be fine,' Hanken said.

Julian seemed to know what Lynley was thinking. He said, 'Work's a balm at the moment. I expect you understand.'

'Need help, Julie?' Samantha asked. To her credit, the offer was gently made.

'Thanks. You can work with the biscuits if you'd like, Sam.

I'm going to rearrange the maze.' He entered the run as Samantha went to fetch the food.

The pups were delighted with this human intrusion into their domain. They stopped playing and gravitated towards Julian, eager for another distraction. He murmured to them, patted their heads, and tossed four balls and several rubber bones to the far end of the run. As the dogs scampered after them, he set to work on the maze, which he disassembled through a series of slots in the wood.

'We've been given to understand that you and Nicola Maiden were engaged to be married,' Hanken said. 'We've been told it was a recent engagement as well.'

'You have our sympathy,' Lynley added. 'It can't be something you particularly want to talk about, but there might be something you can tell us – something you're not even aware of yourself perhaps – that will help in the investigation.'

Julian gave his attention to the sides of the maze, stacking them neatly as he answered. 'I misled Andy and Nan. It was easier at the moment than going into everything. They kept asking if we'd had a row. Everyone kept asking, when she didn't turn up.'

'Misled? Then you weren't engaged to her?'

Julian cast a glance in the direction that Samantha had taken to fetch the dogs' food. He said quietly, 'No. I asked. She turned me down.'

'The feelings weren't mutual?' Hanken asked.

'I suppose they weren't if she didn't want to marry me.'

Samantha rejoined them, lugging a large burlap sack behind her, her pockets bulging with treats for the puppies. She entered the run, saying, 'Here, Julie. Let me help you with that,' when she saw that her cousin was wrestling with a part of the maze that didn't want to give way.

He said, 'I'm coping.'

'Don't be a goose. I'm stronger than you are.'

In Samantha's capable hands, the maze came apart quickly. Julian stood by and looked uncomfortable.

'Exactly when did this proposal occur?' Lynley asked.

Samantha's head turned swiftly towards her cousin. Just as swiftly, it turned away. She industriously began hiding dog biscuits throughout the run.

'On Monday night,' Julian told them. 'The night before she . . . before Nicola went out on the moor.' Abruptly, he went back to his work. He spoke to the maze, not to them, saying, 'I know how that looks. I'm not such a fool that I don't know exactly how it looks. I propose, she turns me down, then she dies. So yes, yes. I know exactly how it bloody well looks. But I didn't kill her.' Head lowered, he widened his eyes as if by doing so he could keep them from watering. He said only, 'I loved her. For years. I *loved* her.'

Samantha froze where she was at the far end of the run, the puppies cavorting round her. It seemed as if she wanted to go to her cousin, but she didn't move.

'Did you know where she'd be that night?' Hanken asked. 'The night she was killed?'

'I phoned her that morning – the morning she left – and we fixed up a date for Wednesday night. But she didn't tell me anything more.'

'Not that she'd be going out hiking?'

'Not that she was going off at all.'

'She had other phone calls before she'd left that day,' Lynley told him. 'A woman phoned. Possibly two women. A man phoned as well. No one gave Nicola's mother a name. Have you any idea who might have wanted to speak with her?'

'None at all.' Julian showed no reaction to the knowledge that one of her callers had been male. 'It could have been anyone.'

'She was quite popular,' Samantha said from her end of the run. 'She was always surrounded by people up here, so she must have had dozens of student friends as well. I expect she got phone calls from them all the time when she was away from college.'

'College?' Hanken asked.

Nicola had just finished doing a conversion course at the College of Law, Julian told them. And he added, 'In London,' when they asked him where she'd studied. 'She was up for the summer working for a bloke called Will Upman. He's got a firm of solicitors in Buxton. Her dad fixed it up for her because Upman's something of a regular at the Hall. And because, I expect, he hoped she'd work for Upman in Derbyshire when she finished her course.'

'That was important to her parents?' Hanken asked.

'It was important to everyone,' Julian replied.

Lynley wondered if *everyone* included Julian's cousin. He glanced her way. She was very busy hiding dog biscuits for the puppies to search out. He asked the obvious next question. How had Julian parted from Nicola that night of the proposal? In anger? Bitterness? Misunderstanding? Hope? It was a hell of a thing, Lynley said, to ask a woman to marry you and to be turned down. It would be understandable if her refusal led to depression or even to an unexpected burst of passion.

Samantha rose from her position at the far end of the run. 'Is that your clever way of asking if he killed her?'

'Sam,' Julian said. It sounded like a warning. 'I was down, of course. I felt blue. Who wouldn't?'

'Was Nicola involved with someone else? Is that why she refused you?'

Julian didn't reply. Lynley and Hanken exchanged a glance. Samantha said, 'Ah. I see where this is heading. You're thinking that Julie came home on Monday night, phoned her up the next day to arrange a meeting, discovered where she'd be that night – which he of course wouldn't admit to you – and then killed her. Well, I can tell you this: That's absurd.'

'Perhaps. But an answer to the question would be helpful,' Lynley noted.

Julian said, 'No.'

'No, she wasn't involved with someone else? Or no, she didn't tell you if she was involved with someone else?'

'Nicola was honest. If she'd been romantically involved with someone else, she would have told me.'

'She wouldn't have tried to protect you from the knowledge, to spare your feelings once you'd made them clear to her?'

Julian gave a rueful laugh. 'Believe me, sparing people's feelings wasn't her way.'

Despite any suspicions he had elsewhere, the nature of Julian's response seemed to prompt Hanken to ask, 'Where were you on Tuesday night, Mr Britton?'

'With Cass,' Julian said.

'The dog? With the *dog*?'

'She was whelping, Inspector,' Samantha said. 'You don't leave a dog alone when she's whelping.'

'You were here as well, Miss McCallin?' Lynley asked. 'Helping out with the delivery were you?'

She caught her lower lip with her teeth. 'It was the middle of the night. Julie didn't get me up. I saw the puppies in the morning.'

'I see.'

'No, you don't!' she cried. 'You think Julie's involved. You've come to trick him into saying something that will implicate him. That's how you work.'

'We work at getting to the truth.'

'Oh right. Tell that to the Bridgewater Four. Only it's three now, isn't it? Because one of those poor sods died in prison. Call a solicitor, Julie. Don't say another word.'

Julian Britton in possession of a solicitor was exactly what they didn't need at the moment, Lynley thought. He said, 'You appear to keep records about the dogs, Mr Britton. Did you record the time of delivery?'

'They don't all pop out at once, Inspector,' Samantha said.

Julian said, 'Cass went into labour round nine at night. She began delivering round midnight. There were six puppies – one was stillborn – so it took several hours. If you want the exact times, I have them in the records. Sam can fetch the book.'

She went to do so. When she returned, Julian said to her, 'Thanks. I'm nearly finished in here. You've been a real help. I'll manage the rest.'

Obviously, he was dismissing her. She appeared to communicate something to him through eye contact only. Whatever it was, he either couldn't or didn't want to receive the message. She cast a moderately baleful look at Lynley and Hanken before she left them. The sound of the dogs barking outside rose then fell as she opened and closed the door behind her.

'She means well,' Julian told them when she was gone. 'I don't know what I'd do without her. Trying to put the whole manor back together . . . It's a hell of a job. Sometimes I wonder why I took it on.'

'Why did you?' Lynley asked.

'There've been Brittons here for hundreds of years. My dream is to keep them here for a few hundred more.'

'Nicola Maiden was part of that dream?'

'In my mind, yes. In her mind, no. She had her own dreams. Or plans. Or whatever they were. But that's fairly obvious, isn't it?'

'She told you about them?'

'All she told me was that she didn't share mine. She knew I couldn't offer her what she wanted. Not at the moment and probably never. She thought it was the wiser course to leave our relationship the way it was.'

'Which was what?'

'We were lovers, if that's what you're asking.'

'In the normal sense?' Hanken asked.

'What's that supposed to mean?'

'The girl was shaved. It suggests . . . a certain sexual whimsicality to the relationship you had with her.'

Ugly colour flared in Julian's face. 'She was quirky. She

185

waxed herself. She had some body piercings done as well. Her tongue. Her navel. Her nipples. Her nose. That's just who she was.'

She didn't sound like a woman who'd be the prospective bride of the impoverished landed gentry. Lynley wondered how Julian Britton had come to think of her as such.

Britton, however, appeared to read the direction his thoughts were taking. He said, 'It doesn't *mean* anything, all that. She just was who she was. Women are like that these days. At least women her age. As you're from London, I'd expect you know that already.'

It was true that one certainly saw just about everything on the streets of London. It would be a myopic investigator who judged any woman under thirty – or over thirty for that matter – on the basis of waxing herself hairless or allowing holes to be needled into her body. But all the same, Lynley wondered at the nature of Julian's comments. There was an eagerness to them that needed probing.

'That's all I can tell you.' Having made that remark, Julian opened the record book that his cousin had brought to him. He flipped to a section behind a blue divider and turned several pages until he found the one he wanted. He turned the book round so that Lynley and Hanken could see it. The page was labelled *Cass* in large block letters. Beneath her name were documented the times of each puppy's delivery, as well as the times that parturition had begun and ended.

They thanked him for the information and left him to continue his work with the harriers. Outside, it was Lynley who spoke first.

'Those times were written in pencil, Peter, the lot of them.'

'I noticed.' Hanken nodded in the direction of the manor house, saying, 'Make quite a team, don't they? "Julie" and his cousin.'

Lynley agreed. He just wondered what game the team was playing.

Chapter Eight

————◆————

Barbara Havers was relieved to be able to leave the claustrophobic confines of the Met headquarters. Once Winston Nkata requested that she get onto the Battersea address of Terry Cole, she wasted little time in dashing for her car. She took the most direct route possible, heading for the river where she followed the Embankment to Albert Bridge. On the south bank of the Thames, she consulted her battered *A to Z* until she found the street she was looking for sandwiched between the two Bridge Roads: Battersea and Albert.

Terry Cole's digs were in a forest green brick-and-bay-windowed conversion set among other similar conversions in Anhalt Road. A line of buzzers indicated that there were four flats in the building, and Barbara pressed the one that had *Cole/Thompson* taped next to it. She waited, glancing round at the neighbourhood. Terraced houses, some in better condition than others, were fronted by gardens. Some were neatly planted, some were overgrown, and more than one appeared to be used as a dumping place for everything from rusting cookers to screenless televisions.

There was no answer from the flat. Barbara frowned and descended the steps. She blew out a breath, not wanting to face another few hours at the computer, and considered her options as she studied the house. A spate of breaking and entering definitely wasn't going to cut the mustard, and she was thinking about a retreat to the nearest pub for a plate of bangers and mash when she noticed a curtain flick in the bay window of the ground floor flat. She decided to have a go at the neighbours.

Next to flat number one was the name Baden. Barbara pressed the buzzer. A tremulous voice came through the speaker almost at once in reply, as if the person in the corresponding flat had been preparing for a visit from the law. Once Barbara identified herself – and cooperatively held up her warrant card so that it could be observed at a distance through the ground floor window – the lock on the door was released. She pushed it open and found herself inside a vestibule that was the approximate size of a chess board. It was chess board in decoration as well: red and black tiles across which innumerable footprints were smudged.

Flat number one opened to the right of the vestibule. When Barbara knocked, she found that she had to go through the procedure all over again. She held her warrant card to the peep hole in the door this time. When it had been studied to the occupant's satisfaction, two dead bolts and a safety chain were released and the door opened. Barbara was faced with an elderly woman who said apologetically, 'One can't be too careful these days, I'm afraid.'

She introduced herself as Mrs Geoffrey Baden and quickly brought Barbara up to speed on the particulars of her life without being asked. Twenty years a widow, she had no children, just her birds – finches, whose enormous cage occupied one complete side of the sitting room – and her music, the source of which seemed to be a piano that occupied the other side. This was an antique upright and its top held several dozen framed pictures of the late Geoffrey throughout his life while its music rack displayed enough hand scored sheet music to suggest that Mrs Baden might be channelling Mozart in her free afternoons.

Mrs Baden herself suffered from tremors. They affected her hands and her head, which shook subtly but unceasingly throughout her interview with Barbara.

'No place to sit in here, I'm afraid,' Mrs Baden said cheerfully when she was done sharing her personal particulars. 'Come through to the kitchen. I've a fresh lemon cake, if you'd like a piece.'

She would have loved a piece, Barbara told her. But the truth was that she was looking for Cilla Thompson. Did Mrs Baden know where Cilla might be found?

'I expect she's working in the studio,' Mrs Baden replied, confiding, 'They're artists, the two of them. Cilla and Terry. Lovely young people, if you don't mind their appearance, which I myself never do. Times change, don't they? And one must change with them.'

She seemed such a gentle, kind soul that Barbara was reluctant to tell her of Terry's death immediately. So she said, 'You must know the two of them well.'

'Cilla's rather shy, I think. But Terry's a dear boy, always popping round with a little gift or surprise. He calls me his adopted Gran, does Terry. He sometimes does the odd job when I need him. And he always stops to ask if I want something from the grocery when he pops out for his shopping. Neighbours like that are hard to come by these days. Don't you agree?'

'I'm lucky that way myself,' Barbara said, warming to the old woman. 'I've good neighbours as well.'

'Then count yourself fortunate, my dear. May I say what a lovely colour your eyes are, by the way? One doesn't see such a pretty blue that often. I expect you've some Scandinavian in your blood. Ancestrally, of course.'

Mrs Baden plugged in the electric kettle and pulled a packet of tea from a cupboard shelf. She spooned leaves into a faded porcelain pot and brought two mismatched mugs to the kitchen table. Her tremors were so bad that Barbara couldn't imagine the woman wielding a kettle of boiling water and, a few minutes later when the kettle clicked off, she hastened to make the tea herself. For this activity, Mrs Baden thanked her graciously. She said, 'One keeps hearing that young people have become virtual savages these days, but that's not been my experience.' She used a wooden spoon to stir the tea leaves round in the water, then she looked up and said quietly, 'I do hope dear Terry's not in some sort of trouble,' as if she'd expected the police to come calling for quite some time, despite her earlier words.

'I'm awfully sorry to tell you this, Mrs Baden,' Barbara said, 'but Terry's dead. He was murdered in Derbyshire several nights ago. That's why I'd like to talk to Cilla.'

Mrs Baden mouthed the word *dead* in some confusion. Her expression became stunned as the full implication behind that word made its way past her defences. 'Oh my goodness,' she said. 'That lovely young boy. But certainly you can't think that Cilla – or even that unfortunate boyfriend of hers – had anything to do with it.'

Barbara filed away the information about the unfortunate boyfriend for future reference. No, she told Mrs Baden, she actually wanted Cilla to let her inside the flat. She needed a look round the place to see if there was anything that might give the police a clue why Terry Cole had been murdered. 'He was one of two people killed, you see,' Barbara told her. 'The other was a woman – Nicola Maiden, she was called – and it may well be that the killings happened because of her. But in any event, we're trying to establish whether Terry and the woman even knew each other.'

'Of course,' Mrs Baden said. 'I understand completely. You have a job to do, as unpleasant as it must necessarily be.' She went on to tell Barbara that Cilla Thompson would be in the railway arches that fronted Portslade Road. That was where she, Terry, and two other artists pooled their resources to have a studio. Mrs Baden couldn't give Barbara the exact address, but she didn't think the studio would be difficult to find. 'One can always ask along the street in the other arches. I expect the proprietors would know whom you're talking about. As to the flat itself . . .' Mrs Baden used a pair of silver tea tongs – their plate worn through in spots – to capture a sugar cube. It took her three tries, because of the shaking, but she smiled with real pleasure when she managed it and she dropped the cube into her tea with a satisfied *plop*. 'I do have a key, of course.'

Brilliant, Barbara thought, and she mentally rubbed her hands together in anticipation.

'It's my house, you see.' Mrs Baden went on to explain that when Mr Baden had passed on, she'd had the house converted as an investment, to provide her with income in her twilight years. 'I let out three flats and live in the fourth myself.' And she added that she always insisted on keeping a key to each of the flats. She'd long ago discovered that the potential of a landlord's surprise visit always kept her tenants on their toes. 'However,' she concluded, sinking Barbara's ship with a nonetheless fond smile, 'I can't let you in.'

'You can't.'

'I'm afraid it would be such a violation of trust, you see, to let you in without Cilla's permission. I do hope you understand.'

Damn, Barbara thought. She asked when Cilla Thompson generally returned.

Oh, they never kept regular hours, Mrs Baden told her. She'd be wisest to run by Portslade Road and make an appointment with Cilla while she was painting. And by the way, could Mrs Baden talk the constable into a slice of lemon cake before she left? One loved to bake but only if one could share one's creations with someone else.

It *would* balance the chocolate donut nicely, Barbara decided. And since immediate access to Terry Cole's flat was going to be denied her, she thought she might as well continue towards her personal dietary goal of ingesting nothing but fat and sugar for twenty-four hours.

Mrs Baden beamed at Barbara's acceptance and sliced a wedge of cake suitable for a Viking warrior. As Barbara fell upon it, the older woman made the sort of pleasant chitchat at which her generation so excelled. Buried within it was the occasional nugget about Terry Cole.

Thus, Barbara gleaned that Terry was a dreamer, not entirely practical – to Mrs Baden's way of thinking – about his future success as an artist. He wanted to open a gallery. But, my dear, the thought that someone might actually want to *buy* his pieces . . . or even those done by his colleagues . . . But then what did an old woman know about modern art?

'His mother said that he was working on a big commission,' Barbara noted. 'Had he mentioned it to you?'

'My dear, he did *talk* about a big project . . .'

'But there wasn't one?'

'I'm not quite saying that.' Mrs Cole made the point hastily. 'I think, in his mind, there truly was.'

'In his mind. You're saying that he was delusional?'

'Perhaps he was . . . Just a little overly enthusiastic.' Mrs Baden gently pressed the tines of her fork against a few cake crumbs and looked reflective. Her next words were hesitant. 'It does seem like speaking ill of the dead . . .'

Barbara sought to reassure her. 'You liked him. That's obvious. And I expect you want to help.'

'He was such a good boy. He couldn't do enough for those he cared for. You'll be hard-pressed to find anyone who'll tell you differently.'

'But . . . ?' Barbara tried to sound supportive and encouraging.

'But sometimes when a young man wants something so desperately, he cuts corners, doesn't he? He tries to find a shorter and more direct route to get to his destination.'

Barbara seized on the final word. 'You're talking about the gallery he wanted to open?'

'Gallery? No. I'm talking about stature,' Mrs Baden replied.

'He wanted to *be* someone, my dear. More than money and goods, he wanted a sense of having a place in the world. But one's place in the world has to be earned, hasn't it, Constable?' She set her fork by her plate and dropped her hands into her lap. 'I feel terrible saying such things about him. He was, you see, so good to me. He gave me three new finches for my birthday. Flowers on Mothering Sunday as well. And only this week, some new piano music . . . So considerate a boy. So generous, really. And helpful. He was so truly helpful when I needed someone to tighten a screw or change a bulb . . .'

'I understand,' Barbara reassured her.

'It's just that I want you to know he had more than one side to him. And this other part – the part in a hurry – well, he would have outgrown that as he learned more about life, wouldn't he?'

'Without a doubt,' Barbara said.

Unless, of course, his hunger for stature was directly related to his death on the moor.

Upon leaving Broughton Manor, Lynley and Hanken stopped in Bakewell for a quick pub meal not far from the centre of town. There, over a filled jacket potato (Hanken) and a ploughman's lunch (Lynley), they sorted through their facts. Hanken had brought with him a map of the Peak District, which he used to make his major point.

'I say we're looking for a killer who *knows* the area,' he said, indicating the map with his fork. 'And I don't see some lag fresh out of Dartmoor Prison taking a crash course in trek-and-track in order to get revenge on Andy Maiden by killing his daughter. That kite won't fly.'

Lynley studied the map dutifully. He saw that hiking trails snaked all across the district, and destinations of interest dotted it. It looked like a paradise for a hiker or camper, but a huge paradise in which the unwary or unprepared walker could easily become lost. He also noted that Broughton Manor was of enough historical significance to be indicated as a point of interest just south of Bakewell and that the manor's land abutted a forest which itself gave way to a moor. Both across the moor and through the forest were a series of footpaths for the hiker, which led Lynley to say 'Julian Britton's family has been here for a few hundred years. I expect he's familiar with the area.'

'As is Andy Maiden,' Hanken countered. 'And he has the look of someone who's been out and about on the land a fair amount. I wouldn't be surprised to learn his daughter inherited her penchant for trekking from him. And he found that car. All night out scouring the whole blasted White Peak, and he managed to find that bloody car.'

'Where was it, exactly?'

Hanken used his fork again. Between the hamlet of Sparrowpit and Winnat's Pass stretched a road that formed the northwest boundary of Calder Moor. A short distance from the track leading southeast towards Perryfoot, the car had been parked behind a drystone wall.

Lynley said, 'All right. I see that it was a lucky shot—'

Hanken snorted. 'Right.'

'—to find the car. But lucky shots happen. And he knew her haunts.'

'He did indeed. He knew them well enough to track her down, do her in, and dash back home with no one the wiser.'

'With what motive, Peter? You can't hang guilt on the man on the strength of his keeping information from his wife. *That* kite won't fly either. And if he's the killer, who's his accomplice?'

'Let's get back to his SO10 years,' Hanken said meaningfully. 'What old lag fresh out of the Scrubs would say no to making a few quid on the side, especially if Maiden made him the offer and guided him personally out to the site?' He forked up a mound of potato and prawns and shovelled them into his mouth, saying, 'It could have happened that way.'

'Not unless Andy Maiden has undergone a transformation in personality since moving here. Peter, he was one of the best.'

'Don't like him too much,' Hanken warned. 'He may have called in markers to get you sent up here for one very good reason.'

'I could take offence at that.'

'My pleasure,' Hanken smiled. 'I've a fancy for seeing a nob cheesed off. But mind you don't think too highly of this bloke. That's a dangerous place to be.'

'Just as dangerous as thinking too ill of the man. In either case, the vision goes to hell.'

'*Touché*,' Hanken said.

'Julian has a motive, Peter.'

'Disappointment in love?'

'Perhaps something stronger. Perhaps an elementary passion. A base one, at that. Jealousy, for instance. Who's this chap Upman?'

'I'll introduce you.'

They finished their meal and returned to the car. They headed northwest out of Bakewell, climbed upwards and traversed the northern boundary of Taddington Moor.

In Buxton, they cruised along the High Street, finding a place to park behind the town hall. This was an impressive nineteenth century edifice overlooking The Slopes, a tree-shaded series of ascending paths, where those who once had come to Buxton to take the waters had exercised in the afternoons.

The solicitor's office was farther along the High Street. Above an estate agent and an art gallery featuring water colours of the Peaks, it was reached by means of a single door with the names Upman, Smith, & Sinclair printed on its opaque glass.

As soon as Hanken sent his card into Upman's office in the hands of an ageing secretary in secretarial twinset and tweeds, the man himself came out to greet them and to usher them into his domain. He'd heard about Nicola Maiden's death.

He'd phoned the Hall to ask where he should send Nicola's final wages for the summer, and one of the dailies there had given him the news. The previous week had been her last in the office, the solicitor explained.

Upman seemed happy enough to cooperate with the police. He deemed Nicola's death 'a damnable tragedy for all concerned. She had tremendous potential in the legal field and I was more than satisfied with her performance for me this past summer.'

Lynley studied the man as Hanken gleaned the background information on the solicitor's relationship with the dead woman. Upman looked like a newsreader for the BBC: picture perfect and squeaky clean. His oak brown hair was greying at the temples, giving him an air of trustworthiness that doubtless served him well in his line of employment. This general sense of reliability was enhanced by his voice, which was deep and sonorous. He was probably somewhere in his early forties, but his casual manner and his easy bearing suggested youth.

He answered Hanken's questions without the slightest indication that he might be uncomfortable with any of them. He'd known Nicola Maiden for most of the nine years that she and her family had lived in the Peak District. Her parents' acquisition of the old Padley Gorge Lodge – now Maiden Hall – had brought them into contact with one of Upman's associates, who handled estate purchases. Through him, Will Upman had met the Maidens and their daughter.

'We've been given to understand that Mr Maiden arranged for Nicola to work for you this summer,' Hanken said.

Upman confirmed this. He added, 'It was no secret that Andy hoped Nicola would practise in Derbyshire when she'd completed her articles.' He'd been leaning against his desk as they spoke, having not offered either detective a chair. He seemed to realise this all at once, however, because he hurried on to say, 'I'm completely forgetting my manners.

Forgive me. Please. Sit. Can we offer you coffee? Or tea? Miss Snodgrass?'

This last he called in the direction of the open door. In its frame the secretary reappeared. She'd donned a pair of large-framed spectacles that gave her the appearance of a timid insect. 'Mr Upman?' She waited to do his bidding.

'Gentlemen?' he asked Lynley and Hanken.

They declined his offer of refreshment, and Miss Snodgrass was dismissed. Upman beamed upon the detectives as they took seats. Then he remained standing. Lynley noted this, raising his guard. In the delicate game of power and confrontation, the solicitor had just scored. And the manoeuvre had been so smoothly handled.

'How did you feel about Nicola becoming employed somewhere in Derbyshire?' he asked Upman.

The solicitor regarded him affably. 'I don't think I felt anything at all.'

'Are you married?'

'Never have been. My line of work tends to give one cold feet when it comes to matrimony. I specialise in divorce law. That generally disabuses one of one's romantic ideals in rather short order.'

'Could that be why Nicola turned down Julian Britton's marriage proposal?' Lynley asked.

Upman looked surprised. 'I'd no idea he'd made one.'

'She didn't tell you?'

'She worked for me, Inspector. I wasn't her confessor.'

'Were you her anything else?' Hanken put in, clearly annoyed at the tenor of Upman's last remark. 'Aside from her employer, naturally.'

From his desk, Upman picked up a palm-sized violin that apparently served as a paper weight. He ran his fingers along its strings and plucked at them as if testing their tuning. He said, 'You must be asking if she and I had a personal relationship.'

'When a man and a woman work at close quarters on a regular basis,' Hanken said, 'these things do happen.'

'They don't happen to me.'

'By which we can take it that you weren't involved with the Maiden girl?'

'That's what I'm saying.' Upman replaced the violin and took up a pencil holder. He began removing those pencils whose lead was too worn, laying them neatly next to his thigh which continued to rest against the desk. He said, 'Andy Maiden would have liked Nicola and me to become involved. He'd hinted as much on more than one occasion, and whenever I was at the Hall for dinner and Nicola was home from college, he made a point of throwing us together. So I saw what he was hoping for, but I couldn't accommodate him.'

'Why not?' Hanken asked. 'Something wrong with the girl?'

'She wasn't my type.'

'What type was she?' Lynley asked.

'I don't know. Look, what does it matter? I'm . . . Well, I'm rather involved with someone else.'

'"Rather involved?"' This from Hanken.

'We have an understanding. I mean, we date. I handled her divorce two years ago, and . . . What does it matter, anyway?' He looked flustered. Lynley wondered why.

Hanken appeared to notice this as well. He began to home in. 'You found the Maiden girl attractive, though.'

'Of course. I'm not blind. She *was* attractive.'

'And did your divorcée know about her?'

'She's not *my* divorcée. She's not my anything. We're seeing each other. That's all there is. And there was nothing for Joyce to know—'

'Joyce?' Lynley asked.

'His divorcée,' Hanken said blandly.

'*And,*' Upman repeated forcefully, 'there was nothing for Joyce to know because there was nothing between us, between Nicola and me. Finding a woman attractive and becoming caught up in something that can't go anywhere are two different things.'

'Why couldn't it go anywhere?' Lynley asked.

'Because we were both involved elsewhere. I am, and she was. So even if I'd thought about trying my luck – which I didn't, by the way – I'd have been signing up for a course in frustration.'

'But she'd turned down Julian,' Hanken interposed. 'That suggests she wasn't as involved as you supposed, that perhaps she'd set her sights on someone else.'

'If so, they weren't set on me. And as for poor Britton, I'd wager that she turned him down because his income didn't suit her. My guess is that she'd got her eye on someone with a hefty bank balance in London.'

'What gave you that impression?' Lynley asked.

Upman considered the question, but he appeared relieved to be himself let off the hook of a possible involvement with Nicola Maiden. 'She had a pager that went off occasionally,' he finally said, 'and once when it did, she asked me would I mind if she phoned London to give someone the number here to ring her back. And he did as much. Time and again.'

'Why would you conclude this was someone with money?' Lynley asked. 'A few long distance phone calls aren't out of the question even for someone strapped for cash.'

'I know that. But Nicola had expensive tastes. Believe me, she couldn't have bought what she wore to work every day on what I was paying her. I'll lay twenty quid on it that if you trace her wardrobe, you'll find it came from Knightsbridge where some poor sod's paying on an account that she was free to use. And that sod's not me.'

Very neat, Lynley thought. Upman had tied all the pieces together with an adroitness that was a credit to his profession. But there was something calculated in his presentation of the facts that made Lynley wary. It was as if he'd known what they would ask him and had already planned his answers, like any good lawyer. From Hanken's expression of mild dislike, it was clear that he'd reached the same conclusion about the solicitor.

'Are we talking about an affair?' Hanken asked. 'Is this a married chap doing what he can to keep the mistress content?'

'I have no idea. I can only say that she was involved with someone, and I expect that someone's in London.'

'When was the last time you saw her alive?'

'Friday evening. We had dinner.'

'But you yourself had no personal relationship with her,' Hanken noted.

'I took her to dinner as a farewell, which is fairly common practice between employers and employees in our society, if I'm not mistaken. Why? Does this put me under suspicion? Because if I'd wanted to kill her – for whatever reason you might have in mind – why would I wait from Friday until Tuesday night to do it?'

Hanken pounced. 'Ah. You seem to know when she died.'

Upman wasn't rattled. 'I did speak to someone at the Hall, Inspector.'

'So you said.' Hanken got to his feet. 'You've been most helpful to our enquiries. If you can just give us the name of Friday night's restaurant, we'll be on our way.'

'The Chequers Inn,' Upman said. 'In Calver. But look here, why do you need that? Am I under suspicion? Because if I am, I insist on—'

'There's no need for posturing at this point in the investigation,' Hanken said.

There was also no need, Lynley thought, to put the solicitor any more on the defensive. He said, 'Everyone who knew the murder victim is a suspect at first, Mr Upman. DI Hanken and I are in the process of eliminating possibilities. Even as a lawyer, I expect you'd encourage a client to cooperate if he wanted to be crossed off the list.'

Upman didn't embrace the explanation, but he also didn't press the issue.

Lynley and Hanken took themselves out of his office and into the street, where Hanken immediately said, 'What a snake,' as they walked to the car. 'Flaming slimy bugger. Did you believe his story?'

'Which part of it?'

'Any of it. All of it. I don't care.'

'As a lawyer, naturally, everything he said was immediately suspect.'

This effected a reluctant smile in Hanken.

'But he gave us some useful information. I'd like to talk to the Maidens again and see if I can get anything out of them that will corroborate Upman's suspicions that Nicola was seeing someone in London. If there's another lover somewhere, there's another motive for murder.'

'For Britton,' Hanken acknowledged. He jerked his head in the direction of Upman's office. 'But what about him? D'you plan to list him among your suspects?'

'Till we check him out, definitely.'

Hanken nodded. 'I think I'm starting to like you,' he said.

Cilla Thompson was in residence at the studio when Barbara Havers tracked it down, three arches away from the dead end of Portslade Road. She had the two big front doors completely open and she was in the midst of what looked like a creative fury, slashing at a canvas with paint as what sounded like African drums emanated rhythmically from a dusty CD player. The volume was high. Against her skin and in her sternum, Barbara could feel the pulsations.

'Cilla Thompson?' she shouted, wrestling her identification from her shoulder bag. 'Can I have a word?'

Cilla read the warrant card and put her paint brush between her teeth. She punched a button on the CD player, choked off the drums, and returned to her work. She said, 'Cyn Cole told me,' and continued to smother the canvas with paint. Barbara sidled round to have a look at her work: It was a gaping mouth out of which rose a motherly-looking woman wielding a teapot decorated with snakes. Lovely, Barbara thought. The painter was definitely filling a vacuum in the art world.

'Terry's sister told you that he was murdered?'

'His mum phoned her from the North as soon as she saw the body. Cyn phoned me. I thought something was up when she rang last night. Her voice wasn't right. You know what I mean. But I wouldn't have guessed ... I mean, like, who would've wanted to snuff Terry Cole? He was a harmless little prick. A bit demented, considering his work, but harmless all the same.'

She said this last with a perfectly straight face, as if all round her were canvases by Peter Paul Rubens and not depictions of countless mouths spilling forth everything from oil slicks to motorway pile-ups. The work of her compatriots wasn't much better from what Barbara could see. The other artists were sculptors like Terry. One used crushed rubbish bins as a medium. The other used rusting supermarket trolleys.

'Yeah. Right,' Barbara said. 'But I s'pose it's all a matter of taste.'

Cilla rolled her eyes. 'Not to someone who's educated in art.'

'Terry wasn't?'

'Terry was a poser, no offence. He wasn't educated in anything, except lying. And he'd got like a first in that.'

'His mum said he was working on a big commission,' Barbara said. 'Can you tell me about it?'

'For Paul McCartney, I have no doubt,' was Cilla's dry reply. 'Depending on what day of the week you happened to have a chat with him, Terry was working on a project that would bring him millions, or getting ready to sue Pete Townsend for not telling the world he had a bastard son – that's Terry, mind you – or stumbling on some secret documents that he planned to sell to the tabloids, or having lunch with the director of the Royal Academy. *Or* opening a top flight gallery where he'd sell his sculptures for twenty thousand a pop.'

'So there was no commission?'

'That's a safe bet.' Cilla stepped back from her canvas to study it. She applied a smear of red to the mouth's lower lip. She followed with a smear of white, saying, 'Ah. Yes,' in apparent reference to the effect she'd attained.

'You're coping quite well with Terry's death,' Barbara noted. 'For having just heard about it, that is.'

Cilla read the statement for what it was: implied criticism. Catching up another brush and dipping it into a glob of purple on her palette, she said, 'Terry and I shared a flat. We shared this studio. We sometimes had a meal together or went to the pub. But we weren't real mates. We were people who served a purpose for each other: sharing expenses so we, like, didn't have to work where we lived.'

Considering the size of Terry's sculptures and the nature of Cilla's paintings, this arrangement made sense. But it also reminded Barbara of a remark that Mrs Baden had made. 'How did your boyfriend feel about the deal, then?'

'You've been talking to Prune-face, I see. She's been waiting for Dan to cut up rough with someone ever since she saw him. Talk about judging a bloke on appearances.'

'And?'

'And what?'

'And has he ever? Cut up rough, that is. With Terry. It's not your everyday situation, is it, when one bloke's girlfriend is living with another bloke.'

'Like I said, we aren't – weren't – living with like in *living* with. Most of the time we didn't even see each other. We didn't hang out with the same group, even. It's, like, Terry had his mates and I have mine.'

'Did you know his mates?'

The purple paint went into the hair of the mouth-sprung

woman who was holding the teapot in Cilla's painting. She applied it in a thick curving line, then she used the palm of her hand to smear it, after which she wiped her palm on the front of her overalls. The effect on the canvas was disconcerting. It rather looked as if Mother had holes in her head. Cilla took up grey next and advanced on Mother's nose. Barbara stepped to one side, not wishing to see what the artist intended.

'He didn't bring them round,' Cilla said. 'It was mostly phone chat and they were mostly women. And they phoned him. Not the other way round.'

'Did he have a girlfriend? A special woman, I mean.'

'He didn't do women. Not that I ever knew.'

'Gay?'

'Asexual. He didn't do anything. Except toss off. And even that's a real maybe.'

'His world was his art?' Barbara offered.

Cilla whooped. 'Such as it was.' She stepped back from her canvas and evaluated it. 'Yes,' she said and turned it round to face Barbara. '*Voila.* Now *that* tells a proper tale, doesn't it?'

Mother's nose was excreting an unsavoury substance. Barbara decided that Cilla couldn't possibly have spoken words more true about her painting. She murmured her assent. Cilla carried her masterwork to a ledge along which half a dozen other paintings rested. From among them, she selected an unfinished canvas of a lower lip harpooned by a hook and carried it to the easel to continue with her work.

'Can I assume Terry didn't sell much?' Barbara asked her.

'He sold sod all,' Cilla said cheerfully. 'But then he wasn't, like, ever willing to put enough of himself into it, was he? And if you don't give your all to your art, your art isn't going to give anything back to you. I put my guts right onto the canvas and the canvas rewards me.'

'Artistic satisfaction,' Barbara said solemnly.

'Hey, I sell. A real gent bought a piece off me not two days ago. Walked in here, took one look, said he had to have his own Cilla Thompson straightaway, and brought out the chequebook.'

Right, Barbara thought. The woman had quite an imagination. 'So if he never sold a sculpture, where did Terry get the beans to pay for everything? The flat. This studio . . .' Not to mention the gardening tools that he appeared to have amassed by the gross, she thought.

'He *said* his money was a payoff from his dad. He had enough of it, mind you.'

'Payoff?' Now *here* was something that could lead them somewhere. 'Was he blackmailing someone?'

'Sure,' Cilla said. 'His dad. Pete Townsend, like I said. As long as old Pete kept the lolly rolling in, Terry wouldn't go to the papers crying, "Dad's rolling in it and I've got sod all." Ha. As if Terry Cole had the slightest hope of convincing anyone he wasn't what he really was: a scam man out for the easy life.'

This wasn't too far from Mrs Baden's description of Terry Cole, albeit spoken with far less affection and compassion. But if Terry Cole had been into a scam, what had it been? And who had been its victim?

There had to be evidence of something somewhere. And there seemed to be only one place where that evidence might be. She needed to have a look through the flat, Barbara explained. Would Cilla be willing to cooperate?

She would, Cilla said. She'd be home by five if Barbara wanted to pop round then. But Constable Havers had better have it straight in her head that whatever Terry Cole had been caught up in, Cilla Thompson had not been part of it.

'I'm an artist. First, last, and always,' Cilla proclaimed. She gave her attention to the lip harpoon.

'Oh, I can see that,' Barbara assured her.

At Buxton police station, Lynley and Hanken parted ways once the Buxton DI arranged for his Scotland Yard associate to pick up a car. Hanken planned to head for Calver, determined to corroborate Will Upman's alleged dinner date with Nicola Maiden. For his part, Lynley set out towards Padley Gorge.

At Maiden Hall, he found that afternoon preparations for the evening meal were going on in the kitchen, which backed onto the car park where Lynley left the police Ford. The bar in the lounge was being restocked with spirits, and the dining room was being set for the evening. There was a general air of activity about the place demonstrating that, as much as possible, life was going on at the Hall.

The same woman who'd intercepted the DIs on the previous afternoon met Lynley just beyond the reception desk. When he asked for Andy Maiden, she murmured 'Poor soul', and left him to fetch the former police officer. While he waited, Lynley went to the door of the dining room, just beyond the lounge. Another woman – of similar age and appearance as the first – was placing slender white candles in holders on the tables. A basket of yellow chrysanthemums sat next to her on the floor.

The serving hatch between dining room and kitchen was open, and from within the latter room came the sound of French, rapidly spoken and with some considerable passion. And then in accented English, 'And no and no and no! I ask for shallots, it means shallots. These are onions for boiling in the pan.'

There was a quiet response that Lynley couldn't catch, then a torrent of French of which he caught only, '*Je t'emmerde.*'

'Tommy?'

Lynley swung round to see that Andy Maiden had come into the lounge, a spiral notebook in his hand. Maiden looked ravaged: He was drawn and unshaven and he wore the clothes he'd had on on the previous evening. 'I couldn't wait for the pension,' he said, voice numb. 'I lived to retire, you know. I put up with the work without a word because it was leading to something. That's what I told myself. And them. Nan and Nicola. A few more years, I'd say. Then we'll have enough.'

Rousing himself to trudge the rest of the way across the lounge to join Lynley seemed to take what few resources he had left. 'And look where it's brought us. My daughter's dead and I've come up with the names of fifteen bastards who'd've willingly killed their own mothers if they'd gain by the act. So why the hell did I think they'd serve their time, disappear, and never bother to go after me?'

Lynley glanced at the notebook, realising what it was. 'You've got a list for us.'

'I read through the night. Three times. Four. And here's where I ended up. D'you want to know?'

'Yes.'

'I killed her. I did. I was the one.'

How many times had he heard that need to take blame? Lynley wondered. A hundred? A thousand? It was always the same. And if there was a glib response that could attenuate the guilt of those who were left behind after violence had done its worst to a loved one, he hadn't yet learned it. 'Andy,' he began.

Maiden cut him off. 'You remember what I was like, don't you? Keeping society safe from the "criminal element", I told myself. And I was good at what I did. I was so *bloody* good. But I never once saw that while I was concentrating on our fucking society, my very own daughter . . . my Nick—' His voice began to waver. 'Sorry,' he said.

'Don't apologise, Andy. It's all right.'

'It'll never be all right.' Maiden opened the notebook and ripped the last page from it. He shoved this towards Lynley. 'Find him.'

'We will.' Lynley knew how inadequate his words were – as would be an arrest in the case – to mitigate Maiden's grief. Nonetheless, he explained that he'd assigned an officer to go through the SO10 records in London, but he'd so far heard nothing. Thus, anything that Maiden provided them with – a name, a crime, an investigation – could well end up halving or quartering the London officer's time on the computer and freeing that officer to pursue likely suspects. The police would be in Maiden's debt for that.

Maiden nodded dully. 'How else can I help? Can you give me something, Tommy . . . something to do . . . because otherwise the nightmare . . .' He ran a large hand through hair that was still curly and thick, albeit quite grey. 'I'm a textbook case. Looking for employment so I can stop going through this.'

'It's a natural response. We all put up defences against a shock till we're ready to deal with it. That's part of being human.'

'This. I'm even calling it *this*. Because if I say the word, that'll make everything real and I don't think I can stand it.'

'You're not expected to cope right now. You and your wife are both owed some time to avoid what's happened. Or to deny what's happened. Or to fall apart altogether. Believe me, I understand.'

'Do you?'

'I think you know I do.' There was no easy way to make the next request. 'I need to go through your daughter's belongings, Andy. Would you like to be present?'

Maiden knotted his eyebrows. 'Her things are in her room. But if you're looking for a connection to SO10, what's Nicola's bedroom got to do with that?'

'Nothing, perhaps,' Lynley told him. 'But we spoke to Julian Britton and Will Upman this morning. There are several details we'd like to explore further.'

Maiden said, 'Good Christ. Are you thinking that one of them . . . ?' and he looked beyond Lynley to the window, seeming to ponder what horrors a reference to Britton and Upman implied.

Lynley said quickly, 'It's too early for anything but guesswork, Andy.'

Maiden turned back, examined him for a long thirty seconds. He finally seemed to accept the answer. He took Lynley to the second floor of the house and led him to his daughter's bedroom, remaining in the doorway and watching as Lynley began going through Nicola Maiden's belongings.

Most of these comprised exactly what one would expect to find in the room of a twenty-five year old woman, and much of it supported points that either Julian Britton or Will Upman had made. A wooden jewellery case contained evidence of the body piercings with which Julian had declared that Nicola had decorated herself: Single gold hoops of varying sizes and without mates suggested rings that the dead girl had worn through her navel, her lip, and her nipple; single studs spoke of the hole in her tongue; tiny ruby and emerald studs with screw tips would have fitted her nose.

The clothes cupboard contained designer clothing: The labels were a Who's Who of haute couture. Upman had declared that she couldn't have dressed herself on what he'd been paying her for her summer's employment, and her clothing fully supported his contention. But there were other indications as well that Nicola Maiden's whims were being fulfilled by someone.

The room was replete with items that could only be associated either with a considerable discretionary income or with a partner eager to prove himself through gifts. An electric guitar took up space in the cupboard, to the side of which were a CD player, a tuner, and a set of speakers that would have set Nicola Maiden back more than a month's wages. A nearby rotating oak stand designed solely for the occupation held two or three hundred CDs. A colour television in one corner of the room was the resting place for a mobile phone. On a shelf beneath the television stand, eight leather handbags were lined up precisely. Everything in the room spoke of excess. Everything also announced that, at least in one respect, Nicola's employer may have been telling the truth. Either that or the girl had come by her money in a way that ultimately led to her death: through drug pushing, blackmail, the black market, embezzlement. But thinking of Upman reminded Lynley of something else that the solicitor had said.

He went to the chest and began sliding open its drawers upon silk underwear and nightgowns, cashmere scarves and designer socks, yet to be worn. He found one drawer devoted solely to the outdoor life, stuffed with khaki shorts, folded jerseys, a small day pack, ordnance survey maps, and a silver flask engraved with the girl's initials.

The bottom two drawers in the chest contained the only items that didn't look as if they'd been purchased in Knightsbridge. But even they were filled to the very top like the others. They were a storage space for woollen sweaters of every possible style and hue, each bearing an identical label sewn into the neckline: *Made with loving hands by Nancy Maiden.* Lynley fingered one of the labels thoughtfully.

He said, 'Her pager's missing. Upman said she had one. Do you know where it is?'

Maiden left his position by the door. 'A pager? Is Will certain about that?'

'He told us that she was paged at work. You didn't know she had one?'

'I never saw her with one. It's not here?' Maiden did what Lynley had done. He examined the items on the top of the chest, then repeated the search through each of the drawers. He went further, however, by taking Lynley's place at the clothes cupboard where he checked the pockets of his daughter's jackets and the waistbands of her trousers and skirts. There were sealed plastic bags of clothing on the bed, and he went through these as well. Finding nothing, he finally said, 'She must have taken it on the hike. It'll be in one of the evidence bags.'

'Why take her pager but leave her mobile phone?' Lynley asked. 'The one would be useless on the moor without the other.'

Maiden's glance went to the television where the mobile

lay, then back to Lynley. 'Then it's got to be here some-where.'

Lynley checked the bedside table. He found a bottle of aspirin, a packet of Kleenex, birth control pills, a box of birthday candles, and a tube of lip balm. He went to the leather handbags beneath the television, opening them, checking each compartment. All of them were empty. As were a satchel, he discovered, a briefcase, and an overnight bag.

'It could be in her car,' Maiden suggested.

'Something tells me not.'

'Why?'

Lynley made no reply. Standing in the middle of the room, he saw the details with a vision that was heightened by the absence of a single, simple possession that could have meant nothing and might have meant everything. Doing so, he was able to see what he hadn't noticed before. There was a museumlike quality to everything round him. Nothing in the room was even remotely out of place.

Someone had been through the girl's belongings.

'Where's your wife this afternoon, Andy?' Lynley asked.

Chapter Nine

When Andy Maiden didn't reply at once, Lynley repeated the question and added, 'Is she in the hotel? Is she somewhere in the grounds?'

Maiden said, 'No. No. She . . . Tommy, Nan's gone out.' His fingers shut into his palms, as if in a sudden spasm.

'Where? Do you know?'

'Onto the moor, I expect. She took the bike, and that's where she generally rides it.'

'On Calder Moor?'

Maiden moved to his daughter's bed and sat heavily on the edge of it. 'You've not met Nancy before this, have you, Tommy?'

'Not that I recall.'

'She means nothing but well, that woman. She gives, and she gives. But there are times when I can't take any longer. Not from her. And not another time.' He looked down at his hands. He flexed his fingers. He raised then dropped his hands to gesture with as he went on. 'She was worried about me. Can you credit it? She wanted to help. All she could think about – or talk about or *do* something about – was getting this numbness out of my hands. All yesterday afternoon she was on at me about them. All last night as well.'

'Perhaps it's her way of coping,' Lynley said.

'But it takes too much concentration for her to cut out the thoughts that she's trying to cut out, d' you see that? It takes every ounce of concentration she has. And I found that I couldn't *breathe* with her round me. Hovering there. Offering cups of tea and heat pads and . . . I began to feel like my skin wasn't even my own any longer, like she couldn't rest till she'd managed to invade my very pores in order to . . .' He paused abruptly and, in that pause, he seemed to evaluate everything he'd said, unguarded, because he shifted gears and his next words were hollow. 'God. Listen to me. Selfish bastard.'

'You've been dealt a death blow. You're trying to cope.'

'She's been dealt the blow as well. But she thinks of *me*.' He kneaded one hand with the fingers of the other. 'She wanted to massage them. That's all it was, really. And God forgive me but I drove her off because I thought I'd suffocate if I stayed in the room with her a moment longer. And now . . . How can we need and love and loathe all at once? What's happening to us?'

The aftershocks of brutality are happening to you, Lynley wanted to reply. But instead he repeated, 'Has she gone to Calder Moor, Andy?'

'She'll be on Hathersage Moor. It's closer. A few miles. The other . . . ? No. She won't be on Calder.'

'Has she ever ridden there?'

'On Calder?'

'Yes. On Calder Moor. Has she ever ridden there?'

'Of course she has. Yes.'

Lynley hated to do so, but he had to ask. Indeed, he owed it both to himself and to his Buxton colleague to ask: 'You as well, Andy? Or just your wife?'

Andy Maiden looked up slowly at this, as if finally seeing the road they were travelling. He said, 'I thought you were pursuing the London angle. SO10. And what goes along with SO10.'

'I *am* pursuing SO10. But I'm after the truth, all of the truth. As you are, I expect. Do both of you ride on Calder Moor?'

'Nancy's *not*—'

'Andy, help me out. You know what the job's like. The facts generally come out one way or another. And sometimes the *how* of their coming out becomes more intriguing than the facts themselves. That can easily divert an otherwise simple investigation, and I can't believe you want that.'

Maiden understood: An attempt at obfuscation could ultimately become more arresting than the information one sought to withhold. 'Both of us ride on Calder Moor. All of us, in fact. But it's too far to bike there from here, Tommy.'

'How many miles?'

'I don't know, exactly. But far, too far. We take the bikes out in the Land Rover when we want to ride there. We park in a lay-by. Or in one of the villages. But we don't ride all the way to Calder Moor from here.' He canted his head in the direction of the bedroom window, adding, 'The Land Rover's still out there. So she won't have gone onto Calder this afternoon.'

Not this afternoon, Lynley thought. He said, 'I did see a Land Rover when I came through the car park.'

Maiden hadn't been a police officer for thirty years without being capable of a simple act of mind reading. He said, 'Running the Hall's a demanding life, Tommy. It drains our time. We take our exercise when we can. If you want to track her on Hathersage Moor, there's a map in reception that'll show you the way.'

That wouldn't be necessary, Lynley told him. If Nancy Maiden had ridden her bike out onto the moors, she probably was seeking some time alone. He was happy enough to let her have it.

Barbara Havers knew that she could have purchased some take-away from Uncle Tom's Cabin, a food stall on the corner of Portslade and Wandsworth Roads. It occupied little more than a niche at the near end of the railway arches, and it looked just the sort of unhygienic place where you could find enough cholesterol-laden grub to guarantee concrete arteries within the hour. But she resisted the impulse – virtuously, she liked to think – and instead took herself to a pub near Vauxhall Station where she indulged in the bangers and mash upon which she'd been meditating earlier. These went down a treat, eased on their way with half a pint of Scrumpy Jack. Sated with the food and drink and satisfied with the information she'd gathered during her morning in Battersea, she returned to the north side of the Thames and skimmed her way along the river. Traffic moved well on Horseferry Road. She was pulling into the underground car park at New Scotland Yard before she'd smoked her second Player.

She had two professional options at this point, she decided. She could return to CRIS and the hunt for a suitable ticket-of-leaver out for the blood of a Maiden. Or she could compile the information she'd gathered so far into a report. The former activity – boring, mind-numbing, and subservient though it was – would demonstrate her ability to take the medicine which certain officers of the law believed she ought to be swallowing. The latter activity, however, appeared to be the one likelier to take them towards an answer in the case. She opted for the report. It wouldn't take that long, it would allow her to set down information in a concrete and thought-provoking order, and it would postpone having to face the glowing screen for at least another hour. She took herself off to Lynley's office – no harm in using the space since it was going empty at the moment, right? – and set to work.

She was thoroughly into it, just coming up to the salient points made by Cilla Thompson concerning Terry Cole's paternity and his propensity towards questionable means of support – BLACKMAIL? she'd just typed – when Winston Nkata strode into the room. He was wolfing down the last of a Whopper, the container of which he tossed into the rubbish. He wiped his hands thoroughly with a paper napkin. He popped an Opal Fruit into his mouth.

'Junk food'll kill you,' Barbara said sanctimoniously.

'But I'll die smiling,' was Nkata's reply. He swung his long leg over a chair and took out his leather-bound notebook as he sat. Barbara glanced at a wall clock and then at her colleague. 'Just how fast're you driving up and down the M1? You're setting land speed records from Derbyshire, Winston.'

He avoided answering, which was answer in itself. Barbara shuddered to think what Lynley would say had he known that Nkata was roaring along in his beloved Bentley at just under the speed of sound. 'Been to the College of Law,' he told her. 'Guv told me to look into the Maiden girl's doings in town.'

Barbara stopped her typing. 'And?'

'She dropped out.'

'She dropped out of law college?'

'That's how it looks.' Nicola Maiden, he told her, had apparently dropped out of law college on the first of May, approaching exam time. She'd done it responsibly, making appointments to see all the appropriate instructors, counsellors and administrators before leaving. Several of them had tried to talk her out of it – she'd been near the top of her class and they'd considered it madness to leave when her successful future in law was assured – but she'd been politely adamant. And she'd disappeared.

'Muffed her exams?' Barbara asked.

'Didn't ever take them. Left before she laid eyes on them.'

'Was she scared? Developing nerves like her dad? Getting ulcers? Losing sleep? Realising she'd have to swot it all in and wasn't up to the challenge?'

'Decided she just didn't fancy the law, was what she told her personal tutor.'

She'd been working for eight months part time at a firm in Notting Hill called MKR Financial Management, Nkata went on. Most of the law students did that sort of thing: worked part time during the day to support themselves, taking instruction at the college in the late afternoons and at night. She'd been offered a full-time place at the Notting Hill firm, and as she liked the work, she decided to take it. 'And that was that,' Nkata said. 'No one at the college heard a word from her since.'

'So what was she doing in Derbyshire if she'd taken a full-time position in Notting Hill?' Barbara asked. 'Was she having a holiday first?'

'Not 'ccording to the guv, and this is where it starts getting dodgy. She was working for a solicitor on a summer job, getting ready for the future and all that bit. That's why he put me onto the College of Law in the first place.'

'So she's employed in finance in London but takes a summer job doing law in Derbyshire?' Barbara clarified. 'That's a new one on me. Does the Inspector know she left law college?'

'Haven't rung him yet. I wanted to have a chat with you first.'

Barbara felt a rush of pleasure at this remark. She shot Nkata a look. As always, his face was ingenuous, pleasant, and perfectly professional. 'Should we ring him, then? The Inspector, I mean.'

'Let's chew on it a bit.'

'Right. Okay. Well, forget what was she was doing in Derbyshire for the moment. The London bit at MKR Financial Management must've brought her some decent dosh, right? Because she wouldn't have been hurting for it at the end of the day had she stayed in law, so why drop out of law college unless there was some decent – and immediate – lolly involved? How does all that sound?'

'I'll go with it for now.'

'Okay. So did she need cash quick? And if so, why? Was she making a big purchase? Paying off a debt? Taking a trip? Wanting to live an easier life?' Barbara thought about Terry Cole and added with a snap of her fingers, 'Ah. How about being blackmailed by someone? By a London someone who zipped up to Derbyshire wanting to know why her payment was late?'

Nkata flipped his hand back and forth, his 'who-knows?' gesture. 'Could just be that the MKR gig looked more exciting than a life of wig-wearing at the Old Bailey. Not to mention more profitable in the long run.'

'What did she do for MKR, exactly?'

Nkata referred to his notes. 'Money management trainee,' he said.

'Trainee? Come on, Winston. She couldn't've dropped out of law college for that.'

'Trainee's where she started round October last year. I'm not saying that's where she ended up.'

'But then what was she doing in Derbyshire working for a solicitor? Had she changed her mind about the law? Was she going to go back to it?'

'If she did, she never told the college.'

'Hmm. That's odd.' As she considered the apparent contradictions in the dead girl's behaviour, Barbara reached for her packet of Players, saying, 'Mind if I do a fag, Winnie?'

'Not in my breathing zone.'

She sighed and settled for a stick of Juicy Fruit, which she found in her shoulder bag adhered to a stub from her local cinema. She picked off the thin shreds of cardboard and folded the gum into her mouth. 'Right. So what else do we know?'

'She left her digs.'

'Why wouldn't she, if she was up in Derbyshire for the summer?'

'I mean she left them permanently. Just like she left the college.'

'Okay. But that doesn't sound like news from the burning bush.'

'Hang on, then.' Nkata reached in his pocket and brought forth another Opal Fruit. He unwrapped it and tucked the sweet into the pocket of his cheek. 'The college had her address

– this is the old one – so I went there and had a chat with the landlady. This is in Islington. She had a bedsit.'

'And?' Barbara encouraged him.

'She moved house – the girl, not the landlady – when she left law college. This was on the tenth of May. No notice given. Just packed her belongings, left behind an address in Fulham to send the post on to, and vanished. Landlady wasn't happy about that. She wasn't happy about the row, either.' Nkata smiled as he offered this last bit of information.

Barbara acknowledged the manner in which her colleague had played out the bits and pieces he'd gathered by cocking a finger at him and saying, 'You rat. Give me the rest, Winston.'

At which Nkata chuckled. 'Some bloke and her. They went at it like paddies in the peace talks, the landlady said. This was on the ninth.'

'The day before she moved house?'

'Right.'

'Violence?'

'No, just shouting. And some nasty language.'

'Anything we can use?'

'Bloke said, "I won't have it. I'll see you dead before I'll let you do it."'

'Now *that's* a nice bit. Dare I hope we have a description of the bloke?' Nkata's expression told her. 'Damn.'

He said, 'But it's something to note.'

'P'rhaps. Or not.' Barbara considered what he'd told her earlier. She said, 'If she moved house right after the threat, why'd the murder come along so much later?'

'If she moved house to Fulham and then left town, he'd have to track her down,' Nkata pointed out. Then he said, 'What'd you get at this end?'

Barbara told him what she'd gathered from her conversations with Mrs Baden and Cilla Thompson. She concentrated on Terry's source of income and on the contrasting descriptions of him as provided by his flatmate and his land-lady. 'Cilla says he never sold a thing and wasn't likely to, and I wouldn't disagree. So then, how did he support himself?'

Nkata thought about this, moving his sweet from one side of his mouth to the other. He finally said, 'Let's phone the guv,' and he went to Lynley's desk where he punched in a number from memory. In a moment the connection went through and he had Lynley on the inspector's mobile. He said, 'Hang on,' and punched another button on the phone. Over the speaker, Barbara heard Lynley's pleasant baritone saying, 'What've we got so far, Winnie?'

Just the sort of thing he would have said to her. She got up and strode to the window. There was nothing to see but Tower Block, of course. It was just something to do.

Winston quickly brought Lynley up to speed on Nicola Maiden's abrupt departure from the College of Law, on her employment at MKR Financial Management, on her moving house without giving notice, on the row that preceded her moving house, and on the particular threat to her life that had been overheard.

'There's apparently a lover in London,' Lynley said in reply. 'Upman's given us that. But not a word about her having left law college.'

'Why'd she keep it a secret?'

'Because of the lover, perhaps.' Barbara could tell from Lynley's voice that he was chewing this over mentally. 'Because of plans they had.'

'Some married bloke, then?'

'Possibly. Check out the financial management firm. He could be there.' Lynley related his own information. He concluded with, 'If the lover in London is a married chap who'd set Nicola up as a permanent mistress in Fulham, it's not the sort of thing she'd want to broadcast in Derbyshire. I can't see her parents feeling pleased with the news. And Britton would have been cut up as well.'

'But what was she doing in Derbyshire in the first place?' Barbara whispered to Nkata. 'Her actions are contradicting themselves all over the map. *Tell* him, Winston.'

Nkata nodded and raised his hand to indicate that he'd heard her. He didn't argue with the inspector's points, however. Instead, he took notes. At the conclusion of Lynley's remarks, he offered the details about Terry Cole. Considering the scope of them in conjunction with the brevity of time Nkata had been back in town, Lynley's comment upon the constable's conclusion was, 'Good God, Winnie. How have you managed all this? Are you working telepathically?'

Barbara turned from the window to get Nkata's attention, but she didn't manage it before he spoke. He said, 'Barb's on to the boy. She did Battersea this morning. She talked to—'

'Havers?' Lynley's voice sharpened. 'Is she with you, then?'

Barbara's shoulders sagged.

'Yeah. She's writing—'

Lynley cut in. 'Didn't you tell me she was going through Maiden's past arrests?'

'She was doing, yeah.'

'Have you completed that search, Havers?' Lynley asked.

Barbara blew out a breath. Lie or truth? she wondered. A lie would serve her immediate purposes, but it would sink her ship at the end of the day. 'Winston suggested I trek out to Battersea,' she told Lynley. 'I was just about to go back to CRIS when he showed up with the information on the girl. I was thinking, sir, that her working for Upman doesn't make sense when you look at the fact that she'd dropped out of law college and had another job in London that she'd apparently taken leave from for some reason. *If* she even had another job at all because we've yet to check that out. And anyway if there's a lover, as you've said, and if she was getting herself ready to be supported by him, why the hell would she be spending a summer working in the Peaks?'

'You need to get back on CRIS,' was Lynley's reply. 'I've had a word with Maiden and he's given us some possibilities to look into from his time with SO10. Take down these names and deal with them, Havers.' He began reciting, spelling when necessary. There were fifteen names in all.

When she had them, Barbara said, 'But, sir, don't you think that this Terry Cole business—'

What he thought, Lynley interrupted, was that as an SO10 officer, Andrew Maiden would have overturned rocks and uncovered slugs, worms, and insects from all walks of life. He could have struck up an acquaintance during his time in undercover who had proved fatal years later. Thus, once Barbara was done looking for the obvious vengeance seekers, she was to read the files again for a more subtle connection: like a disappointed snout whose efforts hadn't been sufficiently rewarded by the police.

'But don't you think—'

'I've told you what I think, Barbara. I've given you an assignment. I'd like you to get on with it.'

Barbara got the message. She said, 'Sir', a polite affirmative. She nodded to Nkata and left the office. But she took no more than two steps from the doorway.

'Get on to the financial management firm,' Lynley said. 'I'm going to have a look at the girl's car. If we can find that pager and if the lover's phoned in, the number will put us on to him.'

'Right,' Winston said and rang off.

Barbara slid back into Lynley's office, sidling along the wall casually as if she'd never had an order to do anything else. 'So who is it who told her in Islington that he'd see her dead before he'd let her do it? The lover? Her dad? Britton? Cole? Upman? Or someone we haven't got onto yet? And what's the *it*, anyway, when it's at home? Settling in to be some heavy punter's fluffy bit on the side? Going for the dosh with a bit of blackmail against the lover – that's always nice, isn't it? Having it off with more than one man? What d'you think?'

Nkata looked up from his notebook as she spoke. His glance went beyond her to the corridor where she'd remained in mild defiance of Lynley's instructions to her. He said, 'Barb . . .' in a monitory fashion. *You heard the guv's order* remained unsaid.

Barbara said breezily, 'There may even be more at MKR Financial Management. Nicola could have been a bird who fancied a regular bonk when she wasn't getting it from the boyfriend in the Peaks and when the London lover was taken up with his wife. But I don't think we want to go at that angle directly at MKR, do you, what with sexual harassment all the rage.'

Nkata didn't miss the plural pronoun. He said, a model of patience and delicacy, 'Barb, the Guv did say you're to get back on to CRIS.'

'Bollocks to CRIS. Don't tell me you think some lag on the loose squared it with Maiden by taking the cosh to his daughter. That's stupid, Winston. It's a waste of time.'

'Might be. But when the 'spector tells you what road to take, you'd be a wise bird to take it. Right?' And when she didn't reply, '*Right*, Barb?'

'Okay, okay.' Barbara sighed. She knew that she'd been given a second chance with Lynley through the good graces of Winston Nkata. She just didn't want the second chance to materialise as a lengthy assignment to sit at the computer. She tried a compromise. 'What about this, then? Let me go with you to Notting Hill, let me work it with you, and I'll do the computer business on my own time. I promise. I give you my word of honour.'

'The guv's not going to go for that, Barb. And he'll be bloody cheesed off when he twigs what you're doing. And then where'll you be?'

'He won't know about it. I won't tell him. You won't tell him.

Look, Winston, I've got a feeling about this. The information we've got is all knotted up and it wants unknotting and I'm good at that. You need my input. You'll need it more once you get more details from this MKR place. I'm promising to do the computer slog – I'm *swearing* to do it – so just let me have a bigger piece of the case.'

Nkata frowned. Barbara waited. She chewed her gum more vigorously.

Nkata said, 'When'll you do it, then? Early morning? Night? Weekends? When?'

'Whenever,' she replied. 'I'll squeeze it in between tea dancing engagements at the Ritz. My social life's a real whirl, as you know, but I think I can carve out an hour here and there to obey an order.'

'He'll be checking to see you're doing what he says,' Nkata pointed out.

'And I'll be doing it. Wearing bells, if necessary. But in the meantime, don't waste my brain and experience by advising me to spend the next twelve hours at a computer terminal. Let me be part of this while the scent's still fresh. You *know* how important that is, Winston.'

Nkata slid the notebook into his pocket and observed her evenly. 'You're a pit bull sometimes,' he said, defeated.

'It's one of my finer attributes,' she replied.

Chapter Ten

Lynley pulled into the car park in front of Buxton police station, untangled his lengthy frame from the small police vehicle, and examined the convex brick façade of the building. He was still astounded at Barbara Havers.

He had suspected that Nkata might put Havers onto the task of tracing Andy Maiden's investigations via computer. He knew the black man was fond of her. And he hadn't forbade it because, in part, he was willing to see if – after her demotion and disgrace – she would complete a simple assignment that she was sure not to like. True to form, she'd gone her own way, proving once again what her superior officer believed to be the case: She had no more respect for a chain of command than a bull had respect for Wedgwood china. No matter that Winston had asked her to see to the Battersea end of things, she'd been given a prior assignment and she very well knew she was supposed to complete it before taking on something else. Christ. *When* would the woman learn?

He ducked inside the building and asked for the officer in charge of evidence from the crime scene. After speaking to Andy Maiden, he'd tracked down Nicola's Saab at the pound where he'd spent a fruitless fifty minutes doing himself what had already been done with exemplary efficiency by Hanken's team: going over every inch of the car, inside and out, stem to stern. The object of his search had been the pager. He'd come up empty-handed. So if Nicola Maiden had indeed left it in the Saab when she'd set off across the moors, the only place remaining to look for it would be among whatever evidence had been taken from her car.

The officer in question was called DC Mott, and he presided over the cardboard boxes, paper bags, plastic containers, clip boards, and record books that constituted the evidence so far linked to the investigation. He gave Lynley the wariest of welcomes into his lair. He was in the middle of tucking into an enormous jam tart onto which he'd just poured a liberal helping of custard and – spoon in hand – he didn't look like a man who wished to be disturbed in the midst of indulging in one of his vices. Munching happily away, Mott leaned back in a metal folding chair and asked Lynley exactly what he wanted to 'mess about with'.

Lynley told the constable what he was looking for. Then hedging his bets, he went on to add that while the pager might well have been left in Nicola Maiden's car, it might also have been left at the crime scene itself, in which case he wouldn't want to limit his search to evidence taken from the Saab. Would Mott mind his having a look through everything?

'Pager, you say?' Mott spoke with the spoon wedged into his cheek. 'Didn't come across nowt like that, 'm afraid.' And he dipped his head to the tart with devotion. 'Best you have a look through the records book first, sir. No sense sifting through everything till you see what we've got listed, is there?'

Fully aware of the degree to which he was treading on another man's patch, Lynley sought the most cooperative route. He found a vacant spot to lean against a metal-topped barrel, and he skimmed through the lists in the records book while Mott's spoon clicked energetically against his bowl.

Nothing in the records book came close to resembling a pager, so Lynley asked if he might have a look through the evidence for himself. Taking time to polish off tart and custard

with gusto – Lynley half expected the man to lick the sides of
the bowl – Mott reluctantly gave Lynley permission to look
through the evidence. Once Lynley managed to obtain a pair
of latex gloves from the DC, he started with the bags marked
Saab. He got only as far as the second bag, however, when DI
Hanken came charging into the evidence room.

'Upman's lied to us, the sod,' he announced, flipping Mott
a cursory nod. 'Not that I'm surprised. Smarmy bastard.'

Lynley went on to the third bag from the Saab. He set it
on the top of the barrel, but he didn't open it, saying, 'Lied
about what?'

'About Friday night. About his supposed—' heavy irony
on the word – 'guv-to-subordinate relationship with our
girl.' Hanken scrambled in his jacket and brought out his
Marlboros, at which Constable Mott said, 'Not in here, sir.
Fire hazard.'

Hanken said, 'Hell,' and shoved them back into his pocket.
He went on. 'They were in the Chequers, all right. I even
had a word with their waitress, a girl called Margery who
remembered them at once. Seems our Upman's taken more
than one dolly bird to the Chequers in the past, and when
he does he asks that Margery serve them. Likes her, she says.
And tips like an American. Bloody fool.'

Lynley said, 'The lie? Did they ask for a room?'

'Oh no. They left, like Upman said. What he failed to tell
us was where they went afterwards.' Hanken smiled thinly,
clearly delighted at having caught the solicitor out. 'They went
from the Chequers to *Chez* Upman,' he announced, 'where the
Maiden girl checked in for a lengthy visit.'

Hanken warmed to his story. Having learned never to
believe the first thing a lawyer said, he'd done a little more
scavenging once he'd spoken to Margery. A brief stint in the
solicitor's neighbourhood had been enough to unearth the
truth. Upman and Nicola Maiden had apparently arrived at the
solicitor's house round eleven forty-five, seen by a neighbour

Elizabeth George

who was taking Rover out for his last-of-the-evening. *And*
they'd been friendly enough with each other to suggest that a
little more existed between them than the employer-employee
relationship depicted by Mr Upman.

'Tongues on the porch,' Hanken said crudely. 'Our Will was
examining her dental work closely.'

'Ah.' Lynley opened the evidence bag and lifted its contents
onto the barrel top. 'And do we know it was Nicola Maiden
Upman was with? What about the divorcée girlfriend? Joyce?'

'It was Nicola all right,' Hanken said. 'When she left – this
was at half past four the next morning – the bloke next door
was taking a piss. He heard voices, had a look out the window,
and got a fine glimpse of her when the light went on in Upman's
car. So—' and here he took out his Marlboros once more –
'what d'you think they were up to for five hours?'

Mott said again, 'Not in here, sir.'

Hanken said, 'Shit,' and returned the Marlboros to their
place.

'Another talk with Mr Upman appears to be in order,'
Lynley said.

The expression on Hanken's face said that he couldn't
wait.

Lynley summarised for his colleague the information that
Nkata and Havers had gleaned in London. He concluded by
saying thoughtfully, 'But no one here in Derbyshire seems to
know that the girl had no intention of completing her law
course. Curious, don't you think?'

'No one knew or someone's lying to us,' Hanken said
pointedly. He seemed to note for the first time that Lynley was
sifting through evidence. He said, 'What're you doing, then?'

'Satisfying myself that Nicola's pager isn't here. D'you mind?'

'Satisfy away.'

The contents of the third bag appeared to be what had come
from the Saab's boot. Among the items lying on the barrel top
were the car's jack, a box spanner, a wheel brace, and a set

228

of screw drivers. Three spark plugs looked as if they'd been rolling round the boot since its factory days, and a set of jump leads were curled round a small chrome cylinder. Lynley lifted this last up and looked it over under the light.

'What've we got?' Hanken asked.

Lynley reached for his glasses and slipped them on. He'd been able to identify every other item that had been taken from the car, but what the cylinder was, he couldn't have said. He turned the object over in his hand. Little more than two inches long, the cylinder was perfectly smooth both inside and out, and either end of it was curved and polished, suggesting that as it was, it was all of a piece. It opened to fall precisely in half by means of a hinge. Each half had a hole bored into it. Through each hole an eyebolt was screwed.

'Looks like something from a machine,' Hanken said. 'A nut. A cog. Something like that.'

Lynley shook his head. 'It hasn't any interior grooves. And if it had, we'd be looking at a machine the size of a space ship, I dare say.'

'Then what? Here. Let me have a look.'

'Gloves, sir,' Mott barked, vigilance in action. He tossed a pair to Hanken, who put them on.

In the meantime, Lynley gave the cylinder a closer scrutiny. 'It's got something on the inside. A deposit of some kind.'

'Motor oil?'

'Not unless motor oil solidifies these days,' Lynley said.

Hanken took it from him and had his own go with it. He turned it in his palm and said, 'Substance? Where?'

Lynley pointed out what he'd seen: a smear in the shape of a small maple leaf lapping over the top – or the bottom – of the cylinder. Something had been deposited there and had dried to the colour of pewter. Hanken scrutinised this, even going so far as to sniff it in a noisy, houndlike fashion. He asked Mott for a plastic sack and said, 'Get this checked out straightaway.'

'Ideas?' Lynley asked him.

'Not off the top of my head,' he replied. 'Could be anything. Bit of salad cream. Smear of mayonnaise from a prawn sandwich.'

'In the boot of her car?'

'She went on a picnic. How the devil do I know? That's what forensics is for.'

There was more than a grain of truth in this. But Lynley felt unsettled by the presence of the cylinder, and he wasn't sure why. He said, attempting delicacy with the request and knowing how it might be interpreted, 'Peter, would you mind if I had a look at the crime scene?'

He needn't have worried. Hanken was hot to get on to other things. 'Go ahead. I'll go after Upman.' He peeled off his gloves and fished out his Marlboros a final time, saying to Mott, 'Don't have a coronary, Constable. I'm not lighting up in here.' And once outside the constable's demesne, he went on happily as he fired up the tobacco. 'You know how it looks, with the girl bonking Upman as well as . . . what've we got so far, two others?'

'Julian Britton and the London lover,' Lynley verified.

'For starters. And Upman'll make a third once I've talked to him.' Hanken inhaled deeply, and with some satisfaction. 'So how d'you suppose our Upman felt, wanting her, having her, and knowing she was giving it out to two other blokes just as happily as she was giving it to him?'

'You're getting ahead of yourself on that one, Peter.'

'I wouldn't put money on it.'

'More important than Upman,' Lynley pointed out, 'how did Julian Britton feel? He wanted to marry her, not to share her. And if, as her mother claims, she always told the truth, what might his reaction have been when he learned exactly what Nicola was up to?'

Hanken mulled this over. 'Britton *is* easier to tag with an accomplice,' he admitted.

'Isn't he just,' Lynley said.

*   *   *

Samantha McCallin didn't want to think, and when she didn't want to think, she worked. She trundled a wheelbarrow briskly down the Long Gallery's old oak floor, kitted out with a shovel, a broom and a dust pan. She stopped at the first of the room's three fireplaces and applied herself to removing the grit, grime, coal dust, bird droppings, old nests, and bracken that over time had fallen down the chimney. In an attempt at disciplining her thoughts, she counted her movements: one-*shovel*, two-*lift*, three-*swing*, four-*dump*, and in this way she emptied the fireplace of what appeared to be fifty years of detritus. She found that as long as she kept up the rhythm, she held her mind in check. It was when she had to move from shovelling to sweeping, that her thoughts began to gallop about.

Lunch had been a quiet affair, with the three of them gathered round the table in a nearly unbroken silence. Only Jeremy Britton had spoken during the meal, when Samantha had placed a platter of salmon in the middle of the table. Her uncle had caught her hand unexpectedly and raised it to his lips, announcing, 'We're grateful for all you've been doing round here, Sammy, my angel. We're grateful for *everything*.' And he'd smiled at her, a long slow meaningful smile, as if they shared a secret.

Which they did *not*, Samantha told herself. No matter the extent to which her uncle had revealed his feelings about Nicola Maiden on the previous day, she'd been successful in keeping hers to herself.

It was necessary, that. With the police crawling about asking questions and gazing at one with open suspicion, it was absolutely crucial that how she felt about Nicola Maiden be something Samantha held close to her heart.

She hadn't hated her. She'd seen Nicola for what she was, and she'd disliked her for it, but she hadn't hated her. Rather, she'd simply recognised her as an impediment to attaining what Samantha had quickly decided she wanted.

In a culture requiring her to find a man in order to define her world, Samantha hadn't come across a decent prospect in the last two years. With her biological clock ticking away and her brother refusing to have so much as a cup of coffee with a prospective female lest he be asked to commit his life to her, she was beginning to feel that the responsibility to extend the immediate family line was hers alone. But she'd been unable to sniff out a mate despite the humiliation of taking out personal ads, joining a dating agency, and engaging in such maritally conducive activities as singing in the church choir. And as a result, she'd felt a growing desperation to Settle Down, which meant, of course, to Reproduce.

At one level she knew it was ridiculous to be so marriage-and-offspring minded. Women in this day and age had careers and lives beyond husband and children, and sometimes those careers and those lives excluded the option of husband and children altogether. But on another level, she believed that she would be failing, somehow, if she made her life's journey forever alone. Besides, she told herself, she *wanted* children. And she wanted those children to have a father.

Julian had seemed so likely a candidate. They'd got on from the first. They'd been such *pals*. They'd achieved a quick intimacy born of a mutual interest in restoring Broughton Manor. And if that interest had been manufactured on her part initially, it had become real quickly enough when she'd understood how passionate her cousin was about his plans. And she could help him with those plans; she could nurse them along. Not only by working at his side, but by infusing the manor with the copious supply of money she'd inherited upon her father's death.

It had all seemed so logical and meant to be. But neither her camaraderie with her cousin, her ample funds, nor her efforts at proving her worthiness to Julian had sparked the slightest degree of interest in him, beyond the affectionate interest one might have had for the family dog.

At the thought of dogs, Samantha shuddered. She would not go in that direction, she thought firmly. Walking that path would lead her inexorably to a consideration of Nicola Maiden's death. And thinking about her death was as intolerable a prospect as was thinking about her life.

Yet the act of trying not to think about her spurred Samantha to think about her anyway. She saw her as she'd seen her last, and she tried to drive the image from her mind.

'You don't like me much do you, Sam?' Nicola had asked her, scanning her face to read what was there. 'Yes. I see. It's because of Jules. I don't want him, you know. Not the way women generally want men. He's yours. If you can win him, that is.'

So frank, she was. So absolutely up front with every word she spoke. Hadn't she ever worried about the impression she was making? Hadn't she ever wondered if someday that relentless honesty was going to cost her more than she was willing to pay?

'I could put in a word for you, if you'd like. I'm happy to do it. I think you and Jules would be good together. A *frightfully* proper sort of match, as they used to say.' And she'd laughed, but it hadn't been malicious. Disliking her would have been so much easier if only Nicola had stooped to ridicule.

But she hadn't. She hadn't needed to when Samantha already knew quite well how absurd her desire for Julian was.

'I wish I could make him stop loving you,' she'd said.

'If you find a way, do it,' Nicola had replied. 'And there'll be no hard feelings. You can have him with my blessing, Sam. It would be for the best.'

And she'd smiled the way she always smiled, so open and engaging and friendly, so completely without the worries of a woman who knew that her looks were nondescript and her talents worthless that smacking her seemed like the only response Samantha could possibly make. Smacking her and

Elizabeth George

shaking her and shouting, 'Do you think it's *easy* being me, Nicola? Do you think I *enjoy* my situation?'

That contact of flesh on flesh, of flesh on bone, was what Samantha had wanted. Anything to remove from Nicola's clear blue eyes the knowledge that in a battle in which Nicola didn't even bother to fight, Samantha McCallin still could not win.

'Sam. Here you are.'

Samantha swung hastily round from the fireplace and saw Julian coming along the gallery in her direction, the afternoon sunlight striking his hair. Her sudden movement spilled several globs of petrified ashes onto the floor. Miniature clouds of griseous dust rose from them.

'You frightened me,' she said. 'How can you walk so quietly on a wooden floor?'

He looked down at his shoes as if in explanation. 'Sorry.' He was carrying a tray with cups and plates on it, and he gestured with it. 'I thought you'd like a break. I've made us tea.'

She saw he'd also cut them each a piece of the chocolate cake she'd made for that evening's pudding. She felt a twinge of impatience at this. Surely, he could have *seen* it hadn't been cut into yet. Surely, he could have *known* it was meant for something. Surely, just for once dear God, he could have drawn one or two conclusions from the facts in hand. But she emptied her shovelful of debris into a wheelbarrow, and said, 'Thanks, Julie. I could do with something.'

She hadn't been able to eat much of the lunch she'd prepared them. Neither, she had noted, had he. So she knew that she was due for some sustenance. She just wasn't sure she could manage it in his presence.

They went to the windows, where Julian set the tray on the top of an old dole cupboard. Leaning their bums against the dusty sill, they each held a mug of Darjeeling and waited for the other to speak.

'It's coming along,' was Julian's offering as he looked the

length of the gallery to the door through which he'd entered. For an overlong time, he seemed to study the grimy, ornate carving of the Britton falcon that surmounted it. 'I couldn't manage any of this without you, Sam. You're a brick.'

'Just what a woman longs to hear,' Samantha replied. 'Thanks very much.'

'Damn. I didn't mean—'

'Never mind.' Samantha took a sip of tea. She kept her eyes on its milky surface. 'Why didn't you tell me, Julie? I thought we were close.'

Next to her, he slurped his tea. Samantha subdued her moue of distaste. 'Tell you what? And we are close. At least, I hope we are. I mean, I want us to be. Without you here, I would have packed it all in a long time ago. You're practically the best friend I have.'

'Practically,' she said. 'That limbo place.'

'You know what I'm saying.'

And the trouble was, she did know. She knew what he was saying, what he meant, and how he felt. She wanted to take him by the shoulders and shake him into an under-standing of what it meant that such an unspoken communi-cation should exist between them. But she couldn't do so, so she settled on trying to ferret out some of the real story of what had occurred between her cousin and Nicola, not really knowing what she'd do with the facts when and if she got them.

'I'd no idea you'd even thought about asking Nicola to marry you. When the police brought it up, I didn't know what to think.'

'About what?'

'About why you hadn't told me. First, that you'd asked her. Then, that she'd said no.'

'Frankly, I hoped she'd reconsider.'

'I wish you had told me.'

'Why?'

'It would have made things . . . easier, I suppose.'

At that, he turned. She could feel his gaze on her, and she grew restive under it. 'Easier? How could knowing I'd asked Nicola to marry me and been turned down have made anything easier? And for whom?'

His words were guarded, careful for the first time, which made her speak guardedly in turn. 'Easier for you, of course. I had the feeling something was wrong all day Tuesday. If you'd told me, I could have given you some support. It can't have been easy, waiting through Tuesday night and Wednesday. I expect you didn't get a minute's sleep.'

Silence for a terribly long moment. Then quietly, 'Yes. That's true enough.'

'Well, we could have talked about it. It helps to talk, don't you think?'

'Talking would have . . . I don't know, Sam. We'd been terribly close, the two of us, in the last few weeks. It felt so good. And I—'

Samantha warmed to the words.

'—suppose I didn't want to do anything that might kill the closeness and drive her off. Not that talking to you would have done that because I know you wouldn't have told her we'd spoken.'

'Naturally,' Samantha said with quiet bleakness.

'I knew she'd be unlikely to reconsider. But I still hoped she would. And it seemed to me that if I said something about what was going on, it would be like bursting a bubble. Idiotic, I know. But there you have it.'

'Putting your hopes into words. Yes. I understand.'

'I suppose the truth is that I couldn't face reality. I couldn't look squarely at the fact that she didn't want me the way I wanted her. I would have done as a friend. As a lover even, when she was in the Peaks. But nothing more than that.' He picked at his wedge of cake with the fork tines. He was, she noted, eating as little as she.

Finally he set his plate on the window sill, then said, 'Did you see the eclipse, by the way?'

She frowned, then remembered. It seemed so long ago. 'No. I didn't go after all. It didn't seem like much fun to wait for it alone. I went to bed.'

'That's just as well. We wouldn't want you lost on the moors.'

'Oh, that's unlikely, isn't it? It was only Eyam Moor. And even if it had been one of the others, I've been out alone enough by now that I always know where I'm—' She stopped herself. She looked at her cousin. He wasn't watching her, but his ruddy natural colouring gave him away. 'Ah. I see. Is that what you think?'

'I'm sorry.' His voice was wretched. 'I can't stop thinking about it. Having the police turn up made everything worse. All I can think about is what happened to her. I can't get it out of my mind.'

'Try doing what I do,' she said past a pounding heartbeat that she heard in her ears. 'There are so many ways to keep one's mind occupied. Try considering, for example, the fact that dogs have been giving birth on their own for a few hundred thousand years. It's remarkable, that. One can think about it for hours. That thought alone can fill up one's head so there's no room left for anything else.'

Julian was immobile. She'd made her point. 'Where were you on Tuesday night, Sam?' he finally whispered. 'Tell me.'

'I was killing Nicola Maiden,' Samantha said, getting to her feet and walking back over to the fireplace. 'I always like to end my day with a spot of murder.'

MKR Financial Management was housed in what looked like a pale pink confection on the corner of Lansdowne Road and St John's Gardens. The decorative icing consisted of woodwork so clean that Barbara Havers imagined a duster-wielding lackey getting up at five in the morning each day to scrub his way from the *faux* columns on either side of the door to the plaster medallions above the porch.

'Good thing we've still got the guv's motor,' Nkata murmured as he pulled up to the pavement across the street from the building.

'Why?' Barbara asked.

'We look like we fit in.' He nodded to a car whose back end was sloping up the drive at one side of the pink confection. It was a Jaguar XJS, silver in colour. It could have been the Bentley's first cousin. A black Mercedes sat in front of the building, locked between an Aston Martin and an antique Bristol.

'We're definitely out of our financial depth,' Barbara said, heaving herself from the car. 'But that's just as well. We wouldn't like to be rich. People with dibs are always dead choked.'

'You believe that, Barb?'

'No. But it keeps me happier to pretend it. Come on. I need some serious financial managing, and something tells me we've come to a place where it can happen.'

They had to ring to get in. No voice inquired as to who'd come calling, but none was necessary since a high tech security system on the building included a video camera placed strategically above the front door. Just in case someone was watching, Barbara took out her warrant card and held it up to the camera. Perhaps in response, the door buzzed open.

An oak-floored entry became a hushed corridor of closed doors with a width of Persian carpet running down it. Off this, Reception consisted of a small room that was heavy on antiques and heavier still on silver framed photographs. There was no one present, just a sophisticated telephone system that appeared to answer calls automatically and send them on their way. This sat on a kidney-shaped desk across whose top were fanned out a dozen brochures with the logo MKR stamped in gold upon them. It was all very reassuring in appearance, just the sort of place one wouldn't mind coming to in order to discuss the delicate matter of one's monetary situation.

Barbara went to investigate the photographs. She saw that the same man and woman were common to them all. He was short, wiry, and angelic in appearance, with a wispy corona of hair round his head, which added to his celestial aura. His companion was taller than he, blonde and as thin as a walking eating disorder. She was beautiful in the fashion of a catwalk model: vacant looking and all cheekbones and lips. The photographs themselves were vintage *Hello!*, featuring their subjects with an assortment of well turned out nobs, politicos, and celebrities. A former Prime Minister stood among them, and Barbara had no trouble identifying opera singers, film stars, and a well-known U.S. Senator.

A door opened and closed somewhere along the corridor. The floor boards creaked as someone walked along the Persian carpet towards Reception. With a click of heels against a bare section of wood, a woman came into the room to greet them. No more than a glance told Barbara that one of the two photographed subjects had herself come to see why the rozzers were calling.

She was Tricia Reeve, the woman said, Assistant Director of MKR Financial Management. How might she be of help to them?

Barbara introduced herself. Nkata did the same. They asked the woman if they could have a few minutes of her time.

'Of course,' Tricia Reeve replied politely, but Barbara couldn't help noticing that the Assistant Director of MKR Financial Management didn't exactly embrace the words *Scotland Yard CID* with the devotion of a member of the faithful. Instead, her glance moved like nervous quicksilver, sliding between the two detectives as if she wasn't certain how to behave. Her wide eyes looked black, but a lengthier look at them revealed that her pupils were so enlarged that they covered all but a thin edge of iris. The effect was disconcerting, but it was also revealing. Drugs, Barbara realised. Tsk, tsk, tsk. No wonder she was jumpy, with the cops on her doorstep.

Tricia Reeve took a moment to inspect her watch. Gold banded, this was, and coruscating expensively in the light. She said, 'I was just about to leave, so I hope this won't take long. I've got to attend a tea at the Dorchester. It's a charity do and as I'm a member of the committee . . . I hope you understand. Is there a problem?'

Murder certainly *was* a problem, Barbara thought. She let Nkata do the honours. For her part, she watched for reactions.

There were none, other than perplexity. Tricia Reeve observed Nkata as if she hadn't heard him correctly. After a moment, she said, 'Nicola Maiden? Murdered?' and then she added most strangely, 'Are you certain?'

'We've had a positive ID from the girl's parents.'

'I meant . . . I meant are you certain she was murdered?'

'We don't think she bashed in her own skull, if that's what you're asking,' Barbara said.

That got a reaction, limited though it was. One of Tricia Reeve's manicured hands reached for the top button of her suit's jacket. It was pin-striped, with a pencil width skirt that showed several miles of leg.

'Look,' Barbara said. 'The College of Law told us that she came to work for you last autumn on a part-time basis that turned to full-time in May. We take it she'd gone on leave for the summer. Is that right?'

Tricia glanced towards a closed door behind the reception desk. 'You'll need to speak to Martin.' She went to the door, knocked once, entered, and shut it behind her without another word.

Barbara looked at Nkata. 'I'm panting for your analysis, son.'

'She's pilled-up like a pharmacist's cupboard,' was his succinct reply.

'She's flying all right. What d'you reckon it is?'

He flipped his hand. 'It's keeping her sweet, whatever she's on.'

It was nearly five minutes before Tricia reappeared. During this time, the phones continued to ring, the calls continued to be routed, and the low murmur of voices came from behind the heavy closed door. When it opened at last, a man stood before them. It was Angel Hair from the photographs, decked out in a well-tailored charcoal suit and waistcoat with the heavy gold chain of a pocket watch slung across his middle. He introduced himself as Martin Reeve. He was Tricia's husband, he told them, Managing Director of MKR.

He invited Barbara and Nkata into his office. His wife was on her way out to tea, he explained. Would the police be needing her? Because as head of fundraising for Children in Need, she had an obligation to her committee to be present at their Autumn Harvest Tea at the Dorchester. It began the season, and had Tricia not been the chairman – 'Sorry, darling, chair*person*—' of the event, her presence wouldn't be so crucial. As it was, however, she happened to have the guest list in the boot of her car. And without that list, the seating plan for the tea couldn't be made. Reeve hoped the police would understand ... He flashed a mouth of perfect teeth in their direction: Straight, white, and capped, they were a testimony to man's triumph over the vicissitudes of dental genetics.

'Absolutely,' Barbara agreed. 'We can't have Sharon Whosis sitting next to the Countess of Crumpets. As long as Mrs Reeve is available later should we need to talk to her ...'

Reeve assured them that both he and his wife understood the gravity of the situation. 'Darling ... ?' He nodded Tricia on her way. She'd been standing hesitantly next to his desk, a massive affair of mahogany and brass with burgundy leather inlaid in the top. At his nod, she made her exit, but not before he stopped her for a goodbye kiss. She was forced to bend to accommodate him. With stilettos on, she was a good eight inches above his height.

That didn't cause them any difficulty, however. The kiss lingered just a bit too long.

Barbara watched them, thinking what a clever move it was on their part. The Reeves were no amateurs when it came to gaining the upper hand. The only question was: Why did they want it?

She could see that Nkata was growing as uncomfortable as they wanted him to be with their unexpected, extended display of affection. Her colleague shifted from one foot to the other as, arms crossed in front of him, he tried to decide where he was supposed to look. Barbara grinned. Because of his impressive height and his equally impressive wardrobe and despite his adolescence spent as chief war counsel with Brixton's most notorious street gang, she sometimes forgot that Winston Nkata was in fact a twenty-five-year-old kid who still lived at home with his mum and his dad. She cleared her throat quietly and he glanced her way. She gave a nod to the wall behind the desk where two diplomas hung. He joined her there.

'Love's a beautiful thing,' she murmured quietly. 'We must show it respect.'

The Reeves eased up on their mouth-to-mouth suction. 'See you later, darling,' Martin Reeve murmured.

Barbara rolled her eyes at Nkata and inspected the two diplomas hanging on the wall. Stanford University and London School of Economics. Both were made out to Martin Reeve. Barbara eyed him with new interest and more than a little respect. It was vulgar to display them – not that Reeve would ever stoop to vulgarity, she thought sardonically – but the bloke was clearly no slouch when it came to brains.

Reeve sent his wife on her way. From his pocket, he took a snowy linen handkerchief, which he used to wipe from his face the leavings of her pale pink lipstick.

'Sorry,' he said with a boyish smile. 'Twenty years of marriage and the fires're still burning. You've got to admit that's not too bad for two middle-agers with a sixteen-year-old son. Here he is, by the way. Name's William. Favours his mom, doesn't he?'

The appellation told Barbara what the Stanford diploma, the antiques, the silver frames, and the careful mid-Atlantic pronunciation had only suggested. 'You're an American?' she said to Reeve.

'By birth. But I haven't been back for years.' Reeve nodded at the photo. 'What d'you think of our William?'

Barbara glanced at the picture and saw a spotty faced boy with his mother's height and his father's hair. But she also saw what she was meant to see: the unmistakable cutaway and striped trousers of a pupil at Eton. La dee dah dah, Barbara thought and handed the picture off to Nkata. 'Eton,' she said with what she hoped was the right degree of awe. 'He must have brains by the bucketful.'

Reeve looked pleased. 'He's a whiz. Please. Sit down. Coffee? Or a drink? But I suppose you don't while you're working, do you? Drink, that is.'

They demurred on everything and got to the point. They'd been told that Nicola Maiden had been employed by MKR Financial Management from October of the previous year.

True enough, Reeve affirmed.

She worked as a trainee?

Equally true, Reeve agreed.

What was that, exactly? What was she training for?

Investment adviser, Reeve told them. Nicola was preparing herself to be able to manage financial portfolios: stocks, bonds, mutual funds, derivatives, offshore holdings . . . MKR managed the investments of some of the biggest hitters in the marketplace. With complete discretion, of course.

Lovely, Barbara told him. It was, then, their assumption that Nicola had remained in his employ until she'd taken a leave of absence to work for a solicitor in Derbyshire for the summer. If Mr Reeve would—

Reeve stopped them going further. He said, 'Nicola didn't take leave from MKR. She quit at the end of April. She was moving home to the North, she said.'

'Moving home?' Barbara repeated. Then what of the forwarding address she'd left with her landlady in Islington? she wondered. An address in Fulham was hardly north of anything save the river.

'That's what she told me,' Reeve said. 'I take it she told others something else?' He offered them an exasperated smile. 'Well, to be frank, that wouldn't surprise me. I discovered that Nicola sometimes played a bit fast and loose with her facts. It wasn't one of her finer qualities. Had she not quit, I'm afraid I would have let her go eventually. I had my . . .' He pressed his fingertips together. 'I had my doubts about her ability to be discreet. And discretion is critical in this line of work. We represent some very prominent players, and as we have access to all their financial data, they have to be able to depend on our ability to be circumspect with our information.'

'The Maiden girl wasn't?' Nkata asked.

'I don't want to say that,' Reeve said hastily. 'Nicola was quick and bright, no mistake about that. But there was something about her that needed watching. So I watched. She had an excellent hand with our clients, which was certainly to her credit. But she had a tendency to be . . . well, perhaps *over-awed* is the best way to put it. She was rather over-awed by the value of some of their portfolios. And it's never a good idea to make how-much-Sir-Somebody-is-worth the topic of your lunchtime conversation.'

'Was there any client with whom she may have had a special hand?' Barbara asked. 'One that extended after business hours?'

Reeve's eyes narrowed. 'What do you mean?'

Nkata took the ball. 'The girl had a lover here in town, Mr Reeve. We're looking for him.'

'I don't know anything about a lover. But if Nicola had one, you'll more likely find him at the College of Law.'

'We've been told that she left the College of Law to work full time for you.'

Reeve looked affronted. 'Officer, I hope you're not suggesting that Nicola Maiden and I—'

'Well, she was a fine looking woman.'

'As is my own wife.'

'I'm wondering if your wife had anything to do with why she left. It's odd, you ask me. The Maiden girl leaves law college to work for you full time, but she leaves you practically the exact same week. Why d'you think she did that?'

'I told you. She said she was moving home to Derby-shire—'

'—where she went to work for a bloke who tells us she had a man in London. Right. So what I'm wondering is whether that London man's you.'

Barbara shot Nkata an admiring glance. She liked that he was willing to cut to the chase.

'I happen to be in love with my wife,' Reeve said. 'Tricia and I have been together for twenty years, and if you think I'd jeopardise everything we have for a one-time romp with a college girl, then you're wrong.'

'There's nothing to suggest it was a one-off,' Barbara said.

'One off or every night of the week,' Reeve countered, 'I wasn't interested in a liaison with Nicola Maiden.' He seemed to stiffen as his thoughts suddenly took another direction. He drew in a shallow breath and reached for a silver letter opener that sat in the middle of his desk. He said, 'Has someone told you otherwise? Has my good name been slandered by someone? I insist on knowing. Because if that's the case, I'll be talking to my solicitor right away.'

He was definitely an American, Barbara thought wearily. She said, 'Do you know a bloke called Terry Cole, Mr Reeve?'

'Terry Cole? C-o-l-e? I see.' As he spoke, Reeve reached for a pen and a pad of paper and scrawled the name. 'So he's the little bastard who's said that—'

'Terry Cole's dead,' Nkata cut in. 'He didn't say anything. He died with the Maiden girl in Derbyshire. You know him?'

'I've never heard of him. When I asked who'd told you . . . Look here. Nicola's dead and I'm sorry she's dead. But I haven't seen her since the end of April. I haven't talked to her since the end of April. And if someone out there is besmirching my good name, I mean to take whatever steps are necessary to rout the bastard out and make him pay.'

'Is that your usual reaction when you're crossed?' Barbara asked.

Reeve set down his pen. 'I think this interview's over.'

'Mr Reeve . . .'

'Please leave. You've had my time and I've told you what I know. If you think I'm going to play police patsy and sit here while you attempt to lead me down the garden path towards some sort of self-incrimination . . .' He pointed at them both. He had, Barbara saw, inordinately small hands, his knuckles cross-hatched with myriad scars. 'You guys need to be less obvious,' he said. 'Now get out of here. *Pronto.*'

There was nothing for it but to accede to his request. Good expatriate Yank that he was, his next move surely was going to be to ring up his solicitor and claim harassment. There was no point pushing anything further.

'Nice work, Winston,' Barbara said when her colleague had unlocked the Bentley and they'd climbed inside. 'You put him on the ropes quick and proper.'

'No sense in wasting our time.' He examined the building. 'I wonder if there's a real Children in Need do going on at the Dorchester today.'

'There must be something going on somewhere. She was dressed up to the nines, wasn't she?'

Nkata looked at Barbara. His glance travelled over her clothes sorrowfully. 'With all respect, Barb . . .'

She laughed. 'All right. What do I know about the nines anyway?'

He chuckled and started the car. Pulling away from the pavement, he said, 'Seat belt, Barb.'

Barbara said, 'Oh. Right,' and turned in her seat to reach for it.

Which was when she saw Tricia Reeve. The Assistant Director of MKR had taken herself nowhere near the Dorchester, as things turned out. She was skulking round the side of the building, hastening up the front steps and heading straight for the door.

Chapter Eleven

———◆———

The moment the cops were out of his office, Martin Reeve pressed the call button that was recessed into one of the shelves on which his collection of Henley photos were arranged. Just as the phony college diplomas were part of the Martin Reeve Story, the Henley photos were a vital piece of the Martin and Tricia Reeve Romance. It was part of their manufactured history that they'd first met at the Regatta years ago. He'd been telling the apocryphal tale of their introduction for so long that he'd begun to believe it himself.

His call was answered in less than five seconds, a record. Jaz Burns entered the room without knocking. 'A real cow, she was,' he said with a smirk. 'Fancy bagging her, Marty. You'd not soon forget it.'

From his lair at the back of the house, Jaz indulged himself in voyeurism with the surveillance equipment in Martin's office; Martin was willing to overlook this, however, in the cause of employing his other talents.

'Follow them,' Martin said.

'The cops? There's a turn around for you. What's up?'

'Later. Get on it now.'

Jaz was astute at reading nuances. He jerked his head in a nod, snatched up the keys to the Jaguar, and slipped soundlessly from the room on cat burglar feet. The door

248

hadn't been closed behind him for more than fifteen seconds, however, when it opened again.

Martin swung round in agitation, saying, 'God damn it, Jaz,' and ready to berate his employee for whatever dawdling had caused him to lose the cops' trail before they'd even begun to lay it. But Tricia, not the sprite-like Burns, stood there, and the expression on her face told Martin that a Scene was coming.

Fuck it, he wanted to say, not now. At the moment he didn't have the resources to soothe Tricia through an attack of the Shrills.

'What are you doing here? Tricia, you're supposed to be at the tea.'

'I couldn't.' She shut the door behind her.

'What do you mean, you couldn't?' Martin asked her. 'You're expected. This has been set up for months. I pulled a dozen strings to get you on that committee, and if you're on the committee you're supposed to turn up. You've got the God damn *list*, Patricia. How're those women supposed to carry on this event – and, by the way, how are *we* supposed to maintain our good name – if you can't be relied upon to show up on time with a seating plan in your possession?'

'What did you tell them about Nicola?'

He blew out a breath on the word *shit*. 'Is that why you're here? Am I clear on that? You've failed in your part to show open support for one of the worthiest causes in the UK because you want to know what I told the cops about a fucking dead bitch?'

'I don't like that language.'

'Which part? Fucking? Dead? Or bitch? Let's get it straight because right at this moment there are five hundred women and photographers from every publication in the country *waiting* for you to appear and God knows you won't be able to manage it if we aren't clear on which part of my language bothers you.'

'What did you tell them?'

'I told them the truth.' He was so irritated that he could almost enjoy the expression of horror that crossed her face.

'*What*?' When she asked, the question was hoarse.

'Nicola Maiden was a trainee financial adviser. She quit last April. If she hadn't quit, I would have fired her.'

Tricia relaxed noticeably. Martin went on. He vastly preferred his wife on edge. 'I'd love to know where the little bitch took herself off to from here, and with any luck, I'll have that information from Jaz within the hour. Cops are nothing if not predictable. If she had a place in London – and my money says she had – then the cops're going to lead us straight to it.'

The tension was, gratifyingly, back in an instant. 'Why d'you want to know? What're you going to do?'

'I don't like disrespect, Patricia. You, of all people, ought to know that. I don't like to be lied to. Trust is the bedrock of any relationship, and if I don't do something when someone screws me over, then it's open season for everyone to take Martin Reeve for all that he's worth. Well, I won't allow that.'

'You had her, didn't you?' Tricia's face was pinched.

'Don't be an idiot.'

'You think I can't tell. You say to yourself, "Dear Trish's doped up to her eyeballs half the time. What could she possibly notice?" But I do. I saw how you looked at her. I knew when it happened.'

Martin sighed. 'You need a hit. Sorry to put it so crudely, my dear. I know you'd prefer to avoid the topic. But the truth of the matter is that you always get weird in the head when you're coming down too fast. You need another hit.'

'I know what you're like.' Her voice was rising, and he wondered idly if he could manage the needle without her cooperation. But how the hell much was she shooting up these days anyway? Even if he could cope with the needle and the syringe, the last thing he needed was his wife carted off in a coma. 'I know how you like to be the *boss*, Martin. And what better way is there to prove you're in charge than to tell some college girl to drop her knickers and then watch how fast she's willing to do it.'

'Tricia, this is such awesome bullshit. Are you listening to yourself?'

'So you had her. And then she walked away. Poof. She was gone. Vanished.' Tricia snapped her fingers. Rather weakly, Martin noticed. 'And that felt nasty, didn't it? And we know how you react when something feels nasty.'

Speaking of which ... Martin itched to strike her. He would have done so had he not been certain that, doped up or not, she'd run straight home to Daddy in an instant with the tale. Daddy would make certain demands if she did that. Detox first. Divorce after that. Neither of which was acceptable to Martin. Marriage into wealth – no matter that the money came from a successful antiques business and hadn't been passed down through successive generations in best blue blood fashion – had garnered for him a degree of social acceptance that he'd never have acquired as a mere immigrant to the country, no matter how successful in business he might be. He had no intention of giving that social acceptance up.

'We can have this discussion later,' he said with a glance at his pocket watch. 'For now, you still have time to get to the tea without thoroughly humiliating yourself or me: Say it was the traffic: a pedestrian hit by a taxi in Notting Hill Gate. You stopped to hold his hand – no, make it a woman and a child – till the ambulance arrived. A hole in your stocking would support the story, by the way.'

'Don't dismiss me like some mindless tart.'

'Then stop acting like one.' He shot the retort back without thinking and immediately regretted it. What possible purpose could be served by escalating an idiotic discussion into a fully blown row? 'Look, sweetheart,' he said, aiming for conciliation, 'let's stop the bickering. We're letting ourselves get thrown by

a simple, routine visit from the cops. As far as Nicola Maiden
goes—'

'We haven't done it in months, Martin.'

He went steadily on. '—it's unfortunate that she's dead, it's
unfortunate that she was murdered, but as we weren't involved
in what happened to her—'

'We. Haven't. Fucked. Since. June.' Her voice rose. 'Are you
listening to me? Are you hearing what I'm saying?'

'I'm doing both,' he replied. 'And if you weren't blitzed most
hours of the day, you'd find your memory improving.'

That, at least and thank God, stopped her. She, after all,
had no more wish than he had to end their marriage. He
served a purpose in her life that was as necessary to her
as the purpose she served was necessary to him: He kept
her supply lines open and her secret safe; she increased his
mobility and garnered from his fellows the sort of deference
one man shows another when that other has possession of
a beautiful woman. Thus, she very much *wanted* to believe.
And in Martin's experience, when people desperately wanted
to believe, they talked themselves into believing just about
anything. In this case, however, Tricia's belief wasn't far from
the truth. He did indeed do her when she was tripped out. She
just didn't know he preferred it that way.

She said in a smaller voice, 'Oh,' and she blinked.

'Yes,' he said. 'Oh. All through June, July, and August. Last
night as well.'

She swallowed. 'Last night?'

He smiled. She was his.

He went to her. 'Let's not let the cops wreck what we have,
Trish. They're after a killer. They're not after us.' He touched
her lips with the battle-weary knuckles of his right hand. Left
hand on her buttocks, he drew her near. 'Now, isn't that right?
Isn't it true that what the police are looking for, they won't
find here?'

'I've got to get off the stuff,' she whispered.

He shushed her and urged her down for a kiss. 'One thing at a time,' he said.

In his room at the Black Angel Hotel, Lynley discarded his suit and tie in favour of jeans, hiking boots, and the old waxed jacket that he generally wore in Cornwall, an ancient possession of his long-dead father. He kept glancing at the telephone as he dressed, alternately willing it to ring and willing himself to make the call from this end.

There had been no message from Helen. He'd excused her silence that morning as a result of her late night with Deborah St James and her probable subsequent lie-in, but he was having difficulty excusing a silence that had apparently continued well into mid-afternoon. He'd even phoned down to reception, asking that they double check his messages, but an extended foray into pigeon holes and rubbish baskets hadn't produced anything different from what he'd had at the beginning: His wife hadn't phoned. Nor had anyone else, for that matter, but silence from the rest of the world didn't concern him. Silence from Helen did.

In the way of people who believe they're in the right, he replayed their conversation of the previous morning. He checked it for subtext and nuance, but no matter how he examined it, he came out on top. The fact was simplicity itself. His wife had been interfering in his professional life, and she owed him an apology She had no business second guessing decisions that he made as part of his work any more than he had a place instructing her how and when she could assist St James in his lab. In the personal arena, they each had a vested interest in knowing the other's hopes, resolutions, and desires. In the world of their individual occupations, they owed each other kindness, consideration, and support. That his wife – as was clearly indicated by her undeniably perverse refusal to phone him – didn't wish to adhere to this basic and reasonable manner of coexisting was a source of disillusionment to him. He'd known Helen for sixteen years. How could he have gone such a time without actually knowing her at all?

He checked his watch. He looked out of the window and made note of the sun's position in the sky. There were several good hours of daylight left, so he had no need to rush off right at the moment. Knowing this, and knowing what he could well do because of this, he procrastinated by checking to make sure he had a compass, a torch, and an Ordnance Survey map tucked into the various pockets of his jacket.

Then, without further employment available, he heaved a sigh of defeat. He walked to the phone and punched in his home number. Might as well leave her a message if she's gone out, he thought. One can only make a point with one's mate for a limited period.

He expected Denton. Or the answerphone. What he didn't expect – because if she was at home, why the devil wasn't she phoning *him* – was to hear his wife's soft voice on the other end of the line.

She said hello twice. In the background, he could hear music playing. It was one of his new Prokofiev CDs. She'd taken the call in the drawing room.

He wanted to say, 'Hello, darling. We parted badly, and I'm longing to make it up with you.' But instead he wondered how the hell she could sit there in London, blissfully enjoying his music, while they were at odds. And they *were* at odds, weren't they? Hadn't he just spent most of his working day successfully avoiding an obsessive contemplation of their disagreement, of everything that had led up to it, of what it indicated about the past, of what it presaged for the future, of what it might lead them to if one of them didn't wake up and realise that . . .

Helen said, 'This is very rude, whoever you are,' and rang off.

Which left Lynley holding a dead receiver and feeling very foolish. Ringing her back at the moment would make him feel even more foolish, he concluded. So that was that. He replaced the receiver, removed the keys to the police car from his suit coat, and left the room.

He drove northeast, cruising along the road that carved a gully between the limestone slopes upon which Tideswell was built. The land formed a natural siphon here. The wind gusted through it like a gushing river, whipping tree limbs and flipping leaves upside down in an unspoken promise of the season's first rain.

At the junction, a handful of honey-coloured buildings marked the hamlet of Lane Head. Here Lynley veered to the west, where the road made a straight, charcoal incision into the moor and drystone walls prevented the accretion of heather, bilberry, and ferns from reclaiming the road and returning it to the land.

It was a wild country. Once Lynley left the last of the hamlets behind, the only signs of life – aside from the vegetation, which was profuse – were the jackdaws and magpies and the occasional sheep that stood serene and cloud like, grazing among the pink and the green.

Stiles provided access to the moor, and signposts marked the routes of public footpaths that had been used for centuries by farmers or shepherds travelling between the far flung hamlets. Hiking and biking trails were a more recent addition to the landscape, however, and these carved through the heather and disappeared towards distant lichen-grey outcrops that formed the remains of prehistoric settlements, ancient places of worship, and Roman forts.

Lynley found the spot a few miles northeast of the tiny hamlet of Sparrowpit, where Nicola Maiden had left her Saab upon setting off into the moor. There, a long and knobby border of wall was interrupted by a white iron gate, its thick skin of crusty paint eaten through in spots by blemishes of rust. When he arrived, Lynley did what Nicola Maiden herself had done: He opened the gate, pulled into a narrow paved lane within, and parked behind the stone wall on a patch of earth.

He consulted the map before getting out of the car. He opened it against the passenger seat and fixed his reading glasses on his nose.

Lynley studied the route he would need to take to get out to Nine Sisters' Henge, making note of landmarks that would be useful in guiding him on his way. Hanken had offered him a detective constable as a guide, but he'd refused. He wouldn't have minded an experienced hiker as an escort, but he preferred not to be accompanied by a member of the Buxton police who could possibly take offence – and report such offence to Hanken – when Lynley scrutinised the crime scene with an attention suggesting that the local CID hadn't done its job.

'It's a last possibility for that blasted pager, and I'd like to eliminate it,' Lynley had told Hanken.

'If it had been there, my boys would have found it,' Hanken had replied, reminding him that they'd done a fingertip search for the weapon, which certainly would have turned up a pager even if it hadn't dislodged a knife from the site. 'But if it puts your mind at rest to do it, then put your mind at rest and do it.' As for himself, he was off after Upman, champing at the bit to confront the solicitor.

Feeling sure of his route, Lynley folded the map and returned his glasses to their case. He put map and glasses in his jacket pockets and climbed out into the wind. He set out southeast, with the collar of his jacket turned up and his shoulders hunched against the gusts that were blowing against him. The stretch of paved lane led in the direction he wanted, so he started out on it, but after less than a hundred yards, it ended in a crumble of aggregate boulders comprising mostly gravel and tar. From there, the going became rougher, an uneven trail of earth and stones, creased by water courses that were skeletally dry from a summer without rain.

The walk took him nearly an hour, and he made it in utter solitude. His route followed stony paths that intersected with other, stonier paths. He brushed through heather, gorse, and fern; he climbed limestone outcrops; he passed the remains of chambered cairns.

He was just coming upon an unexpected fork in the trail when he saw a lone hiker walking his way from the southeast. As he was fairly certain that this was the direction of Nine Sisters' Henge, Lynley remained where he was, waiting to see who had made this late afternoon visit to the scene of the crime. As far as he knew, Hanken still had the stone circle taped off and guarded. So if the hiker was a journalist or press photographer, he would have found little joy in taking an extended walk across the moor.

It wasn't a man, as things turned out. Nor was it either a journalist or a photographer. Instead, as the figure approached, Lynley saw that Samantha McCallin had, for some reason, decided to treat herself to an afternoon hike out to Nine Sisters' Henge.

Apparently, she recognised him at the same instant that he realised her identity because her gait changed its rhythm. She'd been marching along with a whip tail of birch in her hand, flicking it against the heather as she stepped along the path. But seeing Lynley, she chucked the whip tail to one side, squared her shoulders, and came straight at him.

'It's a public place,' she said at once. 'You can tape off the circle and post guards out there, but you can't keep people off the rest of the moor.'

'You're some miles from Broughton Manor, Miss McCallin.'

'Don't killers return to the scenes of their crimes? I'm merely living the part. Would you like to arrest me?'

'I'd like you to explain what you're doing here.'

She looked over her shoulder in the direction from which she'd come. 'He thinks I killed her. Isn't that rich? I speak out in defence of him this morning and by afternoon he's decided *I* did it. It's an odd way to say "Thanks for taking my part, Sam," but there you have it.'

It could have been the wind, of course, but it looked to Lynley as if she'd been crying. He said, 'So what are you doing here, Miss McCallin? You must know that your presence—'

'I wanted to see the place where his fantasy died. My cousin's fantasy.' The wind had loosened hair from her plait, and wispy tendrils of it blew round her face. 'He says, of course, that his fantasy really died on Monday night when he asked her to marry him. But I don't think so. I think as long as Nicola walked the earth, my cousin Julian would have held on to his obsession of having a life with her. Waiting for her to change her mind. Waiting for her to – as he would say – *really* see him. And the funny thing is, if she'd crooked her finger at him just the right way – or even the wrong way, for that matter – he would've interpreted it as the sign he was waiting for, proving to him that she loved him in spite of everything she said and did to the contrary.'

'You disliked her, didn't you?' Lynley asked.

She gave a short laugh. 'What difference does it make? She was going to get what she wanted no matter how I felt about her.'

'What she got was death. She can't have wanted that.'

'She would have destroyed him. She would have sucked out his marrow. She was that sort of woman.'

'Was she?'

Samantha's eyes narrowed as a gust of wind spat chalky bits of earth into the air. 'I'm glad she's dead. I won't lie about that. But you're making a mistake if you think that I'm the only person who'd dance on her grave, given half the chance.'

'Who else is there?'

She smiled. 'I don't intend to do your job for you.'

That said, she stepped past him and walked off down the path, taking the direction he himself had travelled from the northern boundary of the moor. He wondered how she had come to be on the moor at all, as he'd seen no cars parked on the verge when he'd turned off the road. He also wondered if she parked elsewhere either out of ignorance of the presence of the hard packed little plot of land behind the drystone wall or to hide her knowledge of the plot's existence.

He watched her, but she didn't turn back to see if he was doing so. She must have wanted to – it was human nature – and the fact that she didn't spoke worlds about her self-discipline. He himself walked on.

He recognised Nine Sisters' Henge by the separate stone – called the King Stone, according to Hanken – that marked its location within a thick copse of birches. He came at the monument from the opposite side, however, and didn't realise that he was actually upon it till he circled the copse, took a compass reading just beyond it, reckoned that the stone circle had to be nearby, and turned back to see the pockmarked monolith rising beside a narrow path into the trees.

He retraced his steps, hands shoved into his pockets. He found DI Hanken's guard posted a few yards from the site, and he admitted Lynley to it, allowing him to duck beneath the crime scene tape and approach the sentry stone alone. Lynley paused by this – the King Stone – and examined it. It was weather-worn, as one would expect, but it was man-worn as well. At some time in the past, indentations had been carved into the back side of the enormous column. They formed handholds and footholds so that a climber could ascend to the top.

To what use had the stone been put in ancient times, Lynley wondered. As a means of calling a community to assemble? As a look-out post for someone responsible for the safety of shamen performing rituals within the stone circle? As the reredos of an altar for sacrifice? It was impossible to say.

He slapped his hand against it and went under the trees, where the first thing he noticed was that the birches – growing so thickly together – acted as a natural windbreak. When he finally made his way into the prehistoric circle, not a breath of air was even stirring.

His first thought was that it was nothing like Stonehenge, which was when he realised how firmly the word *henge* was rooted in his mind with a particular image. There were standing stones – nine of them, as the place name suggested – but these were far more roughly hewn than he'd expected. There were no lintel stones as there were at Stonehenge. And the external bank and the internal ditch that enclosed the standing stones were far less distinct.

He entered the circle. It was quiet as death. While the trees prevented the wind from reaching into the circle, the stones appeared to prevent the sound of the leaves being rustled from reaching into the circle either. It wouldn't be difficult for someone at night to come upon the monument unheard, then. He – or she or they – would merely have had to know where Nine Sisters' Henge was or to follow a hiker there from a distance in daylight and wait for nightfall. Which in itself would not have been difficult. The moor was vast, but it was also open. On a clear day, one could see for miles.

The circle's interior was moor grass beaten lateral by a summer of visitors to the site, a flat slice of rock at the base of the northernmost standing stone, and the remains of half a dozen old fires built by campers and worshippers. Starting at the circle's perimeter, Lynley began a systematic search for Nicola Maiden's pager. It was a tedious activity, involving an inch by inch scrutiny of the bank, the ditch, the base of each stone, the moor grass, and the fire rings. When he'd completed his inspection of the site without finding a thing and knew he'd next have to trace Nicola's route to the location of her death, he paused to pick out the path of her flight. In doing so, he found his gaze drawn to the central fire ring.

He saw that the ring was distinguished from the rest in three ways. It was fresher – with hunks of charred wood not yet disintegrated into ashes and lumps – it bore the unmistakable marks of having been sifted through by the scenes of crime team, and the stones that encircled it had been disturbed roughly, as if someone had stamped on the fire to put it out and dislodged the barrier in the process. But seeing these stones brought to Lynley's mind the photographs of the dead Terry Cole and the burns that charred one side of the young man's face.

He went to squat by the fire remains, and he thought for the first time about that face and what was indicated by its burnt and bubbling skin. He realised that the extent of the burning suggested that the boy had had a fairly lengthy contact with the fire. But he hadn't been held *down* into the flames, because if he had been, there would have been defensive wounds on his body as he struggled to free himself from someone's grasp. And according to Dr Myles, there had been no such wounds on Terry Cole: no bruising or scratching of his hands or knuckles, no distinctive abrasions on his torso. And yet, Lynley thought, he'd been exposed to the fire long enough to be severely burnt, indeed to have his skin blackened. So how had he got there? There seemed to be only one reasonable answer. Cole must have fallen into the fire. But how?

Lynley rested on his haunches and let his gaze wander round the circle. He saw that a second, narrower path led out of the thicket – opposite the path he'd come in on – and from his position by the fire ring, that path was in a direct line with his vision. This, then, had to be Nicola's route. He pictured the young people on Tuesday night, sitting side by side at the fire. Two killers wait outside the stone circle, unheard and unseen. They bide their time. When the moment is right, they charge towards the fire, each of them taking one of the two others and making short work of them.

It was plausible, Lynley decided. But if that was what happened, he couldn't see why short work hadn't been made of Nicola Maiden. Indeed, he couldn't see how the young woman had managed to get one hundred and fifty yards away from her killer before she was even attacked. While it was true that she could have fled the circle and taken off on the second path that he himself could see cutting through the trees, with the advantage of surprise on the killers' part how had she managed to elude capture for such a distance? She was an experienced hiker, of course, but what did experience really count for in darkness, with someone in a panic and running for her life? And even if she wasn't in a panic, how could her reflexes have been so good or her understanding of what was happening so acute? Surely, it would have taken her at least five seconds to realise that harm was intended her, and that delay would have been her undoing right then, within the circle and not one hundred and fifty yards away.

Lynley frowned. He kept seeing the photograph of the boy. Those burns were important, a critical point. Those burns, he knew, told the real tale.

He reached for a stick – part of the kindling of the fire – and aimlessly shoved it into the ashes as he thought. Nearby, he spotted the first of the dried splatters of blood that had come from Terry Cole's wounds. Beyond those splatters, the dry moor grass was heavily gouged in a zigzagging path that led to one of the standing stones. Slowly, Lynley followed this path. He found that it was speckled with blood for the entire distance.

There were no great gobs of gore, though, and not the sort of blood evidence one would expect from someone bleeding to death from an arterial wound. In fact, as he moved along it, Lynley realised that the trail did not offer the sort of blood evidence one would expect to find from the multiple stab wounds that Terry Cole had had inflicted upon him. At the base of the standing stone, however, Lynley saw that the blood had pooled. Indeed, it had splashed onto the stone itself, leaving tiny rivulets from a height of three feet, dribbling down to the ground below.

Lynley paused here. His gaze moved from the fire ring to the beaten path. In his mind he saw the picture of the boy that the police photographer had taken, his flesh eaten black by the flames. He considered all of it point by point:

Blood by the fire in daubs and splatters.

Blood by the standing stone in pools.

Blood in rivulets from a height of three feet.

A girl running off into the night.

A chunk of limestone bashing in her skull.

Lynley narrowed his eyes and drew a slow breath. Of course, he thought. Why hadn't he seen what had happened from the first?

The address they'd been given in Fulham took Barbara Havers and Winston Nkata to a maisonette in Rostrevor Road. They expected to have to deal with a landlady, custodian, or concierge in order to gain access to Nicola Maiden's rooms. But when they went through the pro forma business of ringing the bell next to the number five, they were surprised to hear a woman's voice on the speaker, asking them to identify themselves.

There was a pause once Nkata made it clear that Scotland Yard CID had come calling. After a moment, the disembodied voice said, 'I'll be down shortly,' in the cultured accent of a woman who spent her free time reading for parts in costume dramas on the BBC. Barbara expected her to appear in full Jane Austen regalia: done up in a slender Regency dress and ringlets round her face. Some five minutes later – 'Where's she coming from, exactly?' Nkata wanted to know, with a glance at his watch, 'Southend-on-Sea?' – the door opened and a twelve-year-old in a vintage Mary Quant mini-dress stood before them.

'Vi Nevin,' the child said by way of introduction. 'Sorry. I'd just got out of the bath and had to pull on some clothes. May I see your identification, please?'

The voice was the same as the woman's on the speaker, and

coming from the pixie-like creature in the doorway, it was quite disconcerting, as if a female ventriloquist were lurking somewhere nearby, throwing her voice into a pre-adolescent child for a bit of a lark. Barbara caught herself sneaking a glimpse round the door jamb to see if someone was hiding there. The expression on Vi Nevin's face said that she was used to such a reaction.

After looking over their warrant cards to her satisfaction, she handed them back and said, 'Right. What can I do for you?' And when they told her that her rooms had been given as a forwarding address for the post from Islington when a student from the College of Law had moved house, she said, 'There's nothing illegal in that, is there? It sounds the responsible thing to do.'

Did she know Nicola Maiden, then? Nkata asked her.

'I don't make a habit of taking up lodgings with strangers,' was her reply. And then glancing from Nkata to Barbara, 'But Nikki isn't here. She hasn't been for weeks. She's up in Derbyshire till next Wednesday evening.'

Barbara saw that Nkata was reluctant to do the dubious honours of announcing death to the unsuspecting yet another time. She decided to show mercy upon him, saying, 'Is there a place we can talk privately?'

Vi Nevin heard something beyond the simple question, as her eyes indicated. 'Why? Have you a warrant or a decree or something? I know my rights.'

Barbara sighed inwardly. What damage the last few revelations of police malfeasance had done to public trust. She said, 'I'm sure you do. But we're not here to conduct a search. We'd like to talk to you about Nicola Maiden.'

'Why? Where is she? What's she done?'

'May we come in?'

'If you tell me what you want.'

Barbara exchanged a glance with Nkata. Oh well, her look told him. There was nothing for it but to give the young woman the nasty news on her own front step. 'She's dead,' Barbara informed her. 'She died in the Peak District three nights ago. Now, may we come in or should we keep talking out here in the street?'

Vi Nevin stared at her. She looked completely uncomprehending. 'Dead?' she repeated. 'Nikki's *dead*? But she can't be. I spoke to her on Tuesday morning. She was going hiking. She isn't dead. She can't be.'

She searched their faces as if looking for evidence of a joke or a lie. Apparently not finding it, she stood back from the door. She said, 'Please come in,' in a hushed and altered voice.

She led them up a flight of stairs to a door that stood gaping on the first floor. This gave into an L-shaped living room, where french windows opened onto a balcony. Below it, water played in a garden fountain, and a hornbeam threw late afternoon shadows on a pattern of flagstones.

At one side of the room, a sleek chrome and glass trolley held at least a dozen bottles of spirits. Vi Nevin chose an unsealed Glenlivet, and she poured herself three fingers in a tumbler. She took it neat, and any lingering doubts that Barbara had had about her age were put to rest when she tackled the whisky.

While the young woman gathered herself together, Barbara took stock of the living situation ... what she could see of it. On the first floor of the maisonette were the living room, the kitchen, and a loo. The bedrooms would be above them, accessed via a staircase that rose along one wall. From where she was standing just inside the front door, she could see to the top of the stairs, as well as into the kitchen. This was fitted out with a surfeit of mod cons: refrigerator with ice maker, microwave oven, espresso machine, gleaming copper bottomed pots and pans. The work tops were granite, and the cupboards and the floor were bleached oak. Nice, Barbara thought. She wondered who was paying for it all.

She glanced at Nkata. He was taking in the low, butter-coloured sofas with their profusion of green and gold cushions tumbling across them. His gaze went from there to the luxurious ferns by the window to the large abstract oil above the fireplace. It was a bloody far cry from Loughborough estate, his expression said. He looked Barbara's way. She mouthed La dee dah. He grinned.

Having downed her drink, Vi Nevin appeared to do nothing more than slowly breathe. Finally, she turned to them. She smoothed back her hair – this was blonde and breast-length – and she fixed it in place with a hairband that made her look like Alice in Wonderland.

She said, 'I'm sorry. No one phoned. I've not had the television on. I had no idea. I talked to her only Tuesday morning and . . . For God's sake, what happened?'

They gave her two pieces of information. Her skull had been fractured. Her death hadn't been an accident.

Vi Nevin said nothing. She looked at them. She didn't move. But a tremor passed through her.

'Nicola was murdered,' Barbara finally said when Vi requested no details. 'Someone beat in her skull with a boulder.'

The fingers of Vi's right hand closed tightly on the hem of her mini dress. She said, 'Sit down,' and motioned them to the sofas. She herself sat rigidly on the edge of a deep armchair opposite, knees and ankles together like a well-trained school-girl. Still, she didn't ask any questions. She was clearly stunned by the information, but she was equally clearly waiting.

What for? Barbara wanted to know. What was going on? 'We're working the London end of the case,' she told Vi. 'Our colleague – DI Lynley – is in Derbyshire.'

'The London end,' Vi murmured.

'There was a bloke found dead with the Maiden girl.' Nkata removed the leather notebook from his jacket and twirled a bit of lead from his propelling pencil. 'Name's Terry Cole. He's got digs in Battersea. You acquainted with him?'

'Terry Cole?' Vi shook her head. 'No. I don't know him.'

'An artist. A sculptor. He's got a studio in some railway arches in Portslade Road. He shares that and a flat with a girl called Cilla Thompson,' Barbara said.

'Cilla Thompson,' she echoed. And shook her head again.

'Did Nicola ever mention either of them? Terry Cole? Cilla Thompson?' Nkata asked.

'Terry or Cilla. No,' she said.

Barbara wanted to point out that there was no Narcissus present, so she could abjure her rôle in the mythical drama, but she thought the allusion might fall on unappreciative ears. She said, 'Miss Nevin, Nicola Maiden's had her skull smashed in. This might not break your heart, but if you could cooperate with us—'

'*Please,*' she said, as if she couldn't bear to hear the news again. 'I haven't seen Nikki since the beginning of June. She went north to work for the summer, and she was due back in town next Wednesday, like I said.'

'To do what?' Barbara asked.

'What?'

'To do what when she got back into town?'

Vi said nothing. She looked at both of them, as if searching the waters for hidden piranhas.

'To work? To take up a life of leisure? To what?' Barbara asked. 'If she was coming back here, she must have intended to do something with her time. As her flatmate, I expect you'd know what that was.'

She had intelligent eyes, Barbara saw. They were grey with black lashes. They studied and assessed while her brain doubtless weighed every possible consequence to every answer. Vi Nevin knew something about what had happened to Nicola; that was a certainty.

If she'd learned nothing else from working with Lynley for nearly four years, Barbara had learned that there were times to play hard ball and times to give. Hard ball produced the intimidation card. Giving offered an exchange of information. Having nothing to use as intimidation with the other woman, the interview was beginning to look like a time to give. Barbara said, 'We know she dropped out of law college round the first of May, telling them she'd taken a full-time job with MKR Financial Management. But Mr Reeve – that's her guv— informed us that she left the company just before that, telling *him* she was moving home to Derbyshire. Yet when she moved house, she gave this address – not a Derbyshire address – to her landlady in Islington. And, from what we've been able to gather, no one in Derbyshire had an inkling that she was up there for anything more than a summer's visit. What does this suggest to you, Miss Nevin?'

'Confusion,' Vi said. 'She hadn't yet made up her mind about her life. Nikki liked to keep her options open.'

'Leaving college, her job? Telling tales unsupported by the facts? Her options weren't open. They were manufactured. Everyone we've talked to has a different idea of what she intended to do with herself.'

'I can't explain it. I'm sorry. I don't know what you want me to say.'

'Did she have a job lined up?' Nkata looked up from his notebook.

'I don't know.'

'Did she have a source of income lined up?' Barbara asked.

'I don't know that either. She paid her share of the expenses here before she left for the summer, and—'

'Why'd she leave?'

'And as it was in cash,' Vi plunged on, 'I had no reason to question her source of income. Really, I'm sorry, but that's all I can tell you.'

Fat chance, Barbara thought. She was lying through her pretty, baby-sized white teeth. 'How did you come to know each other? Are you at the College of Law yourself?'

'We met through work.'

'MKR Financial?' And when Vi nodded, 'What d'you do for them?'

'Nothing any longer. I left in April as well.' What she had done, she told them, was work as Tricia Reeve's personal assistant. 'I didn't much care for her,' she said. 'She's a bit ... peculiar. I handed in my notice in March and left once they found a replacement for me.'

'And now?' Barbara asked.

'Now?' Vi inquired.

'What d'you do now?' Nkata clarified. 'Where d'you work?'

She'd taken up modelling, she told them. It had long been her dream, and Nikki had encouraged her to go for it. She produced a portfolio of professional photographs, which depicted her in a variety of guises. In most of the pictures, she looked like a waif: thin and large eyed with the sort of vacant expression that was currently de rigueur in fashion magazines.

Barbara nodded at the photos, aiming for appreciation but inwardly wondering for a fleeting moment when Rubenesque figures – such as her own, frankly – would ever be in vogue. 'You must be doing well. A place like this ... I don't expect it comes cheap, does it? Is it your own, by the way? This maisonette?'

'It's rented.' Vi gathered up her pictures. She tapped them together and replaced them in their portfolio.

'From who?' Nkata asked the question without looking up from his meticulous note taking.

'Does it matter from whom?'

'Tell us and we'll make up our minds,' Barbara said.

'From Douglas and Gordon.'

'Mates of yours?'

'It's an estate agency.'

Barbara watched as Vi returned the portfolio to its place on a shelf beneath the television. She waited till the young woman had turned back to them before she went on. 'Mr Reeve told us

that Nicola Maiden had a problem with the truth and a bigger
problem keeping her mouth shut about his clients' finances.
He said he was going to sack her when she left.'

'That's not true.' Vi remained standing, arms folded beneath
diminutive breasts. 'If he was going to sack her, which he
wasn't, it would've been because of his wife.'

'Why?'

'Jealousy. Tricia wants to eliminate every woman he looks
at.'

'And he looked at Nicola?'

'I didn't say that.'

'Listen. We know she had a lover,' Barbara said. 'We know
he's in London. Could that have been Mr Reeve?'

'Tricia doesn't give him ten minutes out of her sight.'

'But it's possible?'

'No. Nikki was seeing someone, it's true. But not here. There.
In Derbyshire.' Vi went into the kitchen and returned with a
handful of picture postcards. They depicted various notable
sites in the Peak District: Arbor Low, Peveril Castle, Thor's
Cave, the stepping stones in Dovedale, Chatsworth House,
Magpie Mine, Little John's Grave, Nine Sisters' Henge. Each
was addressed to Vi Nevin, and each bore an identical message:
Oooh la la. This was followed by the initial *N*. That was all.

Barbara handed the postcards over to Nkata. She said to Vi,
'Okay. I'll bite. Clue me in on the meaning behind these.'

'Those are the places she had sex with him. Every time they
did it in a new location, she bought a postcard and sent it along
to me. As a joke.'

'A real scream,' Barbara agreed. 'Who's the bloke?'

'She never said. But I expect he's married.'

'Why?'

'Because aside from the postcards, she never once mentioned
him when we talked on the phone. That's how I'd expect her to
act if she had a relationship that wasn't on the up and up.'

'Made a habit of that, did she?' Nkata set the cards on the

coffee table and made a note in his book. 'She did other married blokes?'

'I didn't say that. Just that I think this one was married. And he wasn't in London.'

But someone was, Barbara thought. Someone had to be. If Nicola Maiden had intended a return to town at the end of the summer, she would have been coming with some means of supporting herself once she got here. With this ultramodern, recently redecorated, plush, posh, and pleasant maisonette having *trysting place* written all over it, how unreasonable was it to assume that a punter deep in dosh had set her up in style to be at his disposal day and night?

That begged the question of what the hell Vi Nevin was doing there. But perhaps that had been part of the deal. A flatmate with whom the mistress could while away the boring hours while waiting for her lord and master to appear.

It was a stretch. But no more than that needed to accommodate the vision of Nicola Maiden as Sir Richard Burton, hiking across the moors to discover new and exciting bonking locations to share with a married lover.

What the hell am I doing in police work, Barbara wondered acerbically, when the rest of the world is having so much fun?

They'd like to have a look at Nicola Maiden's room and belongings, she told Vi Nevin. Somewhere there was going to be concrete evidence that Nicola was up to something, and she was determined to find it.

Chapter Twelve

'**H**e squirmed. The flaming bastard bloody well *squirmed*.'
DI Peter Hanken leaned back in his chair and savoured the
moment, arms locked behind his head. A lit cigarette dangled
from his mouth, and he talked round it with the expertise of a
man long practised in the art. Lynley stood at a set of filing cabi-
nets, spreading out on their tops the photographs of both dead
bodies. He studied these while doing his best to keep clear of
Hanken's tobacco smoke. A former victim to the weed himself,
he found cause for celebration in the fact that he experienced
the smoke as an irritant at long last when months before he
would have queued just to lick Hanken's ashtray. Not that the
other DI was using the ashtray. When the burnt tobacco needed
dislodging, he merely turned his head and let the ashes fall to
the floor. It was a gesture out of character in the otherwise
compulsively neat DI. It spoke of the level of his excitement.

Hanken was recounting his interview with Will Upman. The
gusto with which he told the tale was growing as he reached its
climax. Metaphorically speaking, it seemed. Because according
to Hanken, the solicitor apparently hadn't been able to perform
to his usual standards.

'But he *said* popping his cork doesn't matter to him when
he's with a woman,' Hanken scoffed. 'Said what matters is "the
fun of it all."'

'I'm intrigued,' Lynley said. 'How did you manage to get that admission from him?'

'That he shagged her or that he didn't go the distance once he had her on the skewer?'

'Either. Both.' Lynley selected the clearest picture of Terry Cole's face and set it next to the clearest of the wounds on his body. 'I trust you didn't use thumb screws, Peter.'

Hanken laughed. 'Didn't have to. I just told him what his neighbours had reported, and he sent the white flag straight up the pole.'

'Why had he lied?'

'Claims he hadn't. Claims he would have told us straight out if we'd asked straight out.'

'That's splitting hairs.'

'Lawyers.' The single word said it all.

Will Upman, Hanken had reported concisely, confessed to a single fling with Nicola Maiden and that fling had occurred on her last night in his employ. He'd felt a strong attraction to her for the entire summer, but his position as her employer had prevented him from making a move.

'Being involved elsewhere didn't prevent him?' Lynley clarified.

Not at all. Because how could he be truly, madly, and deeply in love with Joyce – and consequently legitimately 'involved' with her – when he felt so wildly attracted to Nicola? And if he *was* wildly attracted to Nicola, didn't he owe it to himself to see what that attraction was all about? Joyce had been pressing him for a commitment – she'd had her mind set on their living together – but he couldn't take the next step with her, until he cleared his head about Nicola.

'May I assume he dashed off straightaway and proposed to Joyce once his head was cleared with regard to the Maiden girl?' Lynley asked.

Hanken guffawed appreciatively. Upman had oiled the wheels with drinks, dinner, and wine, the DI reported. He took her to his home. More drinks there. Some music. Several cappuccinos. He had candles set up round his bathtub—

'Lord.' Lynley shuddered. The man was a victim of Hollywood cinema.

—and he got her undressed and in the water without any trouble.

'Her wanting it as bad as he did, according to Upman,' Hanken said.

They played in the tub till they looked like prunes, at which point they adjourned to the bedroom.

'Which is where,' Hanken concluded, 'the rocket didn't launch.'

'And on the night of the murder?'

'Where was he, you mean?' Hanken recounted that as well. At lunch on Tuesday, Upman had had another set-to with the girlfriend on the topic of cohabitation. Rather than go home after work and run the risk of a phone call from her, he went for a drive. He ended up at Manchester Airport where he checked into a hotel for the night and had a massage therapist come to his room to relieve him of his tension.

'Even had the receipts to wave in front of me,' Hanken said. 'Seems he intends to claim it as a business expense.'

'You're checking it out.'

'I plan to, as I live and breathe,' Hanken said. 'Your end of things?'

This was where he had to tread carefully, Lynley thought. So far, Hanken hadn't appeared to be wedded irrevocably to any particular scenario. Still, what he was about to suggest was a contravention of the DI's main conjecture. He wanted to lead into it carefully so that his colleague might be open to its logic.

He hadn't found the pager, he said. But he'd had a rather long look round the site and an even longer think about the two bodies. He wanted to propose an altogether different hypothesis to the one they'd been working with. Would Hanken hear him out?

The DI lowered his chair and smashed out his cigarette. Mercifully, he didn't light another. He ran his tongue over his teeth, eyes speculatively fixed on Lynley. He finally said, 'Let's have it,' and settled back as if expecting a lengthy monologue.

'I think we've got one killer,' Lynley said. 'And no accomplice. No phone call for reinforcements when our man—'

'Or woman? Or are you giving that up as well?'

'Or woman,' Lynley replied, and he used the opportunity to inform Hanken of his encounter with Samantha McCallin on Calder Moor.

The other DI said, 'That puts her back in the running, I'd say.'

'She was never out of it.'

'Okay. Go on.'

'No call for reinforcements when the killer saw there were two targets instead of one.'

Hanken folded his hands over his stomach and said, 'Continue.'

Lynley used the photograph of Terry Cole as he did so. Burns on the face but no defensive wounds on the body, Lynley said, indicated that Cole hadn't been held in the fire but rather that he had fallen into it. The damage to his skin indicated that contact with the flames had been more than brief. There was no contusion to the head to suggest that he'd been clubbed, knocked unconscious, and left in the fire. So he had to have been wounded or disabled in some way as he sat by the fire in the first place.

'One killer,' Lynley said, 'goes out there after the girl. When he arrives at the site—'

'Or she,' Hanken cut in.

'Yes. Or she. When he or she arrives at the site, it's to find that Nicola isn't alone. So Cole has to be eliminated. First, because he's capable of protecting her should the killer go after her and second, because he's a potential witness. But the killer faces a dilemma. Does he – or she, yes, I see that, Peter – kill Cole at once and run the risk of losing Nicola if she escapes while he's dispatching Cole? Or does he kill Nicola and run the risk of being thwarted by Cole? He has surprise on his side but that's all he has, aside from his weapon.' Lynley sorted through the photographs and pulled out one that showed the trail of blood most clearly. 'If you consider all that and take into account the deposits of blood at the site—'

Hanken raised his hand to stop the words. He moved his gaze from Lynley to the window and said thoughtfully, 'The killer rushes forward with his knife and wounds the boy in an instant. The boy topples into the fire, where he's burned. The girl takes to her heels. The killer follows.'

'But his weapon is lodged in the boy.'

'Hmm. Yes. I see how it works.' Hanken turned from the window, eyes cloudy as he considered the scene he went on to describe. 'It's dark outside the ring of the fire. The girl's on the run.'

'So does he take the time to remove the knife from the boy or does he take off after the girl straightaway?'

'He goes after the girl. He has to, hasn't he? He dispatches her with three blows to the head, then returns to finish off the boy.'

'By which time, Cole's managed to crawl from the fire to the edge of the stone circle. And that's where the killer finishes him off. The blood tells the tale, Peter. Dripping down the standing stone, pooled on the ground.'

'If you're right,' Hanken said, 'we've got a killer covered in blood. It's night and in the middle of the back of beyond, so he has an advantage there. But eventually, he's going to need something to hide his clothes unless he did the killing in the nude, which isn't likely.'

'He may have brought something with him,' Lynley said.

'Or taken something from the scene itself.' Hanken slapped

his hands against his thighs and got to his feet. 'Let's get the Maidens to take a look at the girl's belongings,' he said.

Barbara fumed, punched her fist into her palm, and paced as Winston Nkata placed the call to Lynley from inside the Prince of Wales pub. They were across the street from Battersea Park and round the corner from Terry Cole's domicile, and while she wanted to grab the phone from Nkata's hand and make a few points more forcefully than Winston was making them, she knew she had to hold her tongue. Nkata was relaying the source of her agitation to their superior officer, and silence on her part was essential lest Lynley realise that she'd left her post at the computer. 'I'll get back to CRIS tonight,' she swore to Nkata when she realised that his reluctance to trot from Fulham to Battersea was directly connected to his worries about her willingness to attend to her assigned duties. 'Winston, on my mum's life, I tell you that I'll sit at the screen till I'm blind. Okay? But later. *Later.* Let's do Battersea first.'

Nkata was relaying to Lynley the results of their visits to Nicola's former employer and to her current flat mate. After reporting on the postcards that Nicola had sent to Vi Nevin and explaining what Vi had claimed their implicit message was, he went on to dwell in particular upon the fact that Nicola's bedroom in the Fulham maisonette had apparently been 'seen to' prior to his laying eyes upon it. 'How many birds you know have nothing that says who they are sitting round?' Nkata asked. 'Man, I say this. That bird Vi kept us waiting on the steps before letting us in 'cause she was shovelling that bedroom clear of something once she heard there were rozzers at the door.'

Barbara winced and held her breath at the plural pronouns. No fool, Lynley. On his end of the line, he jumped at once.

Nkata said in reply with a glance at Barbara, 'What? . . . No. Figure of speech, man . . . Yeah. Believe me, I got that engraved on my soul.' He listened as Lynley apparently relayed how things were playing out in his part of the world. He laughed outright at a piece of information, saying, 'The *fun* of it? Lord, I believe that like the world is flat,' and toyed with the steel tubing of the telephone cord. After a few moments, he said, 'Battersea right now. Barb said that Cole's flatmate'd be in for the evening, so I thought to have a look through his traps. Landlady wouldn't let Barb have a peek earlier and—' He stopped as Lynley interrupted at some length.

Barbara tried to read his expression for an indication of what the inspector was saying. The black man's face was completely blank. She whispered tersely, 'What? *What?*'

Nkata waved her off. 'Following up on those names you gave her,' he said. 'Far as I know, at least. You know Barb.'

'Oh, thanks very much, Winston,' she whispered.

Nkata turned his shoulder and gave her his back. He went on to Lynley, saying, 'Barb said the flatmate says anything's possible. The kid was flush with money – always had a wad of cash – and he never sold a stick of his art. Which isn't hard to believe when you see it. Blackmail's sounding nicer every minute.' Again he listened and he finally said, 'That's why I want to have a recce. There's a connection somewhere. Has to be.'

That they were on the trail of something significant had been spelled out to them in the complete lack of personal detail in Nicola Maiden's Fulham bedroom. Apart from a few articles of clothing and an innocuous line of seashells on the window sill, there was nothing to suggest the room had ever been occupied by a real person. Barbara would have concluded that the Fulham address was a front and that the Maiden girl had never lived there at all had not the evidence of something having been removed betrayed Vi Nevin's use of the time between their speaking to her from the street and her appearance at the front door of the building. Two drawers in the large chest were completely empty, in the clothes cupboard a space on the hanging rail spoke of a few articles hastily deleted, and on top of the chest bare spots devoid of dust indicated that something had stood there until recently.

Barbara saw all of this, but she didn't bother to request a look at Vi Nevin's own bedroom for the missing items. The young woman had been plain enough earlier that she knew her rights under the law, and there was no point in pushing her to exercise them.

But it meant something that she'd performed the expurgation. And only a fool would walk away from the implications.

Nkata rang off and recounted Lynley's end of the investigation. Barbara listened carefully, looking for connections among the pieces of information they were gathering. When he was done, she said, 'The Upman bloke *claims* he stuffed her on a one-off. But he could be Mr Oooh la la from the postcards and be lying through his teeth, couldn't he?'

'Or lying about what it meant when he had her,' Nkata said. 'He could've thought it was something important happening between them. She could've just been doing it for kicks.'

'And when he found out, he did her in? Where was he on Tuesday night, then?'

'Getting a massage near Manchester Airport. For stress, he said.'

Barbara whooped. She slung her bag over her shoulder and jerked her head towards the door. They ducked out into Parkgate Road.

The house that contained Terry Cole's flat was less than five minutes by foot from the pub, and Barbara led Nkata to it. This time when she rang the buzzer next to the tag reading Cole/Thompson, the door catch was released in reply.

Cilla Thompson met them at the top of the stairs. She was dressed for a night out, her metallic silver mini skirt and matching bustier and beret suggesting an imminent audition for a rôle in a feminist *Wizard of Oz*. She said, 'I don't have much time.'

Barbara replied, 'No problem. We don't need much.' She

introduced Nkata and they went inside the flat which, occupying the second floor of the house, had been remodelled into two small bedrooms, a sitting room, a kitchen, and a loo the size of a larder. Not wanting to encounter another Vi Nevin situation, Barbara said, 'We'd like to paw through everything, if that's okay with you. If Terry was into something dodgy, he might have left evidence of it anywhere. He might have hidden it as well.'

Cilla had nothing to hide, she informed them, but she didn't fancy them fingering through her knickers. She'd show them every one of her belongings, but that was the extent of it. They could do whatever serious trolling they wanted to do among Terry's lumber.

The rules established, they began in the kitchen where the cupboards revealed nothing except a predilection for instant macaroni cheese which the flat's occupants appeared to consume by the gross. Several bills lay on the draining board – where what looked like six weeks of crockery was drying – and Nkata examined these and handed them over to Barbara. The telephone bill was respectable but not outrageously high. The electricity usage seemed normal. Neither bill was overdue; neither bill had gone unpaid during the previous billing period. The refrigerator was equally unilluminating. A limp lettuce and a plastic bag of sad-looking Brussels sprouts suggested that the flat's inhabitants hadn't been as conscientious about eating their veggies as they should have been. But there was nothing more sinister inside the appliance than a tin of pea soup that was open and appeared to have been half eaten as it was, straight up with no heating. Barbara's stomach lurched. And she'd thought *her* culinary tastes were questionable.

'We eat out mostly,' Cilla said from the doorway.

'Looks like it,' Barbara agreed.

They moved to the sitting room, where they paused and took in its unusual decor. The room appeared to be a showplace for their art. There were several pieces of the same agricultural nature as the larger efforts that Barbara had seen earlier that day in the railway arch studio, marking them as the work of Terry. The other objects – paintings, these – were the obvious results of Cilla's endeavours.

Nkata – having not seen Cilla's mouth fixation given concrete form earlier – whistled quietly in reaction to the dozen or more oral cavities that were explored on canvas in the sitting room. Screaming, laughing, weeping, speaking, eating, slobbering, vomiting, and bleeding were all featured in graphic detail. Cilla had also explored further fantastic possibilities of the orifice in her paintings: Several mouths had fully grown human beings rising from them, most notably members of the Royal Family.

'Very . . . different,' Nkata commented.

'Munch, however, has nothing to worry about,' Barbara murmured next to him.

There were bedrooms on either side of the sitting room, and they ventured into Cilla's first, with the artist herself leading the way. Aside from a collection of Paddington Bears that overflowed from the top of the chest of drawers and the windowsill onto the floor, Cilla's room didn't present any contradiction to the artist herself. Her wardrobe contained the usual colour-splodged garments one would associate with a painter; the milk crate serving as bedside table held the box of condoms that one would expect of the sexually active and sexually cautious young woman in the depressing days of STDs; a considerable collection of CDs met with Barbara's approval and told Nkata how far out of the loop he was when it came to rock 'n' roll; a number of copies of *What's On* and *Time Out* had pages turned down and galleries with newly mounted shows circled. The walls featured her own art, and the floor had been painted by the artist to reveal more of her singular artistic sensibility. Great flapping tongues dribbled partially masticated food onto naked infants who were defecating onto other great flapping tongues. It was certainly one for Freud.

Cilla said, 'I told Mrs Baden I'd paint over it when I move out,' in apparent response to the detectives' failure to keep their expressions dispassionate. 'She likes to support talent. She says so. You can ask her.'

'We'll take your word for it,' Barbara said.

They found nothing in the bathroom, except a grubby and unhygienic ring round the bath, which Nkata clucked at mournfully. From there, they went to Terry Cole's bedroom with Cilla dogging their heels as if worried that they might nick one of her masterpieces if she didn't keep watch.

Nkata took a post at the chest of drawers, Barbara at the wardrobe. There, she discovered the gripping fact that Terry Cole's preference in colours was black, and he carried this theme out in T-shirts, jerseys, jeans, jackets, and footwear. While Nkata slid open drawers behind her, Barbara began going through the jeans and the jackets, in the hope that they might reveal something cogent. She found only two possibilities among the cinema ticket stubs and crumpled tissues. The first was a scrap of paper with *31–32 Soho Square* written on it in a small, pointed hand, and the second was a business card that had been folded in half over a wad of discarded chewing gum. Barbara prised this open. One could always hope . . .

Bowers was engraved in posh script across the card. In the left-hand corner was an address on Cork Street and a phone number. On the right was a name: Neil Sitwell. The address was W1. Another gallery, Barbara deduced, but she flicked the dried gum onto the bedside table and pocketed the card nonetheless.

'Something here,' Nkata said behind her.

She swung round and saw that he'd taken a humidor from the bottom drawer of the chest. He had it open. 'What?' she said.

He tilted it towards her. Cilla craned forward. She said in a rush, 'That's none of mine, you lot,' when she saw what was in it.

The humidor contained cannabis. Several lids, by the look of it. And from the drawer from which he'd taken the humidor, Nkata pulled out a palm-size bong, rolling papers, and a large freezer bag sealed upon at least another kilo of the weed.

'Ah,' Barbara said. She eyed Cilla suspiciously.

'I said,' Cilla countered. 'I wouldn't've let you go through the flat if I knew he had that stuff, would I? I don't touch it. I don't touch anything that could cock up the process.'

'The process?' Nkata looked quizzical.

'The creative process,' Cilla said. 'My art.'

'Right,' Barbara said. 'God knows you don't want to mess about with that. Wise move on your part.'

Cilla heard no irony. She said, 'Talent's precious. You don't want to . . . like waste it.'

'Are you saying this—' with a nod at the cannabis – 'is why Terry couldn't make it as an artist?'

'Like I told you at the studio, he never put enough into it – his art, that is – to get anything out of it. He didn't want to work at it like the rest of us. He didn't think he had to. Maybe this is why.'

'Because he was high too often?' Nkata asked.

Cilla looked uncomfortable for the first time. She shifted from foot to foot on her platform shoes. 'Look. It's like . . . He's dead and all that and I'm sorry about it. But truth's the truth. His money came from somewhere. This is probably it.'

'There's not much here if he's pushing,' Nkata said to Barbara.

'Maybe he's got a cache somewhere else.'

But aside from a lumpy overstuffed chair, the only other article of furniture in the room that afforded a hiding place was the bed. It seemed too obvious to be likely, but Barbara went through the manoeuvre anyway: She lifted the edge of an old chenille counterpane. Doing so, she exposed the side of a cardboard box that had been shoved beneath the bed.

'Ah,' Barbara said. 'Perhaps, perhaps . . .' She crouched and drew the box towards her. Its flaps were tucked in, but they weren't sealed. She separated them and examined the box's contents.

They were postcards, Barbara discovered, several thousand of them. But they were definitely not the kind that one sent home to the family while on one's yearly hols in regions afar. These postcards weren't for greeting purposes. They weren't for sending messages. They weren't souvenirs. What they were, however, was the first indication of who had killed Terry Cole and why.

A detective constable had been sent to fetch the Maidens to Buxton for their inspection of their daughter's effects. Hanken had pointed out that a mere request for their presence would likely be met with a postponement on their part, since the dinner hour was fast approaching and the Maidens would probably be tied up seeing to the needs of their guests. 'If we want an answer tonight, we fetch them,' Hanken said not unreasonably.

An answer that night would be helpful, Lynley concurred. So while he and Hanken tucked into *rigatoni puttanesca* at the Firenze Restaurant in Buxton market square, DC Stewart went to Padley Gorge to fetch the parents of the dead girl. By the time the DIs had finished their meal and topped it off with two espressos apiece, Stewart had telephoned to Hanken that Andrew and Nan Maiden were waiting at the station.

'Have Mott sign out the girl's belongings to you,' Hanken directed her from his mobile. 'Lay them out in room four and wait for us.'

They were no more than five minutes from Buxton station. Hanken took his time about seeing to the bill. He wanted to make the Maidens sweat if he could, he explained to Lynley. He liked everyone on edge in an investigation because one never knew what a case of nerves could turn up.

'I thought you'd switched your interest to Will Upman?' Lynley remarked to his colleague.

'I'm interested in everyone. I want them all on edge,' Hanken replied. 'It's amazing what people will suddenly remember when the pressure builds.'

Lynley didn't point out that Andy Maiden's experience with SO10 had probably conditioned him to weathering a great deal more pressure than would develop during a quarter of an hour's wait for two colleagues inside a police station. This was, after all, still Hanken's case, and he was proving himself to be an accommodating colleague.

'I'm sorry to have missed you this afternoon,' Lynley told Nan Maiden when she and her husband were ushered into room four where he and Hanken stood on either side of a large pine table. On this, Nicola's possessions had been laid out by DC Stewart, who remained by the door with a notepad in her hand.

'I'd gone out for a bike ride,' Nan Maiden said.

'Andy said you were on Hathersage Moor. Is that a tough ride?'

'I like the exercise. And there're bike trails everywhere. It's not as rough as it sounds.'

'Run into anyone else while you were out there?' Hanken asked.

Andy Maiden's arm went round his wife's shoulders. She replied evenly enough. 'Not today. I had the moor to myself.'

'Go out often, do you? Mornings, afternoons? Nights as well?'

Nan Maiden frowned. 'I'm sorry, are you asking me—' but her husband's grip, tightening on her shoulders, was enough to stop her.

Andy Maiden said, 'I think you wanted us to look through Nicola's belongings, Inspector.'

He and Hanken observed each other across the width of the table. By the door, DC Stewart glanced between them, her pencil poised. Outside the building, a car alarm went off suddenly.

Hanken was the one to blink. He said, 'Have a go,' with a nod at the articles on the table. 'Is there anything missing? Or anything not hers?'

The Maidens moved slowly, inspecting each item displayed. Nan Maiden reached out tentatively and fingered a navy sweater with a strip of ivory defining its neckline.

She said, 'The neck wasn't right . . . the way it lay on her skin. I wanted to change it, but she wouldn't have that. She said, "You made it, Mum, and that's what counts." But I wish I'd fixed it. It would've been no trouble.' She blinked several times. Her breathing altered. 'I don't see anything. I'm sorry. I'm being so little help.'

Andy Maiden put his hand on the back of his wife's neck and said, 'A few moments more, love,' and urged her along the table. He, however, rather than she, was the one to notice what wasn't among the items taken from the scene of the crime. 'Nicola's waterproof,' he told them. 'It's blue, with a hood. It isn't here.'

Hanken shot a glance at Lynley. Corroboration for your theory, his expression said.

'It didn't rain Tuesday night, did it?' Nan Maiden's question was non sequitorial. They all knew that anyone who hiked on the moors had to be prepared for swift changes in weather.

Andy spent the longest time with the implements from the camp site: the compass, the stove, the pot, the map case, the trowel. His forehead creased as he examined everything. Then he finally said, 'Her pocket knife's missing as well.'

It was a Swiss Army knife that had been his own, he told them. He'd given it to Nick as a gift one Christmas when her interest in hiking and camping had first developed. She'd always kept it with the rest of her gear. And she'd always taken it when she went into the Peaks.

Lynley felt rather than saw Hanken looking his way. He

reflected on what the fact of a missing knife might do to their conjecture. He said, 'You're sure of that, Andy?'

'She could've lost it,' Maiden replied. 'But she would have replaced it with another before camping again.' His daughter was an experienced hiker, he explained. Nick didn't take chances on the moors or in the Peaks. She never went out without being prepared. 'Who would try to camp without a knife?'

Hanken asked for a description. Maiden gave him the particulars, listing the features of a multi-use utensil. The largest blade was about three inches, he said.

When the dead girl's parents had completed their task, Hanken asked Stewart to provide them with a cup of tea. He turned to Lynley once the door was shut upon them. 'Are you thinking what I'm thinking?' he asked.

'The blade length matches Dr Myles' conclusions on the weapon used on Cole.' Lynley stared thoughtfully at the items on the table and pondered the spanner that Andy Maiden had inadvertently thrown into the works of his theory. 'It could be a coincidence, Peter. She could have lost it earlier that day.'

'But if she didn't, you know what it means.'

'We have a killer on the moors, tracking Nicola Maiden, and for some reason tracking her without a weapon.'

'Which means—'

'No premeditation. A chance encounter in which things got out of hand.'

Hanken blew out a breath. 'Where the *hell* does that take us?'

'To some serious rethinking,' Lynley said.

Chapter Thirteen

The night sky was awash with stars when Lynley stepped from the entrance porch of Maiden Hall. And because he'd loved the night sky as a boy in Cornwall where, like the sky in Derbyshire, he could see, study, and name the constellations with an ease that was impossible in London, he paused next to the weather-pitted stone pillar marking the edge of the car park and looked to the heavens. He was seeking an answer to what everything meant.

'There must be a mistake with their records,' Nan Maiden had told him with quiet insistence. She was hollow-eyed, as if the last thirty-six hours had dragged from her a life force that would never be replaced. 'Nicola *wouldn't* have left law college. And she certainly wouldn't have left law college without telling us. That wasn't her way. She loved the law. Besides, she'd spent the whole summer working for Will Upman. So why on earth would she have done that if she dropped out of college in . . . Did you say it was May?'

Lynley had driven them home from Buxton and had followed them into the Hall for a final conversation. Because the lounge was still occupied by hotel residents and diners enjoying postprandial coffees, brandy, and chocolates, they'd repaired to an office next to the reception desk. It was overcrowded with the three of them, a room meant for a single person who would work at a computer behind a desk. A fax machine was disgorging a lengthy message when they walked in. Andy Maiden glanced at this and placed the message into a tray that bore a neat sign declaring it to be the repository of reservations.

Neither of the Maidens had known of their daughter's leaving the College of Law. Neither had known that she had moved house to take up residence in Fulham with a young woman called Vi Nevin, whose name Nicola had never mentioned. Neither had known that she'd gone to work full time at MKR Financial Management. Which went far to put a significant dent in Nan Maiden's earlier assertion that her daughter had been the incarnation of honesty.

Andy Maiden had been silent in response to the revelations. But he looked beaten, as if each new piece of knowledge about his daughter was a blow to his psyche. While his wife sought to explain away the inconsistencies in their daughter's actions, he merely seemed to be attempting to absorb them while minimising the additional damage to his heart.

'Perhaps she meant to transfer to a college closer to home.' Nan had sounded pathetically eager to believe her own words. 'Isn't there one in Leicester? Or in Lincoln? And as she was engaged to Julian, she might have wanted to be nearer to him.'

Disabusing Nicola's mother of the notion of an engagement to Julian Britton had been a tougher task than Lynley would have thought possible. Nan Maiden's efforts at elucidation ceased entirely when he revealed Britton's misrepresentation of the facts of his relationship with her daughter. She looked stricken, saying only, 'They weren't . . . ? But then why . . . ?' before falling silent and turning to her husband as if he were capable of giving her an explanation for the inexplicable.

Thus, Lynley reached the conclusion that it wasn't beyond the realm of reason that the Maidens hadn't known of their daughter's possession of a pager. And when Nan Maiden had proved to be as much in the dark as her husband regarding the little device, Lynley had felt inclined to believe her.

Now as he stood in the penumbrous space between the softly lit car park and bright-windowed hotel, Lynley allowed himself a few minutes to ponder in a circumstance in which he also allowed himself a few additional minutes to feel. He'd earlier taken the car keys from Hanken and said, 'Go home to your family, Peter. I'll drive the Maidens back to Padley Gorge,' and it was Hanken, his family, and his words earlier that day that Lynley considered as he remained by the pillar. The DI had said that holding in his arms an infant – one's own child and creation – changed a man irrevocably. He'd said that the pain of losing that child was something beyond his contemplation. What, then, did a man like Andy Maiden feel at this moment: the fabric of him altered so many years ago at his daughter's birth, the substance of him shifting subtly throughout her childhood and adolescence, and the core of him fractured – perhaps irreparably – at her death. And now to pile on top of the loss of her came the additional knowledge that his only child had had secrets from him . . . How, Lynley wondered, must it feel?

The death of a child, he thought, kills the future and decimates the past, making the former an imprisonment that seems interminable, rendering the latter an unvoiced reproach for every moment robbed of its significance by the calls of a parent's career. One didn't recover from such a death. One just grew more adept at stumbling on.

He glanced back at the Hall and saw the distant form of Andy Maiden leave the little office, cross the entrance, and trudge towards the stairs. The light remained on in the room he departed and in the window of that room Nan Maiden's silhouette appeared. Lynley saw the Maidens' separateness and wanted to tell them not to bear their grief in solitude from each other. They'd created their daughter Nicola together and they'd bury her together. So why did they have to mourn her alone?

'*We're all alone, Inspector,*' Barbara Havers had told him once in a similar case in which two parents had been forced to mourn the death of a child. '*And believe me, it's only a bloody illusion that we're anything else.*'

But he didn't want to think of Barbara Havers, of her wisdom or her lack thereof. He wanted to do something to give the Maidens a measure of peace. He told himself that he owed that much, if not to two parents whose suffering was of a kind he hoped never to have to face, then to a former colleague whose service on the force had placed officers like Lynley in his debt. But he also had to admit that he sought to give them peace as a hedge against potential grief in his own future, in the hope that attenuating their present sorrow might prevent him from ever having to experience a similar pain himself.

He couldn't change the basic facts of Nicola's death and the secrets she'd kept from her parents. But he could seek to disprove what information was beginning to look manufactured, wearing the guise of innocent revelation while all the time created to meet the exigency of the moment.

Will Upman, after all, was the person who had mentioned a pager and a London lover in the first place. And who better than Upman – interested in the young woman himself – to fabricate both possessions and relationships to divert the police's attention from himself? He could have been the lover in question, showering gifts upon a woman who was his obsession as well as his employee. And told that she was leaving the law, leaving Derbyshire, and establishing a life for herself in London, how might he have reacted to the knowledge that he would be losing her permanently? Indeed, they knew from the postcards that Nicola sent to her flatmate that she had a lover in addition to Julian Britton. And she would have hardly felt the need to code a message – let alone to arrange for the assignations suggested by the postcards – had the man in question been someone with whom she felt that she could freely be seen.

And then there was the entire question of Julian Britton's place in Nicola's life. If he had actually loved her and had wished to marry her, what would his reaction have been had he discovered her relationship with another man? It was perfectly possible that Nicola had revealed that relationship to Britton as part of her refusal to marry him. If she'd done so, what thoughts – taking up residence in Britton's mind – did he have and where did those thoughts take him on Tuesday night?

An exterior door closed somewhere. Footsteps crunched in gravel, and a figure came round the side of the building. It was a man, wheeling a bicycle. He guided it into a puddle of light that spilled from one of the windows. There, he toed the kick stand downwards and removed from his pocket a small tool which he applied to the base of the bicycle's spokes.

Lynley recognised him from the previous afternoon when, from the lounge window, he'd seen him pedalling away from the Hall as Lynley and Hanken had waited for the Maidens to join them. He was, doubtless, one of the employees. As Lynley watched him, crouched on his haunches next to the bike with a heavy lock of hair falling into his eyes, he saw his hand slip and get caught between the spokes and he heard him cry out, *'Merde! Saloperie de bécane! Je sais pas ce qui me retient de t'envoyer à la casse.'* He leaped up, knuckles shoved to his mouth. He used the sweatshirt he wore to wipe the blood from his skin.

Hearing him speak, Lynley also recognised the unmistakable sound of a cog in the wheel of the investigation clicking into place. He adjusted his previous conjectures and his thinking with alacrity, realising that Nicola Maiden had done more than merely joke with her London flatmate. She'd also given her a clue.

He approached the man. 'Have you hurt yourself?'

The man swung round, startled, brushing the hair from his eyes. *'Bon dieu! Vous m'avez fait peur!'*

'Excuse me. I didn't mean to come out of nowhere like that,'

Lynley said. And he produced his warrant card and introduced himself.

A fractional movement of the eyebrows was the other man's only reaction to hearing the words 'New Scotland Yard.' He replied in heavily accented English – interspersed with French – that he was Christian-Louis Ferrer, master chef of the kitchen and the primary reason that Maiden Hall had been awarded the coveted *étoile Michelin*.

'You're having trouble with your bike. D'you need a lift somewhere?'

No. *Mais merci quand même.* Long hours in the kitchen robbed him of time to exercise. He needed the twice daily ride to keep himself fit. This *vélo de merde* – with a dismissive gesture at the bicycle – was better than nothing to use for that exercise. But he'd have been grateful for *un deux-roues* that was a little more dependable on the roads and the trails.

'Might we chat before you leave, then?' Lynley asked politely.

Ferrer shrugged in classic, Gallic fashion: a simple uplift of the shoulders communicating that if the police wished to speak with him, he'd be foolish to refuse. He'd been standing with his back to the window, but now he shifted position so that his face was in the light.

Seeing him illuminated, Lynley realised that he was much older than he'd looked from a distance on his bicycle. He appeared to be in his mid fifties, with age and the good life incised on his face and grey threaded through his walnut hair.

Lynley quickly discovered that Ferrer's English was fine when it suited him. Of course he knew Nicola Maiden, Ferrer said, calling her *la jeune femme malheureuse.* He had laboured for the past five years to raise Maiden Hall to its current position *de temple de la gastronomie* – did the Inspector happen to know how few country restaurants in England had actually been awarded the *étoile Michelin*? – so of course he knew the daughter of his employers. She had worked in the dining room during all her school holidays ever since he himself had practised his art for *Monsieur Andee,* so naturally he had come to know her.

Ah. Good. How well? Lynley enquired mildly.

At which time Ferrer failed to understand English, although his anxious, polite smile – spurious though it might have been – indicated his willingness to do so.

Lynley switched to what he'd always referred to as his travel-and-survive French. He took a moment to telegraph a silent message of thanks to his fearsome aunt Augusta who'd often decreed – in the midst of a family visit – that *ce soir, on parlera tous français à table et après dîner. C'est la meilleure façon de se préparer à passer des vacances d'été en Dordogne,* thus attempting to polish his rudimentary skills in a language in which he would otherwise only have been able to request a cup of coffee, a beer, or a room with a bath. He said in French, 'Your expertise in the kitchen isn't in doubt, Monsieur Ferrer. What I'd like to know is how well you knew the girl. Her father tells me that all the family are cyclists. You're also a cyclist. Did you have occasion to ride with her?'

If Ferrer was surprised that a barbaric Englishman spoke his language – however imperfectly – he covered it well. He gave no quarter by slowing the pace of his reply, though, forcing Lynley to ask him to repeat the answer, which gave the Frenchman the satisfaction he apparently needed. 'Yes, of course, once or twice we rode together,' Ferrer told him in his native tongue. He had been riding from Grindleford to Maiden Hall on the road and, when she'd heard about this, the young lady had told him of a route through the forest that was rough going, but more direct. She didn't wish him to become lost, so she rode it with him twice to make sure he took all the right paths.

'Grindleford is where you have lodgings?'

Yes. There were not enough rooms here at Maiden Hall to

accommodate those who worked for the hotel and restaurant. It was, as the inspector had no doubt observed, a small establishment. So Christian-Louis Ferrer had a room with a widow called Madame Clooney and her spinster daughter who, if Ferrer's account was to be believed, had designs upon him that were – alas – impossible to gratify.

'I am, of course, married,' he told Lynley. 'Although my beloved wife remains in Nerville le Forêt until such a time as we can be together again.'

This, Lynley knew, was not an unusual arrangement. European married couples often lived separately, one of them remaining with their children in their native country while the other emigrated to seek more gainful employment. However, an innate cynicism that he quickly assessed as having flourished within him through too much exposure to Barbara Havers over the past few years made him immediately suspicious of any man who used the adjective *beloved* in front of the noun *wife*. 'You've been here the entire five years?' Lynley asked. 'Do you get home much, for holidays and such?'

Alas, Ferrer confessed, a man of his profession was best served – as indeed were his beloved wife and dearest children – by spending his holiday time in the pursuit of cooking excellence. And while this pursuit could be done in France – and with far more felicitous results, considering with what licence the word *cuisine* was bandied about in this country – Christian-Louis Ferrer knew the wisdom of thrift. Should he travel back and forth between England and France at holiday time, there would be that much less money to save for the future of his children and the security of his old age.

'It must be difficult,' Lynley said, 'such a long separation from one's wife. Lonely as well, I expect.'

Ferrer grunted. 'A man does what he must do,' he said.

'Still, there must be times when the loneliness makes one long for a connection with someone. Even a spiritual connection with a like-minded soul. We don't live on work alone, do we? And a man like you ... It would be understandable.'

Ferrer crossed his arms in a movement that emphasised the prominence of his biceps and triceps. He was, in so many ways, the perfect image not only of virility but of virility's need to establish its presence. Lynley knew that he was engaging in the worst kind of stereotyping even to think so. But still he allowed himself to think it, and to see where the thinking would lead their conversation. He said with a meaningful, just-between-us-boys shrug, 'Five years without one's wife ... I couldn't do it.'

Ferrer's mouth – full-lipped, the mouth of a sensualist – curved and his eyes became hooded. He said in English, 'Estelle and I understand each the other. It is why we are married for twenty years.'

'So there is the occasional dalliance here in England.'

'Nothing of significance. Estelle, I love. The other ... ? Well, it was what it was.'

A useful slip, Lynley thought. He said, 'Was. It's over, then?'

And Ferrer's face – so swiftly guarded – told Lynley the rest. 'Were you and Nicola Maiden lovers?'

Silence in reply.

Lynley persevered. 'If you and the Maiden girl were lovers, Monsieur Ferrer, it looks far less suspicious if you answer the question here and now, rather than find yourself being confronted with the truth of it gathered from a witness who might have seen the two of you together.'

'It is nothing,' Ferrer said, again in English.

'That's not the assessment I'd make about the possibility of coming under suspicion in a murder investigation.'

Ferrer raised his face and went back to French. 'I don't mean suspicion. I mean with the girl.'

'Are you saying that nothing happened with the girl?'

'I'm saying that what happened was nothing. It meant nothing. To either of us.'

'Perhaps you'd tell me about it.'

Ferrer glanced at the Hall's front door. It stood open to the pleasant night air and within, residents were moving towards the stairs, chatting amiably among themselves. Ferrer spoke to Lynley but kept his gaze on the residents. 'A woman's beauty exists for a man to admire. A woman naturally wishes to augment her beauty to increase the admiration.'

'That's arguable.'

'It is the way of things. It has always been the way. All of nature speaks to support this simple, true order of the world. One sex is created by God to attract the other.'

Lynley didn't point out that the natural order of which Ferrer spoke generally called for the male – not the female – of a species to be more attractive in order to be acceptable as a mate. Instead he said, 'Finding Nicola attractive, you did something to support God's natural order, then.'

'As I say, it meant nothing of a serious nature. I knew this. She knew it as well.' He smiled, not without fondness it seemed. 'She enjoyed the game of it. I could see this in her when first we met.'

'When she was twenty?'

'It is a false woman who doesn't know her own allure. Nicola was not a false woman. She knew. I saw. She saw that I saw. The rest . . .' He gave another quintessentially Gallic shrug. 'There are limits to every communion between men and women. If one remembers the limits, one's happiness within the communion is safeguarded.'

Lynley made the interpretation adroitly. 'Nicola knew you wouldn't leave your wife.'

'She did not require that I leave my wife. She had no interest there, believe me.'

'Then where?'

'Her interest?' He smiled, as if with memory. 'The places we met. The exertion required of me to get to the places. What was left of my energy once I arrived. And how well I was able to use it.'

'Ah.' Lynley considered the places: the caves, the barrows, the prehistoric villages, the Roman forts. Oooh la la, he thought. Or as Barbara Havers might have said, *Bingo, Inspector*. They had Mr Postcard. 'You and Nicola made love—'

'We had sex, not love. Our game was to choose a different site for each meeting. Nicola would pass a message to me. A map sometimes. Sometimes a riddle. If I could interpret it correctly, follow it correctly . . .' Again that shrug. 'She would be there to provide the reward.'

'How long had you been lovers?'

Ferrer hesitated before replying, either doing the maths or assessing the damage of revealing the truth. Finally, he chose. 'Five years.'

'Since you first came to the Hall.'

'This is the case,' he admitted. 'I would, of course, prefer that *monsieur* and *madame* . . . It would only serve to distress them unnecessarily. We were always discreet. We never left the Hall together. We returned first one, then the other later. So they never knew.'

And never had reason to sack you, Lynley thought.

The Frenchman seemed to feel the necessity for a further explanation. 'It was that look she gave me when first we met. You know what I mean. I could tell from the look. Her interest matched my own. There is sometimes an animal need between a man and a woman. This is not love. This is not devotion. This is just what one feels – a pain, a pressure, a need – here.' He indicated his groin. 'You, a man, you feel this as well. Not every woman has an ache that matches that of a man. But Nicola had. I saw that at once.'

'And did something about it.'

'As was her wish. The game of it came later.'

'The game was her idea?'

'Her way . . . It was why I never sought another woman

while in England. There was no need. She had a way to make a simple affair . . .' He sought a word to describe it. 'Magic,' he settled on. 'Exciting. I would not have thought myself capable of fidelity to a mere mistress over five years. One woman had never held me more than three months before Nicola.'

'The game of it was what she enjoyed? That's what kept her tied to the affair with you?'

'The game kept me tied. For her, there was the physical pleasure, naturally.'

There was also the ego, Lynley thought wryly. He said, 'Five years is a long time to keep a woman interested, especially with no hope of any future.'

'Of course, there were the tokens as well,' Ferrer admitted. 'They were small, but all true symbols of my esteem. I have so little money because most of it . . . My Estelle would wonder if the money changed . . . what I send to her, you see . . . if it became less. So there were tokens only, but they were enough.'

'Gifts to Nicola?'

'Gifts, if you will. Perfume. A gold charm or two. It was that kind of thing. This pleased her. And the game went on.' He dug into his pocket and removed the small tool he'd been using on the bicycle spokes. He hunkered down and went at them again, tightening each spoke with infinite patience. He said, 'I shall miss her, my little Nicola. We didn't love. But how we laughed.'

'When you wanted the game to begin,' Lynley said, 'how did you let her know?'

The Frenchman raised his head, his expression puzzled. 'Please?'

'Did you leave her a note? Did you page her?'

'Ah. No. It was the look between us. Nothing else was needed.'

'So you never paged her?'

'Page? No. Why would I when the look was all that . . . ? Why do you ask this question?'

'Because evidently when she was at work in Buxton this past summer, someone paged her and phoned her a number of times. I thought it might have been you.'

'I had no need. But the other . . . He could not leave her alone. The buzzer. Every time it went off. Like a clock's work.'

Corroboration at last, Lynley thought. He clarified with, 'She received pages when you were together?'

'It was the only imperfection in our game, that little pager. Always, she would ring him back.' He tested the bicycle spokes with his fingers. '*Bah*. What was she doing with him? There was so little they could have had together. Sometimes when I think of what she had to experience with him, too young to know the first thing about giving a woman pleasure . . . What a crime against love, him with my Nicola. With him, she endured. With me, she enjoyed.'

Lynley filled in the blanks. 'Are you saying it was Julian Britton who paged her?'

'Always he wanted to know when they could meet, when they could talk, when they could make plans. She would say, "Darling, how extraordinary that you'd page me now. I was just thinking of you. I swear I was. Shall I tell you what I was thinking? Shall I tell you what I'd do if we were together?" And then she would tell. And he would be satisfied. With that. Just *that*.' Ferrer shook his head in disgust.

'Are you certain it was Britton who paged her?'

'Who else? She talked to him as she talked to me. The way one talks to a lover. And he was her lover. Not the same as I, of course, but still her lover.'

Lynley set that area of discussion aside. 'Did she always have the pager with her? Or did she only have it when she was away from the Hall?'

She always had it as far as he knew, Ferrer answered. She wore it at her waist, tucked into the waistband of her trousers or her skirt or her hiking shorts. Why? he wanted to know. Was the pager of some importance in the inspector's investigation?

That, Lynley thought, was indeed the question.

Nan Maiden watched them. She'd moved from the office to the first floor corridor where a bank of windows lined the wall. She stood in the embrasure of one of these windows, someone studying the moonlight striking the trees should any of the residents happen to see her.

Nervously, she fingered the tie-back of the heavy curtains. It caught on the bitten skin round her nails. She watched the two men below in conversation, and she fought the desire – the impulse, the *need* – to run down the stairs with an excuse to join them, to offer explanations and to argue fine points of her daughter's character that might be misconstrued.

'Look, Mum,' Nicola had said, all of twenty years old with the Frenchman's scent clinging to her like the aftertaste of wine gone bad, 'I know what I'm doing. I'm quite old enough to know my own mind, and if I want to fuck a bloke old enough to be my dad, then I'm going to fuck him. It's no one's business but my own and it isn't hurting a soul. So why're you in a state about it?' And she'd gazed at Nan with those clear blue eyes, so frank and open and reasonable. She'd unbuttoned her shirt and stepped out of her shorts, dropping bra and knickers on top of them. As she passed her mother and stepped into the bathtub, Ferrer's scent grew stronger, and Nan gagged upon it. Nicola lowered herself into the bath, sinking up to her shoulders so that the water completely covered her teacup breasts. But not before Nan saw the bruises on them and the marks of his teeth. And not before Nicola saw her see them. She said, 'He likes it that way, Mummy. Rough. But he doesn't actually hurt me. And anyway, I do the same to him. Everything's okay. You're not to worry.'

Nan said, 'Worry? I didn't bring you up to—'

'Mum.' She'd lifted the sponge from the tray and dipped it into the water. The room was steamy and Nan sat on the toilet. She felt dizzy and caught in a world gone mad. 'You brought me up fine,' Nicola said. 'And this isn't about how you brought me up, anyway. He's sexy and he's fun and I like to fuck him. There's no need to make an issue out of something that isn't an issue for either one of us.'

'He's married. You know that. He can't offer you marriage. He wants you for . . . Can't you see it's only sex to him? Free sex without the slightest obligation? Can't you see you're his toy? His little English plaything?'

'It's only sex to me as well,' Nicola said frankly. She brightened as if she suddenly realised why her mother was harbouring such concerns. 'Mum! Were you really thinking I *love* him? That I want to marry him or something like that? Lord, *no*, Mum. I promise you. I just like the way he makes me feel.'

'And when the happiness of being with him makes you long for more and you're not able to have it?'

Nicola picked up her gel soap and applied it to the sponge, dribbling it out like custard over a cake. She looked confused for a moment, then her expression cleared and she said, 'I don't mean *that* kind of feel, that heart kind of feel. I mean physically. The way he makes my body feel. That's all. I like what he does and how I feel when he does it. That's what I want from him and that's what he gives me.'

'Sex.'

'Right. He's quite good, you know.' She'd cocked her head, given an impish grin, and winked at her mother. 'Or do you know already? Have you had him as well?'

'Nicola!'

She squirmed in the water and hung her head appealingly on the side of the tub. 'Mum, it's okay. I wouldn't tell Dad. God, *have* you done it with him? I mean when I'm away at school, he must need someone else to . . . Come on. Tell me.'

Nan had longed to strike her, to mark the lovely elfin face as Christian-Louis had marked the lithe young body. She wanted to take her by the shoulders and shake until her teeth rattled in her head and pebbled from her mouth into the water. She wasn't supposed to *be* like this. Confronted by her mother with the accusation, she was supposed to deny, to break down when the evidence was presented, to plead for forgiveness, or to ask for understanding. But the last thing she was supposed to do was to confirm her mother's worst suspicions with the same ease that might have gone into answering a question about what she'd eaten for breakfast.

'Sorry,' Nicola said when her mother didn't reply to her lighthearted questions. 'It's different for you. I can see that. I shouldn't have intruded. I'm sorry, Mum.'

She'd taken a razor from the bathtub tray and she was applying this to her right leg. It was deeply tanned and long, with well-shaped calves and muscles taut from hiking. Nan watched her run it along her flesh. She waited for a nick, for a scrape, for the blood. None came.

She said, 'What are you, exactly? What do I call you? A scrubber? A slag? A common tart?'

The words didn't wound. They didn't even touch. Nicola set down the razor and gazed at her. 'I'm Nicola,' she said. 'The daughter who loves you very much, Mummy.'

'Don't say that. If you loved me, you wouldn't be—'

'Mum, I made a decision to do this. Eyes wide open and knowing all the facts. I didn't make the decision to hurt you. I made it because I wanted him. And when this ends – because all things do – how I'll feel is *my* responsibility. If I'm hurt, I'm hurt. If I'm not, I'm not. I'm sorry you found out about it because it's obviously upset you. But I'd like you to know that we did try to be discreet.'

The voice of reason, her lovely daughter. Nicola was who Nicola was. She called aces as she saw them and spades the same. And as Nan saw her so vividly – a spectral figure whose image seemed to form on the glass panes of the window at which her mother now stood – she tried not to think, let alone to believe that the girl's forthright honesty was what had killed her.

Nan had never understood her daughter, and she saw that now more clearly than she had done in all the years she'd waited for Nicola to emerge from the chrysalis of her troubled adolescence, fully formed as an adult made in the image and likeness of her progenitors. Thinking of her child, Nan felt settle upon her shoulders the weighty mantle of a failure so profound that she wondered how she would ever be able to continue living. That she had produced such a daughter from her own body ... that the years of self-sacrifice had brought her to this moment ... that the cooking and cleaning and washing and ironing and worrying and planning and giving giving giving had resulted in her feeling like a starfish taken from the ocean and left to dry – and to rot – too far from the water to save herself ... that the sweaters knitted and the temperatures taken and the scraped knees bandaged and the little shoes polished and the clothes kept neat and fresh and sweet had ultimately counted for nothing in the eyes of the single person for whom she lived and breathed ... It was too much to bear.

She'd given the effort of motherhood everything she possessed, and she'd failed entirely, teaching her daughter nothing of substance. Nicola was who Nicola was.

Nan was only grateful that her own mother had died during Nicola's childhood. She would never have to see how Nan had failed where her female forebears had known nothing but success. Nan herself was the embodiment of her mother's values. Born into a time of terrible strife, she'd been schooled in the disciplines of poverty, suffering, generosity, and duty. In war, one did not seek to gratify the self. The self was secondary to the Cause. One's home became a haven for convalescing soldiers. One's food and clothing – and, dear God, even the gifts one received at an eight-year-old's birthday party when the little attendants had been told in advance that the guest of honour had no wants in comparison with what the dear soldiers needed – were gently but firmly removed from one's grasp and passed on to hands worthier than her own. It was a hard time, but it created her mettle on its forge. She had character as a result. This was what she should have passed to her daughter.

Nan had moulded herself in her own mother's image, and her reward had been a cool, unspoken but nonetheless treasured approval communicated by a single nod of the regal head. She'd lived for that nod. It said, 'Children learn from their parents, and you have learned to perfection, Nancy.'

Parents gave their children's world both order and meaning. Children learned who they were – and how to be – at their parents' knees. So what had Nicola seen in her parents that resulted in who and what she had become?

Nan didn't want to answer that question. It brought her face to face with ghouls that she didn't wish to confront. She's so like her father, Nan's inner voice whispered. But no, but *no*. She turned from the window.

She climbed the stairs to the private floor of Maiden Hall. She found her husband in their bedroom, sitting in the armchair in the darkness, his head in his hands.

He didn't look up as she closed the door behind her. She crossed the room to him, knelt by the chair, and put her hand on his knee. She didn't say to him what she wanted to say, that Christian-Louis had burnt pine nuts into tiny lumps of charcoal weeks ago, that the ground floor took hours to lose the acrid scent of the burning, and that he – Andy – hadn't mentioned the odour because he hadn't noticed it in the first place. She didn't say any of this because she didn't want to consider what it implied. Instead, she said, 'Let's not lose each other as well, Andy.'

At that, he looked up. She was struck by how the last days

Elizabeth George

had aged him. His natural vibrancy was gone. She couldn't imagine the man she saw before her jogging from Padley Gorge to Hathersage, skiing hell for leather down Whistler Mountain, or tearing along the Tissington Trail on his mountain bike without raising a sweat. He didn't look as if he'd make it down the stairs, let alone ever be restored to the score of activities in which he'd once engaged.

'Let me do something for you,' she murmured, a hand at his temple to smooth back his hair.

'Tell me what you did with it,' he replied.

Her hand dropped to her side. 'With what?'

'I don't need to spell it out. Did you take it with you onto the moor this afternoon? You must have done. It's the only explanation.'

'Andy, I don't actually know what you—'

'Don't,' he said. 'Just tell me, Nan. And tell me why you said you didn't know she had one. I'd like to know that most of all.'

Nan felt – rather than heard – an odd buzzing in her head. It was very much as if Nicola's pager were somewhere in the room with them. An impossibility, of course. It lay where she had deposited it: deep in a crevice created at the juncture of two pieces of limestone on Hathersage Moor.

'Dearest,' she said, 'I really don't know what you're talking about. Truly. I don't.'

He examined her. She met his gaze. She waited for him to be more direct, to ask with an explicitness of language that she couldn't avoid: She had never been a particularly good liar; she could feign confusion and act ignorant of the facts, but she could do little else.

He didn't ask. Instead, he let his head sink back against the chair, and he closed his eyes. 'God,' he whispered. 'What have you done?'

She made no reply. He'd been invoking God, not her. And God's ways were a mystery, even to the faithful. Yet Andy's

suffering was so excruciating to her that she wanted to give him
an anodyne of some sort. She found it in a partial disclosure.
He could make of it what he would.

'Things need to stay uncomplicated,' she murmured. 'We
need to keep things simple as best we can.'

Chapter Fourteen

━━━━◆━━━━

Samantha came across her uncle Jeremy in the parlour when she was making her final rounds of the night. She'd been checking doors and windows – by virtue of habit rather than by virtue of the fact that the family had anything of value worth burgling at this point – and she'd marched into the parlour with the intention of seeing to the windows in there before she realised that he was present.

The lights were off, but not because Jeremy was sleeping. He was instead running an old eight millimetre film through a projector that clacked and whirred as if on its last legs. The picture itself flickered not on a screen because Jeremy couldn't be bothered setting that up. Rather it moved against a bookshelf, where the curved backs of mildewing volumes distorted the figures whose images had been filmed.

Jeremy lifted his glass and drank. He replaced it with such precision on the table next to his chair that Samantha wondered what he was actually drinking. He turned his head and squinted in her direction as if the light from the corridor were too bright for him. 'Ah. It's you, Sammy. Come to join the resident insomniac?'

'I was checking the windows. I didn't know you were still up, Uncle Jeremy.'

'Didn't you.' The film continued to run. In it, little Jeremy and his Mum were on horseback, Jeremy on a light-coloured pony and Mum on a spirited bay. The horses were cantering towards the camera and Jeremy was grasping the saddle's pommel for all he was worth. He bounced as if his bum had been made of rubber. His little feet had lost the stirrups. The horses halted and Mum dismounted, grabbed her son from the pony and swung him, laughing, round in a circle.

Jeremy turned from his scrutiny of Samantha, giving his attention back to the film. 'You lose your mum, and you're marked forever,' he murmured, taking up his glass once more. 'Did I ever tell you, Sammy—'

'Yes. You did.' Numerous times since her arrival in Derbyshire, Samantha had heard the story that she already knew: his mother's untimely death in a shop in Longnor, his father's rapid remarriage, his own banishment to boarding school at the tender age of seven while his only sister was allowed to remain at home. 'Ruined me,' he'd said time and again. 'Robs a man of his soul and don't you forget it.'

Samantha decided it was best to leave him to his musings and she began to depart the room. But his next words stopped her.

'It's nice to have her out of the way, isn't it?' he asked with absolute clarity. 'Opens things up the way they should be opened up. That's what I think, Sammy. What about you?'

She said, 'What? I don't ... what?' and in her surprise she feigned misunderstanding in a circumstance where no misapprehension was really feasible, especially with the *High Peak Courier* sitting on the floor next to her uncle's chair with its front page headline shouting *Death at Nine Sisters*. So it was foolish to attempt to dissemble with her uncle. *Nicola's dead* was going to be the subtext of every conversation Samantha had with anyone from this time forward, and it would serve her interests far better to become used to Nicola Maiden as a Rebecca-like figure in the background of her life than it would to pretend the other woman had never existed at all.

Jeremy was watching the film, a smile playing round the corners of his mouth as if he found amusement in the sight of his five-year-old self skipping along the path in one of the gardens, dragging a stick along the edge of what was then a well-tended herbaceous border. 'Sammy, my angel,' he said to the screen, and again his voice was remarkable for the unusual clarity of his enunciation, 'how it happened isn't the point. *That* it happened is. And what we're going to do *now* that it's happened is the most important point of all.'

Samantha made no reply. She felt unaccountably rooted to the spot, both trapped and mesmerised by what could destroy her.

'She was never right for him, Sammy. Obvious whenever they were together. She held the reins. And he got ridden. Whenever he wasn't riding her, of course.' Jeremy chuckled at his own joke. 'P'rhaps he would've seen the wrongness of it all at the end of the day. But I don't think so. She'd worked herself under his skin too deep. Good at that, she was. Some women are.'

You're not was what he didn't say. But Samantha didn't need him to say it. Pulling men had never been her forte. She'd always believed that an outright demonstration of her virtues would serve to establish her firmly in someone's affections. Womanly virtues had a longevity to them that sexual allure could never match. And when lust and passion died the death of familiarity, one needed something of substance to take their place. Or so she had taught herself to believe through an adolescence and a young adulthood remarkable for their solitude.

'Couldn't have happened any better,' Jeremy was saying. 'Sammy, always remember this: Things work out the way they're meant to.'

She felt her palms dampening, and she rubbed them surreptitiously against the skirt that she'd donned for dinner.

'You're right for him. The other . . . She wasn't. What you

have to offer, she couldn't touch. She would've brought nothing to a marriage with Julie – aside from the only decent pair of ankles the Brittons have seen in two hundred years – whereas you understand our dream. You can be part of it, Sammy. You can make it happen. With you, Julie can bring Broughton Manor back to life. With her . . . Well. Like I said, things work out the way they're meant to do. They work out quite nicely, in fact. So what we've got to do now—'

'I'm sorry she's dead,' Samantha broke in, because she knew she must say something eventually, and a conventional expression of sorrow was the only statement she could think of at the moment to stop him from going on. 'For Julian's sake, I'm sorry. He's devastated, Uncle Jeremy.'

'Isn't he just. And that's exactly where we begin.'

'Begin?'

'Don't play the innocent with me. And for God's sake, don't be a fool. The way's clear and there're plans to be laid. You've taken enough trouble to woo him—'

'You're mistaken.'

'—and what you've done is lay a decent foundation. But this is the point where we start building on that foundation. Nothing hasty, mind you. No going to his bedroom and dropping your knickers just yet. Everything in good time.'

'Uncle Jeremy. I hardly think—'

'Good. Don't think. Let me do that. You keep it simple from now on.' He raised his glass to his lips and eyed her sharply over its rim. 'It's when a woman *complicates* her plans that her plans get cocked up. If you know what I mean. And I expect you do.'

Samantha swallowed, pinned to his gaze. How was it that an ageing alcoholic – a bloody *drunk*, for the love of God – could manage to discompose her so easily? Except he didn't seem very much like a drunk right now. Flustered, she went to the windows and locked them as had been her intention. Behind her, the film came to an end, and the tail of it slapped noisily against its spool as the projector continued to run. *Kickateck, kickateck, kickateck, kickateck.* Jeremy didn't seem to notice.

'You want him, don't you?' he asked her. 'And don't lie to me about it, because if I'm to help you catch the boy, I want to know the facts. Oh, not all of them, mind you. Just the important one, about you wanting him.'

'He's not a boy. He's a man who—'

'Isn't he just.'

'—knows his own mind.'

'Bollocks, that. He knows his own dick and where he wants to stick it. We just need to see that he learns to want to stick it in you.'

'Please, Uncle Jeremy . . .' It was horrible, inconceivable, humiliating: to be listening to this. She was a woman who'd forged her own path throughout her life, and to place herself in the position of depending on someone other than herself to mould events and people to her wishes was not only foreign to her thinking, it was also foolhardy and it could be dangerous.

'Sammy, my angel, I'm on your side.' Jeremy's voice coaxed, urging her to declare herself in the very same way that one might urge a frightened puppy to come forward from beneath a chair. She found herself turning from the windows. She saw that he was watching her, his eyes hooded and his chin held by fingers adopting a pious attitude of prayer. 'I'm on your side completely and one hundred percent. Only listen, my angel. I need to know exactly what your side is before I take action on your behalf.'

Samantha tried to move her eyes away from him, but she failed completely.

'One little fact, Sammy: You want the boy. Believe me, you don't need to say anything more. Fact is, I don't want to *know* any more. Just that you want him. End of story.'

'I can't.'

'You can. Simple as anything. Three little words. And they

won't kill you. Words, that is. Words don't kill. But I fancy you know that already, don't you?'

She couldn't look away. She wanted to, she was desperate to, and yet she couldn't.

'I want you to have him as bad as you want him,' Jeremy told her. 'Just say the words.'

They came from her at last without volition, as if he drew them from her and she was powerless to stop him. 'All right. I want him.'

Jeremy smiled. 'Don't tell me anything else.'

Barbara Havers felt as if someone had planted minuscule thorns beneath her eyelids. It was her fourth hour into her adventure with the SO10 files on CRIS, and she was mightily regretting her promise to Nkata that she'd work nights and dawns to fulfil her obligations to the assignment given her by Inspector Lynley. She wasn't getting anywhere with this rubbish, aside from becoming aware of her potential for arriving at destinations marked Damaged Retinas and Imminent Hypermetropia.

Following their recce of Terry Cole's flat, Nkata and Barbara had driven to the Yard. There, after transferring the cannabis and the box of postcards to the front seat of Barbara's Mini – to be dealt with later – they had parted ways. Nkata drove off to return the Inspector's Bentley to his home in Belgravia. Barbara reluctantly trudged off to fulfil her promise to Nkata to do her duty in the Crime Recording Information System.

She'd come up with sod bloody all so far, which hardly surprised her. As far as she was concerned, after the discovery of the postcards in the Battersea flat, neon arrows had begun pointing to Terry Cole as the killer's main target – not to Nicola Maiden – and unless there was some manner in which she could tie Cole to Andy Maiden's time in SO10, this business of delving through files was a waste of her time. Only a name leaping off the screen, drooling blood, and screaming 'I'm the one, baby!' was going to convince her otherwise.

Still, she'd known it was in her best interest to comply with Lynley's orders. So for the fifteen names he had given her, she'd read the cases and organised each into arbitrary – albeit useless – categories that she'd called Drugs, Potential for Blackmail, Prostitution, Organised Crime, and Hit Men. Dutifully, she'd placed the names from Lynley's list into these categories and she'd added the prisons to which each malefactor had been sent to while away a few years at Her Majesty's pleasure. She'd tracked down terms of imprisonment and added those to the mix, and she'd begun the process of determining which of the convicts were now on parole. Locating the former lags, however, was something which she knew would be impossible at the time of night. So feeling that she'd been virtuous, obedient, and responsive to her superior's order to return to CRIS, she decided, at half past twelve, to call it a day.

Traffic was light, so she was home before one. With Terry on her mind and a motive for his murder to be fished from the evidence, she scooped up the box of postcards and carried them through the dark garden to her digs.

Inside, her phone was blinking its message light when she shouldered open the door of her bungalow and heaved the cardboard box onto the table. She switched on a lamp, grabbed up a selection of the postcards – which were bundled together with elastic bands – and crossed the room to listen to her calls.

The first was Mrs Flo, telling her that 'Mum looked right at your picture this morning, Barbie dear, and she said your name. Bright and clear as ever was. She said, "This is my Barbie." What do you think of that? I wanted you to know because . . . Well, it *is* distressing when she's got herself into one of her muddles, isn't it? And that silly business about . . . what was she called? . . . Lilly O'Ryan? Well, no matter. She's been right as rain all day. So don't you worry that she's forgotten you because she hasn't. All right, dear? I hope you're well. See you soon. Bye now, Barbie. Bye bye. Bye bye.'

Praise God for small favours, Barbara thought. A day of lucidity weighed against weeks and months of dementia was little enough to celebrate, but she'd learned to take her triumphs in teaspoonfuls when it came to her mother's fleeting moments of coherence.

The second message began with a bright, 'Hello he*llo*,' followed by three breathy notes of music. 'Did you hear that? I'm learning flute. I just got it today after school and I'm to be in the orchestra! They asked me special and I asked Dad would it be okay and he said yes so now I play flute. Only I don't play it very well yet. But I'm practising. I know the scale. Listen.' There followed a clatter as the phone was dropped onto a solid surface. Afterwards came eight highly hesitant notes, breathy like the first. Then, 'See? The teacher says I've a natural talent, Barbara. Do you think so as well?' The voice was interrupted by another, a man's voice speaking quietly in the background. Then, 'Oh. This is Khalidah Hadiyyah. Up front in the ground floor flat. Dad says I forgot to tell you that. I expect you know it's me, though, don't you? I wanted to remind you about my sewing lesson. It's tomorrow and you said you wanted to see what I'm making. D'you still want to go? We c'n have the rest of the toffee apple afterwards, for our tea. Ring me back, okay?' And the phone clunked down at her end of the line.

After which Barbara heard the quiet, well-bred tones of Inspector Lynley's wife. Helen said, 'Barbara, Winston's just returned the Bentley. He told me you're working on the case here in town. I'm so glad, and I wanted to tell you so. I *know* your work will put you back in good standing with everyone at the Yard. Barbara, will you be patient with Tommy? He thinks the world of you, and ... Well, I do hope you know that. It's just that the situation ... what happened this past summer ... it took him rather by surprise. So ... Oh bother. I just wanted to wish you well on the case. You've always worked brilliantly with Tommy, and I know this instance will be no different.'

At which Barbara winced. Her conscience prickled. But she muffled the voice that told her she'd been acting in defiance of Lynley's orders for a good part of the day, and she silently announced that she wasn't defying anyone at all. She was merely taking the initiative, supplementing her assignment with additional activities demanded by the logic of the unfolding investigation.

It was as good an excuse as any.

She kicked off her shoes and flopped onto the day bed, where she pulled the elastic band from the collection of postcards she was carrying. She began to flip through them. And as she did so, she thought of the myriad ways in which Terry Cole's life – as it was unfolding through her investigation of it – was unveiling him as a killer's target while Nicola Maiden's life – no matter how they viewed it – was unveiling her as nothing more than a sexually active twenty-five year old who'd had one or two men in every port and a wealthy lover by the string. And while sexual jealousy on the part of one of those men might have led him to give the girl the chop, he certainly wouldn't have needed to do the job out on the moor, especially when he saw that she was with someone. It would have made more sense for him to wait till he found her alone. Unless, of course, she and Terry had been into something at that moment that made him think they were an item. In which case, blinded by rage and jealousy, he could well have stormed into the stone circle and attacked his rival for the Maiden girl's favours, running her down as well after he'd wounded the boy. But that seemed an unlikely scenario. Nothing Barbara had learned about Nicola Maiden had so far suggested that she'd gone for unemployed teenage boys.

Terry, on the other hand, was turning out to be a field ripe for harvest when it came to activities from which murder could arise. According to Cilla, he'd carried gobs of cash with him, and the postcards that Barbara now arranged on her day bed suggested a field of underworld employment that was rife with violence. Despite what his mother claimed about the big commission that Terry had, despite what Mrs Baden had asserted about the boy's good nature and generosity, it was seeming more and more likely that the real Terry Cole had lived close to if not directly within the underbelly of English life. Tied to that underbelly were drugs, pornography, snuff films, paedophilia, exotica, erotica, and white slavery. Not to mention a hundred tasty perversions, all of which could so easily give rise to a motive for murder.

But in Nicola's case, nearly everything had been accounted for: from her lifestyle in London to her supply of dosh. They still had to discover why she'd gone to work in Derbyshire for the summer, but what on earth could that possibly have to do with her murder?

On the other hand, virtually nothing about Terry Cole's life had made sense at all. Until Barbara had unearthed the postcards.

She gazed upon them in their orderly rows on the day bed and pursed her lips. Come on, she told them, give me something to run with. I know it's here, I know one of you can tell me, I know, I *know*.

She could still hear Cilla Thompson's passionate reaction to seeing the cards: 'He *never* would've told me about this. Never in a hundred years. He was pretending to be an *artist*, for God's sake. And artists spend their time on their art. When they're not creating, they're thinking about creating. They're not crawling round London sticking these up. Art begets art so you expose yourself to art. *This*—' with a contemptuous gesture towards the cards – 'is a life exposed to absolute crap.'

But Terry had never been truly interested in art, Barbara guessed. He'd been interested in something else entirely.

In the first set of postcards, there were forty-five in all. Each, Barbara saw, was different. And no matter how she studied them, categorized them, or attempted to eliminate them one by one, she was finally forced to accept the fact that only the telephone – even at this hour of the night – was going to assist her in sussing out her next move in the investigation.

She set aside any consideration that Terry Cole might be connected to Andy Maiden's past in SO10. She set aside any consideration that SO10 was involved in the case at all.

Instead, she reached for the phone. She knew quite well that – despite the hour – at the other end of the line would be forty-five suspects just waiting for someone to ring them and ask a few questions.

By rising at dawn the next morning and driving to Manchester airport, Lynley managed to catch the first flight to London. It was nine-forty when his taxi left him at the front door of his house in Eaton Terrace.

He paused before entering. Despite the brightness of the morning – with the sun glittering against the transom windows of the houses that lined the quiet street – he felt as if he were walking directly beneath a cloud. His eyes took in the fine white buildings, the wrought iron railings that fronted them without a spot of rust marring their midnight paint, and regardless of the fact that he'd been born into the longest period of peace that his country had ever experienced, he found himself unaccountably thinking of war.

London had been devastated. Night after night the bombs fell upon it, reducing large areas of the metropolis to bricks, mortar, beams, and rubble. The City, the docklands, and the suburbs – both north and south of the river – had sustained the worst of the damage, but no one in the nation's capital had escaped the fear. It was heralded nightly by the sound of the sirens and the whistling of the bombs. It was embodied by explosions, fires, panic, confusion, uncertainty and the aftermath of them all.

Yet London had continued to persevere, renewing itself as

it had done for two thousand years. Boadicea's tribesmen had not vanquished it, neither the plague nor the Great Fire had subdued it, so the firestorm of the Blitz could not have hoped to defeat it. Because out of pain, destruction, and loss it always managed to rise anew.

So perhaps it could be argued that strife and travail could lead one to greatness, Lynley thought, that one's sense of purpose, once tested by adversity, became reliably firm and one's understanding of the world, once questioned in the midst of sorrow and misconception, was forever enhanced. But the thought that bombs ultimately led to peace as a woman's labour led to birth was not enough to dispel the gloom, apprehension, and dread that he was feeling. Good could come out of bad, it was true. It was the hell in between that he didn't want to ponder.

At six that morning, he'd phoned DI Hanken and told him that 'some crucial information uncovered by the London officers working the case' required his presence back in town. He would be communicating with Derbyshire as soon as he followed up on that information, made some sense of it, and saw where it fitted into the whole. To Hanken's logical query about the necessity of Lynley's travelling to London when he had two officers already working there and could – with a simple telephone call – garner two or even two dozen more, Lynley replied that his team had uncovered a few details that were making it look as if London and not Derbyshire was where the facts were leading. It seemed reasonable, he said, for one of the two ranking officers on the case to assess and assemble these facts in person. Would Hanken make available to him a copy of the postmortem report? he asked. He also wanted to hand that document over to a forensics specialist, to see if Dr Myles's conclusion about the murder weapon was accurate.

'If she's made an error about the knife – the length of the blade, for example – I'd like to know that at once,' he said.

Elizabeth George

How would a forensics specialist be able to discern an error in the report without seeing the body, the x-rays, the photographs, or the wound itself? Hanken queried.

This, Lynley told him, was no ordinary specialist.

But he asked for copies of the x-rays and the photographs as well. And a quick stop at the Buxton station on his way to the airport had put everything into his possession.

For his part, Hanken was going to start a search for the Swiss Army knife and the Maiden girl's missing waterproof. He would also be talking personally to the masseuse who'd seen to Will Upman's ostensibly tense muscles on Tuesday night. And if time allowed, he'd pay a call at Broughton Manor to see if Julian Britton's father could confirm his son's alibi or that of his niece.

'Look hard at Julian,' Lynley told him. 'I've found another of Nicola's lovers.' He went on to summarise his previous night's conversation with Christian-Louis Ferrer. Hanken whistled. 'Are we going to be able to find a bloke anywhere who *wasn't* shafting this bird, Thomas?'

'I expect we might be looking for the bloke who thought that he was the only one.'

'Britton.'

'He said he proposed and she refused. But we only have his word for that, don't we? It's a good way to take the spotlight off himself: saying he wanted to marry her when he wanted – and did – something else entirely.'

Now in London, Lynley unlocked the front door and shut it quietly behind him. He called his wife's name. He was half-expecting Helen to be out already – somehow knowing his intention to return without having been told and seeking to avoid him in the aftermath of their earlier disagreement – but as he crossed the entry to the stairs, he heard a door crash shut, a man's voice say, 'Whoops. Sorry. Don't know my own strength, do I,' and a moment later Denton and Helen came towards him from the direction of the kitchen. The former was

320

balancing a stack of enormous portfolios across his arms. The latter was following him, a list in her hand. She was saying, 'I've narrowed things down somewhat, Charlie. And they were willing to part with the sample books till three o'clock, so I'm depending on you to give me input.'

'I hate flowers and ribbons and that sort of rubbish,' Denton said. 'All twee, that is, so don't even show it me. Makes me think of my gran.'

'So noted,' Helen replied.

'Cheers.' Denton saw Lynley then. 'Look what the morning's brought, Lady Helen. Good. You won't be needing me, then, will you?'

'Needing you for what?' Lynley asked.

Helen, hearing him, said, 'Tommy! You're home? That was a quick trip, wasn't it?'

'Wallpaper,' Denton said in reply to Lynley's question. He gestured with the portfolios he was carrying. 'Samples.'

'For the spare rooms,' Helen added. 'Have you looked at the walls in there lately, Tommy? The paper looks as if it hasn't been changed since the turn of the century.'

'It hasn't,' Lynley said.

'Just as I suspected. Well, if we don't get it changed before she gets here, I'm afraid your aunt Augusta will change it for us. I thought we might head her off. I had a look through the books at Peter Jones yesterday, and they were good enough to let me pinch a few at closing time. Just for today, though. Wasn't that kind of them?' She started up the stairs, saying over her shoulder, 'Why're you back so soon? Have you sorted everything out already?'

Denton followed her. Lynley made a third in their little procession, suitcase in his hand. He'd followed some information to London, he told his wife. And there were documents he wanted St James to look over. 'The postmortem. Some photos and x-rays,' he said.

'Arguments among the experts?' she asked, a reasonable

assumption. It wouldn't have been the first time St James had been requested to mediate a dispute among scientists.

'Just some questions in my own mind,' Lynley told her, 'as well as a need to look over some information Winston's managed to gather.'

'Ah.' She glanced over her shoulder and offered him a fleeting smile. 'It's quite nice to have you back.'

The spare rooms in need of refurbishment were on the second floor of the house. Lynley left his suitcase inside the door of their bedroom and then joined his wife and Denton up above. Helen was laying sample sheets of wallpaper out on the bed in the first of the rooms, removing the portfolios from Denton's outstretched arms one at a time and making her selections with infinite care. The younger man was wearing an expression of long suffering patience throughout this activity. But he brightened considerably when Lynley walked into the room.

He said hopefully, 'Here he is. So if you won't be needing me . . . ?' to Lynley's wife.

'I can't stay, Denton,' was Lynley's reply.

The other man drooped.

'A problem?' Lynley said. 'Have you a sweet young thing waiting somewhere today?' It wouldn't be unusual. Denton's pursuit of ladies was the stuff of legend.

'I've the half price ticket booth waiting,' Denton answered. 'I hoped to make it in advance of the crowd.'

'Ah, yes. I see. Theatre. Not another musical, I hope?'

'Well . . .'

Denton looked embarrassed. His love of the spectacles posing regularly as West End theatre soaked up a good part of his wages each month. He was almost as bad as a cocaine addict when it came to greasepaint, dimmed lights, and applause.

Lynley took the portfolios from Denton's arms. 'Go,' he said. 'God forbid that we keep you from experiencing the latest theatrical extravaganza.'

'It's art,' Denton protested.

'So you keep telling me. Go. And if you buy the accompanying CD as usual, I'll ask you not to play it when I'm home.'

'He's a real culture snob, isn't he?' Denton asked Helen, his voice confidential.

'As ever there was.'

She continued laying wallpaper samples out on the bed once Denton had left them. She rejected three samples, replaced them with three others, and took another portfolio from her husband's arms. She said, 'You don't need to stand there holding them, Tommy. You've work to do, haven't you?'

'It can wait a few minutes.'

'This will take far longer than a few minutes, I'm afraid. You know how hopeless I am when it comes to making up my mind about anything. I *had* thought of something rather pretty with flowers. Subdued and calming. You know what I mean. But Charlie's put me off that idea. God forbid we ask him to escort Aunt Augusta into a room he considers twee. What about this one, unicorns and leopards? Isn't it ghastly?'

'But suitable for guests whose visits one wishes to curtail,' Lynley said.

Helen laughed. 'There *is* that.'

Lynley said nothing until she'd made her selections from all the portfolios he was holding. She covered the bed with them and went on to litter most of the floor. All the time he thought how strange it was that two days previously they'd been at odds with each other. He felt neither irritation nor animosity now. Nor did he feel that sense of betrayal that had triggered within him such righteous indignation. He experienced only a quiet surging of his heart towards hers, which some men might have identified as lust and dealt with accordingly but which he knew had nothing to do with sex and everything on earth to do with love.

He said, 'You had my number in Derbyshire. I gave it to Denton. To Simon as well.'

She looked up. A lock of chestnut hair caught at the corner of her mouth. She brushed it away.

'You didn't ring,' he said.

'Was I meant to ring?' There was nothing coy about the question. 'Charlie gave me the number, but he didn't say you'd asked me to—'

'You weren't supposed to ring. But I hoped you would. I wanted to talk to you. You left the house in the middle of our conversation the other morning, and I felt uneasy with the way things were left between us. I wanted to clear the air.'

'Oh.' The word was small. She went to the room's old Georgian dressing table and sat tentatively on the edge of its stool. She watched him gravely, a shadow playing across her cheek where her hair shielded her face from a shaft of sunlight that streamed in through the window. She looked so much like a schoolgirl waiting to be disciplined that Lynley found himself reassessing what he'd believed were his rational grievances against her.

He said, 'I'm sorry about the row, Helen. You were giving your opinion. That's more than your right. I jumped all over you because I wanted you on my side. She's my wife, I thought, and this is my work and these are the decisions that I'm forced to take in the course of my work. I want her behind me, not in front of me blocking my way. I didn't think of you as an individual in that moment, just as an extension of me. So when you questioned my decision about Barbara, I saw red. My temper ran away with me. And I'm sorry for it.'

Her gaze lowered. She ran her fingers along the edge of the stool and examined their route. 'I didn't leave the house because you lost your temper. God knows I've seen you lose it before.'

'I know why you left. And I shouldn't have said it.'

'Said . . . ?'

'That remark. The tautology bit. It was thoughtless and cruel. I'd like to have your forgiveness for having said it.'

She looked up at him. 'They were only words, Tommy. You don't need to ask forgiveness for your words.'

'I ask nonetheless.'

'No. What I mean is that you're already forgiven. You were forgiven at once if it comes to that. Words aren't reality, you know. They're only expressions of what people see.' She bent and took up one of the wallpaper samples, holding it the length of her arm and evaluating it for some moments. His apology, it seemed, had been accepted. But he had the distinct feeling that the subject itself was miles away from being put to rest between them.

Still, following her lead, he said helpfully in reference to the wallpaper, 'That looks like a good choice.'

'Do you think so?' Helen let it fall to the floor. 'Choices are what defeat me. Having to make them in the first place. And having to live with them afterwards.'

Warning flares shot up in Lynley's consciousness. His wife hadn't come into their marriage the most eager of brides. Indeed, it had taken some time to persuade her that marriage was in her interests at all. The youngest of five sisters who'd married in every possible circumstance, from into the Italian aristocracy to on the land to a Montana cattleman, she'd been a witness to the vicissitudes and vagaries that were the offspring of any permanent attachment. And she'd never prevaricated about her reluctance to become a party to what might take from her more than it could ever give. But she'd also never been a woman to let momentary discord prevail over her common sense. They'd exchanged a few harsh words, that was all. Words didn't necessarily presage anything.

Still, he said to counter the implication in her statements, 'When I first knew that I loved you – have I ever told you this? – I couldn't understand how I'd managed to go so long blind to the fact. There you were, a part of my life for years, but you'd always been at the safe distance of a friend. And when I actually *knew* that I loved you, risking having more than your friendship seemed like risking it all.'

'It was risking it all,' she said. 'There's no going back after a certain point with someone, is there? But I don't regret the risk for a moment. Do you, Tommy?'

He felt a rush of relief. 'Then we're at peace.'

'Were we anything else?'

'It seemed . . .' He hesitated, uncertain how to describe the sea change he was experiencing between them. He said, 'We've got to expect a period of adjustment, haven't we? We aren't children. We had lives that were independent of each other before we married, so it's going to take some time to adjust to lives that include each other all the time.'

'Had we.' She said it as a statement, reflectively. She looked up from the wallpaper samples, to him.

'Had we what?'

'Independent lives. Oh, I see that you did. Who would ever argue with that? But as to the other half of the equation . . .' She made an aimless gesture at the samples. 'I would have chosen flowers without a moment's hesitation. But flowers, I'm told by Charlie, are twee. You know, I never actually considered myself hopeless in the arena of interior design. Perhaps I've been kidding myself about that.'

Lynley hadn't known her for more than fifteen years to fail in understanding her meaning now. 'Helen, I was angry. Angry, I'm the first to climb on the highest horse I can find. But as you pointed out, what I said was words. There's no more truth in them than there's truth in suggesting I'm the soul of sensitivity. Which, as you know, I'm not. Full stop.'

As he spoke, she'd begun setting the floral samples to one side. As he finished, she paused. She looked at him, head cocked, face gentle. 'You don't really understand what I'm talking about, do you? But then, how could you? In your position I wouldn't understand what I was talking about either.'

'I do understand. I corrected your language. I was angry

because you weren't taking my side, so I responded as I believed you'd responded: to the form instead of to the substance beneath it. In the process, I hurt you. And I'm sorry for that.'

She got to her feet, sheets of wallpaper held to her chest. 'Tommy, you described me as I am,' she said simply. 'I left the house because I didn't want to listen to a truth I've avoided for years.'

Chapter Fifteen

Women had always been a mystery to him. Helen was a woman. Ergo, Helen would always be a mystery. Or so Lynley thought as he worked his way from Belgravia to Westminster and New Scotland Yard.

He'd wanted to continue their discussion, but she'd said gently, 'Tommy darling, you've come back to London with work to do, haven't you? You must do it. Go on. We'll talk later.'

A man who'd generally managed to obtain what he desired in fairly short order after desiring it, Lynley chafed at any kind of postponement. But Helen was right. He'd already tarried at home longer than he'd originally intended. So he kissed her and set off for the Yard.

He found Nkata on the telephone in his office. He was jotting something into his notebook, saying, 'Describe it for me as best you can, then ... Well, what sort of collar does it have, f'r instance? Are there snaps or a zip? ... Look, *anything* you give me is more than I have right now ... Hmmm? Yeah. Okay. Right. I'll hold ... Put her on as well. Cheers.' He looked up as Lynley entered the room. He began to remove himself from the chair behind the desk.

Lynley waved him back into place. He went round to stand behind him where he could see a column of postcards that had been arranged on his leather blotter. The cards ran along one edge of this, samples of the lot that – according to Nkata – had been taken from Terry Cole's flat.

Lynley saw that punishment was offered on some of the cards; domination was promised on others; still others suggested that one's ultimate fantasies could be fulfilled. Mention was made of bubble baths, massages, video services, torture chambers. Some cards offered the use of animals; a few noted that costumes could be provided. Many had photographs depicting such delights as were on offer from the *Transsexual Black She-Male* or *The Ultimate Domina* or a *Hot Stunning Thai Girl*. In short, there was something for every taste, inclination and perversion. And since the cards looked too fresh from the printer to have spent any time Blu Tacked to the walls of a phone box prior to being collected by a sweaty palmed teenager with masturbation in mind, the only conclusion to be reached from the presence of several thousand of such cards beneath his bed was that Terry Cole had not been a collector but rather a distributor – part of the great machine that peddled sex in London.

This, at least, explained the cash that Cilla Thompson claimed the boy had carried. Card boys who worked quickly enough putting up cards in phone boxes all round central London could earn a substantial living because the going rate was £100 for every five hundred cards the boy managed to place. And the service of a card boy was absolutely essential: Agents of British Telecom removed the cards daily, so they always had to be replaced.

Two of these cards had been isolated from the column on Lynley's blotter and lay in the centre of his desk. One displayed the photo of a putative schoolgirl; one bore only print. Lynley picked them up and examined them – feeling heart sore – as Nkata continued his call.

Shhh was printed across the top of the first. And below the photograph ran the words *Don't Tell Mummy What's On*

After School! The picture itself showed a rucksack with books tumbling out of it and bending from the waist to gather them up was a girl, her bum pointing towards the camera. She wasn't your average schoolgirl: Her pleated skirt was hiked up to display black thong knickers and thigh-high black stockings with lace round the top. She was looking coyly over her shoulder at the camera, blonde hair tousled and tumbling round her face. Beneath her stiletto-heeled shoes was a telephone number with a hand-scrawled *ring me!* next to it.

'Christ,' Lynley whispered. And when Nkata ended his phone call, he said as if an explanation in the light of day would negate the one he'd heard via phone from the constable in the dead of night, 'Take me through the entire situation beginning to end another time, Winnie.'

'Let me fetch Barb. The brainwork was hers.'

'Havers?' Lynley's tone stopped the other man in the action of picking up the phone. 'Winston, I gave an order. I told her I wanted her on the computer. You assured me that's what she was doing. Why's she involved in this end of the investigation?'

Nkata showed his palms, empty and innocent. He said, 'She's not involved. I'd the box of cards in your motor when I came back here last night from Battersea. I called in to see how she was doing on CRIS. She asked to take the cards along with her when she went home. To have a look through them. The rest . . . She can tell you how it played out.'

Nkata's face wore the guileless expression of a child at the knees of Father Christmas, inadvertently declaring that there was more to the story than had been revealed. Lynley sighed. 'Fetch her, then.'

Nkata reached for the phone. He punched in a few numbers and while waiting for the connection, said solemnly, 'She's working CRIS right now. Been there since six this morning.'

'I'll kill the fatted calf,' Lynley replied.

Nkata, not given to Biblical exegesis or allusion, said, 'Right,' uncertainly. And then into the phone, 'Guv's here, Barb.' That was the extent of it.

While they waited for Havers, Lynley examined the second postcard. He didn't want to think of the anguish that lay ahead for the parents of the murdered girl, however, so he gave his attention back to Nkata. 'Anything else this morning, Winnie?'

'I'd a page from the Coles. Missus and the sister. That was the sister I was talking to just now.'

'And?'

'The boy's jacket's missing.'

'Jacket?'

'Right. A black leather jacket. He always wore it when he rode the big bike. When you gave Mrs Cole that list of the kid's effects – those receipts, remember? – the jacket wasn't on it. They think someone pinched it at the station in Buxton.'

Lynley recalled the photographs of the crime scene. He thought about the evidence that he'd looked through in Buxton. Then he said, 'Are they certain about the jacket?'

'Generally wore it, they claimed. And he wouldn't've ridden all the way North in a T-shirt, which's all the covering it looked like he had ... from the receipts, that is. He wouldn't've ever ridden on the motorway in only a T-shirt, they said.'

'It hasn't been cold, though.'

'The jacket was for more'n warmth. It was also protection if he accidentally pranged the bike on the road. Wouldn't get so cut up with the jacket on, they explained. So where is it is what they want to know.'

'It wasn't among his things in the flat?'

'Barb went through his clobber, so she can tell you—' Nkata stopped himself abruptly. He had the grace to look abashed.

'Ah,' Lynley said, the syllable rich with meaning.

'She worked the computer half the night afterwards,' Nkata said hastily.

'Did she indeed? And whose idea was it that she accompany you to the Cole boy's flat?'

Havers' advent saved Nkata from having to reply. She arrived as if on cue, all business with a notebook in her hand. She looked as professionally attired as Lynley had ever seen her.

She didn't flop into the chair in front of his desk as usual. She stood by the open door, her heels pressed against it as if holding her body at respectful attention. To Lynley's question about the jacket, she responded after a moment in which she seemed to be attempting to read her fellow DC's face as if it were a barometer that would enable her to assess the climate in Lynley's office.

'The kid's gear?' she said carefully when Nkata's earnest nod towards Lynley apparently told her it was at least moderately safe to reveal that she'd once again been derelict in her duties. 'Well. Hmmm.'

'We'll deal later with what you were supposed to be doing, Havers,' Lynley told her. 'Was a black leather jacket among the boy's clothes?'

She managed to look uncomfortable, Lynley noted. There was a mercy in that. She licked her lips and cleared her throat. Everything was black, she reported. There were sweaters, shirts, T-shirts, and jeans in his clothes cupboard. But a jacket hadn't been among them, not a leather one at least.

'There was a lighter jacket, though, a windcheater,' she said. 'And a coat. Really long, like something from the Regency period. That was it.' A pause. And then she ventured, 'Why?'

Nkata told her.

'Someone must have taken it from the crime scene,' was her immediate assessment. To which she added, 'Sir,' in Lynley's direction as if the respectful utterance might indicate a newly found reverence for authority.

Lynley thought about what her conjecture implied. Two garments now were missing from the crime scene: a jacket and a waterproof. So were they back to two killers?

'P'rhaps the jacket points the *way* to the killer,' Havers offered, as if reading his mind.

'If our killer's worried about forensic evidence, then he should have stripped the body completely. What does taking only the jacket gain him?'

'Coverage?' Nkata said.

'He'd have had the waterproof to hide the blood on him.'

'But if he knew he had to stop somewhere after the killing – or if he knew he'd be seen on the route back to his digs – he couldn't exactly have a waterproof on. Why would he be wearing it? It wasn't raining on Tuesday night.' Havers still stood at the doorway. And her questions and statement were careful, as if she'd finally and gratifiyingly come to realise just how much a probationary figure she was.

There was sense in her remarks. Lynley acknowledged this with a nod. He went on to the postcards, saying as he used them to gesture with, 'Let me hear it all again.'

Havers shot a look at Nkata as if she expected him to take the bit. He read her meaning and said, 'I could do a quick A to Zed off the top of my head. But I'd miss fifteen letters in between. You take it.'

'Right.' She stayed at the door.

'I'd been thinking how any one of that lot—' with a nod to the cards on Lynley's desk – 'might have a motive to murder Terry Cole. What if he'd been cheating them? What if he collected their cards, took their hundred pounds each, and never put up the cards at all? Or at least not the number he said.' After all, she pointed out, how did a prostitute really know where – or even if – her cards were tacked up, unless she went out personally to check on them? And even if she walked round central London making stops at every phone box she came to, what was to prevent Terry Cole from claiming that the BT contract cleaners were sweeping the boxes free of cards just as fast as he could distribute them?

'So I decided to give each of them a call, to see what they had to say about Terry.' She got very little joy from the calls she'd made, however, and she had just begun to ring the number advertised on the schoolgirl card when she'd given the picture closer scrutiny and realised the girl looked awfully familiar. Fairly certain about her identity, she'd phoned the number on the card and said, 'Is that Vi Nevin, then?' when her call was answered. 'DC Barbara Havers here,' she'd said to the young woman. 'I've one or two points to clear up, if you have the time. Or should I ring you in the morning?'

On the other end of the line, Vi Nevins hadn't even questioned how Havers had come to have her number. She'd merely said in her sculpted RADA voice, 'It's after midnight. Do you know that, Constable? Are you trying to intimidate me?'

'She looks young enough to play the part of a schoolgirl in some punter's sex fantasy,' Havers concluded. 'And from the looks of her digs yesterday, I'd say—' She winced and halted, obviously realising what she'd just revealed about the rest of her activities on the previous day. She added hastily, 'Inspector, listen. I talked Winnie into letting me be part of everything. He really wanted me to stay on the computer, just like you ordered. He's absolutely in the clear on this. It just seemed to me that with two of us doing the interview instead of one, we'd be able to—'

Lynley cut her off. 'We'll talk about that later.' He gave his attention to the second of the two postcards that had been at the centre of his desk. The telephone number was the same as the number on the schoolgirl card. What was on offer was completely different, however.

Nikki Temptation was printed prominently at the top of the second card with the words *Discover the Mysteries of Domination* just beneath the name. And under that suggestion the mysteries themselves were alluded to: a fully equipped torture chamber, a dungeon, a medical room, a school room. *Bring Your Toys Or Use Mine* was the final enticement. The telephone number followed. There was no picture.

'At least we got the reason they left MKR Financial,' Nkata said. 'These birds, they take in anything from fifty quid an hour up to fifteen hundred a night, 'ccording to what my sources say,' he added quickly as if clarification was needed to keep his reputation unbesmirched. 'I had a word with Hillinger in Vice. Those blokes've seen it all.'

Lynley saw – reluctantly – how the various pieces of information they'd been gathering on Nicola Maiden were beginning to fit together. He said, 'The pager was for her clients then, which explains why her parents didn't know she had one but Upman and Ferrer – both of them with whom she'd been intimate – did.'

'You mean she was on the game in Derbyshire as well?' Barbara asked. 'With Upman and Ferrer?'

'Perhaps. But even if she was having them just for the fun of it, she was a business woman who'd want to keep in touch with her regular clients.'

'Giving them phone sex while she was away?'

'It's possible.'

'But *why* was she away?'

That was still the question.

'As to those blokes from the Peaks,' Nkata added, thoughtfully.

'What about them?'

'There was a blow-up in Islington. I'm wondering about it.'

'Blow up?'

'Nicola's landlady in Islington heard her having a row with some bloke,' Havers put in from the doorway. 'In May. Just before she moved house to Fulham.'

'I'm wondering if we finally got ourselves a rock-solid motive to pin to Julian Britton,' Nkata said. 'This bloke said he'd see her dead before he'd let her "do it" . . . something like that. P'rhaps he knew she was planning to leave law college and go on the game.'

'How would he know?' Lynley countered, testing the theory. 'Julian and Nicola were living more than two hundred miles apart. You can't be thinking he came to London, picked up a card in a call box somewhere, phoned the number for a nice session of whips-and-handcuffs, and found Nicola Maiden dressed up to use them. That's more coincidence than one case can bear.'

Havers said, 'He could have come to town for a visit – without telling her in advance, sir.'

Nkata nodded. 'He shows up in Islington and finds his woman tightening the nipple clamps on a bloke who's wearing a leather harness. That'd be something that could cause a row.'

That was, indeed, a potential scenario, Lynley agreed. But another existed as well. 'There's someone else here in town who might have been just as aggrieved to learn about Nicola's career plans. We need to find her London lover.'

'But couldn't that have been just another one of her clients?'

'Phoning as often as Upman and Ferrer both claim? I doubt it.'

Havers said, 'Sir, there's Terry Cole to consider, isn't there?'

'I'm talking about a man who killed her, Constable,' Lynley said, 'not about a man who was killed alongside her.'

'I'm not suggesting Cole as her London lover,' Havers said, her voice uncharacteristically careful. 'I meant Cole as Cole. To look at. To talk about. We've got our connection between them now – Maiden and Cole. Obviously, he was placing cards for her just like he was doing for the other tarts. But he can't have gone all the way to Derbyshire to collect more cards from her to put in call boxes especially since she wasn't in London to take calls from anyone who picked up her cards. So what was he *doing* there in the first place? There must be a further tie between them.'

'Cole's hardly the point at the moment.'

'Hardly the point? How can you say that? He's *dead*, Inspector. Do we need a bigger point?'

Lynley shot her a look. Nkata spoke quickly as if to head off a hovering confrontation. 'What if Cole was sent there to kill her? And he ended up getting killed himself? Or he was trying to warn her about something? Giving her the word to expect some kind of danger.'

'Then why not just phone her?' Barbara countered. 'Does it even make sense that he'd hop on his motorcycle and roar up to Derbyshire to *warn* her about something?' She took a step away from the door, as if getting closer to them could somehow win them to her way of thinking. 'The girl had a pager, Winston. If you're going to argue that Terry trekked all the way up to the Peaks because he couldn't get her by phone, why didn't he just page her? If there was danger that she needed to know about, there was too much of a chance it would get to her before Cole himself did.'

'Which is what happened,' Nkata pointed out.

'Right. The worst happened, and both of them died. *Both* of them. And I say we'd be wise to start thinking of them that way: as a unit, not as a coincidence.'

'And what I say,' Lynley said meaningfully, 'is that your assignment's waiting for you, Havers. Thank you for your input. I'll let you know if I want more.'

'But, sir—'

'Constable?' The way he said the word made it more than her title. At Lynley's desk Nkata stirred. He seemed to be hoping Havers would look his way.

She didn't. The hand holding her notebook fell to her side. Assurance was gone from her voice when she went on. 'Sir, I just think we need to work out exactly what Cole was doing in Derbyshire. When we've got the reason for his trip, we'll have our killer. I can feel that. Can't you?'

'Your feeling has been noted.'

Her bottom teeth chewed at her upper lip. She looked towards Nkata at last, as if hoping for direction. The other DC raised his eyebrows slightly, with a cock of his head towards the office door, perhaps telling her that the course of wisdom suggested she hot foot it back to the computer. She didn't take his meaning to heart. She said to Lynley, 'Can I follow it, sir?'

'Follow what?'

'The Cole end of things.'

'Havers, you have an assignment. And you've been told to return to it. When you've completed your work with CRIS, there's a report I want you to deliver to St James. After you accomplish that, I'll give you another assignment.'

'But don't you see that if he went all the way to Derbyshire to meet with her, there's got to be something more between them?'

Nkata said 'Barb . . .' like a cautious admonition.

'He had wads of dosh,' she persisted. 'Wads of it, Inspector. All right. Okay. It *could* have come from the card business. But he also had cannabis in his flat. *And* a big commission that he talked about. To his mum and sister, to Mrs Baden, to Cilla Thompson. I thought at first he was blowing smoke but since the card boy business can't even begin to explain what he was doing in Derbyshire—'

'Havers, I'm not going to tell you again.'

'But, sir—'

'God damn it. *No.*' Lynley felt the ground fracturing beneath his hold on his temper. The woman's obstinacy was working on him like a match put to dry tinder. 'If you're trying to suggest that someone followed him all the way to Derbyshire with the express intention of slicing open his arteries, that isn't on. Every piece of information we've come across takes us straight to the Maiden girl, and if you can't see that, then you've lost more than merely your rank as a result of your day trip on the North Sea last June.'

Her mouth clamped shut. Her lips thinned like a spinster's hopes. Nkata let out a heavy breath on the word 'damn.'

'Now.' Lynley used the word to gain time. He used the time to bring his temper to heel. 'If you'd like to request a placement with another DI, Havers, be plain about it. There's work to do.'

Five seconds ticked by. Nkata turned from the window. He and Havers exchanged a look that appeared to mean something to them but to Lynley was inscrutable.

'I'm not requesting another placement,' Havers finally said.

'Then you know what to do.'

She shared another look with Nkata. Then she gave her glance to Lynley. 'Sir,' she said politely. And she left the office.

Lynley realised that he hadn't asked her one question regarding her search through the files. But it was a fact that didn't occur to him until he'd replaced Nkata behind his desk. And then he felt that to call her back would be to give her the advantage. Which was something he didn't want to do at that moment.

'We'll take the prostitution angle first,' he told Nkata. 'That could give a man in love one hell of an incentive to kill.'

'It'd be ugly for a bloke, sussing out the fact that his woman's on the game.'

'And being on the game in London suggests the possibility of someone sussing it out here in London as well, wouldn't you agree?'

'I got no argument with that.'

'Then I suggest we begin by tracking the London lover,' Lynley finished. 'And I've a fairly good idea where to start.'

Chapter Sixteen

❮━━━━◆━━━━❯

Vi Nevin took the postcard from Lynley's fingers and, after glancing at it, she set it carefully onto the spotless glass coffee table that served both the buttery sofa and the matching love seat which formed a right angle at one of its corners. She had placed herself on the sofa, leaving the love seat for Lynley and Nkata to crowd onto. Nkata hadn't cooperated with the ploy, however. He'd stationed himself at the door to the maisonette, with his arms crossed and his body proclaiming *no escape*.

'You're the schoolgirl pictured on the card, aren't you?' Lynley began.

Vi reached for the portfolio she'd showed Havers and Nkata on the previous day. She slid this across the coffee table. 'I pose for pictures, Inspector. That's what I do and that's what I get paid for. I don't know who's going to use them for what and I don't really care. As long as I get paid.'

'Are you saying that you're just a model for sexual services that someone else provides?'

'That's what I'm saying.'

'I see. Then what's the purpose of having your phone number on the card if you're not the "schoolgirl" in question?'

Her gaze slid away from him. She was quick, fairly well-educated, well-spoken, and clever, but she hadn't thought quite that far ahead.

'You know, I don't have to talk to you,' she said. 'And what I'm doing's not illegal, so please don't act like it is.'

Explaining the finer points of the law to her wasn't his purpose in coming to see her, Lynley told her. But if she was engaged in prostitution—

'Show me where it says on that card that anyone pays me for *anything*,' she demanded.

If, Lynley repeated, she was engaged in prostitution, then he assumed she knew where the ice was thin and where it was not in her behaviour. That being the case—

'Am I loitering somewhere. Am I soliciting in a public place?'

That being the case, he continued firmly, he would also assume that Miss Nevin was cognisant of how loosely and generously the word *brothel* could be defined by a magistrate with little patience with linguistic gymnastics. He glanced round the maisonette lest she not comprehend the full meaning of his comment.

She said, 'Cops,' dismissively.

'Indeed,' was Lynley's affable reply.

He and Nkata had driven directly to Fulham from New Scotland Yard. They'd found Vi Nevin unloading Sainsbury's carrier bags from a new late model Alfa Romeo and when she'd caught a glimpse of Nkata as he eased his lengthy body from the Bentley, she said, 'Why're you here again? Why aren't you out looking for Nikki's killer? Look, I don't have time to talk to you. I've an appointment in forty-five minutes.'

'Then I expect you'd like us to be gone in advance,' Lynley had said.

She'd flicked a glance at both men, looking for meaning. She said, 'Give me a hand, then,' and passed two loaded carrier bags over to them.

She'd unpacked perishables into a large refrigerator: pâté, Greek olives, prosciutto, Camembert, dolmades ...

'Having a party?' Lynley had asked her. 'Or is the food part of the . . . appointment, perhaps?'

Vi Nevin had shut the refrigerator door smartly and walked into the sitting room where she'd taken up her position on the sofa. There she still sat, a retro-garbed figure in brogues and white socks, turned-up blue jeans, a white shirt with the sleeves rolled up and the collar at attention, a scarf knotted at the throat, and a pony tail. She looked like a refugee from a James Dean film. All that was missing was the bubble gum.

She did not, however, speak like a refugee from a James Dean film. She might have been dressed like a gum-popping devotee of bop, but she spoke like a woman either born to advantage or self-made to appear that way. More likely the latter, Lynley would think as he interviewed her. Every now and then, her careful persona slipped. Just a word here and there or a skewed pronunciation that inadvertently revealed her origins. Still, she wasn't what he would have expected to find at the other end of a phone box postcard advertising sex.

'Miss Nevin,' Lynley said, 'I'm not here to strong arm you. I'm here because a woman's been murdered and if her murder is somehow connected with her source of income—'

'That's where you always head, isn't it? Right to one of our clients. "She's a slag and she got what she was asking for. It's damn lucky she lasted as long as she did, what with her lifestyle and the blokes who take part in it." Which is what you'd like to put an end to, isn't it? The lifestyle. So don't tell me what you do or don't *intend* with regard to my "source of income."' She gazed at him evenly. 'If you only knew how many warrant cards get put to one side when a bloke's in a hurry to climb out of his trousers. Hmph. I could name a few names.'

'I'm not interested in your clients. I'm interested in finding Nicola Maiden's killer.'

'Who, you think, is *one* of her clients. Why won't you admit it? And how do you expect those clients will feel when the cops come calling on them? And what do you think it'll do for business once word gets out that I'm naming names? *If* I know their names to begin with. And I don't, by the way. We go by first names only, and that's not going to help you much.'

Across the room, Nkata took out his notebook, opened it, and said, 'We're happy to take what's on offer, Miss.'

'Forget it, Constable. I'm not that stupid.'

Lynley leaned towards her. 'Then you know how simple it would be for me to shut you down. A uniformed constable walking this street every fifteen minutes would, I think, do some damage to your clients' sense of privacy. As would the word slipped to one or two tabloids who might want to see if anyone worthy of public notice is paying calls on you.'

'You wouldn't dare! I know my rights.'

'None of which preclude the presence of journalists, *paparazzi* looking for everyone from film stars to members of the Royal Family, or your local bobby who's just keeping the streets safe for elderly women walking their dogs.'

'You bloody outrageous—'

'It's a nasty world,' Nkata cut in solemnly.

She glared at both of them. The telephone rang and she jumped to answer it. She said, 'What's your pleasure . . . ?' into the receiver.

Across the room, Nkata looked heavenward.

Vi said, 'Hang on. Let me check my book,' and she flipped through the pages of an engagement diary. 'Sorry. I can't manage that. Someone's already booked . . .' She ran her finger down the page, saying, 'I could do four o'clock . . . How long a session . . . ?' She listened, then murmured, 'Don't I always leave you fit for her afterwards?' And she jotted a reference into her diary. She rang off, stood with her fingers on the telephone as if in thought, her back to them. She sighed and said, 'All right, then,' quietly. She went into the kitchen and returned with an envelope, which she handed over to Lynley.

'This is what you want. I hope it doesn't break your heart to be completely wrong about our clients.'

The envelope had already been unsealed. Lynley slid out its contents: one piece of paper and a single message, assembled from letters that appeared to come from glossy magazines. *Two bitches will die in there own puke. They'll beg for mersey and get nothing but pain.* After reading it, Lynley handed the note to Nkata. The DC looked it over, then raised his head.

'Same as the others left at the scene.'

Lynley nodded. He told Vi Nevin about the other anonymous notes that had been found at the murder site.

'I sent them to her,' she said.

Puzzled, Lynley turned over the envelope and saw it was addressed to Vi Nevin, with a local postmark. 'But this appears identical to those.'

She said, 'I don't mean I sent them to her like this. Without a name. Like a threat. I mean they came to me. Here. At home. They've been coming all summer long. I kept telling Nikki about them when we talked on the phone, but she just laughed them off. So I finally sent them up to her with Terry because I wanted her to see for herself that the situation was escalating and we both needed to start taking some care. Which,' she added bitterly, 'Nikki didn't do. God, why wouldn't she ever *listen*?'

Lynley took the note back from Nkata. He examined it again, then carefully refolded it and stowed it into its envelope. He said, 'Perhaps you'd better start from the beginning.'

'Shelly Platt's the beginning,' was her reply.

Vi went to the window, which overlooked the street. She said, 'We were friends. It was always Shelly and Vi and it had been for years. But then Nikki came along, and I could see it made more sense to set myself up with her. Shelly couldn't cope with that, and she started causing trouble. I knew . . .' Her voice quavered. She halted. Then, 'I *knew* she'd do something eventually. But Nikki never believed me. She just kept laughing it off.'

'It?'

'The letters. And the calls. We hadn't been in this place—' With her hand, she indicated the maisonette – 'two days before Shelly got her hands on the phone number and started ringing. And then sending letters. And then turning up in the street. And then pinching the cards . . .' Vi went to the drinks trolley. An ice bucket stood on it. She lifted this, and from beneath it she took a small stack of postcards which she handed over. 'She said she'd destroy us. She's a nasty little jealous—' She drew a quick breath. 'She's jealous.'

The cards were the same schoolgirl advertisements that Lynley had already seen, except that each had been defaced, with various sexually transmitted diseases scrawled upon it in bright felt pen.

'Terry found those when he was making his regular rounds of the boxes,' Vi said. 'It was Shelly who did it, up to her tricks. She won't be happy till I'm ruined.'

'Tell us about Shelly Platt,' Lynley said.

'She was my maid. We met in *C'est la Vie*. Do you know it? It's a French bakery and caff over by South Ken Station. I had what you might call an arrangement there with the head baker – baguettes, quiches, and tarts in exchange for a few liberties in the gents' – and Shelly was there one morning packing chocolate croissants into her mouth when Alf and I went below stairs. She saw him give me the food afterwards without taking any money from me, and she got interested in what was going on.'

'In order to blackmail you?'

Vi looked grimly amused by the question. 'She wanted to know what she had to do to get her croissants for nothing. Plus, she liked the way I dress – I was doing a Mary Quant that morning – and she wanted a bit of that as well.'

'Your clothes?'

'My whole life, as things turned out.'

'I see. And as your maid, with access to your belongings—'

Vi laughed. At the drinks trolley, she took two cubes of

ice from the bucket and a small tin of tomato juice from the bottom shelf. She deftly mixed herself a Bloody Mary with the precision of long experience. 'She wasn't that kind of maid, Inspector. She was the other kind. She took phone calls from punters and booked their appointments for me.' Vi stirred her drink with a glass rod surmounted by a bright green parrot. She set this neatly on a cocktail napkin and returned to the sofa, where she placed the glass on the coffee table and continued her explanation. She'd been employing a middle-aged Filipino woman to book her clients prior to meeting Shelly Platt in *C'est la Vie*. But everyone employed middle-aged Filipino women as their maids these days, so she thought it might be an added interest to have a teenager acting the part instead. Fixed up, Shelly wouldn't look half bad. And, more importantly, she was so ignorant of the ways of the profession that Vi knew she would be able to pay her a pittance. 'I gave her room, board, and thirty pounds a week,' Vi told them. 'And believe me, that's more than she was getting doing knee tremblers outside Earl's Court Station, which was how she was supporting herself when I met her.'

They were together for nearly three years, she went on. But then Vi met Nikki Maiden and saw how much more was possible if the two of them set up a business together. 'We kept Shelly with us at first. But she hated Nikki because with her there, it wasn't just the two of us any longer. That's the way Shelly is, although I didn't know it when I first took her on.'

'"The way she is?"'

'She gets her hooks into people and thinks she owns them. I should have seen it when she first talked about what had gone on with her boyfriend. She followed him to London from Liverpool, and when she got here and found out he didn't want to *be* her boyfriend any longer, she started her routine: following him everywhere, phoning him constantly, hanging round his flat, sending him letters, bringing him presents. Only I didn't know it *was* her routine, you see. I thought it was a one-off: her reaction to her first love not working out.' She took a stiff gulp of her drink. 'Right bloody fool I was.'

'She did the same to you?'

'I should have seen, obviously. Stan – this was her boyfriend – came to the flat after she'd cut up his car tyres. He was all in a rage, and he must have thought he'd straighten her out. But he was the one who got straightened out.'

'How?'

'She cut him open with a butcher's knife.'

Nkata glanced Lynley's way. Lynley nodded. A killer did generally have a favourite weapon. But why kill Nicola if Shelly's object was Vi? he wondered. And why wait so many months to do it?

Vi seemed to recognise his unspoken questions. She said, 'She didn't know where Nikki was. But she did know Terry was thick with her. If she followed him, it was only a matter of time before he led Shelly right to her.' She tossed down more of the drink, picking up a napkin to dab against the corner of her mouth. 'Murdering little bitch,' she said quietly. 'I hope she rots.'

'"This bitch has had it,"' Lynley murmured, now knowing the source of the note that had been found in Nicola Maiden's pocket. He said, 'We'll need her address, if you have it. And we'll also need a list of Nicola's clients.'

'This isn't *about* clients. I've just told you that.'

'You have. But we've also been told that there was a man in London with whom Nicola had a relationship that was more than you'd expect between a client and . . .' He looked for a euphemism.

'His evening's companion,' Nkata supplied.

'And we may well find him among the men she serviced regularly,' Lynley finished.

'Well, if there was someone, I don't know about him,' Vi said.

'I have trouble believing that,' Lynley said. 'You can't expect me to believe that a flat like this is paid for solely from your earnings in the sex trade.'

'Believe what you want,' Vi Nevin said. Her fingers crept to the scarf at her throat and loosened it quickly.

'Miss Nevin, we're looking for a killer. If he's the man who initially installed Nicola Maiden in this maisonette, then you need to give us his name. Because if he thought he had one kind of arrangement with her only to learn that it was another, he might well have been driven to kill her and I dare say he won't like you hanging on here at his expense now that she's gone.'

'You've had my answer.'

'Is Reeve the bloke?' Nkata asked her.

'Reeve?' Vi reached for her glass again.

'Martin Reeve. MKR Financial Management.'

She didn't drink. Instead she swirled the liquid and watched as it slid across the ice cubes, which rattled against the side of the glass. She finally said, 'I lied about MKR. I've never worked for Martin Reeve. I don't even know him. I just knew about him and Tricia from what Nikki said. And when you asked about him yesterday, I followed your lead. Sorry. I didn't know what you knew. About me. About Nikki. And in my line of work, it doesn't make sense to trust the police.'

'Then how did you two hook up in the first place?' Nkata asked her.

'Nikki and I? We met in a pub. The Jack Horner on the Tottenham Court Road, near her college. She was being chatted up by a bald-headed bloke with a paunch and bad teeth, and once he left her alone, we had a laugh about him. We began to chat and . . .' She shrugged. 'We just got on. Nikki was easy to talk to. Easy to tell the truth to. She was interested in my work and when she knew how much money could be had on the job – more than what she was making at MKR – she decided to try it.'

'You didn't mind the competition?' Lynley asked.

'There wasn't any.'

'I don't understand.'

'Nikki didn't like it straight,' Vi explained. 'She only serviced men if they wanted quirky sex. Costumes, play-acting, domination. I'll do little girls for men who prefer it from twelve year olds without the risk of going to gaol for their pleasure. But that's about as quirky as I get. I'll give hand relief and do oral in addition to the little-girl bit, naturally. Otherwise, what I have on offer is exactly what Nikki couldn't be bothered with: romance, seduction, and understanding. You'd be amazed how little of that goes on between husbands and wives.'

'So between the two of you,' Lynley concluded, sidestepping any discussion of what marriage could do by way of putting a spanner in the works of a relationship, 'you covered all tastes and all inclinations?'

'We did,' she replied. 'And Shelly knew it. So she also knew that I wasn't about to choose her over Nikki if the two of them didn't get on once Nikki and I hooked up, which is why you need to talk to her. Not to some non-existent punter with money enough to give Nikki this place.'

'Where c'n we find this Shelly?' Nkata asked.

Vi didn't have her address. But she'd be easy enough to locate, she said. She was a regular at The Stocks, a club in Wandsworth that 'catered to individuals with specific interests'. She was, Vi added, 'special mates' with the barman.

'If she's not there now, he'll be able to tell you where to find her,' Vi told them.

Lynley examined her from his position on the love seat. He found that, despite the volume of information she'd given them, he still wanted to give her some sort of veracity test. Glibness was one of the essentials for survival in her profession, and the course of wisdom – not to mention the years of rubbing elbows with those who lived on the edge of the law – suggested that he take her word as something less than gospel.

He said, 'Nicola Maiden's movements in the months preceding her death seem at odds with each other, Miss Nevin. Was she using prostitution for a quick source of income to tide her over till her law work was profitable?'

'No law work is as profitable as this,' Vi said. 'At least not when you're young. That's why Nikki dropped out of law college in the first place. She knew she could go back to the law when she was forty. But she couldn't be turning tricks at that age. It made sense to her to get the money while she could.'

'Then why did she spend the summer working for a lawyer? Or was she doing more than merely working for him?'

Vi shrugged. 'You'll have to ask the lawyer.'

Barbara Havers worked the computer till midday. She'd left Lynley's office in the thrall of an effort to maintain such a strict control upon her anger that for an hour at the glowing screen, she'd been completely incapable of assimilating a single piece of information. But by the time she'd read through the seventh report, she'd calmed down. What had been rage metamorphosed into blind intent. No longer was her performance in the investigation a case of redeeming herself in the eyes of a man she'd long respected. It was now a case of proving to them both – to herself as well as to Lynley – that she was right.

She could have dealt with anything other than the professional indifference with which he was making her current assignments. Had she seen the slightest indication on his patrician face of scorn, impatience, disregard or loathing, she could have confronted him and they could have battled openly as they'd battled in the past. But he'd obviously concluded that she was criminally inadequate and hence beneath his notice, and nothing she could say by way of explaining her actions was going to make him think otherwise. Her only option was to prove to him how incorrect his assessment was.

There was a single way to accomplish this. Barbara knew that to do it was to put her entire career on the line. But she also knew that she had no career of value at the moment. And she never again would be able to have one unless she freed herself from the shackles of judgement that were currently binding her.

She began with the idea of lunch. She'd been at the Yard since early morning, and she was due a break. So why not, she thought, take a stroll during the time that was due her? Nowhere was it written that she had to take all her meals in Victoria Street. Indeed, a little walk through Soho would be *just* the ticket to prime her with a bit of exercise before she faced a few more hours sifting through the SO10 cases on CRIS.

She wasn't, however, so wedded to the idea of Soho and exercise that she considered walking there. Time was of the utmost importance. So she toddled out to her Mini in the Yard's underground car park, and she zipped up to Soho via Charing Cross Road.

The crowds were out. In an area of London that blended everything from book shops to skin shows, from street markets offering vegetables and flowers to sex shops selling vibrating dildos and pulsating ersatz vaginas, there would always be crowds on the pavements of Soho. And on a sunny Saturday in September with the tourist season not yet on the wane, those crowds spilled from pavements into the streets, making the going treacherous once one turned off the theatre-oriented congestion of Shaftesbury Avenue and began heading up Frith Street.

Barbara ignored the restaurants that called to her like sirens. She inhaled through her mouth so as to avoid the beguiling fragrances of garlic-laden Italian food that were carried on the air. And she allowed herself a sigh of relief when at last she saw the timbered structure – part arbour and part tool shed – that marked the centre of the square.

She made a circuit once, looking for a place to park. Finding nothing available, she located the building she was seeking and resigned herself to giving half a day's wages to a carpark a short distance from Dean Street. She hoofed it back in the direction of the square, digging from her shoulder bag the address that she'd found on the crumpled bit of paper she'd taken from a pair of Terry Cole's trousers in his flat. She verified the address: *31–32 Soho Square.*

Right, she thought. So let's see what little Terry was up to.

She rounded the corner from Carlisle Street and sauntered to the building. It stood at the southwest corner of the square, a modern structure of brick with a mansard roof and sash windows. A portico supported by Doric columns sheltered the glass-doored entrance, and above this entrance in brass were identified the occupants of the building: Triton International Entertainment.

Barbara knew little enough about Triton, but what she did know was that she'd seen their logo at the end of television dramas and at the beginning of cinema films, which made her wonder if Terry Cole had hoped to have a career as an actor, in addition to his other questionable pursuits.

She tried the door. It was tightly locked. She muttered, 'Damn,' and peered through the tinted glass to see what, if anything, she could deduce by having a look at the lobby of the building. Not much, as she discovered.

It was a marble plane, its surface interrupted by sepia-coloured leather chairs that apparently served as a waiting area. At the plane's centre, a kiosk stood, on which Triton's latest films were advertised. Near to the door curved a chest-high walnut reception station, and across from this a bank of three polished bronze lift doors reflected Barbara's image for her personal viewing pleasure.

On a Saturday, there were no signs of life in the lobby. But as Barbara was about to curse her luck and turn tail for the Yard, one of the lift doors opened and revealed a grey-haired uniformed security guard in the act of zipping his trousers snugly and bobbing to adjust his testicles. He stepped into the lobby, started when he saw Barbara at the door, and waved her off.

'Not open,' he called out. And even from behind the glass, Barbara could hear the glottal stop of the north Londoner, born and bred.

She dug out her warrant card and raised it to the glass. 'Police,' she called in turn. 'Could I have a word, please?'

He hesitated, looking towards an enormous brass-faced clock that hung above a line of celebrity photographs on the wall to the left of the door. He called, 'It's my lunch break.'

'Better still,' Barbara responded. 'It's mine as well. Come on out. I'll buy, if you like.'

'What's this about, then?' He approached the door, but he maintained his distance across a rippled rubber door mat.

'Murder enquiry,' Barbara said. She wiggled her warrant card meaningfully. *Please note*, her gesture told him.

He noted. Then he brought out a ring of what looked like two thousand keys and took his time about inserting the right one in the front door.

Once inside, Barbara got directly to the point. She was investigating the Derbyshire murder of a young Londoner called Terence Cole, she told the guard whose name tag announced him, unfortunately, as Dick Long. Cole had had this address among his things, and she was attempting to uncover the reason why.

'Cole, you say?' the guard repeated. 'Terence the Christian name? Never had nobody here called that. Far as I know. Which isn't saying much as I only work at the weekends, I do. Weekdays I'm Security at the BBC. Doesn't pay much either way, but it keeps me from sleeping rough somewhere.' He pulled on his nostrils and investigated his fingers to see if he'd mined anything of interest.

'Terry Cole had this address among his belongings,' Barbara

said. 'He could have come here passing himself off as an artist, of sorts. A sculptor. Does this sound familiar?'

'No one here's an art buyer. What you want is one of them posh galleries, luv. Over in Mayfair or places like that. Though it *does* look a bit like a gallery in here, eh? What about that? What d'you think?'

What she thought was that she didn't have time to discuss Triton Entertainment's interior decoration. She said, 'Could he have had a meeting with someone at Triton?'

'Or at any of the other companies,' Dick said,

'There're more groups than Triton at this address?' she asked.

'Oh yeh. Triton's only one. They get their name above the door 'cause they take up the most space. T'others don't mind as their rent's lower.' Dick jerked his head in the direction of the lifts and led Barbara to a notice board between two of them. On this she saw names, departments, and lists of companies. They represented publishing, film making, and theatre. It would take hours – perhaps days – to talk to everyone whose name was listed. And to everyone else whose name wasn't included because he or she played a supporting role.

Barbara turned away from the lifts and caught sight of the reception desk. She knew what such a desk meant at the Yard where security was paramount. She wondered if it meant the same here. She said, 'Dick, do visitors sign in?'

'Oh yeh. They do.'

Excellent. 'Can I have a look at the book?'

'Can't do that, Miss . . . er Constable. Sorry.'

'Police business, Dick.'

'Right. But it's locked up at the weekend, like. You can have a try of the desk drawers to make sure, though.'

Barbara did so, slipping behind the walnut counter and pulling on the drawers to no avail. Damn, she thought. She hated having to wait till Monday. She was itching to slap handcuffs on a guilty party and to parade him in front of

Lynley, shouting, 'See? *See?*' And waiting nearly forty-eight hours to take another step closer to the perpetrator of the Derbyshire murders was like asking hounds on the scent of a fox to have a bit of a kip once their quarry was in sight.

There was only one alternative. She didn't much like it, but she was willing to put in the time to give it a try. She said, 'Tell me, Dick, have you a list of the people who work here?'

'Oh, Miss . . . er, Constable . . . as to that . . .' He pulled on his nostrils again and looked uneasy.

'Yes. You do. Right? Because if something's dodgy in part of the building, you need to know who to contact. Yes? Dick, I need that list.'

'I'm not supposed to—'

'—give it out to anyone,' she concluded. 'I know. But you're not giving it out to anyone. You're giving it to the police because someone's been murdered. And you understand that if you don't assist in the enquiry, it might look like you're involved in some way.'

He looked affronted. 'Oh no, Miss. I never been to Derbyshire.'

'But someone here may have been. On Tuesday night. And to be a party to protecting that someone . . . That never looks very good to the CPS.'

'Wha'? You think there's a *murderer* works here?' Dick glanced at the lifts as if expecting them to disgorge Jack the Ripper.

'Could be the case, Dick. Could very well be.'

He thought it over. Barbara let him think. He looked from the lift doors to reception once again. He finally said, 'As it's the police . . .' and joined Barbara behind the reception desk, where he opened what looked like a broom cupboard containing reams of paper and coffee supplies. He took from the top shelf a stapled sheaf of papers. He handed it over. 'These're them,' he said.

Barbara thanked him fervently. He was making his mark for

the cause of justice, she told him. She would need to take a copy of the document with her, though. She was going to have to phone all of the employees listed, and she didn't expect that he wanted her to do so sitting in the empty lobby of the building.

Dick gave his reluctant permission and disappeared for five minutes to make a copy of the paperwork. When he returned, Barbara did her best to stride with dignity – and not dance with delight – out of the building. Maintaining her poise, she didn't take a look at the list until she rounded the corner into Carlisle Street. But once there, she dropped her gaze to it eagerly.

Her spirits plummeted. It was page after page. No fewer than two hundred names were printed.

She groaned at the thought of the job ahead of her.

Two hundred phone calls with no one to help her.

There *had* to be a more efficient way to serve up humble pie for Lynley's dining pleasure. And after a moment's thought, she decided what it might be.

Chapter Seventeen

DI Peter Hanken's plan was to carve an hour out of his Saturday to work on Bella's new swing set, a plan that he had to abandon not twenty minutes after his return from Manchester Airport. He'd got back from the airport by midday, having used up his morning tracking down the Airport Hilton masseuse who had worked on Will Upman on the previous Tuesday night. She'd sounded sultry, sexy, and seductive over the phone when Hanken had spoken to her from the Hilton lobby. But she'd turned out to be a thirteen-stone Valkyrie in medical whites with the hands of a rugby player and hips the width of a lorry's front bumper.

She'd confirmed Upman's alibi for the night of the Maiden girl's murder. He had indeed been 'seen to' by Miss Freda — as she was called — and he'd given her his usual generous tip when she'd finished tenderising his knotted tendons. 'Tips just like a Yank,' she informed Hanken in a friendly fashion. 'Has done from the first, so I'm always glad to see him.'

He was one of her regulars, Miss Freda explained. He made the drive twice a month, at least. 'Lots of stress in his line of work,' she said. Upman's appointment had been for one hour only. She'd seen to the solicitor in his room, from half past seven.

That, Hanken reckoned, gave Upman plenty of time to trot

from Manchester back to Calder Moor afterwards, to dispatch the Maiden girl and her companion easily by half past ten, and to scurry back to the Airport Hilton to resume his stay and firm up his alibi. All of which kept the solicitor in the frame.

And a phone call from Lynley made Upman a principal player, at least to Hanken.

He got the call on his mobile at home, where he'd just laid out the pieces of Bella's swing set on the floor of the garage and was standing back to study them as he counted the number of screws and bolts that had been included in the package. Lynley reported that his officers had tracked down a young woman who was Nicola Maiden's new flatmate, and he himself had just completed an interview with her. She'd maintained that there was no lover in London – an assertion that Lynley appeared to dispute – and she'd also suggested that the police have another chat with Upman if they wanted to know why Nicola Maiden had decided to spend the summer in Derbyshire. To this, Hanken said, 'We only have Upman's word for it that the girl had a lover in the South, Thomas.' To which Lynley replied, 'But it doesn't make sense that she'd drop out of law college yet still spend the summer working for Upman . . . unless the two of them had something going on together. Do you have time to wring more information from him, Peter?'

Hanken was happy – delighted, in fact – to wring away at the smarmy sod, but he sought some firm ground on which to base another interview with the Buxton solicitor, who so far hadn't called on his own lawyer to stand by his side during questioning but was likely to do so should he begin to believe that the investigation was tunnelling in his direction.

'Nicola had a visitor, just before she moved house from Islington to Fulham. This would have been on the ninth of May,' Lynley explained. 'A man. They had an argument. They were overheard. The man said he'd see her dead before he let her do it.'

'Do what?' Hanken asked.

And Lynley told him. Hanken listened to the story with a fair amount of incredulity. Midway through, he said, 'Hell's bells. Damn. Hang on, Thomas. I'll need to take some notes,' and he went from the garage into the kitchen where his wife was supervising his two daughters' lunch while his infant son dozed in a baby carrier set on the work top. Clearing off a space next to Sarah, who'd separated her egg sandwich into halves that she was smearing on her face, he said, 'Right. Go on,' and began jotting down places, activities, and names. He whistled softly as Lynley told the tale of Nicola Maiden's clandestine life as a London prostitute. Dazed, he looked at his own young daughters as Lynley explained the dead girl's speciality. He found that he felt torn by the need to make accurate notes and the desire to crush Bella and Sarah to his heart – grimy with egg and mayonnaise though they were – as if by that action he could ensure that their futures would be blessed with the safety of normalcy. It was, in fact, in consideration of his girls that Hanken said, 'Thomas, what about Maiden?' when Lynley had concluded his remarks by explaining that his next move was going to be to track down Vi Nevin's former flatmate Shelly Platt, sender of the anonymous letters. 'If he somehow found out that his daughter was turning tricks in London ... Can you imagine what that would have done to him?'

'I think it's more profitable to consider what that knowledge would have done to a man who thought he was her lover. Upman and Britton – even Ferrer – seem far more likely than Andy for the rôle of Nemesis.'

'Not when you consider how a father thinks: "I gave her life." What if he also thought her life was his to take away?'

'We're talking about a cop, Peter, a decent cop. An *exemplary* cop without a single black mark on his whole career.'

'Right. Fine. But this situation has sod all to do with Maiden's career. What if he went to London? What if he stumbled on the truth? What if he tried to talk her out of her lifestyle – and I want to be sick even *calling* it a lifestyle – but failed and knew there was only a single way to end it? Because, Thomas, if he didn't end it, the girl's mum would have discovered it eventually and Maiden couldn't abide the thought of what that would do to the woman he loves.'

'That goes for the others as well,' Lynley countered. 'Upman and Britton. They'd want to talk her out of it. And with far more reason. Christ, Peter. Sexual jealousy goes a greater distance than protecting a mother from having to hear the truth about her child. You must see that.'

'He found that car. Out of sight. Behind a wall. In the middle of the God damn bloody White Peak.'

'Pete, the children . . .' Hanken's wife admonished him, delivering glasses of milk to their daughters.

Hanken nodded in acknowledgment as Lynley said, 'I know this man. He doesn't have a violent bone in his body. He had to leave the Yard, for God's sake, because he couldn't stomach the job any longer. So where and when did he develop the capacity – the blood lust – to beat in his own child's skull? Let's do some digging on Upman and Britton – and Ferrer if we have to. They're unknown quantities. There are at least two hundred people at the Yard who can testify that Andy Maiden isn't. Now, the flatmate – Vi Nevin – is insisting we talk to Upman again. She may be temporising but I say we start with him.'

It was, Hanken realised, the logical place to begin. But something about tackling the enquiry from that direction didn't feel right to him. 'Are you personalising this in some way?'

'I might very well ask the same of you,' was Lynley's reply. Before Hanken could argue, the London DI concluded the call with the information that Terry Cole's black leather jacket was missing from the personal effects listed on the receipt that had been handed over to his mother on the previous morning. 'It makes sense to have a thorough look for it among the crime scene evidence before we rally the troops,' he pointed out.

And then, as if he wished to smooth over their disagreement, he added, 'What do you think?'

'I'll see to that at this end,' Hanken said.

The call concluded, he looked at his family: Sarah and Bella shredding their sandwiches and dipping the torn bits of bread into their milk, PJ awakening and beginning to fret for his own lunch, and Hanken's own darling Kathleen unbuttoning her blouse, loosening the nursing bra, and raising their son to her swollen breast. They were a miracle to him, his little family. He would, he knew, go to any extreme to keep them from harm.

'We're richly blessed, Katie,' he said to his wife as she sat at the table where Bella was inserting a carrot stick into her sister's right nostril. Sarah screamed in protest and startled PJ. He turned from his mother's milk and began to wail.

Kathleen shook her head wearily. 'It's all in the definition, I dare say.' She nodded at his mobile. 'Are you off again, then?'

'Afraid so, darling.'

'What about the s-w-i-n-g-s?'

'I'll have the set up in time. I promise.' He took the carrots away from his daughters, grabbed a dish cloth from the sink, and mopped up some of the mess they'd made on the kitchen table.

His wife cooed, crooned and comforted PJ. Bella and Sarah made tentative peace.

After directing DC Mott to paw through everything they'd taken from the murder site and after phoning the lab to make sure Terry Cole's jacket hadn't been accidentally omitted from the list of clothing sent onward for analysis, Hanken set off to duel with Will Upman once more. He found the solicitor in the narrow garage that abutted his home in Buxton. He was casually clad in jeans and a flannel shirt, and he squatted next to a fine looking mountain bike whose chain and gear cluster he was attending to with a hose pipe, a small spray bottle of solvent, and a plastic bristle brush with one end shaped like a crescent.

He wasn't alone. Leaning against the bonnet of his car, her eyes fixed on him with the unmistakable hunger of a woman desperate for commitment, a petite brunette was saying to him, 'You *did* say half past twelve, Will. And I know I'm not mistaken this time,' as Hanken joined them.

Upman said, 'I couldn't have done, darling. I'd always planned to clean the bike. So if you're ready for lunch this early—'

'It isn't early. And it'll be even less early by the time we get there. Damn it. If you didn't want to go, I just wish you'd told me for once.'

'Joyce, did I say . . . did I even bloody *hint* that—' Upman caught sight of Hanken. 'Inspector,' he said, rising and tossing the hose pipe to one side where it burbled water in a gentle stream from the garage out onto the driveway. 'Joyce, this is Inspector Hanken, Buxton CID. Could you deal with the tap for me, darling?'

Joyce sighed and saw to the water. She returned to the car and took up position in front of one of its headlamps. 'Will,' she said. *I've been patient as a saint,* her tone implied.

Upman flashed a smile at her. 'Work,' he said, with a jerk of his head in Hanken's direction. 'Will you give us a few minutes, Joy? Let's forget lunch and have something here. We can drive over to Chatsworth afterwards. Have a walk. Do some talking.'

'I have to pick up the kids.'

'By six. I remember. And we'll manage it. No problem.' Again, the smile. It was more intimate this time, the kind of smile that a man uses when he wishes to suggest to a woman that he and she speak a special language understood only by the two of them. It was mostly the language of bollocks, Hanken decided, but Joyce looked desperate enough to accept the central theme such a language implied. 'Could you make us some sandwiches, darling? While I'm finishing here? There's chicken in the fridge.' Upman didn't mention Hanken's presence or the privacy that Joyce's removal to the kitchen would effect.

Joyce sighed again. 'All right. This once. But I wish you'd start writing down the time when you want me to come over. With the kids, it's not exactly easy to—'

'Will do in future. Scout's honour.' He blew her a kiss. 'Sorry.'

She took it all in. 'Sometimes I wonder why I bother,' she said with absolutely no conviction.

We all know the answer to that, Hanken thought.

When she'd taken herself off to prove herself in the house-wife department Upman went back to his mountain bike. He squatted and sprayed solvent lightly on the gear cluster and along the chain. The pleasant smell of lemons rose round them. He spun the left pedal backwards as he sprayed, running the chain through one revolution round the gears and, when it was soaked, he leaned back on his heels.

'I can't think we have anything more to talk about,' he said to Hanken. 'I've told you what I know.'

'Right. And I've got what you know. I want to hear what you think, this time round.'

Upman took up the plastic brush from the floor. 'About what?' he asked.

'The Maiden girl moved house in London – months ago. She left law college round the same time, and she had no plans to return to her studies. She had, in fact, taken up an entirely new line of work. What do you know about that?'

'About the new line of work? Nothing, I'm afraid.'

'So why was she spending the summer working for you in the sort of job a law student takes in between terms for work experience? It wasn't going to get her anywhere, was it?'

'I don't know. I didn't ask her those questions.' Upman

applied the brush to the bicycle chain, meticulous with his cleaning efforts.

'Did you know she'd left college?' Hanken asked. And when Upman nodded, he said, exasperated, 'God's teeth, man. What's the matter with you? Why didn't you tell us when we spoke to you yesterday?'

Upman glanced his way. 'You didn't ask outright,' he said dryly. And the implication was clear: A man in his right mind never gave answers to questions that the police didn't ask.

'All right. My mistake. I'm asking now. Did she tell you she'd left college? Did she tell you why? And when did she tell you?'

Upman scrutinised the bike chain as he worked upon it, one inch at a time. The grime that resulted from the marriage of off-road dust, dirt, and bicycle lubricant began to liquefy into soapy brown globs, some of which plopped to the floor beneath the bike. 'She phoned me in April,' Upman said. 'Her dad and I had arranged her summer job last year. In December, this was. I let her know then that I was selecting her on the strength of my friendship – well, acquaintance, really – with her father, and I asked her to let me know at once if something more to her taste came along, so I could offer the job to some other student. I'd meant more to her taste in law, but when she phoned in April, she told me she was giving up the practice of law entirely. She'd got another job that she liked better, she said. More money, less hours. Well, don't we all want that?'

'She didn't say what it was?'

'She named a firm in London. I don't remember what she called it. We didn't dwell much on the subject. Just spoke for a few minutes, mostly about the fact that she wouldn't be working for me in the summer.'

'But she ended up here, anyway. So why was that? Did you talk her into it?'

'Not at all. She phoned again a few weeks later and said she'd changed her mind about the job and could she work for me as previously arranged if I hadn't got anyone yet?'

'She'd changed her mind about college?'

'No. She was still leaving college. I asked her that and she told me as much. But I don't think she was ready to tell her parents. They set a lot of store by her achievements. Well, what parent doesn't? And, after all, her dad had gone out of his way to arrange a job for her, and she knew that. The two of them were close, and I think she'd had second thoughts about letting him down when he was getting so much mileage from bragging about her. My daughter the lawyer. You know what I mean.'

'So why did you employ her? If she'd already left college, if she'd made it clear that she wouldn't be returning . . . She wasn't a law student any longer. Why hire her?'

'As I know her dad, I wasn't averse to going along with a little deception to spare his feelings, if only for the time being.'

'Why does that sound like pure cock to me, Upman? You had something going with the Maiden girl, didn't you? This summer job rubbish was nothing but a blind. And you damn well know what she was up to in London.'

Upman withdrew the crescent end of the brush from the bicycle chain. It bled slick soapy residue onto the floor. He looked at Hanken. 'I told you the truth yesterday, Inspector. All right, she was attractive. And she was intelligent. And the thought of having an attractive and intelligent young woman picking up the slack round the office from June till September didn't exactly set my teeth on edge. She would be a visual diversion, I thought. And I'm not a man who's distracted from his own work by a pleasant visual diversion. So when she wanted back in, I was happy to have her. As were my partners, by the way.'

'She had the lot of you hard, then?'

'Hell. Come on. We aren't playing at examine-the-hostile-witness. There's no point to your trying to trap me with slips because I'm not hiding anything. You're wasting your time.'

'Where were you on the ninth of May?' Hanken persisted.

Upman's forehead furrowed. 'The ninth? I'd have to check my diary, but I expect I had meetings with clients, as usual. Why?' He looked over at Hanken and appeared to take an accurate reading from the DI's face. 'Ah. Someone must have gone to London to see Nicola. Is that right? To talk her into – perhaps even to force her into – a scintillating summer in Derbyshire taking depositions from housewives estranged from their husbands. Is that what you think?' He got to his feet and went for the hose pipe. He turned on the tap and brought the nozzle back. He directed a gentle spray at the bike chain, moving it along and watching the muck wash easily away.

'Perhaps that was you,' Hanken told him. 'Perhaps you wanted to keep her from her "other employment". Perhaps you wanted to make sure you got the—' He felt his lip curl – '"visual diversion" you were looking for. Since she was so attractive and intelligent, as you say.'

'You'll have copies of my office diary on Monday morning,' was Upman's even reply.

'Names and phone numbers appended, I hope?'

'Whatever you'd like.' Upman nodded at the house, at the door through which the long-suffering Joyce had disappeared. 'In case you hadn't noticed, I already have attractive and intelligent women in my life, Inspector. Believe me, I wouldn't have gone all the way to London to arrange for another. But if your thoughts are heading in that direction, you might want to consider who didn't have access to such a woman. And I think we both know who that poor sod is.'

Teddy Webster ignored his dad's bark of an order. Since it came from the direction of the kitchen where his parents were still finishing their lunch, he knew he had a good quarter of an hour before the order came a second time. And since his mum had made apple crumble as their sweet for once – a rare occurrence considering that her usual offering was a packet of fig newtons opened without ceremony and tossed into the centre of the table while she was clearing the plates away – that quarter of an hour might stretch to thirty minutes, in which case Teddy would have plenty of time to watch the rest of *The Incredible Hulk* before his father shouted, 'Turn off that damn telly and get yourself out of the house right now! I mean it, Teddy. I want you out in the fresh air. Now. *Now!* Before I make you sorry I've had to repeat myself.'

Saturdays were always like that: a boring, daft repetition of every other boring, daft Saturday since they'd moved to the Peaks. What always happened on Saturdays was this: Dad clumped round the house at half past seven, bellowing about how *fine* it was to be out of the city at *last* and weren't they all just bloody *delighted* to have fresh air to breathe and open *spaces* to explore and their country's *history* and *culture* and *tradition* jumping out at them from every stupid pile of rocks in every dumb field. Only these *weren't* fields, were they? These were *moors* and weren't they all lucky and blessed and ... oh, just bloody *special* to live in a place where they could set off north just beyond their own house and walk for six billion miles at least without ever seeing a single soul? This wasn't a *bit* like Liverpool, was it, kids? *This* was heaven. *This* was Utopia. *This*—

Sucks, Teddy thought. And sometimes he said it, which set his father off and made his mother cry and sent his sister into one of her fits where she started whingeing about how was *she* ever going to go to *drama* school and become a real *actress* if she had to live in the middle of nowhere like some sort of leper?

Which *really* set Dad off at full gallop. And took the heat off Teddy who always used the opportunity to slink to the television and tune in to Fox Kids which, at the moment, was featuring that always wicked moment when pencil dick Dr David Banner got his knickers twisted *just* enough by some ignorant yobbo that he went into one of those very cool fits where his eyes went backwards into his head and his arms and legs popped out of his clothes while his chest swelled up and his buttons flew off and he was beating the shit out of everyone in sight.

Teddy sighed with pure happiness as the Hulk made hash of his most recent tormentors. It was exactly what Teddy wished that he could do to those pea-brain twits who met him at the school gates every morning and shadowed him – taunting, poking, tripping, and shoving – from the moment he set foot inside the school yard. He'd beat them to puke and guts and shit, if he was the Hulk. He'd take them one at a time or all at once. It wouldn't matter because he'd be more than seven feet tall and—

'God damn it, Ted. I want you *out* of here.'

Teddy scrambled to his feet. So deeply into his fantasy had he sunk that he hadn't noticed his dad come into the sitting room. 'It was nearly the end,' he said hastily. 'I wanted to see—'

His father held up a pair of scissors. He grabbed the flex from the back of the telly. 'I didn't bring my family to the country to have them spend their free time with their noses glued to the television. You have fifteen seconds to get out of this house, or the flex gets cut. Permanently.'

'Dad! I just wanted—'

'You need a hearing test, Ted?'

He shot towards the door. But there, he paused. He said, 'What about Carrie? Why doesn't she—'

'Your sister's doing her school prep. Would you like to do yours? Or will you be going outside to play?'

Teddy knew that Carrie was no more doing her school prep than he was preparing to perform brain surgery. But he also knew when he was defeated. He said, 'Play, Dad,' and he trudged outside, giving himself full marks for not sneaking on his sister. She was in her room mooning over *Flicks*, and writing loony love letters to some loonier actor. It was a bloody stupid way to spend her time, but Teddy understood. She had to do *something* to keep the bats from her brain.

Telly did that for him. Watching telly felt good. Besides, what else was there to do?

He knew better than to ask Dad that question, though. When he'd asked it at first – shortly after they'd moved here from Liverpool – the answer had been having a chore assigned to him. So Teddy no longer asked for suggestions when it came to free time. He took himself outside and shut the door, but not before he allowed himself the satisfaction of casting a baleful look over his shoulder as his father retreated into the kitchen.

'For his own good,' were the last words Teddy heard from his dad.

And he knew – with despair – what those four words meant.

They'd come to the country because of him: a fat little kid who wore pebble specs, who had pimples on his legs and braces on his teeth and breasts like a girl, who got bullied in school from day one. He'd overheard the Big Plan when his parents were making it: 'If he's in the country, he'll be able to exercise. He'll want to exercise – boys are like that, Judy – and then he'll lose the weight. He won't have to worry about being seen while he's exercising, the way he does here. And it'll be good for all of us, anyway.'

'I don't know, Frank . . .' Teddy's mum was the doubtful kind. She didn't like disruptions and a move to the country was Disruption Times Ten.

But Teddy's dad had made up his mind, so here they were, on a sheep farm where the sheep and the land were rented out to a farmer who lived in Peak Forest, which was the nearest thing to a town within miles. Except it wasn't a town, it wasn't even a village. It was a handful of houses, a church, a pub, and a grocery, where, if a bloke decided to sneak a packet of crisps for an afternoon snack – even if the bloke *paid* for them, mind you – that bloke's mum was sure to hear about it by six o'clock in the evening. And there'd be hell to pay.

Teddy hated it. The vast empty space that stretched into forever on every side, the great dome of sky that went pewter with fog at a moment's notice, the wind that whipped round the house all night and rattled his bedroom window like aliens trying to get in, the sheep that bleated like something was wrong but ran off the first time you took a step towards them. He just bloody hated the place. And as Teddy left the house and plodded into the yard, a piece of grit – shot by the wind like a missile – flew past his glasses, exploded into his eye, and made him yowl. He *hated* this place.

He removed his glasses and used the hem of his T-shirt against his eye. It stung, it burned, and his sense of grievance grew. Blurry of vision, he stumbled to the back of the house, where the Saturday morning washing was flapping and snapping on the line that was strung from the eaves to a rust-eaten pole near a crumbling drystone wall.

'Pooey, phooey, *poop*,' Teddy muttered. On the ground near the house, he found a long thin branch. He scooped this up, and it became a sword. He used it as he advanced on the washing, a row of his dad's jeans his target.

'Stay where you are,' he hissed at them. 'I'm armed, you lot. And if you think you can take me alive . . . Ha! Take that! And that! And that!'

They'd come from the Death Star to deal with him. They knew that he was the Last of the Jedi. If they could just get him out of the way, the Emperor would be able to Rule the Universe. But they couldn't kill him. AbsoLutely no way. They were under orders to take him captive so that he could be made an Example to All Rebels in the Star System. Well, Ha! And Ha! They would NEVER take him. Because he had a laser sword and *swish swish lash and swish*. But omigod. Hang on now. They had laser *guns*. And they didn't want to capture him at all! They wanted to kill him and ... Eeeeooooowww! He was completely outnumbered! Runrunrun!

Teddy turned and fled, waving his sword in the air. He sought the protection of the drystone wall that fronted the property and edged the road. With a leap, he was over. His heart pounded. His ears throbbed.

Safe, he thought. He'd gone into light speed and left the Imperial Star Troopers behind. He'd landed on an undiscovered planet. They'd never find him here in a zillion years. HE would be an Emperor now.

Whoosh. Something whizzed by on the road. Teddy blinked. The wind pummelled him like an angry ghost's fists, bringing water to his eyes. He couldn't quite see, but still, it looked like ... No. It couldn't be. Teddy peered to the right and to the left. He realised with horror where he'd landed. This wasn't a brand new planet at all. He'd taken himself into Jurassic Park! And what had lightninged by with the fury of hunger driving it was a velociraptor homing in on something for the kill!

Omigod omigod. And he had NOTHING with him. No high powered rifle, no weapon of any kind. Just a stupid old stick and what good would THAT be against a dinosaur with human flesh on its mind?

He had to hide. He had to be invisible. One velociraptor didn't exist without another nearby. And two meant twenty. Or a hundred. A thousand!

Omigod! He tore along the road.

A short distance ahead, he saw his safety. A yellow bin stood in the weeds on the verge. He could hide in there till the danger passed.

Whoosh. Whoosh. More raptors tore by as Teddy flung his body inside the bin. He lowered himself and brought the lid down firmly.

He'd seen what raptors could do to a person, Teddy had. They tore at flesh and sucked out eyeballs and crunched bones like they were McDonald's french fries. And they liked ten-year-old boys the best.

He had to do something. He had to save himself. He crouched within the safety of the bin and tried to come up with a plan.

The bin held the remainder of last year's grit: some six inches of it, left over from the winter when it was used on the road so that car tyres didn't slide on the ice. Teddy could feel the pebbles and shards of it biting into the palms of his hands.

Could he use the grit? Could he make it a weapon? Could he ball it up into a nasty missile that he could throw at the raptors and hurt them enough for them to leave him alone? If he did that, he would then have time to—

His fingers grabbed onto something hard, something buried three inches into the grit. It was slender and palm sized and when he dug round it with his fingers, he was able to free it and to bring it up into the weak light that came through the yellow walls of his hiding place.

Wicked, he thought. What a find. He was saved.

It was a knife.

Julian Britton was doing what he always did at the end of a mountain rescue: he was checking his equipment as he put it away. But he wasn't being as thorough or as careful as he usually was when organising and repacking his gear. His thoughts were far away from ropes, boots, picks, hammers, compasses, maps, and everything else they used when someone got lost or someone else got injured and a team was required to find them.

His thoughts were on her. On Nicola. On what had been and what could have been had she only acted the appropriate part in the drama he'd written for their relationship.

'But I love you,' he'd said to her, and even to his own ears the four words had sounded pathetic and stricken.

'And I love you back,' she'd replied kindly. She'd even taken his hand and held it – palm upwards – as if she intended to place something within it. 'Only it's not enough, the kind of love I feel for you. And the kind of love you want – and *deserve* – to have, Jules ... well, it isn't the sort of love I'm likely to feel for anyone.'

'But I'm good for you. You've said it enough times over the years. That's enough, isn't it? Can't the other sort of love – the sort you're talking about ... can't it grow from there? I mean, we're friends. We're companions. We're ... for God's sake we're *lovers* ... And if that doesn't mean we have something special together ... Hell. What does?'

She'd sighed. She'd looked out of the car window to the darkness. He could see her reflection in the glass. 'Jules, I've become an escort,' she said. 'Do you know what that means?'

The statement and the question had come out of nowhere, so for a moment he'd thought ridiculously of tour guides, travel escorts who stand at the front of a coach and speak into a microphone as the vehicle lumbers round the country-side with tourists crammed into its seats. 'You're travelling?' he'd asked.

'I'm seeing men for money,' she replied. 'I spend the evening with them. Sometimes I spend the night. I go to hotels and pick them up and we do what they want. Whatever they want. Then they pay me. They give me two hundred pounds an hour. Fifteen hundred pounds if I sleep in their beds for the night.'

He stared at her. He heard her clearly, but his brain refused to assimilate the information. He said, 'I see. You have someone else in London, then.'

She said, 'Jules, you're not listening to me.'

'I am. You said—'

'You're hearing. Not listening. Men pay me for companion-ship.'

'To go out on dates.'

'You could call them dates: dinner, the theatre, a gallery

opening or business party when someone wants a nice looking woman on his arm. They pay me for that. And they pay me for sex as well. And depending on what I do to them when it comes to sex, they pay me quite a lot. More than I would ever have imagined possible for fucking a relative stranger, to be honest with you.'

The words were like bullets. And he reacted as he would have done had she fired a volley through his body. He went into shock. Not the normal sort of shock when one's system has undergone a physical trauma like a motor accident or a fall from a barn roof, but the sort of shock that shatters the psyche so that one can only take in a single detail and that detail is usually the least dangerous to one's peace.

So what he saw was her hair, how the light was behind it, and how it shone through individual strands so that she looked like an earthbound angel. But what she was telling him was far from angelic. It was foul and disgusting. And she continued to tell him, and he continued to die.

'No one forced me into it,' she said as she took a boiled sweet from her bag. 'The escort stuff. Or the other. The sex. It was my decision once I saw the possibilities and once I knew how much I had to offer. I started out just having drinks with them. Dinner, sometimes. Or the theatre. All on the up and up, you know: a few hours of conversation and someone to listen, to reply if they wanted, and to look starry-eyed otherwise. But they always asked – every one of them, – if I would do more. At first, I thought no. I couldn't. I didn't *know* them, after all. And I always thought . . . I mean I couldn't imagine doing it with someone that I didn't actually know. But then one of them asked if he could just touch me. Fifty pounds for putting his hand in my knickers and feeling my bush.' A smile. 'When I had a bush. Before . . . You know. So I let him and it wasn't half bad. It was rather funny, in fact. I started laughing – this was inside, not openly, mind you – because it seemed so . . . just so *silly*: this bloke – older than my dad, he was – breathing heavy and going all teary eyed because he had his hand in my crotch. So when he said Touch me back please, I told him that would be fifty pounds more. He said Oh God, anything. So I obliged. One hundred pounds for feeling his willie and letting him poke round my bush with his fingers.'

'Stop.' He'd finally managed the words.

But she was eager to make him understand. They were friends, after all. They'd always been friends. They'd been mates from the moment they'd met in Bakewell: she a seventeen-year-old schoolgirl with an attitude and a strut to her walk that had always said I'm free for the taking only he hadn't seen that until this moment, and he nearly three years her senior, home from university for the holidays and consumed with worry about his father's drinking and a house that was falling down round their ears. But Nicola hadn't seen his worries then. She'd only seen an opportunity for some fun. Which she'd taken happily. He understood that now.

'What I'm trying to explain is that it's a way of life that works for me at the moment. It won't always, of course. But it does, today. And because it does, I'm grabbing it, Jules. I would be every sort of fool if I didn't.'

'You've gone bloody mad,' was his numb assessment. 'London's done this to you. You need to come home, Nick. You need to be with friends. You need help.'

'Help?' She looked at him blankly.

'It's obvious, isn't it? Something's wrong. You can't be in your right mind and be selling your body night after night.'

'Several times a night, generally.'

He'd clutched his head. 'Jesus, Nick . . . You need to *talk* to someone. Let me find a doctor, a psychiatrist. I won't tell anyone why. It'll be our secret. And when you've recovered—'

'Julian.' She drew his hands from his head. 'There's nothing wrong with me. If I thought I was having relationships with these men, there'd be something wrong. If I thought I was on the path to true love, there'd be something wrong. If I was trying to avenge a wrong or hurt someone else or live in a fantasy, I'd need to be carted to the mad house straightaway. But that's not how it is. I'm doing this because I enjoy it, because I'm paid well, because my body has something to offer men and while it's silly to *me* that they'd pay me to get it, I'm perfectly willing to—'

He'd hit her then. God forgive him, but he'd hit her because he was desperate to make her stop. So he struck her in the face with a hard, closed fist, and her head flew back and hit the window.

Then they stared at each other, she with her fingertips at the point where his knuckles had met her face, he with his left hand holding those knuckles and in his ears a high, loud singing like the whining of car tyres caught in a skid. And there was nothing to say. Not a single word to excuse what he'd done, to excuse what she was doing to both of them by the choices she was making and the life she was living. Still, he'd tried.

'Where did this come from?' he'd asked hoarsely. 'Because it had to come from somewhere, Nick. It's not how normal people live.'

'A nasty skeleton in the closet, d'you mean?' she'd replied lightly, fingers still at her cheek. Her voice was the same, but her eyes had changed, as if she was seeing him differently. Like the enemy, he'd thought. And he'd despaired right to the soles of his feet because he loved her so. 'No, Jules. I haven't got any convenient excuses. No one to blame. No one to accuse. Just a few experiences that led to other experiences. Just exactly as I told you. First an escort, then a brief little grope and feel, then . . .' She smiled. 'Then on from there.'

He read the truth of who she was in that instant. 'You must despise us all. Men. What we want. What we do.'

She'd reached for his hand. It was still clenched and she unclenched it. She raised it to her lips and kissed the knuckles that he'd used to bruise her. 'You are who you are,' she said. 'Julian, it's the same for me.'

But he couldn't accept the simplicity of that statement. He railed against it, even now. And he railed against her. And he determined to change her no matter the cost. She *would* see reason, he'd decided. She *would* get help, if that's what it took.

She'd got death instead. A fair trade, some would argue, for what she offered life.

Julian felt numb as he packed his mountain rescue equipment away in its haversack. His mind was swarming with memories, and he was willing to do just about anything to silence the voices in his head.

Distraction arrived in the person of his father, who toddled along the first floor passageway just as Julian was placing his haversack into the old mule trunk. Jeremy Britton clutched a glass in one hand, which was no surprise, and a fan of brochures in the other, which was. He said, 'Ah. M'boy. Here you are, then. Have you a minute for your dad on this fine day?'

His speech was clear, which caused Julian to eye his father's glass curiously. The colourless liquid suggested gin or vodka. But the glass was large enough to hold at least eight ounces of fluid, and since it was three-quarters empty and since Jeremy would have never splashed so meagre an amount into a glass whose volume could have held more, *and* since he wasn't slurring his words, it could only mean that the glass didn't hold either vodka or gin at all. Which in *turn* had to mean . . . Julian rattled his own head mentally. God, he was losing it by leaps and by bounds.

'Sure.' He did his best not to eye the glass or to sniff its contents.

Jeremy knew, though. He smiled, lifted the glass, and said, 'Water. The old local aitch-two-and-oh. I'd nearly forgotten the taste of it.'

The sight of his father drinking water was akin to having a vision of the Ascension into Heaven while hiking on the moor. Julian said, 'Water?'

Elizabeth George

'Best there is. You ever notice, my boy, how the flavour of water taken off our own land tastes sweeter than what you can get from a bottle? Bottled water, I mean,' he added with a smile. 'Evian, Perrier. You know.' He tipped the glass to his mouth and swigged down a mouthful. He smacked his lips. 'Spare a bit of time for your dad? I want to ask your advice, old chap.'

Puzzled, wary, amazed at the change in his father – prompted, it seemed to Julian, by nothing at all – he followed him into the parlour. There, Jeremy sat in his usual chair after pulling another round to face it. He gestured for Julian to take that place. Julian did so, hesitantly.

'Didn't notice at lunch, did you?' Jeremy asked.

'Notice what?'

'Water. Nothing else. That's what I was drinking. Didn't you see?'

'Sorry. I've had things on my mind. But I'm glad of it, Dad. Good for you. Brilliant.'

Jeremy nodded, looking pleased with himself. 'Had a think over the past week, Julie. And here's what it is. I'm going to take the cure. I've been thinking about it since . . . Oh, I don't know since when. And I think it's time.'

'You're going to stop? Drinking? You're going to stop drinking?'

'Enough is enough. I been . . . I've been blotto for something like thirty-five years. Thought I'd try the next thirty-five sober as a judge.'

His father had made this claim before. But he'd usually made the claim when either drunk or hung over. This time he seemed neither. 'You're going to go to AA?' Julian asked. There were meetings in Bakewell, others in Buxton, in Matlock, and in Chapel-en-le-Frith. Julian had phoned each town to get schedules of meetings that were sent to the manor house and then thrown away.

'That's what I want to talk to you about,' Jeremy said. 'How

378

best for me to beat the devil forever this time. Here's what I think, Julie,' and he handed over the fan of brochures he'd been holding, spreading them out on Julian's knees. 'These're clinics,' he said. 'Drying-out houses. You check in for a month – two or three, if you need it – and you take the cure. Proper diet, proper exercise, sessions with the resident shrink. The whole boiling lot. That's where you start. Once you've done the dance steps, you're into AA. Have a look, m'boy. Tell me what you think.'

Julian didn't need to look to know what he thought. The clinics were private. They were expensive. And there was no money to pay for them unless he gave up his work on Broughton Manor, sold off the hounds, and got a proper job. It would be the end of his dream to bring the estate back to life if he sent his father to a clinic.

Jeremy was watching him hopefully. 'I know I could do it this time, m'boy. I feel it in my gut. You know how that is. With a little help, I'll do it. I'll beat the devil at his own game.'

'You don't think AA's enough to help you?' Julian said. 'Because, you see, Dad, in order to send you to a place like this . . . I mean, I can check our insurance, and I will, absolutely. But I rather think they won't pay . . . We have the most basic health insurance, you know. Unless you'd like me to . . .' He didn't want to do it. And the guilt of his reluctance felt like a gouge incised on his soul. But he made himself say it. This was, after all, his father in front of him. 'I could stop work on the estate. I could get a proper job.'

Jeremy reached forward and hastily gathered up the brochures. 'I don't want that. Great Scot, Julie. I don't want that. I want Broughton Manor back in its glory like you do. I won't take you from that, son. No. I'll make do.'

'But if you think you need a clinic—'

'I do. I do. I'd get squared away proper and have a foundation. But if there's no money – and God knows I believe you, boy – then there's no money and that's an end to it.

Perhaps another day . . .' Jeremy stuffed the brochures into his jacket pocket. He gave his gaze moodily to the fireplace. 'Money,' he murmured. 'Damn me if it doesn't always come down to money.'

The parlour door opened. Samantha entered.

Just as if she'd heard her cue.

Chapter Eighteen

<hr />

'Sorry, luvs, members only,' was how Lynley and Nkata were greeted at a lectern at the top of a staircase in Wandsworth. This led into the dark cavity that appeared to be the entrance to The Stocks, and it was being guarded in the early afternoon by a matronly woman doing needlepoint. Aside from her curious ensemble, which consisted of a black leather sheath with a silver zip lowered to her waist and exposing pendulous breasts of an unappealing chicken-skin texture, she could have been somebody's grandmother and she probably was. She had grey hair that looked crimped for Sunday's church services and half-moon glasses at the end of her nose. She looked up over them at the two detectives and added, 'Unless you're wanting to join. Is that it? Here. Have a look, then.' She handed each of them a brochure.

The Stocks, Lynley read, was a private club for discriminating adults who enjoyed the diversion of domination. For a modest yearly fee, they would be offered access to a world in which their most private fantasies could become their most exciting realities. In an atmosphere of light food, drink, and music whilst surrounded by other like-minded enthusiasts, they could live out, witness, or participate in the realisation of mankind's darkest dreams. Their identities and professions would be scrupulously protected by a management committed to complete discretion while their every desire would be seen to by a staff devoted to accommodating their needs. The Stocks was open from noon until four a.m. from Monday to Saturday, bank holidays included. Sundays were given to worship.

The worship of what? Lynley wondered. But he didn't ask. He slipped the brochure into his jacket pocket, smiled affably, said, 'Thank you. I'll keep it in mind,' and took out his warrant card. 'Police. We'd like a word with your barman.'

Black Leather Sheath wasn't exactly Cerberus, but she knew her cue. She said, 'This is a private club for members only, sir. This isn't a disorderly house by any means. No one gets by me without showing his membership card, and when someone wants to join, he must bring with him a picture ID that includes his date of birth. We only give memberships to consenting adults, and our employees are thoroughly vetted for police records prior to being hired.'

When she drew breath, Lynley spoke. 'Madam, if we wanted to close you down—'

'You can't. As I've said, this is a private club. We've got a solicitor from Liberty, so we know our rights.'

Lynley aimed for patience with his reply. 'I'm very glad of that. I find that the average man on the average street is remarkably uninformed. But as you're not in that position yourself, you'll know that if we wanted to close you down or even attempt to do so, we'd hardly present ourselves at the entrance with our identifications. My colleague and I are in CID, not in undercover investigations.'

Next to Lynley, Nkata shuffled on his feet. He was looking as if he didn't quite know where to look. The elderly woman's décolletage was directly in his line of vision, and he'd doubtless never had the opportunity to examine flesh less suitable for examination.

'We're trying to locate someone called Shelly Platt,' Lynley explained to the woman. 'We were told your barman knows her whereabouts. If you'll fetch him, we can talk to him right here. Or we can go below. The choice is yours.'

'He's working,' she said.

'As are we.' Lynley smiled. 'And the sooner we talk to him, the sooner we take our work elsewhere.'

Reluctantly, she said, 'Right,' and punched a number on the phone. She spoke into the receiver but she kept her eyes glued to Nkata and Lynley, as if they'd bolt for the staircase otherwise. She said, 'I got two busies up here wanting to find a Shelly Platt . . . They say you know her . . . No. CID. D'you want to come up or shall I . . . You're sure? Right. Will do.' She replaced the receiver and inclined her head towards the stairs. 'Down you go,' she said. 'He can't leave the bar as we're shorthanded at the moment. He can give you five minutes, he said.'

'His name?' Lynley asked.

'You can call him Lash.'

'Is that Mister Lash?' Lynley enquired soberly.

To which the woman disciplined a smile from twitching her lips. She said, 'You've a pretty enough face, luv, but don't push your luck.'

They descended the stairs into a passageway where red lights hung above bare walls painted black. At the end of this corridor, a black velvet curtain hung over a doorway. And through this, evidently, lay The Stocks.

Music filtered through the velvet like beams of light, not the raucous heavy metal of punk guitars screeching like robots put to the rack but what sounded like a Gregorian devotional chanted by monks on their way to prayer. It was louder than monks would have chanted it, however, as if volume rather than meaning were what was required by the ceremony going on. '*Agnus dei qui tollis peccata mundi?*' the voices sang. As if in answer, a whip cracked like a pistol shot.

'Ah. Welcome to the world of S and M,' Lynley said to Nkata as he drew the curtain to one side.

'Lord, what's my mum goin' t'say to all this?' was the DC's response.

On an early Saturday afternoon, Lynley expected the club to be deserted, but that wasn't the case. Although he suspected that nightfall would bring many more members slithering out from beneath whatever stones they hid during the day, there were still present enough devotees of the dungeon to get an idea of what The Stocks was like when filled to capacity.

Central to the club was the eponymous mediaeval device of public punishment. It had positions for five miscreants, but on this Saturday only one sinner was paying the price for a malefaction: A thickset man with a shiny bald head was being whipped by a barrel-shaped woman shouting, 'Naughty! Naughty! Naughty!' with every blow. He was naked; she wore a black leather corset to which lace stockings were fastened. On her feet were shoes with heels so high that she could have toe danced with very little effort.

Up above them, a light fixture revolved. It was fitted with spots, one of which pooled illumination directly downwards round the stocks, and others which were appendant like arms, and which revolved as the fixture did and slowly illuminated the rest of the action within the club.

'Oh my,' Nkata murmured.

Lynley couldn't fault the DC's reaction.

To the rhythms of the Gregorian chant, several men in dog collars attached to leads were being led round the club by fierce looking women in black body suits or leather G-strings and thigh-high boots. An elderly gentleman in a Nazi uniform was attaching something to the testicles of a naked younger man manacled to a black brick wall while a woman strapped to a nearby rack writhed and shouted 'More!' as a steaming substance was poured from a tin jug onto her bare chest and between her legs. A blowsy blonde in a PVC waistcoat with a cinched-in waist stood arms akimbo on one of the club's tables as a leather-masked man in a metal g-string ran his tongue round the spike heels of her patent leather shoes. And while these activities were going on in nooks, in crannies, and in the open, a costume stall appeared to be doing a satisfactory business with club members who were hiring everything from cardinals' red cassocks to cats o' nine tails.

Next to Lynley, Nkata took out a snowy handkerchief and pressed it quickly to his forehead.

Lynley eyed him. 'For a man who once organised Brixton's knife fights, you've led something of a sheltered existence, Winston. Let's see what Lash has to say for himself.'

The man in question seemed completely oblivious of the activities going on in the club. He didn't acknowledge the presence of the two detectives until he'd counted six shots of gin into a shaker, added vermouth, and dashed into the mix a few splashes of juice from a jar of green olives. He screwed the cap onto the cocktail shaker and began to do the shaking, which was when he looked their way.

As one of the revolving lights hit him, Lynley saw where the man's sobriquet had come from: A ragged scar ran from his forehead and across one of his eyelids, cutting a swathe that had removed the tip of his nose and half his upper lip. *Slash* would probably have been more appropriate since the scar was obviously the legacy of a knife. But he'd no doubt wished to stay with the theme of the club. *Lash* suggested that an element of the voluntary had been involved in his maiming.

Lash looked not at Lynley but at Nkata. Abruptly, he set the cocktail shaker to one side. 'Fuck,' he snarled. 'I should of killed you when I had you, Demon. That ransom idea was bullshit on wheels.'

Lynley looked at his DC curiously. 'You two know each other?'

'We—' Clearly, Nkata was seeking a delicate way of framing the information for his superior officer. 'We met once or twice in the 'lotments near Windmill Gardens,' Nkata said. 'Some years back, this was.'

'Weeding out dandelions from the lettuce patch, I dare say,' Lynley noted dryly.

Lash snorted. 'We 'as doing some weeding, true enough,' he said, and then to Nkata, 'I always wondered where you wanked off to. I might of guessed it'd be to something like this.' He took a step towards them and peered more closely at Nkata. His misshapen lips suddenly parted in what went for his smile. 'You sod!' he cried, giving a bark of happy laughter. 'I *knew* I marked you that night. I swore up and down all that blood wasn't mine.'

'You marked me,' Nkata said congenially, tapping the scar that ran across his cheek. He extended his hand. 'How are you, Dewey?'

Dewey? Lynley wondered.

'Lash,' Dewey said.

'Right, then. Lash. You straight? Or what?'

'Or what,' Lash said and smiled again. He took Nkata's offered hand and shook it, saying, 'I just bloody *knew* I marked you, Deme. You 'as good with a knife. Shit. Just take a look at *this* sodding mug if you don't believe me.' This last was said to Lynley, and then back to Nkata, 'But I was always fast with the razor.'

'True enough,' Nkata said.

'What d'you lot want with Shelly Platt, then?' Lash grinned. 'Can't be looking for her usual.'

'We'd like to talk to her about a murder,' Lynley said. 'Nicola Maiden. Is the name familiar?'

Lash considered this as he poured martinis into four glasses arranged on a tray. He speared on toothpicks two stuffed green olives per glass and plopped them into the cocktails before replying. 'Sheila!' he barked. 'It's up.' And when the barmaid teetered over in platform boots and a fishnet teddy that showed far more than it could ever conceal, he slid the tray to her and turned back to the detectives. 'Great name, Maiden. For this sort of place. I'd of remembered. No. Don't know her.'

'Shelly did, apparently. And now she's dead.'

'Shelly's no killer. A bitch and a tart with a temper like a cobra. But she's never done harm that I ever heard.'

'We'd like to speak to her nonetheless. I understand she's an habitué of the club. If she's not here now, you might want to tell us where we can find her. I can't think you'd like us hanging about till she arrives.'

Lash glanced at Nkata. 'He always talk like that?'

'Born to it, he was.'

'Shit. That must put the mockers on your style.'

'I cope,' Nkata said. 'Can you help us out, Dew?'

'Lash.'

'Lash. Right. I forget.'

'Can,' Lash said. 'For old times and the like. But you didn't hear it from me. That straight?'

'Got it,' Nkata said, and he took out his neat little leather notebook.

Lash grinned. 'Chrisamighty. You *are* legit, eh?'

'Keep it to yourself, mate, won't you?'

'Shit. Demon of Death a cop.' He chuckled. Shelly Platt worked the streets round Earl's Court Station, he said. But at this time of day, they wouldn't find her there. She did the dusk-to-dawn shift and that being the case, they'd find her kipping in what went for her lodgings. He recited the address.

They nodded their thanks and slipped out of the club where, once in the black-walled corridor, they saw that a partitioned section of the passage had been opened. What had appeared to be an expanse of plaster painted in funereal hue was now folded to one side, and in its place was a small shop with a counter stretching its width. Behind this stood a ghoulish woman with purple hair worn in style reminiscent of the *Bride of Frankenstein*. Her lips and eyelids were highlighted in black. Body studs erupted from her face and her ears like a fatal visitation of the king's evil.

'Off your patch, you lot,' the woman said with a smirk as Lynley and Nkata passed her. 'But I c'n make it worth your while calling in, if you've a mind for it.'

Lynley's attention went to the goods she had on offer in her shop. Displayed within was everything from sex toys to pornographic videos. The counter itself was a glass case decorated with an artful arrangement of jars containing *Shaft: The Personal Lubricant* as well as leather and metal devices of various shapes and sizes, upon whose use Lynley didn't care to speculate. But as he passed, he caught sight of one of these devices, and his footsteps slowed, then halted altogether. He squatted in front of the case.

Nkata said, ''*Spector,*' in the agonised tone of a schoolboy whose parent has committed an unforgivable indiscretion.

'Hang on, Winnie,' Lynley said. And to the purple-haired woman, 'What is this, please?'

He pointed and she brought out a chrome cylinder. It was identical to the one he'd found among the items taken from Nicola Maiden's car.

'This,' she said proudly, 'is imported from Paris, this is. Nice, don't you think?'

'Lovely,' Lynley agreed. 'What is it?'

'A ball stretcher.'

'A what?'

She grinned. She brought out a life-size, anatomically correct, male blow-up doll from the floor behind the counter and stood him up, saying to Nkata, 'Hold him upright, will you? He's generally on his back, but in a pinch and for a demo . . . Hey. Grab him by the bum or something. He's not going to bite you, luv.'

'I'll keep mum about it,' Lynley said to Nkata, *sotto voce.* 'Your secret is safe with me.'

'Funny, you are,' Nkata said. 'I never touched any bloke's bum. Plastic or otherwise.'

'Ah. First times are always the most anxiety-laden, aren't they?' Lynley smiled. 'Please help the lady out.'

Nkata winced but did as she'd asked him, hands on the plastic buttocks of the doll who was turned sideways and stood astride the counter.

'Right,' the shop assistant said. 'Watch this, then.'

She took the ball stretcher in hand and unscrewed the two eyebolts on either side of it. This allowed it to open on its hinge so that it could be fastened neatly round the scrotum of the plastic doll, leaving its testicles dangling beneath. Then she took the eyebolts and replaced them, explaining that the dom screwed them in as far as the sub wanted, increasing the pressure on the scrotum, until the sub asked for mercy or said whatever predetermined word had been agreed upon to cease the torture. 'You c'n hang weights here as well,' she said pleasantly, indicating the loops of the eyebolts. 'It all depends on what you like and how much it takes to get you ready for relief. Most blokes generally want beatings as well. But then, that's blokes, isn't it? Sh'll I wrap one up for you?'

Lynley fought back a smile at the thought of presenting Helen with such a souvenir of his day's activity. 'Perhaps another time.'

'Well, you know where to find us,' she told him.

Out on the street once more, Nkata breathed out a gusty sigh. 'Never thought I'd see something like that. Whole place gave me the wim-wams, man.'

'"Demon of Death?" Who would think that someone meeting Mister Lash for a bout of knife play would go faint at the sight of a little torture?'

Nkata's lips twitched. Then he grinned outright. 'You call me Demon in public, man, our relationship is finished.'

'I do stand advised. Come along, then.'

It was, Barbara Havers decided, ridiculous to trek all the way back to the Yard once she'd bought her lunch off a cart selling stuffed pita bread at the end of Walker's Court. After all, Cork Street was so close at hand. Indeed, tucked just to the northwest of the Royal Academy, Cork Street was nothing more than a hop, skip, and jump from the car park where Barbara had deposited her Mini prior to seeking out 31–32 Soho Square. And since she was going to have to pay for a full hour of parking time whether she used the full hour or not, it seemed much more admirably economical to trot over to Cork Street right then while she was in the area rather than to return at the end of the day when she'd dutifully – not to mention uselessly – slogged through a few more hours at the computer terminal.

She dug out the business card that she'd found in Terry Cole's flat and confirmed the name of the gallery that was engraved on it. *Bowers*, it read, with an address on Cork Street. And *Neil Sitwell* beneath that. Time to see what Terry Cole had wanted or hoped for when he'd collected the card.

She sauntered along Old Compton Street, crossed over into Brewer Street, and dodged the Saturday shoppers, the traffic surging up from Piccadilly Circus, and the tourists seeking the Café Royal on Regent Street. She found Bowers without any difficulty because an enormous lorry parked directly in front of it in Cork Street was blocking traffic and incurring the ire of a taxi driver who was shouting imprecations at two men unloading a crate onto the pavement.

Barbara ducked inside what appeared to be not a gallery – as she'd originally supposed from the card, the address printed upon the card, and Terry's artistic aspirations – but instead an auction house not unlike Christies. Apparently, an auction was in some stage of preparation and the goods on offer were being unloaded from the lorry that was parked outside. These were paintings in ornate gilt frames, and they were everywhere: stacked in crates, propped against counters, hanging on walls and lying on the floor. Stepping around them and among them, blue-smocked employees with clipboards in their hands made notations which seemed to relegate each piece to areas signposted with the words Frame Damage, Restoration, and Suitable.

Behind a counter, a glass noticeboard was hung with posters that advertised past and future auctions. In addition to paintings, the house had sold to the highest bidder everything from farms in the Irish Republic to silver, jewellery, and *objets d'art.*

Bowers was much larger than it looked from the street, where two windows and a door suggested entrance to a humbler establishment. In reality, inside one room appeared to open into another and that one to another, all the way to the top of Old Bond Street. Barbara wandered through, looking for someone who could point her in the direction of Neil Sitwell.

Sitwell turned out to be the major-domo of the day's activities. He was a rotund figure with a rug on his head that made him look like a bloke wearing yesterday's road kill. When Barbara came upon him, he was on his haunches inspecting a frameless painting of three hunting dogs capering beneath an oak tree. He'd placed his clipboard on the floor and stuck his hand completely through a large rip in the canvas that ran from the right corner like a bolt of lightning. Or a commentary on the work itself, Barbara thought: It looked to her like a fairly dismal effort.

Sitwell withdrew his hand and called out 'Take this to Restoration. Tell them we'll want it in six weeks,' to a youngish assistant who was rushing by with several other paintings stacked in his arms.

'Right, Mr Sitwell,' the boy called back. 'Will do in a tick. These're going to Suitable. I'll be right back.'

Sitwell shoved himself to his feet. He nodded at Barbara and then at the painting he'd been inspecting. 'It'll go for ten thousand.'

'You're joking,' she said. 'Is it the painter?'

Elizabeth George

'It's the dogs. You know the English. Can't abide them myself. Dogs, that is. What can I do for you?'

'I'd like a word, if there's a place we can talk.'

'A word about what? We're overwhelmed at the moment. And we've two more deliveries coming in this afternoon.'

'A word about murder.' Barbara offered him her identification. Presto. His attention was hers.

He ushered her up a cramped stairway, where his office occupied a cubbyhole overlooking the showrooms. It was furnished simply, with a desk, two chairs, and a filing cabinet. Its only decorations – if they could be called such – were the walls. These had been covered with cork board from floor to ceiling and on them were pinned and stapled a veritable history of the enterprise in which Mr Sitwell worked. It appeared that the auction house had a distinguished past. But like a less noticed child in a home of high-achieving siblings, it needed to shout about itself to be heard above the notoriety given to Sotheby's and Christie's.

Barbara brought Sitwell quickly up to speed with regard to the death of Terry Cole: A young man – found dead in Derbyshire – had evidently kept a business card with Neil Sitwell's name on it among his belongings, she said. Would Mr Sitwell have any idea why that was the case?

'He was something of an artist,' Barbara added helpfully. 'A sculptor. He banged about with gardening tools and farming implements. For his sculptures, I mean. That's how you might have met him. P'rhaps at a show ... Does this sound familiar?'

'Not in the least,' Sitwell said. 'I attend openings, naturally. One likes to keep abreast of what's current in the art world. It's rather like honing one's instincts for what will sell and what won't. But that's my avocation – following the latest trends – not my main line of work. Since we're an auction house, and not a gallery, I'd've had no reason to give a young artist my business card.'

'Because you don't auction modern art, you mean?'

'Because we don't auction work by unestablished artists. For obvious reasons.'

Barbara mulled this over, wondering if Terry Cole had attempted to present himself as an established sculptor. This seemed unlikely. And while Cilla Thompson had claimed the sale of at least one of *her* rebarbative pieces, it didn't seem likely that an auction house would be trying to win her over by wooing her flatmate instead. 'Could he have come by here – or even met you elsewhere – for another reason, then?'

Sitwell templed his fingertips beneath his chin, 'We've been looking for a qualified picture restorer for the past three months. As he was an artist—'

'I'm using the word in its broadest sense,' Barbara cautioned the man.

'Right. I understand. Well, as he *considered* himself an artist, perhaps he knew something about restoring pictures and came here for an interview with me. Hang on.' He wrestled a black engagement diary from the top middle drawer of his desk. He began going back through the pages, running his index finger down the days as he examined the appointments listed for each. 'No Cole, Terry or Terence, I'm afraid. No Cole at all.' He turned next to a dented metal box in which index cards were filed behind dog-eared alphabetical dividers. He explained that it was his habit to keep the names and addresses of individuals whose talents he'd deemed useful to Bowers in one way or another and perhaps Terence Cole was among those individuals ... But no. His name wasn't among those on the index cards either. He was terribly sorry, Neil Sitwell said, but it didn't appear that he was going to be able to assist the detective constable with her enquiry at all.

Barbara tried a last question. Was it possible, she asked, that Terry Cole had come across Mr Sitwell's business card in another way? From what she'd learned from speaking to the boy's mother and sister, he had dreams of opening his own art gallery. So perhaps he'd run into Mr Sitwell somewhere, got into a conversation with him, and found himself on the receiving end of one of Mr Sitwell's cards with an invitation to call in sometime for a chat and some advice . . .

Barbara said it all encouragingly, without much hope of striking gold. But when she said the words, 'opening his own art gallery', Sitwell held up an index finger as if a memory had been jarred loose in his brain.

'Yes. Yes. The art gallery. Of course. I remember. It was because you first said he was a sculptor, you see. The young man never identified himself as a sculptor when he came to see me. Or even an artist, for that matter. He only confided that he hoped—'

'You remember him?' Barbara broke in eagerly.

'It seemed like a rather dubious plan for someone who spoke so—' Sitwell glanced at her and quickly shifted gears – 'Well, who dressed so . . .' Sitwell hesitated altogether, caught between the devil and the deep blue sea. Clearly, he realised that he was bordering on giving offence. Barbara's accent betrayed her origins, which were very nearly identical to those of Terry Cole. And as to her manner of dress, she didn't need a full-length mirror to tell her she was no candidate for *Vogue*.

'Right. He wore black all the time and had a working class accent,' Barbara said. 'Goatee. Cropped hair. A black ponytail.'

Yes. That was the chap, Sitwell confirmed. He'd been at Bowers the previous week. He'd brought along a sample of something that he thought the house might wish to auction. The proceeds of such an auction, he'd confided, would help him fund the gallery that he wished to open.

A sample of something to auction? Barbara's first thought went to the box of call girl cards that she'd found beneath Terry Cole's bed. Stranger things had been sold to the public. But she wasn't sure she could name any of them.

'What was it? Not one of his sculptures?'

'A piece of sheet music,' Sitwell replied. 'He said he'd read about someone selling a handwritten Lennon and McCartney song – or a notebook of lyrics, something like that – and he'd hoped to sell a packet of music he had in his possession. The sheet he showed me was part of that packet.'

'Lennon and McCartney music, d'you mean?'

'No. This was a piece by Michael Chandler. The boy told me he'd got a dozen more and was hoping for an auction. I expect he was imagining a scene in which several thousand fans of musical theatre queue up for hours, hoping for the chance to pay twenty thousand pounds for a sheet of paper on which a dead man once made a few pencil smudges.' Sitwell smiled, offering Barbara the sort of expression he must have offered Terry: one of tolerant and paternalistic derision. She itched to smack him. She restrained herself.

'So the music was worthless?' Barbara asked.

'Not at all.' Sitwell went on to explain that the music might have been worth a fortune, but it made no difference because it belonged to the Chandler estate no matter how it happened to come into Terry Cole's possession. So Bowers couldn't auction it off unless the Chandler estate authorised a sale. In which case, the money would go to the surviving Chandlers anyway.

'So how *did* the music come to be in his possession?'

'Oxfam? Jumble sale? I don't know. People sometimes toss out valuable belongings without realising, don't they? Or they shove them away in a suitcase or a box and the suitcase or box falls into someone else's hands. At any rate, the boy didn't say and I didn't ask. I did offer to track down the solicitors for the Chandler estate and turn the music over to them, to pass on to the widow and children. But Cole preferred to do that himself, hoping – he said – that there'd be a reward, at least, for handing over found property.'

'Found property?'

'That's what he called it.'

The only question the boy had at the end of their meeting

was to enquire how best to find the Chandler solicitors. Sitwell had directed him to King-Ryder Productions since – as everyone who'd been even moderately conscious for the last two decades knew – Michael Chandler and David King-Ryder had been partners until Michael Chandler's death. 'I suppose I should have pointed him towards the King-Ryder estate as well, come to think of it,' Sitwell said contemplatively, adding 'Poor sod,' in apparent reference to David King-Ryder's suicide earlier that summer. 'But as the production company's still up and running I thought it made sense to start with them.'

What, Barbara thought, an intriguing wrinkle. She wondered if it was on the blanket of the murder or part of another bed entirely.

Into her silence, Sitwell waxed apologetic. He was sorry he couldn't be more helpful. There'd been nothing sinister about the boy's visit. Nothing exceptional about it, either. Sitwell had forgotten altogether that he'd ever met him and he still couldn't say how Terry Cole had come to have his business card because he still couldn't recall ever handing him one.

'He took one,' Barbara said and indicated a card holder on Sitwell's desk with a nod of her head.

'Oh. I see. I don't exactly remember him doing so, but I suppose he might have. I wonder why.'

'For his chewing gum,' she told him, thinking, And thank God for that.

She made her way back out to the street. There, she dug out of her bag the roster of employees that Dick Long had given her at 31–32 Soho Square. The list was alphabetical by employee surname. It included the office telephone number of the person in question, the home address and phone number, and the organisation for which each individual worked.

Barbara scanned the list till she'd come up with what she was looking for.

King-Ryder Productions, she read next to the tenth name down.

Bingo, she thought.

Security was non-existent at Shelly Platt's address. She lived not far from Earl's Court Station, in a conversion that had once been protected by the sort of door whose lock could be released by a resident pushing a buzzer from within an individual flat. Now, however, the door stood open. When, in an automatic response to seeing it ajar, Lynley paused to examine its locking mechanism, he saw that while the door itself had the requisite parts, the jamb that surrounded it had been destroyed sometime in the past. The door was still capable of swinging shut, but it caught upon nothing. *Burgle At Will* could have been the building's epigraph.

There was no lift, so Lynley and Nkata headed for the stairs at the far end of the ground floor corridor. Shelly lived on the fourth floor, which gave both men an opportunity to assess their physical condition. Nkata's was better, Lynley discovered. His lips had never so much as tasted tobacco. That abstinence – not to mention the man's insufferable youth – showed. But Nkata was considerate enough to mention neither. Although the blasted man *did* pretend to pause on the second floor mezzanine to admire what passed for a view and to give Lynley a breather, which he would have been damned before taking in front of his subordinate.

There were two flats on the fourth floor, one facing the street and one overlooking what lay behind the building. Shelly Platt lived in this latter accommodation, which proved to be a small bed-sit.

They had to rap on the door several times to get a response from within. When it was finally opened the length of an insubstantial security chain, a squinting face with sleep-modified orange hair peered out at them.

'Wha'? Oh. Two of you, is it? No offence, luv. I don't do black. Not prejudiced, mind you. Jus' a deal I got with a three-way girl who's getting on in years. I c'n give you her number, if you want.' The girl had the distinctly adenoidal accent of a woman who'd spent her formative years just north of the Mersey.

'Miss Platt?' Lynley asked.

'When I'm conscious.' She grinned. Her teeth were grey. 'Don't get your type round here much. Wha' d'you have in mind?'

'Conversation.' Lynley produced his warrant card and reacted quickly with his foot when she sought to slam the door. 'CID,' he told her. 'We'd like a word, Miss Platt.'

'You lot woke me up.' She was suddenly aggrieved. 'You c'n come back later when I've had me kip.'

'I doubt you want us to do that,' Lynley told her. 'Especially if you're in the midst of an engagement later. That could put a damper on business. Let us in, please.'

She said, 'Oh fook it,' then slid the chain off the door. She left them to open it for themselves.

Lynley pushed it inward to reveal a single room with a sash window covered by the sort of beaded curtain one usually found in doorways. Beneath this window, a mattress on the floor served as a bed, and Shelly Platt shuffled to this on bare feet and then walked across it to a heap of denim that turned out to be a pair of overalls. These she pulled on over what little she was wearing: an extremely faded T-shirt printed with the instantly recognisable face of the *Les Miserables* street urchin. She scooped up a pair of moccasins and slid her feet into them. The moccasins had been beaded at one time, but what was left of their decoration consisted of tiny turquoise baubles that trailed along behind her on strings when she walked.

The bed was unmade, its counterpane an Indian bedspread of yellow and orange, its single blanket a striped affair of purple and pink with a well-frayed satin border. Shelly left this behind and walked across the room to a wash basin where she filled a pan. This she set on one of the burners of a hot plate that stood atop a scarred chest of drawers.

There was only a single seat in the room: a black futon
marked with stains, which were all of a similar grey hue.
Like clouds, these took a variety of shapes. One could use the
imagination and see in them everything from unicorns to seals.
Shelly nodded towards the futon as she padded back to the bed.
'You c'n park it there if you want,' she said indifferently. 'One
of you'll have to stand.'

Neither of them moved towards the grubby bit of furniture.
She said, 'Suit yourselves, then,' and plopped down on the
mattress, snatching up one of its two pillows which she cradled
against her stomach. She kicked out of the way another heap
of clothing – a red PVC mini skirt, black net stockings with
a suspender belt still attached, and a green top that appeared
to carry stains of a colour similar to those on the futon. She
observed Lynley and Nkata emotionlessly, from eyes that were
notable for their lifelessness, as well as for the skin beneath
them, which gave her the unappealing addicted-to-heroin look
that fashion magazines had been featuring in their models
lately. 'Well? What d'you lot want? You said CID, not vice.
So this i'n't nothing to do with business, is it?'

Lynley removed from his jacket pocket the anonymous letter
that Vi Nevin had shown them earlier in the day. He handed
it over. Shelly made much of giving it a thorough perusal,
sucking in on her lower lip and pinching it between her teeth
thoughtfully.

As she did so, Nkata flipped open his notebook and adjusted
the lead in his propelling pencil while Lynley gathered information by allowing his glance the freedom of wandering round
the room. It possessed two notable features, aside from the
unmistakable odour of sexual intercourse which was barely
covered by the scent of jasmine incense recently burned. One
was an old travelling trunk that was open upon its contents of
black leather garments, manacles, masks, whips and the like.
The other was a collection of photographs that were pinned
to the walls. These were of two subjects only: a youngish lout

usually pictured with an electric guitar slung somewhere about his person and Vi Nevin in a variety of poses from seductive to playful: childlike of body and coy of face.

Shelly saw Lynley looking at these when she raised her head from studying the anonymous letter. She said, 'So? Wha' of it, anyway?' in apparent reference to what she was holding.

'Did you send it?' Lynley asked her.

'I can't *believe* she'd call the cops on this. Wha' a flaming div *she's* turned out.'

'So you did send it? And others like it?'

'I di'n't say that, did I?' Shelly flung the letter to the floor. She sprawled on her stomach and unearthed a gaily printed box from beneath several yellowed copies of the *Daily Express.* It contained chocolate truffles which she picked through to find one to her liking. She used her tongue against its entire surface before easing it slowly into her mouth. Her cheeks moved like bellows as she made much of sucking it. She offered a moan of putative pleasure.

Across the room, Nkata looked like a man who'd just begun wondering how his day could possibly get worse.

'Where were you on Tuesday night?' It was largely a pro forma question. Lynley couldn't imagine this girl having the wits – not to mention the strength – to dispatch two able-bodied young adults, no matter what Vi Nevin thought otherwise. Nonetheless, he asked it. There was never any way to know how much information might be obtained by a simple show of police suspicion.

'Where I always am,' she replied, easing herself down so that she was propped on one elbow with her hand supporting her lank-haired orange head. 'I hang about Earl's Court Station ... so I c'n give directions to anyone lost when he gets off the tube, natcherly—' this with a smirk – 'I was there last night. I'll be there tonight. I was there on Tuesday night as well. Why? Vi saying something different, is she?'

'She's saying you sent her letters. She's saying you've stalked her for a number of months.'

'Listen to her,' Shelly said derisively. 'This's a free country last time I looked. I c'n go where I want an' if she just happens to be there, it's too bloody bad. For *her*, that is. *I* don't give a fook one way or th'other.'

'Even if she's with Nicola Maiden?'

Shelly said nothing in reply, merely fingering through her chocolates for another piece. She was skeletally thin beneath her overalls, and the unappealing condition of her teeth gave mute testimony to how she managed it despite a diet of truffles. She said, 'Bitches. Users, those two are. I should of seen it sooner, only I thought being mates meant something to certain people. Which, of course, it di'n't. I hope they pay for how they treated me.'

'Nicola Maiden has done,' Lynley told her. 'She was murdered on Tuesday night. Have you someone who can verify your whereabouts between ten and midnight, Miss Platt?'

'Murdered?' Shelly sat up straight. 'Nikki Maiden murdered? How? When? *I* di'n't ever . . . You saying she was *murdered*? Fook. Hell. I got to ring Vi. I *got* to ring Vi.' She popped to her feet and went to the telephone which, like the hot plate, was on the chest of drawers. There, the water in the pan had begun to boil, which offered Shelly a moment's distraction in her quest to contact Vi Nevin. She carried the pan to the basin where she poured some of the water into a lavender cup, saying, '*Murdered*. How is she? Vi's okay, right? No one did nothing to Vi, did they?'

'She's fine.' Lynley was curious about the sudden change in the young woman: what it said about her, what it said about the case.

'She asked you to come and tell me, di'n't she? Fook. Poor kid.' Shelly opened a cabinet above the wash basin and took from it a jar of Gold Blend, a second jar of coffee creamer, and a box of sugar. She excavated in the coffee creamer for a grimy-looking spoon. She used it to measure everything into her cup, stirring vigorously between each measurement and dipping the spoon liberally into the next ingredient. She performed each step without drying the utensil. By the end, it was thickly coated with an unappetising patina the colour of mud. 'Well, steady on, anyway,' she said, having apparently used the coffee-making time to reflect upon the information Lynley had brought to her. 'It's not like I'm going to run right over, am I, no matter *what* she wants. She did wrong by me, and she bloody well knows it and she can just *ask* me nice if she wants me back. And I might not go, mind you. I got my pride.'

Lynley wondered if she'd heard his earlier question. He wondered if she understood what his having asked it implied: not only about her place in the investigation into Nicola Maiden's murder but also about the state of her relationship with Vi Nevin. He said, 'Your having sent threatening letters puts you under suspicion, Miss Platt. You do understand that, don't you? So you're going to need to produce whoever can verify your whereabouts on Tuesday night between ten and midnight.'

'But Vi knows I'd never . . .' Shelly frowned. Something apparently made its way into her consciousness, like a mole burrowing towards the roots of a rose bush. Her face illustrated what her mind was assembling: If the police were standing there in her bedsit, putting the frighteners on her about Nikki Maiden's death, there could be only one reason for their visit and only one person who'd pointed them towards her. 'Vi sent you to me, didn't she? Vi . . . sent . . . you . . . to . . . *me*. Vi thinks *I* took Nikki for an airing. Fook. That bitch. That rotten little *bitch*. She'll do *anything* to get back at me, won't she?'

'To get back for what?' Nkata asked. The guitar-wielding lout leered over his shoulder from an overlarge photograph, tongue hanging out. A line of studs pierced it. A silver chain dangled from one of the studs, looping across his cheek to a ring in his ear. 'To get back at you for what?' Nkata repeated patiently, his pencil poised and his face all interest.

'For sneaking to Prongbreath Reeve, that's for what,' Shelly declared.

'MKR Financial Management?' Nkata asked. 'Martin Reeve?'

'As ever bloody was.' Shelly marched over to the mattress, her coffee mug in her hand, unmindful of the hot liquid that sloshed onto the floor. She squatted, rooted for a truffle, and plopped it into the mug along with the coffee. Another chocolate she popped into her mouth. She sucked energetically and with intense concentration. This appeared to be directed – at long last – at the moderate peril of her situation. 'Okay, so I told him about *everything*,' she announced. 'So bloody what? He had a *right* to know they were lying to him. Oh, he didn't *deserve* to know, little wanker that he is, but since they were doing to him what they did to *me* and since they were going to *keep* bloody doing it to everyone else in sight as long as they could get away with it, then he had a right to know. Because if people just use other people like that, then they bloody ought to *pay*. One way or another, they bloody ought to pay. Just like the punters, is what I say.'

Nkata looked like a man who was listening to Greek and attempting to write a translation in Latin. Lynley didn't feel a great deal more clarity at his end. He said, 'Miss Platt, what are you talking about?'

'I'm talking about Prongbreath Reeve, I am. Vi and Nikki milked him like a cow and when their pockets were full—' Obviously, she wasn't a woman who clung to the unity of her figurative language – 'they did a bunk on him. Only they made sure they took their punters with them when they scarpered. They were setting themselfs up to cost the Prong dear by going into business for themselfs, Nikki and Vi were, and I didn't think it was fair. So I told him.'

'So Vi Nevin did work for Martin Reeve?' Lynley asked Shelly.

'Course she did. Both of them did. Tha's how they met.'

'Did you work for him as well?'

She snorted. 'Not bloody likely that. Oh I tried, I did. Right when Vi got hired, I tried. But *I* wasn't the type he was looking for, Prongbreath said. *He* wanted *refinement*, he said. He wanted his girls to make *conversation* and know which *fork* to use with the *fish knife* and watch an *opera* without falling asleep and go to a *drinks party* on the arm of some ugly fat bloke who wants to pretend she's his girlfriend for a night and—'

'I think we've got the idea,' Lynley cut in. 'But let me make sure so there's no confusion: MKR is an escort service.'

'Posing as a financial management firm,' Nkata added.

'Is that what you're saying?' Lynley asked Shelly. 'Are you saying that both Nicola and Vi worked for MKR as escorts until they broke away to form their own business? Is that right, Miss Platt?'

'Right as rain,' she asserted. 'Right as a bleeding hurricane. He hires girls, does Martin, and he calls them trainees for some flaming money business that don't even exist in the first place. He sits them down with a slew of books they're supposed to study from to learn the "business", and after 'bout a week he asks them will they do him a favour and act like the date of one of MKR's big clients in town for a conference and wanting to go to dinner. He'll pay them *extra*, he says, if they'll do it just this once. And just this once turns into just another time and by the time they figger what MKR's *really* about they're seeing they can make a lot more dosh acting like dates for Korean computer salesmen or Arab oil blokes or American politicos or ... whoever than they could ever make doing whatever else they was doing when they came to work for Prongbreath in the first place. And they can make even *more* if they give their *companion* a bit more than their *company* for the evening. Which is when the Prong introduces them to what his business *really* is. Which has sod all to do with investing anyone's money anywhere, believe you me.'

'How did you learn all this?' Lynley asked.

'Vi brought Nikki home once. They were talking. I listened. Vi got hired by the Prong different, and they were telling their stories to each other to compare.'

'Vi's was?'

'Different, like I said. She was the only escort he ever hired from the street. The rest were students. College girls who wanted to work part time. But Vi worked the game by sticking up her card in call boxes—'

'With you as her maid?'

'Yeah. Tha's right. And Prongbreath picked up one of her cards, liked the look of her – I s'pose he didn't have another girl who could look ten years old like Vi can when she sets her mind to it – and he rang her up. I booked him in like I always did, but when he showed up, he wanted to talk *business*.' She lifted her coffee and drank, examining Lynley over the rim. She said, 'So Vi went to work for him.'

'And ceased to need you,' Lynley said.

'I stuck by her, though. Cooking meals, doing laundry, keeping the flat nice. But then she wanted to take up with Nikki as her mate and her partner, and I was out. Just like that.' She snapped her fingers. 'One day I was washing her knickers. The next day I was pulling mine down to give ten-pound-pokes to blokes waiting to catch the District Line to Ealing Broadway.'

'Which was when you decided to inform Martin Reeve what they were up to,' Lynley noted. 'It was a good provocation for you to seek revenge.'

'I didn't hurt no one!' Shelly cried. 'If you want someone likely to do someone else in – I mean, to kill them – then you look at Prongbreath, not at me.'

'Yet Vi doesn't point the finger at him,' Lynley said. 'Which you think she would do if she suspected him of anything. How do you account for that? She even denies knowing him.'

'Well, she would do, wouldn't she?' Shelly declared. 'If that bloke even knew she sneaked on him to the cops about . . .

like . . . well, about his escort business, on top of her *already* using him to build up a list of clients and then doing a runner to set up in business on her own . . .' Shelly drew a breath as well as a thumb across her neck in a mime of throat slitting. 'She wouldn't last ten minutes after he found out, Vi wouldn't. The Prong don't like to be crossed, and he'd see to it she paid for crossing.' Shelly seemed to hear what she was saying and to realise all of the possibilities that could grow out of it. Nervously she looked towards the door, as if expecting Martin Reeve to come barrelling through it, ready to wreak vengeance upon her for the sneaking that *she* had just done.

'If that's the case,' Lynley said, 'if Reeve is indeed responsible for Nicola Maiden's death – which is what, I assume, you're suggesting when you talk about people paying when they double cross him—'

'I never said!'

'Understood. You didn't say it directly. I'm drawing the inference.' Lynley waited for her to give a sign of comprehension. She blinked. He decided that would do. He said, 'If we infer that Reeve's responsible for Nicola Maiden's death, why would he have waited so long to kill her? She left his employ in April. It's now September. How do you account for the five months he waited to take his revenge?'

'I never told him where they were.' Shelly said it proudly. 'I pretended I didn't know. I reckoned he was owed the tale of what they were up to, but he was on his own to track them down. And tha's what he did. Depend on it.'

Chapter Nineteen

───────◆───────

DI Peter Hanken had just got back to his office after his conversation with Will Upman when the news came in that a ten-year-old schoolboy called Theodore Webster playing hide-and-seek on the road between Peak Forest and Lane Head had found a knife buried in a grit dispenser. It was a good-size pocket knife, replete with blades and the sort of miscellaneous gewgaws that made its inclusion in the equipment of a camper or a hiker de rigueur. The boy might have kept it hidden away for years for his own use – so his father reported – had its blades not been impossible to open without someone's assistance. Because of this, he'd taken the knife to his father for help, thinking that a few drops of oil would take care of the problem. But his father had seen the dried blood that was crusting the tightly closed knife, and he'd recalled the story of the Calder Moor murders that had filled the front page of the *High Peak Courier*. He'd phoned the police immediately. It might not be the knife that had been used on one of the two Calder Moor victims, Hanken was told via his mobile by the WPC who'd taken the call, but the DI might want to have a look at it himself prior to its being sent onward to the lab. Hanken declared that he'd take the knife to the lab himself, so he barrelled north to the A623 and headed southeast at Sparrowpit. This course bisected Calder Moor, running at a forty-five degree angle from its northwest edge, which was defined by the road along which the Maiden girl's car had been parked.

At the site, Hanken examined the grit dispenser in which the weapon had been found. He made a note of the fact that a killer – depositing a knife therein – could then have proceeded on his way to a junction not five miles distant at which he could have turned either due east then north for Padley Gorge or immediately south towards Bakewell and Broughton Manor, which lay a mere two miles beyond it. Once Hanken had confirmed this bit of data with a quick look at the map, he went on to examine the knife itself in the kitchen of the Websters' farmhouse.

It was indeed a Swiss Army model, and it now lay in an evidence bag on the car seat next to him. The lab would conduct all the necessary tests to ascertain whether the blood on both the blades and the case was Terry Cole's, but prior to those tests, another less scientific identification could give the investigators a valuable piece of information.

Hanken found Andy Maiden at the bottom of the drive leading up to the Hall. The former SO10 officer was apparently installing a new sign for the establishment, an activity that involved a wheelbarrow, a shovel, a small concrete mixer, several lengths of flex, and an impressive set of floodlights. The old sign had already been removed and lay disassembled beneath a lime tree. The new one – in all its ornate, hand-carved and hand-painted splendour – waited nearby to be mounted on a sturdy oak post.

Hanken parked on the verge and studied Maiden, who was working with a fierce expenditure of energy, as if the replacement of the sign had to be accomplished in record time. He was sweating heavily, the damp forming rivulets on his muscled legs and plastering his T-shirt to his torso. Hanken noted that he was in remarkable physical condition, looking like a man who had the strength and endurance of a boy in his twenties.

'Mr Maiden,' he called as he shoved his door open. 'Could I have a word, please?' And then more loudly when there was no reaction, 'Mr Maiden?'

Maiden slowly turned from his work, revealing his face. Hanken was struck by what his expression revealed of his mental state. If the other man's body could have belonged to a bloke of a younger generation, his face was ancient. Maiden looked as if the only thing keeping him going was the mindlessness of the moment's exertion. Ask him to do anything but labour and sweat, and the shell of the man that he had become would be blasted to fragments like a friable carapace hit by a hammer.

Hanken experienced a dual reaction to the sight of the former SO10 officer: an immediate surge of sympathy that was swiftly replaced by the recollection of an important detail. As an undercover cop, Andy Maiden knew how to play a rôle.

Hanken slid the evidence bag into his jacket pocket and joined Andy Maiden on the drive. Maiden watched him, expressionless, as he approached.

Hanken nodded at the sign that Maiden was preparing to hang, admiring the artistry with which it had been crafted and saying, 'Nicer than the Cavendish's, I think.'

'Thanks.' But Maiden hadn't spent thirty years with the Met to think that the detective inspector in charge of the investigation into his daughter's murder had come to chat about the manner in which Maiden Hall was advertising its presence. He dumped a mound of concrete into the hole he'd dug, and he sank his shovel into the earth nearby. He said, 'You've news for us,' and he appeared to be attempting to read Hanken's face for the answer in advance of hearing it.

'A knife's been found.' Hanken brought the other policeman into the picture with a brief explanation of how it had come into the hands of the police.

'You'll want me to look at it,' Maiden said, a step ahead of him.

Hanken brought out the plastic evidence bag and rested it with the knife in his palm. Maiden didn't ask to hold it himself. Rather, he stood gazing at it as if the case, the folded blades, or the blood upon both could give him an answer to questions he wasn't yet willing to ask.

'You mentioned that you gave her your own knife,' Hanken said. 'Could this be it?' And when Maiden nodded, 'Is there anything about the knife that you gave her that distinguishes it from others of the same type, Mr Maiden?'

'Andy? Andy?' A woman's voice grew louder as the woman herself descended from the Hall, walking through the trees. 'Andy darling, here. I've brought you some—' Nan Maiden stopped abruptly when she saw Hanken. 'Excuse me, Inspector. I had no idea you were . . . Andy, I've brought you some water. The heat. You know. Pellegrino's all right, isn't it?'

She thrust the water at her husband. She touched the back of her fingers to his temple, saying, 'You aren't overdoing it, are you?'

He flinched.

Hanken felt a stirring on the back of his neck, like a spirit's caress against his skin. He looked from husband to wife, assessed the moment that had just passed between them, and knew he was fast approaching the time to ask the question no one had given voice to yet.

He said first, after nodding a hello to Maiden's wife, 'As to anything that might differentiate the knife you gave your daughter from other similar Swiss Army knives . . . ?'

'One of the blades of the scissors broke off a few years ago. I never replaced it,' Maiden said.

'Anything else?'

'Not that I recall.'

'After you gave the knife – possibly this one – to your daughter, did you buy another for yourself?'

'I have another, yes,' he said. 'Smaller than that, though. Easier to carry about.'

'You have it with you?'

Maiden reached into the pocket of his cut-off jeans. He brought out another model of a Swiss Army knife and handed it over. Hanken examined it, using his thumbnail to prise open its largest blade. Two inches appeared to be its length.

Nan Maiden said, 'Inspector, I don't understand what Andy's knife has to do with anything.' And then, without a pause for response, 'Darling, you haven't had lunch yet. Can I bring you a sandwich?'

But Andy Maiden was watching Hanken open the knife and take the measure of each of its blades. Hanken could feel the former officer's eyes upon him. He could sense the intent behind the gaze that fixed itself on his fingers.

Nan Maiden said, 'Andy? Can I bring you . . . ?'

'No.'

'But you must eat something. You can't keep—'

'No.'

Hanken looked up. Maiden's replacement knife was too small for the murder weapon. But that didn't obviate the necessity for asking the question that both of them knew he would ask. He had, after all, admitted to helping his daughter pack her camping gear into her car on Tuesday. And he himself had given her the knife that he himself had later declared to be missing.

'Mr Maiden,' he said, 'where were you on Tuesday night?'

'That's a monstrous question,' Nan Maiden said quietly.

'I suppose it is,' Hanken agreed. 'Mr Maiden?'

Maiden glanced in the direction of the Hall above them, as if what he was about to say needed an accompanying corroboration that would be supplied by the Hall's existence. 'I was having some eye trouble on Tuesday night. I went upstairs early because my vision kept tunnelling. It gave me a scare, so I had a lie down to see if that would help take care of it.'

Tunnel vision? Hanken wondered incredulously. *That* was certainly an alibi and a half.

Maiden obviously inferred Hanken's thoughts from the expression on his face. He said, 'It happened during the evening meal, Inspector. One can't mix drinks or serve dinners if one's field of vision is reduced to the size of a five pence coin.'

'It's the truth,' Nan asserted. 'He went upstairs. He was resting in the bedroom.'

'What time was this?'

Maiden's wife answered for him. 'The first of our guests had gone through for their starters. So Andy must have left round half past seven.'

Hanken looked at Maiden for confirmation of the time. Maiden frowned, as if he were conducting a complex inner dialogue with himself.

'How long were you up there in your bedroom, then?'

'The rest of the evening, the night,' Maiden said.

'Your vision didn't improve. Is that it?'

'That's it.'

'Have you seen a doctor? Seems to me that a problem like that could be cause for real concern.'

'Andy's had a few turns like this,' Nan Maiden said. 'They pass. He's fine as long as he rests. And that's what he was doing on Tuesday night. Resting. Because of the vision.'

'I'd expect, though, that a condition like that wants looking at. It could lead to something far worse. A stroke, perhaps? Chances are one would think of a stroke straightaway. I'd want to call the ambulance as soon as I had the first symptoms.'

'It's happened before. We know what to do,' Nan Maiden said.

'Which is what, exactly?' Hanken enquired. 'Ice packs? Acupuncture? Full body massage? Half a dozen aspirin? What is it you do when it looks like your husband might be having a stroke?'

'It isn't a stroke.'

'So you left him alone to his bed rest, did you? From half

past seven in the evening until . . . what time might that have been, Mrs Maiden?'

The care the couple took not to look at each other was as obvious as would have been a sudden collapse into each other's arms. Nan Maiden said, 'Of course I didn't leave Andy alone, Inspector. I looked in on him twice. Three times, perhaps. During the evening.'

'And the times?'

'I have no idea. Probably at nine. Then again round eleven.' And as Hanken looked towards Maiden, she continued by saying, 'It's no use asking Andy. He'd fallen asleep, and I didn't wake him. But he was there in the bedroom. And there he stayed. All night. I hope that's all you want to ask in the matter, Inspector Hanken, because the very idea . . . the thought that . . .' Her eyes grew bright as she directed them towards her husband. He looked in the direction of the U-shaped gorge, whose south end could be glimpsed where the road curved to the north. 'I hope that's all you want to ask,' she said simply, and there was a quiet dignity to her words.

Still, Hanken said, 'Do you have any idea what your daughter planned to do with her life once she returned to London from her summer in Derbyshire?'

Maiden watched him steadily, though his wife looked away. 'No,' he said. 'I don't know.'

'I see. And you're certain of that? Nothing you want to add? Nothing you want to explain?'

'Nothing,' Maiden said, and to his wife, 'You, Nancy?'

'Nothing,' she said.

Hanken gestured with the evidence bag in which the knife lay. 'You know the routine, Mr Maiden. Once we have a report with all the particulars from forensic, I'll probably need another chat with you.'

'I understand,' Andy Maiden said. 'Do your job, Inspector. Do it well. That's all I ask.'

But he didn't look at his wife.

They seemed to Hanken like strangers on a railway platform, tied in some way to a departing guest that neither wanted to admit to knowing.

Nan Maiden watched the inspector drive off. Without realising that she was doing it, she began to gnaw at what was left of the fingernails on her right hand. Next to her, Andy set the bottle of Pellegrino she'd brought him into a depression that his heel had made in the soft earth round the concrete-filled hole. He hated Pellegrino. He scorned every kind of water that touted itself as offering more benefit than a full glass of the spring water from their own well. She knew that. But when she'd looked from the window of the first floor mezzanine when through the trees she'd seen the car pull onto the verge and watched the police inspector clamber out, a bottle of water was the only excuse she could think of to get her down the hillside quickly enough to intercept him. So now, she bent for the water and wiped off the grime where the earth clung like an eruption of scabies to the condensation that had formed on the bottle.

Andy fetched the thick oak pole from which the new Maiden Hall sign would hang. He sank it upright into the ground and held it into position with four sturdy timbers. He shovelled the rest of the concrete round it.

When will we talk? she wondered. When will it be safe to say the worst? She tried to tell herself that thirty-seven years of marriage made conversation unnecessary between them, but she knew there was little truth to that. It was only in the halcyon days of courting, engagement, and newlywed excitement that a look, a touch, or a smile sufficed between a man and a woman. And they were decades away from those halcyon days. They were more than thirty years and one devastating death away from that time when words were secondary to the knowledge of one's partner that was as immediate and as natural as breathing.

Silently, Andy packed the concrete round the post. Carefully, he scraped the remains of the mixture from the bucket until there was nothing left. He gave his attention next to the floodlights. Nan clasped the bottle of Pellegrino to her bosom and turned away to climb back to the Hall.

'Why did you say that?' her husband asked.

She turned back to him. 'What?'

'You know. Why did you tell him you looked in on me, Nancy?'

The bottle felt sticky under her palm. It felt hard against her breast. She said, 'I did look in on you.'

'You didn't. We both know it.'

'Darling, I did. You were asleep. You must have dozed off. I had a quick look in the door and then went back to work. I'm not surprised you didn't hear me.'

He stood with the floodlights in his hands. She wanted to go to him, to swaddle his body with the kind of protection that would dispel the demons and drive off the despair. But she just stood there, a few feet above him on the slope, holding a bottle of Pellegrino which both of them knew he would never drink.

'She was the why of it,' he said quietly. 'Every journey in life reaches an end. But if you're lucky, it has another beginning inside of it. Nick was the why. Do you understand, Nancy?'

Their gazes locked on each other for a moment. His eyes – which she'd studied for thirty-seven years of love and frustration and laughter and fear and delight and anxiety – spoke a message to her that was unmistakable in its existence but incomprehensible in its meaning. Nan's body quivered with a chill of fear, with the belief that she couldn't afford to understand anything that the man she loved would try to tell her from this moment on.

'I've something to see to in the Hall,' she said. She began to climb the slope beneath the lime trees. She felt the cool air of the shadows as if the tree leaves were spilling it like a soft fall of rain. It touched her cheeks first, then slid to her shoulders, and the movement of the coolness against her skin was what prompted her to turn back to her husband for a final question.

'Andy,' she said. The volume of her voice was as normal. 'Can you hear me from here?'

He didn't respond. He didn't look up. He didn't do anything save place the first floodlight in position on the ground beneath the pole that would hold the new sign for Maiden Hall. 'Oh God,' Nan whispered. She turned and continued her climb.

After the conversation she'd had with her uncle Jeremy on the previous evening, Samantha had done what she could to stay out of his way. She'd had to see him at both breakfast and lunch, naturally, but she'd avoided eye contact and conversation with him and as soon as she'd finished eating, she'd cleared her plates from the table and cleared herself from the room.

She was out in the older courtyard, preparing to wash what looked like a good fifty years of grime from those windows that were still glazed, when she noticed her cousin. He was sitting at the desk in his office, just across the cobbles from where she was unreeling a lengthy hose pipe. She paused to observe him, admiring how the autumn light fell in the open window of the office and struck the top of his bent head so that his hair was burnished to a rusty gold. As she watched, she saw him rub the worry lines on his forehead, and that told her instantly what he was doing, although it didn't tell her why.

He was very good with figures, so he was going over the accounts, as he did every week, making an evaluation of what went for the income, assets, and investments of his family's estate. He'd be looking at everything: what came in from the sale of the harrier puppies and what went out to keep the kennel running; what amassed from the rents accrued across the estate and what bled from the profits to keep all of the farm buildings in usable condition; what income was provided by the tournaments and fêtes held at Broughton Manor and what costs were accrued from the normal wear and tear that occurred when one's property was used by others; what interest came in from invested capital and how much of that capital leeched away when a month's expenditure exceeded its profits.

When he was done with that, he would go on to examine the books in which he meticulously recorded every pound that was spent on the renovation of Broughton Manor itself, and then he would refresh his memory about the debts that also comprised part of the Britton Family Financial Picture. When he was finished, he would have a fair idea of how things stood, and he could lay any plans that needed to be laid for the coming week.

So Samantha wasn't surprised to see him looking over the books. She was, however, surprised to see him at them for the second time in four days.

As she watched, she saw him plunge one hand back through his hair. He entered some figures into an antique adding machine and from across the courtyard, Samantha could hear the whir and click of the old calculator as it lumbered through its sums. When the answer was produced, Julian ripped the tape from the back of the machine and studied it for a moment. Then he crumpled the tape into a ball and threw it over his shoulder. He went back to the books again.

Seeing this, Samantha felt her heart tugged. She wondered if there had ever been a man as responsible as Julian. A child less mindful of his family's history and his personal duty would have decamped from this nightmare of an ancestral home long ago. A child less loving would have left his father to swill his way to delirium tremens, cirrhosis of the liver, and an early grave. But her cousin Julian wasn't that sort of child. He felt the ties of blood and the obligations of heritage. Both were burdens. But he bore them with dignity. Had he approached them any other way, Samantha wouldn't have come to care for him so deeply. In his struggle, she'd learned to see a strength of purpose which was closely attuned to her own way of living.

They were right for each other, she and her cousin. No matter that the blood relationship was a close one, cousins had formed alliances before and in the process had enriched the family from which they both sprang.

Formed an alliance. What a way to label it, Samantha thought wryly. And yet hadn't things been so much more sensible during that period when marriages came about for just that reason? There was no talk of true love in the days of political and financial match making, no aching, longing, and pining until one's true love happened to come along. What there was, instead, was a steadiness and devotion that grew from an understanding of what was *expected* of one. No illusions, no fantasy. Just an agreement to bind one's life to another in a situation in which both parties had much to gain: money, position, property, authority, protection, and authentication. Perhaps that last, most of all. One wasn't complete until one married; one wasn't married until the match was consolidated through coition and legitimised through reproduction. Simple. There were no expectations of romance, passion, and exquisite surrender. There was just the steady, lifelong assurance that one's mate was actually that which the agreeing parties had earlier defined him to be.

Sensible, Samantha decided. And in a world in which men and women were partnered to each other in that fashion, she knew that agents of herself and Julian would long ago have reached an understanding.

But they didn't live in that world. And the world they did live in was one suggesting that a permanent soul mate was one little strip of celluloid away: boy meets girl, they fall in love, they have their troubles which are resolved by Act III, fade to black, and the credits roll. That world was maddening because Samantha knew if her cousin adhered to a belief in that sort of love, she was doomed to failure. *I'm here,* she found herself wanting to shout, hose pipe in hand. *I have what you need. Look at me.* Look *at me.*

As if he'd heard her silent cry, Julian glanced up at just that moment and caught her watching him. He leaned forward and swung the casement window fully open. Samantha crossed the courtyard to join him.

'You're looking grim. I couldn't help noticing. You caught me trying to design a cure for what ails you.'

'D'you think I have a future in counterfeiting?' he asked. The sun was shining directly on his face and he squinted into it. 'That may be the only answer.'

'Do you think so?' she asked lightly. 'No rich young thing waiting for seduction on your horizon?'

'It doesn't look like it.' He saw her observing the mass of documents and account books that were spread on his desk, certainly a far greater number than he usually went through when doing his sums for the coming week. 'Trying to see where we stand,' he explained. 'I was hoping to wring about ten thousand pounds out of . . . well, out of nothing, I'm afraid.'

'Why?' She noted the downhearted cast of his face and hastened to add, 'Jules, is there an emergency of some sort? Is something wrong?'

'That's just the hell of it. Something's right. Or something could be *made* right. But there's not enough liquid cash to do much more than see us through to the end of the month.'

'I hope you know that you can always ask me . . .' She hesitated, not wanting to offend him, knowing that he was as proud a man as he was responsible. She put it another way. 'We're family, Julie. If something's come up and you'd like some money . . . it wouldn't even be a loan. You're my cousin. You can have it.'

He looked horrified. 'I didn't mean you to think—'

'Stop it. I'm not thinking anything.'

'Good. Because I couldn't. Not ever.'

'Fine. We won't discuss it. But please tell me what's happened. You look really cut up.'

He blew out a breath. He said, 'Oh bugger it,' and in a quick movement, he climbed onto the desk and out of the window to join her in the courtyard. 'What're you up to? Ah. Windows. I see. Have you any idea how long it's been since they've had a wash, Sam?'

'When Edward chucked it all in for Wallis? Fool that he was.'

'That's a fair bet.'

'Which part of it? The guess itself? Or chucking it all in for her?'

He smiled resignedly. 'I'm not sure at this point.'

Samantha didn't say what came first to her mind: that he wouldn't have answered in such a way a week ago. She merely gave a few moments' consideration to what such an answer implied.

Companionably, they went at the windows. The old glazing was set into lead in far too fragile a fashion to blast away at it with the hose pipe, so they were reduced to a painstaking process of soaking away the grime with rags, one single pane at a time.

'This'll take till our dotage,' Julian noted grimly after ten minutes of silent cleaning.

'I dare say,' Samantha replied. She wanted to ask him if he was prepared for her to stay round the manor that long, but she let the thought go. Something serious was on his mind, and she had to get to it, if only to prove to him her abiding concern for all aspects of his life. She sought a way in, saying quietly, 'Julie, I'm sorry about your worries. On top of everything else. I can't do anything about ... well ...' She found that she couldn't even say her name. Not here and now. Not to Julian. 'About what's happened in the last few days,' was what she settled on. 'But if there's ever anything else that I can do ...'

'I'm sorry,' he replied.

'Of course you are. How could you be anything else but sorry?'

'I mean I'm sorry for what I said . . . how I acted . . . when I questioned you, Sam. About that night. You know.'

She gave particular attention to a window pane that was crusted with guano, which had dripped from a hundred years of birds' nests tucked into a crevice above them. 'You were upset.'

'I didn't need to accuse you, though. Of . . . of whatever.'

'Of murdering the woman you loved, you mean.' She looked his way. The ruddy colour in his face had heightened.

'Sometimes it seems like I can't get a rein on the voices inside my head. I start talking and whatever the voices have been shouting pops out. It's nothing to do with what I believe. I'm sorry.'

She wanted to say, 'But she wasn't good for you anyway, Julie. Why did you never see that she wasn't good for you? And when will you see what her death can mean? To you. To me. To us. Julie.' But she didn't say it because to say it would be to reveal what she couldn't afford – or even bear – to reveal to him. 'Accepted,' she said instead.

'Thanks, Sam. You're a brick,' he said.

'Again.'

'I mean—'

She flashed him a smile. 'It's okay. I understand. Hand me the hose pipe. These need dousing now.'

A burble of water was all they could risk against the old windows. Sometime in the future it would be necessary to have all the lead replaced or what was left of the ancient windows would definitely be destroyed. But that was a conversation for another time. With his present money worries, Julian didn't need to hear Samantha's prescription for saving another part of the family home.

He said, 'It's Dad, actually.'

She said, 'What?'

'What's on my mind. Why I've been going through the books. It's Dad.' And then he explained, ending ruefully with, 'I've been waiting for years for him to choose sobriety—'

'All of us have waited.'

'—and now he's done that, I got all caught up in trying to come up with a way to seize the moment before it passes. I know the truth of the matter. I've read enough about it to understand he has to do it for himself. He has to *want* it. But if you could have seen him, heard how he was talking ... I don't think he's had a drink all day, Sam.'

'Hasn't he? No, I suppose he hasn't.' And she thought of her uncle as he'd been last night: slurring not a word and coaxing from her an admission that she didn't want to make. She felt a stillness come over her, one in which she knew that she too could seize the moment – could use it and mould it – or let it pass. She said carefully, 'Perhaps he does want it this time, Julie. He's getting older. Facing his ... well, his mortality.' His *mortality*, she thought, not his death. She wouldn't use that word because in this instance it was crucial to maintain a delicate balance in the conversation. 'I expect everyone comes face to face with ... well, with the knowledge that nothing goes on forever. Perhaps he's feeling older all at once and he wants to sort himself out while he still has the chance.'

'But that's just it,' Julian said. '*Does* he have a chance? How can he do it without help when he's never been able to do it before? And now that he's finally *asked* for help how can I fail to give it? Because I want to give it. I want him to succeed.'

'We all do, Julie. The family. We want that.'

'So I went through the books. Because of the health insurance we have. I don't even need to read the small print to know there's no way ...' He examined the pane he was working on, scraping his fingernail against the glass.

Nails on a chalkboard. Samantha shuddered. She turned her head from the sound.

Which was when she saw him, where he always was. He stood at the window in the parlour. He watched her talking to his son. And as she watched him watching her, Samantha saw her uncle raise his hand. One finger touched his temple and then his hand dropped. He might have been smoothing his hair from his face. But the reality was that the gesture looked very much like a mock salute.

Chapter Twenty

'We got in straightaway yesterday,' Nkata said, when no entry buzzer answered their ringing of the bell next to the white front door. 'Could be they got word 'bout us from the Platt bird and did a runner. What d'you think?'

'I didn't get the impression that Shelly Platt had any sympathy for the Reeves, did you?' Lynley rang the bell at MKR Financial Management another time. 'She seemed happy enough to put a spanner in their works so long as no trail led back to her. Do the Reeves live here as well as run their business from here, Winnie? It looks like a residence to me.' Lynley moved back from the door, then descended the stairs to the pavement. While the candy floss building appeared uninhabited, he had the distinct sensation of being watched from within. It could have been his impatience to get Martin Reeve under his thumb for a thorough grilling, but something suggested to him a form just out of sight behind the sheer curtains of a second floor window. Even as he stood gazing up at it, the curtain twitched. He called up, 'Police. It's in your interests to let us in, Mr Reeve. I'd rather not have to phone Ladbroke Grove police station for their assistance.'

A minute passed during which Nkata leaned on the bell and Lynley walked to the Bentley to phone the Ladbroke Grove station. This apparently did the trick, for as he was speaking to the duty sergeant, Nkata called, 'We're in, 'spector,' and shoved the door open. He waited for Lynley just inside the hall.

The building was quiet, the air bearing a faint odour of lemons: from polish, perhaps, used to maintain an impressive Sheraton wardrobe in the corridor. As Lynley and Nkata shut the door behind them, a woman descended the stairs.

Lynley's first thought was that she looked like a doll. In fact she looked like a woman who'd spent considerable time and energy – not to mention money – in moulding herself into a remarkable duplicate of Barbie. She wore black Lycra from head to toe, displaying a body so outrageously perfect that only imagination and silicone could have produced it. This had to be Tricia Reeve, Lynley thought. Nkata had done a fine job of describing her.

Lynley introduced himself, saying, 'We'd like a word with your husband, Mrs Reeve. Will you fetch him for us, please?'

'He's not here.' She'd stopped at the lowest step on the stairs. She was tall, Lynley saw, and she'd made herself taller by refusing to descend completely to their level.

'Where's he gone, then?' Assiduously, Nkata prepared to take down the information.

Tricia's hand was on the staircase railing, long skeletal fingers encumbered by rings. She had a formidable grip upon the oak: Her diamonds glittered as her arm trembled with the force she was applying. 'I don't know.'

'Try out a few ideas on us,' Nkata said. 'I'll take them all down. We're happy to check 'round for him. We got the time.'

Silence.

'Or we could wait here,' Lynley said. 'Where might we do that, Mrs Reeve?'

Her glance flickered. Blue eyes, Lynley saw. Enormous pupils. Nkata had told him that she was a user. It appeared that she was spiked up right now. 'Camden Passage,' she said, her pale tongue coming out to lick bee-stung lips. 'There's a dealer there. Miniatures. Martin collects. He's gone to look at what's been brought in from an estate sale last week.'

'The name of the dealer?'

'I don't know.'

'Name of the gallery? The shop?'

'I don't know.'

'What time d'he leave?' Nkata asked.

'I don't know. I was out.'

Lynley wondered in what sense she was using *out*. He had a fairly good idea. He said, 'We'll wait for him, then. Shall we show ourselves into your reception room? Is it this door, Mrs Reeve?'

She followed them, saying quickly, 'He's gone to Camden Passage. From there to meet some painters who're working on a house of ours in Cornwall Mews. I've the address. Shall I give it to you?'

The switch to cooperation was far too swift. Either Reeve was in the house or she'd come up with a plan to put him on the alert to their search for him. That would be easy enough. Lynley couldn't imagine a man of Reeve's description wandering the byways of London without a mobile phone in his possession. The moment he and Nkata were out the front door and on his trail, Reeve's wife would be at the phone to warn him.

'I think we'll wait all the same,' Lynley said. 'Join us, Mrs Reeve. I can phone the Ladbroke Grove station for a female constable if you're feeling uncomfortable alone with us. Shall I do that?'

'No!' With her right hand, she clasped her left elbow. She looked at her watch and the muscles in her neck convulsed as she worked her way through a swallow. She was coming down, Lynley speculated, and checking to see when she could next hit up with relative safety. Their presence was an obstacle that thwarted her need, and that might be useful. She said insistently, 'Martin isn't here. If I knew more, I'd tell you. But the fact is, I don't.'

'I'm unconvinced,' Lynley said.

'I'm telling you the truth!'

'Tell us another, then. Where was your husband on Tuesday night?'

'On Tuesday ... ?' She looked honestly confused. 'I have no ... He was here. With me. He was here. We spent the evening in.'

'Can anyone confirm that?'

The question obviously rang alarm bells for her. She said in a rush, 'We went for a curry at the Star of India on Old Brompton Road round half past eight.'

'So you weren't in, then.'

'We spent the rest of the evening here.'

'Did you book a table at the restaurant, Mrs Reeve?'

'The maitre d' will remember us. He and Martin had words because we hadn't booked in advance and they didn't want to let us have a table at first, even though there were several vacant when we got there. We had a meal. Then we came home. That's the truth. On Tuesday. That's what we did.'

It would be easy enough to confirm their presence at the restaurant, Lynley thought. But how many maitre d's would recall on what *particular* day they'd had a row with a demanding customer who'd failed to book and also thus failed to provide himself with a reliable alibi? He said, 'Nicola Maiden worked for you.'

She said, 'Martin didn't kill Nicola! I know that's why you've come, so don't let's pretend otherwise. He was with me on Tuesday night. We went to the Star of India for a meal. We were home by ten, and we stayed in the rest of the evening. Ask our neighbours. Someone will have seen us either going out or coming back. Now do you want the address of the mews house or not? Because if not, I'd like you to leave.' Another agitated glance at her watch.

Lynley decided to press her. He said to Nkata, 'We're going to need a warrant, Winnie.'

Tricia cried, 'What for? I've told you everything. You can phone the restaurant. You can talk to our neighbours. How can you get a search warrant when you haven't bothered to see if I'm telling you the truth in the first place?' She sounded horrified. Better yet, she sounded afraid. The last thing she wanted, Lynley expected, was to have a team of police going through her belongings, no matter what they were looking for. She may have had no hand in the death of Nicola Maiden, but possession of narcotics wasn't going to go down a treat with the CPS, and she knew that.

'We sometimes cut corners,' Lynley said pleasantly. 'This looks like a good time to do so. We've a murder weapon missing as well as a piece of clothing from the dead girl and the boy, and if either article turns up in this house, we'll want to know why.'

'Sh'll I phone, then, Guv?' Nkata enquired blandly.

'Martin didn't kill Nicola! He hasn't seen her in months! He didn't even know where she was! If you're looking for someone who might have wanted to see her dead, there are plenty of men who—' She stopped herself.

'Yes?' Lynley asked. 'Plenty of men?'

She brought up her left arm to cradle her right elbow, just as her right had been cradling her left. She walked the length of the reception room and back.

Lynley said, 'Mrs Reeve, we know exactly what MKR Financial Management is fronting. We know that your husband hires students to work as escorts and prostitutes for him. We know that Nicola Maiden was one of those students and that she left your husband's employ along with Vi Nevin to set up in business on her own. The information we have right now can lead directly to charges against you and your husband, and

I expect you're well aware of that. So if you'd like to avoid being charged, tried, sentenced, and locked up, I suggest you cooperate straightaway.'

She looked rigid. Her lips hardly moved when she said, 'What do you want to know?'

'I want to know about your husband's relationship with Nicola Maiden. Pimps are known for—'

'He isn't a pimp!'

'—frequently displaying displeasure if one of their stable decides to break away from them.'

'That's not what it's like. That's not how it was.'

'Really?' Lynley asked. 'How was it, then? Vi and Nicola decided to start their own business, which cut out your husband. But they did so without informing him. He can't have liked that very much, once he sussed it out.'

'You're getting it wrong.' She went to the ornate desk and out of a drawer she took a packet of Silk Cut. She shook one out and lit it. The phone began to ring. She glanced down at it, reached forward to press a button, stopped herself at the final moment. After twenty double rings, it was silent. But less than ten seconds later it started up again. She said, 'The computer should be getting that. I can't think why . . .' And with an uneasy look in the direction of the police, she snatched up the receiver and said tersely, 'Global,' into it. Then after a moment of listening, and spoken in the most pleasant of tones she said, 'It depends what you want, actually . . . Yes. That shouldn't be a problem at all. May I have your number, please? I'll ring you back shortly.' She scribbled on a paper. That done, she looked up defiantly as if to say, 'Prove it,' to what Lynley was thinking about the conversation that she'd just had.

He was happy to oblige her. 'Global,' Lynley said. 'That's the name of the escort agency, Mrs Reeve? Global what? Global Dating? Global Desires? What?'

'Global Escorts. And providing an educated escort to a businessman in town for a conference isn't illegal.'

'Living off immoral earnings however, is. Mrs Reeve, do you really want the police to take possession of your account books? Assuming, of course, that there are account books for MKR Financial Management in the first place? We can do that, you know. We can ask for documentation of every pound you've made. And once we're through with our bit of research, we can hand everything over to the Inland Revenue so that their chaps can make certain you've donated your fair share to the support of the government. How does that sound to you?'

He gave her time to ponder. The telephone went again. After three double rings, it switched onto another line with a soft click. An order being taken elsewhere, Lynley thought. By mobile, remote control, or satellite. Wasn't progress a wonderful thing.

Tricia seemed to reach some sort of realisation. Obviously, she knew that Global Escorts and the position of the Reeves were compromised at this point: One word from Lynley to the Inland Revenue or even to the local police station's Vice boys, and the Reeves' entire way of life was on the chopping block. And that didn't even begin to address what could happen to them once a search of the premises unearthed whatever mood altering substance was squirrelled away somewhere in the house, waiting to work its magic on Tricia. All this knowledge seemed to settle upon her, like soot from a fire she'd lit herself.

She gathered herself together. She said, 'All right. If I give you a name – if I give you *the* name – it can't have come from me. Is that understood? Because if word gets out about an indiscretion committed at this end of the business . . .' She let the rest of the sentence hang.

Indiscretion was a unique way of labelling it, Lynley thought. And why in God's name did she think that she was in any position to bargain with him? He said, 'Mrs Reeve, the business – as you call it – is finished.'

'Martin,' she said, 'won't see it that way.'

'Martin,' Lynley countered, 'will find himself held on charges if he doesn't.'

'And Martin will ask for bail. He'll be out on the street in twenty-four hours. Where will you be by then, Inspector? No closer to the truth, I expect.' She might have looked like Barbie, she might have sautéed part of her brain in drugs, but somewhere along the line she'd learned a bit about bargaining and she was doing it now with a fair amount of expertise. Lynley reckoned that her husband would have been proud of her. She had no legal leg to stand on and she stood there anyway, pretending she had. He had to admire her *chutzpah*, if nothing else. She said, 'I can give you a name – *the* name, as I've said – and you can go on your way. I can say nothing and you can search the house, cart me off to gaol, arrest my husband, and be not an inch closer to Nicola's killer. Oh, you'll have our books and our records. But you can't expect that we're so stupid as to list our punters by name. So what will you gain? And how much time will you lose?'

'I'm prepared to be reasonable if the information's good. And in the time it takes me to ascertain the information's viability, I would assume you and your husband would be considering where to relocate your business. Melbourne comes to mind, what with the change in law.'

'That might take some time.'

'As will the verification of information.'

Tit for tat. He awaited her decision. She finally made it and took up a pencil from the top of the desk. 'Sir Adrian Beattie,' she said as she wrote. 'He was mad about Nicola. He was willing to pay her whatever she wanted if he could keep her all to himself. I don't expect he much liked the thought of her expanding her business, do you?'

She handed over the address. It was in the Boltons.

It appeared, Lynley thought, that they had the London lover at last.

* * *

When Barbara Havers found the note on her door upon her arrival home that evening, she remembered the sewing lesson with a jolt. She said, 'Bloody hell. *Damn* it,' and berated herself for having forgotten. True, she was involved in a case, and Hadiyyah would surely understand that. But Barbara hated to think that she might have been the cause of disappointment to her little friend.

You are cordially invited to view the work of Miss Jane Bateman's Beginning Seamstresses, the note announced. It was meticulously printed in a childish hand that Barbara well recognised. A drooping cartoonish sunflower was sketched on the bottom. Alongside this was the date and time. Barbara made a mental note to enter both on her calendar.

She'd put in another couple of hours at the Yard after her conversation with Neil Sitwell. She'd been champing at the bit to start phoning the numbers of every employee listed under King-Ryder Productions on the roster she'd been given earlier, but she trod the path of caution lest Inspector Lynley turn up and demand to know what she'd gathered from the Yard computer. Which was sod bloody all in spades, of course. To hell with him, she'd begun to think during her eighth cumulative hour at the terminal. If he wanted a flaming report on every bleeding individual with whom DI Andrew Maiden might have rubbed elbows in his years undercover, she'd damn well give it to him by the shovelful. But the information was going to get him bugger all that would lead him to the Derbyshire killer. She would have bet her *own* life on that.

She'd left the Yard round half past four, stopping at Lynley's office to drop off a report and a personal note. The report made her point, she liked to think, without stooping to rub his nose or otherwise dabble in the obvious. *I'm right, you're wrong, but I'll play your stupid game* were not words that she needed to say to him. Her time would come, and she thanked her stars that the manner in which Lynley was orchestrating the case actually left her more of a free hand then he realised. The personal note that she left with the report assured Lynley in the most polite of terms that she was taking to Chelsea the postmortem file prepared by Dr Sue Myles in Derbyshire. Which was what Barbara did as soon as she left New Scotland Yard.

She found Simon St James and his wife in the back garden of their Cheyne Row house, where St James was watching Deborah crawl on her hands and knees along the brick path edging a herbaceous border that ran the length of the garden wall. She had a pump action sprayer that she was dragging along as she moved, and every few feet she stopped and energetically attacked the ground with a rainfall of pungent insecticide.

She was saying, 'Simon, there are *billions* of them. And even when I spray, they keep moving about. Lord. If there's ever a nuclear war, ants will be the only survivors.'

St James, reclining on a chaise longue with wide-brimmed hat shading his face, said, 'Did you get that section by the hydrangeas, my love? It looks as if you missed that bit by the fuchsia as well.'

'Honestly. You're maddening. Would you rather do this yourself? I hate to be disturbing your peace of mind with such a slapdash effort.'

'Hmm.' St James appeared to consider her offer. 'No. I don't think so. You've been getting so much better at it recently. Doing anything well takes practice, and I hate to rob you of the opportunity.'

Deborah laughed and mock-sprayed him. She caught sight of Barbara just outside the kitchen door. She said, 'Brilliant. Just what I need. A witness. Hullo, Barbara! Please take note of which partner is slaving away in the garden and which is not. My solicitor will want a statement from you later.'

'Don't believe a word she says,' St James said. 'I've only this moment sat down.'

'Something about your posture says you're lying,' Barbara told him as she crossed the lawn to the chaise longue. 'And your father-in-law just suggested that I light a stick of dynamite under your bum, by the way.'

'Did he?' St James enquired, frowning at the kitchen window through which Joseph Cotter's form could be seen moving round.

'Thanks, Dad,' Deborah called out in the direction of the house.

Barbara smiled at their quiet, fond sparring. She pulled up a deck chair and sank into it. She handed over the file to St James, saying, 'His Lordship would like you to make a study of this.'

'What is it?'

'The Derbyshire postmortems. Both the girl and the boy. The inspector'd tell you to have the closer look at the data on the girl, by the way.'

'You wouldn't tell me that?'

Barbara smiled grimly. 'I think my thoughts.'

St James opened the file. Deborah crossed the lawn to join them, trailing the spray pump behind her. 'Pictures,' St James warned her.

She hesitated. 'Bad?'

'Multiple stab wounds on one of the victims,' Barbara told her.

She blanched and sat on the chaise longue near to her husband's feet. St James gave the photographs a glance only, before he placed them face down on the lawn. He flipped through the report, pausing to read here and there. He said, 'Is there something particular that Tommy's looking for, Barbara?'

'The inspector and I aren't communicating directly. I'm currently his gofer. He told me to bring you the report. I tugged my forelock and did his bidding.'

St James looked up. 'Things still bad between you? Helen did tell me you were on the case.'

'Marginally,' she said.

'He'll come round.'

'Tommy always does,' Deborah added. Husband and wife exchanged a look. Deborah said uneasily, 'Well. You know.'

'Yes,' St James said after a moment and with a brief, kind smile in her direction. Then to Barbara, 'I'll have a look at the paperwork, Barbara. I expect he wants inconsistencies, anomalies, discrepancies. The usual. Tell him I'll phone.'

'Right,' she said. And then she added delicately, 'I'm wondering, Simon . . .'

'Hmm?'

'Could you phone me as well? I mean, if you unearth something.' When he didn't reply at once, she rushed on with, 'I know it's irregular. And I don't want to get you into a bad spot with the inspector. But he won't tell me much and it's always, "Get back to the computer, Constable," if I make a suggestion. So, if you were willing to keep me in the picture . . . I mean, I know he'd be cheesed off if he knew, but I swear I'd never tell him that you—'

'I'll phone you as well,' St James interrupted. 'But there may be nothing. I know Sue Myles. She's nothing if not thorough. Frankly, I don't see why Tommy wants me to look her work over in the first place.'

Neither do I, Barbara wanted to tell him. Still, his promise to phone her buoyed her spirits, so she ended the day in far better a frame of mind than she'd begun it.

When she saw Hadiyyah's note, however, an unhappy twinge pricked at her mood. The little girl had no mother to speak of – at least no mother who was present or likely to become present any time soon – and while Barbara didn't expect to take her mother's place, she had struck up a friendship with Hadiyyah that had been a source of pleasure to them both. Hadiyyah had hoped that Barbara would attend her sewing lesson that afternoon. And Barbara had failed her. It didn't feel good.

So when she'd dropped her bag on the dining room table

and listened to her messages – Mrs Flo reporting on her mum, her mum reporting on a jolly trip to Jamaica, Hadiyyah telling her she'd left a note on the door and did Barbara find it? – she wandered up to the front of the big Edwardian house where the ground floor flat's french windows were open from the sitting room onto the flagstones of the area and within the room itself, a child's voice was declaring, 'But they don't *fit*, Dad. Honest.'

Hadiyyah and her father were just inside, Hadiyyah seated on a cream puff shaped ottoman and Taymullah Azhar kneeling next to her like a lovesick Orsino. The object of their attention appeared to be the shoes that Hadiyyah was wearing. These were black lace-ups of school-uniform appearance, and Hadiyyah was squirming round in them as if they were a new device for extracting information from double agents.

'My toes're all squished up. My toe knuckles *hurt*.'

'And you are certain this pain has nothing to do with the desire to follow a fad of fashion, *khushi*?'

'Dad,' Hadiyyah's tone was martyred. 'Please. These're *school* shoes, you know.'

'And as we both recall,' Barbara said from the flagstones, 'school shoes are never cool, Azhar. They always defy fashion. That's why they're school shoes.'

Father and daughter looked up, Hadiyyah crying out, 'Barbara! I left you a note. On the door. Did you get it? I stuck it with Sellotape,' and Azhar leaning back on his heels to give his daughter's shoes a more objective scrutiny. 'She says they no longer fit,' he told Barbara. 'I myself am not convinced.'

'Arbitration is called for,' Barbara said. 'May I . . . ?'

'Come in. Yes. Of course.' Azhar rose in his formal fashion and made a gesture of welcome.

The flat was fragrant with the smell of curry. Barbara saw that the table was neatly laid for dinner, and she said quickly, 'Oh. Sorry. I wasn't thinking about the time, Azhar. You've not eaten yet, and . . . D'you want me to come back later? I just saw Hadiyyah's note and thought I'd pop round. You know. The sewing lesson this afternoon. I'd promised her . . .' She brought herself up short. *Enough*, she thought.

He smiled. 'Perhaps you'll join us for our meal.'

'Oh gosh, no. I mean, I haven't eaten yet, but I wouldn't want to—'

'You must!' Hadiyyah said happily. 'Dad, say that she must. We're having chicken biryani. And dal. *And* Dad's special veg curry, which Mummy cries when she eats 'cause it's so spicy. She says, "Hari, you make it far too *hot*," and her eye make-up runs. Doesn't it, Dad?'

Hari, Barbara thought.

Azhar said, 'It does, *khushi*.' And to Barbara, 'It will be our pleasure if you join us, Barbara.'

She thought, Better run, better hide. But, nonetheless, she said, 'Thanks. I will, then.'

Hadiyyah crowed. She pirouetted in her ostensibly too tight shoes. Her father watched her gravely and said with meaning, 'Ah. As to your feet, Hadiyyah . . .'

'Let me check them,' Barbara interposed quickly.

Hadiyyah flew to the ottoman and plopped down upon it. She said, 'They pinch and they pinch. Even then, Dad. Really.'

Azhar chuckled and disappeared into the kitchen. 'Barbara will decide,' he told his daughter.

'They really pinch *awfully*,' Hadiyyah said. 'Feel how my toes're scrunched up in front.'

'I don't know, Hadiyyah,' Barbara said, probing the toe-caps tentatively. 'What'll you replace these with? More of the same?'

The little girl didn't reply. Barbara looked up. Hadiyyah was sucking her lip.

'Well?' Barbara asked. 'Hadiyyah, have they changed the style of shoe you can wear with your uniform?'

'These're so *ugly*,' she whispered. 'I feel like I've got *boats* on my feet. The new shoes're slip-ons, Barbara. They've the loveliest leather braid round the top and the sweetest little tassle dangling over the toes. They're a bit 'spensive, which is why not everyone has them yet, but I *know* I could wear them forever if I got them. I really could.' She looked so hopeful, brown eyes the size of old tuppence pieces.

Barbara wondered how her father managed to deny her anything. She said in her position of arbiter, 'Will you go for a compromise?'

Hadiyyah's brow scrunched as effectively as had her toes. She said, 'What's compromise?'

'An agreement in which both parties get what they want, just not exactly how they expected to get it.'

Hadiyyah thought this over, bouncing her lace-up-clad feet against the ottoman. She said, 'All right. I s'pose. But they're really pretty shoes, Barbara. If you saw them, you'd understand.'

'Doubtless,' Barbara said. 'You've probably noticed what a fashion hound I am.' She heaved herself to her feet. With a wink at Hadiyyah, she called into the kitchen, 'I'd say she's got several months in these, Azhar.'

Hadiyyah looked stricken. She wailed, 'Several *months*?'

'But she'll definitely need another pair before Bonfire Night,' Barbara said meaningfully. She mouthed *compromise* in Hadiyyah's direction and watched the little girl do the mental maths from September to November. Hadiyyah looked pleased when she'd counted up the weeks.

Azhar came to the kitchen door. He'd tucked a tea towel into his trousers to serve as an apron. In his hand he held a wooden spoon. 'You can be that exact with your shoe analysis, Barbara?' he asked soberly.

'Sometimes my talents amaze even myself.'

* * * *

Curry in the kitchen was just another thing that Azhar appeared to do effortlessly. He accepted no assistance, even with the washing up, saying, 'Your presence is the gift you bring to our meal, Barbara. We require nothing else of you,' to her offers of help. Nonetheless, she bullied her way to clearing the dining table, at least. And while he was scrubbing and drying in the kitchen, she entertained his daughter, which was her pleasure.

Hadiyyah pulled Barbara into her bedroom once the table was cleared, declaring that she had 'something special and secret to show', a just-between-us-girls revelation, Barbara assumed. But instead of a collection of film star photos or a few pencilled notes passed to her at school, Hadiyyah pulled from beneath her bed a carrier bag whose contents she lovingly eased out onto her counterpane.

'Finished today,' she announced proudly. 'In sewing class. I was s'posed to leave it for the display – did you get my invitation to the sewing show, Barbara? – but I told Miss Bateman I'd bring it back nice and clean but that I *had* to have it to give to Dad. 'Cause he wrecked one pair of trousers already. When he was cooking dinner.'

It was a bib apron. Hadiyyah had crafted it from pale chintz on which was printed an endless pattern of mother ducks leading their broods towards a pond with a stand of reeds. The mother ducks all wore identical bonnets. Their little ones each carried a different beach-going utensil under a tiny wing.

'D'you think he'll like it?' Hadiyyah asked anxiously. 'The ducks're so sweet, aren't they, but I s'pose for a man ... I especially love ducks, see. Dad and I feed them at Regent's Park sometimes. So when I saw this material ... But I expect I could've chosen something more mannish, couldn't I?'

The thought of Azhar encased in the apron's folds made Barbara want to smile, but she didn't. Instead she examined the zigzagging seams and the hem with its lopsided, loving hand stitching. She said, 'It's perfect. He'll love it.'

'D'you think so? It's my first project, see, and I'm not very good. Miss Bateman wanted me to start with something simpler, like a hankie. But I knew what I wanted to make 'cause Dad wrecked his trousers like I said and I knew he didn't want to wreck any more trousers cooking. Which's why I brought this home to give to him.'

'Shall we do that now, then?' Barbara asked.

'Oh no. It's for tomorrow,' Hadiyyah said. 'We've a special day planned, Dad and I. We're to go to the sea. We're to pack a picnic lunch and eat on the sand. I'll give it to him then. As a thank you for taking me. And afterwards, we'll ride the roller coaster on the pier, and Dad'll play the crane grab for me. He's quite good at the crane grab, is Dad.'

'Yes. I know. I saw him work it, remember?'

'That's right. You did,' Hadiyyah said brightly. 'Would you like to come with us to the sea, then, Barbara? It'll be such a special day. We're taking a picnic lunch. And we'll go to the pleasure pier. And there's the crane grab as well. I'll ask Dad if you can come.' She scampered to her feet, calling, 'Dad! Dad! Can Barbara—'

'No!' Barbara interrupted hastily. 'Hadiyyah, no. Kiddo, I can't go. I'm in the middle of a case and I've got mountains of work. I shouldn't even be here right now, with all the calls I should've been making before bed. But thanks for the thought. We'll do it another time.'

Hadiyyah stopped, door knob in hand. 'We're going to the pleasure pier,' she coaxed.

'I'll be with you in spirit,' Barbara assured her. And she thought about the resilience of children and she marvelled at their capacity for taking what came. Considering what had occurred the last time Hadiyyah had been to the sea, Barbara wondered that she wanted to go again. But children aren't like adults, she thought. What they can't endure, they simply forget.

Chapter Twenty-one

'Least we're running round incognito,' was DC Winston Nkata's announcement as they pulled into the Boltons, a small neighbourhood shaped like a rugger ball, sandwiched between the Fulham and Old Brompton Roads. It consisted of two curving, leafy streets that formed an oval round the central church of St Mary the Boltons, and its predominant characteristics were the number of security cameras that were mounted on the exterior walls of the mansions and the ostentatious display of Rolls-Royces, Mercedes Benzes, and Range Rovers that were tucked behind the iron gates of many of the properties.

When Lynley and Nkata pulled into the Boltons, the street lamps had not yet switched on and the pavements were largely deserted. The only sign of life came from a cat who slunk along the gutter in pursuit of another slinking feline and a Filipina – dressed in the anachronistic black-and-white garb of a housemaid – who tucked a handbag under her arm and slid into a Ford Capri across the street from the house that Lynley and Nkata were seeking.

Nkata's remark was in reference to Lynley's Bentley, as perfectly at home in this neighbourhood as it had been in Notting Hill. But other than being in possession of the car, the two detectives couldn't have been more out of place in the area: Lynley for his choice of occupation, so unlikely in a man whose family could trace its roots back to the Conqueror and whose more recent ancestors would have considered the Boltons a step down from their usual haunts, and Nkata for the obvious Caribbean-via-south-of-the-river sound of his voice.

'Don't 'spect they see much rozzer action here,' Nkata said as he stood surveying the iron railings, the cameras, the alarm boxes, and the intercoms that appeared to be the feature of every dwelling. 'But it makes you wonder what the point is – all that money – if you got to wall yourself up to enjoy it.'

'I wouldn't disagree,' Lynley said, and he accepted an Opal Fruit from the detective constable's portable stash, unwrapping it and carefully folding the paper into his pocket so as not to foul the pristine footpath with litter. 'Let's see what Sir Adrian Beattie has to say.'

Lynley had recognised the name when Tricia Reeve had spoken it in Notting Hill. Sir Adrian Beattie was the UK's answer to Christian Barnard. He'd performed the first heart transplant in England and he'd successfully kept performing them round the world for the last several decades, establishing a record of success that had assured his place in medical history and guaranteed his wealth. This latter was on display in the Boltons: Beattie's home was a fortress of glacially white walls and gridiron windows with a front gate barring entrance to anyone who couldn't provide its inhabitants with an acceptable identity through an intercom from which a disembodied voice demanded 'Yes?' in a tone suggesting that not just any answer would do.

Assuming that *New Scotland Yard* would have a cachet unavailable to the simple word *police*, Lynley used their place of employment along with their ranks when he identified himself and Nkata. In reply, the gate clicked ajar. By the time Lynley and Nkata had mounted the six front steps, the door had been opened by a woman wearing an incongruous cone-shaped party hat.

She introduced herself as Margaret Beattie, daughter of Sir Adrian. The family were having a birthday party at the moment, she explained hastily, unhooking the hat's elastic strap from her chin and removing the cone from her head. Her daughter was this very evening celebrating the happy negotiation of five years among her fellow men. Was there something wrong in the neighbourhood? Not a burglary, she hoped. And she glanced past them anxiously, as if breaking and entering in the Boltons were a daily occurrence that she might inadvertently encourage by holding the front door open for longer than necessary.

They were there to see Sir Adrian, Lynley explained. And no, their visit had nothing to do with the neighbourhood and its vulnerability to professional thieves.

Margaret Beattie said doubtfully, 'I see,' and admitted them into the house. She said that if they'd wait in her father's study upstairs, she would fetch the man himself. 'I hope it won't take too long, what you've come to see him about,' she said with the sort of gentle smiling insistence a well-bred woman always uses to imply what she wants without stating it directly. 'Molly's his favourite grandchild and he's told her she can have him all to herself tonight. He's promised to read her a whole chapter of *Peter Pan*. He asked her what she wanted for her birthday, and that was it. Remarkable, don't you think?'

'Quite.'

Obviously pleased, Margaret Beattie beamed, directed them to the study, and went seeking her father.

Sir Adrian's study was on the first floor of the house, at the top of a wide staircase. Decorated with burgundy leather armchairs and fitted with forest green carpet, the room contained a plethora of volumes from the medical to the mundane, and it acted as a silent testimony to the two disparate aspects of Sir Adrian's life. The professional side was represented by medallions, certificates, awards, and mementos as diverse as antique surgical instruments and centuries' old engravings of the human heart. The personal side showed itself in dozens of photographs. They stood everywhere – on the mantelpiece, tucked into random spaces in the bookshelves, lined up like dancers ready to high kick across the top of the desk. Their subjects were the doctor's family: on holiday, at home, at school, and through the years. Lynley picked up one picture and examined it as Nkata bent to scrutinise the antique instruments that were arranged on the top of a dwarf break-front bookcase.

The doctor had four children, it seemed. In the picture Lynley held, Beattie posed among them and among their spouses, a proud paterfamilias with his wife standing next to him and eleven grandchildren clustered about him like tiny beads of oil round a larger central drop that seeks to absorb them. The occasion of the photograph had been a Christmas celebration, with each of the children holding a gift and Beattie himself decked out as Father Christmas sans beard. Everyone in the picture was either smiling or laughing, and Lynley wondered how their expressions would have read should Sir Adrian's liasion with a dominatrix have become public – or even familial – knowledge.

'Detective Inspector Lynley?'

Lynley swung round at the sound of the pleasant tenor. It should have been voiced by a younger man, but it came from the rotund surgeon himself who stood in the doorway, a *papier mâché* captain's hat on his head and a fluted glass of champagne in his hand. He said, 'We're about to toast our little Molly. She's going to open her presents. Can this wait another hour?'

'I'm afraid not.' Lynley replaced the photograph and introduced Nkata, who reached in his jacket pocket for his notebook and pencil.

Beattie saw this with apparent consternation. He entered the room and shut the door behind him. 'Is this a professional call? Has something happened? My family . . .' He looked in the direction from which he had come and dismissed whatever it was that he'd intended to say. Bearing bad news about a member of his family could not be the reason that the police had come calling. His family members were all in his house.

'A young woman called Nicola Maiden was murdered in Derbyshire on Tuesday night,' Lynley told the surgeon.

In reply, Beattie was stillness itself, waiting incarnate. His eyes were on Lynley. His surgeon's hands – an old man's hands that still looked as nimble as the hands of a man three decades younger – neither trembled, grasped the glass more tightly, nor moved in any visible way. His glance went to Nkata, dropping to the little leather notebook in the DC's big palm, then back to Lynley.

Lynley said, 'You knew Nicola Maiden, didn't you, Sir Adrian? Although perhaps you knew her by her professional name only: Nikki Temptation.'

Beattie advanced across the forest green carpet and set his champagne glass upon the desk with studied care. He placed himself behind the desk in a high back chair and canted his head at the leather armchairs. He finally said, 'Please sit, Inspector. You as well, Constable.' And when they had done so, he went on with, 'I've not seen a paper. What happened to her, please?'

It was the sort of question that a man who was used to being in charge might have asked of a subordinate. In reply, however, Lynley sought to communicate which of them would be controlling the direction of the conversation. He said evenly, 'You did know Nicola Maiden, then.'

Beattie's fingers folded round each other. Two of them, Lynley saw, had nails that were blackened, both of them deformed by some sort of fungus that apparently grew rampant beneath them. It was a disconcerting sight in a man of medicine, and Lynley wondered why Beattie didn't do something about it.

'Yes. I knew Nicola Maiden,' Beattie said.

'Tell us about your relationship.'

Behind gold-framed spectacles, the eyes were wary. 'Am I a suspect?'

'Everyone who knew her is a suspect.'

'You said Tuesday night.'

'I did say that, yes.'

'I was here on Tuesday night.'

'In this house?'

'Not here. But in London. At my club in St James's. Shall I arrange for corroboration, Inspector? That's the word I want, isn't it? *Corroboration.*'

Lynley said, 'Tell us about Nicola. When did you see her last?'

Beattie reached for his champagne and drank. To gain time, to still nerves, to quench sudden thirst. It was impossible to tell. 'The morning of the day before she left for the North.'

'This would be last June?' Nkata asked. And when Beattie nodded, Nkata added, 'In Islington?'

'Islington?' Beattie frowned. 'No. Here. She came to the house. She always came to the house when I ... when I needed her.'

'Your relationship was sexual, then,' Lynley said. 'You were one of her clients.'

Beattie turned his head away from Lynley, looking towards the mantelpiece with its copious display of family photos. 'I expect you know the answer to that question. You'd hardly have come calling on a Saturday evening had you not been told exactly where I fitted in Nikki's life. So, yes, I was one of her clients if that's what you'd like to call it.'

'What would you call it?'

'We had a mutually beneficial arrangement. She provided an indispensable service. I paid her generously for it.'

'You're a man with a high public profile,' Lynley pointed out. 'You've a successful career, a wife and children, grandchildren and all the external trappings of a fortunate life.'

'I've all the internal trappings as well,' Beattie said. 'It *is* a

446

fortunate life. So why would I risk losing it by having a liaison with a common prostitute? That's what you want to know, isn't it? But that's just the point, you see, Inspector Lynley. Nikki wasn't common in any way.'

Music started somewhere in the house, a furious and proficient playing on a piano. Chopin, it sounded like. Then the tune broke off abruptly amid some shouting, to be replaced by a spritely Cole Porter piece that was accompanied by exuberant voices not bothering to aim for the appropriate key. 'Call me irresponsible, call me unreliable,' the group partly howled, partly laughed, partly sang. 'But it's undeniably TRUE ...' Much guffawing and good-natured derision followed this: the happy family in celebration.

'So I'm learning,' Lynley agreed. 'You're not the first person to mention the fact that she was a cut above the ordinary. But actually, why you were willing to risk everything with an affair—'

'That's not what it was.'

'With an arrangement, then. Why you'd risk everything for that isn't what I want to know. I'm more interested in discovering exactly what you'd be willing to do to safeguard what you have – these external and internal trappings of your life – if the continuing possession of them was threatened in some way.'

'Threatened?' Beattie's voice was too perplexed for Lynley to believe the reaction was ingenuous. Surely the man knew how much he put at jeopardy by having a prostitute operating on the periphery of his life.

'Every man has enemies,' Lynley told him. 'Even you, I dare say. Should someone untrustworthy have found out about your arrangement with Nicola Maiden, should someone have decided to harm you by revealing that arrangement, you would have lost a great deal, and not all of it tangible.'

'Ah. I do see: the traditional outcome of societal defiance. "Who steals my purse,"' Beattie murmured. Then he went on more conversationally, giving Lynley the oddest sensation that they might have been discussing the next day's weather forecast. 'That couldn't have happened, Inspector. Nikki came to the house, as I said. She dressed conservatively, carried a brief case, and drove a Saab. To all appearances, she was arriving to take dictation or to help plan a party. And as our encounters took place well away from windows, there was absolutely nothing for anyone to see.'

'She herself didn't wear a blindfold, I expect.'

'Of course she didn't. She could hardly do that and be of any satisfactory service to me.'

'So you'll no doubt agree that she might have been in possession of certain details about you. Details which, if revealed, could confirm a story – perhaps one sold to a tabloid? – that would prove whatever facts she might choose to lay before a public for whom gossip can never be salacious enough.'

Beattie said, sounding pensive, 'Good God.'

'So corroboration is in order, as you guessed,' Lynley said. 'We'll need the name of your club.'

'Are you suggesting that I killed Nikki because she wanted more from me than I was paying? Or because I'd decided I didn't need her any longer and she was threatening to go public if I didn't keep paying her?' He tossed back a final mouthful of his champagne, afterwards giving a rueful laugh and shoving the glass away. He lumbered to his feet, saying, 'Mother of God, if that had only been the case. Wait here please.' And he left the room.

Nkata rose quickly in response. 'Guv, sh'll I . . . ?'

'Wait. Let's see.'

'He could be on the phone setting up his alibi.'

'I don't think so.' Lynley couldn't have explained why he had that feeling, save the fact that there was something decidedly odd in Sir Adrian Beattie's reactions, not only to the news of Nicola Maiden's murder but also to the logical implication that his involvement with her had vast potential to destroy everything he appeared to value.

When Beattie returned some two minutes later, he brought with him a woman whom he introduced to the detectives as his wife. Lady Beattie, he titled her and then to the woman herself, 'Chloe, these men are here about Nikki Maiden.'

Lady Beattie – a thin woman with Wallis Simpson hair and skin made shiny by too many facelifts – reached for the triple strand of pearls that were slung round her neck like souvenir golf balls. She said, 'Nikki Maiden? She's not in some kind of trouble, I hope.'

'Unfortunately, she's been murdered, my dear,' her husband said, and he placed a hand at her elbow, perhaps on the chance that she'd find the news distressing.

Which she apparently did, saying, 'Oh my God. Adrian—' and reaching for him.

He slid his hand down her arm and took her own, clucking at it with what looked to Lynley like genuine tenderness. 'Awful,' he said. 'Ghastly, rotten. These policemen have come because they think I might be involved somehow. Because of the arrangement.'

Lady Beattie disengaged her hand from her husband's. She raised a shapely eyebrow, saying, 'But isn't it much more likely that Nikki could have hurt you, and not the opposite? She didn't allow anyone to dominate her, did she? I remember her being quite specific about that the very first time we interviewed her. "I won't be the bottom," is exactly what she said. "I only tried it once, and I found it revolting." And then she pardoned herself, thinking she might have offended you. I remember that perfectly, don't you, dear?'

'I don't expect she was killed during a session,' Beattie told his wife. 'They've said it was in Derbyshire, and she'd got that summer job with the solicitor, you remember.'

'And in her free time she didn't . . . ?'

'That was only in London, as far as I know.'

'I see.'

Lynley found himself feeling as if he'd just stepped through the looking glass. He glanced at Nkata and saw that the DC, his face a study in stupefaction, felt the same. Lynley said, 'Perhaps you'd explain the arrangement to us, Sir Adrian, Lady Beattie. The background will allow us to see what we're dealing with.'

'Of course.' Lady Beattie and her husband were pleased as punch to give a full account of Sir Adrian's sexual proclivities. Lady Beattie sat gracefully on a sofa near the fireplace, while the men went back to their original positions. And while her husband outlined the exact nature of his relationship with Nicola Maiden, she added salient details wherever he forgot them.

He'd met Nicola Maiden round the first of November the previous year, perhaps nine months after his Chloe's arthritis had become too painful in her fingers and hands for her to be able to perform the rites of discipline that they'd learned to enjoy throughout their marriage. 'We thought at first that we'd simply go without,' Sir Adrian said. 'The pain, I mean. Not the sex itself. We thought we'd just cope. Be traditional and all that. But it wasn't long before we saw that my need . . .' He paused, as if seeking an abbreviated way to explain that would not take them through the cob-webbed labyrinth of his psyche. 'It *is* a need, you see. My personal need. You must understand that if you're to understand anything.'

'Go on,' Lynley said. He shot a look at Nkata. The DC had resumed his scrupulous note taking although his expression was telegraphing *Oh Lord, what's my mum going to say 'bout this* as eloquently as if he were speaking it.

Realising that Sir Adrian's need was going to have to be met if the Beatties wanted to continue their own sexual relations, they'd sought someone young, healthy, strong and – most importantly – entirely discreet to minister to him.

'Nicola Maiden,' Lynley said.

'Discretion was – is – critical,' Sir Adrian said. 'For a man in my position.' Obviously, he couldn't select a dominatrix blindly by choosing someone from a phone box card or a magazine advert. He could hardly ask friends and colleagues for recommendations. And going to an S & M club – or even to one of the lesser flesh pits in Soho in the hope of meeting a likely candidate – wasn't a wise option since there was always the chance of being seen, being recognised, and consequently being subjected to the sort of tabloid treatment guaranteed to cause excruciating agonies to his children, the spouses of his children, and their offspring. 'And to Chloe, of course,' Sir Adrian added with a nod. 'For while she knew – has always known, in fact – about the hunger, her friends and relations don't know. And I expect she'd like to keep it that way.'

'Thank you, darling,' Chloe said.

So Sir Adrian had contacted an escort service – Global Escorts, to be precise – and through that institution had ultimately met Nicola Maiden. Their first interview – consisting of tea, scones, and satisfactory conversation – had been followed by a second in which the initial deal had been struck.

'Deal?' Lynley asked.

'When her services would be required,' Chole explained. 'What they would entail and what she would be paid for them.'

'Chloe and I talked to her together for both interviews to make the arrangements,' Sir Adrian said. 'It was crucial that she understand there would be nothing gained by holding over my head a liaison potentially painful to my wife.'

'Because it wasn't painful,' Chloe said. 'At least not to me.'

'Will you show them the chamber, darling?' Sir Adrian asked his wife. 'I'll pop down to the children and let them know we'll be with them before too much longer.'

'Of course,' she replied. 'Come with me, Inspector, Constable.' And as gracefully as she'd sat, she rose, leading them to the door and up two flights of stairs as Sir Adrian went off to have a few words with his partying offspring. They were, ironically, crooning 'I Get No Kick from Champagne'.

Lady Beattie showed them up to the top floor of the house. From deep within an old clothes press that stood in the narrow corridor there, she took a key, which she used on one of the doors. She swung it open, preceded the police into the room, and switched on a low-wattage light.

'He actually only wanted discipline at first,' she explained, 'which, while I found it a bit odd, frankly – I was able to give him. Rulers on the palm, paddles on the bottom, the strap against the back of his legs. But after a few years, he wanted more and when it got to the point that I wasn't strong enough . . . Well, he's already explained that, hasn't he. At any rate, here's where they had their sessions – where he and I had them as well when I was able.'

The chamber, as they'd called it, had been fashioned out of several of the erstwhile servants' bedrooms. By knocking out walls, padding them, installing a ventilation system that obviated the use of windows – which were themselves shuttered against potential outside curiosity – the Beatties had created a fantasy world that was part headmaster's office, operating theatre, dungeon, and mediaeval torture chamber. A line of cupboards had been fitted under the eaves, and Lady Beattie opened these to display the various costumes and devices of discipline, as she called them, that had been used on Sir Adrian.

It was clear why the Maiden girl had brought nothing with her to the house save her desire to be useful to Sir Adrian and to be paid well for her usefulness: The costumes in the cupboards ranged from a heavy wool nun's habit to a prison guard's uniform complete with truncheon. There was, of course, the more traditional garb associated with the S & M game: PVC getups of red or black, leather teddies and masks, high-heeled boots. And the instruments of Sir Adrian's discipline, tidily arranged like the antique surgical instruments in the study, also explained why she'd been able to make her calls so lightly burdened. Everything necessary for discipline, pain, and humiliation had been collected and housed together.

From his years in policing, Lynley knew that he should by now have seen it all. But every time he thought he had, something in life caught him by surprise. And in this case, it wasn't so much the presence of the chamber in the Beatties' house that took his breath away. It was the attitude to it taken by the couple themselves, particularly the wife. She might have been showing them a state-of-the-art kitchen.

She seemed to realise this. Watching Lynley from her position in the doorway, observing Nkata wandering the length of the room with an expression on his face that suggested how actively his imagination was supplying him with images of the uses to which the costumes and the equipment were put, she said quietly, 'I wouldn't have had it this way, had I been given a choice. One does expect a traditional marriage. But loving someone means compromise occasionally. And once he explained why it was so important to him . . .' She gestured at the room with a hand whose knuckles were enlarged from the disease that had necessitated Nicola Maiden's entrance into the Beatties' private world. 'Need is just need. So long as judgement remains apart from it, need has no real power to hurt us.'

'Did you mind another woman seeing to the need?'

'My husband loves me, I've never had any doubt about that.'

Lynley wondered.

Sir Adrian rejoined them, saying to her, 'You're wanted below, darling. Molly's not to be denied her presents another five minutes.'

'But will you—'

They communicated in that way peculiar to couples who'd been married for more than a generation. 'As soon as I finish here. It won't be long.'

When she'd left them, Sir Adrian waited for a moment before

he said quietly, 'There's part, of course, that I'd rather Chloe didn't know. It would only hurt her unnecessarily.'

Nkata made his notebook ready as Lynley thought about what the surgeon's statement implied. He said. 'You paged her – Nicola – throughout the summer. But as she couldn't have serviced you from Derbyshire, I've a feeling your "arrangement" was something more than you wanted to say in front of your wife.'

'You're very good, Inspector.' Beattie closed the chamber door. 'I was in love with her. Not at first, naturally. We didn't know each other. But within a month or two, I realised how strongly I was feeling about her. Initially I told myself it was only addiction: A new woman doing the discipline heightened my excitement, and I wanted that excitement more and more often. But it went beyond that in the end because she was far more than I expected. So I wanted to keep her. More than anything in the world, I wanted that.'

'To keep her as your wife?'

'I love Chloe. But there's more than one kind of love in a man's life – which you may know already or will come to know eventually – and selfishly I hoped to experience it.' He dropped his gaze to the deformed nails at the end of his fingers. He said, 'I felt sexual love for Nikki, the sort that has to do with physical possession. Animal craving. My love for Chloe, on the other hand, is the stuff of our history. When I knew I had this other love for Nikki – this sexual thing that I found I couldn't get out of my mind the more we met – I told myself it was natural to feel it. She was meeting a tremendous need of mine. And no matter what I wanted, she was willing to do it to me. But when I saw there was so much more to her than domination . . .'

'You became reluctant to share her with other men.'

Beattie smiled. 'An intuitive leap. Yes, you *are* very good.'

Nicola visited the Boltons at least five times a week, Beattie told them. And he explained the frequency of their sessions to Chloe by talking about the heightened stress of his work as younger doctors and advances in medicine had increased his level of anxiety to the point that only discipline could relieve it. And the truth wasn't so far from that, anyway.

'I told her that when the craving came upon me, I wanted her available to gratify it at once,' he said.

'But the reality was more complicated than that?'

'The reality was infinitely simple. I couldn't deal with imagining Nikki doing to others and being to others – what she was doing and being to me. Thinking of her with anyone else – whoever they might have been – was a quick descent into hell. And I didn't expect that, to *feel* that way about a tart. But then, when I took her on, I didn't know how much more than a tart she was going to be.'

Without his wife's knowledge, he'd offered Nicola a special deal. He would pay to keep her – and pay her more than she'd ever dreamed of being paid – in whatever situation she fancied for herself: a flat, a house, a hotel suite, a country cottage. He didn't care, just so long as she promised him that her time would be kept open solely for him. 'I claimed that I didn't want to stand in a queue or book an appointment any longer,' Beattie explained. 'But if I wanted her available to me at any hour, I had to place her in a position where she was free.'

The maisonette in Fulham gave her that position. And since Nicola always came to Sir Adrian and not the reverse, it was of little account to him that she asked to be allowed a flatmate as company for the periods of time when he didn't want her services. 'That was fine with me,' he told them. 'All I wanted was her to be available whenever I phoned. And for the first month, that's what she was. Five or six days a week. Sometimes twice a day. She'd arrive within an hour of being paged. She'd stay as long as I wanted her to be here. The arrangement worked well.'

'But then she returned to Derbyshire. Why?'

'She claimed that she needed to honour a commitment to

work for a solicitor up there, that she'd only be gone for the summer. I was a fool in love, but not so much of a fool as to believe that. I told her I wouldn't go on paying for the Fulham place if she wasn't going to be in town for me.'

'But she went anyway. She was willing to risk losing what she had from you. What does that suggest?'

'The obvious. I knew that if she was returning to Derbyshire despite what I was paying her to be here in London, there had to be a reason and the reason was money. Someone there was paying her more than I was. Which meant, of course, another man.'

'The solicitor.'

'I accused her. She denied it. And I have to admit that an ordinary solicitor couldn't have afforded her, not without an independent source of income. So it was someone else. But she wouldn't name him, no matter what I threatened. "It's only for the summer," she kept saying. And I kept bellowing, "I don't bloody care."'

'You quarrelled.'

'Bitterly. I withdrew my support. I knew she'd have to go back to the escort service – or perhaps even to the street – if she wanted to keep the maisonette when she returned to London, and I was betting that she wouldn't want to do that. But I bet wrong. She left me anyway. And I lasted four days before I was on the phone, ready to give her anything to return to me. More money. A house. God, even my name.'

'But she wouldn't return.'

'She didn't mind being on the street, she said. Casually, this was. As if I'd asked her how she was finding Derbyshire. "We've got cards printed and Vi's are already out there," she said. "Mine'll be out there as well when I get back to town. I have no hard feelings about what's happened between you and me, Ady. And anyway, Vi says the phone's ringing day and night, so we'll be fine."'

'Did you believe her?'

'I accused her of trying to drive me mad. I railed. Then I apologised. Then she played up to me on the phone. Then I wanted her desperately and couldn't bear to think of what she was giving him, whoever he was. Then I railed at her again. Stupid. Bloody stupid. But I was desperate to have her back. I would have done anything—' He stopped, seeming to realise how his words could be interpreted.

Lynley said, 'On Tuesday night, Sir Adrian?'

'Inspector, I didn't kill Nikki. I couldn't have harmed her. I haven't even seen her since June. I'd hardly be standing here telling you all this if I'd . . . I couldn't have hurt her.'

'Your club's name?'

'Brooks's. I met a colleague there for dinner on Tuesday. He'll confirm, I dare say. But my God, you won't tell him that I . . . No one knows, Inspector. It's something that's between Chloe and me.'

And anyone Nicola Maiden chose to tell, Lynley thought. What would it mean to Sir Adrian Beattie to have his most closely guarded secret held over his head like Damocles' sword? What would he do if threatened with exposure?

'Did Nicola ever introduce you to her flatmate?'

'Once, yes. When I gave her the keys to the maisonette.'

'So Vi Nevin, the flatmate, knew about the arrangement?'

'Perhaps. I don't know.'

But why even take the *risk* of someone knowing? Lynley wondered. Why allow a flatmate into the mix and face the dangers inherent in an outsider's having knowledge of a sexual proclivity that could cause such humiliation to a man in Beattie's position?

Beattie himself seemed to read the questions in Lynley's eyes. He said, 'Do you know what it feels like to be that desperate for a woman? So desperate that you'll agree to anything, do anything to have her? That's what it was like.'

'What about Terry Cole? How did he fit in?'

'I don't know a Terry Cole.'

Lynley tried to gauge the level of veracity in the statement. He couldn't do so. Beattie was too good at maintaining his expression of guilelessness. But that alone increased Lynley's suspicion.

He thanked the surgeon for his time, and he and Nkata took their leave, giving Beattie back into the arms of his family. Incongruously, the man had kept his *papier mâché* captain's hat on throughout their interview. Lynley wondered if the wearing of that hat kept him firmly anchored in his family life or acted as a spurious symbol of a devotion that he did not feel.

Once out on the street, Nkata said, 'My sweet Lord. What people get themselves into, 'spector.'

'Hmm. Yes,' Lynley agreed. 'And what they get themselves out of as well.'

'You don't believe his story?'

Lynley answered indirectly. 'Talk to the people at Brooks's. They'll have records showing when he was there. Then head over to Islington. You've seen Sir Adrian Beattie in the flesh. You've seen Martin Reeve as well. Talk to the Maiden girl's landlady, the neighbours. Let's see if anyone can recall glimpsing either of those gentlemen there on the ninth of May.'

'Asking a lot, Guv. Four months back.'

'I've faith in your powers of interrogation.' Lynley disarmed the Bentley's security system, saying over the car's roof, 'Climb in. I'll drop you at the tube.'

'What's on for yourself?'

'Vi Nevin. If anyone can confirm Beattie's story she's going to be the one.'

Azhar wouldn't hear of Barbara walking the seventy or so yards alone to her bungalow at the bottom of the garden. She might be mugged, raped, accosted, or attacked by a cat with a proclivity for thick ankles.

So he tucked his daughter into her bed, scrupulously locked the door of his flat, and ushered Barbara round the side of the house. He offered her a cigarette. She accepted and they paused to light up, the flaring match emphasising the contrasting colours of their skin as she held the cigarette to her lips and he sheltered the flame near to her mouth.

'Nasty habit,' she said conversationally. 'Hadiyyah's after me all the time to stop.'

'After me as well,' Azhar said. 'Her mother is – at least she was – quite a militant non-smoker, and Hadiyyah has apparently inherited not only Angela's dislike of tobacco but also her crusading spirit.'

It was the most Azhar had yet said about the mother of his child. Barbara wanted to ask him whether he'd informed his daughter that her mother was gone for good or if he was still holding firmly to the fairy tale of Angela Weston's holiday in Canada, one which had now extended itself for nearly five months. But she said nothing beyond, 'Yeah. Well. You're her dad, and I expect she'd like to keep you round for a few more years.' They followed the path that led to her digs.

'Thanks for the dinner, Azhar. It was lovely. When I get beyond re-heating pizza, I want to return the favour, if you'll let me.'

'That would be a pleasure, Barbara.'

She expected him to turn back for his flat – her own small hovel being well in view so there was little chance that she'd get into trouble in a five second saunter down the rest of the garden path. But he continued to walk along with her in his quiet way.

They reached her front door. She hadn't locked it and, when she swung it open, Azhar frowned and said that her sense of security was not as heightened as it ought to be. She said Yeah, but she hadn't intended to stay for dinner. And thank you for that meal, by the way. You are a brilliant cook. Or have I said that already?

Azhar politely pretended that she hadn't mentioned his cooking expertise until that moment, after which he insisted that he be allowed inside to make certain there were no unwanted visitors lurking in the shower or under the day bed. Having examined the bungalow to his satisfaction, Azhar advised her to lock her door carefully when he left. But then he didn't leave. Instead, he glanced at the dining room table where Barbara had deposited her belongings upon arriving home from work. These consisted of her shapeless old shoulder bag and a manila folder into which she'd tucked the roster of employees from 31–32 Soho Square, her own surreptitiously duplicated copy of the postmortem that she'd delivered to St James, and the rough draft of the report she'd crafted for Lynley, delineating the information she'd gleaned from reading the SO10 files of Andy Maiden.

Azhar said, 'This new investigation keeps you busy. You must be gratified to be back among your colleagues.'

'Yeah,' Barbara said. 'It was a long patch of waiting. Regent's Park and I were becoming a bit more acquainted than I'd thought we might be when it all began.'

Azhar drew in on his cigarette, watching her over it and then through the smoke. She never liked it when he looked at her this way. It was a look that always left her wondering what was supposed to happen next.

She said, 'Thanks again for the meal.'

'Thank you for sharing it with us.' But still he made no move to leave and she realised why when he finally said, 'The letters D and C, Barbara. They're an indication of rank in the police force, are they not?'

Her heart sank. She wanted to divert the conversation they were about to have, but she couldn't think of a quick way to do so. So she said, 'Yeah. Generally. I mean I suppose it depends on what they're attached to, those letters. Like Washington, D.C. That's not a rank. But of course, it's not a police force, either.' She smiled. Far too brightly, she decided.

'But attached to your name. DC. Detective Constable. Yes?'

Damn, Barbara thought. But what she said was, 'Oh. Yeah. Right.'

'Then you've been demoted. I saw the letters on that note that the gentleman left for you. I thought at first there was some sort of mistake but as you've not been working with Inspector Lynley—'

'I don't always work with the inspector, Azhar. Sometimes we take different parts of a case.'

'Do you.' But she could see he didn't believe the story. Or at least that he thought there was something more to it. 'Demotion. And yet there's been no reduction in the force, has there? I believe you told me that earlier, didn't you? And if that's the case, it seems that you must be avoiding a truth. With me, that is. I find myself wondering why.'

'Azhar, I'm not avoiding anything. Hell. We don't exactly live in each other's knickers, do we?' Barbara said and then found her face blazing with the implication of an intimacy which she hadn't intended. Bloody hell, she thought. Why was conversation with this man such a minefield? 'I mean, we don't do a lot of job talk, you and I. We never have done. You teach your classes at the university. I saunter round the Yard and try to look indispensable.'

'Demotion is serious in any profession. And in this case, I expect that it comes from your time in Essex, doesn't it? What happened there, Barbara?'

'Whoa. How'd you make *that* jump?'

He crushed out his cigarette in an ashtray from which at least ten dog ends of Players protruded from the burnt tobacco like burgeoning vegetables. He regarded her. 'I am correct in the surmise, am I not? You were disciplined because of your work in Essex last June. What happened, Barbara?'

'It's sort of a private situation.' She temporised, 'I mean, you know, it's a personal thing. Why d'you want to know?'

'Because I find myself in a state of confusion about British law, and I wish to understand it better. How can I be of assistance to my people when they have legal difficulties if I don't clearly see how the laws of your country are applied to the individual who breaks them?'

'But this wasn't a case of breaking a law,' Barbara said. And that, she told herself, was merely a mild prevarication. After all, she hadn't been defending herself against a charge of assault or attempted murder, so law-wise, she'd always been in the clear.

'Nonetheless, as you are my friend – at least I hope that you are—'

'Of course I am.'

'Then perhaps you'll help me to understand more about your society.'

Bollocks, Barbara thought. He understood more about British society than she herself did. But she could hardly take the discussion in that direction where it would soon enough crumble into a verbal Punch and Judy of Yes you do. No I don't. So she said, 'It's nothing much. I had a row with the DCI in charge of the case out in Essex, Azhar. We were in the middle of a chase. And the one thing an underling isn't supposed to do is to question an order in the middle of a chase. That's what happened and that's why I lost my rank.'

'For questioning an order.'

'I tend to question more forcefully than the average bird,' she said airily. 'It's a habit that I learned in school. I'm short. I get lost in a crowd if I don't make myself heard. You ought to hear me order a pint of Bass in the Load of Hay when the football crowd's watching an Arsenal match on the telly. But when I used the same approach with DCI Barlow, she didn't much like it.'

'Yet to lose your rank . . . It's a draconian measure, certainly. Are you being made an example of? Can you not protest it? Is there not a union or organisation who might represent you aggressively enough to—'

'In a situation like this,' Barbara cut in, 'it's best not to make waves. Let the smoke clear, you know. Let sleeping dogs lie.' She groaned inwardly, the Queen of Cliché. 'Anyway, when enough time passes, it'll sort itself out. The situation. You know.' She smashed her own cigarette among the others, putting an end to their discussion. She waited for him to bid her goodnight.

Instead, he said, 'Hadiyyah and I go to the seaside tomorrow.'

'She told me. She's looking forward to it. The pleasure pier, especially. And she's expecting a big win from the crane grab, Azhar, so I hope you've been practising with the pincers.'

He smiled. 'She asks for so little. And yet life appears to give her so much.'

'P'haps that's why,' Barbara pointed out. 'If you don't spend your time looking for something particular, what you end up finding suits you just fine.'

'Wise words,' he acknowledged.

Wisdom's cheap, Barbara thought. She rustled in the manila folder on the table and brought out the roster of names from Soho Square. Duty was calling, her action told him. And Azhar was nothing if not astute at drawing inferences from unspoken implications.

The journey from Sir Adrian Beattie's home to Vi Nevin's maisonette was little more than a cruise down the Fulham Road in rather light traffic. It didn't take long But it was long enough for Lynley to consider what he'd heard from Beattie and what he felt about what he'd heard. After years in CID, he realised that there was no real place in the investigation for him to be dwelling upon what he felt about anyone's revelations, least of all Sir Adrian's. But he found that he couldn't help himself. And he justified the direction his thoughts were taking by declaring them natural: Sexual deviance was as much a curiosity as a two-headed kitten. One might shudder at the sight of such an anomaly. But one still looked at it.

And that's what he was doing: looking at the deviant behaviour for its anomaly quotient first, and then evaluating the possibility that sexual deviance in itself was the relevant detail that would allow him to unearth Nicola Maiden's killer. The only problem he was having with attempting to use sexual deviance as a means of finding a killer was that he was discovering himself incapable of moving beyond the mere presence of the deviance in the first place.

Why was this? he wondered. Was he titillated by it? Sententiously condemnatory? Intrigued? Appalled? Seduced? What?

He couldn't have said. He knew it existed, of course: what some would call the dark side of desire. He was aware of at least some of the theoretical frameworks that students of the psyche had constructed to explain it. Depending upon what school of thought one wished to enroll in, sado-masochism could be considered an erotic blasphemy born of sexual dissent; an upper class vice growing out of spending one's formative years in boarding schools where corporal punishment was the order of the day – and the more ritualised the better; a defiant reaction to a rigidly conservative upbringing; an expression of personal loathing for the simple possession of sexual drives; or the sole means of physical intimacy for those whose terror of the mere prospect of intimacy was greater than their willingness to overcome it. But what he didn't know was why, at the moment, the thought of deviancy was eating away at him. And it was the *why* of that eating that plagued his mind.

What has all this to do with love? Lynley had wanted to ask the surgeon. What did being bruised, beaten, bloodied, and humiliated have to do with the ineffable and – yes, all right, it was absurdly romantic but he'd use the term anyway – *transcendent* joy that was attached to the act of possessing and of being possessed by another person? Wasn't that joy the outcome to which sexual partners ought to aspire when they engaged in intercourse? Or was he too new a newlywed to be making any assessments at all about what went for devotion between consenting adults? And did sex have anything to do with love anyway? And should it, for that matter? Or was that where everyone went wrong in the first place, assigning an importance to a bodily function that should have no more importance than cleaning one's teeth?

Except that direction of thought was sophistry, wasn't it. One didn't *need* to clean one's teeth. One didn't even feel the need. And it was the *feeling* of that need – the slow building up of a tension at first subtle and ultimately impossible to ignore – that told the real tale in life. Because it was that *feeling* of need which led to a hunger that insisted upon gratification. And it was the desire for gratification that caused one to abjure everything that rose up to forbid the satiety one sought: One willingly disregarded honour, responsibility, tradition, fidelity, and duty in pursuit of one's passion. And why? Because one *wanted*.

If he cast himself back more than twenty years, Lynley could see how the wanting had rent his own family. Or at least how he himself had allowed the wanting – which he had then only imperfectly understood – to rend it. Honour had bound his mother to his father. Responsibility and tradition had tied her to the family home and to the more than two hundred and fifty years of Asherton countesses who had overseen its maintenance and its glory. Duty had demanded that she concern herself with her husband's failing health and her children's welfare. And fidelity had required that she do it all without openly, inwardly, or privately acknowledging that she herself might want something different – or at least something more – than the lot she'd chosen as an eighteen-year-old bride. She'd coped with everything well until disease began to gnaw at her husband. Even then, she'd managed to hold together life as the family had always known it, until the very act of *having* to cope, of having to act a rôle instead of simply being able to live it, had made her long for rescue. And rescue had come, if only temporarily.

Bitch, whore, tart, he'd called her. And he would have struck her – the mother he'd adored – had she not struck him first, and with a violence, a frustration, and an anger that had given to the blow a force which split open his upper lip.

Why had he reacted so violently to the knowledge of her infidelity? Lynley wondered now as he braked to avoid a pack of cyclists who were negotiating the right turn onto North End Road. He watched them idly – all business in their helmets and Spandex – and considered the question, not only for what it revealed about his adolescence but also for what its answer implied about the case in hand. The answer, he decided, had to do with love and with the insidious and often unreasonable expectations that always seemed to attach themselves to the very fact of loving. How often we want the love object to be an extension of ourselves, he thought. And when that doesn't happen – because it never can – our frustration demands that we take action to alleviate the turmoil we feel.

But, he realised, there was more than one kind of turmoil that was becoming apparent in the relationships that Nicola Maiden had had. While thwarted desire played a part in her life – and very possibly in her death – he couldn't overlook the place that was occupied by jealousy, revenge, avarice, and hate. All those crippling passions caused turmoil. Any one of them could drive someone to murder.

Lynley found that Rostrevor Road was a mere half mile south of Fulham Broadway, and the door of Viola Nevin's building was propped open when he climbed the steps. A hand-lettered sign on the jamb explained why, as did the noise coming from a ground floor flat, whose door was also propped open. *Tildy and Steve's Digs At The Rear* were the words written out in multi-coloured felt pen on a sheet of heavy paper. *Smoke Outside, Please!* was the request made beneath.

The noise from within was considerable as the partygoers were enjoying the musical talents of an unidentifiable group of males who were gutturally advising members of their sex to use her, abuse her, have her, and lose her, all to the accompaniment of percussion and brass. None of this sounded particularly mellifluous in combination, Lynley decided. He was getting older – and, alas, stuffier – than he thought. He headed for the stairs and dashed upwards.

The corridor lights were on a timer, with a push button at the bottom of the stairs. There were windows on the landing, but as darkness had fallen, these did very little to dispel the gloom once one climbed above the ground floor of the building. So Lynley punched for the lights on Vi Nevin's floor and strode towards her door.

She hadn't been willing to tell the truth about how she'd come to meet Nicola Maiden in the first place. She hadn't been willing to name the man who had originally financed the rooms in which she lived. There were probably a score of other facts that she could part with, if the psychological thumbscrews were applied with enough finesse.

Lynley felt up to the task of applying them. Although Vi Nevin was nobody's fool and unlikely to be tricked into revealing information, she was also living at the edge of the law and, like the Reeves, she'd be willing to compromise if compromise was what would keep her in business.

He rapped sharply on her door. There was a brass knocker, so he knew she'd be able to hear his knock despite the music and shouting from the party below. However, there was no answer from within, which upon reflection, was hardly a circumstance worthy of suspicion since it was a Saturday night and – whether she was out servicing a client or otherwise engaged – a woman away from home on a Saturday night was nothing to raise the alarm about.

He removed one of his cards from his jacket, put on his glasses, and slid a pen from his pocket to leave her a note. He wrote and returned the pen to his pocket. He fixed the card to the door at the height of the knob.

And then he saw it.

Blood. An unmistakable thumbprint upon the doorknob. A second smear some eight inches higher, rising at an angle on the door from the jamb.

'Christ.' Lynley used his fist against the door. 'Miss Nevin?' he called. Then he shouted, 'Vi Nevin!'

There was no answer. There was no sound from within.

Lynley pulled his wallet from his trouser pocket, extracted a credit card, and applied it to the old Banham latch.

Chapter Twenty-two

———❖———

'Do you have any idea what you've done? Any idea at all?'

How long had it been since she'd shot up? Martin Reeve wondered. And could he hope against unlikely hope that the pathetic smack-head had hallucinated the encounter and not actually lived it in the first place? Strictly speaking, that was possible. Tricia *never* answered the door when he wasn't in. Her paranoia was far too advanced for that. So why the hell would she have answered it this time, when nearly everything that comprised their lifestyle was sitting at the edge of a cliff just waiting for someone to make a wrong move and send it hurtling down to the boulders below?

But he knew the answer to that question well enough. She would have answered the door because she was brainless, because she couldn't be trusted to think in a straight line from action to consequence of action for five minutes, because if anyone on the face of the earth even prompted her to think that her pipeline of dope was in danger of being stopped up in some way, she would do *anything* to prevent that happening, and answering a door was the least of that anything: She would sell her body, she would sell her soul, she would sell them both down the God damn river. Which was, apparently, what the airheaded bitch had actually managed to do while he was out.

He'd found her in their bedroom nodding away in her white wicker rocker next to the window, with a sword's width of illumination from the streetlight outside falling across her left shoulder and gilding her breast. She was completely nude, and an oval cheval mirror, drawn near to the rocker, reflected the ghostly perfection of her body.

He'd said, 'What the hell are you doing, Tricia?' not entirely unpleasantly since he was, after twenty years of marriage to the woman, quite used to finding his wife in an array of conditions: from dressed to the nines in a little designer number that cost a small fortune, to tucked up in bed at three o'clock in the afternoon wearing a Babygro and sucking on a bottle of *piña colada*. So at first he'd thought she'd arranged herself for his delectation. And while he hadn't been in the mood to fuck her, he'd still been capable of acknowledging that the money he'd spent on Beverly Hills surgeons had been cash invested with visually enjoyable results.

But that thought had died like a candle's flame in a draught when Martin saw how far his wife was gone on the stuff. While her shit-induced semi-somnolence generally inspired him to take her in that master-of-the-rag-doll fashion which he vastly preferred when coupling with any woman openly willing to receive his ministrations, the afternoon and evening hadn't worked out according to his plans, and he knew the workings of his body and his mind well enough to realise that if he roused himself to take another woman today – especially one who wouldn't put up a gratifying fight against him – it wasn't going to be a female whose range of response was similar to that of a bottle of plasma. That would hardly provide him with the distraction he'd been looking for.

So at first, he'd dismissed both her and the possibility of receiving a coherent answer to the question he'd asked her. And he'd ignored her altogether when she'd murmured, 'Got t'go t'Melbourne, Marty. Got t'get's there straight away.' Typical strung out nonsense, he'd thought. He went into the bathroom, turned on the shower to heat up, and lathered his hands beneath the tap, soothing both his knuckles and his face with the creamy soap that Tricia favoured.

By the window, she spoke again, this time louder so as to be heard over the rush of water. 'S' I made some calls. T'see wha' iss cost us to go. Soon's we can, Marty. Babe? You hear tha'? Got t'go t'Melbourne.'

He went to the doorway, drying his hands and face gently on a towel. She saw him, smiled, and ran her manicured fingers up her thigh, across her stomach, and teasingly round her nipple. The nipple hardened. She smiled wider. Martin did neither. 'I wonder 'bout the heat in 'Stralia,' she said. 'I know you don't much fancy heat. Bu' we got go t' Melbourne 'cause I promised him.'

Martin had begun to take her more seriously at that. It was the *him* that caught his attention. 'What are you talking about, Tricia?'

She said with a pout, 'No' list'ning, Marty. I *hate* it when you don't listen to me.'

Martin knew the importance of keeping his voice pleasant, at least for the moment. 'I *am* listening, darling. Melbourne. The heat. Australia. A promise. I've heard it all. I just don't understand how it fits together and what it relates to. Perhaps if you'll explain . . . ?'

'What it *relates* to—' She waved airily round the room at everything and at nothing. Then she shifted gears abruptly in that Jekyll-Hyde move so common to loadies, saying scornfully, 'You soun' like *such* a poof, Marty. P'rhaps if you'll 'xplain . . .'

Martin's reservoir of patience was nearly depleted. Another two minutes of verbal blind man's buff and he was likely to throttle her. He said, 'Tricia, if you've something of importance to relate, tell me. Otherwise, I'm taking a shower. All right?'

'Ooohhh,' she mocked. 'He's taking a shower. And I 'spect we know why if we sniff him up. We know what we'll smell.

So who was it this time? Which one of the *ladies* di' you have today? An' don' lie 'bout it, Marty, 'cause I know what's what with you 'n' the girls. They tell me, y'know. They even *complain*. Which, I 'spect, you'd never think of them doing, would you?'

For a moment Martin considered believing her. God knew there were times when the act of simply demanding and taking what wasn't on offer *wasn't* enough to satisfy him. Every now and then events piled one upon the other in such a way that only a certain level of ferocity was able to compensate him for his lack of control over the countless daily irritations that swirled around him like gnats. But Tricia didn't know that beyond a shadow of a doubt and there wasn't a single girl in his stable who'd be stupid enough to tell her. So Martin turned away from his wife without making a response to her remark. He stripped off his shirt in preparation for his shower.

She said from the bedroom, 'So say bye-bye. Bye-bye to all this. You ready to do that, Marty?'

He unzipped his trousers and let them drop to the floor. He peeled off his socks. He made no reply.

She went on, calling, 'He said if we wen' t' 'Stralia, you and me, he'd keep his mug shut 'bout the bus'ness. So I 'spect that's what we got to do.'

'He.' Martin re-entered the bedroom, clad only in his shorts. 'He?' he said again. 'Tricia, *he?*' Within his gut, a roiling began: a nascent nausea suggesting that something previously inconceivable might actually have happened in the hours during which he'd left his wife alone in the house.

'Righ',' she said. 'Just like a chocolate bar, he was. And just as sweet, I 'spect, if I'd wanted t' try him. He di'n't come with that cow this time round, so I could've, I s'pose. Only he di'n't come alone.'

Jesus, Martin thought. They'd come back, the bastards. And they'd got into the house. And they'd talked to his air-head nitwit of a wife.

He strode over to the rocker. He knocked her hand from her breast. 'Tell me,' he said sharply. 'The police were here. Tell me.'

She said, 'Hey!' in protest and reached for her nipple again.

He caught her fingers in his hand. He squeezed them till the bones ground together like brittle twigs. He said, 'I'll cut it off. You like that pretty tit of yours, I think. You wouldn't want it to go missing, would you? So tell me right now or I won't answer for the consequences.' And just to make certain she understood – he moved his clasp from her fingers to her hand and then to her wrist. A good twist, he'd found long ago, was worth a hundred lashes. And more importantly, it didn't leave a significant mark to show Mummy and Daddy later.

Tricia cried out. He increased the torque. She shrieked, 'Marty!' He said, 'Talk.' She tried to slither from the rocker to the floor, but he had the better position and he straddled her. An arm across her throat and he had her head flung back into the wicker chair. 'Do you want more?' he asked. 'Or is this enough?'

She opted for the second. She told the story. He listened with mounting incredulity, wanting so much to pound in his wife's face that he wasn't quite sure how he'd possibly keep himself from doing it. That she'd let the cops in the house in the first place bordered on the absolutely fantastic. That she'd spoken to them about the escort service ventured into the unbelievable. But that she'd actually given them the *name* and *address* of Sir Adrian Beattie – just blithely handed it over without even considering what it meant to break the confidence of a man whose peculiar needs had been serviced by Global Escorts in the past and whose same peculiar needs would want servicing by Global Escorts anew now that the Maiden tart was finally out of the way – constituted such an act of insanity that Martin didn't know how he could contain his fury.

So he said, 'Do you have *any* idea what you've done?' as his insides tightened like a wrung-out rag. 'Any idea at all?' and he grabbed her by the hair, and jerked her head back viciously.

'Stop it! Tha' hurts. Marty! Stop!'

'Do you know what you've done, you stupid little cunt? Have you any idea how thoroughly you've finished us?'

'No! Hurts!'

'Oh darling, I'm glad of it.' And he yanked her head so far back that he could count the muscles down the front of her neck. 'You're worthless, beloved,' he said into her ear. 'You're trash in a bun, little wife of mine. If your father had just half a dozen fewer connections, I'd throw you on the street and be done with you.'

She began to cry at that. She was afraid of him, had always been so, and that knowledge usually acted like an aphrodisiac upon him. But not tonight. Tonight, on the contrary, he wanted to kill her.

'They were going to arrest you,' she cried. 'Wha' was I s'posed to do? Just let it happen?'

He moved his other hand up her throat and settled it under her jaw, thumb on one side and index finger on the other. This grip *could* cause a mark or two, he thought. But by God, she was such an exceptional imbecile that the consequences of damaging her seemed almost worth it. 'Oh were they?' he said, again into her ear. 'And upon what charge?'

'Marty, they knew. They knew ever'thing. They knew about Global and Nicola and about Vi and her going off on their own. *I* di'n't tell them any of that. But they *knew*. They asked where you were on Tuesday night. I told them the res'rant, but it wasn't enough. They were going t' search and get our books and give them to the Inland Revenue and charge you with keeping a disorderly house and—'

'Stop babbling!' He pressed thumb and index finger more deeply into her skin to emphasise his point. He needed time to think what to do and he wasn't going to be able to manage it with her spewing nonsense like a vomiting cat.

All right, he thought, one hand still in Tricia's hair and the other at her throat. The worst had happened. His dearly beloved – possessing all the presence of mind of a melting ice cube – had been the one to parry with the cops on their second go in Lansdowne Road. That was unfortunate, but it couldn't be helped now. And Sir Adrian Beattie, not to mention the thousands he was willing to spend in a single month just to gratify the more eccentric of his urges, was undoubtedly lost to them. He might take others with him, if he was willing to spread the word to his fellow puling bottoms that his name and inclinations had been made known to the police by a source hitherto irreproachable. *But* there was a saving grace: The cops had nothing on Martin Reeve in the long run, did they? Just the blathering of a smack user whose credibility was about as unimpeachable as a con man's in the act of selling eighteen carat 'gold' necklaces at Knightsbridge Station.

They might come to arrest him, Martin thought. Well frigging *let* them. He had a solicitor who'd have him out of the slammer so fast, the cell bars might have been coated with axle grease in anticipation of his rapid departure. And *if* he ever had to stand in front of a magistrate or *if* he was ever charged with something other than introducing gentlemen with a taste for quirky encounters to appealing and intelligent young women willing to take an active part in those encounters, he had in his possession a list of clients from so many lofty positions of influence, that the multitudinous strings that could be pulled on his behalf would make the Met, the Inns of Court and the Old Bailey look like puppet conventions.

No. He had nothing to worry about in the long run. And he was as likely to have to go to Australia as to the moon. Things might be a little unpleasant for a while. Certain newspaper editors might have to be paid to quash a story here and there. But that would be the extent of it, aside from the cash he'd also probably have to pay out to his solicitor. And *that* likely – and significant – expenditure pissed him off in a very big way.

So much so, in fact, that when he thought about it, when he added it all up, when he dwelt for so much as a nanosecond on the fucking *cause* of all these added aggravations Jesus he just wanted to crush in her face break open her nose blacken her eyes ram himself into her when she was dry and unwilling and likely to scream and beg him to stop so that just for a moment he'd be so supreme that no one no one no one in his life would ever again look at him and think he was less than or smaller than or weaker than or God God God how he wanted to hurt her and mutilate everyone else who said *Martin Reeve* without *Mister* in front of it who smiled from faces with eyes of derision who crossed his path without stepping aside who dared to even *think*—

Tricia had ceased moving. She wasn't thrashing. Her legs were motionless. Her arms had gone limp.

Martin looked down at her, down at his hand whose thumb and index finger made a half circle high on his wife's throat.

He jumped up, jumped off her, backed away in a rush. She was white in the moonlight, as still as marble.

'Tricia,' he said hoarsely. 'God damn you. Bitch!'

Lynley's credit card was sufficient to slide the latch of the lock from its housing. The maisonette's door swung open. Inside, all was darkness. There was no sound save what drifted upwards from the drinks party going on in the ground floor flat.

'Miss Nevin?' Lynley called.

There was no response.

The light from the corridor provided a glowing parallelogram on the floor. In it, a large cushion lay, half in and half out of its yellow cover of fine brocade. Next to this, a pool of spilled liquid had soaked into the carpet in an alligator shape while just beyond, the drinks trolley stood upended and surrounded by its bottles, its decanters – now unstoppered and emptied – its glasses, and its jugs.

Lynley reached for a switch on the wall to the right of the door. He flipped it on. Recessed lights sprang to life in the ceiling, revealing the extent of the chaos beneath them.

From what he could see from the doorway, the maisonette was in ruins: sofa and love seat overturned with cushions torn from their covers, pictures off the walls and looking as if they'd been broken deliberately across someone's knee, stereo system and television flung to the floor and destroyed – the backings on everything from the speakers to the television hacked away – a portfolio ripped into two pieces with its photographs left scattered round the room. Not even the fitted carpet had escaped, jerked back from the wall with the sort of strength that spoke of a rage long anticipated and fully indulged.

The devastation in the kitchen was similar: crockery lying shattered on the white tiled floor, shelves swept clean of every object which now lay where it had apparently fallen, either on work tops or broken beneath them. The refrigerator had been dealt with as well, if only in part: everything from the freezer was dewing with moisture among the rest of the detritus while the contents of the crisping drawers were smashed like victims of runaway lorries, leaving smears of their juices on the tiles, in the grout, and against the cupboard doors.

From the ruins of a bottle of ketchup and a jar of mustard, footprints led from the kitchen towards the outer corridor. One of them was perfectly formed, as if brushed onto the tiles with dark orange paint.

Along the ascent of the stairs, pictures torn from the walls had met a fate similar to those in the sitting room, and as he climbed, Lynley felt the burning of a slow hard anger begin in the middle of his chest. It mixed there, however, with the chill of fear. And he found himself praying that the condition of the maisonette meant Vi Nevin had been absent from the building when the intruder – so obviously bent upon harming her – had taken out his frustration on her possessions.

He called her name again. Again there was no reply. He

flicked on the light in the first of the bedrooms. Illumination fell upon utter ruin. Not one stick of furniture had been left untouched.

He murmured, 'Christ.' Which was when the pulsation from the music below ceased abruptly as, perhaps, a new selection of entertainment was made.

And then, in that sudden quiet, he heard it. A scrabbling, like rodents running on wood. It came from the bedroom in which he was standing, from behind the bed's mattress which canted drunkenly against one of the walls. In three strides he was to it. He shoved it aside. He said, 'Jesus,' and bent to the battered form whose hair – so long, so Alice-in-Wonderland blonde where it wasn't blood-soaked – told him that Viola Nevin had indeed been at home when vengeance had come calling in Rostrevor Road.

The scrabbling had come from her fingernails, plucking spasmodically at the white baseboard which was splodged with her blood. And the blood itself came from her head, particularly from her face which had been bashed repeatedly, destroying the little girl prettiness that had been her hallmark and her stock in trade.

Lynley held her small hand. He didn't want to take the risk of moving her. Had he been willing to do so, he would have grabbed her up once he'd phoned for help and cradled her battered body until the ambulance arrived. But he couldn't tell how – or if – she was injured internally, so he simply held onto her hand.

The ensanguined weapon lay nearby, a heavy hand mirror. It appeared to have been fashioned from some sort of metal, but now it was crimson with gore and made repulsive with strands of blonde hair and small bits of flesh. Lynley closed his eyes briefly when he saw it. Having observed far worse crime scenes and far more grievously wounded victims in his time with the police, he could not have said why an object as simple as a hand mirror affected him so, except that the mirror was such an innocent object, really, a piece of feminine vanity that suddenly made Vi Nevin more of a living presence to him than she had been before. Why? he wondered. And even as he asked himself the question, he saw Helen with just such a mirror in her own hand, examining the way she'd arranged her hair, saying, 'It's hopeless. I look like a curled up hedgehog. Lord, Tommy. How can you love a woman who's so utterly useless?'

And Lynley wanted her to be there in that moment. He wanted to hold her, as if the simple, primitive act of holding his wife could safeguard all women from every possible harm.

Vi Nevin moaned. Lynley tightened his grip on her hand.

'You're safe, Miss Nevin,' he told her, although he doubted that she could either hear or understand him. 'An ambulance is coming. Just hold on until it gets here. I won't leave you. You're safe. You're really quite safe.'

He noticed for the first time that she was dressed for her work: She wore a schoolgirl's uniform with the skirt hiked high up on her thighs. Beneath it, tiny bits of black lace served as her knickers, and lacy stockings were fastened to a matching suspender belt. She had knee socks on over the stockings. She wore regulation schoolgirl shoes on her feet. It was doubtless an ensemble designed to titillate, with Vi Nevin presenting herself to her client as the bashful schoolgirl he desired.

God, Lynley wondered. Why did women make themselves so vulnerable to men who could harm them? Why did they ever involve themselves in a pursuit that was guaranteed to destroy, if not in one way then certainly in another?

The first of the sirens shattered the night as the ambulance made the turn into Rostrevor Road. Moments later below stairs, the door to the maisonette crashed open.

'Up here,' Lynley shouted.

And Vi Nevin stirred. 'Forgot ...' she murmured. 'Likes honey. Forgot.'

And then the bedroom filled with paramedics while below on the street more sirens sounded as the local police arrived.

While in the building itself, a selection of music having apparently been made, the musical score to *Rent* began playing. The ensemble sang their paean to love.

Chapter Twenty-three

I t was part blessing and part curse that a good number of the forensic scientists at the police lab were lads and lasses of insatiable curiosity. The blessing rose from their willingness to work days, nights, weekends, and holidays if they were intrigued enough by evidence that was presented for their evaluation. The curse rose from one's personal knowledge of the existence of the blessing. For realising that the forensic lab employed scientists whose inquisitive natures prompted them to remain at their microscopes when saner individuals were at home or out on the town, one felt obliged to gather the information that those scientists were so willing to provide.

Thus on a Saturday night, DI Peter Hanken found himself not in the bosom of his family in Buxton but rather standing before a microscope while Miss Amber Kubowsky – chief evidence technician of the moment – waxed enthusiastic on what she'd discovered about the Swiss Army knife and the wounds that had been made on the body of Terry Cole.

The blood on the knife – she was happy to confirm as she went at her scalp with the rubber end of a pencil, as if wishing to erase something that was scribbled on her skull – was indeed Cole's. And, upon carefully prising apart the knife's various blades and devices, she'd been able to ascertain that the left blade of the scissors was, as reported by Andy

Maiden, broken off. Thus, the ineluctable conclusion one would normally reach was that the knife in question not only inflicted the wounds found upon Terry Cole's body, but also bore a marked resemblance to the knife that Andy Maiden had allegedly passed on to his daughter.

'Right,' Hanken said.

She looked pleased at his affirmation of her remarks. She said, 'Have a look at *this*, then,' and nodded towards the microscope.

Hanken squinted through the lens. Everything Miss Amber Kubowsky had said was so achingly obvious that he wondered at her level of excitement. Things must be as bland as yesterday's porridge in the laboratory – not to mention in her life – if the poor lass got herself worked up over this. 'What exactly am I supposed to be looking for?' he asked Miss Kubowsky, raising his head and gesturing at the microscope. 'This doesn't much look like a scissor blade to me. Or blood for that matter.'

'It isn't,' she said happily. 'And that's the point, DI Hanken. That's what's so damned intriguing about *everything*.'

Hanken glanced at the clock on the wall. He'd been working nonstop for more than twelve hours, and before the day was through he still wanted to coordinate his information with whatever was being accumulated at the London end of the case. So the last thing he wanted was a guessing game with a frizzy-haired forensic technician.

He said, 'If it's not the blade and it's not Cole's blood, why am I looking at it, Miss Kubowsky?'

'It's nice you're so polite,' she told him. 'Not every detective has your manners, I find.'

She was going to find out a hell of a lot more if she didn't start elucidating, Hanken thought. But he thanked her for the compliment and indicated that he'd be happy to hear whatever else she had to tell him as long as she told him post haste.

'Oh! Of course,' she said. 'That's the scapula wound you're looking at there. Well, not all of it. If you magnified the whole thing it would be twenty inches long, probably. This is just a portion of it.'

'The scapula wound?'

'Right. It was the biggest gash on the boy's body, did the doctor say? On his back? The boy, not the doctor, that is.'

Hanken recalled Dr Myles's report. One of the wounds had chipped the left scapula and come near to one of the heart's arteries.

Miss Kubowsky said, 'I wouldn't have bothered with it normally, except I saw on the report that the scapula – that's one of the bones in the back, did you know? – had a weapon mark on it, so I went ahead and compared the mark with the knife blades. With all the knife blades. And what do you know?'

'What?'

'The knife didn't make that mark, Inspector Hanken. No way, not for a minute, uh-uh, and forget it.'

Hanken stared at her. He tried to assimilate the information. More, he wondered if she'd made a mistake. She looked so scatty – her lab coat had half its hem hanging down and a coffee stain on its front – that it was hardly beyond the realm of possibility that she was less than proficient in her own line of work.

Amber Kubowsky apparently not only saw the doubt on his face but also understood the necessity for dispelling it. When she went on, she'd become perfect science, speaking in terms of x-rays, blade widths, angles, and micro millimetres. She didn't complete her remarks until she was certain he understood the import of what she was saying: The tip of the weapon that had pierced Terry Cole's back, chipped his scapula, and scored the bone was not shaped like the tip of any of the Swiss Army knife's blades. While the knife blades' tips were pointed – obviously, because how could they be knife blades if they *weren't* pointed, she asked reasonably – they broadened out at an entirely different angle from the weapon that had marked the bone in Terry Cole's back.

Hanken whistled tonelessly. She'd given an impressive recitation, but he had to ask. 'Are you sure?'

'I'd swear to it, Inspector. We would've all missed it if I didn't have this theory about X-rays and microscopes that I won't go into at the moment.'

'But the knife made the other wounds on the body?'

'Except for the scapula wound. Yes. That's right.'

She had other information to impart, as well. And she took him to another area of the lab where she held forth on the topic of a pewter-like smear she'd also been asked to evaluate.

When he'd heard what Amber Kubowsky had to say on this final subject, Hanken headed immediately for a phone. It was time to track down Lynley.

Hanken rang the other DI's mobile and found Lynley in the casualty ward of Chelsea and Westminster Hospital. Lynley brought him up to speed tersely: Vi Nevin, Nicola's Fulham flatmate, had been brutally attacked in the maisonette that she and Nicola Maiden had shared.

'What's her condition?'

There was noise in the background, someone shouting, 'Over here!' and the increasingly loud howl of an ambulance's double-note siren.

'Thomas?' Hanken raised his voice. 'What's her condition? Have you got anything from her?'

'Nothing.' Lynley finally replied from London. 'We haven't been able to manage a statement yet. We can't even get close. They've been working on her for an hour.'

'What do you think? Related to the case, what's happened?'

'I'd say that's likely.' Lynley went on to catalogue what he'd learned since their last conversation, beginning with his interview of Shelly Platt, continuing with a précis of his experience at MKR Financial Management, and ending with his meeting with Sir Adrian Beattie and his wife. 'So we've managed to unearth the London lover, but he's got an alibi – still to be confirmed, by the way. Even if he hadn't an alibi, I have to say I can't see him slogging across the moors to knife one victim and chase down the other. He must be over seventy.'

'So Upman was telling the truth,' Hanken said, 'at least in regard to the pager and those phone calls that the Maiden girl took while she was at work.'

'It looks that way, Peter. But Beattie claims there had to be someone in Derbyshire supplying her with money or she wouldn't have gone there in the first place.'

'Upman can't be making that much from his divorcées. He said he wasn't in London in May by the way. He said his daily diary could prove it.'

'What about Britton?'

'He's still on my list. I got waylaid by the Swiss Army knife.' Hanken brought Lynley up to date in that respect, adding the news about the scapula wound. Another weapon, he told Lynley, had evidently been used upon the boy.

'Another knife?'

'Possibly. And Maiden's got one. He even produced it for my inspection.'

'You aren't thinking Andy's fool enough to show you one of the murder weapons, Peter. He's a cop; not a cretin.'

'Wait. When I saw it at first I didn't think Maiden's knife could have been used on the boy because the blades are too short. But I was thinking of the other wounds then, not the blow to the scapula. How far is the scapula beneath the skin, anyway? And if Kubowsky dismissed one Swiss Army knife for the scapula wound, does it follow that none other could have done the job?'

'We're back to motive, Peter. Andy hasn't got one. But every other man in her life – not to mention one or two women – has.'

'Don't be so quick to dismiss him,' Hanken objected, 'because there's more. Listen to this. I've identification on the substance we found on that odd chrome cylinder from the boot of her car. What d'you think it is?'

'Tell me.'

'Semen. And there were two *other* semen deposits on it as well. We've two from secretors – that's counting the one you and I saw – and the other not. The only thing Kubowsky couldn't tell me is what the damn cylinder is in the first place. I've never seen anything like it and neither has she.'

'It's a ball stretcher,' Lynley told him.

'A *what*?'

'Hang on, Pete.' At the other end of the line, Hanken heard the rumble of male voices with continued hospital noises as counterpoint. Lynley got back to him saying, 'She'll pull through, thank God.'

'Can you get to her?'

'Unconscious at the moment.' And then to someone else, 'Round-the-clock protection. No visitors without first clearing them with me. And ask for their IDs if anyone shows up . . . No. I have no idea . . . Right.' Then he was back. 'Sorry. Where was I?'

'A ball stretcher.'

'Ah. Yes.'

Hanken listened as his colleague explained the device of torture. He felt his own testicles shrink in response.

'My guess is that it rolled out of one of her cases when she was en route to or from a client while she worked for Reeve,' Lynley concluded. 'It could have been in the boot of her car for months.'

Hanken reflected on this and saw another possibility. He knew Lynley would fight it, so he broached the subject with care. 'Thomas, she might have used it in Derbyshire. Perhaps on someone who's not admitting it.'

'I don't see either Upman or Britton going in for the whips

and chains routine. And Ferrer seems more likely to use something on his women, rather than vice versa. Who else is there?'

'Her dad.'

'Christ. Peter, that's sick.'

'Isn't it just. But the whole S and M scene's sick and from what you've just told me, its major players look normal as hell.'

'There is *no* way—'

'Just listen.' And Hanken reported his interview with the dead girl's parents, including Nan Maiden's interruption of that interview and Andy Maiden's feeble alibi. 'So who's to say beyond doubt that Nicola wasn't servicing her dad along with everyone else?'

'Peter, you can't keep reinventing the case to fit your suspicions. If she was servicing her father – which, by the way. I would go to the rack protesting – then he can't have killed her because of her lifestyle which – as you recall – was your earlier position.'

'Then you agree he has a motive?'

'I agree that you're twisting my words.' A new spate of noise then ensued: sirens and a babble of voices. It sounded to Hanken as if the other DI were conducting their conversation in the middle of a motorway. When the noise abated slightly, Lynley said, 'There's still what happened to Vi Nevin to consider. What happened tonight. If that's related to the doings in Derbyshire, you've got to see that Andy Maiden isn't involved.'

'Then who?'

'My money's on Martin Reeve. He had a bone to pick with both women.'

Lynley went on to say that their best hope was having Vi Nevin regain consciousness and name her attacker. Then they would have immediate grounds to drag Martin Reeve into the Met where he belonged. 'I'll stay for a while to see if she comes to,' he said. 'If she doesn't in an hour or two, I'll have them ring me the moment her condition changes. What about you?'

Hanken sighed. He rubbed his tired eyes and stretched to ease the tension he was feeling in the muscles of his back. He thought of Will Upman and his stress management massages at the Manchester Airport Hilton. He could have done with one of those himself.

'I'll get on to Julian Britton,' he said. 'Truth to tell, though, I can't see him as anyone's killer. He wouldn't be putting up with that dad of his if he was anything other than a softie at heart.'

'But if he believed he had powerful cause to kill her . . . ?' Lynley asked.

'Oh, to be sure,' Hanken agreed. 'Someone believed he had powerful cause to kill Nicola Maiden.'

The doctor had given her sleeping pills but Nan Maiden hadn't taken them after the first night. She couldn't afford to be less than vigilant, so she did nothing to encourage slumber. When she went to bed at all, she dozed. But most of the time she either walked the corridors in a corporeal haunting or sat in the overstuffed armchair in their bedroom and watched her husband's fitful rest.

This night, her pyjama-clad legs curled beneath her and a hand-knitted blanket drawn round her shoulders, Nan huddled into the armchair and observed her husband thrashing round in the bed. She couldn't tell if he was really asleep or just feigning sleep, but in either case, it didn't matter. The sight of him there roused within her a complicated tangle of emotions more important to consider at the moment than the authenticity of her husband's repose.

She still wanted him. Odd after all these years that she still felt desire for him in the same old way, but she did. And that desire had never abated for either of them. Rather it seemed to have increased over time, as if the length of their marriage had somehow seasoned the passion they felt for each other. So she'd noticed when Andy first stopped turning to her at night. And she'd noticed when he stopped reaching for and claiming her with the assurance and familiarity that were born of their long and happy marriage.

She dreaded what that change meant.

It had happened once before – this loss of interest on Andy's part in what had always been the most vital area of their relationship – and so long ago that Nan liked to believe she'd nearly forgotten it had happened at all. But that wasn't really the truth of the matter, and Nan could admit that much in the safety of darkness as her husband did or did not sleep some six feet away from her.

He'd been undercover in a drugs operation. Seduction had been called for as the drama played out. Remaining true to his assigned rôle required him to accept all advances made in his direction, no matter the nature those advances took. And when several of them were overtly sexual . . . What else could he do that would keep him in character? he asked her later. How else could he act so as not to betray the entire operation and endanger the lives of the officers involved?

But he took no pleasure from any of it, he'd said as he confessed to her. There had been *nothing* for him in the firm young beautiful flesh of girls young enough to be his daughters. What he'd done, he'd done because it had been required of him, and he wanted his wife to grasp that fact. There was no joy in such an act of coupling. There was only getting through the act itself, which was robbed of feeling when it was done without love.

They were lofty words. They demanded of an intelligent woman her compassion, forgiveness, acceptance, and understanding. But they were also words which made Nan wonder at the time why Andy had felt it necessary to confess his transgression to her at all.

But she'd learned the answer to that question through the

years as she slowly developed a knowledge of her husband's ways that she'd not thought possible to possess about anyone other than herself. And she'd seen the alterations that had come upon him whenever he was untrue to who he actually was. Which was why SO10 had ultimately become such a nightmare: because he was forced, day in and day out and month after month, to be someone who he simply was not. Required by his job to live through great periods of untruth, his mind, his soul, and his psyche would not permit dissimulation without making a demand for some sort of payment from his body.

That payment had shown itself in ways that had been extremely easy to ignore at first, to label as an allergic reaction to something or the initial harbinger of approaching old age. The tongue grows old so the food stops tasting right and the only way to give it flavour is to soak it in sauce or blizzard it with pepper. And what did it really mean when one failed to catch the subtle scent of night blooming jasmine? Or the musty odour of a country church? Those little occasions of sensory deprivation were easy to ignore and overlook.

But then the more serious deprivations began – the sort that couldn't be ignored without risk to one's well being. And when the doctors and the specialists had run their tests, tried out their diagnoses, and finally shrugged their shoulders in a maddening combination of fascination, perplexity, and defeat, the psychiatric warriors had boarded the ship of Andy's condition, setting sail like Vikings towards the uncharted waters of her husband's psyche. There was never a name applied to what ailed him, just an explanation of the human condition as some people experienced it. So he fell apart by inches and degrees, with confession the only means by which he could put his life in order once again, reclaiming who he was through an act of purgation. But ultimately, all the diary writing, analysing, discussing, and confessing were not enough to make him completely well.

Unfortunately, considering the type of work he does, your

husband simply can't live a dichotomous life, she was told after months and years of visiting doctors. Not, that is, if he wishes to be completely integrated as an individual.

She'd said, What? A dichotomous . . . What?

Andrew can't live a life of contradictions, Mrs Maiden. He can't compartmentalise. He can't assume an identity at odds with his central persona. It's the adoption of a succession of identities that appears to be causing this failure of part of his nervous system. Another man might find that sort of life exciting – an actor, for example, or at the other extreme a sociopath or a manic-depressive – but your husband does not.

But isn't it just like playing dressing up? she'd asked. When he's under cover, I mean.

With enormous attendant responsibility, she'd been told, and even more enormous stakes and costs.

She'd thought at first how lucky she was to be married to such a man. And in all the years since he'd taken his retirement from New Scotland Yard, the future that they'd worked upon in Derbyshire had obliterated every one of the lies and the complicated subterfuges that Andy had been forced to make part of his life in the past.

Until now.

She should have realised when he hadn't noticed those burnt pine nuts in the kitchen, despite the way the smell had permeated the air of the Hall like overloud music played enthusiastically and in every wrong key. She should have realised then that something was wrong. But she hadn't noticed because everything had been right for so many years.

'Can't say . . .' Andy murmured from the bed.

Nan leaned forward anxiously. She whispered, 'What?'

He turned, burrowing his shoulder into the pillow. 'No.' It was sleep talk. 'No. No.'

Nan's vision went blurred as she watched him. She cast back through the last four months in a desperate attempt to find something that she might have done to alter this ending that they had reached. But she could only come up with having had the courage and the willingness to ask for honesty in the first place, which had not been a realistic option.

Andy turned again. He punched his pillow into shape and flopped from his side onto his back. His eyes were closed.

Nan left her chair and went to the bed, where she sat. She reached forward and brushed her fingertips across her husband's forehead, feeling his skin both clammy and hot. For thirty-seven years, he'd been at the centre of her world, and she wasn't about to lose her world's centre at this autumnal date in her life.

But even as she made that determination, Nan knew that life as she currently experienced it was filled with uncertainties. And it was in her uncertainties that her nightmares lay, another reason for her refusal to sleep.

Lynley unlocked his front door just after one in the morning. He was exhausted and heavy of heart. It was difficult to believe that his day had begun in Derbyshire, and more difficult to believe that it had ended in the encounter he'd just experienced in Notting Hill.

Men and women possessed limitless potential to astonish him. He'd long ago accepted that fact, but he realised now that he was getting weary of the constant surprises they had to offer. After fifteen years in the CID, he wanted to be able to say he'd seen it all. That he hadn't – that someone could still do something to amaze him – was a fact that weighed in his gut like a boulder. Not so much because he couldn't understand a person's actions but because he continually failed to anticipate them.

He'd remained with Vi Nevin until she regained consciousness. He'd hoped she'd be able to name her attacker and thus provide him with an immediate reason for arresting the bastard. But she'd shaken her swollen, bandaged head and her blackened eyes had gone liquid as Lynley questioned her. All he was able to glean from the injured woman was that she'd been set upon too suddenly to manage a clear look at her assailant. Whether that was a lie that she told to protect herself was something that Lynley couldn't discern. But he thought he knew, and he cast about for a way to make it easier for her to say the necessary words.

'Tell me what happened, then, moment by moment, because there may be something, a detail you recall, that we can use to—'

'That's quite enough for now.' The sister in charge of casualty intervened, her blunt Scot's face a picture of steely determination.

'Male or female?' Lynley pressed the injured woman.

'Inspector, I believe I made myself clear,' the sister snapped. And she hovered protectively over her childlike patient, making what seemed like unnecessary adjustments to bedclothes, pillows, and drips.

'Miss Nevin?' Lynley prodded, nonetheless.

'Out!' the sister said as Vi murmured, 'Inspector. A man.'

Upon hearing that, Lynley decided enough identification had been established. She wasn't, after all, telling him anything that he didn't already know. He'd merely wanted to eliminate the possibility that Shelly Platt – and not Martin Reeve – had come calling on her old flatmate. Having done that much, he felt justified in taking matters to the next level.

He'd begun that process at the Star of India in Old Brompton Road, where a conversation with the *maître d'* established that Martin Reeve and his wife Tricia – both of whom were regulars in the restaurant – had indeed taken a meal there earlier in the week. But no one could say on what evening they'd occupied their table by the window. The waiters were evenly divided between Monday and Tuesday while the *maître d'* himself seemed able only to recall that which he had written evidence of in his reservations folder.

'I see they did not book,' he said in his lilting voice. 'Ah, one must book at the Star of India to guarantee a seating.'

'Yes. She claims they didn't book,' Lynley told him. 'She said that was the cause of a row between you and her husband. On Tuesday night.'

'I do not row with the customers, sir,' the man had said stiffly. And the offence he took at Lynley's remark had coloured the rest of his memory.

The indefinite nature of the corroboration from the Star of India gave Lynley the impetus to call upon the Reeves, despite the hour. And as he drove to do so, he fixed in his mind the image of Vi Nevin's ruined face. When finally he'd negotiated his way to the top of Kensington Church Street and made the turn into Notting Hill Gate, he was feeling the sort of slow burning anger that made it easy for him to persist at the doorbell of MKR Financial Management when no one answered his initial ring.

'Do you have *any* idea what time it is?' was Martin Reeve's greeting to him upon jerking open the door. He didn't even need to identify himself for Lynley to know who he was. The overhead light which illuminated his face and glowed brightly against four fresh, deep scratches on his cheek told the tale well enough.

He strong-armed Reeve backwards into the entry corridor of the house. He muscled him into the wall – easy enough to do since the pimp was so much smaller than Lynley had anticipated – and held him there with one cheek pressed into the tastefully striped wallpaper.

'Hey!' Reeve protested. 'What the *hell* do you think you're—'

'Tell me about Vi Nevin,' Lynley demanded, wrenching his arm.

'Hey! If you think you can barge in here and—' Another wrench. Reeve howled. 'Fuck you!'

'Not even in your dreams.' Lynley pressed up against him and jerked his arm upwards. He spoke into his ear. 'Tell me about your afternoon and your evening, Mr Reeve. Give me every detail. I'm done in and I need a fairy tale before I go to bed. Oblige me. Please.'

'Are you out of your fucking *mind*?' Reeve twisted his head towards the stairs. He shouted, 'Trish ... Tricia ... Trish! Phone the cops.'

'Nice try,' Lynley said, 'but the cops have already arrived. Come along, Mr Reeve. Let's talk in here.' He shoved the smaller man in front of him. Inside the reception office, he threw Reeve into a chair and switched on a light.

'You'd better have an eighteen carat reason for this,' Reeve snarled. 'Because if you don't, you can anticipate a lawsuit the likes of which you've never seen in this country.'

'Spare me the threats,' Lynley replied. 'They might work in America, but they're not going to get you a cup of coffee here.'

Reeve massaged his arm. 'We'll see about that.'

'I'll count the moments till we do. Where were you this afternoon? This evening as well? What happened to your face?'

'What?' The word was spoken incredulously. 'D'you think I'll actually *answer* those questions?'

'If you don't want this building boarded up by the vice squad, I expect you'll give me chapter and verse. And don't push me, Mr Reeve. I've had a long day, and I'm not a reasonable man when I'm tired.'

'Fuck you.' Reeve turned his head to the door and shouted, 'Tricia! Get your ass down here. Phone Polmanteer. I'm not paying through the nose for his sorry butt—'

Lynley grabbed a heavy ash tray from the reception desk and hurled it at Reeve. It skimmed past his head and slammed into a mirror, shattering it.

'Jesus!' Reeve shouted. 'What the *hell*—'

'Afternoon and evening. I want the answers. Now.'

When Reeve didn't reply, Lynley advanced on him, grabbed the collar of his pyjama top, yanked him backwards into the chair and twisted the collar till it was tight round his neck. 'Tell me who scratched you, Mr Reeve. Tell me why.'

Reeve made a choking sound. Lynley found that he liked it.

'Or shall I fill in the blanks myself? I dare say I know the dramatis personae.' Another twist with each name as he said, 'Vi Nevin. Nicola Maiden. Terry Cole. Shelly Platt as well, if we get down to it.'

Reeve gasped, 'F . . . king . . . out . . . of . . . *mind.*' His hands clawed his throat.

At which Lynley released him, flinging him forward like a discarded rag. 'You're trying my patience. I'm beginning to think a phone call to the local station isn't a bad idea. A few nights with the boys in the Ladbroke Grove lock-up might be just what we need to oil your tongue.'

'Your ass is history. I know enough people who'll—'

'I've no doubt of that. You probably know people from here to Istanbul. And while every one of them would doubtless rise to your defence were you brought up on charges of pandering, you're going to find that assaulting women doesn't go down such a treat among the big public profiles. Not when you think of the fodder they'd be giving the tabloids if word got out that they came to your aid. As it is, they're going to find it a delicate enough business lending you a hand once I run you in as a pimp. To expect more from them . . . I wouldn't be so unwise, Mr Reeve. Now answer the question. What happened to your face?'

Reeve was silent, but Lynley could see his mind working. The other man would be assessing what facts the police had. He hadn't lived on the periphery of the law for as long as he had without acquiring some knowledge about the law's application to his own life. He would surely know that, had Lynley possessed anything solid – like an eyewitness or the signed statement of his victim – he would have made an immediate arrest. But he would also know that he had fewer options when caught up in a dicey situation.

Reeve said, 'All right. It's Tricia. She's on the shit. I came home from looking in on two of my girls whose work's fallen off. She was smacked out. I lost it. Jesus. I thought she was dead. I got physical with her, slapped her around, part fear and part anger. And I found out she wasn't as out of it as I'd thought. She got physical back.'

Lynley didn't believe a word. He said, 'You're trying to tell me that your wife – strung out on drugs – did that to your face?'

'She was upstairs in a nod, the worst she's been in months. I couldn't deal with it on top of the girls and their troubles. I can't be everyone's daddy. So I lost it. Like I said.'

'What troubles?'

'What?'

'The girls. Their troubles.'

Reeve looked towards the reception desk and upon it the display of brochures that ostensibly advertised MKR's financial services. 'I know you know about the business. But you probably don't know what lengths I go to to keep them healthy. Blood tests every four months, drug screening, physical exams, balanced diet, exercise . . .'

'A real drain on your financial resources,' Lynley noted dryly.

'Hell. I don't care what you think. This is a service industry and if someone doesn't offer it, someone else will. I'm not apologising for it. I supply clean, healthy, educated girls in a pleasant environment. Any guy who spends time with one of them gets value for his money and no threat of disease to take home to the ball-and-chain. And that's what I was uptight about when I got home: two girls with trouble.'

'Disease?'

'Genital warts. Chlamydia. So I was pissed off. And then

when I saw Tricia, I snapped. That's it. If you want their names, addresses, and numbers, I'm happy to oblige.'

Lynley watched him carefully, wondering if it was all a calculated risk on the part of the pimp or an actual coincidence that he'd bear his wife's defensive marks on his face on the very same evening that Vi Nevin had been attacked. He said, 'Let's have Mrs Reeve down here to tell her side of the story, then.'

'Oh come on. She's asleep.'

'That didn't appear to bother you a moment ago when you were howling for her to phone the police. And Polmanteer . . . your solicitor, is that? We can still phone him, if you'd like.'

Reeve stared at Lynley, disgust and dislike on his features. He finally said, 'I'll get her.'

'Not alone, I'm afraid.' The last thing Lynley wanted to do was give Reeve an opportunity to coerce his wife into supporting his story.

'Fine. Then come along.'

Reeve led the way up two flights of stairs to the second floor. In a bedroom overlooking the street, he walked to a bed the size of a playing field and switched on the bedside lamp. Light from it fell upon the form of his wife. She lay on her side, curled foetally, deeply asleep.

Reeve flipped her onto her back, grabbed her under the armpits, and pulled her upright. Her head lolled forward like a rag doll's. He tipped her backwards and propped her up against the headboard. 'Good luck,' he said to Lynley with a smile. He pointed out a string of nasty bruises round her throat, saying, 'I had to get rougher than I wanted with the bitch. She was out of control. I thought she'd kill me.'

Lynley jerked his head away from the woman, indicating he wanted Reeve to back off. Reeve did so. Lynley took his place at the bed. He reached for Tricia's arm, saw the angry tracks of injections, felt for a pulse. As he did this, she heaved in a deep breath, making his gesture unnecessary. Lightly, he slapped her face. 'Mrs Reeve,' he said. 'Mrs Reeve. Can you wake up?'

Reeve moved behind him and before Lynley realised what he intended, he'd grabbed a vase of flowers, tossed the blooms to the floor, and dashed the water across his wife's face. 'God damn it, Tricia. Wake up!'

'Stand *back*,' Lynley ordered.

Tricia's eyes fluttered open as the water dripped down her cheeks. Her dazed glance went from Lynley to her husband. She flinched. That reaction said it all.

Lynley said through his teeth, 'Get out of here, Reeve.'

'Fuck that,' Reeve said. And he went on tersely, 'He wants you to tell him we fought, Tricia. That I went after you and you went after me. You remember how it happened. So tell him that you went for my face and he'll clear the hell out of our house.'

Lynley surged to his feet. 'I said get out!'

Reeve stabbed a finger at his wife. 'Just tell him. He can see we fought when he looks at us, but he's not about to take my word unless you tell him it's the truth. So *tell* him.'

Lynley threw him from the room. He slammed the door. He returned to the bed. There, Tricia sat as he'd left her. She made no move to dry herself.

There was an en suite bathroom, and Lynley went to this and fetched a towel. He used it gently against her face, against her damaged neck, against her sopping chest. Tricia looked at him numbly for a moment before she turned her head and gazed at the door through which he'd ejected her husband.

He said, 'Tell me what happened between you, Mrs Reeve.'

She turned back to him. She licked her lips.

'Your husband attacked you, didn't he? Did you fight back?' It was a ludicrous question and he damn well knew it. How, he wondered, could she possibly have done so? The last thing heroin users were good for was a vigorous round of self-defence. 'Let me phone someone for you. You need to get out of here. You must have a friend. Brothers or sisters? Parents?'

'No!' She grabbed his hand. Her grip wasn't strong, but her nails – long and as artificial as the rest of her – dug into, his flesh.

'I don't believe for a moment that you put up a fight against your husband, Mrs Reeve. And my failure to believe that is going to make things difficult for you once your husband bails himself out of custody. I'd like to get you out of here before all that happens, so if you'll give me a name of someone to phone . . .'

'Arrest?' she whispered, and she seemed to be making a monumental effort to clear her head. 'You'll . . . arrest? But you said—'

'I know. But that was earlier. Something's happened this evening that makes it impossible for me to keep my word. I'm sorry, but I have no choice in the matter. Now, I'd like to phone someone for you. Will you give me a number?'

'No. *No.* It was . . . I hit him. I did. I tried . . . bite.'

'Mrs Reeve. I know you're frightened. But try to see that—'

'I scratched him. My nails. His face. Scratched. *Scratched.* Because he was choking me and I wanted him . . . stop. Please. Please. I scratched . . . face. I made him bleed. I did.'

Lynley saw her rising agitation. He cursed silently: He cursed Reeve's slippery and successful insinuation of himself into the interview with his wife; he cursed his own damnable inadequacies, the largest of which was the loss of temper that always obscured his vision and clouded his thinking. As it had done on this night.

Now, in his house in Eaton Terrace, Lynley reflected on everything. His sense of grievance and his need to avenge Vi Nevin had got in his way, allowing Martin Reeve to out-manoeuvre him. Tricia's fear of her husband – probably in combination with a heroin addiction which he no doubt fed – had prompted her at long last to confirm Reeve's every word. Lynley still could have run the soulless little rat into the nick for six or seven hours of interrogation, but the American hadn't got where he was by being ignorant of his rights. He was guaranteed legal representation, and he would have claimed it before he'd left the house. So what would have been gained was a sleepless night for everyone concerned. And in the end, Lynley would have found himself no closer to an arrest than he'd been upon his arrival in London that morning.

But things had ended in Notting Hill the way they had ended because of a miscalculation on Lynley's part, and he had to admit that. In his anxiety to have Tricia Reeve conscious, cognizant, and coherent enough to take part in a conversation, he'd allowed her husband enough time in her presence to give her the script she needed in her interview with Lynley. Thus, he'd lost whatever advantage he might have established over the other man in arriving at his home in the dead of night. It was a costly mistake, the sort of error that was made by an earnest but rank beginner.

He wanted to tell himself that the miscalculation was the product of a long day, a misguided sense of chivalry, and out-and-out exhaustion. But the disquiet in his soul, which he'd begun feeling the moment he saw the card with Nikki Temptation's advertisement on it, spoke of another source altogether. And because he didn't wish to consider either the source or the implications of the source, Lynley descended to the kitchen where he rooted round in the refrigerator until he found a container of leftover paella, which he thrust into the microwave.

He fetched a Heineken to go with his makeshift meal, and he cracked it open and carried it to the table. He dropped wearily into one of the chairs and took a deep swig of the lager. A slim magazine lay next to a bowl of apples, and while he waited for the microwave to work its magic on his food, Lynley reached in his pocket for his spectacles and had a look at what turned out to be a souvenir theatre programme.

Denton, he saw, had managed to prevail over the masses who were attempting to obtain tickets to the season's hottest show in the West End. The single word *Hamlet* made a bold graphic design in silver on an ebony cover, along with a rapier and the words *King-Ryder Productions* tastefully arranged above the play's title. Lynley shook his head with a chuckle as he flipped through the pages of glossy photographs. If he knew Denton, the next few months in Eaton Terrace were going to be an endless exposure to whatever melodies from the pop opera resonated within his stage-struck soul. As he recalled, it had taken nearly nine months for Denton to stop warbling 'The Music of the Night' at the drop of a hat.

At least this new production wasn't Lloyd-Webber, he thought with some gratitude. He'd once considered homicide the only viable alternative to having to listen to Denton crooning the main – and what seemed like the *only* – melody from *Sunset Boulevard* for weeks on end.

The microwave signalled, and he scooped out the container and dumped its contents unceremoniously onto a plate. He tucked into his late night meal. But the action of forking up the food, chewing, and swallowing was not enough to divert his thoughts, so he cast about for something else to distract him.

He found it in the consideration of Barbara Havers.

She must have managed to gather something useful by now, he thought. She'd been on the computer since the morning, and he could only assume that he'd finally pounded into her skull the message that he expected her to continue at CRIS until she had something valuable and viable to report.

He reached for the phone that sat on the work top and, mindless of the hour, he punched in her number. The line was engaged. He frowned and looked at his watch. Christ. Who the hell would Havers be talking to at one-twenty in the morning? No one that he could name, so the only conclusion was that she'd taken her phone off the hook, the bloody woman. He dropped his own receiver into the cradle and gave idle thought to what he was going to do with Havers. But going down that path only promised him a tempestuous night, which would do nothing to improve his performance in the morning.

So he finished his meal with his attention on the *Hamlet* programme once again, and he thanked Denton silently for having provided him with a diversion. The photographs *were* good. And the text made interesting reading. David King-Ryder's suicide was still fresh enough an event in the public consciousness to give an air of romance and melancholy to anything associated with his name. Besides, it was no arduous task, having to gaze upon the voluptuous maiden who'd been cast as the production's Ophelia. And how clever of the costume designer to have her go to her death in a gown so diaphanous as to make the wearing of it practically unnecessary. Back-lit, she stood poised to drown herself, a creature already caught between two worlds. The gauzy gown claimed her soul for heaven while her earthbound body chained her – in all her sensual beauty – firmly to the earth. It was the perfect combination of—

'Are you actually *leering*, Tommy? Married three months and I've already caught you leering at another woman?' Helen stood in the doorway, blinking, sleep tousled, tying her dressing gown belt at the waist.

'Only because you were asleep,' Lynley said.

'That reply came too readily. I expect you've used it a bit more often than I'd like to know.' She padded across the room to him, looked over his shoulder, placing one slender cool hand on the back of his neck. 'Ah. I see.'

'A little light reading with dinner, Helen. Nothing more than that.'

'Hmm. Yes. She's beautiful, isn't she?'

'She? Oh. Ophelia, you mean? I hadn't really noticed.' He flipped the programme closed and took his wife's hand, pressing her palm against his mouth.

'You make a poor liar.' Helen kissed his forehead, disengaged her hand from his, and went to the refrigerator where she took out a bottle of Evian. She leaned against the work top as she drank, watching him fondly over the top of her glass. 'You look ghastly,' she noted. 'Have you eaten today? No. Don't answer. That's your first decent meal since breakfast, isn't it?'

'Am I meant to answer or not?' he asked reasonably.

'Never mind. I can read it all over your face. Why is it, darling, that you can forget to eat for sixteen hours while I can't manage to put food from my mind for ten simple minutes?'

'It's the contrast between pure and impure hearts.'

'Now *that's* a new slant on gluttony.'

Lynley chuckled. He rose. He went to her and took her into his arms. She smelled of citrus and sleep, and her hair was as soft as a breeze when he bent his head to press his cheek against it. 'I'm glad I woke you,' he murmured and he settled into their embrace, finding within it enormous comfort.

'I wasn't asleep.'

'No?'

'No. Just making an attempt but not getting very far with it, I'm afraid.'

'That's not like you.'

'It isn't. I know.'

'Something's on your mind, then.' He released her and looked down at her, smoothing her hair away from her face. Her dark eyes met his and he made a study of them: what they revealed and what they tried to hide. 'Tell me.'

She smiled gently and touched his lips with the tips of her fingers. 'I do love you,' she said. 'Much more than when I married you. More, even, than I loved you the first time you took me to bed.'

'I'm glad of it. But something tells me that's not what's on your mind.'

'No. That's not what's been on my mind. But it's late, Tommy. And you're far too exhausted for conversation. Let's go to bed.'

He wanted to do so. Nothing sounded better than sinking his head into a plump down pillow and seeking the soothing oblivion of sleep with his wife, warm and comforting, by his side. But something in Helen's expression told him that would not be the wisest course to take at the moment. There were times when women said one thing when they meant another, and this appeared to be one of those times. He said, half truth and half lie, 'I *am* done in. But we've not talked properly today, and I won't be able to sleep till we do.'

'Really?'

'You know me.'

She searched his face and seemed satisfied with what she saw. She said, 'It's really nothing much. Mental gymnastics, I suppose. I've been thinking all day about the lengths people go to when they want to avoid confronting something.'

A shudder passed through him.

'What?' she asked.

'Someone walking on my grave. What brought all this up?'

'The wallpaper.'

'Wallpaper?'

'For the spare rooms. You remember. I narrowed the choices down to six – which seemed quite admirable, considering what a muddle I was in about having to choose in the first place – and I spent all afternoon pondering them. I pinned them to the walls. I set furniture in front of them. I hung pictures round them. And still, I couldn't make up my mind.'

'Because you were thinking of this other?' he asked. 'About people not confronting what they need to confront?'

'No. That's just it. I was consumed with wallpaper. And making a decision about it – or rather finding myself incapable of *making* a decision – became a metaphor for living my life. Do you see?'

Lynley didn't. He was too wrung out to see anything at all. But he nodded, looked pensive, and hoped that would do.

'You would have chosen and had done with it. But I couldn't

do that, no matter how hard I tried. Why? I finally asked myself. And the answer was so simple: because of who I am. Because of who I was moulded to be. From the day of my birth to the morning of my wedding.'

Lynley blinked. 'Who you were moulded to be?'

'Your wife,' she said. 'Or the wife of someone exactly like you. There were five of us and each of us – every *one* of us, Tommy – was assigned a rôle. One moment we were safe in our mother's womb and the next we were in our father's arms and he was looking down at us saying, "Hmmm. Wife of a count, I think." Or "I dare say she'll do as the next Princess of Wales." And once we knew what rôle he'd assigned us, we played along. Oh, we didn't have to, of course. And God knows neither Penelope nor Iris danced to the music he'd written for them. But the other three – Cybele, Daphne, and I – why, the three of us were nothing more than warm clay in his hands. And once I realised that, Tommy, I had to take the next step. I had to ask why.'

'Why you were warm clay.'

'Yes. *Why*. And when I asked that question and took a hard look at the answer to it, what do you expect the answer was?'

His head was spinning and his eyes burned with fatigue. Lynley said, reasonably enough, he thought, 'Helen, what does this have to do with wallpaper?' and knew a moment later he'd failed her in some way.

She released herself from his embrace. 'Never mind. This isn't the moment. I *knew* that. I can see you're exhausted. Let's just go to bed.'

He tried to regroup. 'No. I want to hear this. I admit that I'm tired. And I got lost following all the dancing warm clay. But I want to talk. And to listen. And to know . . .' To know what? he wondered. He couldn't have said.

She frowned at him, a clear warning sign that he should have heeded and did not. 'What? The dancing warm clay? What are you talking about?'

'I'm talking about nothing. It was stupid. I'm an idiot. Forget it. Please. Come back. I want to hold you.'

'No. Explain what you meant.'

'Helen, it was nothing. It was just an inanity.'

'Just an inanity rising from my conversation.'

He sighed. 'I'm sorry. You're right. I'm done in. When I get like this, I say things without thinking. You said that two of your sisters didn't dance to his tune while the rest of you did, which made you warm clay. I took that and wondered how warm clay could dance to his music and ... Sorry. It was a stupid remark. I'm not thinking right.'

'And I'm not thinking at all,' she said. 'Which, I suppose, shouldn't come as a surprise to either of us. But that's what you wanted, isn't it?'

'What?'

'A wife who couldn't think.'

He felt as if she'd slapped him. 'Helen, that's not only bloody nonsense. It's an insult to us both.' He went to the table for his plate and cutlery, which he carried to the sink. He rinsed them, spent far too much time watching the water swirl round the drain, and finally said on a sigh, 'Damn.' He turned to her. 'I'm sorry, darling. I don't want us to be at odds with each other.'

Her face softened. 'We aren't,' she said.

He went back to her, pulled her to him once again. 'Then what?' he asked.

'I'm at odds with myself.'

Chapter Twenty-four

———◆———

Trying to pin down the individual whom Terry Cole had gone to see at King-Ryder Productions hadn't been as easy as Barbara Havers had anticipated after her conversation with Neil Sitwell, even with the list of employees in her possession. Not only were there three dozen of them listed, but on a Saturday night most of those three dozen had not been at home. They were, after all, theatre people. And theatre people – so she discovered – were not in the habit of vegetating blissfully under their own roofs when they could be out on the town. So it had been after two in the morning before she'd tracked down Terry Cole's contact at 31–32 Soho Square: Matthew King-Ryder, son of the deceased founder of the theatrical production company.

He'd agreed to see her – 'after nine, if you don't mind. I'm completely fagged out' – at his home in Baker Street.

It was half past nine when Barbara found the address that had been listed along with Matthew King-Ryder's name and phone number. It was a mansion block, she saw, one of those enormous brick Victorian structures that – at the end of the nineteenth century – had signalled an alteration in lifestyle from the spacious and gracious to the more understated and the somewhat confined. Relatively speaking, of course. Compared to Barbara's hovel, King-Ryder's flat was a virtual palace although it *did* appear to be one of those ill-thought out conversions of a larger flat in which cross ventilation and natural lighting had been sacrificed to the cause of lining someone's pockets with monthly rental payments.

Or such was Barbara's assessment of the flat when Matthew King-Ryder admitted her to it. He asked her to 'excuse the mess, please. I'm getting ready to move house,' in reference to a pile of rubbish and bin bags waiting for the mansion block's cleaners outside his front door, and he led her down a short and badly lit corridor to a sitting room. There, gaping cardboard boxes displayed books, silver cups, and various ornaments indifferently wrapped in newspaper, and framed photographs and theatrical posters leaned in stacks against the walls, waiting for a similar disposition. 'I'm finally entering the world of property ownership,' King-Ryder confided. 'I've got enough for the house, but not enough for the house *and* the removal men. So it's a bit of a do-it-yourself job. Hence the mess. Sorry. Here. Have a seat.' He swept a stack of theatre programmes to the floor. 'Would you like a coffee? I was just about to make some for myself.'

'Sure,' Barbara said.

He went to the kitchen which lay just beyond a dining nook. A hatch had been crafted into one of the walls, and he spoke through this casually as he dumped a measure of coffee beans into a grinder. 'I'll be south of the river, which won't be as convenient for getting to the West End. But it's a house, not a flat. And it has a decent garden and, more important, it's freehold. And it's mine.' He canted his head and grinned in her direction. 'Sorry. I'm rather excited. Thirty-three and I've finally got a mortgage. Who knows? It'll probably be marriage next. I like it strong. The coffee, that is. 'S that okay with you?'

Strong was fine by her, Barbara told him. The more caffeine the better, as far as she was concerned. Idly, she flipped through one of the stacks of framed photos near to her chair as she waited. Most of them depicted the same familiar individual posing through the years alongside a score of even more familiar theatrical faces.

'This your dad?' Barbara called out conversationally – albeit unnecessarily – over the gravelly roar of the coffee grinder.

King-Ryder glanced through the hatch and saw what she was doing. 'Oh,' he said. 'Yeah. That's my dad.'

The two men had looked very little alike. And Matthew had been blessed with all the physical advantages that nature had denied his father. While father had been short and froglike of face with the exophthalmic eyes of a thyroid patient, the jowls of a *bon viveur*, and the facial warts of a fairy-tale villain, son had been blessed with greater stature, with an aristocratic nose, and with the sort of skin, eyes and mouth that women would pay plastic surgeons handsomely to possess.

'You didn't look much alike,' Barbara said. 'You and your dad.'

From the kitchen Matthew shot her a regretful smile. 'No. He wasn't much to look at, was he? And he knew it, unfortunately. Took a lot of bullying when he was a boy. I think that's why he kept going after new women through the years: to prove something to himself.'

'Too bad about his death. I was sorry to hear . . . well, you know.' Barbara felt uncomfortable. What did one say about an unaccountable suicide, after all?

Matthew nodded, but made no reply. He went back to his coffee making, and Barbara went back to the pictures. She saw that only one of them featured father and son together: an ancient school photo in which a small Matthew stood with a silver cup in his hand and an enraptured smile like a blaze on his face while his father held a rolled up programme of some kind and frowned with an inner preoccupation. Matthew was proudly clad in athletics kit with a leather strap diagonally bisecting his torso in the fashion of a soldier from World War I. David was clad in his own version of uniform, a well-cut business suit that spoke of a score of important meetings he was missing.

'He doesn't look too happy in this shot,' Barbara noted, removing the picture from the stack and studying it.

'Oh. That. Sports day at school. Dad really hated it. He was about as athletic as an ox. But Mum was good at pushing the guilt buttons when she could get him on the phone, so he generally turned up. He didn't much like it. And he was good at letting one know when he didn't much like doing what he was doing. Typical artist, he was.'

'That must have hurt.'

'Not really. They were divorced by then – my parents – so my sister and I took what we could get of his time.'

'Where is she now?'

'Isadora? She does costume design. For the RSC mostly.'

'You've both followed in his footsteps, then.'

'Isadora more than me. Like Dad, she's on the creative end. I'm just a number cruncher.' He returned to the sitting room, bearing an old tin tray on which he'd placed mugs of coffee, a jug of milk, and some sugar cubes on a saucer. He balanced this on the top of a stack of magazines that sat on an ottoman and went on to explain that he had been his late father's business manager and agent. He negotiated contracts, tracked royalty money from the numerous productions of his father's work all round the globe, sold rights to future productions of the plays, and kept his fingers on the pulse of expenditure when the company mounted a new pop opera in London.

'So your work doesn't end with your father's death.'

'No. Because his work – the music itself, that is – doesn't actually end, does it? As long as his operas are being mounted somewhere, my work will continue. Eventually, we'll reduce the staff at the production company, but someone will have to keep tabs on all the rights. And there'll always be the fund to look after as well.'

'The fund?'

Matthew plunked three sugar cubes into his mug and stirred it with a ceramic-handled spoon. His father, he explained, had established a foundation some years ago to fund creative artists. The money was used to send actors and musicians to school, to back new productions, to launch new plays by unknown playwrights, to support lyricists and composers who were just starting their careers. With David King-Ryder's death, all monies accrued from his work would go into that fund. Aside from a bequest to his fifth and final wife, the David King-Ryder Fund was the sole beneficiary of King-Ryder's will.

'I didn't know that,' Barbara said, impressed. 'Generous bloke. Nice of him to give others a leg up.'

'He was a decent man, my dad. He wasn't that much of a father when my sister and I were young, and he didn't believe in hand outs or in coddling anyone. But he supported talent wherever he found it if the artist was willing to work. And that's a brilliant legacy, if you ask me.'

'Too bad, what happened. I mean ... you know.'

'Thanks. It was ... I still don't understand it.' Matthew examined the rim of his coffee mug. 'What was so bloody strange was that he had a hit ... after all those rotten years. The audience went wild before the curtain call began, and he was *there*. He saw it. Even the critics were on their feet. So the reviews were going to be like a miracle. He *had* to have known.'

Barbara knew the story. Opening night of *Hamlet*. A brilliant success after years of failure. No note left behind to explain his actions, the composer/lyricist offed himself with a single shot to the head while his wife was having a bath in the very next room.

'You were close to your dad,' Barbara noted, seeing the grief still evident in Matthew King-Ryder's expression,

'Not as a child, or an adolescent. But in the final years, I was, yes. I *was*. But obviously, not close enough.' Matthew blinked and took a gulp of his coffee. 'Right, then. Enough.

You've come on business. You said you wanted to see me about
Terence . . . That boy in black who came to see me in Soho.'

'Yes. Terence Cole.' Barbara gave Matthew the facts in
anticipation of his verifying them. 'Neil Sitwell – he's the
head muckety over at Bowers in Cork Street – said he sent
him to you with a piece of handwritten music by Michael
Chandler that he'd come across. He figured you'd know how
Terry could contact the solicitors for the Chandler estate.'

Matthew frowned. 'He did? That's extraordinary.'

'You wouldn't know how to contact those solicitors?' Barbara
asked. That hardly seemed credible.

Matthew hastened to correct her. 'Obviously, I know the
Chandler solicitors. I know the Chandlers themselves, if it
comes down to it. Michael had four children and they're all
still in London. As is his widow. But the boy didn't mention
Bowers when he came to see me. He didn't mention a Neil
Sitwell either, for that matter. And most importantly, he didn't
mention any music.'

'He didn't? Then why did he ask to see you?'

'He said he'd heard about the Fund. Well, he would have
done, wouldn't he, since it got a lot of press when Dad died.
Cole hoped for patronage. He brought me some photos of
his work.'

Barbara felt as if cobwebs were filling her skull, so unprepared had she been for this information. 'Are you sure?'

'Of course I'm sure. He had a portfolio with him and I
thought at first he was hoping for financial support while
he studied to be a set or costume designer. Because, like I
said, those are the people the Fund supports: artists who're
connected with the theatre in one way or another. Not artists
in general. But he didn't know this. Or he misunderstood. Or
he'd misread the details somewhere . . . I don't know.'

'Did he show you what he had in the portfolio?'

'Pictures of his work, most of it pretty awful. Gardening
tools bent this way and that. Rakes and hoes. Trowels split

into sections. I don't know much about modern art, but from what I could see, I'd say he needed to think about another profession.'

Barbara mused. When, she asked, had the visit from Terry Cole occurred?

Matthew thought for a moment and left the room to fetch his diary, which he carried back to the sitting room, open upon his palm. He hadn't recorded the visit since the Cole boy hadn't phoned for an appointment in advance. But it had been a day when Ginny – his father's widow – had been in the office and he had made note of that. Matthew gave Barbara the date. It was the very day of Terry Cole's death.

'Of course, I didn't tell him what I actually thought of his work. There would have been no point in that, would there? And besides he seemed so earnest about it.'

'Cole never mentioned music? A piece of sheet music? Or Michael Chandler? Or even your dad?'

'Not at all. Of course, he knew who my father was. He did say that. But that could have been merely because he was hoping to get some money off the Fund. Oiling his way with the odd compliment or two, if you know what I mean. But that was it.' Matthew sat down again, closed his diary, and took up his mug. 'Sorry. I haven't helped much, have I?'

'I don't know,' Barbara replied thoughtfully.

'May I ask why you're collecting information on the boy? Has he done something . . . ? I mean, you *are* the police.'

'Something's been done to him. He was murdered the same day he saw you.'

'The *same* . . . ? God. That's nasty. You're on the trail of his killer?'

Barbara wondered about that. It had certainly *felt* like a trail. It had looked like, smelled like, and acted like a trail. But for the first time since Inspector Lynley had directed her back to the Criminal Record Information System with the order to explore Andrew Maiden's past cases for a potential connection to his daughter's death, and for the first time since she'd rejected that line of enquiry as useless to the case, she was forced to wonder if she was following a fox or a herring, cured and dyed. She couldn't have said.

So she dug her car keys out of her bag and told Matthew King-Ryder she would be in touch if she had further questions. And if he should happen to recall anything more from his time with Terry Cole . . . She handed over her number. Would he phone? she asked him. One never knew what detail might work its way out of memory when one least expected it.

Certainly, Matthew King-Ryder told her. And in case Terry Cole had unearthed the name of the Chandler solicitors without the aid of King-Ryder, he wanted the police to have the name of the firm and their telephone number. He flipped to the back of his diary, accessed a directory, and ran his finger down a page of names and numbers. Finding the one he wanted, he recited the information. Barbara took it down in her dog-eared notebook. She thanked the young man for his cooperation and wished him luck in his move south of the river. He saw her to the door. In the manner of all wise Londoners, he bolted it behind her.

Alone in the corridor outside his flat, Barbara considered what she'd heard and she pondered how – and if – the information she was gathering fitted into the puzzle of Terry Cole's death. Terry had talked about his big commission, she recalled. Could he have been speaking about his hopes for a grant from the King-Ryder Fund? She'd leapt to the conclusion that his visit to King-Ryder must have had to do with the Michael Chandler music in his possession. But if he'd been informed that the music was worthless to him, why would he have gone to the trouble of tracking down solicitors and turning the music over to Chandler's family? Certainly, he might have hoped for a reward from the Chandlers. But even if he'd been given one, could it possibly have matched an artistic grant from King-Ryder which would have allowed him to pursue his unlikely career in sculpting? Hardly, Barbara decided. Far better to make an attempt to impress an established benefactor with his talent than to hope for the generosity of unknown people grateful to have their own property returned.

Yes. There was sense in this. And chances were that Terry Cole had shrugged off every consideration of making money from Chandler's handwritten score once he knew how necessary were the kindness and generosity of strangers to the successful fulfilment of his ambition. After speaking to Sitwell, he'd probably chucked the music out or taken it home and left it somewhere among his things. Which, of course, begged the question of why she and Nkata hadn't come across it when they'd searched the flat. But would they even have noticed a sheet of music among his gear? Especially when one considered the bombardment their senses had taken with the art of both the occupants of the flat.

Art. There was a point of connection for all the details in the case, she thought. Art. Artists. The King-Ryder Fund. Matthew had said that grants were given only to artists connected with the theatre. But what was to prevent an artist *switching* to the theatre just to cut in on some money? If Terry Cole had twigged to this idea, if he'd actually presented himself as a designer and not a sculptor, if indeed his big commission was in reality a fraud perpetrated against a fund that was intended as a lasting memorial to a giant of the theatre . . .

No. She was getting ahead of herself. She was mixing too many possibilities into the brew. She was going to give herself a headache, and she was going to turn cloudy water to mud. She needed to think, to get out in the air, to have a brisk walk in Regent's Park so she could sort out everything that was piling up in—

Barbara's thoughts stopped their tumble as her gaze settled on the collection of rubbish outside King-Ryder's door. She hadn't paid it any attention on the way in, but now she did. They'd talked about artists, about not knowing much about modern art. And what she saw outside King-Ryder's door intruded upon her notice because they'd had that conversation.

A canvas was among the rubbish that King-Ryder was discarding. It leaned with its face against the wall, rubbish bags piled up against it.

Barbara looked left and right. She made the decision to see what went for art – discarded or otherwise – to Matthew King-Ryder. She eased the rubbish bags away from the canvas and eased the canvas away from the wall.

'Bloody hell,' she whispered when she saw what she'd uncovered: A grotesque blonde woman, her huge mouth gaping open to display a cat defecating on her tongue.

Barbara had seen a dozen or more variations on this questionable theme already. She'd seen and talked to the artist as well: Cilla Thompson, who'd announced proudly that she'd sold a painting 'to a gent with good taste only last week.'

Barbara examined the closed door to Matthew King-Ryder's digs. A chill ran through her. A killer lived within, she decided. And she determined then and there that she was just the rozzer who would bring him to justice.

Lynley found Barbara Havers' report on his desk when he arrived at the Yard at ten o'clock that morning. He read the summaries and conclusions she'd developed regarding the files she'd explored on CRIS, and he took note of the implication of grievance which coloured her choice of words. At the moment, though, he couldn't afford to give weight to her thinly veiled criticism of the orders he'd given her. The morning had already been a wrenching one, and he had other more pressing matters on his mind than a DC's unhappiness with her assignment.

He'd taken a detour from his normal route from Eaton Terrace to Victoria Street, dropping down to Fulham where he checked on Vi Nevin's condition at the Chelsea and Westminster Hospital.

The young woman's doctors had granted him quarter of an hour with her. But she'd been deeply sedated and during that time she hadn't stirred. A plastic surgeon had arrived to examine her, which necessitated the removal of her bandages, and she slept through this activity as well.

In the midst of the surgeon's attention to her friend, Shelly Platt arrived at the hospital in a linen trouser suit and sandals, her orange hair hidden beneath a wide-brimmed raffia hat and her eyes concealed by a pair of sunglasses. With the excuse of offering sympathy upon the death of Nicola Maiden, she'd been phoning Vi repeatedly since Lynley's visit to her Earl's Court bed-sit. Unable to raise her, she'd finally gone to Rostrevor Road where the attack on her old flatmate was the talk of the neighbourhood.

'I got t' see her!' was what Lynley heard from within as the plastic surgeon studied the ruin of Vi's face and talked quietly about bones shattered like glass, skin grafts and scar tissue with the disinterested air of a man more suited to medical research than to the treatment of patients. Recognising the glottal stops if not the voice itself coming from the corridor, Lynley excused himself and went out to find Shelly Platt trying to elbow past the police guard and a nurse from the floor.

'He did it, di'n't he?' Shelly Platt cried when she saw him. 'I tol' him and he found her, di'n't he? He *did*. And he *got* her just like I thought he would. And now he'll come for me if he knows I tol' you the truth about his business. How is she? How's Vi?? Lemme *see* her. I got to.'

Her voice rose towards hysteria, and the nurse asked if 'this creature' was a relative of the patient. Shelly took off her sunglasses, exposing bloodshot eyes that she rolled towards Lynley in mute appeal.

'She's her sister,' Lynley informed the nurse, guiding Shelly by the arm. 'She's allowed inside.'

Within, Shelly threw herself at the bed, where another nurse was replacing Vi Nevin's bandages as the plastic surgeon washed his hands at the basin and then departed. Shelly began to cry. She said, 'Vi. Vi. Vi, baby doll. I di'n't mean none of it. Not one single word,' and she took up the limp hand that lay on the bedclothes and pressed it to her heart as if the beating within her bony chest would somehow confirm what she was saying. 'Wha's the matter with her?' she demanded of the nurse. 'Wha've you *done* to her?'

'She's sedated, Miss.' The nurse pursed her lips in disapproval as she put the final bit of tape on the gauze.

'But she'll be all right, won' she?'

Lynley glanced at the nurse before saying, 'She'll recover.'

'Bu' her face. All them bandages. Wha's he *done* t' her face?'

'That's where he beat her.'

Shelly Platt wept harder. 'No. *No.* Oh Vi. I'm that sorry. I di'n't *mean* no real harm on you. I was cheesed off, tha's all. You know how I am.'

The nurse crinkled her nose at this display of emotion. She left the room.

'She's going to need plastic surgery,' Lynley told Shelly when they were alone. 'And then . . .' He sought a clear but compassionate way of explaining to the girl what the future was likely to hold for Vi Nevin. 'There's a very good chance she's going to find her professional options narrower than they were before.' He waited to see if Shelly would understand without a more graphic explanation. Unpretty as she was but still on the game, she would have to know what facial scars presaged for a woman who'd earned her substantial keep by playing Lolita for her clients.

Shelly moved an anguished gaze from Lynley to her friend. 'I'll take care of her, then. F'm now on, and every single minute. I'll take care of my Vi.' She kissed Vi's hand and clutched it harder and wept harder still.

'She needs to rest now,' Lynley told her.

'I'm not leaving Vi till she knows I'm here.'

'You can wait with the constable. I'll see to it that he allows you in the room once an hour.'

Shelly parted with Vi's hand only reluctantly. In the corridor, she said, 'You'll go after him, won' you? You'll cart him off to the nick straightaway?' And it was those two questions that haunted Lynley all the way to the Yard.

Martin Reeve had it all in the attack on Vi Nevin: motive, means, and opportunity. He had a lifestyle to maintain and a wife whose drug habit needed feeding. He couldn't afford to lose any income. If one girl managed to leave him successfully, there was nothing to prevent another girl – or ten girls – from following suit. And if he allowed that to happen, he'd soon be out of business altogether. Because the two necessary participants in prostitution are the prostitutes themselves and their willing punters. Pimps are expendable. And Martin Reeve was aware of that fact. He would rule over his women by example and fear: by illustrating the extremes he was willing to go to to protect his domain and by implying – through those extremes – that what happened to one girl could easily happen to another. Vi Nevin had served as an object lesson for the rest of Reeve's women. The only question was whether Nicola Maiden and Terry Cole were object lessons as well.

There was one way to find out: get Reeve to the Yard without a solicitor in tow and outsmart him once he was present. But to do that, Lynley knew that he was going to need to outmanoeuvre the man, and his options in that particular realm were limited.

Lynley looked for a means of manipulation in the photographs of the maisonette, which the police photographer had rushed to him that morning. He studied in particular a shoe print on the kitchen floor, and he wondered if the pattern of hexagons on the shoe's sole was rare enough to count for something. Certainly, it ought to be sufficient to get a warrant. And, warrant in hand, three or four officers could tear apart MKR Financial Management and find evidence of Reeve's true business dealings, even if he'd been clever enough to rid himself of the shoes with those hexagonally marked soles. Once they had that evidence, they'd be in a position to intimidate the pimp. Which was exactly where Lynley wanted to be.

He looked through more of the pictures, tossing them one by one onto his desk. He was still in the process of examining them for something useful when Barbara Havers charged into his office.

'Holy hell,' she said without preamble, 'wait till you hear what I've got, Inspector.' And she began to chatter about an auction house on Cork Street, someone called Sitwell, Soho Square, and King-Ryder Productions. 'So I saw this painting when I left his digs,' she concluded triumphantly. 'And believe me, sir, if you'd got a glimpse of Cilla's work in Battersea, you'd agree it's a hell of a lot more than a simple coincidence that I'd stumble across *anyone* in God's creation who'd actually bought one of her disgusting pieces.' She flopped into one of the chairs in front of his desk and scooped up the photographs. She said, giving them a cursory examination, 'King-Ryder's our boy. And you can write that in my blood if you'd like to.'

Lynley observed her over the top of his spectacles. 'What led you in that direction? Is there a connection between Mr King-Ryder and Maiden's SO10 time that you've uncovered? Because in your report you didn't mention . . .' He frowned, wondering and not liking his wondering. 'Havers, how did you get on to King-Ryder?'

She kept up a resolute study of the pictures as she replied. But she spoke in a rush. 'It was like this, sir. I found a business card at Terry Cole's flat. An address as well. And I thought . . . Well, I know I should have turned it over to you straightaway, but it slipped my mind when you sent me back to CRIS. And as things turned out, I had a bit of free time yesterday when I finished the report and . . .' She hesitated, her attention still on the pictures. But when she finally looked up, her expression had altered, less sure now than when she'd strode into the room. 'Since I had that card and the address, I went over to Soho Square and then down to Cork Street and . . . Inspector, gosh. What *difference* does it make what led me to him? King-Ryder's lying and if he's lying, we both know there's just one reason why.'

Lynley placed the rest of the pictures on his desk. He said: 'I'm not following this. We've established the connection between our two victims: prostitution and the advertisement of prostitution. We've developed an understanding of another possible motive: a common pimp's vengeance for an act of betrayal by two girls in his stable, one of whom – by the way – he beat up last night. No one can confirm that pimp's alibi for Tuesday night, other than his wife whose word doesn't appear to be worth the breath she uses to speak it. What we have left to root out is the missing weapon, which may very well be sitting somewhere in Martin Reeve's house. Now, all of that being established, Havers, and established – I'd like to add – through doing the sort of police work you appear to be avoiding these days, I'd be grateful if you would list the facts that allow you to argue a case for Matthew King-Ryder as our killer.'

She didn't reply, but Lynley saw the ugly flush begin to splodge her neck.

He said, 'Barbara, I'm hoping your conclusions are the result of foot work and not intuition.'

Havers' colour deepened. 'You always say that coincidence doesn't exist when it comes to murder, Inspector.'

'So I do. But what's the coincidence?'

'That painting. The Cilla Thompson monstrosity. What's he doing with a painting by Terry Cole's flatmate? You can't argue he's bought it to hang on his wall when it was out with his rubbish, so it's *got* to mean something. And I think it must mean—'

'You think it means he's a killer. But you have no motive for his committing this killing, have you?'

'I've just begun. I only went to see King-Ryder initially because Terry Cole had been sent there by this bloke Neil Sitwell. I didn't *expect* to uncover one of Cilla's paintings by his door, and when I did, I was gobsmacked. Well, who wouldn't be? Five minutes earlier and King-Ryder was telling me that Terry Cole came to talk to him about a grant. I leave the flat, trying to adjust my thinking to the new information, and there's this painting in the rubbish that tells me King-Ryder has a connection to this killing he's not talking about.'

'A connection to the killing?' Lynley allowed his scepticism to underscore the words. 'Havers, all you've uncovered at the moment is the fact that King-Ryder may have a connection to someone who's connected to someone who's been murdered in the company of a woman with whom he has no connection at all.'

'But—'

'No. No *but*, Havers. No *and* and no *if*, if it comes down to it. You've been fighting me every inch of the way on this case, and that's got to stop. I've assigned you a task, which you've largely ignored because you don't like it. You've gone your own way to the detriment of the team—'

'That's not fair!' she protested. 'I did the report. I put it on your desk.'

'Yes. And I've read it.' Lynley rooted out the paperwork. He picked it up and used it to emphasise his words as he went on. 'Barbara, do you think I'm stupid? Do you suppose I'm incapable of reading between the lines of what's posing as the work of a professional?'

She lowered her eyes. She was still holding some of the photographs of Vi Nevin's destroyed home, and she fastened her gaze upon these. Her fingers whitened as her grasp on them tightened, and her colour deepened its revealing hue.

Thank God, Lynley thought. He finally had her attention. He warmed to his theme. 'When you're given an assignment, you're expected to complete it. Without question or argument.

And when you complete it, you're expected to turn in a report that reflects the dispassionate language of the disinterested professional. And after that, you're expected to await your next assignment with a mind that remains open and capable of assimilating information. What you're not expected to do is create a disguised commentary on the wisdom of the investigation's course should you happen to disagree with it. This—' he slapped her report against his palm – 'is an excellent illustration of why you're in the position you're in right now. Given an order that you neither like nor agree with, you take matters into your own hands. You go your own way with complete disregard for everything from the chain of command to public safety. You did that three months ago in Essex, and you're doing it now. When any other DC would be toeing the line in the hope of redeeming his name and reputation if not his career, you're still pig-headedly trotting along on whatever path pleases you most at the moment. Aren't you?'

Head still lowered, she made no reply. But her breathing had altered, becoming shallow with the effort to hold back emotion. She seemed, at least for the moment, suitably chastened. He was gratified to see it.

'All right,' he said. 'Now hear me well. I want a warrant to tear Reeve's house apart. I want a team of four officers to do the tearing. I want from that house a single pair of shoes with hexagons on the soles and every scrap of evidence you can find on the escort service. May I put you on this and be assured that you'll carry through as directed?'

She made no reply.

He felt exasperation plague him like a cloud of gnats. 'Havers, are you listening to me?'

'A search.'

'Yes. That's what I said. I want a search warrant. And when you've got it, I want you on the team that goes to Reeve's house.'

She raised her head from the pictures. 'A bloody search,' she said, and her face was unaccountably altered now, bright with a smile. 'Yes. *Yes.* Bloody hell, Inspector. By holy God. That's absolutely it.'

'That's what?'

'Don't you see?' She crumpled one of the pictures in her excitement. 'Sir, don't you see? You're thinking of Martin Reeve because his motive's been established and it's so bloody obvious that any other motive is small beer in comparison. And because his motive's so *out* there for you, everything you come across ends up getting attached to it, whether it belongs attached or not. But if you forget about Reeve for a moment, you can see in these pictures that—'

'Havers.' Lynley fought against the tide of his own incredulity. The woman was unquashable, unsinkable, and entirely ungovernable. For the first time he wondered how he'd ever managed to work with her at all. 'I'm not going to repeat your assignment after this. I'm going to give it to you. And you're going to do it.'

'But I only want you to see that—'

'No! God damn it! Enough. Get the warrant. I don't care what you have to do to get it. But get it. Put together a team from CID. Go to that house. Tear it apart. Bring me shoes with hexagonal markings on the sole and evidence of the escort service. Better yet, bring me a weapon that could have been used on Terry Cole. Is that clear? Now *go.*'

She stared at him. For a moment, he believed she would actually defy him. And in that moment, he knew how DCI Barlow must have felt out on the North Sea in pursuit of a suspect and having her every decision second-guessed by a subordinate who was incapable of keeping her opinions to herself. Havers was damned lucky Barlow hadn't been the officer with the gun in that boat. Had the DCI been armed, that North Sea chase might have come to a very different conclusion.

Havers rose. Carefully, she placed the photographs of Vi

Nevin's maisonette on his desk. She said, 'A warrant, a search. A team of four officers. I'll see to it, Inspector.'

Her tone was measured. It was utterly polite, deeply respect-ful, and completely proper.

Lynley chose to ignore what all of that meant.

Martin Reeve's palms itched. He pressed his fingernails into them. They began to burn. Tricia had backed him when he needed her to back him with that butthole of a cop, but he couldn't depend on her to hold to the story. If someone promised her enough of the beast at a moment when her stash was low and she wanted to crank up, she'd say or do anything. All the cops had to do was to get her alone, get her away from the house, and she'd be butter on their toast in less than two hours. And he couldn't watch over her every frigging minute of every God damn day for the rest of their lives to make sure that didn't happen.

Whattaya wanna know? Gimme the stuff.

Just sign on the line, Mrs Reeve, and you'll have it.

And it would be done. No. Better. *He* would be done. So he had to firm up his story.

On the one hand, he could muscle a lie from someone who already knew firsthand what could come from refusing his request. On the other hand, he could demand the truth from someone else who might take an appeal for common veracity as a sign of weakness. Go the first way, and he ended up owing a favour, which handed the reins of his life to someone else. Go the second way, and he looked like a pantywaist who could be dissed without fear of reprisal.

So the situation was a basic no-win: Caught between a rock and a hard place, Martin wanted to find enough dynamite to blast a passageway while keeping the damage from falling stones to a minimum.

He went to Fulham. All his current troubles had their genesis there, and it was there that he was determined to find the solutions as well.

He got into the building on Rostrevor Road the easy way: He rang each bell in rapid succession and waited for the fool who would buzz him inside without asking him to identify himself over the intercom.

He dashed up the stairs, but at the landing he paused. A sign was affixed to the maisonette's door and even from where he stood, he could read it. Crime Scene, it announced. Do Not Enter.

'Shit,' Martin said.

And he heard the cop's low, terse voice once again, as clearly as if he were on the landing as well. '*Tell me about Vi Nevin.*'

'Fuck,' Martin said. Was she dead?

He dug up the answer by descending the stairs and knocking up the residents of the flat directly beneath Vi Nevin's front door. They'd been giving a party on the night before, but they hadn't been too occupied with their guests – or too smashed – to take note of the arrival of an ambulance. Much had been done by the paramedics to shield the shrouded form they carried out of the building, but the haste with which they removed her and the subsequent appearance of what had seemed like a score of policemen who began asking questions throughout the building suggested that she'd been the victim of a crime.

'Dead?' Martin grabbed onto the young man's arm when he would have turned back into his flat to catch up on more of the sleep of which Martin's appearance at his door had robbed him. 'Wait. Damn it. Was she dead?'

'She wasn't in a body bag,' was the indifferent reply. 'But she might've popped her clogs in hospital during the night.'

Martin cursed his luck and, back in his car, got out his *London Streetfinder*. The nearest hospital was the Chelsea and Westminster on the Fulham Road, and he drove there directly. If she was dead, he was done for.

The nurse in casualty informed him that Miss Nevin had been moved. Was he a relative? she asked

An old friend, Martin told her. He'd been to her home and discovered there'd been an accident ... some sort of trouble ...? If he could see Vi and set his mind at rest that she was all right ... So that he in turn could let their mutual friends and her relatives know ...? He should have shaved, he thought. He should have worn the Armani jacket. He should have prepared for an eventuality beyond the simple knocking on a door, gaining admittance and coercing cooperation.

Miss Schubert — for such was the name on her identification badge — eyed him with the open animosity of the overworked and the underpaid. She consulted a clipboard and gave him a room number. He didn't miss the fact that when he thanked her and headed towards the elevators, she reached for a phone.

Thus, he wasn't entirely unprepared for the sight of a uniformed constable seated outside the closed door of Vi Nevin's room. He was, however, completely unprepared for the appearance of the orange-haired harpy in a crumpled pantsuit who was sitting next to the cop. She leapt to her feet and came hurtling in Martin's direction the moment she saw him.

She shrieked, 'It's 'im, it's 'im, it's *'im!*' She flew at Martin like a starving hawk with a rabbit in sight, and she sank her talons into the front of his shirt and screeched, 'I'll kill you. Bastard. *Bastard!*'

She shoved him into the wall and butted him with her head. His own head flew back and smacked against the edge of a notice board. His jaw clamped shut. Teeth sinking into his tongue, he tasted blood. She'd ripped the buttons from his shirt and gone for his neck when the constable finally managed to pull her off. Whereupon she began screaming, 'Arrest him! He's the one! Arrest him! Arrest him!' and the constable asked for Martin's i.d. He somehow dispersed a small crowd that had gathered at the end of the corridor to watch the unfolding scene, a minor kindness for which Martin was grateful.

The woman held at arm's length from him, Martin was able to recognise her at last. It was the hair colour that had thrown him off. When they'd met – when she'd come for her first and only interview at MKR – she'd been black-haired. Otherwise, she was little changed. Still skeletal, still sallow skinned, with very bad teeth, even worse breath, and the body odour of three-day-old halibut.

'Shelly Platt,' he said.

'You did it! You tried to kill her!'

Martin wondered how his day could possibly get worse. He had his answer a moment later. The constable studied his identification, still holding Shelly in a death lock grip. He said, 'Miss, Miss, one thing at a time,' and he took her with him while he went to the phone at the nurses' station and punched in a number.

'Look,' Martin called to him. 'I only want to know if Miss Nevin's all right. I spoke to someone in casualty. I was told she'd been transferred here.'

'He wants to kill her!' Shelly cried.

'Don't be an idiot,' Martin responded. 'I'd hardly show up in the middle of the day and present my i.d. if I planned to kill her. What the hell happened?'

'As if you don't know!'

'I just need to talk to her,' he told the constable when he was returned his i.d. and refused admittance. 'That's all. It probably won't take five minutes.'

'Sorry,' was the reply.

'Look. I don't think you understand. This is an urgent matter and—'

'Aren' you going t'*arrest* him?' Shelly demanded. 'Wha's he have t'*do* to her before you lot cart him off to the nick?'

'Will you at least shut her up long enough for me to explain to you that—'

'Orders're orders,' the constable said, and he loosened his grip on Shelly Platt just enough to indicate to Martin that a temporary retreat was called for.

He made that retreat with as much grace as he could muster, considering that the orange-haired termagant had raised enough ruckus for him to become the cynosure of the entire hospital floor. He returned to the Jaguar, threw himself inside, and flicked its air conditioning on full blast with every vent pointing at his face.

Shit, he thought. Fuck, hell, shit. He had little doubt about who had been on the receiving end of that constable's phone call, so he'd put himself in line for another visit from the cops. He considered what sort of light he was going to shine upon his trip to the Chelsea and Westminster Hospital. 'Getting corroboration for my story last night' hardly seemed credible when one considered from whom he was attempting to wrest corroboration in the first place.

He jerked the car into gear and roared out of the car park. On the Fulham Road once more, he pulled down the sun visor and used the recessed mirror within it to examine the damage Shelly Platt had done to him. Jesus, she was a vicious little cat. She'd managed to draw blood on his chest when she'd grabbed his shirt. He'd be wise to get a tetanus shot pronto.

He cut up Finborough Road, heading for home and considering what options were available to him now. It appeared that there was no way he was going to get close to Vi Nevin any time soon and, since the cop on guard in front of her room had no doubt phoned that goon who'd dropped by Lansdowne Road in the middle of the previous night, it also appeared that there was no way he was going to get close to her any time at all. At least not while the cops were doing their bloodhound bit on the Maiden whore's killing and *that* might go on for months. He had to develop another plan to get corroboration for his alibi, and he found his mind feverishly coming up with one scenario only to dismiss it and come up with another.

On the Exhibition Hall side of Earl's Court Station, he stopped for a traffic light. He waved off a street urchin who wanted to wash his windscreen for fifty p, and he observed a hooker in negotiations with a potential client by the underground entrance. He made an instant evaluation of her in a knee jerk reaction to the sight of her Bandaid-size skirt of magenta Spandex, her black polyester blouse with its plunging neckline and its senseless ruffles, her stiletto heels and her fishnet stockings: She was a hand-or-mouth bitch only, he decided. Twenty-five pounds if the john was desperate; no more than ten if she and her coke habit were working the street together.

The light changed, and as he drove off, Martin's sense of grievance against the police began to grow in him. He was doing the whole shitting city one *hell* of a favour, he decided, and no one – least of all the cops – seemed to realise or appreciate that. His girls didn't clutter up the sidewalks making deals with clients, and they sure as hell didn't pollute the landscape by dressing like something out of an adolescent's wet dream. They were refined, educated, attractive, and discreet, and if they *did* take money for engaging in the odd sexual encounter or two and if they *did* pass on a percentage to him who made it possible for them to be in the company of wealthy and successful men who were willing to recompense them richly for their services, who the hell cared? Who the hell did it hurt? No one. The bottom line was that sex had a place in men's lives that it did not have in the lives of women. For men it was a signature act, primal and necessary to their identity. Their wives grew tired of it or bored by it, but the men did not. And if someone was prepared to provide those men with access to women who welcomed their attentions, women willing to allow their bodies to be the soft and pliable wax into which those men poured their juices not to mention left the indelible impression of their very characters, why couldn't money be exchanged for such a service? And why couldn't someone – like himself – with the organisational skills and the vision to recruit exceptional women for the entertainment of exceptional men be allowed to make a living doing it?

If the laws had been written by visionaries like himself and not by a group of spineless jerks who were more concerned with being able to feed at the public trough than they were with being even marginally realistic about activities participated in by consenting adults, Martin thought, then he wouldn't have been in the position he was in at this very moment. He wouldn't be scrambling for someone who could vouch for his whereabouts and get the police off his back because the police would never have been on his back in the first place. And even if they *had* come calling and had asked their questions and made their demands, they wouldn't have had a single thing to hold over his head to gain cooperation because he wouldn't have been living just the other side of the law in the first place.

And what sort of country was it, anyway, where prostitution was legal but living off prostitution wasn't? What was prostitution but a means of livelihood? And who the hell were they kidding trying to regulate it from Westminster when three-quarters of those hypocrites who planted their asses on those leather benches were screwing their eyeballs out with any secretary, student, or parliamentary assistant who appeared even remotely willing?

Fuck it, the entire situation made him want to punch holes through walls. And the more he thought of it, the angrier he became. And the angrier he became, the more he focused on the cause of all his current troubles. Forget Maiden and Nevin, he realised: They were taken care of, after all. They hadn't been the ones to spill their miserable guts to the cops. Tricia, on the other hand, remained to be dealt with.

He spent the rest of the drive considering how best to do this. What he came up with wasn't pleasant, but when was it pleasant when a notable figure on the social scene loses his wife to heroin despite his best efforts to save her from herself and to shield her from the displeasure of her family and the censure of an unforgiving public?

He felt his mood lift. His lips curved upward, and he began to hum. He made the turn from Lansdowne Walk into Lansdowne Road.

And there he saw them.

Four men were mounting the front steps to his house, with PLAINCLOTHES COPS written all over them. They were beefy, tall, and designed to tyrannise. They looked like gorillas in fancy dress.

Martin hit the accelerator. He swerved into the drive and left a patch of rubber where he made the turn. He was out of the Jaguar and up the steps in their wake before they had a chance to ring the bell. 'What do you want?' he demanded.

Gorilla One removed a white envelope from the pocket of a leather bomber jacket. 'Search warrant,' he said.

'Search for what?'

'Are you opening the door or are we breaking it down?'

'I'm phoning my solicitor.' Martin shoved past them and unlocked the door.

'Whatever you want,' Gorilla Two said.

They followed him inside. Gorilla One gave instructions as Martin raced for the phone. Two of the cops were right on his heels and into his office. The other two pounded up the stairs. Shit, he thought, and he shouted, 'Hey! My wife's up there!'

'They'll say hello,' Gorilla One said.

As Martin frantically punched in the phone number, One began removing books from the shelves and Two went for a filing cabinet. 'I want you fuckers out of here,' Martin told them.

'Right,' said Two, 'I'm not surprised.'

'And we all want something,' said One with a smirk.

Upstairs, a door crashed back against a wall. Muffled voices accompanied the noise of furniture being roughly shoved round a room. In Martin's office, the cops made their search with a minimum of effort and a maximum of mess: They strewed books on the floor, took pictures from the walls, and emptied the filing cabinet in which Martin kept scrupulous records for the escort service. Gorilla Two bent and, with cigar-stub fingers, began sifting through them.

'Shit,' Martin hissed, receiver to his ear. Where was that fucker Polmanteer?

On the other end of the line, the phone at his solicitor's home double rang four times. His answer machine clicked on. Martin cursed, disconnected, and tried the solicitor's mobile. Where would he be on a Sunday, for God's sake? The slimy bastard couldn't have gone to church.

The mobile brought him no better results. He slammed down the receiver and rooted in his desk for the solicitor's card. Gorilla Two elbowed him to one side. He said, 'Sorry, sir. Can't let you remove—'

'I'm not removing a fucking thing! I'm looking for my solicitor's pager.'

'Wouldn't keep it in your desk, would he?' One asked from the shelves where he continued his work. Books thunked to the floor.

'You know what I mean,' Martin said to Two. 'I want the number of his pager. It's on a card. I know my rights. Now step aside or I won't be responsible—'

'Martin? What is it? What's going on? There're men in our room and they've emptied the wardrobe and . . . What's going on?'

Martin spun round. Tricia was in the doorway, unshowered, undressed, and unpainted. She looked like the hags who sat on their sleeping bags and begged for money in the subway at Hyde Park Corner. She looked like a smack head.

His hands started to burn once again. He dug his nails into his palms. Tricia had been the single cause of his every difficulty for the last twenty years. And now she was the cause of his downfall.

He said, 'God damn it. God *damn* it. You!' And he plunged across the room. He grabbed her by the hair and managed to ram her head against the doorjamb before the cops were on him. 'Stupid cunt!' he shouted as they dragged him off her. And then to the police, 'All right. All *right*,' as he shook off their hold on him. 'Call your asshole boss. Tell him I'm ready to deal.'

Chapter Twenty-five

———◆———

It was nearly midday before Simon St James was able to give his time to the Derbyshire postmortem reports that Lynley had sent him via Barbara Havers. He wasn't sure what he was supposed to be looking for. The examination of the Maiden girl appeared in order. The conclusion of epidural haematoma was consistent with the blow to her skull. That it had been administered by a right-handed person attacking her from above was consistent with the hypothesis that she'd been running and had tripped – or been tackled – in her flight across the moor in the darkness. Apart from the blow to her head and the scrapes and contusions one would expect to find after a rough fall on uneven ground, there was nothing on her body that suggested anything curious. Unless, of course, one wanted to consider the extraordinary number of holes she'd had pierced in everything from her eyebrows to her genitals as a point of interest. And that hardly seemed a reasonable route to go when driving needles through various body parts had long ago become one of the relatively few acts of defiance left to a generation of young people whose parents had already engaged in them all.

From his reading of the Maiden report, it seemed to St James that all the bases had been covered: from the time, cause, and mechanism of death to the evidence – or lack thereof – of a struggle. X-rays and photographs had been duly taken, and the body had been examined from top to bottom. The various organs had been studied, removed, and commented upon. Samples of body fluids had been sent to toxicology for their findings. At the end of the report, the opinion was stated briefly and clearly: The girl had died as the result of a blow to the head.

St James went through the findings once more, to make sure he hadn't missed any pertinent detail. Then he turned to the second report and immersed himself in the death of Terence Cole.

Lynley had phoned him with the information that one of the wounds on the boy hadn't been inflicted by the Swiss Army knife that had apparently been responsible for the others, including the fatal piercing of the femoral artery. After reading through the basic facts in the report, St James gave a more careful scrutiny to everything related to this particular wound. He noted its size, its position on the body, and the marking left on the bone beneath it. He stared at the words and then walked contemplatively to the window of his lab, where he watched as Peach rolled blissfully below him in a patch of garden sunlight, exposing her furry dachshund belly to the twelve o'clock heat.

The Swiss Army knife, he knew, had been found in a grit dispenser. Why hadn't the secondary weapon been left in the same place? Why cache one weapon but not the other? Those questions of course belonged in the realm of the case detectives and not the scientists, but he believed they needed to be asked nonetheless.

Once they were asked, there seemed to be only two possible answers: Either the second weapon identified the killer too closely to be left at the scene or the second weapon *had* been left at the scene and the police had mistaken it for something else.

If the first supposition was the case, he could be of no

assistance in the matter. If the second was the case, a more detailed study of the crime scene evidence was in order. He had no access to that evidence and he knew he wouldn't be welcome in Derbyshire to finger through it. So he returned to the postmortem report and he sought anything within it that might give him a clue.

Dr Sue Myles hadn't missed a thing: from the insects that had taken up residence in and on both of the bodies during the hours they'd lain undiscovered on the moor to the leaves, flowers, and twigs that had become caught up in the hair of the girl and the wounds on the boy.

It was this final detail – a sliver of wood some two centimetres long found on the body of Terence Cole – that St James closed in on curiously. The sliver had been sent on to the lab for analysis, and someone had appended a note in pencil in the margin of the report, identifying it. From a phone call, probably. When officers were pressed, they didn't always wait for official word from the police lab before they moved on.

Cedar, someone had printed neatly in the margin. And next to it in parentheses the words *Port Orford*. St James was no botanist, so Port Orford illuminated nothing for him. He knew it was unlikely that he'd be able to track down on a Sunday the forensic botanist who'd identified the wood, so he gathered up his paperwork and descended the stairs to his study.

Deborah was within, absorbed in the *Sunday Times* Magazine. She said, 'Trouble, love?'

He replied, 'Ignorance. Which is trouble enough.'

He found the book he was looking for among the dustier of his volumes. He began leafing through the pages as Deborah joined him by the shelves.

'What is it?'

'I don't know,' he said. 'Cedar. And Port Orford. Mean anything to you?'

'Sounds like a place. Port Isaac, Port Orford. Why?'

'A sliver of cedar was found on Terence Cole's body. The boy on the moors.'

'Tommy's case?'

'Hmm.' St James flipped to the back of the book and ran his finger down the index under *cedar*. 'Atlas, blue, Chilean Incense. Did you know there were so many kinds of cedar?'

'Is it important?'

'I'm beginning to think it could be.' He ran his gaze further down the page. And then he saw the two words *Port Orford*. They were listed as a variety of the tree.

He turned to the indicated page, where first he took note of the picture which featured a sample of the coniferous tree's foliage and then read the entry itself. 'This is curious,' he said to his wife.

'What?' she asked, sliding her arm through his.

He told her what the postmortem had claimed: that a wooden sliver identified by the forensic botanist as Port Orford cedar had been found in one of the wounds on Terence Cole's body.

Deborah looked thoughtful as she shrugged back a heavy mass of her hair. 'Why's that curious? They were killed out of doors, weren't they? Out on the moors?' And then her eyes widened. 'Oh yes. I do see.'

'Exactly,' St James said. 'What kind of moor has cedars growing on it? But it's more curious than that, my love. This particular cedar grows in America, in the States. Oregon and northern California, it says.'

'The tree could have been imported, couldn't it?' Deborah asked reasonably. 'For someone's garden or for a park? Or even a greenhouse or conservatory. You know what I mean: like palm trees or cactuses.' She smiled, her nose wrinkling. 'Or is that cacti?'

St James walked to his desk and put the book down. He lowered himself slowly into his chair, thinking. 'All right. Let's say it was imported for someone's garden or a park.'

'Of course.' She was with him, tagging her own thought on to his. 'That still begs the obvious question, doesn't it? How did a cedar tree meant for someone's garden or a park get to the moor?'

'And how did it get to a part of the moor that's nowhere near someone's garden or a park in the first place?'

'Someone planted it there for religious reasons?'

'More likely no one planted it at all.'

'But you said . . .' Deborah frowned, 'Oh yes. I see. I suppose the forensic botanist must have made an error, then.'

'I don't think so.'

'But, Simon, if there was only a sliver to work with—'

'That's all a good forensic botanist would need.' St James went on to explain. Even a fragment of wood, he told her, bore the pattern of tubes and vessels that transported fluids from the bottom to the top of a tree. Soft wood trees – and all conifers, he told her, are among the soft woods – are less developed evolutionarily and consequently easier to identify. Placed under microscopic analysis, a sliver would reveal a number of key features that distinguish its species from all other species. A forensic botanist would catalogue these features, plug them into a key – or a computer identification system, for that matter – and derive from the information and the key an exact identification of the tree. It was a faultlessly accurate process, or at least as accurate as any other identification made from microscopic, human, and computer analysis.

'All right,' Deborah said slowly and with some apparent doubt. 'So it's cedar, yes?'

'Port Orford cedar. I think we can depend on that.'

'And it's a piece of cedar that's not from a tree growing in the area, yes?'

'Yes as well. So we're left with asking where that piece of cedar came from and how it came to be on the boy's body.'

'They were camping, weren't they?'

'The girl was, yes.'

'In a tent? Well, what about a tent peg?

'She was hiking. I doubt it was that kind of tent.'

Deborah crossed her arms and leaned against the desk, considering this. 'What about a camp stool, then? The legs, for instance.'

'Possibly. If a stool was among the items at the site.'

'Or tools. She would have had camping tools with her. An axe for wood, a trowel, something like that. The sliver could be from one of the handles.'

'Tools would have to be lightweight, though, if she was carrying them in a rucksack.'

'What about cooking utensils? Wooden spoons?'

St James smiled. 'Gourmets in the wilderness?'

'Don't laugh at me,' she said, laughing herself. 'I'm only trying to help.'

'I've a better idea,' he told her. 'Come along.'

He led her upstairs to the laboratory where his computer hummed quietly in a corner near the window. There, he sat down and, with Deborah at his shoulder, he accessed the internet, saying, 'Let's consult the Great Intelligence online.'

'Computers always make my palms sweat.'

St James took her palm, unsweaty, and kissed it. 'Your secret's safe with me.'

In a moment the computer screen came to life, and St James selected the search engine he generally used. He typed the word *cedar* into the search field and blinked with consternation when the result was some six hundred thousand entries.

'Good Lord,' Deborah said. 'That's not very helpful, is it?'

'Let's narrow out options.' St James altered his selection to *Port Orford Cedar*. The result was an immediate change to one hundred and eighty-three. But when he began to scroll through the listing, he saw he'd come up with everything from an article written about Port Orford, Oregon, to a treatise on wood rot. He sat back, reflected for a moment, and typed in the word *usage* after *cedar*, adding the appropriate inverted commas and addition signs. That gleaned him absolutely nothing at all. He switched from *usage* to *market* and hit the return. The screen altered and gave him his answer.

He read the very first listing and said, 'Good God,' when he saw what it was.

Deborah, whose attention had drifted towards her darkroom, came back to him. 'What?' she said. 'What?'

'It's the weapon,' he said and pointed to the screen.

Deborah read for herself and drew in a sharp breath. 'Shall I get in touch with Tommy?'

St James considered. But the request to study the post-mortem reports had been relayed to him from Lynley via Barbara. And that served as sufficient indication of a chain of command, which gave him the excuse he needed in order to attempt to make peace where there was strife.

'Let's track down Barbara,' he told his wife. 'She can be the one to take the news to Tommy.'

Barbara Havers zoomed round the corner of Anhalt Road and hoped her luck would hold for another few hours. She'd managed to find Cilla Thompson in her railway arch studio applying her talents to a canvas on which a cavernous mouth with tonsils like bellows opened upon a three-legged girl skipping on a spongy-looking tongue. A few questions had been enough to ascertain fuller information about the 'gent with good taste' who'd purchased one of Cilla's masterworks the previous week.

Cilla couldn't remember his name off the top of her head. Come to think of it, she reported, he'd never told her. But he'd written her a cheque which she'd photocopied, the better – Barbara thought – to prove to the world of artistic doubting Thomases that she'd actually managed to sell a canvas. She had that photocopy taped to the inside of her wooden paintbox, and she showed it off willingly, saying, 'Oh yeah, the bloke's name's right here. Gosh. Look at this. I wonder if he's any relation?'

Matthew King-Ryder, Barbara saw, had paid an idiotically exorbitant amount for one dog of a painting. He'd used a cheque drawn on a bank in St Helier on the island of Jersey. *Private Banking* was embossed above his name. He'd scrawled the amount as if he'd been in a hurry. As perhaps he had been, Barbara thought.

How had Matthew King-Ryder happened to turn up in Portslade Street? she'd asked the artist. Cilla herself would admit, wouldn't she, that this particular row of railway arches wasn't exactly heralded throughout London as a hotbed of modern art.

Cilla shrugged. She didn't know how he'd happened upon the studio. But obviously, she wasn't the sort of girl who looked at a gift horse cross-eyed. When he'd shown up, asked to have a look about, and demonstrated an interest in her work, she was as happy as a duck in the sun to let him browse right through it. All she could report in the end was that the bloke with the chequebook had spent a good hour looking at every piece of art in the studio—

Terry's as well? Barbara wanted to know. Had he asked about Terry's art? Using Terry's name?

No. He just wanted to see *her* paintings, Cilla explained. All of them. And when he couldn't find anything he liked, he asked if she had any others tucked away that he could see. So she'd sent him round to the flat, having phoned Mrs Baden and told her to show him up when he arrived. He went straight there and made his selection from one of those paintings. He sent her a cheque promptly by post on the following day. 'Gave me the asking price as well,' Cilla said proudly. 'No dickering about it.'

And that point alone – that Matthew King-Ryder had gained access to the digs of Terry Cole, for *whatever* reason – made Barbara push the accelerator floorward as she whipped through Battersea back to Cilla's flat.

She didn't give a thought to what she was supposed to be doing instead of reversing into a parking space at the end of Anhalt Road. She'd got the search warrant as directed, and she'd pulled together a team. She'd even met them in front of Snappy Snaps in Notting Hill Gate and put the whole kettle of them in the picture on what the Inspector wanted them to look for in Martin Reeve's home. She'd merely omitted the information that she was supposed to accompany them. It was easy enough to justify this omission. The team she'd assembled – two members of which were amateur boxers in their free time – could shake up a house and intimidate its inhabitants far better if they had no female presence diluting the threat implied by their imposing physiques and their tendency to communicate in monosyllables. Besides, wasn't she killing two birds – three or four, perhaps – by sending officers to Notting Hill to shake up and shake down the Reeves without her? While they were doing that, she would be using the time to see what information could be harvested from the Battersea end of things. Delegation of responsibility and the mark of an officer with leadership potential, she called the situation. And she pushed from her mind the nasty little voice that kept trying to call it something else.

She pressed the bell for Mrs Baden's ground floor flat. The faint sound of hesitantly played piano music halted abruptly. The sheer curtains in the bay window flicked an inch to one side.

Barbara called out, 'Mrs Baden? Barbara Havers again. New Scotland Yard CID.'

The buzzer sounded to release the lock. Barbara scurried inside.

Mrs Baden said graciously, 'Goodness me. I'd no idea detectives were expected to work on Sundays. I hope they give you the time to go to church.'

She herself had attended the early service, the woman confided without waiting for a response from Barbara. And afterwards, she'd joined a meeting of the wardens in order to put forward her opinions on the subject of establishing bingo nights to raise money to replace the roof of the chancel. She was in favour of the idea although in general she didn't approve of gambling. But this was gambling for God, which was altogether different from the sort of gambling that lined the secular pockets of casino owners who made their fortunes by offering games of chance to the avaricious.

'So I've no cake to offer you, I'm afraid,' Mrs Baden concluded regretfully. 'I took the rest with me to serve at the wardens' meeting this morning. It's far more pleasant engaging in debate over cake and coffee than over grumbling stomachs, don't you agree? Especially—' and here she smiled at her witticism – 'when grumbling enough is already going on.'

For a moment Barbara looked at her blankly. Then she recalled her previous visit. 'Oh, the *lemon* cake. I expect that went down a real treat with the wardens, Mrs Baden.'

The elderly woman lowered her gaze shyly. 'I think it's important to make a contribution when one's part of a congregation. Before these dreadful shakes of mine began—' Here, she held up her hands whose tremors today were making her look like the victim of an ague – 'I used to play the organ at services. I liked the funerals best, frankly, but of course I wouldn't have admitted that to the wardens, as they might have found my taste a bit macabre. When the shakes started, I had to give all that up. Now I play the piano instead for the infants' school choir where it doesn't much matter if I hit a wrong note from time to time. The children are quite forgiving about that. But I suppose people at funerals have far less reason to be understanding, don't they?'

'That makes sense,' Barbara agreed. 'Mrs Baden, I've just seen Cilla.' She went on to explain what she'd learned from the artist.

As she spoke, Mrs Baden went to the old upright piano at one side of the room, where a metronome was tick-tocking rhythmically and a timer whirred. She ceased the metronome's movement and turned off the timer. She put the piano's bench back into place, tapped several sheets of music neatly together, replaced them on their holder, and sat with her hands folded, looking attentive. Across from the piano, the finches twittered in their enormous cage as they flew from one perch to another. Mrs Baden glanced at them fondly as Barbara went on.

'Oh yes, he was here, that gentleman Mr King-Ryder,' Mrs Baden said when Barbara had concluded. 'I recognised his name when he introduced himself, of course. I offered him a piece of chocolate cake, but he didn't accept, didn't even step over my threshold. He was quite intent on seeing those pictures.'

'Did you let him into the flat? Terry and Cilla's, I mean.'

'Cilla phoned me and said that a gentleman was coming round to look at her pictures and would I unlock the door for him and let him see them? She didn't give me his name – the silly child hadn't even asked him, can you imagine? – but as there's not generally a queue of art collectors ringing my bell and asking to see her work, when he showed up, I assumed he was the one. And anyway, I didn't let him stay in the flat alone. At least not until I'd checked with Cilla.'

'So he was alone upstairs? Once you'd checked with her?' Barbara rubbed her hands together mentally. Now, at last, they were getting somewhere. 'Did he ask to be alone?'

'Once I took him up to the flat and when he saw how very many paintings are in it, he said that he'd need some time to really *study* them before he made his selection. As a collector, he wanted—'

'Did he say he was a collector, Mrs Baden?'

'Art is his abiding passion, he told me. But as he isn't a wealthy man, he collects the unknowns. I remember that especially because he talked about the people who'd bought Picasso's work before Picasso was ... well, before Picasso was Picasso. "They just went on faith, and left the rest to art history," he said. He told me that he was doing the same.'

So Mrs Baden had left him alone in the flat upstairs. And for more than an hour he'd contemplated Cilla Thompson's work until he'd made his choice.

'He showed it to me after he'd locked up and returned the key,' she told Havers. 'I can't say I *understood* his choice. But then ... well, I'm not a collector, am I? Aside from my little birds, I don't collect anything at all.'

'Are you sure he was up there as long as an hour?'

'More than an hour. You see, I practise my piano in the afternoons. Ninety minutes every day. Not very much use at this point, of course, with my hands getting so bad. But I believe in trying no matter what. I'd just wound up the metronome and set the timer when Cilla rang to say he'd be coming. I decided not to start my practice till he'd come and gone. I deplore interruptions ... but of course, please don't take that personally, dear. This conversation is an exception to the rule.'

'Thanks. And ... ?'

'And when he said he wanted to take his time having a good long look at the paintings, I decided to go ahead with my practice. I'd been at it – not very successfully, I'm afraid – for an hour and ten minutes when he knocked at my door a second time. He had a painting under his arm, and he asked would I tell Cilla that he'd be sending her a cheque in the post. Oh my goodness.' Mrs Baden suddenly straightened, one hand at her throat where a quadruple strand choker of knobbly beads circled her crepey neck. 'Did he not send Cilla that cheque, my dear?'

'He sent the cheque.'

The hand dropped. 'Thank heavens. I'm so relieved to know it. Granted, I was terribly preoccupied with my music that day because I wanted to play at least one piece for dear Terry by the end of the week. After all, it was a sweet present. Not my

birthday or Mothering Sunday or anything and there he was
. . . Not that I'd *expect* something on Mothering Sunday from
a boy not my son, mind you, but he was a dear and always
so generous, and I felt I ought to show him how much I
appreciated his generosity by being able to play it. But it hadn't
been going well at all – my practice, that is – because my eyes
aren't what they used to be and reading music that's been
hand-written is rather a problem. So I was quite preoccupied,
you see. But the young man – Mr King-Ryder, this is – seemed
honest and truthful, so when it came to taking his word about
a cheque, why, I didn't once think that he might be untruthful.
And I'm glad to know that he wasn't.'

Barbara only half heard her final comments. She was trans-
fixed, instead, by the woman's earlier words. She said, 'Mrs
Baden,' quite slowly, drawing in a breath carefully, as if to do
it with too much energy might frighten away the facts which
she believed she was about to coax from the older woman. 'Are
you telling me that Terry Cole gave you some piano music?'

'Certainly, my dear. But I believe I mentioned that the other
day when you were here. Such a lovely boy, Terry. Such a *good*
boy, really. He was always willing to do the odd job or two
round the house if I needed him. He fed my little birds if I was
out as well. And he loved to wash windows and hoover the
rugs. At least that's what he always said.' She smiled gently.

Barbara dragged the old woman away from her carpets and
back to the topic. 'Mrs Baden, do you still have that music?'
she asked.

'Well, certainly, I do. I have it right here.'

Lynley had Martin Reeve delivered to one of the Yard's
interview rooms. He'd refused to talk to him on the phone
when DC Steve Budde from the search warrant team had
placed a call to the Yard from the pimp's Notting Hill home,
relaying Reeve's offer to strike a deal. Reeve, Budde said, wished

to produce information that might be valuable to the police in exchange for the opportunity to emigrate to Melbourne, a city that Reeve appeared newly eager to embrace. What did DI Lynley want done about the matter? Scotland Yard, Lynley said, didn't make deals with killers. He told DC Budde to relay that message and to bring the pimp in.

As Lynley had hoped, Reeve arrived without his solicitor in tow. He was haggard, unshaven and wearing jeans and a boxy Hawaiian shirt. This gaped open on a pallid chest, the sanguinolent path of someone's fingernails still fresh upon it.

'Call off your goons,' Reeve said without preamble when Lynley joined him. 'This dickhead's pals—' with a jerk of his head at DC Budde – 'are still trashing my house. I want them out of there or I'm not cooperating.'

Lynley nodded Constable Budde into a seat against the wall, where he assumed a watchful position. The DC was the size of Big Foot, and the metal chair creaked beneath him.

Lynley and Reeve took places at the table where Lynley said, 'You're not in a position to make demands, Mr Reeve.'

'The fuck I'm not. I am if you want information. Get those assholes out of my house, Lynley.'

In response, Lynley put a fresh cassette into the tape player, pushed the record button and gave the date, the time, and the names of everyone present. He recited the formal caution for Reeve's benefit, saying, 'Are you waiving your right to a solicitor?'

'Jesus. What is this? D'you guys want the truth or a tapdance?'

'Just answer me, please.'

'I don't need a solicitor for what I'm here for.'

'The suspect waives his right to legal representation,' Lynley said for the record. 'Mr Reeve, were you acquainted with Nicola Maiden?'

'Let's cut to the chase, all right? You know I knew her. You know she worked for me. She and Vi Nevin quit last spring, and I haven't seen either one of them since. End of story. But that's not what I'm here to talk—'

'How long was it after their departure before Shelly Platt informed you that the Maiden girl and Viola Nevin had set themselves up privately in prostitution?'

Martin Reeve's eyes became hooded. 'Who? Shelly what?'

'Shelly Platt. You can't be denying that you know her. According to my man at the hospital, she recognised you the moment she saw you this morning.'

'Lots of people recognise me. I get around. So does Tricia. Our faces must be in the papers once a week.'

'Shelly Platt states that she told you about the two girls' going into business for themselves. You can't have liked that. It can't have done much to enhance your reputation as a man with his stable under control.'

'Look. If a flatbacker wants to go it alone, I could give a shit, all right? They find out soon enough how much work and money's involved in attracting the calibre of clients they're used to. Then they come back, and if they're lucky and I'm in the mood, I take them back. It's happened before. It'll happen again. I knew it would happen to Maiden and Nevin if I waited them out long enough.'

'And if they didn't want back in? If they were more of a success than you anticipated? What then? And what can you do to prevent the rest of your girls from trying their luck as independents?'

Reeve leaned back in his chair. 'Are we here to talk about the pussy game in general or do you want some straight answers to last night's questions? Your choice, Inspector. But make it quick. I don't have the time to sit here and chew the fat with you.'

'Mr Reeve, you're not in a bargaining position. One of your girls is dead. The other – her partner – has been beaten and left for dead. Either this is a remarkable coincidence or the events are related. The link appears to be you and their decision to leave you.'

'Which makes them not my girls any longer,' Reeve said. 'I'm not involved.'

'So you'd like us to believe that a call girl can leave you, set herself up in business in competition with you, and not expect any reprisal. Free market economy, with the spoils going to him or her with the superlative product. Is that it?'

'I couldn't have put it better.'

'The best man wins? Or the best woman, for that matter?'

'The first precept of business, Inspector.'

'I understand. So you'll have no objection to telling me where you were yesterday while Vi Nevin was being assaulted.'

'As my half of the deal, I'm happy to tell you. Once I learn what your half's going to be.'

Lynley felt weary with the pimp's manoeuvring. 'Put him on the charge sheet,' he said to DC Budde. 'Assault and murder.' The constable rose.

'Hey! Wait a minute! I came here to talk. You offered a deal to Tricia yesterday. I'm claiming it today. All you need to do is put it on the table so we both know what we're agreeing to.'

'That's not how things work.' Lynley got to his feet.

DC Budde took the pimp's arm. 'Let's go.'

Reeve shook him off. 'Fuck that shit. You want to know where I was? All right. I'll tell you.'

Lynley sat again. He hadn't switched the recorder off, and the pimp in his agitation hadn't noticed. 'Go on.'

Reeve waited until Budde had returned to his seat. He said, 'Keep a collar on Rufus. I don't like being manhandled.'

'We'll take note of that.'

Reeve rubbed his arm as if contemplating a future suit charging police brutality. He said, 'All right. I wasn't at home yesterday. I went out in the afternoon. I didn't get back till night. Nine or ten o'clock.'

'Where were you, then?'

Reeve looked as if he was calculating the damage he was about to inflict upon himself. He said, 'I went there. I admit it. But I wasn't there when—'

For the record, Lynley said, 'You went to Fulham? To Rostrevor Road?'

'She wasn't there. I'd been trying to track them down all summer, Vi and Nick. When those two cops – the black and the dumpy broad with chipped front teeth – came round for a chat with me on Friday, I had a feeling they could lead me to Vi if I played it right. So I had them followed. I went back the next day.' He grinned. 'Something of a turn-around, huh? Tailing the cops instead of the reverse.'

'For the tape, Mr Reeve: You went to Rostrevor Road yesterday.'

'And she wasn't there. No one was there.'

'Why did you go to see her?'

Reeve examined his nails. They looked freshly buffed. His knuckles, however, were swollen and bruised. 'Let's say I went to make a point.'

'In other words, you beat Vi Nevin.'

'No way. I said I didn't get the chance. And you sure as hell can't arrest me for what I *wanted* to do. *If* I even wanted to beat her in the first place, which I'm not admitting to, by the way.' He adjusted his position in his chair, more comfortable now, more sure of himself. 'Like I said, she wasn't there. I went back three times during the afternoon, but my luck didn't change and I started getting antsy. When I get like that ...' Reeve used his fist against his palm, sharply. 'I *do*. I act. I don't go home like a limp dick pantywaist and wait for somebody else to screw me over.'

'Did you try to find her? You must have had a list of her clients, at least those she serviced when she worked for you. If she wasn't at home, it stands to reason that you'd begin a search for her. Especially if you were – how did you put it? – getting antsy.'

'I said I *do*, Lynley. I *act* when I'm getting riled, okay? I wanted to make a point with the whore and I couldn't do it and that pissed me off. So I decided to make a point with someone else.'

'I don't see how that served your needs.'

'It served my needs of the moment just fine because I started thinking it was time to put a tighter rein on the rest of them. I don't want them even beginning to think about taking a page from the Nikki-Vi book. Whores think men are cocksuckers. So if you want to run them, you'd better be willing to do what it takes to keep their respect.'

'It takes violence, I'd assume.' Lynley marvelled at Reeve's hubris. How could the pimp not know he was digging his own grave with every sentence he spoke? Did he actually think he was ameliorating his position with his declarations?

Reeve went on. He'd begun paying visits to his employees during the afternoon, he said, surprise visits that were designed to reinforce his authority over them. He appropriated their bank books, diaries, and bills with the intention of comparing them to his own records. He listened to messages on their answer machines to learn if they'd encouraged their clients to bypass Global Escorts when booking a session. He went through their wardrobes checking for clothing that revealed a higher income than he was shelling out to them. He examined their supplies of condoms, lubricating jellies, and sex toys to see if everything matched what he knew of each girl's clientele.

'Some of them didn't like what I was doing,' Reeve said. 'They complained. So I straightened them out.'

'You beat them.'

'Beat them?' Reeve laughed. 'Hell no. I fucked them. That's what you saw on my face last night. I call it fingernail foreplay.'

'There's another word for it.'

'I didn't rape anyone, if that's where you're heading. And there's not a single one among them who'll say that I did. But if you want to bring them in – the three I fucked – and grill them, go right ahead and do it. I've come to give you their names anyway. They'll back my story.'

'I'm sure they will,' Lynley said. 'Obviously, the woman who doesn't is inclined to experience your brand of ... What did you call it? Straightening out?' He got to his feet and ended the taped interview. He said to DC Budde, 'I want him charged. Get him to a telephone because he'll be howling for his solicitor before we've even begun to—'

'Hey!' Reeve jumped up. 'What're you doing? I didn't touch either one of those cunts. You've got nothing on me.'

'You're a pimp, Mr Reeve. I have your own admission of that on tape. It's a decent start.'

'You offered a deal. I'm here to collect it. I'm talking and then I'm clearing out to Melbourne. You put that on the table for Tricia and—'

'And Tricia may collect it if she chooses to do so.' Lynley said to Budde, 'We'll want to send a team from vice back to Lansdowne Road. Phone over there and tell Havers to wait till they arrive.'

'Hey! Listen to me!' Reeve came round the table. DC Budde grabbed his arm. 'Get your fucking hands *off*—'

'She's probably had time to pull together enough evidence to hold him on an immoral earnings charge,' Lynley told Budde. 'That'll do for now.'

'You assholes don't know who you're dealing with!'

DC Budde tightened his grip. 'Havers? Guv, she's not in Notting Hill. Jackson, Stille, and Smiley're doing the search. You want me to track her down anyway?'

Lynley said, 'Not there? Then where—'

Reeve struggled against Budde. 'I'll have your *butts* for this.'

'Steady on, mate. You're not going anywhere.' Budde said to Lynley, 'She met us there and handed over the warrant. Do you want me to try to—'

'*Fuck* this shit!'

The door to the interview room swung open. ''Spector?' It was Winston Nkata. 'Need some help in here?'

'It's under control,' Lynley said, and to Budde, 'Get him to a phone. Let him call his solicitor. Then get on the paperwork to charge him.'

Budde danced Reeve past Nkata and down the corridor. Lynley remained by the table, fingers on the tape recorder for want of something to ground himself through touch. If he did anything else without taking time to consider the consequences of every possible action, he knew he'd regret it eventually.

Havers, he thought. Christ. What was it going to take? She'd never been the easiest officer to work with, but this was outrageous. It was beyond comprehension that she'd defied a direct order after what she'd already been through. Either she had a death wish or she'd lost her mind. No matter which it was, though, Lynley threw up his hands. He'd reached the end of his tether with the woman.

'—took some time to track down which clamping unit works the area, but it paid off big,' Nkata was saying.

Lynley looked up. 'Sorry,' he said. 'I was miles away. What've you got, Winnie?'

'I checked Beattie's club. He's in the clear, I went on to Islington,' Nkata said. 'I had a talk with the neighbours at the Maiden girl's old digs. No one matched up any visitors with Beattie or Reeve, even when I showed them pictures. Found one of each bloke at the *Evening Standard*, by the way. Always helps to have snouts in the newspaper offices.'

'But no joy in that direction?'

'Not to speak. But while I was there, I saw a clamped Vauxhall sitting on double yellow. Which got me to thinking 'bout other possibilities.'

Nkata reported that he'd phoned all the London clamping agencies to see which of them served the Islington streets. It was a shot in the dark, but since no one he'd spoken to had been able to identify either Martin Reeve or Sir Adrian Beattie as visitors to Nicola Maiden's bedsit prior to her removal to Fulham, he decided to see if anyone clamped in the area on the ninth of May might match up with anyone connected to Nicola Maiden.

'And that's where I struck gold,' he said.

'Well done, Winnie,' Lynley said warmly. Nkata's initiative had long been one of his finest qualities. 'What did you get?'

'Something dicey.'

'Dicey? Why?'

'Because of who got clamped.' The DC looked suddenly uneasy, which should have been a warning. But Lynley didn't see it and, at any rate, he was distracted by feeling too decidedly positive about how things had gone with Martin Reeve.

'Who?' he asked.

'Andrew Maiden,' Nkata said. 'Seems he was in town on the ninth of May. He got clamped round the corner from Nicola's digs.'

Lynley felt a tight sickness in the pit of his stomach as he closed his front door and began to climb the stairs. He went to his bedroom, pulled out the same suitcase he'd brought back from Derbyshire on the previous day, and opened it on the bed. He started to pack for the return journey, tossing in pyjamas, shirts, trousers, socks, and shoes without giving a thought to what he'd actually need when he got there. He packed his shaving gear and rooted out an unopened tube of toothpaste among Helen's body lotions and face creams.

His wife came in as he was closing the lid on a packing job that would have sent Denton into fits. She said, 'I thought I heard you. What's happened? Are you off again so soon? Tommy darling, is something wrong?'

He set the suitcase on the floor and cast about for an explanation. He went with the facts without attaching an interpretation to them. 'The trail's leading back to the North,' he told her. 'Andy Maiden appears to be involved.'

Helen's eyes widened. 'But why? How? Lord, that's terrible. And you admired him so, didn't you?'

Lynley told her what Nkata had discovered. He related what the DC had learned earlier about the argument and the threat heard in May. He added to that what he himself had put together from his interviews with the SO10 officer and his wife. He finished with the information that Hanken had passed along on the phone. What he didn't embark on was a monologue dealing with the probable reason that Andy Maiden had requested one DI Thomas Lynley – a notable washout from SO10 – as the Scotland Yard officer sent north to assist in the investigation. He would face that subject later, when his pride could stand it.

'It made sense to me at first to look at Julian Britton,' he said in conclusion. 'Then at Martin Reeve. I stuck with one and then the other and ignored every detail that pointed anywhere else.'

'But, darling, you may still be right,' Helen said. 'Especially about Martin Reeve. He has more of a motive than anyone, hasn't he? And he *could* have tracked Nicola Maiden to Derbyshire.'

'And out onto the moor as well?' Lynley said. 'How could he possibly have managed that?'

'Perhaps he followed the boy. Or had the boy followed by someone else.'

'There's nothing to say Reeve even knew the boy.'

'But he may have learned about him through the phone box cards. He's someone who watches the competition, isn't he? If he found out who was placing Vi Nevin's cards and began to have him trailed just as he had Barbara and Winston trailed to Fulham ... Why couldn't he have tracked down Nicola that way? Someone could have been following the boy for weeks, Tommy, knowing he'd lead the way to Nicola.'

Helen warmed to her theory. Why, she asked, could someone employed by Reeve to trail the boy not have followed him out of London, up to Derbyshire, and onto the moors to meet Nicola? Once the girl was located, a single phone call to Martin Reeve from the nearest pub would have been all that it took. Reeve could have ordered the murders from London at that point, or he could have flown up to Manchester – or driven to Derbyshire in less than three hours – and gone out to the ancient stone circle to settle them himself.

'It doesn't *have* to be Andy Maiden,' she concluded.

Lynley touched her cheek with his fingers. 'Thank you for being my champion.'

'Tommy, don't discount me. And don't discount yourself. From what you've told me, Martin Reeve has a motive carved out of marble. Why on earth would Andy Maiden kill his daughter?'

'Because of what she became,' Lynley replied. 'Because he couldn't talk her out of becoming it. Because he couldn't stop her by means of reasoning, persuasion, or threat. So he stopped her the only other way he knew.'

'But why not just have her arrested? She and the other girl—'

'Vi Nevin.'

'Yes. Vi Nevin. There were two of them in business. Doesn't it constitute a brothel if there're two? Couldn't he merely have phoned an old friend in the Met and brought her down that way?'

'With all his former colleagues knowing what she'd become? What his own daughter had become? He's a proud man, Helen. He'd never go for that.' Lynley kissed her forehead then her mouth. He picked up his suitcase. 'I'll be back as soon as I can.'

She followed him down the stairs. 'Tommy, you're harder on yourself than anyone I know. How can you be certain that you're not just being hard on yourself now? And with far more disastrous consequences?'

He turned to answer his wife, but the doorbell rang. The ringing was insistent and repeated, as if someone outside was leaning on the bell.

Their caller turned out to be Barbara Havers, and when Lynley set his suitcase by the door and admitted her into the house, she charged past him with a thick manila envelope in her hand, saying, 'Holy hell, Inspector, I'm glad I caught you. We're one step closer to paradise.'

She greeted Helen and went into the drawing room where she plopped onto a sofa and spilled the contents of her envelope onto a coffee table. 'This is what he was after,' she said obscurely. 'He spent over an hour at Terry Cole's flat pretending to look at Cilla's paintings. She thought he was in love with her work.' Havers ruffled her hair energetically, the signature gesture of her excitement. 'But he was *alone* in that flat, Inspector, and he had plenty of time to search it stem to stern. He couldn't find what he wanted, though. Because Terry had given it to Mrs Baden when he'd realised he wasn't going to be able to flog it at a Bowers' auction. And Mrs Baden just gave it to me. Here. Have a look.'

Lynley stayed where he was, by the door to the drawing room. Helen joined Barbara and glanced through the copious sheets of paper that she'd dumped from the envelope.

'It's music,' Barbara told him. 'A whole slew of music. A whole bloody slew of *Michael Chandler* music. Neil Sitwell at Bowers told me he sent Terry Cole to King-Ryder Productions to get the name of the Chandler solicitors. But Matthew King-Ryder denied the whole thing. *He* said Terry came to get an artistic grant from him. So why the hell has *no one* we've talked to said a single word about Terry and a grant?'

'You tell me,' Lynley said evenly.

Havers ignored – or didn't notice – the tone. 'Because King-Ryder is lying his head off. He followed him. He trailed

Terry Cole round London everywhere he went, trying to get his mitts on this music, Inspector.'

'Why?'

'Because the milk cow's dead.' Havers sounded triumphant. 'And King-Ryder's only hope of keeping the ship floating for a few more years was to be able to produce another hit show.'

'You're mixing your metaphors,' Lynley remarked.

'Tommy.' Helen's expression carried an unspoken entreaty. She knew him better than anyone after all and unlike Havers, she'd noted his tone. She'd also noted his unchanged position at the door of the room, and she knew what that meant.

Oblivious, Havers continued with a grin. 'Right. Sorry. Anyway. King-Ryder told me that his dad's will leaves all the profits from his current productions to a special fund that supports theatre types. Actors, writers, designers. That sort. His last wife gets a bequest, but she's the sole beneficiary. Not a penny goes to Matthew or his sister. He'll have some sort of position as chairman or leader or whatever of the fund, but how can that compare to the lolly he'd be gathering if he mounted another of his dad's productions? A *new* production, Inspector. A posthumous production. A production not governed by the terms of the will. There's your motive. He had to get his maulers on this music and eliminate the only person who knew Michael Chandler – and not David King-Ryder – had written it.'

'And Vi Nevin?' Lynley enquired. 'How does she fit into the picture, Havers?'

Her face grew even brighter. 'King-Ryder thought Vi had the music. He hadn't found it at the flat. He hadn't found it when he followed Terry Cole and offed him and tore that camp site apart looking for it. So he came back to London and paid a call on Vi Nevin's flat when she was out. He was tearing it apart looking for that music when she surprised him.'

'That flat was destroyed. It wasn't searched, Havers.'

'No way, Inspector. The pictures show a search. Look at

them again. Things're thrown round and opened up and shoved onto the floor. But if someone wanted to put Vi out of business, he'd spray paint the walls. He'd slice up the furniture and cut up the carpets and punch holes in the doors.'

'And he'd batter her face in,' Lynley injected. 'Which is what Reeve did.'

'King-Ryder did it. She'd *seen* him. Or at least he thought she'd seen him. And he couldn't take a chance that she hadn't. For all he knew, she was wise to the music's existence, too, because she knew Terry as well. At any rate, what does it matter? Let's haul him in and hold his feet to the flame.' For the first time, she suddenly seemed to see the suitcase that stood in the doorway. She said, 'Where're you going, anyway?'

'To make an arrest. Because while you were larking round London, DC Nkata – in compliance with orders – was doing the footwork he'd been assigned to in Islington. And what he's uncovered has sod all to do with Matthew King-Ryder or anyone else with that surname.'

Havers blanched. Next to her, Helen set a sheet of the music, which she'd been inspecting, onto the pile. She raised a cautionary hand, resting it at the base of her throat. Lynley recognised the gesture but ignored it.

He said to Havers, 'You were given an assignment.'

'I got the warrant, Inspector. I set up a team for the search, and I met them. I told them what they—'

'You were directed to be a part of that team, Havers.'

'But the thing is that I believed . . . I had this gut feeling—'

'No. There is no *thing*. There is no gut feeling. Not in your position.'

Helen said, 'Tommy . . .'

He said, 'No. Forget it. It's done. You've defied me every inch of the way, Havers. You're off the case.'

'But—'

'Do you want chapter and verse?'

'Tommy.' Helen reached in his direction. He could see that

she wanted to intercede between them. She so hated his anger. For her sake, he did his best to control it.

'Anyone else in your position – demoted, having barely escaped criminal prosecution – and with your history of failure in CID—'

'That's low.' Havers' words sounded faint.

'—would have toed every line that was drawn from the instant AC Hillier pronounced sentence.'

'Hillier's a pig. You know it.'

'Anyone else,' he went doggedly on, 'would have dotted every *i* in sight and double crossed every *t* for good measure. In your case, all that was asked of you was a bit of research through some SO10 cases, research which you had to be ordered back to on more than one occasion in the last few days.'

'But I did it. You got the report. I did it.'

'And after that, you went your own way.'

'Because I *saw* those pictures. In your office. This morning. I *saw* that the flat in Fulham had been searched, and I tried to tell you, but you wouldn't hear me out. So what could I do?' She didn't wait for an answer, doubtless knowing what he would say. 'And when Mrs Baden handed over that music and I saw who'd written it, I knew we'd found our man, Inspector. All right. I should have gone with the team to Notting Hill. You told me to go, and I didn't. But can't you please look at how much time I ended up saving us? You're about to trot back up to Derbyshire, aren't you? I've saved you the trip.'

Lynley blinked. He said, 'Havers, do you actually think I give credence to this nonsense?'

Nonsense. She mouthed the word, rather than to speak it.

Helen looked from one of them to the other. She dropped her hand. Expression regretful, she reached for a sheet of the music. Havers looked at her, which sparked Lynley's anger. He *wouldn't* have his wife put into the middle.

'Report to Webberly in the morning,' he told Havers. 'Whatever your next assignment is, get it from him.'

'You aren't even looking at what's in front of you,' Havers said, but she no longer sounded argumentative or defiant, merely mystified. Which angered him more.

'Do you need a map out of here, Barbara?' he asked her.

'Tommy!' Helen cried.

'Sod you,' Havers said.

She rose from the sofa with a fair amount of dignity. She took up her tattered bag. As she moved past the coffee table and sailed out of the room, five sheets from the Chandler music fluttered to the floor.

Chapter Twenty-six

The Derbyshire weather matched DI Peter Hanken's mood: grim. While a silver sky dissolved into rain, he navigated the road between Buxton and Bakewell, wondering what it meant that a black leather jacket was missing from the evidence taken from Nine Sisters' Henge. The missing waterproof had been easy to explain. The missing jacket was not. For a single killer did not need two articles of clothing to cover up the blood from a chopped up victim.

He hadn't made the search for Terry Cole's missing leather jacket entirely unassisted. DC Mott had been with him, a flapjack in his hand. As evidence officer, Mott's presence was essential. But he did little enough to help with the search. Instead, he munched loudly and appreciatively with much smacking of lips and pronounced that he'd 'never seen no black leather jacket, Guv', throughout Hanken's inspection.

Mott's record keeping had been vindicated. There was no jacket. That message transmitted to London, Hanken set out for Bakewell and Broughton Manor. Jacket or no, there was still Julian Britton to clear off or keep on their list of suspects.

As Hanken cruised over the bridge that spanned the River Wye, he unexpectedly entered another century. Despite the rain that was continuing to fall unabated like a harbinger of grief to come, a fierce battle was going on round the manor house. On the hillside that descended to the river, five or six dozen Royalist soldiers, wearing the varied colours of the Monarch and the nobility, were flailing swords with an equal number of armoured and pot-helmeted Parliamentarians. On the meadow beneath them, more armoured soldiers were rolling cannon into position while on a far slope a pistol-wielding division of helmeted infantry made for the south gate of the manor house with a battering ram trundling along among them.

The Cavaliers and the Roundheads were re-fighting a battle of the Civil War, Hanken concluded. Julian Britton was engaged in yet another means of raising money for the restoration of his home.

A seventeenth-century milkmaid standing beneath a Burberry umbrella waved Hanken to a makeshift car park a short distance from the house. There, various other players in the reenactment drama were milling about in the guise of royals, peasants, farmers, noblemen, surgeons, and musketeers. Eating from a soup tin in the door of a caravan, ill-fated King Charles – a bloody bandage round his head – chatted up a wench who was carrying a basket of bread getting soaked by the rain. Not far away, a black-garbed Oliver Cromwell struggled out of his armour, attempting the feat without untying the lacing. Dogs and children dashed in and out of the crowd while a snack stall did a thriving business in whatever they could serve that was hot and steaming.

Hanken parked and asked where the Brittons were hiding. He was directed to a viewing area within the third of the manor's ruined gardens. There, on the southwest side of the house, a stalwart crowd huddled on makeshift stands and deck chairs to watch the unfolding reenactment from beneath a motley mushrooming of umbrellas.

To one side of the viewers, a lone man sat on a tripod stool of the type used at the turn of the century by artists or hunters on safari. He wore an antique tweed suit and an old pith helmet, and he sheltered himself from the rain with a striped umbrella. He watched the action with a collapsible telescope. A walking stick lay by his feet. Jeremy Britton, Hanken thought, dressed as always in his forebears' clothing.

Hanken approached him. 'Mr Britton? You won't remember me. DI Peter Hanken. Buxton CID.'

Britton half-turned on the stool. He'd aged greatly, Hanken thought, since their sole encounter at the Buxton police station five years in the past. Britton had been drunk at the time. His car had been broken into on the High Street while he was 'taking the waters' – undoubtedly a euphemism for his imbibing something stronger than the town's mineral water – and he was demanding action, satisfaction, and immediate vengeance upon the ill-dressed and worse-bred hooligans who'd violated him so egregiously.

Looking at Jeremy Britton now, Hanken could see the results of a lifetime spent in drink. Liver damage showed in the colour and texture of Britton's skin and in the cooked-egg-yolk look of his eyes. Hanken noted the Thermos on the far side of the camp stool on which Britton was sitting. He doubted it contained either coffee or tea.

'I'm looking for Julian,' Hanken said. 'Is he taking part in the battle, Mr Britton?'

'Julie?' Britton squinted through the rain. 'Don't know where he's gone off to. Not part of this, though.' He waved at the drama below. The battering ram was mired in the mud and the Cavaliers were taking advantage of this blip on the screen of the Roundheads' plans. Swords drawn, a crush of them were swarming down the slope from the house to fend off the Parliamentary forces. 'Julie never did like a good dust up like this,' Britton said, slipping slightly with *dust*. He'd added an *h*. 'Can't think why he agrees to let the grounds be used this way. But it's great fun, what?'

'Everyone seems to be fully involved,' Hanken agreed. 'Are you a history buff, sir?'

'Nothing like it,' Britton said and shouted down at the soldiers, 'Traitors be damned! You'll burn in hell for harming one hair on the head of God's anointed.'

Royalist, Hanken thought. Odd position for a member of the gentry to have taken at the time, but not unheard of if the gentleman in question had no political ties to Parliament. 'Where can I find him?'

'Carried off the field, sporting a head wound. No one could 'cuse the poor sod of not having his share of courage, could they?'

'I meant Julian, not King Charles.'

'Ah. Julie.' With an irresolute grip, Britton fixed his telescope towards the west. A fresh band of Cavaliers had just arrived by coach. That vehicle was disgorging them on the far side of the bridge, where they were racing to arm themselves. Among them an elaborately clad nobleman appeared to be shouting directions. 'Shouldn't allow that, you ask me,' Britton commented. 'If they aren't here on time, they should forfeit, what?' He swung back to Hanken. 'The boy was here, if tha's why you've come.'

'Does he get to London much? With his late girlfriend living there, I expect—'

'Girlfriend?' Britton blew out a contemptuous breath. 'Rubbish. *Girlfriend* says there's give and take involved. There was none of that. Oh, he wanted it, Julie. He wanted *her*. But she wasn't having anything from him, other than a shag if the mood was on her. If he'd only used the eyes God gave him, he would've seen that from the first.'

'You didn't like the Maiden girl.'

'She had nothing to add to the brew.' Britton looked back at the battle, shouting, 'Watch your backs, you blighters!' at the Parliamentary soldiers as the Cavaliers forded the River Wye and began charging wetly up the hillside towards the house. A man of easy allegiance, Hanken thought.

He said, 'Will I likely find Julian in the house, Mr Britton?'

Britton watched the initial clash as the Cavaliers reached those of the Roundheads who were straggling behind in the effort to free the battering ram from the mud. Suddenly, the tide of the battle shifted. The Roundheads looked outnumbered three to one. 'Run for your lives, you idjits,' Britton shouted. And he laughed with glee as the rebels began to lose the uneasy purchase they had on their footholds. Several men went down, losing their weapons. Britton applauded.

Hanken said, 'I'll try him inside.'

Britton stopped the detective as he turned to depart. 'I was with him. On Tues'ay night, you know.'

Hanken turned back. 'With Julian? Where? What time was this?'

'In the kennels. Don't know the time. Proba'ly round eleven. A bitch was delivering. Julie was with her.'

'When I spoke to him, he made no mention of your being there, Mr Britton.'

'He wouldn't've done. Didn't see me. When I saw what he was about, I lef' him to it. I watched for a bit from the doorway – something special about the birthing process, no matter who's delivering, don't you think? – then I went off.'

'Is that your normal routine? To visit the kennels at eleven at night?'

'Don't have a normal routine at all. Do what I want when I want.'

'What took you to the kennels, then?'

Britton reached in his jacket pocket with an unsteady hand. He brought out several heavily creased brochures. 'Wanted to talk to Julie about these.'

They were, Hanken saw, all leaflets from clinics that offered programmes for alcoholics. Smudged and dog-eared, they looked like refugees from the Oxfam book section. Either Britton had been fingering them for weeks on end or he'd found them secondhand somewhere in anticipation of a moment just like this.

'Want to take the cure,' Britton said. ''Bout time, I think. Don't want Julie's kids to have a sot for a granddad.'

'Julian's thinking of marrying, is he?'

'Oh, things're brewing in that direction.'

Britton extended his hand for the brochures. Hanken bent towards the umbrella to give them back.

'He's a good boy, our Julie,' Britton said, taking the leaflets and stuffing them back in his jacket pocket. 'Don't you forget it. He'll make a good father. And I'll be a granddad he can be proud of.'

There was at least a fragment of doubt to that. Britton's breath could have been lit with a match, so heavily was it laden with gin.

Julian Britton was conferring with the reenactment's organisers on the roof top battlements when DI Hanken appeared. He'd seen the detective in conversation with his father and he'd watched as Jeremy produced his treatment brochures for the other man's inspection. He knew how unlikely it was that Hanken had come to Broughton Manor to have colloquy on the subject of alcoholism with his father, so he wasn't unprepared when the policeman finally tracked him down.

Their conversation was brief. Hanken wanted to know the exact last date that Julian had been in London. Julian took him down to his office where his diary lay among the discarded account books on his desk, and he handed it over. His record keeping was faultless, and the diary showing that his last trip to London had been at Easter, in early April. He'd stayed at the Lancaster Gate Hotel. Hanken could phone to verify because the number was next to the hotel's name in his diary. 'I always stay there when I'm in town,' Julian said. 'Why do you want to know?'

Hanken answered the question with one of his own. 'You didn't stay with Nicola Maiden?'

'She only had a bedsit.' Julian coloured. 'Besides, she preferred me to stay in a hotel.'

'But you'd gone to town to see her, hadn't you?'

He had.

It had been stupid really, Julian told himself now as he watched Hanken work his way back through the Cavaliers that crowded the courtyard, bunched under awnings and umbrellas as they prepared for the next phase of the battle. He'd gone to London because he'd sensed a change in her. Not only because she hadn't come to Derbyshire for Easter – as had been her habit during every holiday while she was at university – but because at each of their meetings from the autumn onwards, he'd felt a greater distance developing between them than had existed at the meeting before. He suspected another man, and he'd wanted to know the worst first hand.

He gave a bitter brief laugh as he thought of it now: that trip to London. He'd never asked her directly if there was someone else because at heart he hadn't wanted to know. He'd allowed himself to be satisfied with the fact that his surprise visit hadn't caught her out with someone else and that a surreptitious look in the bathroom cupboards, the medicine cabinet, and her chest of drawers hadn't turned up anything a man might keep there for mornings after nighttime assignations. On top of that, she'd made love with him. And, hopeless numbskull that he'd been at the time, he'd actually thought that her lovemaking meant something.

But it was just a part of her line of work, he realised now. Just part of what Nicola did for money.

'All's clear with the coppers, Julie my boy.'

Julian swung round to see that his father had joined him in the manor office, apparently having had enough of the rain, the reenactment, or the company of other spectators. Jeremy had a dripping umbrella hanging over his arm, a camp stool in one hand, and a Thermos in the other. His great uncle's telescope poked from the breast pocket of his grandfather's jacket.

Jeremy smiled, looking pleased with himself. 'Gave you an alibi, son. Concrete as the motorway, it was.'

Julian stared at him. 'What did you say?'

'Told the copper I was with you an' the new pups on Tuesday. Saw them pop out and saw you catch them, I said.'

'But, Dad, I never said you were there! I never told them . . .' Julian sighed. He began sorting through the account books. He stacked them in order of year. 'They're going to wonder why I never mentioned you. You see that, don't you? *Don't* you, Dad?'

Jeremy tapped a trembling finger to his temple. 'Thought that out in advance, my boy. Said I never disturbed you. There you were acting the part of midwife and I didn't like to break your concentration. Said I went to talk to you 'bout getting off the drink. Said I went to show you these.' Once more, Jeremy produced the brochures.

''nspired, wasn't it? You already saw them, see? So when he asked you 'bout them, you tol' him, right?'

'He didn't *ask* me about Tuesday night. He wanted to know when I'd last been to London. So no doubt he's wondering why you took the trouble to give me a damn alibi, when he wasn't even asking for one.' Past his exasperation Julian suddenly realised the implication behind what his father had done. He said, 'Why *did* you give me an alibi, Dad? You know I don't need one, don't you? I *was* with the dogs. Cassie *was* delivering. And anyway, how did you know to tell them that?'

'Your cousin tol' me.'

'Sam? Why?'

'She says the police're looking at you funny, and she doesn't like that. "As if Julie would raise his hand against anyone, Uncle Jeremy," she says. All righteous anger, she is, Julie. Quite a woman. Loyalty like that . . . It's something to behold.'

'I don't need Sam's loyalty. Or your help, for that matter. I didn't kill Nicola.'

Jeremy shifted his glance from his son to the desktop. 'No one's saying you did.'

'But if you think you have to lie to the police, that must mean ... Dad, do you think I killed her? Do you honestly *believe* ... Jesus.'

'Now, don't get worked up. You're red in the face, and I know what that means. I didn't say I thought anything. I don't think anything. I just want to ease the way a bit. We don't have to take life as it comes so much, Julie. We can do something to shape our destinies, y'know.'

'And that's what you were doing? Shaping my destiny?'

He shook his head. 'Selfish bastard. I'm shaping my own.' He indicated the brochures by lifting them to his heart. 'I want to dry out. It's time. I want it. But God knows and I know: I can't do it alone.'

Julian had been round his father long enough to recognise a manipulation when he heard one. The yellow flags of caution went up. 'Dad, I know you want to get sober. I admire you for it. But those programmes ... the cost ...'

'You c'n do this for me. You c'n do it knowing I'd do it for you.'

'It isn't as if I don't want to do it for you. But we haven't the funds. I looked through the books again and again and we just haven't got them. Have you thought about phoning Aunt Sophie? If she knew what you intend to do with the money, I expect she'd lend—'

'Lend? Bah!' Jeremy swept the notion aside with the brochures he held. 'Your aunt'll never go for that. "He'll stop when he wants to stop" is what she thinks. She won't lift a finger to help me do it.'

'What if I phone her?'

'Who're you to her, Julie? Just some relative she's never seen, come begging for a handout from what her own husband worked hard to make. No. You can't be the one to do the asking.'

'If you spoke to Sam, then.'

Jeremy waved the idea off like a gnat. 'Can't ask her to do that. She's been giving us too much as it is. Her time. Her effort. Her concern. Her love. I can't ask her for anything more, and I won't.' He heaved a sigh and shoved the brochures back into his pocket. 'Never mind, then. I'll soldier on.'

'Then I could ask Sam to speak to Aunt Sophie. I could explain.'

'No. Forget it. I c'n bite the bullet. I've done it before . . .'

Too many times, Julian thought. His father's life spanned more than five decades of broken promises and good intentions come to nothing. He'd seen Jeremy give up drink more times than he could remember. And just as many times, he'd seen Jeremy return to the bottle. There was more than a simple grain of truth in what he said. If he was going to beat the beast this time, he was not going to go into battle alone.

'Look, Dad. I'll talk to Sam. I want to do it.'

'Want to?' Jeremy repeated. 'Really *want* to? Not think you *have* to because of whatever you owe your old man?'

'No. Want to. So I'll ask her.'

Jeremy looked humbled. His eyes actually filled with tears. 'She loves you, Julie. Fine woman like that and she *loves* you, son.'

'I'll speak to her, Dad.'

The rain was still falling when Lynley turned up the drive to Maiden Hall.

Barbara Havers had actually provided him with a few minutes' distraction from the turmoil he felt over what he'd learned about Andy Maiden's presence in London. Indeed, he'd managed to exchange the turmoil for an anger over Barbara's defiance that hadn't been the least palliated by Helen's gentle attempt to wring reason from the constable's behaviour. 'Perhaps she misunderstood your orders, Tommy,' she'd said once Havers had taken herself away from Eaton Terrace. 'In the heat of the moment, she might have assumed you didn't intend her to be part of the Notting Hill search.'

'Christ,' he'd countered. 'Don't defend her, Helen. You heard what she said. She knew what she was supposed to do and she chose not to do it. She went her own way.'

'But you admire initiative. You always have done. You've always told me that Winston's initiative is one of the finest—'

'God damn it, Helen. When Nkata takes matters into his own hands, he does it *after* he's completed an assignment, not before. He doesn't argue, whinge, or ignore what's in front of him because he thinks he's got a better idea. And when he's been corrected – which is damn seldom, by the way – he doesn't make the same mistake twice. One would think that Barbara would have learned something this summer about the consequence of defying an order. But she hasn't. Her skull is lead.'

Helen had carefully gathered together the sheets of music that Barbara had left behind. She placed them, not in the envelope, but in a pile on the coffee table. She said, 'Tommy, if Winston Nkata and not Barbara Havers had been in that boat with DCI Barlow . . . If Winston Nkata and not Barbara Havers had taken up that gun . . .' She'd gazed at him earnestly. 'Would you have been so angry?'

His response had been both swift and hot. 'This isn't a bloody issue of gender. You know me better than that.'

'I do know you, yes,' had been her quiet reply.

Still, he'd considered her question more than once during the first one hundred miles of the drive to Derbyshire. But every way he examined his possible responses both to the question and to Havers' incredible act of insubordination on the North Sea, his answer was the same. Havers had engaged in assault, not initiative. And nothing justified that. Had Winston Nkata been wielding the weapon – which was as risible an image as Lynley could invent – he would have reacted identically. He knew it.

Now, as he pulled into the car park of Maiden Hall, his anger had long since abated, to be replaced by the same disquiet of spirit that had descended upon him when he'd learned about Andy Maiden's visit to his daughter. He stopped the car and gazed at the hotel through the rain.

He didn't want to believe what the facts were asking him to believe but he drew in what resolve he could muster and reached in the back seat for his umbrella. He walked through the rain across the car park. Inside the hotel, he asked the first employee he saw to fetch Andy Maiden. When the former SO10 officer appeared five minutes later, he came alone.

'Tommy,' he greeted him. 'You've news? Come with me.'

He led the way to the office near reception. He carefully shut the door behind them.

'Tell me about Islington in May, Andy,' Lynley said without preamble because he knew that to hesitate was to offer the other man an opening into his sympathy that he couldn't afford to allow. 'Tell me about saying "I'll see you dead before I let you do it."'

Maiden sat. He indicated a chair for Lynley. He didn't speak until Lynley was seated and even then he seemed to go inward for a moment, as if he was gathering his resources before he replied.

Then he said, 'The wheel clamp.'

To which Lynley replied, 'No one could ever accuse you of being an incompetent cop.'

'The same could be said of you. You've done good work, Tommy. I always believed you'd shine in CID.'

If anything, the compliment was like a slap in the face, hearkening as it did to all the now obvious reasons that Andy Maiden had chosen him – blinded as he was by admiration – to come to Derbyshire. Lynley said steadily, 'I have a good team. Tell me about Islington.'

They were finally upon it, and Maiden's eyes bore so much anguish that Lynley found he still – even now – had to steel himself against a rush of pity towards his old friend. 'She asked to see me,' Maiden said. 'So I went.'

'Last May. To London,' Lynley clarified. 'You went to Islington to see your daughter.'

'That's right.'

He'd thought Nicola wanted to make arrangements to move her belongings back to Derbyshire for the summer, preparatory to taking her holiday job with Will Upman as they'd arranged in December. So he'd driven the Land Rover instead of flying or taking the train, the better to be able to haul things home if she was willing to part with them a few weeks before her classes ended at the College of Law.

'But she didn't want to come home,' Maiden said. 'That's not why she'd called me to London. She wanted to tell me her future plans.'

'Prostitution,' Lynley said. 'Her set up in Fulham.'

Maiden cleared his throat roughly and whispered, 'Oh God.'

Even hardening himself against empathy, Lynley found he couldn't force the man to lay out the facts that he'd gathered that day in London. So he did it for him: Lynley went through everything as he himself had learned it, from Nicola's employment first as a trainee then as an escort at MKR Financial Management to her partnership with Vi Nevin and her choice of domination as her speciality. He concluded with 'Sir Adrian believes there could be only one reason why she came north for the summer instead of remaining in London: money.'

'It was a compromise,' Maiden said. 'She did it for me.'

They'd argued bitterly, but he'd finally got her to agree to work for Upman during the summer, at least to *try* the law as a career. By paying her more than she would have made remaining in London, he said, he garnered her cooperation. He'd had to take out a bank loan to raise the sum she demanded as recompense, but he considered it money well spent.

'You were that confident that the law would win her over?' Lynley asked. The prospect hardly seemed likely.

'I was confident that Upman would win her over,' Maiden replied. 'I've seen him with women. He has a way. I thought he and Nicola ... Tommy, I was willing to try anything. The right man, I kept thinking, could bring her to her senses.'

'Wouldn't Julian Britton have been a better choice? He was already in love with her, wasn't he?'

'Julian wanted her too much. She needed a man who'd seduce her but keep her guessing. Upman seemed right for the job.' Maiden appeared to hear his own words because he flinched a moment after he'd made the declaration, and he began to weep. 'Oh God, Tommy. She drove me to it.'

And Lynley was at last face to face with what he hadn't wanted to see. He'd turned away from the potential guilt of this man because of who he had been at New Scotland Yard, while all the time who he had been at New Scotland Yard illuminated his culpability as nothing else could. A master of deception and dissimulation, Andy Maiden had spent decades moving in that netherworld of undercover where the lines between fact and fantasy, between illegality and honour first become blurred and ultimately become altogether non-existent.

'Tell me how it happened,' Lynley said stonily. 'Tell me what you used besides the knife.'

Maiden dropped his hand. 'God in heaven ...' His voice was hoarse. 'Tommy, you can't be thinking ...' Then he appeared to reflect back over what he'd said, as if to locate the exact point of misunderstanding between them. 'She drove me to bribery. To *paying* her to work for Upman so that he could win her ... so that her mother would never discover what she was ... because it would have destroyed her. But no. *No.* You can't think I killed her. I was here the night she died. Here in the hotel. And ... my God, she was my only child.'

'And she'd betrayed you,' Lynley said. 'After all you'd done for her, after the life you'd given her—'

'No! I loved her. Do you have children? A daughter? A son? Do you know what it is to see the future in your child and know you'll live on no matter what happens just because she herself exists?'

'As a whore?' Lynley asked. 'As a woman on the game who makes her money paying house calls on men she whips into submission? "I'll see you dead before I let you do it." Those were your words. And she was returning to London next week, Andy. You'd bought yourself only a reprieve from the inevitable when you paid her to work in Buxton.'

'I didn't! Tommy, listen to me! I was *here* on Tuesday night.'

Maiden's voice had risen and a knock sounded on the door. It opened before either man could speak. Nan Maiden stood there. She looked from Lynley to her husband. She didn't speak.

But she didn't need to say a word in explanation of what Lynley read on her face. She knows what he did, he thought. My God, she's known from the first.

'Leave us,' Andy Maiden cried out to his wife.

'I don't think that will be necessary,' Lynley said.

Barbara Havers had never been to Westerham, and she discovered soon enough that there was no easy way to get there from the St James home in Chelsea. She'd made a quick run to the St Jameses upon leaving Eaton Terrace – why not, she'd thought, since she was in the area so close to the King's Road, a short jaunt down which would take her to Cheyne Row – and she'd been dead eager to let off steam to the couple who, she very well knew, were most likely to have also experienced Inspector Lynley's brand of priggish irrationality first hand at one time or another. But she hadn't had a chance to tell her story. For Deborah St James had answered the door, given an inexplicable happy shout in the direction of the study, and pulled her inside the house like a woman greeting someone unexpectedly back from the war.

'Simon, look!' she'd announced. 'Isn't this just *meant*?'

And the meeting between the three of them had been the spur that sent Barbara into Kent. To get there, however, she'd had to battle the maze of unmarked streets that made the words *south of the river* synonymous with a sojourn in hell. She'd got lost on the far side of Albert Bridge, where one moment of inattention resulted in twenty minutes of exasperation driving round Clapham Common in a futile search for the A205. Once she'd found it and worked her way over to Lewisham, she'd begun wondering about the efficacy of using the internet to locate one's expert witnesses.

The witness in this case lived in Westerham, where he also ran a small business a short distance away from Quebec House. 'You won't be able to miss it,' he'd told her on the telephone. 'Quebec House sits at the top of the Edenbridge Road. It's got a sign at the front. It's open today – Quebec House – so there'll probably be the odd coach in the car park. I'm less than five hundred yards to the south.'

So he was, she found, in a clapboard construction that bore the sign 'Quiver Me Timbers' above its door.

His name was Jason Harley, and his business shared room with his house, the original home having been halved by a wall that ran down its middle like Solomon's judgement. An overly wide door had been set into this wall, and it was through this door that Jason Harley rolled himself in the high performance wheelchair of a marathon athlete when Barbara rang the bell outside the shop door.

'You're Constable Havers?' Harley asked.

'Barbara,' she said.

He tossed back a mass of hair that was blond, very thick, and straight as a ruler. 'Barbara, then. Lucky you caught me at home. I usually shoot on Sundays.' He rolled himself back and beckoned her inside, saying, 'Make sure the sign stays on *closed*, won't you? I've got a local fan club that likes to drop by when they see I'm open.' He made this last remark ironically.

'Trouble?' Barbara asked him, thinking of louts, hooligans, and what torments they could inflict on a paraplegic.

'Nine-year-old boys. I spoke at their school. Now I'm their hero.' Harley grinned affably. 'So. How can I help you, Barbara? You said you wanted to see what I have?'

'Right.'

They'd found him on the internet, where his business had a web page, and his proximity to London had been the deciding factor in Barbara's selection of him as her expert witness. On the phone, which rang in his house as well as in his shop, Jason Harley had told her he wasn't open on Sundays, but when she'd explained the reasons behind her call, he'd agreed to see her.

Now she stood in the close confines of Quiver Me Timbers, and she glanced over its merchandise: the fibreglass, yew, and carbon of Jason Harley's trade. Racks stood against walls. Display cases lined the shop's single wide aisle. An assembly area spanned the farther end. And central to everything was a maple stand in which a ribboned medal was encased in glass. It was an Olympic gold, Barbara saw when she examined the medal. Not only in Westerham was Jason Harley somebody.

When she gave her attention back to him, she saw he was watching her. 'I'm impressed,' she said. 'Did you do it from your chair?'

'Could have done,' he told her. 'Would do today, as well, if I had a bit more free time to practise. But I wasn't in a chair back then. The chair came later. After a hang-gliding accident.'

'Rough,' she said.

'I cope. Better than most, I dare say. Now. How can I help you, Barbara?'

'Tell me about cedar arrows,' she said.

* * *

Jason Harley's Olympic gold medal represented the culmi-
nation of years of competition and practice. Years of competition and practice gave him rare expertise in the field of
archery. His hang-gliding accident had forced him to consider
how he might put his athletic prowess and his knowledge to use
in order to support himself and the family he and his girlfriend
wished to have. The result was his shop, Quiver Me Timbers,
where he sold the fine carbon arrows shot by modern bows
made of fibreglass or laminae of wood and where he handmade
and sold the wooden arrows that were used with the traditional
long bows for which English archery had historically been
known, from the Battle of Agincourt onwards.

In his shop, he also provided his customers with the
accoutrements of archery: from the complicated hand and
body pieces worn by archers to the arrow heads – called
piles, he told Barbara – that differed depending upon the
use to which the arrow was being put.

What about shooting a nineteen-year-old boy in the back?
Barbara wanted to ask the archer. What kind of pile would you
need for that? But she went at it slowly, knowing that she was
going to need a volume of information to heave at Lynley in
order to make the slightest dent in his armour against her.

She asked Harley to tell her about the wooden arrows
he made, particularly the arrows that he crafted from Port
Orford cedar.

Cedar arrows were the only ones he made at all, he corrected
her. The shafts came to him from Oregon. There they were
individually weighed, graded, and subjected to a bending test
prior to being shipped. 'They're dependable as hell,' he told
her, 'which is important because when the pull weight of the
bow is high, you need an arrow that's made to withstand it.
You *can* get arrows of pine or ash,' he went on after a moment
during which he handed her a finished cedar arrow for her
inspection, 'some from local wood and some from Sweden.
But the Oregon cedar's more easily available – because of the

quantity, I suppose – and I expect you'd find every archery shop in England sells it.'

He shepherded her to the back of his shop where his work area was. There, set at the height of his waist, a mini assembly line allowed him to move easily from the round saw that cut the slot in the arrow's shaft to the fletching jig where the cock and shaft feathers were glued into position. Araldite kept the pile in place. And, as he'd said before, the pile differed depending on the use to which the arrow would be put.

'Some archers prefer to make their own arrows,' he told her in summation. 'But as it's a labour intensive job – well, I suppose you can see that for yourself, can't you – most of them find an arrow maker they like and they buy their arrows from him. He can make them distinctive in any way they prefer – within reason, of course – so long as they tell him what they want as a means of identification.'

'Identification?' Barbara asked.

'Because of the competitions,' Harley said. 'That's mostly what long bows are used for these days.'

There were, he explained, two types of competitions that long bow archers engaged in: tournament shooting and field shooting. With the former, they shot at traditional targets: twelve dozen arrows fired at bulls' eyes from varying distances. For the latter, they shot in wooded areas or on hillsides: arrows fired at animals whose images were depicted on paper. But in either case, the only way a winner could be determined was by the individual identification marks that were made upon the arrow that was fired. And every competitive archer in England would be certain that his arrows could be distinguished from the arrows of every other archer who also competed. 'How else could they tell whose arrow hit the target?' Harley asked reasonably.

'Right,' Barbara said. 'How else.'

She'd read the postmortem report on Terry Cole. She knew from her conversation with St James that Lynley had been told of a third weapon beyond the knife and the stone they'd already identified as having been used on the victims. Now, with that third weapon as good as identified, she began to see how the crime had occurred.

She said, 'Tell me, Mr Harley – how fast can a good archer – with a decade or more of experience, let's say – get off successive arrows at a target? Using a long bow, that is.'

He considered the question thoughtfully, fingers pulling at his lower lip. 'Ten seconds, I'd guess. At the most.'

'As long as that?'

'Let me show you.'

She thought Harley intended to demonstrate for her himself. But instead, he fetched a quiver from the display rack, slid six arrows into it and motioned Barbara to come to his chair. 'Right handed or left?' he asked her.

'Right.'

'Okay. Turn around.'

Feeling a little foolish, she allowed him to slide the quiver onto her body and adjust the strap across her torso. 'Suppose the bow's in your left hand,' he explained when he had the quiver in place. 'Now reach back for the arrow. Only one.' When she had it – and not without a bit of unfamiliar groping – he pointed out that she would next have to position it on the Dacron string of the bow. Then she would have to draw the string back and take aim. 'It's not like a gun,' he reminded her. 'You have to reload and re-aim after every shot. A good archer can do it in just under ten seconds. But for someone like you – no offence—'

Barbara laughed. 'Give me twenty minutes.'

She looked at herself in the mirror that hung on the door through which Jason had earlier rolled himself into the shop. Standing there, she practised reaching back for the arrow. She imagined herself with a bow, and she tried to picture the target in front of her: not a bull's eye or a paper animal, but a living human being. Two of them, in fact, sitting next to a fire. That would have been the only light.

He didn't shoot the girl because he wasn't after the girl, she thought. But he had no other weapon with him, and he was desperate to kill the boy, so he had to use what he'd brought and hope the shot would kill him because – with another person present – he wasn't going to have the chance to fire off another at Cole.

So what had happened? The shot hadn't gone true. Perhaps the boy had moved at the last moment. Perhaps, aiming for the neck, he'd hit lower, on the back instead. The girl, realising someone in the darkness was trying to harm them, would have jumped to her feet and tried to flee. And since she was running and since it was dark, the bow and arrow were useless against her. So he'd have hunted her down. He'd have dispatched her and gone back for the boy.

Barbara said, 'Jason, if you were shot in the back with one of these arrows, what would you feel? Would you know you'd been hit? By an arrow, I mean.'

Harley gave his attention to the rack of bows as if the answers were hidden among them. 'I expect you'd feel a terrific blow at first,' he said slowly. 'Rather like you'd been hit with a hammer.'

'Could you move? Stand?'

'I don't see why not. Until you realised what had happened to you, of course. And then you'd probably go into shock. Especially if you reached back and felt the shaft sticking out of you. God. That would be grim. That would be enough to make you—'

'Faint,' Barbara said. 'Pass out. Fall over.'

'Right,' he agreed.

'And then the arrow would break off, wouldn't it?'

'Depending on the way you fell, it might do.'

Which would, she concluded silently, possibly leave a sliver of wood behind when the killer – anxious to remove the one thing from the body that could ultimately identify him to the police – pulled the remainder of the arrow from the victim's back. But he wouldn't have been dead – Terry Cole – at that point. Just in shock. So the killer would have to finish him off once he returned from pounding in the girl's skull. He had no weapon with him other than the long bow. His only choice was to find a weapon there at the campsite.

And having done that, with the boy safely stabbed, he himself was free to search for what he assumed Terry Cole had with him: the Chandler music. The source of a fortune denied him by the terms of his father's will.

There was only a final point to clarify with Jason Harley. She said, 'Jason, can an arrow's tip—'

'The pile,' he corrected her.

'The pile. Can it pierce human flesh? I mean, I always thought arrows had to have rubber ends or something if you took them out in public.'

He smiled. 'Suction cups, you mean? Like on kids' bows-and-arrows?' He rolled past her and behind one of the display cases where he took out a small box and emptied it on the low glass counter. These, he told her, were the piles used at the end of the cedar arrows. The most common for field archery was the bodkin head. Barbara could test its sharpness if she wanted to.

She did so. The metal piece was cylindrical in keeping with the arrow's shape, but it also narrowed to a nasty four-sided point that would be deadly when propelled with force. As she was pressing this tip into her finger experimentally, Harley chatted on about the other piles he sold. He laid out broadheads and hunting heads and explained their use. Finally, he separated from them the mediaeval reproductions.

'And these,' he concluded, 'are for demonstrations and battles.'

'Battles?' Barbara asked incredulously. 'People actually shooting *arrows* at each other?'

'Not real battles, of course, and when the fighting begins, the arrows are fitted out with rubber bunts on the end so they're not dangerous. They're reenactments, the battles are. A slew of weekend warriors gather together in the grounds of some castle or great house and play soldiers. It goes on all over the countryside.'

'People travel to reenactments, do they? With bows and arrows in the boots of their cars?'

'Just like that. Yes they do.'

Chapter Twenty-seven

The rain was unrelenting. The wind had joined it. In the car park of the Black Angel Hotel, both the wind and the rain played a sodden game with the top layer of rubbish in an overloaded skip. The wind lifted and hurled cardboard boxes and old newspapers into the air; the downfall plastered both to the windscreens and wheels of the empty cars.

Lynley climbed from the Bentley and raised his umbrella against the late summer storm. He hurried with his suitcase in hand round the side of the building and through the front door. A coat rack just within the entrance sprouted the dripping coats and jackets of a dozen or more Sunday patrons whose shapes Lynley could see through the translucent amber glass of the upper half of the hotel bar's door. Next to the rack a good ten umbrellas stood in an elongated iron stand and glistened wetly under the light of the entrance porch where Lynley stamped the damp from his shoes. He hung his coat among the others, shoved his umbrella in with the rest, and went through the bar to reception.

If the proprietor of the Black Angel was surprised to see him back so soon, the man gave no indication. The tourist season, after all, was nearly at an end. He would be happy enough for whatever custom came his way in the coming months. He handed over a key – Lynley was depressed to see it was for the same room he'd had earlier – and asked if the inspector wanted his bags taken up or would he rather see to them himself? Lynley handed over his suitcase and went to the bar for a meal.

Sunday lunch was long since finished, but they could do him a cold ham salad or a filled jacket potato, he was informed, as long as he wasn't overly particular about the potato's filling. He said that he wasn't and asked for both.

When the food was in front of him, however, Lynley found that he wasn't as hungry as he'd thought. He dipped into the potato with its thatch of cheddar but when he brought the loaded fork to his mouth, his tongue thickened at the thought of having to swallow anything solid, chewed or not. He lowered the fork and reached for the lager. Getting drunk was still an option.

He wanted to believe them. He wanted to believe them not because they were able to offer him the slightest bit of evidence in support of their statements but because he didn't want to believe anything else. Cops went bad from time to time, and only a fool denied that fact. Birmingham, Guildford, and Bridgewater were only three of the cases that had numbers attached to them – six, four, and four respectively – in reference to defendants convicted on spurious evidence, interrogation room beatings, and manufactured confessions with signatures forged. Each conviction had been the result of police malfeasance for which not a single excuse could possibly be made. So there were bad cops: whether one called them overly zealous, outright tendentious, thoroughly corrupt, or simply too indolent or ignorant to do the job the way the job was supposed to be done.

But Lynley didn't want to believe that Andy Maiden was a cop who'd gone bad. Nor did he even want to believe that Andy was simply a father who'd reached the end of his tether in dealing with his child. Even now, after meeting Andy, after watching the interplay between the man and his wife and having to evaluate what every word, gesture, and nuance between them meant, Lynley found that his heart and mind were still in conflict over the basic facts.

Nan Maiden had joined them in the airless little office behind reception in Maiden Hall. She'd shut the door. Her husband had said, 'Nancy, don't bother. The guests . . . Nan, you're not needed in here,' and cast a beseeching look at Lynley in an unspoken request that Lynley did not grant. For needed was exactly what Nan Maiden was if they were to get to the bottom of what had happened to Nicola on Calder Moor.

She said to Lynley, 'We weren't expecting anyone else today. I told Inspector Hanken yesterday that Andy was at home that night. I explained—'

'Yes,' Lynley agreed. 'I've been told.'

'Then I don't see what further good can come from more questions.' She stood stiffly near the door, and her words were as rigid as her body when she went on. 'I know you've come for that, Inspector: questioning Andy instead of offering us information about Nicola's death. Andy wouldn't look like that – like he's being chewed up inside – if you hadn't come to ask him if he actually . . . if he went onto the moor so that he could—' And there her voice faltered. 'He was *here* on Tuesday night. I *told* Inspector Hanken that. What more do you want from us?'

The absolute truth, Lynley thought. He wanted to hear it. More, he wanted them both to face it. But at the last moment when he could have revealed to her the real nature of her daughter's life in London, he didn't do it. The truth about Nicola would come out eventually – in interrogation rooms, in legal depositions, and in the trial – but there was no reason to drag it out now, like a grinning skeleton forced from a cupboard that the girl's mother didn't even know existed. If nothing else, he could honour Andy Maiden's wishes in that matter, at least for now.

He said, 'Who can support your statement, Mrs Maiden?

DI Hanken told me that Andy had gone to bed early in the evening. Did someone else see him?'

'Who else would have seen him? Our employees don't go into the private part of the house unless they're instructed to do so.'

'And you didn't ask one of them to check on Andy during the evening?'

'I checked on him myself.'

'So you see the difficulty, don't you?'

'No, I don't. Because I'm telling you that Andy didn't . . .' She clenched her fists at her throat and squeezed her eyes shut. 'He didn't kill her!'

So the words were said at last. But even as they were said the one logical question that Nan Maiden might have asked went completely unspoken. She never said the words, 'Why? Why would my husband have killed his own daughter?' And that was a telling omission.

Lynley said, 'How much did you know about your daughter's plans for her future?' to both of them, giving Andy Maiden the opportunity of revealing to his wife the worst there was to know about their only child.

'Our daughter has no future,' Nan answered. 'So her plans – whatever they might have been – are completely irrelevant.'

'I'll arrange to take a polygraph,' Andy Maiden said abruptly. Lynley saw in his offer how keen he was to keep his wife from hearing an account of their daughter's London life. 'That can't be so difficult to set up, can it? We can find someone . . . I want to take one, Tommy.'

'Andy, no.'

'I'll arrange for both of us to take one, if you like,' Maiden said, ignoring his wife.

'Andy!'

'How else can we make him see that he's got it all wrong?' Maiden asked her.

'But with your nerves,' she said, 'with the state you're in . . . Andy, they'll turn you and twist you. Don't do it.'

'I'm not afraid.'

And Lynley could see that he wasn't. Which was a point he clung to all the way back to Tideswell and the Black Angel Hotel.

Now, with his meal in front of him, Lynley considered that lack of fear and what it might mean: innocence, bravado, or dissimulation. It could be any one of the three, Lynley thought, and despite everything he'd learned about the man, he knew which one he still hoped it was.

'Inspector Lynley?'

He looked up. The barmaid stood there, frowning down at his uneaten meal. He was about to apologise for ordering what he hadn't been able to consume when she said, 'You've a call from London. The phone's behind the bar if you want to use it.'

The caller was Winston Nkata, and the constable's words were urgent. 'We got it, Guv,' he said tersely when he heard Lynley's voice. 'Postmortem showed a piece of cedar found on the Cole boy's body. St James says the first weapon was an arrow. Shot in the dark. The girl took off running, so he couldn't shoot at her. Had to chase her down and cosh her with the boulder.'

Nkata explained: exactly what St James had seen on the postmortem report, how he had interpreted the information, and what he – Nkata – had learned about arrows and long bows from a fletcher in Kent.

'Killer would've taken the arrow with him from the scene because most long bows're used in competitions,' Nkata finished, 'and all the long bow arrows're marked to identify them.'

'Marked in what way?'

'With the shooter's initials.'

'Good God. That puts a signature on the crime.'

'Isn't that true. These initials c'n be carved or burned into the wood or put on with transfers. But in any case, at a crime scene, they'd be as good as dabs.'

'Top marks, Winnie,' Lynley said. '*Excellent* work.'

The DC cleared his throat. 'Yeah. Well. Got to do the job.'

'So if we find the archer, we've got our killer,' Lynley said.

'Looks that way,' Nkata agreed, and he asked the next logical question: 'You talk to the Maidens, 'spector?'

'He wants to take a polygraph.' Lynley told him about his interview with the dead girl's parents.

'Make sure he gets asked if he plays the Hundred Years War on his free afternoons.'

'Sorry?'

'That's what they do with long bows. Competitions, tournaments, and reenactments. So is our Mister Maiden fighting the French for a lark up there in Derbyshire?'

Lynley drew in a breath. He felt as if a weight had been lifted from his shoulders at the very same moment as a fog bank cleared from his brain. 'Broughton Manor,' he said.

'What?'

'Where I'll find a long bow,' Lynley explained. 'And I've a very good idea who knows how to shoot it.'

In London, Barbara watched as Nkata rang off. He looked at her sombrely.

'What?' She felt a vice round her heart. 'Don't tell me he didn't *believe* you, Winnie.'

'He believed me.'

'Thank God.' She looked at him more closely. He seemed so grave. 'Then what?'

''S your work, Barb. I don't like taking credit.'

'Oh. That. Well, you can't think he'd have listened to me if I'd phoned him with the news. It's better this way.'

'Puts me in a better light than you. I don't much like it when I've done nothing to get there.'

'Forget it. It was the only way. Leave me out of it so his nibship can keep his knickers from twisting. What's he going to do?'

She listened as Nkata related Lynley's plans to seek the long bow at Broughton Manor. She shook her head at the futility of his thinking. 'He's on a goose chase, Winnie. There's not going to be a long bow in Derbyshire.'

'How c'n you be so sure?'

'I can feel it.' She gathered up what she'd brought into Lynley's office. 'I may phone in with the 'flu for a day or two, but you didn't hear that from me. Okay?'

Nkata nodded. 'What'll you be up to, then?'

Barbara held up what Jason Harley had given her before she left his shop in Westerham. It was a lengthy mailing list of individuals who received his quarterly catalogues. He'd generously handed this over, along with the records of everyone who had placed orders with Quiver Me Timbers in the last six months. He'd said, 'I don't expect these will be much help because there're plenty of archery shops in the country that your man might've ordered his arrows from. But if you'd like to have a go, you're welcome to take them.'

She'd jumped at the offer. She'd even taken along two of his catalogues for good measure. For some Sunday evening light reading, she'd thought as she'd tucked them into her bag. As things were now, she certainly had Sweet F.A. else to do.

'What about you?' she asked Nkata. 'The inspector give you another assignment?'

'Sunday night off with my mum and dad.'

'Now *there's* an assignment.' She saluted him and was about to stride off when the phone rang on Lynley's desk. She said, 'Uh-oh. Forget Sunday night, Winston.'

'Hell,' he grumbled and reached for the phone.

His side of the conversation consisted of: 'No. Not here.

Sorry . . . Up in Derbyshire . . . DC Winston Nkata . . . Yeah. Right. Pretty much, but it's not 'xactly the same case, I'm 'fraid . . .' A lengthier pause as someone went on and on, followed by, 'She is?' and a smile. Nkata looked at Barbara and, for some reason, gave her a thumbs up. 'Good news. Best news there is. Thanks.' He listened a moment longer and looked at the wall clock. 'Right. Will do. Say thirty minutes? . . . Yeah. Oh, we definitely got someone who can take a statement.' He rang off a second time and nodded at Barbara. 'That's you, Barb.'

'Me? Hang on, Winnie, you've got no rank to pull on me,' Barbara said in protest, seeing her Sunday evening plans go down the sewer.

'Right. But I don't think you want to miss out on this.'

'I'm off the case.'

'I know that. But 'cording to the guv this isn't exactly on the case any longer, so I don't see why you don't take it yourself.'

'Take what?'

'Vi Nevin. She's fully conscious, Barb. And someone's got to take a statement from her.'

Lynley phoned DI Hanken at home, where he found him sealed within his small garage, apparently trying to make sense of instructions to assemble a child's swing set. 'I'm not a bloody God damn *engineer*,' he fumed and seemed grateful for anything that promised to take him away from a hopeless endeavour.

Lynley brought him into the picture. Hanken agreed that an arrow and its bow looked likely as their missing weapon. 'Explains why it wasn't stowed in that grit dispenser with the knife,' he said. 'And if it's initials that we're going to find on the arrow, I've a good idea whose they're likely to be.'

'I recall your telling me about the various ways Julian Britton makes money at Broughton Manor,' Lynley acknowledged. 'It looks like we're finally closing in on him, Peter. I'm heading over there now to have a—'

'Heading over? Where the hell *are* you?' Hanken demanded. 'Aren't you in London?'

Lynley was fairly certain in which direction Hanken would run when he learned why Lynley had returned so quickly to Derbyshire, and his fellow DI did not disappoint him. 'I *knew* it was Maiden,' Hanken exclaimed at the end of Lynley's explanation. 'He found that car on the moor, Thomas. And there's no way in hell he would have found it had he not known where she'd be in the first place. He *knew* she was on the game in London and he couldn't deal with it. So he gave her the chop. It was the only way – I dare say – that he could keep her from spilling the news to her mum.'

This was so close to what Maiden's actual desires were that Lynley felt chilled by Hanken's perspicacity. Still, he said, 'Andy's said he'll arrange to take a polygraph. I can't think he'd make an offer like that if he had Nicola's blood on his hands.'

'The hell he wouldn't,' Hanken countered. 'This bloke's an undercover cop, let's not forget. If he hadn't been able to lie with the best of them, he'd be a dead man now. A polygraph taken by Andy Maiden's going to be nothing more than a joke. On us, by the way.'

'Julian Britton's got the stronger motive,' Lynley said. 'Let me see if I can shake him up.'

'You're playing right into Maiden's hands. You know that, don't you? He's working you like you're wearing the same school tie.'

Which they were, in a manner of speaking. But Lynley refused to be blinded by their history. He refused to be blinded in either direction. It was as foolhardy to believe beyond doubt that Andy Maiden was the killer as it was to ignore the possible guilt of someone with a stronger motive.

Hanken rang off. Lynley had made the phone call from his

hotel room, so he took five minutes to unpack his belongings before heading out to Broughton Manor. He'd left his umbrella and trench coat below in the entrance when he'd gone upstairs to place the call, so after leaving his room key on the reception desk, he went to fetch them.

The Black Angel's earlier patrons had mostly departed, he saw. There were only three umbrellas left in the stand and, apart from his own coat, only a single jacket remained on the coat rack.

Under other circumstances, a jacket on a coat rack wouldn't have caught his attention. But as he endeavoured to untangle the hook of his umbrella from the gaping ribs of another, he knocked the jacket from its spot on the rack and thus felt obliged to pick it up from the floor.

The fact that the garment was black leather didn't strike him at first. It was only when the silence and darkness of the previously occupied hotel bar told him all the patrons were gone that he realised the jacket had no owner.

He looked from the darkened bar door to the black leather jacket, feeling a tingling along his scalp. He thought, No, it can't be. But even as his mind formed the words, his fingers contacted the jacket's stiffened lining – stiffened the way only one substance can render an otherwise soft material stiff because the substance itself does not so much dry as coagulate . . .

Lynley dropped his umbrella. He took the jacket nearer to the entry porch's window where he could better examine it under the light. And there he saw that in addition to that unnamed substance which had altered the texture of the lining, the leather was damaged in another way. A hole – perhaps the size of a five pence coin – had pierced the back.

Apart from knowing that the lining of the jacket had once been soaked with blood, Lynley did not need to be a student of anatomy also to know that the hole in the jacket matched up precisely with the left scapula of the unfortunate person who'd been wearing it.

Nan Maiden found him in his lair near their bedroom. He'd left the office as soon as the detective was out of the hotel, and she hadn't followed him. Instead, she'd spent nearly an hour straightening the lounge after the last of the Sunday guests and setting up the dining room for residents and others who would be requiring a light Sunday supper. When she'd completed these tasks, checked the kitchen to see that the evening's soup was being prepared, and given directions to several American hikers who were apparently intent upon reenacting *Jane Eyre* at North Lees Hall, she went in search of her husband.

Her excuse was a meal: She hadn't seen him eat for days and if he went on like this, he would certainly fall ill. The reality was something rather different: Andy couldn't be permitted to carry through his plan to be questioned with electrodes attached to his body. None of his responses could possibly be accurate when one considered the condition he was in.

She loaded a tray with anything he might find tempting. She included two drinks for him to choose from, and she climbed the stairs to make her offering.

He was sitting at the desk and before him was a shoe box with its lid off and its contents spread across the secretaire drawer that was pulled out and open. Nan said his name, but he didn't hear her, so engrossed was he with the papers that had been in the box.

She approached. Over his shoulder she could see that he was looking at a collection of letters, notes, drawings, and greeting cards spanning nearly a quarter of a century. What had occasioned each one was different, but their source was the same. They represented every drawing or other communication that Andy had received from Nicola throughout her life.

Nan put the tray down next to the comfortable old over-stuffed chair where Andy sometimes read. She said, 'I've brought you something to eat, darling,' and was unsurprised when he didn't reply. She didn't know if he could not hear her or if he merely wished to be alone and wasn't willing to say so. But in either case, it didn't matter. She would make him hear her and she would not leave him.

She said, 'Please don't take that lie detector test, Andy. Your condition isn't normal, and it hasn't been for months. I'm going to ring that policeman in the morning and tell him you've changed your mind. There's no sin in that. You're perfectly within your rights. He'll know it.'

Andy stirred. In his fingers he held a child's gawky drawing of 'dady gets out of his bath' that had provoked in both of them such fond laughter so many years ago. But now the sight of that little girl's rendering of her naked father – complete with a penis hilariously out of proportion – caused a shudder in Nan, followed by a shutting down of some basic function in her body and a shutting off of some essential emotion in her heart. 'I'll take the polygraph.' Andy set the drawing to one side. 'It's the only way.'

She wanted to say, 'The only way to what?' And she would have done had she been more prepared to hear the answer. Instead she said, 'And what if you fail?'

He turned to her then. He held an old letter between his fingers. Nan could see the words *Dearest Daddy* in Nicola's bold, firm hand. 'Why would I fail?' he asked.

'Because of your condition,' she answered. Too quickly, she thought. Far far too quickly. 'If your nerves are going bad, they're going to send out incorrect readings. The police will take those readings and misinterpret them. The machine will say your body's not working. The police will call it something else.'

They'll call it guilt. The sentence hung between them. It seemed to Nan suddenly that she and her husband were occupying different continents. She felt that she was the one who'd created the ocean between them, but she could not take the risk of diminishing its size.

Andy said, 'A polygraph measures temperature, pulse, and respiration. There won't be a problem. It's nothing to do with nerves. I want to take it.'

'But why? Why?'

'Because it's the only way.' He smoothed the letter against the top of the secretaire drawer. He traced *Dearest Daddy* with his index finger. 'I wasn't asleep,' he said to her. 'I tried to sleep but I couldn't because I was so unnerved when my sight went bad. So why did you tell them you checked on me, Nancy?' And then he looked up and held her gaze with his.

'I've brought you something to eat, Andy,' she said brightly. 'There's simply got to be something here to tempt you. Should I spread some paté on a piece of baguette?'

'Nancy,' he said, 'tell me the truth. Please tell me the truth.'

'She was wonderful, wasn't she?' Nan Maiden whispered instead, gesturing to the memories of Nicola that her husband had taken from their storage place. 'Wasn't our little girl just the best?'

Vi Nevin wasn't alone in her room when Barbara Havers arrived at Chelsea and Westminster Hospital. Sitting next to her bed with her head pressed into the mattress like an orange-haired supplicant at the feet of a heavily bandaged goddess was a girl with limbs like bicycle spokes and the wrists and ankles of an anorectic. She looked up as the door swung shut behind Barbara.

'How'd you get in?' she demanded, rising and adopting a defensive stance with her inadequate body placed between the interloper and the bed. 'That cop out there i'n't s'posed to let *anyone—*'

'Relax,' Barbara said, excavating in her bag for identification. 'I'm one of the good guys.'

The girl sidled forward, snatched Barbara's warrant card, and read it: one eye on the card and the other on Barbara lest she make any precipitate moves. On the bed behind her, the patient stirred. She murmured, ''S okay, Shell. I saw her already. With the black th'other day. You know.'

Shell – who said she was Vi's best friend on earth Shelly Platt who meant to take care of Vi till the end of time and don't you forget it – returned Barbara's identification and slunk back to her seat. Barbara rustled out a notepad and a chewed Biro and pulled the room's other chair into a position from which she and Vi Nevin could see each other.

She said, 'I'm sorry about the beating. I got one myself a few months ago. Rotten business, but at least I could point the finger at the bastard. Can you? What d' you remember?'

Shelly went to the head of the bed, taking Vi's hand in her own and beginning to stroke it. Her presence was an irritant to Barbara, like a sudden case of contact dermatitis, but the young woman in the bed seemed to take comfort from it. Whatever helps, Barbara thought. She sat with biro poised.

Beneath the bandages, what could be seen of Vi Nevin's swollen face was her eyes, a small portion of her forehead, and a stitched-up lower lip. She looked like a victim of the sort of explosive that threw off shrapnel. She said in a voice so faint that Barbara strained to hear it, 'Had a punter coming. Old bloke, this is. Likes honey on him. I coat him first . . . You know? Then I lick it off.'

What a treat, Barbara thought. She said, 'Right. You say honey? Brilliant. Go on.'

Vi Nevin did so. She said she'd readied herself for her appointment in the schoolgirl costume that her client preferred. But when she'd brought out the honey jar, she'd realised that there wouldn't be enough to baste all the body parts he usually requested. 'Plenty for the prong,' Vi said with the frankness of a professional. 'But if he wanted more, I needed to have it to hand.'

'I've got the picture,' Barbara told her.

At the head of the bed, Shelly eased a skinny thigh onto the mattress. She said, 'I c'n tell it, Vi. You'll wear yourself out.'

Vi shook her head and continued the story. There was little enough of it.

She'd popped out for the honey before her client's arrival. When she'd returned, she'd transferred the honey into its regular jug and she'd assembled a tray with the linens and other assorted goodies – all of which appeared to be either edible or potable – that she used in her regular sessions with the man. She'd been carrying the tray into the sitting room when she'd heard a sound from one of the bedrooms upstairs.

All *right*, Barbara thought. Her interpretation of the pictures taken at the Fulham crime scene was about to be confirmed. But to be absolutely sure, she clarified with, 'Was it your client? Had he arrived ahead of you?'

'Not him,' Vi said. The remark was breathed, rather than spoken.

Shelly said to Barbara, 'You c'n see she's knackered. That's enough for now.'

'Hang on,' Barbara told her. 'So a bloke was upstairs, but he wasn't a client? Then how'd he get in? You hadn't bolted the door?'

Vi raised the hand that Shelly wasn't clutching. It rose two inches off the bed and fell back. She reminded Barbara, 'Only popped out for honey. Ten minutes is all.' So she saw no reason to bolt it. When she heard the noise above stairs, she explained, she went to investigate and found a bloke in her bedroom. The room itself was a shambles.

'You saw him?' Barbara asked.

Only a shadowy glimpse of him as he lunged at her, Vi explained.

Fine, Barbara thought, because a glimpse might well do

it. She said, 'That's good. That's brilliant, then. Tell me what you can. Anything at all. A detail. A scar. A mark. Anything,' and she summoned into her mind the image of Matthew King-Ryder's face to match it up with whatever Vi Nevin said.

But what Vi gave her was a description of Everyman: medium height, medium build, brown hair, clear skin. And while it fitted Matthew King-Ryder to a tee, it also fitted at least seventy percent of the male population.

'Too fast,' Vi murmured. 'Happened too fast.'

'But it *wasn't* the client you'd been expecting? You do know that?'

Vi's lips curved, and she winced as they pulled against their stitches. 'Eighty-one, that bloke is. On his best day ... can't even manage the stairs.'

'And it wasn't Martin Reeve?'

She shook her head.

'One of your other clients? An old boyfriend, perhaps?'

'She *said*—' Shelly Platt interrupted hotly.

'I'm clearing the decks,' Barbara told her. 'It's the only way. You want us to nick whoever assaulted her, right?'

Shelly grumbled and petted Vi's shoulder. Barbara tapped the pen against her notebook and considered their options.

They could hardly cart Vi Nevin to an identity parade and even if that were possible, they had – at the moment – no reason in hell to trot Matthew King-Ryder into the local nick to stand in one. So they needed a picture, but it would have to come from a newspaper or a magazine. Or from King-Ryder Productions on some sort of spurious excuse. Because one hint that they were on to him, and King-Ryder would weigh down his long bow and arrows with concrete and dump them into the Thames faster than you could say Robin Hood's Merry Men.

But getting a photo was going to take some time because they needed the real thing – sharp and clear – and not something sent over to the hospital via fax. And fax or otherwise, where the hell were they going to get a photo of Matthew King-Ryder at – here Barbara looked at her watch – half past seven on a Sunday evening? There was no way. It was stab-in-the-dark time. She drew a deep breath and took the plunge. 'D'you know a bloke called Matthew King-Ryder by any chance?'

Vi said the unexpected. 'Yes.'

Lynley held the jacket by its satin lining. It had most likely been touched by a dozen people since being removed from Terry Cole's body on Tuesday night. But it had been touched by the killer as well, and if he hadn't realised that fingerprints could be lifted from leather nearly as easily as they could be lifted from glass or painted wood, there was an excellent chance that he'd left an unintentional calling card upon the garment.

Once the proprietor of the Black Angel understood the import of Lynley's request, he fetched all the employees to the bar for some questions post haste. He offered the inspector tea, coffee, or other refreshment to go along with his queries, seeking to be helpful with the sort of anxiety to please that generally struck people who found themselves inadvertently living on the county line between murder and respectability. Lynley demurred at all refreshment. He just wanted some information, he said.

Showing the jacket to the hotel's proprietor and its employees didn't get him anywhere, however. One jacket was much like another to them. None could say how or when the garment that Lynley was holding had appeared at the hotel. They made suitable noises of horror and aversion when he pointed out the copious amount of dried blood on the lining and the hole in the back, and while they looked at him with properly mournful expressions when he mentioned the two deaths on Calder Moor, not an eyelash among them so much as fluttered at the suggestion that a killer might have been in their midst.

'I reckon someone left that thing here. Tha's what happened. No mistake about it,' the barmaid said.

'Coats hanging on the rack all winter long,' one of the room maids added. 'I never notice them one day to the next.'

'But that's just it,' Lynley said. 'It isn't winter. And until today, I dare say there hasn't been rain enough for macs, jackets, or coats.'

'So what's'r point?' the proprietor said.

'How could all of you fail to notice a leather jacket on a coat rack if the leather jacket is hanging there alone?'

The ten employees who were gathered in the bar shrugged, looked sheepish, or appeared regretful. But no one could shed any light on the jacket or how it had come to be there. They came in to work through the back door, not through the front, they told him. They left the same way. Besides, things often got left behind at the Black Angel Hotel: umbrellas, walking sticks, rain gear, rucksacks, maps. Everything ended up in lost property and until things got there, no one paid them much mind.

Lynley decided on a full frontal approach. Were they acquainted with the Britton family? he wanted to know. Would they recognise Julian Britton if they saw him?

The proprietor spoke for everyone. 'We all know the Brittons at the Black Angel.'

'Did any of you see Julian on Tuesday night?'

But no one had.

Lynley dismissed them. He asked for a carrier bag in which to stow the jacket and while one was being fetched for him, he walked to the window, watched the rain fall, and thought about Tideswell, the Black Angel, and the crime.

He himself had seen that Tideswell abutted the eastern edge of Calder Moor, and the killer – vastly more familiar with the White Peak than Lynley – would have known that as well. So in possession of a jacket with an incriminating hole that would have told the tale of the crime in short order had it been found on the scene, he had to get rid of it as soon as possible. What could have been easier than stopping at the Black Angel Hotel on his way home from Calder Moor, knowing as an habitué of the bar, that coats and jackets accumulated for whole seasons before anyone thought to have a look at them.

But could Julian Britton have managed to hang up the leather jacket in the entrance without being seen by anyone inside? It was possible, Lynley thought. Risky as the devil, but possible.

And at this point, Lynley was willing to accept what was possible. It kept what was probable out of his thoughts.

Barbara leaned forward in her chair, saying, 'You know him? Matthew King-Ryder. You *know* him?' and trying to keep the excitement from her voice.

'Terry,' Vi murmured.

Her eyelids were getting heavy. But Barbara pressed the young woman anyway, against the rising protestations of Shelly Platt. 'Terry knew Matthew King-Ryder? How?'

'Music,' Vi said.

Barbara felt immediately deflated. Damn, she thought. Terry Cole, the Chandler music, and Matthew King-Ryder. There was nothing new in this. They were nowhere again.

Then Vi said, 'Found it in the Albert Hall, Terry.'

Barbara's eyebrows knotted. 'The Albert Hall? Terry found the music there?'

'Yeah. Under a seat.'

Barbara was gobsmacked. She tried to get her mind round what Vi Nevin was telling her even as Vi continued to talk.

In the course of his job, Terry put up cards regularly in South Kensington phone boxes. He always did this work at night, since there was less likelihood of finding himself on the receiving end of police aggro after dark. He'd been on his regular rounds in the neighbourhood of Queen's Gate when the phone in one of the boxes rang.

'On the corner of Elvaston Place and one of the mewses, this was,' Vi said.

For a lark, Terry answered to hear a male voice say, 'The package is in the Albert Hall. Circle Q, Row 7, Seat 19,' after which the line went dead.

The mysterious nature of the call piqued Terry's interest. The word *package* – with its intimations of either a money drop, a drug drop, or a dead letter box – clinched the deal. Since he was so close to Kensington Gore where the Royal Albert Hall looked over the south border of Hyde Park, Terry went to investigate. A concert audience was just leaving so the Hall was open. He tracked down the seat high in one of the balconies and found a package of music beneath it.

The Chandler music, Barbara thought. But what the bloody hell was it doing *there*?

He thought at first that he'd been sent off on a fool's errand intended for whatever fool was supposed to answer that phone on the corner of Elvaston Place. And when he'd met up with Vi to collect a fresh batch of cards, he'd told her about his brief adventure.

'I thought there might be money to be made,' Vi told Barbara. 'So did Nikki when we told her about it.'

Shelly dropped Vi's hand abruptly, saying, 'I don't want to hear nothing about that bitch.'

To which Vi replied, 'Come on, Shell. She's dead.'

Shelly flounced over to the chair she'd been sitting on earlier. She plopped down and began to sulk, arms crossed over her bony chest. Barbara speculated briefly on the uneasy future of a relationship between two women when one of them was so perilously dependent. Vi ignored the demonstration of pique.

They all had ambitions, she told Barbara. Terry had his Destination Art and Vi and Nikki had plans to start up a first class escort business. They also had a need to support themselves once Nikki broke with Adrian Beattie. Both operations depended upon an infusion of cash and the music looked like a potential source of it. 'See, I remembered when Sotheby's – or whoever it was – was set to auction a piece by Lennon and McCartney. And *that* was just one single sheet that was supposed to fetch a few thousand quid. This was a whole packet of music. I said Terry ought to try to sell it. Nikki offered to do the research and find the right auction house. We'd split the money when the music sold.'

'But why cut you in?' Barbara asked. 'You and Nikki. It was Terry's find, after all.'

'Yeah. But he was soft on Nikki,' Vi said simply. 'He wanted to impress her. This was the way.'

Barbara knew the rest. Neil Sitwell at Bowers had opened Terry's eyes to copyright law. He'd handed over the address for 31–32 Soho Square and informed the boy that King-Ryder Productions would put him in touch with the Chandler solicitors. Terry had gone to Matthew King-Ryder with the music in hand. Matthew King-Ryder had seen it and had realised how he could use it to make himself the fortune that his father's will denied him. But why not just buy the music from the boy right then? she wondered. Why kill him to get it? Better yet, why not just buy the rights to the music from the Chandler family? If the production that resulted from the music was anything like the King-Ryder/Chandler productions from the past, there would have been plenty of lolly to go round in royalties even if fifty percent of it went to the Chandlers.

Vi was saying, '—couldn't get the name,' when Barbara roused herself from her thoughts. She said, 'What? Sorry. What did you say?'

'Matthew King-Ryder didn't give Terry the solicitor's name. Didn't even give him a chance to ask for it. He booted him out of his office as soon as he saw what Terry'd brought with him.'

'When he saw the music.'

She nodded. 'Terry said he went red-faced and called security. Two guards came up straightaway and threw him out.'

'But Terry had gone there just for the Chandler solicitor's address, hadn't he? That's all he wanted from Matthew King-Ryder? He didn't want money? A reward or something?'

'Money's what we wanted the Chandlers to give him. Once we knew the music couldn't be auctioned.'

A nurse came into the room then, a small square tray in her hand. A hypodermic needle lay on it. Time for pain medication, the woman said.

'One last question,' Barbara said. 'Why did Terry go up to Derbyshire on Tuesday?'

'Because I asked him to,' Vi said. 'Nikki thought I was being a fool about Shelly—' Here the other woman raised her head. Vi spoke to her, rather than to Barbara. 'She kept sending these letters and hanging about and I was getting scared.'

Shelly raised a thin hand and pointed to her chest. 'Of me?' she asked. 'You was scared of *me*?'

'Nikki laughed them off when I told her about them. I thought if she *saw* them herself, we could plan to take care of Shelly some way. I wrote Nikki a note and asked Terry to take it and the letters up to her. Like I said, he was soft on her. Any excuse to see her. You know what I mean.'

The nurse interposed at this juncture, saying, 'I really must insist,' and holding up the syringe.

'Yeah, okay,' Vi Nevin said.

Barbara stopped for groceries on her way back to Chalk Farm, so it was after nine by the time she got home. She unpacked her booty and stashed it within cupboards and the miniature fridge of her bungalow. All the time in her mind she picked through the information that Vi Nevin had given her. Somewhere within their interview was buried the key to everything that had happened: not only in Derbyshire but also in London.

Surely, she thought, a mere assembling of the information in the right order would tell her what she needed to know.

With a plate of reheatable *rogan josh* from the grocery's pre-cooked section – of which Barbara had quickly become an habitué nonpareil when she'd moved to the neighbourhood – she settled herself at her tiny dining table next to the bungalow's front window. She accompanied her meal with a lukewarm Bass and laid her notebook next to the coffee mug from which she was reduced to drinking since several days of crockery, cutlery, and glassware had piled in her kitchen's diminutive sink. She took a gulp of the ale, forked up a portion of the lamb, and flipped to the notes from her interview with Vi Nevin.

Once the pain medication had been administered, the patient had drifted off to sleep, but not before answering a few more questions. In her rôle of Argos watching over Io, Shelly Platt had protested Barbara's continued presence. But Vi, lulled into a drug-induced ease, had murmured responses cooperatively until her eyes had closed and her breathing had deepened.

Reviewing her notes, Barbara concluded that the logical place to begin in developing a hypothesis about the case would have to be with the telephone call that Terry Cole had intercepted in South Kensington. That event had set all others in motion. It also stimulated enough questions to suggest that an understanding of the phone call – what had prompted it and what exactly had arisen from it – would lead inexorably to the evidence that would allow her to nab Matthew King-Ryder as a killer.

Although it was now September, Vi Nevin had been quite clear about the fact that Terry Cole had intercepted the phone call in South Kensington in the month of June. She couldn't give the exact date, but she knew it was early in the month because she'd collected her new cards at the beginning of the month and she passed them to Terry on the same day that she picked them up. It was then that he told her about the curious call.

Not the beginning of July? Barbara enquired. Not August? Not even September?

June it was, Vi Nevin insisted. She remembered because they'd recently moved house to Fulham – she and Nikki – and since they were setting themselves up in business away from MKR Financial Management, they would need the cards to advertise and this batch was the first of them. She'd wanted Terry to put up her own as soon as possible so that she could continue to build her clientele, and she'd even given Nikki's cards to Terry too, telling the boy to hold onto them until the autumn when he was to place them in boxes the day before Nikki returned.

But why, then, had it taken Terry so long to go to Bowers with the music he'd found?

First, Vi informed her, because she didn't tell Nikki straight-away about Terry's find. And second, because once she *did* tell Nikki and the plan was hatched among them to try to make some money from the music, it took some time for Nikki to research the best auction houses available to handle a sale of the sort they imagined. 'Didn't want to pay lots of sellers' fees,' she murmured, eyelids heavy. 'Nikki thought 'f a country auction first. She made phone calls. Talked to people who knew.'

'And she came up with Bowers?'

''S right.' Vi turned on her side. Shelly raised the blanket round her charge's shoulders and tucked her in, up to her neck.

Now, munching her *rogan josh* in her Chalk Farm bungalow, Barbara reflected on that telephone call yet another time. No matter which way she considered it, however, she arrived at the same conclusion. The call had to have been intended for Matthew King-Ryder, who failed to be there at the designated hour to receive it. Hearing the single word *yeah* spoken by a male voice – by Terry Cole's voice – the caller had assumed that his message about the Albert Hall was being received by the right person. And since whoever had possession of the Chandler music wished to remain anonymous – why else make a phone call to a call box? – it seemed reasonable to conclude that something illegal was involved somewhere along the line. In any case, the caller *thought* he'd passed the music along to King-Ryder, who'd no doubt paid a significant sum to get his mitts on it. With that sum in hand – probably paid in advance and in cash – the caller faded into the fog of obscurity, leaving King-Ryder out of the money, out of the music, and out of the picture as well. So when Terry Cole had dropped into his office flashing a page of the Chandler score Matthew King-Ryder must have thought he was being deliberately ridiculed by someone who had already double-crossed him. Because if he'd arrived in South Kensington just one minute late for that telephone call, he'd have stood around for hours waiting for that phone to ring and assuming he'd been had.

He'd want revenge for that. He'd also want that music. And there was only one way to have both.

Vi Nevin's story supported Barbara's contention that Matthew King-Ryder was the man they were looking for. Unfortunately, it wasn't evidence, and without something more solid than conjecture Barbara knew that she had no case to lay before Lynley. And laying before him irrefutable facts was going to be the only way she could ever redeem herself in his eyes. He'd seen her defiance as further proof of her indifference to a chain of command. He needed to see that same defiance as the dynamism that brought down a killer.

Pondering this, Barbara heard her name called from outside the bungalow. She looked up to see Hadiyyah skipping down the path that led to the back garden. The motion-detecting lights came on as she passed beneath them. The effect wasn't unlike a dancer being spotlit as she flew across the stage.

'We're back, we're back, we're back from the sea!' Hadiyyah sang out. 'And look what Dad won me!'

Barbara waved at the little girl and closed her notebook. She went to the door and opened it just as Hadiyyah was finishing a pirouette. One of her long plaits had come loose from its restraining ribbon and was beginning to unravel, trailing a tail of silver satin like a comet in the sky. Her socks were droopy and her T-shirt was stained with mustard and ketchup, but her face was radiant.

'We had such fun!' she cried. 'I wish and I wish that you could've come, Barbara. We went on the roller coaster and the sailing ships and the airplane ride, and – oh, Barbara, wait'll you hear – I got to drive the train! We even went to the Burnt House Hotel and I visited Mrs Porter for a bit, but not all day because Dad fetched me back. We ate our lunch on the beach and after we went paddling in the sea but the water was *so* cold that we decided to go to the arcade instead.' She gulped for breath.

'I'm surprised you're still standing after a day packed like that.'

'I slept in the car,' Hadiyyah explained. 'Almost all the way home.' She thrust her arm forward and Barbara saw that she was carrying a small stuffed frog. 'See what Dad won me at the crane grab, Barbara? He's ever so good at the crane grab.'

'It's nice,' Barbara told her with a nod at the frog. 'Good to practise with while you're young.'

Hadiyyah frowned and inspected the toy. 'Practise with?'

'Right. Practise. Kissing.' Barbara smiled at the little girl's confusion. She put her hand on her tiny shoulder, ushered her to the table, and said, 'Never mind. It was a daft joke anyway. I'm sure dating will've improved enormously by the time you're ready to try it. So. What else have you got?'

What she had was a plastic bag whose handles were tied to one of the belt loops in her shorts. She said, 'This is for *you*. Dad won it as well. At the crane grab. He's ever so—'

'Good at the crane grab,' Barbara finished for her. 'Yeah. I know.'

'Because I already said.'

'But some things bear repeating,' Barbara told her. 'Hand it over, then. Let's see what it is.'

With some effort, Hadiyyah untangled the bag's handles and presented it to Barbara. She opened it to find inside a small plush red velvet heart. It was trimmed with white lace.

'Well. Gosh,' Barbara said. She set the heart on the dining table and felt her face growing hot.

'Isn't it lovely?' Hadiyyah gazed upon the heart with no little reverence. 'Dad won it at the crane grab, Barbara. Just like the frog. I said, "Get her a froggie, Dad, so she'll have one as well and they can be friends." But he said, "No. A frog won't do for our friend, little *khushi*." That's what he calls me.'

'*Khushi*. Yeah. I know.' Barbara felt a rapid pulse in her fingertips. She stared at the heart like the votary of a saint in the presence of relics.

'So he aimed for the heart instead. It took him three tries to get it. He could've got the elephant, I suppose, because *that* would've been a lot easier. Or he could've got the elephant *first* to get it out of the way and given it to me, except I already have an elephant, and I suppose he remembered that, didn't he? But anyway he wanted the heart. I expect he might've brought it to you himself, but I wanted to and he said that was all right as long as your lights were on and you were still up. *Was* it all right? You look a bit peculiar. But your lights were on. I saw you in the window. Should I not have given it to you, Barbara?'

Hadiyyah was watching her anxiously. Barbara smiled and put an arm round her shoulders. 'It's just so nice that I don't know what to say. Thanks. And thank your dad for me, won't you? Too bad expertise with the crane grab isn't a highly marketable skill.'

'He's ever so—'

'Good. Right. I've seen that first hand, if you recall.'

Hadiyyah recalled. She rubbed her stuffed frog against her

cheek. 'It's extra special to have a souvenir of a day at the sea, isn't it? Whenever we do something special together, Dad buys a souvenir for me, did you know? So I'll remember what a fine time we had. He says that's important. The remembering part. He says the remembering is just as important as the doing.'

'I wouldn't disagree.'

'Only, I wish you could've come. What did you *do* today?'

'Work, I'm afraid.' Barbara gestured at the table where her notebook lay. Next to it sat the mailing list and the catalogues from Quiver Me Timbers. 'I'm still at it.'

'Then I mustn't stay.' She retreated towards the door.

'It's okay,' Barbara said hastily. She realised how much she'd been longing for company. 'I didn't mean—'

'Dad said I could only visit for five minutes. He wanted me to go straight to bed but I asked if I could bring you your souvenir and he said, "Five minutes, *khushi*." That's what he—'

'Calls you. Right. I know.'

'He was ever so nice to take me to the sea, wasn't he, Barbara?'

'The nicest there is.'

'So I must listen when he says, "Five minutes, *khushi*." It's a way of saying thank you to him.'

'Ah. Okay. Then you'd better scoot.'

'But you *do* like the heart?'

'Better than anything in the world,' Barbara said.

Once the child had left, Barbara approached the table. She walked gingerly, as if the heart were a diffident creature who might be frightened away by sudden movement. With her eyes on the red velvet and the lace, she felt for her shoulder bag, rooted out her cigarettes, and set a match to one. She smoked moodily and she studied the heart.

A frog won't do for our friend, little khushi.

Never had nine words seemed so portentous.

Chapter Twenty-eight

Hanken treated the black leather jacket with something akin to reverence: He donned latex gloves before handling the carrier bag into which Lynley had deposited the garment, and when he laid the jacket onto one of the tables in the empty dining room of the Black Angel Hotel, he did it with the sort of ecclesiolatry that was generally reserved for religious services.

Lynley had phoned his colleague shortly after his futile interview with the Black Angel's employees. Hanken had taken the phone call at dinner and vowed he'd be in Tideswell within the half hour. He was as good as his word.

Now he bent over the leather jacket and examined the hole in the back of it. Fresh looking, he noted to Lynley, who stood across the table from him and watched the other DI scrutinise each millimetre of the perforation's circumference. Of course, they wouldn't know for certain until the jacket was placed under a microscope, Hanken continued, but the hole appeared recent because of the condition of the surrounding leather, and wasn't it going to be a treat if forensic came up with even a microscopic amount of cedar right on the edge of that hole?

'Once we have a match on that blood with Terry Cole's, any more cedar is academic, isn't it?' Lynley pointed out. 'We've got the sliver from the wound, after all.'

'We have,' Hanken said. 'But I like my cake with icing.' He bagged the jacket after examining its blood-soaked lining. 'This'll do to get us a warrant, Thomas. This'll do a flaming *treat* to get us a warrant.'

'It'll make things easier,' Lynley agreed. 'And the fact that he allows the manor to be used for tournaments and the like ought to be enough to allow us to—'

'Hang on. I'm not talking about a warrant to shovel through the Brittons' territory. This—' Hanken lifted the bag – 'gives us another nail to pound into *Maiden's* coffin.'

'I don't see how.' And then, when he saw that Hanken would expatiate on his reasons for seeking a warrant to search Maiden Hall, Lynley said quickly, 'Hear me out for a moment. Do you agree that a long bow's probably our third weapon?'

'When I compare that suggestion to the hole in this jacket, I do,' Hanken said. 'What're you getting at?'

'I'm getting at the fact that we already know a place where long bows have probably been used. Broughton Manor's been the site for tournaments, hasn't it? For reenactments and fêtes, from what you've told me. That being the case and Julian being the man who hoped to marry a woman who – as we know – betrayed him in Derbyshire *alone* with two other men, why would we want to search Maiden Hall?'

'Because the dead girl's dad was the man who threatened her in London,' Hanken countered. 'Because he was shouting that he'd see her dead before he'd let her do what she wanted to do. Because he took out a bloody *bank* loan to bribe her into living the way he wanted her to live, and she pocketed that money, played the game by his rules for three short months, and then said, "Right. Well, thanks a bundle for the loot. It's been great fun, Dad, but I'm off to London to squeeze blokes' bollocks for a living. Hope you understand." And he didn't. Understand, that is. What dad would?'

Lynley said, 'Peter, I know it looks bad for Andy . . .'

'Any way you play it, it looks bad for Andy.'

'But when I asked the hotel employees if any of them knew the Brittons, the answer was yes. Frankly, it was more than yes. It was "we know the Brittons by sight." Now why would that be?' Lynley didn't wait for Hanken to respond. 'Because they come here. Because they drink in the bar. Because they eat in the dining room. And it's easy enough for them to do that because Tideswell's practically on a direct route between Broughton Manor and Calder Moor. And you can't go charging off to search Maiden Hall without stopping to consider what all of that means.'

Hanken kept his gaze fixed on Lynley as he spoke. When Lynley had finished his polemic, he said, 'Come with me, lad,' and led his colleague to the reception counter of the hotel where he asked for a map of the White and Dark Peaks. He took Lynley through to the bar and opened this map on a table top in the corner.

Lynley wasn't mistaken, he acknowledged. Tideswell sat on the east edge of Calder Moor. A decent hiker with murder in mind could start out from the Black Angel Hotel, climb to the top of the town, and set off across the moor to Nine Sisters' Henge. It would take a few hours, considering the size of the moor, and it wouldn't be as efficient as simply following the route the girl herself had taken from the site just beyond the hamlet of Sparrowpit. But, it could be done. On the other hand, that same killer could arguably have accomplished everything by car: parking in the same spot where Nicola had left her Saab behind the stone wall and, after the killings, returning home by way not only of the Black Angel Hotel but also by way of the hamlet of Peak Forest near which he got rid of the knife.

'Exactly,' Lynley said. 'That's my point exactly. So you do see—'

But, Hanken argued, if his colleague would take a closer look at the map, he would see that the *same* short detour of less than two miles that their killer would have taken to drop the leather jacket at the Black Angel and then proceed homeward to the south towards Bakewell and Broughton Manor was the *identical* short detour of less than two miles that their killer would have taken to drop the leather jacket at the Black Angel and then proceed homeward to the *north* to Padley Gorge and Maiden Hall.

Lynley followed the two routes that Hanken indicated. He had to admit that the other DI had a point. He could see how their killer – having left the murder site, having driven through Peak Forest to dump the knife in the grit dispenser, having detoured briefly to Tideswell to place the jacket where it would hang unnoticed – could then have driven onwards to the junction that marked Wardlow Mires. From there, one road led towards Padley Gorge and the other towards Bakewell. And when means and opportunity aligned for two suspects in an investigation, the police were bound by everything from logic to ethics to look first at the stronger suspect. So a search of Maiden Hall was called for.

The event would be hell for Andy and his wife, but Lynley had to conclude that it was unavoidable. Still, a remnant of the old loyalty towards Andy prompted him to ask Hanken for a single assurance. The Maidens wouldn't be told, of course, what it was that the police were looking for in their search of Maiden Hall. It stood to reason, therefore, that there was no need to make any further discussion of Nicola's London life part of that inspection.

'You're only postponing the inevitable, Thomas. Unless Nan Maiden's dead before we make an arrest and go to trial, she's eventually going to know the worst about the girl. Even – and I don't believe this, but let's say it for the moment – even if Dad didn't chop her. If Britton did the business on her . . .' Hanken made an aimless gesture with his hand.

The worst will still out, Lynley finished silently. He knew that. But if he couldn't save his former colleague from the humiliation of a formal search of his home and his business, at least he could spare him for the moment the added grief of having to be witness to the suffering of the only person left in his world.

'We'll set it for tomorrow,' Hanken said, folding the map and taking up the bag with its incriminating contents. 'I'll take this to the lab. You get some sleep.'

It was hardly a directive he'd be able to comply with, Lynley thought.

Although she wasn't involved in the investigation and thus had less cause than her husband for turmoil, in London, Lynley's wife also slept fitfully and awakened in a thoughtful mood on the following morning. Sleeping fitfully was an anomaly for Helen. Generally, she sank into something resembling unconsciousness shortly after her head touched her pillow, and she remained in that condition until morning. Thus, Helen found the fact of having slept poorly a sure indication that something was vexing her, and she didn't have to excavate very far into her psyche to uncover what that something was.

Tommy's reactions to and dealings with Barbara Havers had been, for the last few days, like a very small splinter festering beneath the surface of Helen's skin: something that she didn't necessarily have to confront in her normal routine, but something that was both troubling and painful when brought to her awareness. And brought to her awareness it had been – in neon lights, actually – during her husband's final confrontation with Barbara.

Helen understood Tommy's position: He'd given Barbara a series of directives, and Barbara had been less than cooperative in carrying them out. Tommy had seen this as an acid test which his former partner had failed; Barbara had seen this as an unfair punishment. Neither of them wished to acknowledge the other's point of view, and Barbara was the one who stood upon the less solid ground when it came to arguing her perspective. So Helen found no difficulty in admitting that

Tommy's ultimate reaction to Barbara's defiance of his orders was justified, and she knew his superior officers would agree with the action he'd taken.

But that same action, when viewed in conjunction with his earlier decision to work with Winston Nkata and not Barbara Havers, was what bothered Helen. What, she wondered as she rose from her bed and donned her dressing gown, was really at the heart of her husband's animus towards Barbara: the fact that she had defied him or the fact that she was a *woman* who'd defied him? Of course, Helen had asked him a variation on this very question prior to his departure on the previous day, and unsurprisingly he'd hotly denied the fact that gender had anything to do with his reaction. But didn't Tommy's entire history give the lie to any denial he might make? Helen wondered.

She washed her face, ran a brush through her hair, and thought about the question. Tommy had a past that was littered with women: women he'd wanted, women he'd had, women with whom he'd worked. His very first lover had been a school friend's mother with whom he'd carried on a tumultuous affair for more than a year, and, prior to his relationship with Helen, his most passionate attachment of the heart had been to the woman who was now the wife of his closest friend. Aside from that latter connection, all Tommy's associations with women had one characteristic in common as far as Helen could see: It was Tommy who directed the course of the action. The women cooperatively went along for the ride.

This exercise of command was simple for him to gain and maintain. Myriad women over the years had been so taken by his looks, his title, or his wealth that giving over to him not only their bodies but also their minds had seemed of little consequence in comparison with what they hoped they'd be getting in return. And Tommy had become used to this power. What human being wouldn't?

The real question was why he'd grasped the power that

very first time with that very first woman. He'd been young, it was true, but although he could have chosen to meet that lover and every lover that followed her on a playing field that he himself made level despite the woman's reluctance or inability to insist upon that levelling, he had not done so. And Helen was certain that the *why* of Tommy's sway over women was behind his difficulties with Barbara Havers.

But Barbara was *wrong*, Helen could hear her husband insisting, and there's no damn way you can twist the facts to make them read that she was right.

Helen couldn't disagree with Tommy on that. But she wanted to tell him that Barbara Havers was only a symptom. The disease, she was certain, was something else.

She left the bedroom and descended to the dining room, where Denton had assembled the breakfast she preferred. She helped herself to eggs and mushrooms, poured a glass of juice and a cup of coffee, and set everything on the dining table, where her morning's copy of the *Daily Mail* lay next to her cutlery and Tommy's *Times* lay just beneath it. She flipped through the morning post idly as she added milk and sugar to her coffee. She set the bills to one side – no reason to spoil her breakfast, she thought – and she also set aside the *Daily Mail* upon whose front page the latest decidedly unattractive royal paramour was being acclaimed as looking 'radiant at the annual Children in Need tea'. No reason, Helen thought grimly, to spoil her entire *day* as well.

She was just opening a letter from her oldest sister – its postmark from Positano telling her that Daphne had prevailed over her husband in terms of where to spend their twentieth wedding anniversary – when Denton came into the room. 'Good morning, Charlie,' Helen said to him cheerfully. 'You've excelled with the mushrooms today.'

Denton didn't return her greeting with similar enthusiasm.

He said, 'Lady Helen . . .' and hesitated – or so it seemed to Helen – somewhere between confusion and chagrin.

'I hope you're not going to scold me about that wallpaper, Charlie. I phoned Peter Jones and asked for another day. Truly, I did.'

Denton said, 'No. It's not the wallpaper,' and he lifted the manila envelope he was holding, bringing it level with his chest.

Helen set down her toast. 'What is it, then? You look so . . .' How *did* he actually look? she asked herself. He looked quite agitated, she concluded. She said, 'Has something happened? You've not received bad news, have you? Your family's well, aren't they? Oh Lord, Charlie, have you got yourself into trouble with a woman?'

He shook his head. Helen saw that a duster hung over his arm, and the pieces fell into place: He'd been doing a spot of cleaning up, she realised, and no doubt he wished to lecture her on the messier of her habits. Poor man. He couldn't decide how best to begin.

He'd come from the direction of the drawing room, and Helen recalled that she hadn't picked up those sheets of music that Barbara had left upon her abrupt departure on the previous afternoon. Denton wouldn't like that, Helen thought. He was so like Tommy in his neatness.

'You've caught me out,' she confessed, with a nod at the envelope. 'Barbara brought that yesterday for Tommy to look at. I'm afraid I forgot all about it, Charlie. Will you believe me if I promise to do better next time? Hmm, I suppose not. I'm promising that constantly, aren't I?'

'Where did you get this, Lady Helen? This . . . I mean, this . . . ?' And Denton gestured with the envelope as if he had no words to describe what it contained.

'I've just told you. Barbara Havers brought it. Why? Is it important?'

As an answer Charlie Denton did the unexpected. For

the first time since Helen had known the man, he drew a chair out from beneath the dining table and, completely unbidden, he sat.

'The blood matches,' was Hanken's terse announcement to Lynley. He was phoning from Buxton, where he'd just got the word from the forensic lab. 'The jacket's the boy's.'

Hanken went on to tell him that they were moments away from getting a warrant to search Maiden Hall. 'I've six blokes who can find diamonds in dog shit. If he's stashed the long bow there, we'll find it.' Hanken went on to grouse about the fact that Andy Maiden had had more than enough time since the night of the murders to rid himself of the bow in three dozen locations round the White Peaks, which made their job of finding it doubly difficult. But at least he didn't know they'd twigged that an arrow was the missing weapon, which gave them the advantage of surprise if he hadn't rid himself of the rest of his equipment.

'We don't have the slightest indication that Andy Maiden's an archer,' Lynley pointed out.

'How many parts did he play undercover?' was Hanken's riposte. He rang off with, 'You're in if you want to be. Meet us at the Hall in ninety minutes.'

Heavy of heart, Lynley hung up the phone. Hanken was right in his pursuit of Andy. When virtually every piece of information that was gathered led to one particular suspect, you proceeded with that suspect. You didn't ignore what was in front of you because you didn't care to see it. You didn't avoid thinking the unthinkable because you couldn't disengage your mind from the past and a memory of your twenty-fifth year and an undercover operation that you had so longed to be a part of. You did what you had to do as a professional.

Yet even though Lynley knew that DI Hanken was following procedures as they were meant to be followed in his search of Maiden Hall, he still found himself thrashing round in the quagmire of evidence, facts, and conjectures, seeking something that would vindicate Andy. It was, he stubbornly continued to believe, the least he could do.

There appeared to be only one usable fact: that Nicola's waterproof had been missing from among her belongings at Nine Sisters' Henge. Alone in his room with the morning sounds of the hotel rising round him, Lynley considered that item and what its absence from the murder scene meant.

They'd originally thought that the killer had taken the waterproof and worn it to cover his blood-stained clothes. But if he had called in at the Black Angel Hotel on Tuesday after the murder, he would hardly have done so wearing a waterproof on a fine summer's night. He wouldn't have been willing to run the risk of standing out, and there wasn't much that would have been more conspicuous than a man walking round in rain gear in the midst of Derbyshire's long spell of perfect weather.

To make certain, however, Lynley rang down to the Black Angel's proprietor. A single question – shouted round the ground floor from one employee to another – was sufficient for Lynley to be assured that nothing like that had been played out at the hotel on any night in recent memory. What, then, had become of the waterproof?

Lynley began to pace the room. He reflected on the moor, the murders, and the weapons, and he dwelt upon the mental image he'd constructed of how the crimes had been carried out.

If the killer had taken the garment from the scene but had not *worn* it from the scene, there seemed to be only two possibilities for its use to him: either the waterproof had been fashioned into some sort of carrier for transporting something from the henge when the killer left or the waterproof had been used in some way by the killer during the commission of the crime.

Lynley dismissed the first prospect as unlikely. He went on to the second possibility. When he lined up all he knew about the killings, what he'd assumed about the killings, and what he'd discovered at the Black Angel Hotel, he finally saw the answer.

The killer had incapacitated the boy with an arrow. He'd then gone after the fleeing girl and dispatched her without much trouble. Returning to the henge, he'd seen that the boy's wound was serious but not mortal. He'd cast about for a quick way of doing him in. He could have stood the boy up – firing squad fashion – and made of him a modern St Sebastian, but the boy would hardly have cooperated in that plan. So the killer had torn through the equipment at the site and found the knife and the waterproof. He'd put on the latter to protect his clothes while he was knifing the boy. Thus he could enter the Black Angel Hotel with impunity later.

A blood-stained waterproof couldn't be left hanging with the black leather jacket, however. The blood on the jacket had soaked into its lining, where it was camouflaged by the material's colour. So the jacket might have taken months to be noticed. But a blood-stained poncho would not be so easily overlooked.

Yet the killer *had* to get rid of it. And sooner, rather than later. So where . . . ?

Lynley continued to pace as he pictured that night, the killings, and their aftermath.

The knife had been left along the killer's escape route. It was easy enough to bury in a few inches of grit in a roadside container, a process that would probably have taken no more than thirty seconds. But the poncho couldn't be buried there because there wasn't enough grit to do the job and, besides that, on a public road even at night it would have been sheer idiocy to stop for the length of time it would have taken to bury something so bulky in a roadside container.

Yet something very *like* a roadside container would have

worked well as a depository for a garment, something that had an everyday use, something that one saw without thinking about, and something on the way to the hotel where – the killer knew – a black leather jacket could be stowed in plain sight with no one the wiser for ages . . .

A pillar box? Lynley wondered. But he dismissed the possibility almost as soon as he considered it. Aside from the fact that the killer wouldn't have wanted to go to the effort of cramming the waterproof inch by inch into the slot for letters, the post was collected every day.

Someone's rubbish bin? But there again he encountered virtually the same problem. Unless the killer managed to bury it at the bottom of someone's dustbin, the first time the bin's owner wished to empty a bag of rubbish, the waterproof would be found. Unless, of course, the killer managed to find a bin that was constructed in such a way that rubbish already within it couldn't be seen when someone deposited more. A bin in a public park might have worked for this, one where refuse was shoved through an opening in the cover or the side. But where on the route from Calder Moor to Tideswell did such a park with such a container exist? That's what he needed to find out.

Lynley descended the stairs and got from reception the same map of the Peaks that Hanken had used on the previous evening. Upon examining the area, the closest Lynley could come to a public park was a nature reserve near Hargatewall. He frowned when he saw how far off the direct route it was. It would have taken the killer a number of miles out of his way. But it was worth a try.

The morning outside was much like the previous day: grey, windy, and rainy. But unlike the previous day when Lynley had arrived, the Black Angel's car park was virtually deserted since it was far too early for even the most inebriated of the hotel's regular patrons to be bellying up to the bar. So with his umbrella raised and the collar of his waxed jacket turned up, Lynley dodged puddles and hurried round the side of the building to the only spot that he'd been able to find for the Bentley on the previous afternoon.

Which was when he finally saw what he'd seen without acknowledging upon his arrival.

The spot he'd found for the Bentley had been vacant yesterday because it would always be the last spot chosen to park one's car. No one with half a care for his car's paint job would park it right next to an overloaded skip that was even now, in the wind and the rain, erupting with refuse.

Of *course*, Lynley thought as the grinding of gears behind him spoke of a lorry's approach.

As it was, he made it to the rubbish-filled skip just a stride ahead of the local dustmen who'd arrived to pick up the Black Angel's week's worth of garbage.

Samantha heard the noise before she saw her uncle. The sound of bottles clinking together echoed on the old stone stairway as Jeremy Britton descended to the kitchen where Samantha was doing the washing up from breakfast. She glanced at her watch, which she'd set on a shelf near the kitchen's deep sink. Even by Uncle Jeremy's standards, it seemed too early in the day to be drinking.

She scoured the frying-pan in which she'd cooked the morning's bacon, and she tried to ignore her uncle's presence. Footsteps shuffled behind her. The bottles continued to clank. When she could no longer avoid doing so, Samantha glanced round to see what her uncle was doing.

Jeremy had a large basket crooked over his arm. Into this he'd deposited perhaps a dozen bottles of spirits. They were mostly gin. He began going through the dole cupboards that they used for storage in the kitchen, rustling through their contents to pull out more bottles. These were miniatures, and he took them from the flour bin, from the containers of rice and spaghetti and dried beans, from among the assorted tins of fruit, from deep within the storage space for pots and pans. As the collection grew in the basket on his arm, Uncle Jeremy clanked and rattled round the kitchen like the Ghost of Christmas Past.

He murmured, 'Going to do it this time.'

Samantha put the final pot on the drying rack and pulled the plug on the water in the sink. She dried her hands on the front of her apron and watched. Her uncle looked older than he had done since she'd been in Derbyshire. And the tremors that were jerking his body didn't help the overall impression he gave of serious illness in the offing.

She said, 'Uncle Jeremy? Are you ill? What's wrong?'

'Coming off it,' he replied. 'It's the bloody devil. Gives you sweet temptation, then sends you to hell.'

He'd begun to perspire and in the kitchen's meagre light, his skin looked like a lemon coated with oil. With hands that didn't want to do what he commanded, he eased the loaded basket onto the draining board. He clutched at the first of the bottles. Bombay Sapphire, his one true love. He unscrewed the top and upended the bottle into the sink. The smell of gin rose up like leaking gas.

When the bottle was empty, Jeremy broke it against the lip of the sink. 'No more,' he said. 'Through with this poison. I swear. No *more*.'

Then he began to cry. He cried with dry hard sobs that shook his body worse than the absence of alcohol in his veins. He said, 'I can't do it alone.'

Samantha's heart went out to him. 'Oh, Uncle Jeremy. Here. Let me help. Here. I'll hold the basket, shall I? Or shall I open the bottles for you?' She took one out – Beefeaters this time – and offered it to her uncle.

'It'll kill me,' he cried. ''S what it's doing already. Look at me. Just look.' And he held up his hands to show her what she'd already seen: their terrible shaking. He grabbed the Beefeaters and broke the bottle against the lip of the sink without emptying it first. Gin splashed on both of them. He grabbed another. 'Rotten,' he wept. 'Drove three of 'em off but that wasn't enough. No. No. He'll not be content till the last one's gone.'

Samantha sorted through this. His wife and the Britton children, she decided. Julian's sister, brother, and mother had fled the manor ages ago, but she couldn't believe that Julian would ever desert his father. She said 'Julian loves you, Uncle Jeremy. He won't leave you. He wants the best for you. You must see that's why he's been working so hard to bring the manor back,' as Jeremy dumped another half litre of gin into the sink.

'He's a wonderful boy. Always was. And I won't, I won't, I won't. No longer.' And another bottle's contents joined the others. ''S working so hard to make this place something, and all the while his sot of a dad's drinking everything away. But no more. No more.'

The kitchen sink was rapidly filling with glass, but that didn't matter to Samantha. She could see that her uncle was in the throes of a conversion so important that one or two kilos of broken glass were of small account in comparison. She said, 'Are you giving up drinking, Uncle Jeremy? Are you seriously giving up drinking?' She had her doubts about his sincerity, yet bottle after bottle went the way of the first. When Jeremy was finished with the lot of them, he leaned over the sink and began to pray with an earnestness that Samantha could feel in her bones.

He swore on the lives of his children and his future grandchildren that he would not take another drop of drink. He would not, he said, be an advertisement for the evils of life-long inebriation. He would walk away from the bottle here and now and he would *never* look back. He owed that much, if not to himself, then to the son whose love had kept him here in the rotting family home when he could have gone elsewhere and lived a decent, wholesome, normal life.

'Hadn't been for me, he'd be married now. Wife. Kids. A life. An' I took that from him. I did it. *Me*.'

'Uncle Jeremy, you mustn't think that. Julie loves you. He knows how important Broughton Manor is to you at the end of the day, and he wants to make it a home again. And anyway, he's not even thirty yet. He's got years and years to have a family.'

'Life's passing him by,' Jeremy said. 'An' it'll go right by him while he struggles at home. An' he'll hate me for that when he wakes up and sees it.'

'But this *is* life.' Samantha placed a comforting hand on her uncle's shoulder. 'What we're doing here, at the manor, everyday. This is life, Uncle Jeremy.'

He straightened from the sink, reaching in his pocket as he did so, bringing out a neatly folded handkerchief and honking into it before he turned to her. Poor man, she thought. When had he last wept? And why were men so embarrassed when they finally broke with the force of a reasonable emotion?

'I want to be part of it again,' he said.

'Part of it?'

'Life. I want life, Sammy. This—' He made a gesture towards the sink. – 'This is a denial of everything living. I say enough.'

Odd, Samantha thought. He suddenly sounded so strong, as if nothing stood between him and his hope of sobriety. And just as suddenly she wanted that for him: the life he imagined for himself, happy in his home, occupied and surrounded by his darling grandchildren. She could even see them, those lovely grandchildren still unconceived. She said, 'I'm so glad, Uncle Jeremy. I'm so terribly terribly *glad*. And Julian . . . Julie'll be so delighted. He'll want to help you. I know he will.'

Jeremy nodded, his gaze fixed on her. 'You think so?' he said hesitantly. 'After all these years . . . with me . . . like this?'

'I know he'll help,' she said. 'I just know it.'

Jeremy straightened his clothes. He blew his nose noisily once again and folded his handkerchief back into his pocket. He said, 'Y' love him, don't you, girl?'

Samantha shuffled her feet.

'You're not like the other. You'd do anything for him.'

'I would,' Samantha said. 'Yes, I would.'

When Lynley arrived in Padley Gorge, the search of Maiden Hall was in full swing. Hanken had brought six constables with him, and he'd deployed them economically as well as thoroughly. Three of them were searching the family's floor, the residents' floor, and the ground floor of the Hall proper. One was searching the outbuildings on the property. Two others were searching the grounds. Hanken himself was coordinating the effort, and when Lynley pulled to a stop in the car park he found his fellow DI smoking moodily beneath an umbrella near a panda car as the family-floor constable made his report.

'Get out with the others on the grounds, then,' Hanken was instructing him. 'If there're any signs of digging round here, I want you lot on it like hounds down a foxhole. Understand? And don't ignore where Maiden planted that new road sign.' The constable trotted off in the direction of the slope that fell away towards the road. There, Lynley could see two other policemen pacing along evenly beneath the trees in the rain.

'Nothing so far,' Hanken told Lynley. 'But it's here somewhere. Or something related to it is. And we'll find it.'

'I've got the waterproof,' Lynley said.

Hanken raised an eyebrow and tossed his cigarette onto the ground. 'Have you indeed? That's good work, Thomas. Where'd you find it?'

Lynley told him about the thought process that had led him to the skip. Under a week's worth of rubbish from the hotel, he'd found the rain gear by relying upon a pitchfork

Elizabeth George

and the patience of the dustmen who'd arrived just behind him to collect the skip's contents.

'You don't look much like you've been doing skip-sifting,' Hanken told him.

'I showered and changed,' Lynley admitted.

The rubbish in the skip – piled up on the waterproof for nearly a week – had ultimately protected it from the rain, which might otherwise have washed away any evidence left upon it. As it was, the plastic garment hadn't been touched by anything other than coffee grounds, vegetable peelings, plate scrapings, old newspapers, and crumpled tissues. And since it had been turned inside out anyway, even these had only smeared its insides, giving it the appearance of a discarded tarpaulin. Its exterior had been largely untouched, so the blood splatters on it remained as they had been on the previous Tuesday night: mute witnesses to what had occurred inside Nine Sisters' Henge. Lynley had bundled the waterproof into a supermarket carrier bag. It was, he said, in the boot of the Bentley.

'Let's have it, then.'

'First,' Lynley said with a nod at the Hall, 'are the Maidens here?'

'We don't need an i.d. on the waterproof if it's got the kid's blood on it, Thomas.'

'I wasn't asking professionally. How are they taking the search?'

'Maiden claims he's found some bloke in London who can do a lie detector on him. Runs a business called Polygraph Professionals, or something like that.'

'If he's willing—'

'Bollocks,' Hanken cut in irritably. 'You know that polygraphs are worth sod all. So does Maiden. But they make one hell of a delaying tactic, don't they? "Please don't arrest me. I've got a polygraph organised." Bugger that for a lark. Let's have the waterproof.'

Lynley handed it over. It was turned inside out, as it had

been upon his discovery of it. But one of its edges was exposed, where the blood made a purple deposit in the shape of a leaf.

'Ah,' Hanken said when he saw it. 'Yes. We'll get this over to forensic, then. But I'd say it's all over bar the shouting.'

Lynley didn't feel so certain. But why, he wondered. Was it because he couldn't believe Andy Maiden had killed his own daughter? Or was it because the facts truly led elsewhere? 'It looks deserted,' he said with a nod at the Hall.

'Due to the rain,' Hanken told him. 'They're inside, though. The lot of them. Most of the guests're gone, it being Monday. But the Maidens are here. As are the employees. Except for the chef. He generally doesn't show up till after two, they said.'

'Have you spoken to them? The Maidens?'

Hanken appeared to read the underlying meaning because he said, 'I haven't told the wife, Thomas,' and then transferred the bag to the front seat of the panda car. 'Fryer!' he shouted in the direction of the slope. The family-floor constable looked up, then came at a trot when Hanken gestured him over. 'The lab,' he said with a jerk of his head towards the car. 'Drive that bag over for a work-up on the blood. See if you can get the job done by a girl called Kubowsky. She doesn't let grass grow, and we're in a hurry.'

The constable looked happy enough to be out of the rain. He removed his lime-coloured windcheater and hopped into the car. In less than ten seconds he was gone.

'We're just going through the motions,' Hanken said. 'The blood's the boy's.'

'Doubtless,' Lynley agreed. Still, he looked towards the Hall. 'D'you mind if I have a word with Andy?'

Hanken eyed him. 'Can't accept it, can you?'

'I can't get away from the fact that he's a cop.'

'He's a human being. Governed by the same passions as the rest of us,' Hanken said. Mercifully, Lynley thought, he didn't add the rest: Andy Maiden was better than most people at doing something about those passions. Instead, Hanken said, 'Mind you remember that,' and strode off in the direction of the outbuildings.

Lynley found Andy and his wife in the lounge, in the same alcove where he and Hanken had first spoken to them. They weren't together this time, however. Rather they sat, silent, on the opposing sofas. They were in identical positions: leaning forward with their arms resting just above their knees. Andy was rubbing his hands together. His wife was watching him.

Lynley wiped from his mind the Shakespearean image that was invoked by Andy's attention to his hands. He said his former colleague's name. Andy looked up.

'What're they looking for?' he asked.

Lynley didn't miss the pronoun or its implication of a distinction between himself and the local police.

He said, 'How are you both doing?'

'How do you expect we're doing? It's not enough that Nicola's been taken from us. But now you come and tear apart our home and our business without having the *decency* to tell us why. Just waving a filthy piece of paper from a magistrate and barging inside like a group of hooligans with—' Nan Maiden's anger threatened to give way to tears. She clenched her hands in her lap and, in a movement not unlike her husband's, she beat them together as if this would allow her to maintain a poise she'd already lost.

Maiden said, 'Tommy?'

Lynley gave him what he could. 'We've found her water-proof.'

'Where?'

'There's blood on it. The boy's most likely. We assume the killer wore it to protect his clothes. There may be other evidence on it. He'd have pulled it on over his hair.'

'Are you asking me for a sample?'

'You might want to arrange for a solicitor.'

'You can't think he did this!' Nan Maiden cried. 'He was

here. Why in God's name won't you believe me when I say he was here?'

'Do you think I need a solicitor?' Maiden asked Lynley. And both of them knew what he was really asking: *How well do you know me, Thomas?* And: *Do you believe I am as I appear to be?*

Lynley couldn't reply in the way Maiden wanted. Instead he said, 'Why did you ask for me specifically? When you phoned the Yard, why did you ask for me?'

'Because of your strengths,' Maiden replied. 'Among which was always honour first. I knew that I could depend on that. You'd do the right thing. And, if it came down to it, you'd keep your word.'

They exchanged a long look. Lynley knew its meaning. But he couldn't risk being made a fool of. He said, 'We're approaching the end, Andy. Keeping my word or not isn't going to make a difference then. A solicitor's called for.'

'I don't need one.'

'Of course you don't need one,' his wife agreed quietly. 'You've done nothing. You don't need a solicitor when you've nothing to hide.'

Andy's gaze dropped back to his hands. He went back to massaging them. Lynley left the lounge.

For the next hour, the search of Maiden Hall and its environs continued. But at the end of it, the five remaining constables had come up with nothing that resembled a long bow, the remains of a long bow, or any item related to archery. Hanken stood in the rain with the wind whipping his mac round his legs. He smoked and brooded, studying Maiden Hall as if its limestone exterior were hiding the bow in plain sight. His search team waited for further instructions, their shoulders hunched, their hair flattened against their skulls and their eyelashes spiked by the rain. Lynley felt vindicated by Hanken's lack of success. If the other DI was going to suggest that Andy Maiden as their killer had removed every last bit of archery-related evidence from his home – without knowing they'd connected one of the two killings to archery in the first place – he was prepared to do battle on that front. No killer thought of everything. Even if that killer was a cop, he was going to make a mistake and that mistake would hang him eventually.

Lynley said, 'Let's go on to Broughton Manor, Peter. We've got the team, and it won't take long to get a second warrant.'

Hanken roused himself. He said, 'Get back to the station,' to his men. And then to Lynley when the constables had departed, 'I want that report from SO10. The one your man in London put together.'

'You can't still be thinking that this is a revenge killing. At least not one connected with Andy's past.'

'I don't think that,' Hanken said. 'But our boy-with-a-past might have used that past in a way we've not considered yet.'

'How?'

'To find someone willing to do a nasty spot of work for him. Come along, Inspector. I've a mind to have a look through the records at your Black Angel Hotel.'

Chapter Twenty-nine

Although they'd been thorough, the police had also been moderately gentle in their treatment of the Maidens' personal belongings and the Hall's furnishings. Andy Maiden had seen far worse searches in his time, and he tried to take comfort from the fact that his brother policemen hadn't decimated his dwelling in their search. Still, the Hall had to be put back into order again. When the police had left, Andy, his wife, and their staff each took a separate section to straighten.

Andy was relieved that Nan had agreed to this reasonable plan of action. It kept her away from him for a while. He hated himself for wanting to be away from her. He knew she needed him, but with the departure of the police, Andy found himself desperate for solitude. He had to think. He knew he wouldn't be able to do so with Nan hanging over him, displacing her grief by locking her mind on the fruitless endeavour of caring for him. He didn't want his wife's care right now. Things had gone too far for that.

The wheel of Nicola's death was coming closer and closer to breaking them both, Andy realised. He could protect Nan from it while the investigation was on-going, but he didn't know how he could continue to do so once the police made an arrest. That they were getting closer to doing just that had been made only too evident by his brief conversation with

Lynley. And in Tommy's suggestion that Andy ask for his solicitor's help, there was fair indication of exactly what the detectives' next move would be.

Tommy was a good man, Andy thought. But there was only so much you could ask of a good man. When that good man's limit was reached, you had to place your confidence in yourself.

This was a principle that his daughter had seen. Blended with her insatiable desire to be gratified – *now* – whenever she had an inclination towards something, her reliance on herself before others had led her down her chosen path.

Andy had long known that his daughter's ambition in life was, simply expressed, never to go without. She'd seen the economies her parents had employed both to save towards the purchase of a country home and to channel funds to Andy's father whose pension didn't cover his profligate ways. And more than once, especially when met with her parents' refusal to accede to one of her demands, she'd announced that *she* would never find herself in a position of having to scrimp and save and deny herself life's simple pleasures, eschewing them for such barren activities as repairing sheets and pillowcases, turning collars on shirts, and darning socks. 'You'd better not end up like Granddad, Dad,' she'd said to Andy on more than one occasion. ''Cause I plan to spend all my money on me.'

Yet it really wasn't avarice that dominated her behaviour. Rather it seemed to be a profound vacuity at the heart of her that she sought to fill with material possessions. How often he'd tried to explain to her mankind's essential dilemma: We are born of parents and into families so we have connections, but we're ultimately alone. Our primitive sense of isolation creates a void within us. That void can be filled only through the nurturing of spirit. 'Yes, but I *want* that motorbike,' she'd respond as if he hadn't just attempted to explain to her why the acquisition of a motorbike would not soothe a spirit whose singular needs were restless for acknowledgment. Or that guitar, she'd reply. Or that set of gold earrings, that trip to Spain, that flashy car. 'And if there's money enough to buy it, I don't see why we shouldn't. What's spirit got to do with whether one has the money to buy a motorbike, Dad? Even if I wanted to, I can't spend money on my spirit, can I? So what am I supposed to do with money if I've ever got it? Throw it away?' And she'd list those individuals whose achievements or position garnered them vast reserves of cash: the royal family, erstwhile rock stars, business magnates, and entrepreneurs. 'They've got houses and cars and boats and planes, Dad,' she would say. 'And they're never alone, either. And they don't look like they've got some big hollow in the pit of their stomachs, if you ask me.' Nicola was a persuasive supplicant when she wanted something, and nothing he could say was sufficient to make her see that she was merely observing the exterior lives of these people whose possessions she so admired. Who they were inside – and what they felt – was something that no one but them could know. And when she acquired what she had begged to possess, she wasn't able to see that it satisfied her only briefly. Her vision was occluded from this knowledge because what stood in the way was always the desire for the next object that she believed would soothe her soul.

And all of this – which would have made any child difficult to rear – was combined with Nicola's natural propensity for living life on the edge. She'd learned that from him, from watching him shift from persona to persona over the years of undercover work and from listening to the tales told by his colleagues over family dinners when they'd all drunk too much wine. Andy and his wife had kept from their daughter the other side of those acts of bravado that so regaled her: She never knew the personal price her father paid as his health crumbled beneath his mind's inability to divide itself into separate arenas serving who he was and who his work forced him to pretend to be. She was supposed to see her dad as strong, complete, and indomitable. Anything else would shake her foundations, they assumed.

Thus, Nicola had thought nothing of it when it came to telling him the truth about her future plans. She'd phoned and asked him if he would come to London. 'Let's have a chick-and-Dad date,' she'd said. Delighted to think that his beautiful daughter would want to spend special time with him, he'd gone to London. They'd have their date – whatever she wanted to do, he told her – and he'd cart some of her belongings back to Derbyshire for her summer's employment. It was when he'd looked round her neat bedsit and rubbed his hands together and asked what she wanted him to load into the Land Rover that she told him the truth.

She began with, 'I've changed my mind about working for Will. I've had another think about law as well. That's what I wanted to talk to you about, Dad. Although,' with a smile and God how lovely she was when she smiled, 'our date was wonderful. I've never been to the Planetarium before.'

She made them tea, sat him down with a plate of sandwiches that she took from a Marks & Spencers container, and said, 'Did you ever get into the bondage scene when you were undercover, Dad?'

He'd thought at first that they were making polite conversation: an ageing father's reminiscences prompted by his daughter's fond questions. He hadn't done much in S & M, he told her. That would have been handled by another division at the Yard. Oh, he'd had to go into the S & M clubs and shops a few times, and there was that party where an idiotic bloke dressed as a schoolgirl was being whipped on a cross. But that had been the extent of it. And thank God for that because there were some things in life that left one feeling too filthy for a simple bath to cure, and sadomasochism was at the top of his list.

'It's just a lifestyle, Dad,' Nicola told him, reaching for a ham sandwich and chewing it thoughtfully. 'After all you've seen, I'm surprised you'd condemn it.'

'It's a sickness,' he said to his daughter. 'Those people have problems they're afraid to face. Perversion looks like the answer while all the while it's only part of what ails them.'

'So you *think*,' Nicola reminded him gently. 'The reality could be something different, though, couldn't it? An aberration to you might be perfectly normal to someone else. In fact, you might be the aberration in their eyes.'

He supposed this was the case, he admitted. But wasn't normality determined by the numbers? Wasn't that what the word *norm* meant in the first place? Wasn't the norm decided by what the most people did?

'That would make cannibalism normal, Dad, among cannibals.'

'Among cannibals, I suppose it is.'

'And if a group among the cannibals decides it doesn't like eating human flesh, are they abnormal? Or can we say they have tastes that might have undergone a change? And if someone from our society goes out and joins the cannibals and discovers he has a taste for human flesh that he wasn't aware he had, is he abnormal? And to whom?'

Andy had smiled at that. He'd said, 'You're going to make a very fine lawyer.'

And that comment had led them to hell.

'As to that, Dad,' she'd begun, 'as to the law . . .'

She'd started with her decision not to work for Will Upman, to remain for the summer in London instead. He'd thought at first that she meant she'd found a placement more to her liking with a firm in town. Perhaps, he'd thought hopefully, she's got herself established at one of the Inns of Court. That wasn't where he dreamed she'd end up, but he wasn't blind to the compliment such a position paid to his daughter. He'd said, 'I'm disappointed, of course. Your mum will be as well. But we always looked at Will as a fallback if nothing better turned up. What has?'

She told him. He thought at first that she was joking,

although Nicola had never been a child to joke when it came to what she wanted to do. In fact, she'd always stated her intentions exactly as she stated them that day in Islington: Here's the plan, here's why, here's the intended result.

'I thought you ought to know,' she'd concluded. 'You have a right since you were paying for law college. And I'll pay you back for that, by the way.' Again, that smile, that sweet and infuriating Nicola smile which had always partnered whatever she announced as a fait accompli. *I'm running away,* she'd tell her parents when they'd refused an unreasonable request. *I won't be here after school today. In fact, I'm not going to school at all. Don't expect me for dinner. Or for breakfast tomorrow. I'm running away.* 'I should have the money to pay you before the end of summer. I would have had it already but we had to buy supplies and they cost quite a lot. Would you like to see them, by the way?'

He'd continued to believe it was some sort of joke. Even when she'd brought out her equipment and explained the use of each obscene item: the leather whips, the braces studded with small chrome nails, the masks and manacles, the shackles and collars. 'You see, Dad, some people just can't get it off unless there's pain or humiliation involved,' she told her father, as if he hadn't spent years exposed to just about every kind of human aberration. 'They want the sex – well, that's natural, isn't it? I mean don't we all want it? – but unless it's connected to something degrading or painful, they either don't get satisfaction from it or they can't even do it in the first place. And then there are others who seem to feel the need to atone for something. It's like they've committed a sin, and if they take their medicine like they're supposed to – six of the best to naughty little boys and all that – they're happy, they're forgiven, and they get on with their business. They go home to the wife and kiddies, and they feel, well, they feel . . . I suppose it sounds awfully odd to say it, but they seem to feel refreshed.' She appeared to read something on her father's face, then, that creased her own because she reached across the table at which they sat and earnestly covered Andy's clenched fist with her hand. 'Dad, I'm always the dom. You *do* know that, don't you? I wouldn't ever let someone do to me what I do to . . .' Well, I'm just not interested. I do it because the money's fabulous, it's just beyond belief, and while I'm young and nice looking and strong enough to do eight or nine sessions a day . . .' She smiled an impish smile, as she reached for the final object to show him. 'The pony tail's the most ridiculous, actually. You can't imagine how silly a seventy-year-old bloke looks when he's got this thing hanging out of his . . . well, you know.'

'Say it,' he'd said to her, finding his voice at last.

She'd looked at him blankly, the black plastic plug with its black leather streamers dangling from her lovely slender hand. 'What?'

'The word. Hanging from his what? If you can't say it, how can you do it?'

'Oh. *That.* Well, I only don't say it because you're my dad.'

And that admission had shattered something within him, some last vestige of control and an outdated restraint born of lifelong repression. 'Arsehole,' he'd shouted. 'It hangs from his God damn arsehole, Nick.' and he swept from the dining table all the devices of torture that she'd assembled for him to see.

Nicola realised – finally – that she'd pushed him too far. She backed away from him as he let his rage, incomprehension, and despair take whatever form they chose. He upended furniture, broke crockery, and ripped her legal books from their bindings. He'd seen the fear in her, and he'd thought of the times that he could have inspired it in the past and had chosen not to. And that enraged him further until the roaring destruction he visited upon her bed-sit reduced his daughter to a cowering heap of the silk, suede and linen that comprised her clothing. She huddled in the corner with her arms over her head, and that wasn't enough for him. He hurled her filthy equipment at her and bellowed, 'I'll see you dead before I let you do it!'

It was only later, when he had time to think in the way that Nicola thought, that he realised there was another route to dissuading his daughter from her newly chosen vocation. There was the route of Will Upman and the possibility that he would do to her what he had the reputation for doing to so many other women. So he'd phoned her two days after his London visit and he'd offered her the deal. And Nicola, seeing that she could make more money in Derbyshire than in London, was willing to compromise.

He'd bought time, he thought. And they didn't discuss what had occurred between them that day in Islington.

For Nancy's sake, Andy spent the summer trying to pretend that everything would work out well in the end. Should Nick return to the College of Law in the autumn, in fact, he'd be willing to go to his death acting as if Islington had never happened at all.

'Don't tell your mother any of this,' he'd said to his daughter when they made their arrangements.

'But, Dad, Mummy—'

'*No.* God *damn* it, Nick, I'm not going to argue. I want your word to keep silent about all of this when you come home. Is that perfectly clear? Because if one whisper reaches your mother, you'll not have a penny from me, and I mean it. So give me your word.'

She did. And if there was any saving grace in the ugliness of Nick's life and the horror of her death, it was that Nancy had been spared the knowledge of what that life had become.

But now that knowledge threatened to bring further destruction into Andy's world. He'd lost his daughter to degradation and defilement. He wasn't about to lose his wife to the anguish and grief of learning about it.

He saw that there was only one way to stop the wheel of Nicola's death in the midst of its cycle of destruction. He knew he had the means to stop it. He could only pray that, at the last moment, he would also have the will.

What did it matter that yet another life would pay the forfeit? Men had died for less if the cause was good. So had women.

By Monday midmorning Barbara Havers had increased her knowledge of archery by several degrees. In the future, she'd be able to discuss with the best of them the merits of mylar instead of feathers for fletchings or the differences among long, compound, and recurve bows. But as to getting any closer to pinning the William Tell award on Matthew King-Ryder's jacket . . . she'd not had a breath of luck in that.

She'd been through Jason Harley's mailing list. She'd even tracked down by telephone every name from the list with a London address, to see if King-Ryder was using a pseudonym. But after three hours, she was nowhere with the list, and the catalogue – while improving her backlog of trivia for those moments at lah-de-dah drinks parties when one racked one's brain for something to add to the conversation – had gained her nothing. So when her phone rang and it was Helen Lynley on the line, inviting her to Belgravia, Barbara was happy to accept the invitation. Helen was nothing if not scrupulous about her mealtimes, and it was drawing towards lunch with nothing in the fridge but more reheatables in the *rogan josh* line. Barbara knew she could do with a change.

She arrived at Eaton Terrace within the hour. Helen herself answered the door. She was, as usual, perfectly turned out in neat tan trousers and a forest green shirt. Seeing her, Barbara felt like a lump of mouldy cheese on the doorstep. Since she'd called in ill to the Yard, she'd dressed with even less care than was her norm. She wore an oversize grey T-shirt over black leggings and she was sockless in her red high-top trainers.

'Don't mind me. I'm travelling incognito,' she said to Lynley's wife.

Helen smiled. 'Thanks for coming so quickly. I would have come to you, but I thought you might want to be in this part of town when we've finished.'

Finished? Barbara thought. Wonderful news. Then lunch *was* in the offing.

Helen beckoned Barbara inside, calling out, 'Charlie? Barbara is here. Have you had lunch, Barbara?'

'Well. No,' Barbara said, and she added, 'I mean not exactly,' because brutal honesty strong-armed her into admitting that having toast with Chicken Tonight creamy garlic sauce on it for her elevenses might be considered an early lunch in some quarters.

'I've got to go out – Pen's coming up from Cambridge sans children this afternoon and we've promised ourselves a meal in Chelsea – but Charlie can do you a sandwich or a salad if you're feeling light-headed.'

'I'll survive,' Barbara told her, although even to herself she sounded doubtful.

She followed Helen into the house's well-appointed drawing room where she saw that the breakfront cabinet which housed Lynley's stereo system was standing open. All of its various components were lit, and a CD's jacket lay splayed on the tuner. Helen beckoned Barbara to sit, and she took the same place she'd taken on the previous afternoon before Lynley had thrown her off the case.

She said, 'I take it the Inspector made it back to Derbyshire in one piece?' as a conversational opener.

Helen said, 'I'm awfully sorry about the row between you two. Tommy is . . . well, Tommy's just Tommy.'

'That's one way of putting it,' Barbara admitted. 'The mould was smashed after he was poured into it, that's for sure.'

'We have something we'd like you to listen to,' Helen said.

'You and the Inspector?'

'Tommy? No. He knows nothing about this.' Helen seemed to read something on Barbara's face because she hastened to add, rather obscurely, 'It's just that we weren't certain how best to interpret what we had. So I said, "Let's phone Barbara, shall we?"'

'We,' Barbara said.

'Charlie and I. Ah. Here he is. Play it for Barbara, will you please, Charlie?'

Denton greeted Barbara and passed to her what he carried into the room: a tray on which sat a plate displaying a succulent-looking breast of chicken nestled in an arrangement of tri-coloured pasta. A glass of white wine and a roll accompanied this. A linen napkin cocooned cutlery in an artistic fashion. 'Thought you might be able to do with a bite,' he told her. 'I hope you like basil.'

'I consider it the answer to a young girl's prayer.'

Denton grinned. Barbara tucked in as he went to the cabinet. Helen joined Barbara on the sofa as Denton fiddled with buttons and dials, saying, 'Have a listen to this.'

Barbara did so, munching Denton's excellent chicken and, as an orchestra began something heavy on the woodwinds, she thought that there were certainly worse ways to spend an afternoon.

A baritone began singing. Barbara caught some, but not all, of the words:

. . . to live, to live, to live onward or die
the question lingers in the mind till mankind questions why
to die, to die, to end the aching heart
to never more be shocked and scored as flesh accepts its part
in what it is to be a man, vows made in haste, afraid
why not take death into my breast, eternal sleep within
my grave
to sleep, that sleep, the terrors waiting there
what dreams may come to men asleep who think without a
care
that they've escaped the whips, the scorns that time brings
those

who live
That sleep allows a peace to grow within a man who can't
forgive . . .

'It's nice,' Barbara said to Denton and Helen. 'It's terrific in
fact. I've never heard it.'

'Here's why.' Helen handed over the very same manila
envelope that Barbara herself had brought to Eaton Terrace.

When she slid the stack of papers out, Barbara saw that
they were the hand-scored music Mrs Baden had given her.
She said, 'I don't get it.'

'Look.' Helen directed Barbara's attention to the first of the
sheets. In very short order, Barbara found herself following
along with what the baritone was singing. She read the song's
title at the top of the page 'What Dreams May Come,' and she
took in the fact that the song had been written in his own hand
with his very own signature scrawled across the top: Michael
Chandler.

Her first reaction was a plummeting of her spirits. She said,
'Damn,' as her theory of the motive behind the Derbyshire
murders was shot straight to hell. 'So the music's already been
produced. That puts a serious screw in my thinking.' For there
was certainly no point in Matthew King-Ryder's rubbing out
Terry Cole and Nicola Maiden – not to mention beating up
Vi Nevin – if the music he was purportedly after had already
been produced. He couldn't mount a brand new production
with old music. He could only mount a revival. And that
was nothing worth killing over since the profits of a revival
of anything by Chandler and King-Ryder would be governed
by the terms of his father's will.

She started to toss the music onto the coffee table, but Helen
laid a hand on her arm. 'Wait,' she said. 'I don't think you
understand. Charlie? Show her.'

Denton handed over two items: One was the jacket of the CD
that was playing; the other was a souvenir theatre programme
of the type that generally set one back rather considerably in

the lolly department. *Hamlet* was emblazoned on both the CD and the programme. And on the CD were the additional words: *Lyrics and Music by David King-Ryder*. Barbara stared at this latter announcement for a number of seconds as she came to terms with everything it meant. And its meaning boiled down to a single lovely fact: She finally had Matthew King-Ryder's real motive for murder.

Hanken was adamant. He wanted the Black Angel Hotel's records and he wasn't going to be pleasant to be around until he got them. Lynley could accompany him on the expedition or he could tackle Broughton Manor by himself, which Hanken didn't advise since he'd done nothing to get a warrant to search Broughton Manor and he didn't think the Brittons would take to their collective bosom anyone sifting through the muck and dross of a few hundred years of their family history.

'It's going to take a team of twenty to go through that place,' Hanken said. 'If we have to, we'll do it. But I'll put money on it we won't have to.'

They had the hotel records in their possession in extremely short order. While Lynley phoned London to track down Nkata for a fax of Havers' SO10 findings, Hanken took the hotel's registration cards through to the bar where pork with apple sauce was on offer for lunch. When Lynley joined him with the fax of Havers' report, the other DI was dipping into the day's speciality with one hand and going through the registration cards with the other. A second plate – steaming with a similar meal – was set opposite him, a pint of lager next to it.

'Thanks,' Lynley said, handing over the report.

'Always go with the speciality of the day,' Hanken advised him and nodded at the paperwork Lynley was holding. 'What've we got?'

Lynley didn't think they had anything, but he remembered three names that he had to admit, even beyond his own prejudices in the matter, bore looking into. One of them was a former snout of Maiden's. Two others were secondary shadowy figures who'd operated at the periphery of Maiden's investigations but never served time at their monarch's pleasure. Ben Venables was the snout. Clifford Thompson and Gar Brick were the others.

On their way back to the Black Angel, Hanken had perfected a new theory. Maiden, he said, had far too much nous to be such a fool as to kill his own daughter personally, no matter how much he wanted her dead. He'd have hired the job out to one of the blighters from his past, and he'd have then misdirected the police by telling them it was a vengeance killing to keep them focused on the louts either in prison or on parole while all the others who'd rubbed elbows with Maiden but had no reason to revenge themselves upon him would escape police notice. It was a clever ploy. So Hanken wanted that SO10 report to see if any names on it matched up with anyone who'd registered at the hotel.

'You see how it could happen, don't you?' Hanken asked Lynley. 'All Maiden would need to do after hiring this bloke would be to put him in the picture where the girl was camping.'

Lynley wanted to argue, but he didn't. Andy Maiden, of all people, would understand how risky it was to arrange a contract killing. That he might have done so to rid himself of a child whose lifestyle he found intolerable was an unthinkable proposition. If the man had wanted to eliminate Nicola because he couldn't force her to change her ways, he wouldn't have looked for someone else to do the job, especially someone who might break easily under interrogation and point the finger back at him. No. If Andy Maiden had wanted to eliminate his daughter, Lynley knew, he would have done so himself. And they had sod all as evidence to suggest that he'd done it.

Lynley picked at his food as Hanken read the report. The other DI wolfed down his own meal. He finished the report and the meal simultaneously and said, 'Venables, Thompson, and Brick,' in an impressive show of reaching the same conclusion as Lynley himself had drawn. 'But I say we check them all against the records.'

Which was what they did. They took the records for the previous week and checked the names of all the hotel's residents during that time against the names that were in Havers' report. As the report covered more than twenty years of Andy Maiden's police experience, the project took some time. But the end of their endeavour left them in the same position as they'd been in in the beginning. No names matched.

It was Lynley who pointed out that someone coming to kill Nicola Maiden would hardly have registered in a local hotel and used his own name. Hanken saw the reason in this. But rather than use it to dismiss altogether the idea of a hired killer who'd stayed at the hotel and left the jacket and waterproof behind, he said obscurely, 'Of course. Let's get on to Buxton.'

But what about Broughton Manor? Lynley wanted to know. Were they going to let that slide in favour of . . . what? A chase for someone who might not exist?

'The killer exists, Thomas,' Hanken replied as he stood. 'And I've an idea we'll track him down through Buxton.'

Barbara looked at Helen and said, 'But why'd you phone me? Why not the inspector?'

Helen said, 'Thank you, Charlie. Will you see about getting those wallpaper books back to Peter Jones? I've made my choice. It's marked.'

Denton nodded, saying, 'Will do,' and took himself up the stairs after switching off the stereo and removing his CD.

'Thank God Charlie loves West End extravaganzas,' Helen said when she and Barbara were alone. 'The more I get to know him, the more invaluable I find he's becoming. And who would have thought that might be the case, because when Tommy and I married, I wondered how I'd feel having my husband's valet – or whatever Charlie Denton actually is, – lurking about like a nineteenth century retainer. But he's indispensable. As you've just seen.'

'Why, Helen?' Barbara asked, not put off by the other woman's light remarks.

Helen's face softened. 'I love him,' she said. 'But he's not always right. No one is.'

'He won't like your having shared this with me.'

'Yes. Well. I'll deal with that as it comes.' Helen gestured to the music. 'What do you make of it?'

'In light of the murder?' And when Helen nodded, Barbara considered all the possible answers. David King-Ryder, she recalled, had killed himself on the opening night of his production of *Hamlet*. From his son's own words, she'd heard that King-Ryder had to have known that very same evening that the show was a smashing success. Nonetheless, he'd killed himself, and when Barbara blended this fact not only with the real authorship of the music and lyrics but also with the story that Vi Nevin had told her about how the music had come to be in Terry Cole's hands, she could arrive at only one conclusion: Someone out there had known that David King-Ryder had not written either the music or the lyrics to the show he was mounting under his own name. That person had known because that same person had somehow got his hands on the original score. And considering that the phone call intercepted by Terry Cole in Elvaston Place had been made in June when *Hamlet* debuted, it seemed reasonable to conclude that that phone call had been intended not for Matthew King-Ryder – hot to produce a show that would not be governed by the terms of his father's will – but for David King-Ryder himself, who was desperate to get that music back and to hide from the world the simple fact that it wasn't his work.

Why else would King-Ryder have killed himself unless he'd

arrived at the phone box just five minutes too late to receive that call? Why else would he have killed himself unless he believed that – despite having paid off a blackmailer who was supposed to phone him with directions where to 'pick up the package' – he was going to be blackmailed *ad infinitum*? Or, worse yet, he was going to be exposed to the very tabloids who'd slagged him off for years? Of *course*, he'd kill himself, Barbara thought. He'd have had no way of knowing that Terry Cole received the phone call intended for him. He'd have had no way of knowing how to make contact with the blackmailer to see what had gone wrong. So once that phone call hadn't come through in that phone box on Elvaston Place when he managed to get there, he'd have thought he was cooked.

The only question was: Who had blackmailed David King-Ryder? And there was only one answer that was remotely reasonable: his own son. There was evidence for this, if only circumstantial. Surely, Matthew King-Ryder had known before his father's suicide that he stood to get nothing when David King-Ryder died. If he was to head the King-Ryder fund – and he'd admitted as much when Barbara spoke to him – he would have had to be told about the terms of his father's will. So the sole way he had to get his hands on some of his father's money was to extort it from him.

Barbara explained all this to Helen, and when she was finished, Lynley's wife asked, 'But have you any evidence? Because without evidence . . .' Her expression said the rest, You're done for, my friend.

Barbara tossed the question round in her head as she finished her lunch. And she found the answer in a brief review of her visit to King-Ryder in his Baker Street flat.

'The house,' she said to Lynley's wife. 'Helen, he was moving house. He said he'd finally got the money together to buy himself a property south of the river.'

'But south of the river . . . ? That's not exactly . . .' Helen looked distinctly uncomfortable, and Barbara liked her for her reluctance to draw attention to Lynley's considerable wealth. One would need brass by the bucketful to buy even a cupboard in Belgravia. On the other hand, south of the river – where the lesser mortals bought their homes – would not present such a problem. King-Ryder could have saved enough to buy a freehold there. Barbara accepted that.

Nonetheless she said, 'There's no other explanation for what King-Ryder's been up to: lying about what happened when Terry Cole went to his office, searching Terry's flat in Battersea, buying one of Cilla Thompson's monstrosities, going to Vi Nevin's digs and trashing them. He's got to get his hands on that music, and he's willing to do anything. His dad's dead, and he's to blame. He doesn't want the poor bloke's memory shot to bits as well. He wanted some of his lolly, sure. But he didn't want him destroyed.'

Helen considered this, smoothing her fingers along the crease in her trousers. 'I see how you're fitting it together,' she admitted. 'But as to proof that he's even a blackmailer, let alone a killer ... ?' She looked up and opened her hands as if to say, *Where is it?*

Barbara thought about what she had on King-Ryder besides what she knew about the terms of his father's will: Terry had been to see him; he had searched Terry's flat; he'd gone to the studio on Portslade Road ... 'The cheque,' she said. 'He wrote Cilla Thompson a cheque when he bought one of her nightmare-in-the railway-arches paintings.'

'All right,' Helen said cautiously. 'But where does that take you?'

'To Jersey,' Barbara said with a smile. 'Cilla made a copy of the cheque – probably because she's never sold a thing in her life and, believe me, she's going to want to remember the occasion since it's never likely to happen again. That cheque was drawn on a bank in St Helier. Now why would our boy be banking in the Channel Islands unless he had money to hide, Helen? Like a major deposit of a few thousand quid –

maybe a few hundred thousand quid bled out of his dad to keep a blackmailer's mug plugged – that he didn't want anyone asking questions about? There's your evidence.'

'But still it's all supposition, isn't it? How can you prove anything? You can't get into those bank records, can you? So where do you go from here?'

That was certainly a problem, Barbara thought. She could prove nothing.

There was that footprint in the muck in Vi Nevin's flat, of course, that shoe sole with its hexagonal markings. But if such a shoe sole proved to be as common as toast on the breakfast table, what did that add to the investigation? Of course, King-Ryder would have left trace evidence all over Vi Nevin's flat. But he wasn't likely to cooperate if the coppers asked him for a few strands of hair or a vial of blood for a DNA match-up. And even if he gave them everything from his toe jam to his dental floss, that did nothing to pin him to the Derbyshire murders unless the rozzers had a packet of trace evidence left at the scene up there as well.

Barbara knew she'd be more than just off the case and demoted if she phoned up DI Lynley for a little confab about the Derbyshire evidence. She'd defied his orders; she'd gone her own way. He'd thrown her off the investigation. What he'd do if he discovered she'd put herself back *on* the investigation did not bear thinking of. So to bring King-Ryder down she had to go it more or less alone. There was only the small point of trying to figure out how to do it.

'He's been clever as the dickens,' Barbara said to Helen, '– this bloke's no slouch in the brains department – but if I can come up with a way to get a step ahead of him . . . If I can use something that I know from everything I've gathered . . .'

'You've got the music,' Helen pointed out. 'Which is what he's wanted from the first, isn't it?'

'He sure as bloody hell searched high and low for it. He tore apart that camping site. He went through the flat in Battersea.

He ripped up Vi's maisonette. He spent enough time in the studio with Cilla to suss out whether there was a hiding place there. I'd say we're safe in assuming he's after that music. And he knows it wasn't with Terry, Cilla, or Vi.'

'But he also knows it's somewhere.'

True, Barbara thought. But where and with whom? Who was it that King-Ryder didn't know, who would convince the man that the music had switched hands more than once and that he – King-Ryder – would have to come forward to get that music? And how the bloody hell could the act of just coming forward for some music – which he could deny knowing about once he saw it – also serve as the act that betrayed him as a killer?

Bloody hell, Barbara thought. It felt as if her brain were undergoing nuclear meltdown. What she needed was to talk to another professional. What she needed was a flaming good confab with someone who could not only see all the tentacles of this octopus crime but could also step forward, offer the solution, be part of the solution, and defend himself against King-Ryder should everything go to hell in an instant.

Inspector Lynley was the obvious choice. But he was out of the question. So she needed someone like him. She needed his clone.

Barbara caught herself up and smiled. 'Of course,' she said.

Helen raised an eyebrow. 'You've got an idea?'

'I've got a bloody inspiration.'

It wasn't until one o'clock that Nan Maiden realised her husband was missing. She'd been occupied with putting the ground floor of Maiden Hall back in order – as well as with supervising the straightening of each of the guest rooms – and she'd been making such an effort to act as if unexpected police searches were part of the normal routine that she hadn't noticed when Andy disappeared.

When he wasn't in the house, she first assumed he was in

the grounds. But when she asked one of the kitchen boys to take a message out to Mr Maiden offering him lunch, the boy told her that Andy had gone off in the Land Rover not half an hour before.

'Oh. I see,' Nan said, and she tried to look as if this were perfectly reasonable behaviour under the circumstances. She even tried to tell herself as much: because it was inconceivable that Andy would have gone off without a word to her after what they both had been through.

She'd said, 'A search?' to DI Hanken's unmoving face. 'But a search for what? We've got nothing . . . we're hiding nothing . . . You'll find nothing . . .'

'Love,' Andy had said. He'd asked to see the search warrant and, once he'd seen it, he'd handed it back. 'Go on, then,' he told Hanken.

Nan wouldn't consider what they were looking for. She wouldn't consider what their presence meant. When they left empty-handed, she felt such relief that her legs wobbled and she had to sit down quickly or risk crumpling to the floor.

Her easing of nerves at the failure of the police to find what they were looking for quickly gave way to anxiety, however, when she learned that Andy was gone. Hanging over their heads was his declared willingness to find someone in the country who would give him a polygraph.

That's where he's gone, Nan decided. He's found someone to give him that bloody test. This search of the Hall pushed him to it. He means to have the test and prove himself to everyone by having it witnessed by someone from the investigation.

She had to stop him. She had to make him see that he was playing into their hands. They'd come with a warrant to search the premises knowing that such an action would unnerve him, and it had done so. It had unnerved them both.

Nan tore at her fingernails anxiously. Had she not felt momentarily faint, she could have *gone* to him, she told herself. They could have talked. She could have drawn him to her and soothed his sore conscience and . . . No. She would not think of that. Not of conscience. Never of conscience. She would only think of what she could do to turn the tide of her husband's intentions.

She realised that there was a single possibility. She couldn't risk using the phone in reception, so she went upstairs to the family floor to use the phone by their bed. She had the receiver in her hand, ready to punch in the number, when she saw the folded piece of paper on her pillow.

The message from her husband comprised one sentence. Nan Maiden read it and dropped the phone.

She didn't know where to go. She didn't know what to do. She ran from the bedroom. She clattered down the stairs with Andy's note clutched in her hand and so many voices inside her head shouting for action that she couldn't make out one coherent word that would tell her what step to take first.

She wanted to grab each person she saw: on the residents' floor, in the lounge, in the kitchen, at work on the grounds. She wanted to shake them all. She wanted to shout Where is he help me what is he doing where has he gone what does it mean that he's . . . oh God don't tell me because I know I know I know what it means and I've always known and I don't want to hear it to face it to feel it to somehow come to terms with what he's . . . no no no . . . help me find him *help* me.

She found herself running across the car park before she knew she'd even gone there, and then she understood that her body had taken control of a mind that had ceased to function. Even as she realised what she was meant to do, she saw that the Land Rover wasn't there. He'd taken it himself. He'd intended to leave her powerless.

She wouldn't accept that. She spun and tore back into the hotel, where the first person she saw was one of her two Grindleford women – and why on earth had she always thought of them as the Grindleford women as if they had no names of their own? – and she accosted her.

Nan knew she looked deranged. She certainly felt deranged. But that couldn't matter.

She said, 'Your car. Please,' which was as much as she could manage because she found that her breathing was erratic.

The woman blinked. 'Mrs Maiden? Are you ill?'

'The *keys*. Your car. It's Andy.'

Blessedly, that was message enough. Within moments, Nan was behind the wheel of a Morris so old that its driver's seat consisted of a thin layer of stuffing covering springs.

She revved the engine and took off down the incline. Her only thought was to find him. Where he'd gone and why he'd gone there was something she would not begin to dwell upon.

Barbara found that it was no mean feat convincing Winston Nkata to get involved. It had been one thing for him to invite her into the investigation when she had been just another DC waiting for an assignment while he himself trekked off to Derbyshire with Lynley. It was quite another for *her* to ask *him* to join her in a part of that same investigation once she'd been drop-kicked out of it. Her suggested little bout of hounds-chasing-the-fox wasn't authorised by their superior officer. So when she spoke to Nkata, she felt a little like Mr Christian, while her fellow DC didn't sound much like a man who wanted to take a cruise on the *Bounty*.

He said, 'No way, Barb. This's dodgy as hell.'

She said, 'Winnie. It's a single phone call. And this's your lunch hour anyway, isn't it? Or it could be your lunch hour, couldn't it? You've got to eat. So just meet me there. We'll have a meal in the neighbourhood. We'll have anything you'd like. My treat. I promise.'

'But the guv—'

Elizabeth George

'—won't even have to know if it comes to nothing,' Barbara finished for him and then she added, 'Winnie, I need you.'

He hesitated. Barbara held her breath. Winston Nkata wasn't a man who rushed in with fools, so she gave him the time to think about her request from every possible angle. And while he did his thinking, she prayed. If Nkata didn't enter into her plan, she had no idea who else might be willing to.

He finally said, 'Guv asked for a fax of your report from CRIS, Barb.'

'See?' she replied. 'He's still barking up that bloody stupid tree and there's nothing in the branches. It's *nowhere*, Winnie. Come on. Please. You're my only hope. This is it. I *know* it. All I need from you is a single little phone call.'

She heard him sigh the sole word *damn*. Then, 'Give me a half hour,' he said.

'Brilliant,' she said and began to ring off.

'Barb.' He caught her. 'Don't make me regret this.'

She took off to South Kensington. After cruising up and down every street from Exhibition Road to Palace Gate, she finally found a place to park in Queen's Gate Gardens and walked over to the corner of Elvaston Place and Petersham Mews, which was where the only phone boxes on Elvaston Place were located. There were two of them, and they were hung with at least three dozen of the sort of advertising postcards that Barbara had found beneath Terry Cole's bed.

Nkata, having to travel the greater distance from Westminster, had not yet arrived, so Barbara took herself across Gloucester Road to a French bakery she'd spied on one of her circum-navigations of the neighbourhood in search of a parking space. Even from the street and inside her car, she'd smelled the siren fragrance of chocolate croissants. With time to kill in the wait for Winston, she decided there was no point to ignoring her body's desperate cry for the two basic food groups she'd so far denied herself that day: butter and sugar.

Twenty minutes after her own arrival in the South Kensington neighbourhood, Barbara saw Winston Nkata's lanky body coming up the street from the direction of Cromwell Road. She shoved the rest of her croissant into her mouth, wiped her fingers on her T-shirt, threw down the remains of a Coke, and dashed across the street just as he reached the corner.

'Thanks for coming,' she said.

'If you're solid on this bloke, why don't we just nick him?' Nkata asked, adding, 'You've got chocolate on your chin, Barb,' with the nonchalance of a man who'd long ago become familiar with the worst of her vices.

She used her T-shirt to take care of the problem. 'You know the dance. What've we got for evidence?'

'Guv's found that leather jacket, for one.' Nkata gave her the details on Lynley's discovery at the Black Angel Hotel.

Barbara was glad enough to hear them, especially since they supported her conjecture that an arrow had been one of their killer's weapons. But Nkata had been the one to pass along the arrow information to Lynley, and Barbara knew that if he were now to phone the inspector another time and say, 'By the way, Guv, why don't we haul in this bloke King-Ryder and get his dabs while we grill him about leather jackets and trips to Derbyshire,' Lynley was going to see the name *Havers* written all over the suggestion, and he'd order Nkata to back off so far that he'd be in Calais before he stopped.

Nkata wasn't a bloke to defy anyone's orders for love or money. And he certainly wouldn't undergo a sudden person-ality change for Barbara's benefit. So they had to keep Lynley out of it at all costs, until the birdcage was built and King-Ryder was sitting inside it singing.

Barbara explained all of that to Nkata. The other DC listened, without comment. At the end, he nodded. But he said, 'I still hate to go at it with him not knowing.'

'I know you do, Winnie. But I don't see how he's given us any other choice. Do you?'

Nkata had to admit not. He said, with a nod to the call boxes, 'Which one do I use, then?'

Barbara said, 'It doesn't matter for the moment, so long as we keep both of them vacant once you've made the call. But I'd go for the one on the left. It's got a brilliant card for Tantalising Transvestites in case you're looking for excitement some evening.'

Nkata rolled his eyes. He went into the booth, fished for some coins, and made the call. Over his shoulder, Barbara listened to his side of the conversation. He did West Indian Yobbo from south of the river. Since that was the voice of his first twenty years of life, it was a stellar performance.

The script was simplicity itself once he got Matthew King-Ryder on the phone: 'I think I got a package you want, Mistah King-Ryder,' Nkata said and listened for a moment. 'Oh, I 'xpect you know which package I mean . . . Albert Hall ring any special bells? Hey, no way, mon. You need the proof? You know the phone box. You know the number. You want the music? You make the call.'

He rang off and looked at Barbara. 'Bait's on the hook.'

'Let's hope for a bite.' Barbara lit a cigarette and walked the few feet to Petersham Mews where she leaned against the wing of a dusty Volvo and counted fifteen seconds before pacing back to the call box then once again to the car. King-Ryder would have to think before he acted. He would have to assess the risks and the payoffs of picking up the phone in Soho and betraying himself. This would take some minutes. He was anxious, he was desperate, he was capable of murder. But he wasn't a fool.

More seconds ticked by. They turned into minutes. Nkata said, 'He's not going for it.'

Barbara waved him off. She looked away from the phone boxes, up Elvaston Place in the direction of Queen's Gate. Despite her own disquiet, she found that she could still picture how it had happened on that night three months ago: Terry

Cole roaring up the street on his motorcycle, hopping off to Blu Tack a fresh batch of postcards into the two phone boxes which were doubtless part of his regular route. It takes him a few minutes; he has a number of cards. As he's sticking them up, the telephone rings and, on a whim, he picks it up to hear the message intended for David King-Ryder. He thinks, Why not see what that's all about? and he goes to do so. Less than half a mile on his Triumph, and he's in front of the Albert Hall. In the meantime, David King-Ryder arrives, five minutes too late, perhaps even less. He parks in the mews, he strides to the phone, he begins his wait. A quarter of an hour passes. Perhaps more. But nothing happens, and he doesn't know why. He doesn't know about Terry Cole. Eventually, he thinks he's been had. He believes he's ruined. His career – and his life – are fodder for a blackmailer who wants to destroy him. They are, in short, history.

One single minute late would be all that it took. And how easy it was to be late in London when so much depended upon the traffic. There was never really a way to know whether a drive from Point A to Point B would take fifteen minutes or forty-five. And perhaps King-Ryder hadn't been trying to get from A to B in town at all. Perhaps he'd been coming in from the countryside, on the motorway where anything could happen to throw a spanner into one's plans. Or perhaps he'd had car trouble, a dead battery, a flat tyre. What did the precise circumstance matter? The only fact that counted was that he'd missed the call. The call made by his son. The call not so different from the one which Barbara and Nkata were waiting for now.

Nkata said, 'It's dead in the water.'

Barbara said, 'God *damn* it.'

And the telephone rang.

Barbara threw her cigarette smouldering into the street. She leaped towards the phone box. It wasn't the same box from which Nkata had made the call in the first place, but the box standing next to it. Which could, Barbara thought, mean nothing or everything since they'd never known which of the two had been the one where Terry Cole had intercepted the call.

Nkata lifted the receiver on the third ring. He said, 'Mistah King-Ryder?' as Barbara held her breath.

Yes, yes, yes, she thought when Nkata gave her a thumb's up. At last they were in business.

'God damn bloody computers! What's the point of having them if they break down daily? You tell me that, damn you.'

WPC Peggy Hammer had apparently heard this demand from her superior officer many times before. 'It's not actually broken, sir,' she said with admirable patience. 'It's just like the other day. We're off line for some reason. I expect the problem's somewhere in Swansea. Or I suppose it could be in London, if it comes down to it. Then there's always our own—'

'I'm not asking for your analysis, Hammer,' Hanken snapped. 'I'm asking for some action.'

They'd brought into the Buxton incident room the stack of registration cards from the Black Angel Hotel with what had seemed like simple instructions which would allow them to gather information in a matter of minutes: Get on line to the DVLA in Swansea. Feed in the numbers on the plates of each car whose driver had stayed at the Black Angel Hotel within the last two weeks. Get the name of the legal owner of that car. Match that name to the registrant on the hotel card. Purpose: to see if anyone had checked into the hotel using a false name. Corroboration for that possibility: one name on the registration card, a different name in the DVLA's system indicating ownership of the vehicle. It was a simple task. It would take a few minutes because the computers were fast and the registration cards – considering the size of the hotel and the number of rooms it had – were not innumerable. It would have been fifteen minutes of labour, maximum. If the sodding system had worked for bloody once.

Lynley could see all of this reasoning going on in DI Hanken's mind. And he felt his own share of frustration. The source of his agitation was different, however: He couldn't loosen Hanken's mind from the lock it had on Andy Maiden.

Lynley understood Hanken's reasoning. Andy had motive and opportunity. Whether he also had the slightest idea how to use a long bow made no difference, if someone who had checked into the Black Angel Hotel under a false name possessed that ability. And until they discovered whether any false identities had been used in Tideswell, Lynley knew that Hanken wasn't about to move on to another area of enquiry.

That logical area was Julian Britton. That logical area had *always* been Britton. Unlike Andy Maiden, Britton had everything they were looking for in their killer. He had loved Nicola enough to want to marry her, and on his own admission, he'd visited her in London. How likely was it that he'd never come across something that had clued him in to her real life? Beyond that, how likely was it that he'd never had the slightest idea he wasn't her only Derbyshire lover?

So Julian Britton had motive in spades. He also had no solid alibi for the murder night. And as for being able to shoot a long bow, he'd doubtless seen long bows aplenty at Broughton Manor during tournaments, reenactments, and the like. How much of a stretch was it to posit that Julian knew how to use one?

A search of Broughton Manor would tell that tale. Julian's fingerprints – matched to whatever prints forensic managed to pull off the leather jacket – would put a full stop to the piece. But Hanken wasn't about to budge in that direction unless the Black Angel's records proved a dead end. No matter that Julian could have planted that jacket at the Black Angel. No matter that he could have thrown that waterproof into the skip. No matter that doing this would have taken him five minutes off the direct route from Calder Moor to his home. Hanken would deal exhaustively with Andy Maiden and until he had done, Julian Britton might as well not exist.

When he was faced with the computer misfiring, Hanken soundly cursed modern technology. He tossed the registration cards at WPC Hammer and ordered her onto that antique means of communication: the telephone. 'Ring Swansea and tell them to do it by hand if they bloody have to,' he snapped.

To which Peggy Hammer said, 'Sir,' in meek compliance.

They left the incident room. Hanken was fuming that all they could 'bloody well do now' was wait for WPC Hammer and the DVLA to come up with the information they needed and Lynley was wondering how best he could turn the spotlight onto Julian Britton when a departmental secretary tracked them down to tell them that Lynley was being asked for in the reception area.

'It's Mrs Maiden,' she said. 'And I ought to warn you she's in something of a state.'

She was. Ushered into Hanken's office a few minutes later, she was panic personified. She was clutching a crumpled piece of paper in her hand and when she saw Lynley, she cried out, 'Help me!' And to Hanken, 'You *forced* him! You wouldn't leave it. You *couldn't* leave it. You didn't want to see that he'd eventually do something ... He'd do ... He'd *do* ... Something ...' And she brought her fist with the crumpled paper in it up to her forehead.

'Mrs Maiden,' Lynley began.

'You *worked* with him. You were his friend. You know him. You knew him. You must do something because if you don't ... if you can't ... Please, *please.*'

'What the hell's going on?' Hanken demanded. He had, obviously, little enough sympathy for the wife of his number one suspect.

Lynley went to Nan Maiden and took her hand in his own.

He lowered her arm and gently removed the note from her fingers. She said, 'I was looking . . . I went out looking . . . But I don't know where and I'm so afraid.'

Lynley read the words and felt a chill of apprehension.

I'm taking care of this myself Andy Maiden had written.

Julian had just finished weighing Cass's puppies when his cousin came into the room. She'd evidently been looking for him because she said happily, 'Julie! Of course. How silly of me. I should have thought of the dogs at once.'

He was using the aniseed oil on Cass's teats, readying her puppies for the twenty-four hour test of their sense of smell. As harriers, they had to be excellent trackers.

Cass growled uneasily when Samantha entered. But she soon settled when Julian's cousin adjusted her voice to the soothing tone that the dogs were more used to.

Sam said, 'Julie, I had the most extraordinary encounter with your father this morning. I thought I'd be able to tell you round lunchtime, but when you didn't turn up . . . Julie, have you eaten anything today?'

Julian hadn't been able to face the breakfast table. And his feelings hadn't much changed by lunch. So he'd busied himself with work instead: inspections of some of the tenant farmers' properties, researching in Bakewell what hoops one had to jump through when making changes in a listed building, throwing himself into the myriad chores in the kennels. Thus, he'd been able to ignore everything that wasn't directly related to whatever he designated as the immediate task in hand.

Sam's appearance inside the kennel made any further efforts at distraction impossible. Nonetheless, in an effort to avoid the conversation he'd promised himself that he'd have with her, he said, 'Sorry, Sam. I got caught up in work round here.' He tried to sound apologetic. And, in fact, he *felt* apologetic when it came down to it because Sam was working her heart out at Broughton Manor. The least he could do to demonstrate his gratitude, Julian thought, was to show up for meals in acknowledgment of her efforts.

He said, 'You're holding us together, and I know it. Thanks, Sam. I'm grateful. Truly.'

Sam said warmly, 'I'm happy to do it. Honestly, Julie. It's always seemed such a shame to me that we've never had much of a chance to ...' She seemed to sense the need to change gears. 'It's amazing when you think that if our parents had only mended their fences, you and I could have ...' Another gear change. 'I mean, we're *family*, aren't we. And it's sad not to get to know the members of your very own family. Especially when you finally *do* get to know them and they turn out to be ... well, such fine people.' She fingered the plait that hung long and thick over her shoulder. Julian noticed for the first time how neatly it was braided. He saw that it very nearly caught the light.

He said, 'Well, I'm not always what I should be when it comes to saying thanks.'

'I think you're great.'

He felt himself colour. It was the curse of his complexion. He turned from her and went back to the dog. She asked what he was doing and why, and he was grateful that an explanation of aniseed oil and cotton swabs provided them a means to get past an awkward moment. But when he'd said all there was to be said, he and his cousin were back in that awkward moment again. And again Samantha was the one to save them.

She said, 'Oh Lord. I've completely forgotten why I wanted to talk to you. Your dad. Jules, it's remarkable what's happened.'

Julian rubbed the oil on Cass's last swollen teat and released the dog to her puppies as his cousin related what had occurred between herself and Jeremy. She concluded with, 'It was every bottle, Julian. Every bottle in the house. And he was *crying* as well.'

'He did tell me he wants to give up,' Julian said. And out of strict fairness and a resolve to be truthful, he added, 'But he's said that before.'

'Then you don't believe him? Because he was . . . Julie, really, you should have seen him. It was like desperation came on him all at once. And, well, frankly, it was all about you.'

'Me.' Julian replaced the aniseed oil in the cupboard.

'He was saying that he'd ruined your life, that he'd driven off your brother and sister—'

That was certainly true enough, Julian thought.

'—and that he'd finally come to understand that if he didn't mend his ways, he'd drive you off as well. Of course, I told him that you'd never leave him. After all, anyone can see you're devoted. But the point is that he wants to change. He's *ready* to change. And I've been looking for you because . . . Well, I had to tell you. Aren't you pleased? And I'm not making up a word of what happened. It was bottle after bottle. Gin down the drain and bottle smashed in the sink.'

Julian knew at heart that there was more than one way to look at what his father had done. True as it might be that he wanted to get off the drink, like all good alcoholics he could also be doing nothing more than positioning his players where he wanted them. The only question was *why* he might be positioning his players at this precise moment.

On the other hand, what if this time his father did mean what he said? Julian wondered. What if a clinic and whatever it was that could follow a clinic would be enough to cure him? How could he – the only child Jeremy had left with enough concern to do something about the situation – begin to deny him that opportunity? Especially when it would take so damn little to obtain the opportunity for him.

Julian said, 'I'm finished in here. Let's walk back to the house,' in a bid for time to gather his thoughts.

They left the kennels. They started down the overgrown lane. He said, 'Dad's talked about giving up booze before. He's even done it. But he only makes it for a few weeks. Well . . . once it must have been three and a half months. But apparently now he's come to believe—'

'That he can do it,' Samantha finished the thought for him and linked her arm with his. She squeezed gently and said, 'Julie, you should have seen him. If you had done, you'd know. I think that the key to success this time round is if we can come up with a plan that will help him. Obviously, it's done no good in the past to pour out the gin, has it?' She gave him an earnest gaze, perhaps seeking to see if she'd somehow offended him by pointing out what he'd done in earlier years to attempt to wean his father from the booze. 'And we can't exactly stop him going into an off-licence, can we?'

'Not to mention barring him from every hotel and pub from here to Manchester.'

'Right. So if there's a way . . . Julian, surely we can put our heads together and come up with something.'

Julian saw that his cousin had just given him the perfect opportunity to speak to her about the money for the clinic. But the words that went with that opportunity were large and unpalatable, and they stuck in his throat like a piece of bad meat. How could he ask her for money? For that *much* money? How could he say, Could you give us ten thousand quid, Sam? Not lend us, Sam – because there wasn't a snowball's chance in the Sahara that he'd be able to repay her anytime soon – but *give* us the money. Lots of it. And soon before Jeremy changes his mind. Please make an investment in a yammering drunk who's never kept his word in his life.

Julian couldn't do it. Despite his promises to his father, he found that – face to face with his cousin – he couldn't even begin to try.

As they reached the end of the lane and crossed the old road to make for the house, a silver Bentley pulled round the side of the building. It was followed by a panda car. Two uniformed constables emerged first, peering round the grounds as if they

670

expected ninja warriors to be lurking in the bushes. Out of the Bentley climbed the tall blond detective who'd first come to Broughton Manor with Inspector Hanken.

His cousin laid a hand on Julian's arm. Through it, he could feel how she'd stiffened.

'Make sure the house is secure,' DI Lynley said to the constables, whom he introduced as PCs Emmes and Benson. 'Then do the grounds. It's probably best to start with the gardens. Then go on to the kennel area and the woods.'

Emmes and Benson ducked inside the courtyard gate. Julian watched, astonished. Samantha was the one who said, 'Hang on, you lot,' and her tone was angry. 'What the hell are you doing, Inspector? Do you have a warrant? What right have you to barge into our lives and—'

'I need you inside the house,' Lynley told her. 'Quickly. And now.'

'What?' Samantha sounded incredulous. 'If you think we're going to jump just because you say so, you'd better think again.'

Julian found his voice. 'What's going on?'

'You can see what's going on,' Samantha said. 'This twit has decided to search Broughton Manor. He's not got a single reason in hell to tear things apart, aside from the fact that you and Nicola were involved. Which, apparently, is some sort of crime. I want to see your warrant, Inspector.'

Lynley came forward and took her by the arm. She said, 'Get your hands off me,' and tried to shake his grip.

He said, 'Mr Britton's in danger. I'd like him out of sight.'

Samantha said, 'Julian? In danger?'

Julian blanched. 'In danger from what? What's going on?'

Lynley said that he'd explain everything once the constables had ascertained that the house was safe. Inside, the three of them retired to the long gallery which was, Lynley said when he saw it, an environment that could be well controlled.

'Controlled?' Julian asked. 'From what? And why?'

So Lynley explained. His information was limited and direct, but Julian found that he couldn't begin to absorb it. The police believed that Andy Maiden had taken matters into his own hands, Lynley told him, which was always a risk if a member of a police officer's family became the victim of a violent crime.

'I don't understand,' Julian said. 'Because if Andy's coming here . . . here to Broughton Manor . . .' He tried to come to terms with the implication behind what the inspector had told him. 'Are you saying that Andy's coming *after* me?'

'We're not certain whom he's after,' Lynley replied. 'Inspector Hanken's seeing to the safety of the other gentleman.'

'The other . . . ?'

'Oh my God.' Samantha was standing next to Julian and immediately she dragged him away from the long gallery's diamond-paned windows. 'Julian, sit down. Here. The fireplace. It's out of sight from the grounds and even if someone barges into the room, we'll be too far away from the doors . . . Julie . . . *Julian*. Please.'

Julian allowed himself to be led, but he felt dazed. He said, 'What are you saying, exactly?' to Lynley. 'Does Andy think I might have . . . *Andy?*'

Absurdly, childishly, he wanted to cry. Suddenly the last six terrible days since – heart brimming with love – he'd asked Nicola to marry him came crashing down like a landslide, and he could not bear another single thing: He was utterly defeated by this final fact that the father of the woman he'd loved might actually believe he had killed her. How strange it was: He hadn't been defeated by her refusal when he'd offered marriage; he hadn't been defeated by the revelations she'd made to him that night; he hadn't been defeated by her disappearance, his part in the search for her, her actual death. But this simple thing – her father's suspicion – was for some reason the final straw. He felt the tears coming and the thought of weeping in front of this stranger, in front of his cousin, in front of anyone, burned in his throat.

Samantha's arm went round his shoulders. He felt her rough kiss against his temple. 'You're all right,' she told him. 'You're safe. And who bloody cares what anyone thinks. I know the truth. And that's what matters.'

'What truth is this?' DI Lynley spoke from the window where he appeared to be waiting for a sign that the police constables had completed their securing of the house. 'Miss McCallin?' he said when Samantha didn't answer.

'Oh shut up,' she returned acerbically. 'Julian didn't kill Nicola. Neither did I. Neither did anyone else in this house, if that's what you're thinking.'

'So what truth is it that you're talking about?'

'The truth about Julian. That he's fine and good and that fine and good people don't go about murdering one another, Inspector Lynley.'

'Even,' DI Lynley said, 'if one of them is less than fine and good?'

'I don't know what you're talking about.'

'But I expect Mr Britton does.'

She dropped her arm from his shoulders. Julian could feel her searching his face. She said his name more hesitantly than she had yet done, and she waited for him to clarify the detective's remarks.

And even now he could not do so. He could see her still – so much more alive than he himself had ever once been, *grasping* life. He could not speak a single word against her, no matter the cause he had for doing so. In the measure and judgement of their everyday world, Nicola had betrayed him, and Julian knew that if he told the tale of her London life as she'd revealed it to him, he could call himself the deeply wronged party. And so he would be seen by everyone he and Nicola had known. And there was indeed some satisfaction to be taken from that. But the truth of the matter would always be that only in the eyes of those who possessed the mere facts could he ever be seen as a man with a grievance. Those who knew Nicola as she truly was and had always been would know he'd brought his grief upon himself. Nicola had never once lied to him. He'd merely blinded himself to everything about her that he hadn't wanted to see.

She wouldn't have cared half a fig if he told the real truth about her now, Julian realised. But he wouldn't do so. Not so much to protect her memory but to protect the people who had loved her without knowing all that she was.

'I don't know what you're talking about,' Julian told the London detective. 'And I don't understand why you can't leave us alone to get on with our lives.'

'I won't be doing that until Nicola Maiden's killer is found.'

'Then look somewhere else,' Julian said. 'You won't find him here.'

At the far end of the room, the door opened and a constable escorted Julian's father into the long gallery. He said to Lynley, 'I found this one in the parlour, sir. PC Emmes has gone on, into the gardens.' Jeremy Britton disengaged his arm from DC Benson's hand. He looked confused by the turn of events. He looked frightened. But he didn't look drunk. He came to Julian and squatted before him.

He said, 'You all right, my boy?' and although the words were ever so slightly slurred, it occurred to Julian that the enunciation was prompted by Jeremy's honest concern for him and not the result of his addiction to drink.

This realisation made his heart suddenly warm. Warm to his father, warm to his cousin, and warm to the connections implied by *family*. He said, 'I'm okay, Dad,' and he made room for Jeremy on the floor by the fireplace. He did this by scooting closer to Sam.

In response, she returned her arm to his shoulders. 'I'm so glad of that,' she said.

Chapter Thirty

━━━◆━━━

Barbara chose a venue that Matthew King-Ryder would know intimately: the Agincourt Theatre where his father's production of *Hamlet* was being mounted. But after Nkata passed this message on to King-Ryder from the phone box in South Kensington, he made it clear that he wasn't about to let his fellow DC meet with a killer alone.

'Are you a convert to King-Ryder-as-killer, then?' Barbara asked her colleague.

'Seems like only one reason he'd know the number of this phone box, Barb.' Nkata sounded mournful, however, and when he went on, Barbara understood why. 'Can't think why he'd go after his own dad. Makes me wonder, that.'

'He wanted more lolly than his dad left for him. He saw only one way to get it.'

'But how'd he come by that music in the first place? His dad wouldn't've told him, would he?'

'Tell your own son – tell *anyone*, in fact – that you're plagiarising your old mate's work? I don't think so. But he was his dad's manager Winnie. He must have come across that music somewhere.'

They walked to Barbara's car in Queen's Gate Gardens. Nkata had told King-Ryder to meet him at the Agincourt half an hour from the moment he rang off. 'You're there too early and I'm not showing my face,' he had warned King-Ryder. 'You just thank your lucky stars I'm willing to negotiate on your own turf, mon.'

King-Ryder was to see to it that the stage door was unlocked. He was also to see to it that the building was unoccupied.

The drive into the West End took them less than twenty minutes. There, the Agincourt Theatre stood next to the Museum of Theatrical History, on a narrow side street off Shaftesbury Avenue. Its stage door was opposite a line of skips serving the Royal Standard Hotel. No windows over-looked it, so Barbara and Nkata could enter the Agincourt unobserved.

Nkata took a position in the last row of the stalls. Barbara placed herself off stage, in the deep darkness provided by a bulky piece of scenery. Although the traffic and the pedestrians outside the theatre had made a din that seemed to run the length of Shaftesbury Avenue, inside the building it was tomb-silent. So when their quarry entered by the stage door some seven minutes later, Barbara heard him.

He did everything as Nkata had instructed him. He closed the door. He made his way to the backstage area. He flipped on the working lights. He walked to centre stage. He stood pretty much where Hamlet would probably lie dying in Horatio's arms, Barbara realised. It was such a nice touch.

He looked out into the darkened theatre and said, 'All right, damn you. I'm here.'

Nkata spoke from the back, where the shadows obscured him. 'So I see.'

King-Ryder took a step forward and said unexpectedly in a high, pained voice, 'You killed him, you filthy bastard. You *killed* him. Both of you. *All* of you. And I swear to God, I'll make you pay.'

'I didn't do no killing. I done no travelling to Derbyshire lately.'

'You know what I'm talking about. You killed my father.'

Barbara frowned as she heard this. What the hell was he on about?

'Seems like I heard that bloke shot himself,' Nkata said.

King-Ryder's fists clenched. 'And why? Just why the hell do you think he shot himself? He needed that music. And he would have had it – every sodding sheet of it – if you and your mates hadn't got in the way. He shot himself because he thought . . . he *believed* . . . My father believed . . .' And then his voice broke. 'You *killed* him. Give me that music. You *killed* him.'

'We need to make ourselfs an arrangement first.'

'Come into the light where I can see you, then.'

'Don't think so. What I figure is this: What you can't see, you don't know how to hurt.'

'You're mad if you think I'll hand over a wad of money to someone I can't even see.'

'Expected your dad to do the same, though.'

'Don't mention him to me. You're not fit to speak his name.'

'Feeling guilty?'

'Just give me that music. Step up here. Act like a man. Hand it over.'

'It's going to cost you.'

'Fine. What?'

'What your dad had to pay.'

'You're mad.'

'Nice little packet of dosh that was,' Nkata said. 'I'm happy to take it off your hands. And play no games, mon. I know the amount. I'll give you twenty-four hours to have it here, in cash. I 'spect things take longer when St Helier's involved, and I'm an understanding kind of bloke, I am.'

The mention of St Helier took things too far. Barbara saw that in King-Ryder's body language: the back suddenly stiffening as every nerve ending went on the alert. No ordinary yobbo in an ordinary scam would have known about that bank in St Helier.

King-Ryder moved away from centre stage. He peered into the darkness of the stalls. Warily, he said: 'Who the hell are you?'

Barbara took the cue.

'I think you know the answer to that, Mr King-Ryder.' She stepped out of the darkness. 'The music's not here, by the way. And to be honest, it probably never would have surfaced at all had you not killed Terry Cole to get it back. Terry had given it to his neighbour, the old lady, Mrs Baden. And she hadn't the least idea what it was.'

'You,' King-Ryder said.

'Right. Do you want to come quietly, or shall we have a scene?'

'You've got *nothing* on me,' King-Ryder said. 'I didn't say a damn thing that you can use to prove I lifted a finger to hurt anyone.'

'Somewhat true, that.' Nkata came forward down the centre aisle of the theatre. 'But we've got ourselves a nice leather jacket up in Derbyshire. And if your dabs match up with the dabs we pull off it, you're going to have one hell of a time dancing your way out of the dock.'

Barbara could almost see the wheels spinning wildly in King-Ryder's skull as he dashed through the options: fight, flight, or surrender. The odds were against him – despite one of the opposition being a woman – and while the theatre and the surrounding neighbourhood provided myriad places to run to and to hide, even had he tried to flee, it was only a matter of time before they nabbed him.

His posture altered again. 'They killed my father,' he said obscurely. 'They killed Dad.'

It was when Andy Maiden hadn't materialised at Broughton Manor within two hours that Lynley began to doubt the conclusions he'd drawn from the note that the man had left in Maiden Hall. A phone call from Hanken – informing him of Will Upman's complete security – further solidified Lynley's doubts.

'There's been no sign of him here, either,' Lynley told his colleague. 'Pete, I'm getting a bad feeling about this.'

His bad feeling grew ominous when Winston Nkata phoned from London. He had Matthew King-Ryder at the Yard, Nkata told him in a rapid recitation that offered no opportunity for interruption. Barbara Havers had developed a plan to nab him, and it had worked like a charm. The bloke was ready to talk about the murders. Nkata and Havers could lock him up and wait for the inspector or they could have at him themselves. What were Lynley's wishes?

'It was all about that music Barb found in Battersea. Terry Cole got between the music and what was supposed to happen to the music, and King-Ryder's dad blew his brains out over it. Matthew was avenging himself for the death, so he claims. 'Course, he wanted that music back as well.'

Lynley listened blankly. Nkata talked about the West End, the new production of *Hamlet*, phone boxes in South Kensington, and Terry Cole. When he had finished and he repeated his question – did the inspector want them to wait until his return to take Matthew King-Ryder's statement? – Lynley said hollowly, 'But Winston, what about the girl? Nicola. What about her?'

'Just in the wrong place at the wrong time,' Nkata replied. 'King-Ryder killed her because she was there. When the arrow hit Terry, she saw him with the bow. Barb says she saw a picture in his flat, by the way: Matthew as a kid posing with Dad on Sports Day at school. She thinks he was wearing a quiver, she says. She saw the strap of it running across his chest. I 'spect if we get a warrant, we'll find that long bow in his digs. D'you want me to get on to that, as well?'

Lynley said, 'How was Havers involved?'

'She grilled Vi Nevin when the girl came to last night. She

got most of the details from her.' Lynley could hear Nkata draw a deep breath to hurry on. 'Since Nevin didn't seem like part of the case, 'spector . . . because of that Islington business . . . the threat . . . the wheel clamp and Andy Maiden and all . . . I told her to do it. I told Barb to talk to her. If things come down to reprimands, I'll take the rap on that.'

Lynley felt stunned by the amount of information Nkata had passed on to him, but he found the voice to say, 'Well done, Winston.'

'I just went along with Barb, 'spector.'

'Then well done to Constable Havers as well.'

Lynley rang off. He found that his movements were slower than normal and he knew that surprise – shock – was the cause. But when he'd finally managed to take in the extent of what had occurred in London during his absence, he felt apprehension descend like a cloud.

After her appearance at the Buxton police station, Nancy Maiden had gone home to await word of her husband's whereabouts. Stubbornly refusing the offer of the companionship of a female constable until Andy turned up, she'd said, 'Find him. *Please*,' to Lynley as she'd left the station. And her eyes had tried to communicate something that she wouldn't put into words.

So now Lynley was forced to reflect upon another meaning behind Andy Maiden's disappearance, a meaning that might have nothing at all to do with taking a rough sort of justice into his own hands.

He realised the challenge that a search for Andy Maiden presented. If he'd learned nothing else in the past few days, he'd come to know that the Peak District was vast: crosshatched by hiking trails, distinguished by utterly different topographical phenomena, and marked with five hundred thousand years of man's habitation upon it. But when he considered the desperate state that Andy had been in when they'd last spoken and he combined this state with the words *I'm taking care of this myself,* the dread that he felt was enough to tell Lynley where his search should begin.

He told the Brittons and Samantha McCallin to remain in the long gallery with their police guards until further notice. He left them there.

He sped north from Broughton Manor towards Bakewell, propelled by an urgency born of dread. If Andy hadn't intended to 'take care of this' with a confrontation with his daughter's killer, there was only one other way that Lynley could imagine him putting a period to the curse of the last few days.

Andy believed that the investigation was heading unstoppably in his direction, and everything Lynley and Hanken had done and said at their last two meetings with the man had communicated that brutal fact. Should he be arrested for his daughter's murder – should he even be questioned more thoroughly about his daughter's murder – the truth of Nicola's life in London would come out. He'd already demonstrated the extremes to which he was willing to go in order to keep the truth of that life hidden. What better way to hide it forever than by simultaneously limning himself as his daughter's killer and removing himself from the reach of justice? There would hardly be need for further investigation into Nicola's life if one of the suspects not only confessed but also demonstrated the veracity of his confession.

Lynley tore across the district to Sparrowpit and flew along the country road beyond it to the white iron gate, behind which lay the unbroken expanse of Calder Moor. A Land Rover stood at the far end of the truncated lane that led onto the moor. Directly behind it was a rusting Morris.

Lynley set off at a jog along the muddy, rut-filled footpath. Because he did not wish to consider the extreme Andy might have gone to in order to keep Nicola's secrets from her mother he concentrated on the one recollection that had bound him to the other man for more than ten years.

Wearing a wire is the easy part, boy-o, Dennis Hextell had told him. Opening your mouth without sounding like you've got starch in your knickers is something else. Hextell had despised him, had patiently anticipated his failure to portray himself undercover as anything other than what he was: the privileged son of a privileged son. Andy Maiden, on the other hand, said, Give him a chance, Den. And when that chance had resulted in an entire lorry of Semtex – intended as bait – hijacked by the very people it was intended to entrap, the message *Americans don't use the word* torch, *Jack* arrived at the Met within the same hour and served as illustration of how a single syllable can cost lives and destroy careers. That it hadn't destroyed Lynley's was owing to Andy Maiden. He'd taken the stricken young officer aside after the subsequent Belfast bombing and said, 'Come in here, Tommy. Talk to me. Talk.'

And Lynley had done, eventually. He had poured out his guilt, his confusion, and his sorrow in a manner that ultimately told him how badly he needed a figure to act the rôle of parent in his life.

Andy Maiden had stepped into that part without ever questioning why Lynley had needed him so desperately to do so. He'd said, 'Listen to me, son,' and Lynley had listened, in small part because the other man was his superior officer, in large part because no one before had ever used the word *son* when speaking to him. Lynley came from a world where people recognised their individual places in the social hierarchy and generally kept to them or felt the consequences of failing to do so. But Andy Maiden was not such a man. 'You're not cut out for SO10,' Andy had told him. 'What you've been through proves that, Tommy. But you *had* to go through it to know, d'you understand? And there's no sin in learning, son. There's only sin in refusing to take what you've learned and doing something with it.'

That guiding philosophy of Andy Maiden's life reverberated now in Lynley's mind. The SO10 officer had used it to map his entire career, and there was very little in the past few days of their re-acquaintance to reassure Lynley that Andy wouldn't follow that same philosophy today.

Lynley's fears drove him towards Nine Sisters' Henge. When he reached it, the place was silent, except for the wind. This gushed and ceased and gushed in great gusts like air from a bellows. It blew from the west off the Irish Sea and promised more rain in the coming hours.

Lynley approached the copse and entered. The ground was still damp from the morning's rain, and the leaves fallen from the birches made a spongy padding beneath his feet. He followed the path that led from the sentry stone into the middle of the copse. Out of the wind, only the tree leaves susurrating provided sound aside from his own breathing, which was harsh with exertion.

At the final moment, he found that he didn't want to approach. He didn't want to see, and more than anything he didn't want to know. But he forced himself forward into the circle. And it was at the circle's centre that he found them.

Nan Maiden half-sat and half-knelt, her legs folded beneath her and her back to Lynley. Andy Maiden lay, one leg cocked and the other straight out, with his head and shoulders cradled in his wife's lap.

The rational part of Lynley's mind said, *That would be where all the blood is coming from, from his head and his shoulders.* But the heart of Lynley said, *Good God no,* and wished what he saw as he circled round the two figures was only a dream: a nightmare coming, as all dreams come, from what lies within the subconscious and cries for scrutiny when one is most afraid.

He said, 'Mrs Maiden. Nancy.'

Nan raised her head. She'd bent to Andy, so her cheeks and her forehead were splodged with his blood. She wasn't weeping and perhaps, beyond tears at this point, she hadn't wept at all. She said, 'He thought he'd failed. And when he found that he couldn't make things good again . . .' Her hands tightened on her husband's body, trying to press close the gash in his neck where the blood had throbbed out of him, bathing his clothes and pooling beneath him. 'He had to do . . . something.'

Lynley saw that a blood-spattered paper lay crumpled on the ground next to her. On it, he read what he'd expected to see: Andy Maiden's brief and apocryphal confession to the murder of a daughter he had deeply loved.

'I didn't want to believe, you see,' Nan Maiden said, gazing down at her husband's ashen face and smoothing back his hair. 'I *couldn't* believe and live with myself. And continue to live with him. I saw that something was terribly wrong when his nerves went bad, but I couldn't think he'd ever have hurt her. *How* could I think it? Even now. How? Tell me. How?'

'Mrs Maiden . . .' What could he say? Lynley wondered. She was too much in shock at the moment to comprehend the scope of what lay behind her husband's actions. Right now, her horror – born of her husband's putative murder of their daughter – was quite enough for her to contend with.

Lynley squatted next to Nan Maiden and put his hand on her shoulder. 'Mrs Maiden,' he said. 'Come away from here. I've left my mobile in the car and we're going to need to phone the police.'

'He is the police,' she said. 'He loved that job. He couldn't do it any longer because his nerves wouldn't take it.'

'Yes,' Lynley said, 'yes. I've been told.'

'Which is why I *knew*, you see. But still I couldn't be sure. I could never be sure, so I didn't want to say. I couldn't risk it.'

'Of course.' Lynley tried to urge her to her feet. 'Mrs Maiden, if you'll come—'

'Because, you see, I thought if I could just protect him from ever having to know . . . That's what I wanted to do. But it turns out that he knew about everything anyway, didn't he, so we could actually have *talked* about it, Andy and I. And if we'd talked about it . . . Do you see what that means? If we'd talked, I could have stopped him. I know it. I hated what she was doing – at first I thought I'd die from the knowledge of it – and if I'd known that she'd told *him* what she was doing as well . . .' Nan bent to Andy again. 'We would have had each other. We could have talked. I would have said the right words to stop him.'

Lynley dropped his hand from her shoulder. He'd been listening all along, but he suddenly realised that he hadn't been hearing. The sight of Andy – his throat slashed open by his own hand – had clouded all his senses save his vision. But he finally heard what Nan Maiden was saying. Hearing, he finally understood.

'You knew about her,' he said. 'You *knew*.'

And a yawning chasm of responsibility opened up beneath him as he saw the part he himself had played in Andy Maiden's purposeless death.

'I followed him,' Matthew King-Ryder said.

They'd taken him to an interview room where he sat at one side of a Formica topped table while Barbara Havers and Winston Nkata sat on the other side. In between them at one end of the table, a tape player whirred, recording his answers.

King-Ryder appeared defeated by more than one aspect of his present situation. His future sealed by the existence of a leather jacket and the presence of a sliver of Port Orford cedar in the wound of one of his victims, he had apparently turned to a review of some of the unpleasant realities that had led him to this juncture. Those past realities joined with his future prospects to alter him appreciably. Upon his entry into the interview room, the vengeance-fuelled anger that had defined his arrival at the Agincourt Theatre had become the devastated submission of the fighter who faces surrender.

He told the first part of his story in a monotone. This was the background against which he laid out the grievance that had prompted him to blackmail his own father. David King-Ryder, worth so many millions that it took the services of a team of accountants to keep track of all his money, had decided to put his fortune into a fund for creative artists upon his death, leaving not a penny of it to his own children. One of these children accepted the terms of the King-Ryder will with the resignation of a daughter who knew only too well that it would be profitless to argue against such a course of action. The other child – Matthew – had sought a way round the situation.

'I'd known about the *Hamlet* music for years, but Dad didn't know that,' Matthew told them. 'He wouldn't have known since he and my mother were long divorced when Michael wrote the score, and he never realised that Michael had kept in touch with us. He was actually more like a dad to me than Dad was, Michael Chandler. He played the score for me – parts of it, that is – when I visited him for tea at half terms and holidays. He wasn't married then, but he wanted a son and I was happy enough for him to act the part of my father.'

David King-Ryder hadn't thought the *Hamlet* score had much potential, so upon Michael Chandler's completion of it, the partners had filed it away twenty-two years ago. There it had remained – buried among the King-Ryder/Chandler memorabilia in the offices of King-Ryder Productions in Soho. Thus, when David King-Ryder had presented it as his latest effort, Matthew had instantly recognised not only the music and the lyrics but also what they represented to his father: a final attempt to salvage a reputation that had been all but destroyed by two successive and expensive failures as a solo act once his longtime partner had drowned.

It hadn't taken much effort for Matthew to find the original score. And once he had it in his hands, he saw how he could make some money from it. His father wouldn't know who had the score – anyone from the production offices could have nicked it from the files if they'd known where to look – and because his reputation was paramount to him, he'd pay whatever was asked to get the music back. In that way, Matthew would have the inheritance his father's will denied him.

The scheme had been simple. Four weeks before the opening of *Hamlet*, Matthew had sent a page of the score to his father's home with an anonymous blackmail note. If one million pounds wasn't paid into an account in St Helier, the score would be sent to the biggest tabloid in the country just in time for opening night. Once the money was in the bank, David King-Ryder would be informed where to pick up the rest of the music.

'When I had the money, I waited till a week before the opening,' Matthew told them. 'I wanted him to sweat.'

He phoned his dad then and told him to go to the phone boxes in South Kensington and wait for further instructions. At ten o'clock, he told him, David King-Ryder would be informed where the music could be found.

'But Terry Cole answered the phone that night, not your dad,' Barbara said. 'Why didn't you recognise the different voice?'

'He said "yeah," that's all,' Matthew told her. 'I thought he was nervous, in a hurry. And he sounded like someone who was expecting the call.'

In the days that followed, he'd seen that his father was agitated about something, but he'd assumed that King-Ryder was in a state about having had to pay out one million pounds. He'd had no way of knowing that his father was daily growing more frantic as the phone call he kept hoping to receive – from the blackmailer who, he believed, had failed to contact him at Elvaston Place – did not materialise. As the premier of *Hamlet* approached, David King-Ryder had started to see himself in the power of someone who was either going to bleed him dry with more demands for money over the years or ruin him forever by releasing Michael Chandler's music to the tabloids.

'When he hadn't heard by opening night and the production was such a success . . . You know what happened.'

Matthew sheltered his face with his hands, then. He said, 'I didn't *mean* him to die. He was my *dad*. But I thought it wasn't fair that all his money . . . every penny of his money except that measly bequest to Ginny . . .' He lowered his hands, spoke to them rather than to Barbara and Winston. 'He *owed* me something. He hadn't been much of a father to me. He owed me at least this much.'

'Why didn't you just ask him for it?' Nkata asked.

Matthew breathed out a bitter laugh. 'Dad worked to be who and where he was. He expected me to do the same. And I always did – I worked and I worked – and I would have kept *on* working. But then I saw that he was going to take a shortcut to his own success through Michael's music. And I decided that if he could take a shortcut, so could I. And it would have come all right in the end if that *bloody* little bastard hadn't come along. And then when I saw that he intended to use the music and to play the same rotten game with me, I had to do something. I couldn't just sit there and let it happen.'

Barbara frowned. Everything until that moment had fitted perfectly into the picture. She said, 'Play the same game? What?'

'Blackmail,' Matthew King-Ryder said. 'Cole walked into my office with that smirk on his face and said, "I got something here that I need your help with, Mr King-Ryder," and as soon as I saw it – a single sheet just like I'd sent to my dad – I knew *exactly* what that little shit had in mind. I asked him how he came to have it in his possession, but he wouldn't tell me. So I threw him out. But I followed him. I knew he wasn't in it alone.'

On the trail of the music, he'd followed Terry Cole to the railway arches in Battersea, and from there to his flat on Anhalt

Road. When the boy had gone inside the studio, Matthew had taken a chance and riffled through the saddlebags hanging from his motorcycle. When he'd found nothing, he knew he had to continue following till the kid led him either to the music or to the person who had the music.

It was when he'd followed him to Rostrevor Road that he'd first believed he was on the right trail. For Terry had emerged from Vi Nevin's building with a large manila envelope, which he'd placed in his saddlebag. And that, Matthew King-Ryder had believed, had to contain the music.

'When he took to the motorway, I'd no idea where he was going. But I was committed to seeing things through. So I followed him.'

And when he'd seen Terry and Nicola Maiden having their meeting out in the middle of nowhere, he'd been convinced that they were the principals behind his father's death and his own misfortune. His only weapon was the long bow he had in his car. He went back for it, waited till nightfall, then dispatched them both.

'But there was no music at the camp site,' Matthew said. 'Just an envelope of letters, pasted-up letters from magazines and newspapers.'

So he'd had to keep looking. He had to find that score to *Hamlet*, and he'd returned to London and searched in those places Terry had led him.

'I didn't think of the old woman,' he said finally.

'You should have accepted when she offered you cake,' Barbara told him.

Once more, Matthew's glance fell to his hands. His shoulders shook. He began to cry.

'I didn't *mean* harm to come to him. I swear to God. If he'd only just said he'd *leave* me something. But he wouldn't do that. I was his son, his only son, but I wasn't meant to have anything. Oh, he said I could have his family pictures. His bloody piano and his guitar. But as for the money . . .

any of the money ... a single penny of his God damn
money ... Why couldn't he see that it made me worth
nothing to be overlooked? I was supposed to be grateful
just to be his son, just to be alive on account of him. He'd
give me a job but for all the rest ... No. I had to make
it entirely on my own. And it wasn't fair. Because I loved
him. All the years when he failed, I still loved him. And if
he'd continued to fail, it wouldn't have made a difference.
Not to me.'

His distress seemed real. Barbara wanted to feel sorry for
him, but she found that she couldn't as she realised how
much he *wanted* her pity. He wanted her to see him as
a victim of his father's indifference. No matter that he'd
destroyed his father for one million pounds, no matter that
he'd committed two brutal murders. They were meant to feel
sorry that circumstances beyond his control had forced his
hand, that David King-Ryder hadn't seen fit to leave him the
money in his will which would have precluded the crimes' ever
happening in the first place.

God, Barbara thought, there it was: the malaise of their time.
Do it to Julia. Hurt someone else. Blame someone else. But
don't hurt or blame me.

She wouldn't begin to buy that line of thinking. Any pity
Barbara might have mustered for the man was erased by two
senseless deaths in Derbyshire and the image of what he'd done
to Vi Nevin. He'd pay for those crimes. But a prison term –
no matter its length – didn't seem enough recompense for
blackmail, suicide, murder, assault, and the aftermath of each.
She said, 'You might want to know the truth of the matter
about Terry Cole's intentions, Mr King-Ryder. In fact, I think
it's important that you know.'

And so she told him that all Terry Cole had wanted was a
simple address and telephone number. In fact, had Matthew
King-Ryder offered to take the music off his hands and pay
him handsomely for bringing it to the offices of King-Ryder

Productions, the boy would probably have been thrilled to the dickens.

'He didn't even know what it was,' Barbara said. 'He hadn't the slightest idea in the world that he'd put his hands on the music to *Hamlet.*'

Matthew King-Ryder absorbed this information. But if Barbara had hoped she was dealing him a mortal blow that would worsen his coming life in prison, she was disabused of that notion when he replied. 'He's at fault for my father's suicide. If he hadn't interfered, my dad would be alive.'

Lynley reached Eaton Terrace at ten that night. He found his wife in the bathroom, sunk in a fragrant citrus froth of bubbles. Her eyes were closed, her head cradled in a towelling pillow, and her hands – garbed incongruously in white satin gloves – rested on the spotless stainless steel tray that spanned the width of the bath and held her soaps and her sponges. A CD player sat on a shelf amid a clutter of Helen's unguents, potions, and creams. Music emanated from it. A soprano sang.

They lay him – gently and softly – in the cold cold ground,
they lay him – gently and softly – in the cold cold ground.
And here am I, a child without a light, to see me through the
coming storm,
oh, hold me near and tell me
I am not alone.'

Lynley reached for the off button. 'Ophelia, I expect, once Hamlet's killed Polonius.'

Helen splashed in the tub behind him. 'Tommy! You frightened me to death.'

'Sorry.'

'Have you just got in now?'

'Yes. Tell me about the gloves, Helen.'

'The gloves?' Helen's glance shifted to her hands. 'Oh! The

gloves. It's my cuticles. I'm giving them a treatment. It's a combination of heat and oil.'

'That's a relief,' he said.

'Why? Had you noticed my cuticles?'

'No. But I thought you were anticipating a future as Queen of England, which would mean our relationship has come to an end. Have you ever seen the Queen *without* her gloves?'

'Hmm. I don't think I have. But you don't suppose she actually *bathes* with them on, do you?'

'It's a possibility. She may loathe human contact even with herself.'

Helen laughed. 'I'm so glad you're home.' She peeled off the gloves and plunged her hands into the water. She settled back against her pillow and regarded him. 'Tell me,' she said gently. 'Please.'

It was her way, and Lynley hoped it would always be her way: to read him so swiftly and to open herself to him with those three simple words.

He pulled a stool over to the side of the bath. He took off his jacket, dropped it onto the floor, rolled up his sleeves, and reached for one of the sponges and some soap. He took her arm first and ran the sponge down its slender length. And as he bathed her, he told her everything. She listened in silence, watching him.

'The worst of it all is this,' he said in conclusion to his tale, 'Andy Maiden would still be alive if I'd stuck to procedure when we met yesterday afternoon. But his wife came into the room, and instead of questioning her about Nicola's life in London – which would have revealed that she'd known about it even longer than Andy – I held back. Because I wanted to help him protect her.'

'When she didn't need his protection at all,' Helen said. 'Yes. I see how it happened. How dreadful. But, Tommy, you were doing the best you knew at the time.'

Lynley squeezed the sponge and let the soapy water run

against his wife's shoulders before he returned the sponge to its tray. 'The best I knew at the time was to stick to procedure, Helen. He was a suspect. So was she. I didn't treat either one of them that way. Had I done so, he wouldn't be dead.'

Lynley couldn't decide what had been worst: seeing the bloody Swiss Army knife still clutched in Andy's stiffened hand, trying to get Nancy Maiden away from her husband's corpse, hiking back to the Bentley with her in tow and every moment fearing that her shock would give way to a raving grief which he would not be able to handle, waiting – endlessly, it seemed – for the police to arrive, facing the corpse a second time and this time without Andy's wife present to deflect his attention from his former colleague's manner of death.

'Looks like the knife he showed me,' Hanken had said, observing it on the ground.

'It would be, wouldn't it,' was Lynley's only reply. Then, passionately, 'Blast it. God *damn* it, Peter. It's all my fault. If I'd showed them every one of my cards when they were *both* with me . . . But I didn't. I *didn't.*'

Hanken had nodded at his team then, directing them to bag the body. He'd shaken a cigarette from his packet and offered the packet to Lynley. He'd said, '*Take* one, God damn it. You need it, Thomas,' and Lynley had complied. They'd left the ancient stone circle but remained by the sentry stone, smoking their Marlboros. 'No one operates by rote,' Hanken said. 'Half of this job is intuition, and that comes from the heart. You followed your heart. In your position, I can't say I would have done differently.'

'Can't you?'

'No.'

But Lynley had known the other man was lying. Because the most important part of the job was knowing when to follow your heart and when to do so would lead to disaster.

'Barbara was right from the first,' Lynley told Helen as she rose from the tub and took the towel he extended to her. 'Had

I even seen *that* this wouldn't have happened because I'd have stayed in London and reined back the Derbyshire end of things while we brought down King-Ryder.'

'If that's the case,' Helen said quietly as she wrapped the towel round her body, 'then I'm equally to blame for what's happened, Tommy.' And she told him how Barbara had come to be tracking down King-Ryder once she'd been thrown off the case. 'I could have phoned you when Denton told me about the music. I didn't make that choice.'

'I doubt I would have listened, if I'd known that what you were telling me was going to prove Barbara right.'

'As to that, darling ...' Helen took up a small bottle of lotion, which she began to smooth against her face and her neck. 'What is it, really, that's bothered you about Barbara? About this North Sea business and her firing that gun. Because I know you know she's a fine detective. She may go her own way now and again, but her heart is always in the right place, isn't it?'

And there it was again, that word *heart* and everything it implied about the underlying reasons behind a person's actions. Hearing his wife use it, Lynley was reminded of another's use of it so many years ago, of a woman weeping and saying to him, 'My God, Tommy, what's become of your heart?' when he refused to see her, to speak to her even, in the aftermath of discovering her adultery.

And then he finally knew. He understood for the very first time and the understanding made him recoil from who he had been and what he had done for the last twenty years. 'I couldn't control her,' he said quietly, far more to himself than to his wife. 'I couldn't mould her into the image I'd had of her. She went her own way and I couldn't bear it. He's dying, I thought, and she should damn well *act* like a wife whose husband is dying.'

Helen understood. 'Ah. Your mother.'

'I thought I'd forgiven her long ago. But perhaps I haven't

forgiven her at all. Perhaps she's always there – in every woman I have to deal with – and perhaps I keep trying to make her be someone she doesn't want to be.'

'Or perhaps you've simply never forgiven yourself for not being able to stop her.' Helen set down her lotion and came to him. 'We carry such emotional baggage, don't we, darling? And just when we think we've finally unpacked, there it all is again, waiting in front of our bedroom door, ready to trip us when we get up in the morning.'

She'd had her head wrapped in a turban, and she took this off and shook her hair out. She hadn't completely dried herself, so drops of water glistened on her shoulders and gathered in the hollow of her throat.

'Your mother, my father,' she said as she took his hand and pressed it to her cheek. 'It's always someone. I was all in a muddle because of that ridiculous wallpaper. I'd decided that if I hadn't become the woman my father intended me to be – the wife of a man in possession of a title – I'd have known my own mind with regard to that paper. And because I didn't know my own mind, I blamed him. My father. But the truth of the matter is that I could always have gone my own way, as Pen and Iris did. I could have said no. And I didn't. I *didn't* because the path laid out was so much easier and so much less frightening than forging my own would have been.'

Lynley smoothed her cheek fondly with the back of his fingers. He traced her jaw and the length of her long and lovely neck.

'Sometimes I hate being a grown up,' Helen told him. 'There's so much more freedom in being a child.'

'Isn't there,' he agreed. He put his fingers to the towel that wrapped her body. He kissed her neck and then went on. 'But there's more advantage in adulthood, I think.'

He loosened the towel and drew her to him.

Chapter Thirty-one

At the sound of her alarm the next morning, Barbara Havers rolled out of bed with a blazing headache. She stumbled to the bathroom where she rattled round for several aspirin and fumbled with the handles of the shower. Bloody Hell, she thought. She'd obviously been leading much too exemplary a life in the last few years. As a result, she'd become grossly out of condition in the partying arena.

It hadn't even been *that* much of a celebration. After they'd finished taking Matthew King-Ryder's statement, she and Nkata had gone out for a minor frolic. They'd only visited four pubs and neither one of them had drunk the truly hard stuff. But what they'd drunk had been enough to do the trick. Barbara felt as though a lorry had driven over her head.

She stood under the shower and let the water beat against her until the aspirin began to take effect. She scrubbed her body and washed her hair, swearing off everything even remotely alcoholic on week nights henceforth. She thought about phoning Nkata to see if he was experiencing a morning-after as well. But she considered how his mother would react to her favourite child's receiving a phone call from an unknown woman before seven in the morning, and she abandoned the idea. No need to worry Mrs Nkata about her darling Winnie's purity of flesh and spirit. Barbara would see him at the Yard soon enough.

Her morning ablutions performed, Barbara padded over to her wardrobe and pondered what sartorial statement she could make today. She opted for discretion and pulled out a trouser suit that she hadn't thought to wear for at least two years.

She sailed it on to the rumpled bed and went to the kitchen. The electric kettle plugged in and watermelon Pop Tarts in the toaster, she towelled her hair dry and threw on her clothes. She turned on the Radio 4 morning news to hear that road works were delaying traffic into the City, there was a pile up on the M1 just south of junction four, and a burst water main on the A23 had created a lake to the north of Streatham. It was another day of commuting hell.

The kettle clicked off, and Barbara toddled to the kitchen to spoon some coffee powder into a mug decorated with a caricature of the Prince of Wales: chinless head, bulbous nose, and flapping ears sitting on a diminutive tartan-clad body. She grabbed her Pop Tarts, plopped them onto a kitchen towel, and carried this well-balanced nutritional masterpiece over to the dining table.

The velvet heart sat in the centre where Barbara had placed it when Hadiyyah had presented it to her on Sunday evening. There it waited for her reflections upon it, a self-satisfied little Valentine of sorts, edged with white lace and filled with implication. Barbara had avoided thinking about it for more than thirty-six hours, and since she'd not seen either Hadiyyah or her father during that time, she'd been able to skip mentioning it in all conversations as well. But she couldn't exactly do that forever. Good manners, if nothing else, demanded that she make some sort of remark to Azhar the next time she saw him.

What would it be? After all, he was a married man. True, he wasn't living with his wife. True, the woman he'd been living with *since* he'd been living with his wife was not his wife. True, *that* woman had apparently done a permanent runner, leaving behind a charming eight-year-old girl and a serious – albeit thoughtful and kind – thirty-five-year-old man in need of adult female companionship. However, none of that went any distance towards making the situation into something that could be addressed easily under the time-honoured rules of etiquette. Not that Barbara had ever bothered to concern herself with the time-honoured rules of etiquette. But that was because she'd never really been in a spot where rules applied. Not man-woman rules, that is. And not man-woman-child rules. And certainly not man-wife-nonwife-child-additionalwoman rules. But still, when she next saw Azhar, she needed to be prepared. She needed to have something quick, useful, direct, meaningful, casual, and reasonable to say. And it had to spring from her tongue spontaneously, as if the thought that prompted it had come upon her that instant.

So ... What would it be? *Thanks awfully much, old bean ... Just what are your intentions? ... How sweet of you to think of me.*

Bloody hell, Barbara thought, and crammed the rest of her Pop Tart into her mouth. Human relationships were murder.

A sharp knock sounded once on her door. Barbara started and looked at her watch. It was far too early for religious zealots to be out on the streets, and the British Gas meter reader had been the social highlight of her previous week. So who ... ?

Chewing, she got to her feet. She opened the door. Azhar was standing there.

She blinked at him and wished she'd taken her rehearsal of grateful remarks more seriously. She said, 'Hullo. Er ... Morning.'

He said, 'You returned quite late last night, Barbara.'

'Well ... yeah. The case was tied up. I mean it was tied up as much as these things can be tied up when we make an arrest. Which is to say that the materials have to be drawn together still, in order to give them to the CPS. But as for the actual investigation—' She forced herself to stop. 'Yeah. We made an arrest.'

He nodded, his face serious. 'This is good news.'

'Good news. Yes.'

He looked beyond her. She wondered if he was trying to suss out whether she'd celebrated the investigation's conclusion with a chorus line of dancing Greek boys who were still lounging somewhere within. But then she remembered her manners and said, 'Oh. Come in. Coffee? I've only got instant, I'm afraid,' and she added, 'this morning,' as if every other day she stood in the kitchen furiously grinding beans.

He said no, he couldn't stay long. Just a moment, in fact, because his daughter was dressing and he would be needed to plait her hair.

'Right,' Barbara said. 'But you don't mind if I . . . ?' And she indicated the electric kettle, using her Prince of Wales mug to do so.

'No. Of course. I have interrupted your breakfast.'

'Such as it is,' Barbara admitted.

'I would have waited until a time more convenient, but I found this morning that I could no longer do so.'

'Ah.' Barbara went to the kettle and switched it on, wondering about his gravity and what it portended. While it was true that he'd been grave at their every meeting all summer, there was something added to his gravity this morning, a way of looking at her that made her wonder if she had Pop Tart frosting on her face somewhere. 'Well, have a seat if you'd like. And there're fags on the table. You're sure about the coffee?'

'Perfectly. Yes.' But he helped himself to one of her cigarettes and watched her in silence as she made her second cup of coffee. It was only when she joined him at the table – the velvet heart like an unmade declaration between them – that he spoke again. 'Barbara, this is difficult for me. I am uncertain how to begin.'

She slurped her coffee and tried to look encouraging.

Azhar restlessly reached for the velvet heart. 'Essex.'

'Essex,' Barbara repeated helpfully.

'Hadiyyah and I were at the seaside on Sunday. In Essex. As you know,' he reminded her.

'Yeah. Right.' Now was the moment to say *Thanks for the heart*, but it wouldn't come out. 'Hadiyyah told me what a good time you had. She mentioned you dropped in at the Burnt House Hotel as well.'

'She dropped in,' he clarified. 'That is to say that I took her there to wait with the good Mrs Porter – you remember her I believe—'

Barbara nodded. Sitting behind her zimmer frame, Mrs Porter had looked after Hadiyyah while her father acted as liaison between the police and a small but restless Pakistani community during the course of a murder enquiry. 'Right,' she said. 'I remember Mrs Porter. Nice of you to go to see her.'

'As I said, it was Hadiyyah who visited Mrs Porter. I myself visited the local police.'

At this, Barbara felt her defences rising. She wanted to make some sort of remark that would derail the conversation they were about to have, but she couldn't think of one quickly enough because Azhar went on.

'I spoke to Constable Fogarty,' he told her. 'Constable Michael Fogarty, Barbara.'

Barbara nodded. 'Yeah. Mike. Right.'

'He's the weapons officer for the Balford-le-Nez police.'

'Yeah. Mike. Weapons. That's right.'

'He told me what happened on the boat, Barbara. What DCI Barlow said about Hadiyyah, what she intended, and what you did.'

'Azhar—'

He rose. He walked to the day bed. Barbara grimaced to see that she'd not yet made it and the loathsome happy face T-shirt she wore at night was still lying in a tangle with the sheets. She thought for a moment that he intended to straighten the bed

– he *was* the most compulsively neat person she'd ever met – but he turned to face her. She could see his agitation.

'How do I thank you? What can I say that could possibly thank you for the sacrifice you have made for my child?'

'No thanks are needed.'

'This is not true. DCI Barlow—'

'Em Barlow was born with ambition, Azhar. That bollocksed up her judgment. It didn't mess with mine.'

'But as a result, you have lost your position. You have been disgraced. Your partnership with Inspector Lynley – whom I know you esteem – has been dissolved, has it not?'

'Well, things between us aren't exactly peachy,' Barbara agreed. 'But the inspector's got rules and regulations on his side so he's within his rights to be cheesed off at me.'

'But this ... All this is due to what you did ... to your protection of Hadiyyah when DCI Barlow wanted to leave her, when she called her a "Paki brat" and was indifferent to her drowning in the sea.'

He was so distressed that Barbara wished fervently that Constable Michael Fogarty had been taken ill on Sunday, absenting himself from the Essex police station and leaving DCI Barlow the only one present who could – and would – give a seriously sanitised account of the North Sea chase that had ended with Barbara firing a weapon at her. As it was, she could only be grateful for the single fact that Fogarty, in making his report to Azhar, had mercifully not included the *God damn* that Emily Barlow had used before the words *Paki brat* that day.

'I didn't think about the consequences,' Barbara told Azhar. 'Hadiyyah was what was important that day. And she's still what's important. Full stop.'

'I must find a way to show what I feel,' he said, despite her words of reassurance. 'I must not let you think that your sacrifice—'

'Believe me, it wasn't a sacrifice. And as to thanks ...

Well, you've given me a heart, haven't you? And that'll do fine.'

'A heart?' He looked confused. Then he followed the direction of Barbara's extended hand and saw the heart that he'd won from the crane grab game. 'That. The heart. But that is nothing. I only thought of the words on it, Barbara, and how you might smile when you saw them.'

'The words?'

'Yes. Did you not see . . . ?' And he came to the table and flipped the heart over. On its obverse side – which she'd have seen well enough if she'd had the courage to examine the damn thing when Hadiyyah had given it to her – was embroidered *I ♥ Essex*. 'It was a joke, you see. Because after what you went through in Essex, you can, of course, hardly love it. But you did not see the words?'

'Oh *those* words,' Barbara said hastily with a hearty *ha ha* that was designed to illustrate the degree of her complicity in his little joke. 'Yes. The old *I love Essex* routine. Just about the last spot on earth that I want to return to. Thanks, Azhar. This's far better than a stuffed elephant, isn't it?'

'But it's not enough. And there's nothing else that I can give you in thanks. Nothing that is equal to what you gave me.'

Barbara remembered what she'd learned about his people: *lenā -denā*. The giving of a gift that was equal to or greater than the one which had been received. It was the way they indicated their willingness to engage in a relationship, an overt manner of declaring one's intentions without the indelicacy of speaking them openly. How sensible they were, the Asians, she thought. Nothing was left to guesswork in their culture.

'Your *wanting* to find something of equal value is what counts, isn't it?' Barbara asked him. 'I mean, we can make the *wanting* to find something count if we want to, can't we, Azhar?'

'I suppose we can,' he said doubtfully.

'Then consider the equal gift given. And go and plait Hadiyyah's hair. She'll be waiting for you.'

He looked as if he might say more, but instead he came to the table and crushed out his cigarette. 'Thank you, Barbara Havers,' he said quietly.

'Cheers,' she replied. And she felt the ghost of a touch on her shoulder as he passed her on the way to the door.

When it was shut behind him, Barbara chuckled wearily at her boundless folly. She picked up the heart and balanced it between her thumbs and index fingers. *I love Essex,* she thought. Well, there were worse ways he could have joked with her.

She dumped the rest of her coffee in the sink and quickly did her few morning chores. Teeth cleaned and hair combed, with a smudge of blusher on each cheek in a bow to femininity, she grabbed her shoulder bag, locked the door behind her, and sauntered up the drive towards the street.

She went out of the front gate but halted when she saw it.

Lynley's silver Bentley was parked in the driveway.

'You're off your patch, aren't you, Inspector?' she asked him as he got out of the car.

'Winston phoned me. He said you'd left your car at the Yard last night and took a taxi home.'

'We'd tossed back a few drinks and it seemed the better course.'

'So he said. It was wise not to drive. I thought you might like a ride into Westminster. There are problems on the Northern Line this morning.'

'When aren't there problems on the Northern Line?'

He smiled. 'So . . . ?'

'Thanks.'

She slung her shoulder bag into the passenger seat and climbed inside. Lynley got in beside her, but he didn't start the car. Instead, he took something from his jacket pocket. He handed it over.

Barbara looked at it curiously. He'd given her a registration card for the Black Angel Hotel. It wasn't a blank card, however, which might have inspired her to think that he was offering her a holiday in Derbyshire. Rather, it was filled in with a name, an address, and other pertinent information about car types, number plates, passports, and nationalities. It had been made out to an M. R. Davidson who had listed an address in West Sussex and an Audi as the vehicle that had carried him or her to the North.

'Okay,' Barbara said. 'I'll bite. What is it?'

'A souvenir for you.'

'Ah.' Barbara anticipated his starting the Bentley. He didn't do so. He merely waited. So she said, 'A souvenir of what?'

He said, 'DI Hanken believed that the killer stayed at the Black Angel Hotel the night of the murders. He ran the cards of all the hotel guests through the DVLA to see if any of them were driving cars that were registered to a name different from the name they had put on the card. That was the one that didn't match up.'

'Davidson,' Barbara said, examining the card. 'Oh yes. I see. David's son. So Matthew King-Ryder stayed at the Black Angel.'

'Not far from the moor, not far from Peak Forest where the knife was found. Not far, as it turns out, from anything.'

'And the DVLA showed this Audi as registered to him,' Barbara concluded. 'And not to an M.R. Davidson.'

'Things happened so quickly yesterday that we didn't actually see the report from the DVLA till late in the afternoon. The Buxton computers were down, so the information had to be compiled by phone. If they hadn't been down . . .' Lynley looked through the windscreen, sighed and spoke meditatively, 'I want to believe that the blame lies with technology, that had we only got our hands on the DVLA information quickly enough, Andy Maiden would still be alive.'

'*What?*' Barbara breathed the word, astounded. 'Still be alive? What happened to him?'

Lynley told her. He spared himself nothing, Barbara saw. But then, that was his way.

He concluded with, 'It was a considered decision on my part, not to talk directly about Nicola's prostitution when her mother was present. It was what Andy wanted and I went along. Had I simply done what I should have done . . .' He gestured aimlessly. 'I let my feelings for the man get in the way. I made the wrong decision, and as a result he died. His blood is on my hands as indelibly as if I'd wielded the knife.'

'That's being a little rough on yourself,' Barbara said. 'You didn't exactly have time to ponder the best way to handle things once Nan Maiden barged into your interview.'

'No. I could *see* that she knew something. But what I thought she knew – or at least believed – was that Andy had murdered their daughter. And even then, I didn't bring the truth to light because *I* couldn't believe he'd murdered their daughter.'

'And he hadn't,' Barbara said. 'So your decision was right.'

'I don't think you can separate the decision from the outcome,' Lynley said. 'I'd thought so before, but I don't think so now. The outcome exists *because* of the decision. And if the outcome is an unnecessary death, the decision was wrong. We can't twist the facts into a different picture, no matter how much we'd like to do so.'

It sounded like a conclusion to Barbara. She treated it as such. She reached for her seat belt and pulled it round her. She was about to fasten it when Lynley spoke again.

'You made the right decision, Barbara.'

'Yeah, but I had the advantage over you,' Barbara said. 'I'd talked to Cilla Thompson in person. You hadn't. I'd talked to King-Ryder in person as well. And when I saw that he'd actually bought one of her gruesome paintings, it was easy for me to reach the conclusion that he was our man.'

'I'm not talking about this case,' Lynley said. 'I'm talking about Essex.'

'Oh.' Barbara felt herself grow unaccountably small. 'That,' she said. 'Essex.'

'Yes. Essex. I've tried to separate the decision you made that day from its outcome. I kept insisting that the child might have lived had you not interfered. But you didn't have the luxury to make calculations about the boat's distance from the child and someone's ability to throw a life belt to her, did you, Barbara? You had an instant in which to decide what to do. And because of the decision you made, the little girl lived. Yet given the luxury of *hours* to think about Andy Maiden and his wife, I still made the wrong decision in their case. His death's on my shoulders. The child's life is on yours. You can examine the situations any way you want to, but I know which outcome I'd prefer to be responsible for.'

Barbara looked away, in the direction of the house. She didn't quite know what to say. She wanted to tell him that she had lain away nights and paced away days waiting for the moment when he'd say he understood and approved what she'd done that day in Essex, but now that the moment had finally come, she found that she couldn't bring herself to say the words. Instead, she muttered, 'Thanks. Inspector. Thanks,' and she swallowed hard.

'Barbara! Barbara!' The cry came from the flagstone area in front of the ground floor flat. Hadiyyah was standing there, not on the stones but on the wooden bench in front of the french windows to the flat she shared with her dad. 'Look, Barbara!' she crowed and danced a little jig. 'I got my new shoes! Dad said I didn't have to wait till Guy Fawkes. Look! Look! I got my new shoes!'

Barbara lowered her window. 'Excellent,' she called. 'You're a picture, kiddo.'

Kiddo whirled and laughed.

'Who is that?' Lynley asked next to her.

'That's the child in question,' Barbara replied. 'Let's go, Inspector Lynley. We don't want to be late for work.'

Acknowledgments

Those familiar with Derbyshire and the Peak District will attest to the fact that Calder Moor does not exist. I ask their pardon for the liberties I've taken in moulding the landscape to fit the needs of my story.

I extend my most sincere thanks to the people who assisted me in England during my research for and my writing of *In Pursuit of the Proper Sinner*. Without them, I would not have been able to take on the project. In the North, I thank Inspector David Barlow in Ripley and Paul Rennie of Outdoor Pursuits Services in Disley for putting me in the picture with regard to Mountain Rescue; Clare Lowery, at the police forensic science lab in Birmingham, for a crash course in forensic botany; Russell Jackson of Haddon Hall, for a behind-the-scenes look at a fourteenth century architectural jewel. In the South, I thank Chief Inspector Pip Lane in Cambridge for his assistance in enhancing my understanding of virtually every area of policing, from the Criminal Reporting Information Service to search warrants; James Mott in London for the helpful background on London's College of Law; Tim and Pauline East in Kent for information on and a demonstration of modern archery; Tom Foy in Kent for a lesson in arrow making and a heightened understanding of the crime in this novel; and Bettina Jamani in London for the most extraordinary sleuthing skills I've ever encountered. I would also like to thank my editor at Hodder & Stoughton in London, Sue Fletcher, for enthusiastically embracing a project set in her own backyard and for lending me Bettina Jamani whenever I needed her. And I extend my gratitude to Stephanie Cabot at William Morris Agency for her willingness to crawl through Soho sex shops with me.

In France, I am deeply indebted to my French translator, Marie-Claude Ferrer, not only for the additional written and visual information she supplied me on S & M but also for her willingness to find a dominatrix – Claudia – who would consent to an interview.

In the United States, I thank Dr Tom Ruben for the medical information he always supplies; my longtime editor at Bantam, Kate Miciak, not only for throwing down the gauntlet of challenge with four simple but maddening words, 'I see two bodies', but also for her willingness to talk through endless plotting sessions as I brought those two bodies to the written page; my wonderful assistant Dannielle Azoulay without whose myriad services I could not have spent the hours I needed to spend at the word processor; and my writing students for keeping me sharp and honest in my approach to the craft.

Last, I extend my gratitude to Robert Gottlieb, Marcy Posner, and Stephanie Cabot of William Morris Agency: literary agents *extraordinaire*.